DRIVIN' WOMAN

THE MACMILLAN COMPANY
NEW YORK · BOSTON · CHICAGO · DALLAS
ATLANTA · SAN FRANCISCO
MACMILLAN AND CO., LIMITED
LONDON · BOMBAY · CALCUTTA · MADRAS
MELBOURNE
THE MACMILLAN COMPANY
OF CANADA, LIMITED
TORONTO

Drivin' Woman

by

ELIZABETH PICKETT CHEVALIER

NEW YORK

THE MACMILLAN COMPANY

1944

Set up and electrotyped.
Eleventh printing.

A
PRINTED IN THE UNITED STATES OF AMERICA
* * *

TO MY HUSBAND

Give fools their gold, and knaves their power;
Let fortune's bubbles rise and fall;
Who sows a field, or trains a flower,
Or plants a tree, is more than all.

—WHITTIER

NOTE

Tugger Blake, Stone Moncure, Ben Piper, Henry Morris, Tom Coyle and other leading characters have no actual counterpart or prototype in the period covered by this novel. The definite plan of the author, consistently carried out, was to make Blake and these other characters composites of prominent men in the tobacco trade, in Wall Street and in industry generally during the time of this story.

DRIVIN' WOMAN

Chapter 1

In that opaque land between sleep and wakefulness, she wrestled anxiously with the giant of her future. How could she, a girl—single-handed—restore the old way of life to Virginia in time to assure suitable marriages to herself and her three younger sisters?

Consciousness tightened. Again she was America Collier Moncure, aged eighteen. She lay in her tester bed and listened while a robin proclaimed aggressively beyond her front windows that spring had come again to a grey land of defeat. Late April, 1865, had dawned on Golden Hill, stronghold of the Ephraim Collier clan in Charlotte County, on the south side of Virginia where the Cavalier English from the Tidewater and the Scotch-Irish Presbyterian colonists from Pennsylvania had met a century before to form a new county purely agrarian, without cities or towns or even crossroads industries.

Between the bird notes, America was hoping to hear the clash of hot-water cans or a thud of fallen kindling which might announce Hattie's approach up the parlor stairs. Until last year, America had never risen without Mammy or a black girl to light her fire in winter, pour her bath and lay out her clothes. America swung down from her bed, dashed behind the washstand screen and poured water from the handsome Canton pitcher into its matching bowl. As she scrubbed, she caught glimpses of herself in the red lacquer mirror above the washstand. Stripped of daytime shabbiness, she bent a youthful Venus to dry her slender feet. On top of her head she had twisted her curls, glossy as a fresh-shucked chestnut, and made them fast with locust thorns. They formed a Romanesque frame for her heart-shaped face, familiar yet strange in its new gravity of leadership. Thoughtful eyes, changeable in hue as the running colors of the sea, and set wide apart, challenged her world grown apathetic in defeat. Her mouth was both invitation and warning to every man who gazed at her.

Out from behind the screen again, she surveyed her work clothes. Her bedraggled petticoats and calico dress were buttoned with gourd seed. Four years ago she would have quickened with shame to see a recovered runaway go to the fields as ragged and mud-stained as she appeared. Brushing down her curls, she refused to consider how life at Golden Hill had shrunk during four years of war. Hard work and good management, she preferred to think, could restore plenty within half that time. She must hurry, hurry! Two years were all she had to give, if she was not to break the family tradition that Collier women married before they were twenty.

She did not minimize the difficulties ahead. In the good years past, black man power under white leadership had reared cabin and mansion and had wrested abundance from red clay fields once so fertile, then tired and now dormant again under a tangle of oak scrub, vines and creepers. All about her, the neglected land was awakening to nature's annual rebirth. Yet on a thousand Golden Hills, who was left to get into the lead of the spring work? White leadership had vanished from Virginia, had dripped red into streams ruddy before sunset, had soaked into trampled wheat fields, been blown skyward from exploding land mines. The soft-spoken Virginia men who had husbanded an agrarian way of life to its well nigh perfect flowering were dead or had come home gutted of pride, grey ghosts of their former selves, gaunt skeletons who wanted only to whisper of dead heroes and Marse Robert. In the Babylons behind the great houses, only the old and the very young, the helpless and the infirm, remained. Emancipation had sent the able-bodied blacks cakewalking up and down the roads, some with bundles, many empty-handed, all resolved never to work again.

It was spring. Peace was here at last. She was young. And Golden Hill needed her. Beside these considerations, what was the loss of slaves, the defeat of the Confederacy, even death itself?

Scorning face curls, America grasped her candle saucer and ran downstairs. White mist was curling like jasmine around the single-story columns of the front porch. The double parlors slept in their memories. Unlocking the back-hall door, America stepped out onto the rear porch and across the flagstones. Halfway to the cook-cabin door, she felt hoarfrost bite through the paper wads in her boot soles. As she entered, a mountain of faded calico heaved itself up from among the pots on the hearth and swung around to reveal the morose face of Flora, Pembroke's wife and head cook at Golden Hill. America demanded cheerfully what was to be had for breakfast.

"Hawg meat. Good hawg meat, black wid peppah an' white wid salt!"

"Auntie, you know I hope to sell it for taxes. Surely some of these Yankees who've rushed to Charlotte Court House will want to buy country meat."

"Wid army rations tuh burn, w'at makes you think any highfalutin Damyankee ud lay aout money foah aour scrawny half-spiled meat?"

Salt-hunger, America realized, lay at the bottom of Flora's apparent disloyalty. Without rebuke, the girl turned her back on the watching negress, and opened the kitchen press. It was spicy with past bounties, but all save one of the squat stone jars were empty.

"Make us some more of your good hot pones," America suggested. "There's sugared honey left."

"Ain't I tol' you I pukes corn bread widaout salt?" Flora unleashed the full force of her disappointment. "Heah I's biled a hunnerd kittles ob dirty water off de smokehaouse flo' tuh git me some salt. Does you lemme habe a pinch in mah pone? No, missy-ma'am! You takes hit away an' locks hit up till you's ready tuh kill dat ol' shoat an' pigs you cotched daown in de swamp. Dat's all right, I sez tuh mahself, mah salt 'll taste all de bettah on dem slat-sides. An' naow you stands dar an' tells me you means tuh sell my meat tuh rich white folkses in taown, while we starve!"

"You don't look starved," America retorted callously, and stepped outside.

Was it her own salt-hunger, or the ordinary variety which the entire South was experiencing, America wondered, that made her remember how the back yard had looked during the lavish hog-killings of her childhood? Boughs of the cedars which screened the house servants' quarters from Golden Hill's rear windows, had dripped with sixty to eighty fat white carcasses cooling out on chill November nights, and had provided safe roosts for generations of chickens, guineas, ducks, geese, turkeys and peafowl which kept the yard nipped of every spear of grass. On this April morning the lush sod was greening under a web of rime. At the pump of a yard cistern, Ol' Uncle with his long switch saw to it that the 'ninnies washed themselves properly.

America stepped thoughtfully up the stairs of the high rear porch. The three-storied rectangular Georgian house, of unpainted brick mellowed into a ruddy brown, was identical front and rear. A third small white porch at the south rear corner of the mansion led down to terraced flower gardens where the finest boxwood in Charlotte County was already as large as the parent maze from which it had been slipped at Williamsburg. Out of the lifting mist emerged the great trees which had suggested the plantation's name. Pushing westward from Williamsburg by order of the House of Burgesses to establish a magazine for the more convenient storage of firearms and powder in the threatened French and Indian wars, Colonel Ephraim Collier had first come at sunset to the sugar-loaf knoll studded with red oaks glowing against a golden goosefeather sky. Here, he had vowed, as soon as this frontier was made safe, he would establish his future manor overlooking virgin forests which could be cleared into lavish fields. Through three wars Golden Hill had stood. Negotiating the rotting porch floor, America entered the second-floor dining room.

Hattie, Flora's harelipped youngest daughter, was warming herself before the fire she had just blown into flame. The black girl arose with the agility of a truant hound which has learned to keep out of its master's way until its absence has been forgotten. Watching America's skirts under downcast eyes, Hattie began to set one of the Sheraton tables. Its twin stood against the wall. Even if Brother Ephraim is spared to us, thought America, how long will it be before Golden Hill again needs a double table in the dining room? After thumping with an umbrella spine and handle on the ceiling, to awaken her sisters sleeping in the chamber above, America tapped on the closed door of the adjacent family room. Within its shuttered privacy Mrs. Moncure struggled with grief and migraine. The household aroused, America produced her keys, unlocked one of the Adam presses flanking the carved mantel and carried a covered dish of honey to the table. Access to the serving pantry was through sliding panels in the dining-room walls. Concealed within the Adam cupboards, when shut, these panels banished servants' voices and inelegant odors of food.

In due time Mrs. Moncure appeared, sat down at the foot of the table and awaited with anticipatory pleasure for her family of girls to assemble. America found it hard to believe that this tragic-eyed aging stranger in her rusty widow's weeds, cheerful though she tried to be, was her own radiant mother, the beloved Miss Jincy who had ruled a plantation and borne with laughter seven babies between trips to Washington, the expanding West and Richmond, whither her husband's public duties had taken them. Of her loveliness little remained except the deeper beauty of bone contours and of a transcendent spirit. Numbed by the loss of husband, father and two sons, she now left Golden Hill's management to America. With a twinkle, she remarked:

"I see we lived through the night, daughter—"

"But the Yankees might have come! Besides, I got the garden plowed."

"It distresses me to have you shoulder responsibility at an age when I knew only gaiety and pleasure," sighed Mrs. Moncure. "When may we have the silver in use again? Coffee just isn't coffee unless it's sipped from a silver spoon."

"There's no rye to parch. I reminded Teena to borrow a little more from Cap'n Oglethorpe, but she forgot."

"What's that you're saying about me, Sister Merry?" came Palestine's vibrant challenge from the inside steps which opened down into the family room.

Charming as a birch tree in spring, Palestine floated into the dining room and took her place at the breakfast table. Arabia, nine, and Andorra, four, came thundering after her. Radford Moncure, tied in Washington with Government duties following his and Jincy's bridal trip around the world, had named their girls for the distant lands which they longed to revisit.

"Ma, Hattie didn't build me a fire this morning," Palestine launched into immediate complaint. "Were you out at all hours with the colored troops, Harriet Anne? Have you been to Richmond, or did you merely oversleep?"

"Dar warn't no kindlin' chopped," giggled the maid, flattered that pretty Miss Teeny should think any black boy, much less one of General Weitzel's dusky heroes, would want to skylark with a harelipped country wench like herself.

"Can't you make the 'ninnies do chores any longer, Sister Merry?" Palestine unwisely broadened her attack. "Surely you ought to make them do something, since I see they've eaten us out of house and home. Ma, when is Sister Merry going to give us something fit for breakfast? I declare, if I wasn't invited out so much, I'd starve!"

America regarded Palestine coldly. In her eyes was more than the annoyance of Martha, who realizes that she is being outdistanced by a younger, prettier Mary.

"Where did you get that dress?"

"I—I made it over yesterday. Cornelia Oglethorpe fitted it on me. How does it look, ma?" chattered Palestine, and rose to display herself with breath sucked in to flatten her stomach, and palms firm on tiny hip bones.

"Did you take that dress out of Cousin Tan's trunk in the garret?"

"Ma, make her stop talking to me as if I were a 'ninny!"

"Did you, Palestine?"

"It serves her right for leaving her belongings all over the county!"

"Next time you are in Charlotte Court House, present yourself before Cousin Tanis, tell her what you have done and beg her permission to keep the dress," Mrs. Moncure pronounced mild judgment. "Where are you going in your new finery?" she continued with an approving smile. She liked to see Palestine prettily dressed and rushing in and out to parties. It gave her a momentary illusion that nothing had changed.

"Day-spending. At the Carringtons'. The Major has agreed to swap his old hunter for one of our work mules. Does it make any difference which one I take?"

"Well, of all the gall!" the inelegant words burst from America's lips. "After Ol' Uncle got rheumatism hiding those mules in the swamp, and I gentled them myself so we can pitch a crop, you talk about swapping one for a wind-broken bag o' bones Sherman wouldn't steal!"

"Then you find me something better to ride! Achates stumbles so, I vow I'm afraid to mount him."

"You stay home and do your share for once, instead of gallivanting around like a Richmond belle!"

"Girls, cease your chit-chat," interposed Mrs. Moncure. "Hattie, I hear someone on the side porch."

A thunderous knock behind her brought America erect in her chair. With a startled glance at Mrs. Moncure, she arose and opened the door. On the threshold stood a lank man with a recently healed scar across his right cheek. He was decently dressed, like a clergyman, in black Prince Albert and wide-brimmed hat, but America felt no reassurance in his presence. Behind him out of the mist loomed blue-clad shoulders, long Yankee faces below dripping Union kepis.

"Is this the Moncure place?" demanded the black-coated man in a nasal Yankee voice.

"This—this is Golden Hill," America temporized.

She tried instinctively to shut the door. Into the aperture was thrust a stocky leg, clad in boots so glossy they must belong to an officer. Looking up, America gazed into the stolid blue eyes of a young lieutenant in charge of the squad. With a grunt, he shoved the door open and strode in, his revolver drawn. Troopers followed and arranged themselves without zest into escort formation. With the ostentation of a man who mistakes military punctilio for personal deference, the frock-coated civilian stepped inside. He began immediately to appraise the contents of the handsome room as a Vermont storekeeper might take swift inventory of a bankrupt competitor's stock.

From the foot of the table, Mrs. Moncure came forward with a whisper of taffeta petticoats. The younger Moncure girls sat galvanized in their chairs. At the press, Hattie held in a slackening grip a tray with a plate of corn bread on it. The plate began to slide. It fell, broke noisily, and scattered the golden pones, but nobody noticed.

"Sir, your display of firearms is unwarranted," Mrs. Moncure's composed voice addressed the officer. "You see us, defenseless women, living alone with such of our people as have elected to remain. To whom do I owe this unmannerly intrusion?"

"We rode north with Sherman, ma'am. We're heading home for Pennsylvania. Yonder's the man you'd best talk to," answered the lieutenant and waggled his revolver at the scarred civilian, who introduced himself grudgingly, as if he would have preferred to accomplish his mission incognito.

"Anthony Mudston, ma'am. From reliable sources at Charlotte Court House—"

"From Mr. Cushman, sir? Nobody else in town would stoop to speak to you." America found her tongue.

"It has come to my ears," Mudston went on as if he had not heard America, "that Union Army mules are being spirited away at night from their picket lines. Four of them have been traced to this farm."

"Sir, do we look like gypsy horse thieves who would visit a Yankee camp at night?" America answered him scornfully. Here was no formidable enemy. Here stood an ordinary enough Yankee, a vulgar tradesman for all his pompous speech, good clothes and that sly air of unpleasant unctuousness which at first had put her in mind of an undertaker.

"The Bureau of Refugees, Freedmen and Abandoned Lands, authorized in March by Congress, ma'am"—Mudston continued to ignore America by addressing his remarks to Mrs. Moncure—"is going to need every mule we can locate to resettle the freedmen onto the land. You will see the wisdom of surrendering these animals without forcing me to appeal to the military, so ably represented by Lieutenant Eppich, here."

"Do you intend to confiscate our mules and take them back to Pennsylvania with you, sir?"

Before he could resent America's question, the panel in the left press was shot back. Flora's moon face appeared in it like the tar-baby in a circus concession.

"Mistis, de lane's swarmin' wid Damyankees!" she cried, and her eyes bulged. " 'Foah de Lawd, boss, I nebber seed jew in dar!"

"Lieutenant, hadn't you better step around back and make sure she doesn't give the alarm? You of the glib tongue"—Mudston pointed a forefinger at America—"show him the way."

"Pem—you Pem!" screeched Flora, disappearing as if a lucky hit had dropped her. Beyond the partition sounded lumbering footsteps, then a shout: "Git away wid dem mules, Pem! Damyankees is heah tuh take 'em."

"Outside, miss," Lieutenant Eppich ordered.

In the back yard stood more soldiers, holding horses. Before she realized how many sharp eyes were watching her, America sent a quick glance towards the scene of her frantic labors yesterday, the plowed garden acreage that came up to the yard fence.

"There's no need to hurry, now. The boys have located 'em," declared the lieutenant.

Down the stable lane through the broken mist, Union troopers came leading the four mules. On them jingled the gear America had galled her fingers to mend. An undersized corporal was prodding Pembroke before him at pistol point.

From the rear porch, Mudston strode across the yard to where America stood with Lieutenant Eppich.

"There's not a thing in there worth taking!" His complaint belied the handle of Andorra's porringer sticking out of his coat pocket. "Where d'you suppose they've hid the stuff?"

At the moment, the lieutenant appeared too preoccupied in examining his revolver to reply. Pembroke and the corporal arrived in time to hear Mudston's query. With a too casual question, the terrier-faced Yankee corporal asked America:

"What you got planted in that garden patch, miss?"

"We intend to grow potatoes there, when the ground warms."

"You do, eh? Suppose we found some ham 'n' table silver, we could set right down to breakfast."

"I don't understand you—"

"Dumb like a fox, ain't she, sir?" the corporal appealed to Mudston.

"Precisely what I was thinking myself, Justin. Soldier, hand me your saber!" As if in actual command of the platoon, the civilian faced the troopers clattering into the yard. "Company, halt—dismount!"

Lieutenant Eppich, Pennsylvania farm boy that he was, felt he had put up with about all he could stand from Anthony Mudston. Eppich had first encountered Mudston before Atlanta, when the young private was on burial-squad duty.

Caught red-handed by Eppich in a situation which looked mighty like looting the dead, Mudston had told a smooth story about a two-year search for a long-lost brother turned Confederate. Eppich felt no immediate concern to report a suspicion which he could not prove. His stripes followed. When he met up with Mudston in South Carolina, the civilian had an unhealed slash from a bowie-knife across his cheek, as if some wounded Johnnie Reb had had strength enough left to resent having his watch lifted. Overcome with war-weariness, Eppich had held his phlegmatic peace. Later, he found himself a lieutenant, and ordered to Charlotte Court House. On the steps at the local commandant's headquarters, Eppich met Mudston. What a whopping contribution the stinking ghoul must have made to the Union League, to reap this plum of an appointment as future head of the Freedmen's Bureau in Charlotte County!

"Draw sabers—form ranks to charge on foot!" Mudston was shouting.

With questioning glances at their lieutenant, the troopers reined in, swung from their saddles. The expressions on their weather-beaten faces indicated that they were in no mood for horseplay and especially from a civilian, regardless of how much pull he could exert in Washington. Mudston jerked open the garden gate, charged into the garden and with his saber began to stab at the plowed ground. After a dozen experimental thrusts the point met resistance. America and her mother exchanged despairing glances. Mudston scratched like a mongrel unearthing a bone, and rose up with a sack-covered ham.

A shout of belated understanding burst from the troopers. They swarmed into the garden and began to stab for buried treasure. Steel struck metal. With a gleeful oath, a soldier dug up and held aloft the kidney-shaped Sheffield tray which had been an heirloom in the Collier family for more than a hundred years.

"Finders keepers!" he yelled, and with the tray under his arm shifted ground to stab for more.

"Come on, Lieutenant! Let's git ours before it's too late," exclaimed the corporal named Justin.

"You go. I'll stand by the horses."

"Seems to me you've gotten mighty squeamish since Georgy! But suit yerself."

"Boss-man, haow's we gwine pitch a crop effen you take aour mules 'n' meat?" spoke up Ol' Uncle, plaintively.

"We understand your commanding general at Appomattox let our soldiers take their horses home to do the spring plowing," Mrs. Moncure followed the old negro's plea. "You yourself look like a farmer, sir—surely you can appreciate our plight? These mules were raised on this plantation. My daughter and servant gentled them."

"Uncle, you won't need to work any more soon as Mudston gets his Bureau going good," Lieutenant Eppich answered the ex-slave first. That was the trouble with these Rebel women: show them a little consideration and they try to make a man forget his duty. "As for you, ma'am, the Vindictives in Congress aim to take the land away from you Seceshers and give it to the smokes."

"Sir, that's a sorry joke."

"By God, it's no joke! A little honest work would do you lazy Virginians good."

With their arms full, Mudston and several troopers were returning to their horses for blankets in which to wrap their loot. The heirlooms of a rich past were gone, America realized; but there was still the barren future to consider.

"I beg you, sir," she cried, and extended her palms blistered by the plow handles. "Leave us our four mules, so that we can pitch a crop for ourselves and our dependents. It's two full weeks since peace was signed. What right have you to forage and steal, now?"

"Don't you start telling us what we can or can't do, you Rebel brat!" answered a hatchet-faced trooper, looking up from the ham he was lashing behind his saddle.

"Ambrose, that's no way to speak to a lady," rebuked Lieutenant Eppich.

"If we paid you Virginians in like coin for what you did to Honest Abe, we'd line every one of you up against that meat-house wall!" declared Mudston, viciously.

" 'He who takes the sword, shall perish by the sword,' " America flung at him.

"You're a sassy piece, ain't you, now?" commented Justin, without malice.

"Merry, guard your tongue!" whispered Mrs. Moncure.

"In Georgy, we had ways o' coolin' hotheads like you—"

"Shoot me then, you brave men who delight to war on women and children!"

Mudston had finished tying his prizes onto the rear of his saddle. Preparing to mount his tall horse, he swung around and stared, as if he were seeing America for the first time. High-spirited and lovely, she stood with arms outflung against the south wall of the woodshed. Gazing at her, Mudston's face sharpened with desire, then relaxed into an unpleasant, purposeful smile. Knee uplifted to mount, he changed his mind, kicked his foot free of the stirrup and came towards the girl, caught in the hypnotism of her own melodrama.

"Merry, run for the swamp!"

At the note of desperation in her mother's voice, America awoke to her own danger. With a gasp of terror, she eluded Mudston's clumsy reach for her, dodged under the startled heads of several horses and ran towards the orchard slope beyond the house servants' quarters. Row after row of fruit trees in the first mist of early bloom extended parallel to the garden. As she ran under the boughs, America heard the drone of working bees, saw their weathered hives, observed that the brisk April breeze, which had cleared the morning fog, was carrying an occasional petal like a snowflake towards the garden. One by one, as she passed, America pushed over the beehives.

With a sibilant rush, the angered insects spiraled out.

Flying with the wind, they first attacked the troopers in the garden. Cursing and shouting, the men ran for the yard carrying what they could and followed by visible streaks of the aroused bees. Lieutenant Eppich ran to the cook cabin for shelter, but Flora slammed the door in his face. Horses neighed and plunged. Kepis beat at shoulders and haunches in a futile attempt to drive off America's winged cohorts. The squad then abandoned the field. Grasping what they could carry, they mounted their frantic animals and went pelting down the carriageway with the confiscated mules clattering behind them.

Mudston, a poor horseman at best, was trying to mount his frantic steed, which reared and circled squealing with pain as the bees attacked him. Shielding his puffing face with his arm, Mudston gained his saddle and turned to shout a last vengeful promise before his mount lunged away with him:

"You damn' Rebels, I'll be back tonight an' burn you out if it's my last act alive!"

The encounter brought on an immediate attack of Mrs. Moncure's migraine. America put a vinegar compress on her mother's eyes, closed the inside shutters of the family room and tiptoed out to the back yard. Idle as a beauty in a fashion print, Palestine sat on the steps and watched while the others collected what meat and silver the Yankees had abandoned in their flight. Baby Andorra had recovered her porringer and was placidly eating corn pone and milk from it which Arabia had brought from the dining room.

Palestine felt that Mudston's promise had been the empty threat of a bully. Between bites of corn bread, she insisted on recounting a tale she had heard just yesterday at the Oglethorpes':

"Cornelia's Aunt Blossom was in Columbus when Sherman's men came through. She had to walk the streets all night carrying a baby on each arm and, over her back, a burlap sack containing the family silver. She got so tired she was ready to drop and let the fire rage over her, when a handsome young Yankee lieutenant—it might have been this self-same one!—stepped up and offered to help. She couldn't trust him with the babies, so she handed over the silver. Of course she never expected to see it again. Imagine her surprise the next day, when the Yankee hunted her up in the refugee camp and returned the sack to her—without a spoon missing!"

"Auntie, what do you think?" America appealed to Flora, who sat a glum Buddha among the pieces of meat she had recovered. The air of offended dignity which the huge black woman wore, America realized, was only the screen of her inner turmoil. Flora relaxed sufficiently to declare:

"My idee ud be tuh move intuh taown dis veree mo'hning—tuh Miz Tan's right acrost from de Cote House."

"You've been saying the Yankees ud get us every night since the war started!" jeered Palestine.

"Missy-ma'am, does you recollec' de cabin in de holler whar youah gran'pap used tuh make he peach an' chirry brandy?"

"The stillhouse, Ol' Uncle? By the big spring with the beegum tree—"

"Dat's de one. Effen I war you, I'd put in mah day movin' w'at's needed daown dar."

"You believe he'll come back, don't you, Ol' Uncle?" whispered America, her eyes darkening with despair. "So do I. And if we lose Golden Hill, it will be my fault because I indulged my ungovernable temper!"

"If I has tuh lib in de stillhouse de res' ob mah days, ever' night I'll git daown in de dust tuh thank de Lawd you bested him," came Flora's staunch support.

"Auntie, how can you encourage Sister Merry in her tantrums like that?"

"Shet youah mouf, chil'. Ever' time you speaks, you shows haow bird-brained you is."

"Sister Merry, I won't stay here and be insulted!" declared

Palestine, with pretty indignation. Springing to her feet, she bade one of the 'ninnies saddle and fetch Achates around to the front stile.

"Teena, you can't go off now, when there's so much to do before sundown!" protested America.

"Don't you go disturbing my room! I never saw such chicken hearts as you four, in all my born days."

After they had watched her spring-green skirts eddy around the back-hall doorway, they sat in apathetic silence. They heard her mount, and clatter over stones of the carriage drive. The *rat-tat-tat* of Achates' running walk diminished down the hill.

"Hit wouldn't sur-prise me none tuh see de Lawd smack her daown foah dat," Flora delivered herself heavily of her opinion. "I knowed dis mo'hnin', when I seed mah cheer spin araound free times on hits lef' hin' laig, we all was in foah trubble."

"Dat's a pow'ful sign," agreed Pembroke. "Hit's most as bad as tuh dream you seed a pot o' gold a-sinkin' intuh de groun' undah a grapevine."

The day passed in desperate, hurried toil. By midafternoon, furniture and bedding, kitchen utensils, tubs, china and farming tools had gone down the hill. America saved two trunks in which to pack what she could of Golden Hill's objects of art. Only the bees, she now realized, had saved them this morning from Yankee search of the entire house.

The big double parlors lay in the twilight of closed shutters. Where slats were missing or broken, fingers of light pointed at polished floors, satinwood and marquetry furniture, and tall gilt mirrors crowned with soaring eagles. Here and there in dark corners winked oxblood cloisonné, glowed mother-of-pearl. Each rarity, every exquisite expression of alien culture, was the prize of some ancestral jaunt, was treasure brought home from foreign shores by tender hands long since turned to dust.

America approached the rear windows, threw open the shutters to admit the sunset. Golden light flooded the parquet floor, regilded the French chairs and faded yellow brocade on the walls. Here she had advanced, a terrified small girl of five, to meet the Indian chieftain in buckskins, wampum and eagle feathers whom her father, then head of the newly organized Interior Department, had brought down from Washington to show how a favored son of the White Father lived in his Virginia lodge.

"Step forward and shake hands with our guest, dear," Miss Jincy had smilingly urged.

America had shot her mother a glance of shocked surprise. Didn't ma realize Indians scalped little girls? The roomful of adults were looking expectantly at her. From the Indian's clifflike face, she felt his searching scrutiny. On knees that seemed to flow like water, she came forward, curtsied and extended a small hand which she could not prevent from trembling visibly.

"Nicketai!"

"What's he saying, Radford?"

"Pretty little girl," she heard her father's amused translation.

"Nicketai!" repeated the Indian. "Strong here," he added and thumped his own bronze barrel chest.

"The chief says you're a brave little girl, America. You may go, now."

America knelt at the French cabinet and began to wrap in damask towels the collection of hand-painted fans which had come down from a French ancestress. Why hadn't the discerning savage, himself a suppliant for all his fine feathers, warned her that courage was not enough? Nor foresight. Nor labor. For weeks before Appomattox, ever since she had come on the rogue sow and her grown pigs in the swamp and had coaxed them home with corn the family could ill spare, she had schemed and toiled and driven others to her will, as she had done today. Now she knelt at the end of her strength, weak with hunger and despair. Yet nothing which she could contrive or dare further could preserve past tonight this beauty so short-lived in brutish hands, so enduring in tender ones.

Flanked by rhododendron and laurel, the stillhouse squatted at the head of the hollow. Ribs of living rock rose sheer behind it. From under the broad slab of granite which formed its foundation, gushed a perpetual stream of bright cold water which overflowed the beegum tree felled across the head of the hollow, and dropped down the ledges to Rough Creek in the valley below. Three log cabins, each twenty feet square and built in a row with one common inside wall, formed the weather-beaten dwelling. Wind and rain had penetrated the mossy roof, so that the split logs, laid in mud to form a puncheon floor, felt spongy to America's heels. Beetles and spiders scurried in all directions and up the mildewed walls every time she carried in a chair or set a portrait down. Above each room was a loft formed by poles floored over with loose planking, on which Pembroke unrolled feather ticks.

Shining with damp and decay as the stillhouse was, nevertheless it afforded living space. Mrs. Moncure's bed almost filled the right cabin. The middle must serve as family room below; above were sleeping quarters for the Moncure girls. In the left cabin, which boasted the only fireplace, Flora unpacked pots and skillets, screwed in roasting spits. She and Pembroke would have to sleep on pallets on the cook hearth. Ol' Uncle established himself overhead with his brood, the 'ninnies left behind in '63 by the general exodus of Moncure slaves.

Twilight shut down early under the hill. The sound of running water deepened. Strangely uncomfortable, the Moncures pulled chairs up to Grandpa Ephraim's bottling shelf, which served well enough for a table. On Haviland china, Pembroke placed before them fried ham and steaming hominy grits. America had forgotten that salt meat could taste so good.

"I'll step up the hill and wait for Teena," Mrs. Moncure broke the silence of complete exhaustion.

"I'll go with you, if somebody will watch Andorra," Arabia denied her fear.

"We'll all go, except you children. Ol' Uncle will stay with you." America rewarded her little sister with false optimism: "And next week we'll move everything back up into the house and laugh about camping down here in the hollow."

The night was clear of fog. A single star trembled like a tear on the horizon above the dark mass of trees on the hilltop. Single file, they trudged along tracks cut by the farm sled into the wet sod. Every time she had strained on the ropes to drag the heavy sled, America had pictured Achates idly fighting the first blue bottles of the season under the Carringtons' hitching tree, while Palestine acted the la-de-da young lady in the parlors.

America stepped out of line to tie a shoelace. As she passed Flora to rejoin her mother, the girl whispered:

"What's that you've got in your hand, auntie?"

"Mah co'hn knife. No Damyankee's gwine buhn Golden Hill widaout me carvin' his gizzard fust."

They passed through the gap in the fence where Pembroke had laid down the rails. In the garden, the heavy fragrance of hyacinths rose to meet them like ghosts of happier springs. Through the boxwood maze, they approached the unlighted house. As a dying face takes on majesty when the tides of life recede, darkness and its approaching doom intensified in America's eyes the beauty of the old brick mansion. Evidence of decay which daylight revealed to distress her, was not visible in the luminous gloom. Mass and contour alone stood out in strength and grace.

Mrs. Moncure, lifting her bedraggled skirts, mounted the stone steps and sat down on one of the benches flanking the fanned doorway. America dropped onto the top step, with her back against a column. Pembroke and Flora sat below her. The calm of the April night held them quiet, as if suspended above all power to experience the catastrophe which each felt the precious fleeting minutes were bringing closer. Within the hour of the Yankees' departure, America had realized that no power remained in Charlotte County, in all Virginia prostrate after Appomattox, to save Golden Hill from the consequences of her own rash act, should Mudston return to make good his threat. Over the beehives, she had stood at the crossroads of this encounter, possessed for a few brief seconds with power to choose whether or not to surrender part to save the greater whole. Surrender was not in her nature. Her passionate choice had been made without thought of reckoning. Tomorrow, on the other side of whatever experience tonight might bring, she would find herself a free agent again, until faced with another crisis at a farther crossroads.

"I hear Teena coming," announced Mrs. Moncure.

"She's riding fast. She's scared. She ought to be."

"Only de good Lawd keeps her safe comin' home dis haour ob de night!"

They watched the young horsewoman rise into view and approach the stile. Pembroke heaved himself up to take Achates. Uncertain of her reception, yet with confidence restored by her safe arrival, Palestine stepped up the flagstones.

"Howd'ye, everybody! Ma, I'm sorry I'm late. Three of us girls rode into town this afternoon, and what do you think? They've shot John Wilkes Booth. He was hiding in a barn, and they set it afire to make him come out. Is supper over?"

"Two hours ago. I'm distressed to hear about Mr. Booth. Your father and I saw him once in Baltimore."

"Auntie, d'you suppose you could find me some cold corn bread and a glass of milk?"

"You hear't youah maw say we's done et two haours back. Ever'thing's put away daown de holler."

"Merry, you haven't actually moved down there?"

"What did you hear about the soldiers, Teena? Are they still in town?"

"Nobody's seen hide nor hair of them. They're well on their way to Richmond by now."

"Dey's hidin' in de woods or under de kivered bridge coolin' der bee stings," chuckled Ol' Uncle, who had approached unobserved and now took Pembroke's place on the lower step. "Dat pore white trash ain't gwine let taown folkses see w'at we done tuh 'em."

Palestine moved uneasily. Suppose, instead of taking the short cut up the creek, she had come clattering down the pike as usual and Mudston had pounced upon her from under the covered bridge? The thought alone made goosepimples start out on her arms. To banish the horrible idea, she began to chatter gaily:

"Everybody in town's talking about the New York Jew who's opened a junk yard on Court Street. He's offered to pay Federal money for horse bones, which he expects to grind into fertilizer. Cannon balls and lead 'll bring top prices. Dick Oglethorpe said he'd rather chip old bricks in Richmond than be a ghoul."

"Teena, spare us!"

"I'm surprised you don't want to hear more about Mr. Booth, Sister Merry."

"We's got bonfires ob aour own tuh puzzle ovah, chil'," Flora declared, crushingly.

"Well, nobody's going to find me sleeping in that wretched cabin, catching my death of cold!" declared Palestine, disappointed that her best conversational efforts had been spent to no effect. "I'm going up to my room and get a good rest. Good-night, ma. Sister Merry, you might call me if the Yankees come."

"Good-night, daughter."

They listened to her progress up the inside stairs. A door slammed, but the petulant sound was too trivial to stir the depths of their foreboding. Mrs. Moncure sighed, like a breeze ruffling the surface of despair:

"Sometimes I wonder if Teena will ever outgrow her young and thoughtless ways. Nobody'd know her for your sister, America."

"At least she hasn't cost you Golden Hill!"

"Life has set you a hard lesson, daughter. But we'll not lose courage yet."

Too miserable to want to talk, America prevailed on Mrs. Moncure to lie down on the couch in the rear hall. Flora moved up one step so that America might lay her head in the negress' lap. The girl's thoughts, like tired soldiers, continued to trudge down and up the hill under the drive of her resolve to save all she could. One more load, Pem. There's light for one more load—

"W'at dat?" demanded Flora, moving.

America sat up with a jerk. Far away below the hill beat the unmistakable pulse of horses' hoofs on a country turnpike.

"Dey's a-comin'," pronounced Ol' Uncle. "Nobody but Yankees got dat many hosses lef'."

"Call ma," whispered America, rising. "I'll get Teena."

As she ran up the stairs, America was surprised to discover how calm she felt. The certainty of Golden Hill's doom, approaching in the crescendo of horses' hoofs, seemed easier to bear than had been the day's dreadful anticipation. Palestine, in deep sleep, was hard to arouse. America pulled her out of bed, propelled her down the stairs and out onto the porch steps where Mrs. Moncure had taken quiet command:

"Wait at the gap in the fence below the flower garden, girls. Flora, you and Pembroke take good care of them. Ol' Uncle, will you stay with me?"

"No use nobody stayin' but me. Dar ain't nuffin nobody kin do."

The clatter of hoofs warned them that the time for words had passed. With backward glances at the aged ex-slave, they hurried into the protecting gloom of the boxwood maze. America paused to watch some twenty horsemen emerge from the well of the carriage road. Mudston's white shirt and collar below the funereal hat made him easily distinguishable. At the stile they dismounted, tied their bridle reins over the hitching board. Rowdy laughter proclaimed that several had been drinking. They swept up the flagstones towards the white-headed old negro on the step, like a gusty wind descending on a dandelion pod in full seed. America recognized the nasal voice of the little corporal called Justin:

"Ain't you up purty late, uncle? Where's that sorrel top?"

"Mah folks all done gone tuh taown, boss."

"None of the Moncure women passed through the covered bridge," answered Mudston, truculently. "Search the house, men."

The soldiers' lighted candles flickered like will-o'-the-wisps from room to room, then clustered on the front porch.

"Looks like a sou'wester struck the place." America identified the next voice as that belonging to the long-faced trooper named Ambrose.

"Two of you men go 'round back, and see if you can locate a can of coal oil," ordered Mudston.

"Boss-man, ain't jew got fine big haouses up Norf whar you comes from? Dissa haouse am olduh dan all you sojers put to-gedder. Hit ain't done nuffin agin you all."

"There's something in what he says, Mudston," Lieutenant Eppich's voice came to the anxious listeners in the boxwood maze. "It does seem a shame to burn down another fine old house like this one, where people have been living and dying maybe since Revolutionary days."

"Yassuh, boss! An' befoah den—"

"What d'you say, men?" Lieutenant Eppich swung in appeal to his troop. "Shall we let these women off? Remember, we're starting home tonight."

"I'm agreeable—if I had a souvenir to take to my old woman!"

"Take everything you can carry, but let's not leave them without shelter," cried the young officer, his voice breaking with relief.

"Sure, the war's over!" called another voice, from the rear.

"Suits me," agreed Justin. "Besides, I kinda liked that sorrel top."

"Gen'nemen, Mistis Merry nevah meant no hahm," Ol' Uncle put in his persuasive oar. "She's jest tellsome by nature."

Behind the boxwood, America smiled at her mother. Their

pleasure in Golden Hill's seeming deliverance was short-lived. Mudston's indignant voice rang across the lawn:

"Lieutenant Eppich! I consider your attitude inexcusably lax and bordering on downright treason. Your detail to Charlotte Court House ends tomorrow, else I should most assuredly report you to Washington. All those with me for stamping out this vipers' nest tonight, step forward! And now, Ambrose, while our co-patriots prepare the torch, let's you and me go locate that coal-oil can."

The first flames showed in the front parlor. As the glow brightened, despairing eyes behind the boxwood watched the soldiers moving inside around the bonfire they had lighted. As at some gala event, marking the crest of lavish hospitality, the firelight streamed across the lawns. It flooded the stile so that America could see the cavalry horses swinging uneasily about the halter rings. Their eyes and burnished gear occasionally caught a high light. It shone on the boxwood between lawn and garden. The lighted side appeared bright as Paris green, the dark side was velvet black with grotesque shadows. It imparted false color to Mrs. Moncure's pinched face. She crouched before shivering Palestine and the others at the first terrace, screened from view by a ragged clump of boxwood which had once been the carefully pruned moon-and-star piece. All saw the lanky silhouette of Mudston throw on the fire armfuls of feminine finery which, powder-dry from years of storage, shot ceilingwards in greedy flames. Heat drove the soldiers out to watch the destruction they had kindled.

"That was my wedding dress," whispered Mrs. Moncure. "I had to leave it hanging in the press, to empty that last trunk for you, Merry."

"My new green dress!" exclaimed Palestine suddenly, as if she had just awakened to a realization of what was taking place.

"Hush, Teena. Do you want them to hear you?"

"Sister Merry, you've got to do something about my new green dress—about my other things!"

"You told me not to touch your room, while you went gadding."

"Then I'll save them, myself!"

While they stared, Palestine dodged around Flora's bulk, evaded her mother and ran towards the burning house. In her pale nightdress, she put America in mind of a silly white moth fluttering across the lawn. Mudston saw her and raised an immediate shout:

"That smoked 'em out! Come on, men—any of you who're a-minded to have a little fun!"

"The first man to follow will be court-martialed!" rang out Lieutenant Eppich's voice.

"Teena, come back!" wailed Mrs. Moncure.

The cries stopped Palestine. Too late she realized her peril. Turning, she lifted her skirts and started running towards the boxwood. Fleeter than her pursuer, she had gained the cockle-shell path when she tripped on the hem of her nightgown. Mudston sprinted, and with a grunt of triumph fell upon her before Palestine could regain her feet. His dark coat blotted out her dim form.

As Palestine stumbled, America heard her mother gasp with horror. Then Flora panted:

"Lemme at dat hawg!"

In Flora's hand, the two-foot blade of the corn knife shone ruddy with firelight reflected from the soaring flames. America wrenched the knife from the negress' hand and leaped past her mother. On the path, Palestine screamed and fought the laughing Yankee who knelt across her twisted body. With his back towards America, Mudston tried to pin Palestine's desperate clawing hands to earth. A second glance told America that to avoid striking her sister, she must aim high. Raising the corn knife in both hands, she swung like a diminutive fury at Mudston's scrawny neck.

The blow met resistance, the knife handle was deflected from her grasp. Thrown momentarily off balance, America recovered herself and stared aghast at what she had done. Palestine's face, throat and shoulders where her nightdress had been ripped, shone with bright crimson. Her eyes were shut, her screaming mouth reminded America of some blood-stained goddess of the French Revolution, as she struggled to push off Mudston's body that flopped like a monstrous, half-decapitated fowl. The blade of the corn knife was buried in the curve of Mudston's neck, above his right shoulder. He uttered no sound. The knife-handle jerked crazily to his dying reflexes.

The sight turned America's stomach. She thought she was going to faint, struggled against it, and was swept with hideous nausea. Leaning for support against the boxwood, she watched her mother and Pembroke pull the still screaming Palestine to her feet. Flora on one side of the frenzied girl, Mrs. Moncure on the other, Pembroke with his palm across her mouth from behind, they hustled her towards the saving darkness of garden and hillside.

As Palestine's muffled screams receded, America became conscious of the roar of the fire. The flames had reached the upper rooms of Golden Hill. On the other side of the boxwood, she heard a Yankee voice:

"Damned if he ain't takin' her down the hill! Who does he think wants to spy on him, the dirty—"

"Lieutenant, give the word an' we'll go pull him off."

"And get busted out of the army on trumped-up charges? Mudston's got more influence at Washington than you think," declared Lieutenant Eppich.

"Where d'you suppose those two old niggers went?" spoke up another voice, unhappily. "Why don't they help her?"

"You know how niggers light out at the first smell o' danger."

"Maybe they went to call the neighbors. This affair won't read any too good at Headquarters."

"And Mudston 'll lay the whole dirty business on us, you mark my words."

"To your horses, men!" Lieutenant Eppich's voice hardened. "Mudston—oh, Mudston!" he shouted, cupping his hands towards the boxwood hedge. "We can't wait any longer for you. The neighbors may be here any minute now."

America watched the soldiers run across the lawn to their horses. Two by two, the cavalrymen dropped down into the well of the carriage road. Tethered to a stile-ring, Mudston's horse swung frantically and nickered.

"Miz Merry! Whar is you all?"

Ol' Uncle's skullcap of white wool, with his anxious face shining blue in the fire glare, showed around the big oak tree. A moment later, he was beside America, whispering:

"Thank de Lawd you's safe! I feart dat war you screamin'. I war tryin' tuh steal a gun."

"That was Palestine."

"Did he—did he—"

"I got there first. Uncle, what shall I do? I—I killed him."

She could not look again. She heard Ol' Uncle suck in his breath, then exhale it in an angry question:

"Ain't I slit de t'roat ob ever' hawg killt on dis place come ever' black frost?"

"But he was a man—with a soul. Do you suppose he had a family? What will the Yankees do to me when they find out? They tried to burn poor Mr. Booth in a barn, Teena said. What shall I do, Ol' Uncle?"

"I kin say I done hit. Looks lak niggers is gwine git off easier dan white folks from naow on."

"Uncle, I couldn't let you hang for me!"

"Why not, missy? You is young, I is old. Mah life's goin' up wid Golden Hill."

"Hush, you're talking foolish. Let me think—"

Stepping carefully past the dark body sprawled on the cockleshells, she walked to the edge of the lawn. A mighty torch against billowing yellow clouds shot with flame, Golden Hill burned straight up in the draft caused by its once proud elevation. Cook cabin and icehouse, woodshed and servants' quarters were ablaze.

"Look, uncle! The fire's comin' this way—to the quarters. Why can't we drag—him—into Pem's cabin? Logs burn forever. Come on!"

They ran to Mudston's body. The greedy hands, America noticed, had clawed at the path. They still gripped more cockleshells than they could hold. Her eyes averted, America seized the feet, Ol' Uncle took the arms. It was all they could do to drag Mudston's body across the brilliantly lighted yard to Pembroke's cabin. Up the puncheon step they struggled and into the single room with its deep-throated fireplace. America felt the heat from the burning roof push down upon her head. Looking up, she saw the great stone chimney bulging in towards them.

"Uncle, the chimney's falling in!" she screamed.

Clutching each other, they leaped doorwards. Roof and chimney crashed like thunder, the fiery air seemed to explode behind them. They found themselves prostrate on the ground outside, glad to cling momentarily to the cool wet earth. Ol' Uncle's snowy cap of wool, his solemn bushy eyebrows and lashes were mostly singed off. Tears from his heat-inflamed eyes had furrowed his cheeks until he looked like an age-shriveled monkey. America began to beat at the patches of sparks which were spreading on his ragged coat. So Pembroke found them. Extinguishing the fire, they got the old negro to his feet.

"W'at dat?" Pembroke whispered, as a scream split the orchestration of the fire.

"It's that horse over there," gasped America.

The scream rose again. Through the partial curtain of flame which had been the stile, they saw Mudston's horse lunging as it struggled to free its head from the bridle reins, looped over the hitching board. As they watched, the suffering animal reared straight up, its pale belly showing, and fell over backwards. A moment later, they heard its mad hoofs pounding down the carriage road off the hill.

"He done slip de bridle," declared Pembroke, and grasped America firmly by the arm. "Stop dem hystir-rics, an' come on daown de hill befoah you goes plumb crazy—lak pore Miz Teeny."

CHAPTER 2

AMERICA put the thought of what she had done resolutely from her mind. She could not so easily deny the presence of three dots dipping and soaring against the bright April sky, or banish the odor that began to pervade the ruined hilltop. Leaning on her hoe, America reflected with bitterness that the fire which had destroyed everything of worth on Golden Hill, must have passed over the one thing she had wanted destroyed and which, if discovered under the chimney stones, could destroy her.

In the flower garden the hyacinths and jonquils hung pale, drained of green by the blasting heat. Of the boxwood, nothing remained except a pattern of charred roots and white ash among the cockleshell paths, one of which had been carefully scraped. Ol' Uncle had also raked the embers of the stile for the blackened remnants of Mudston's bridle, which he hid under his coat as he limped away to bury it. The great oaks near the house had burned to snaggle-teeth. Only four tall chimneys and several cross partitions of the gutted mansion's walls stood swaying, a hazard to the curious who might want to rake the debris.

Fear of discovery held America during daylight hours at the scene of her violence. Her active mind prodded her to dispose of Mudston's body before its presence could be sniffed out by some Yankee friend from Charlotte Court House or by Lieutenant Eppich's successor. Yet her senses balked at the gruesome undertaking. Other pressing considerations claimed her time and strength. If taxes were to be paid next year, she must pitch some kind of money crop. She had tobacco seedlings pushing up plant-bed cotton near the stillhouse. The only plowed ground on Golden Hill was the several acres adjoining the back yard, the former vegetable garden wherein she had unwisely buried the family plate. While Pembroke dragged down the clods with grunting Achates, America laid off rows in anticipation of a "season," that period of blessed damp following heavy rains when earth and air remain sufficiently humid for tobacco seedlings to be drawn from the plant bed and set out into the wet field rows. In southeastern Virginia, since Jamestown, tobacco in hand has been tax money.

A third reason kept America on the hilltop. Her presence in the crowded cabin below apparently slowed her sister's recovery. Palestine's experience with Mudston appeared to have wiped her brain clean of all power to think and remember. Acquiescent as a young child, she moved about the stillhouse or sat in the warm sunshine outside, the lovely shell of her former wilful self. Only when she gazed at America, her empty mind was stirred with troubled memories. Whimpering, she had to be led away by Mrs. Moncure into the cabin where they slept, and soothed with gentle reassurances that she was in no danger, that they were safe in the familiar pineapple bed.

April passed in intermittent, windy flashes of sunshine and rain. Fence corners and thickets glowed with laurel and dogwood, were melodious with nesting birds. Across the bright blue sky, fleecy clouds raced like celestial lambs at play. Everywhere the abandoned countryside, with neglected fields in the foreground cut by busy little streams and the ever present fringe of dark forest on the rolling horizon, quickened with hope for another and better harvest. Life could get on, America discovered with some surprise, in cabin as in mansion. Straightening in the furrow to push her goober-vine hat back from her flushed face, she wondered if some day in a stifling Federal prison in Washington or from the scaffold on which Mrs. Surratt might also hang, she would not look back in agony and remember this sunny May morning in the tobacco patch, with the free wind cooling her forehead and the old black man, who would die for her, safe within sight? Clasp the happy moment to your heart, her soul whispered, for the times are in flux; and who knows when, if ever, joy may show her winsome face to you again?

Pembroke, a house servant, leaned on his hoe and sniffed elaborately. He was about to voice his olfactory diagnosis when America interposed:

"When do you think our tobacco plants will be ready, Pem? We don't want them to get spindly."

"Dey's yoder things 'round heah needs puttin' in de groun' wuss," snorted the butler, and squinted up at the sky where the buzzards swung with seraphic grace.

You wouldn't be so quick to sniff, America thought as she continued viciously chopping clods, if you knew what you smell and where it's buried. Under your own chimney stones! What did Pem suppose they had done with Mudston's body, while he was scurrying in safe irresponsibility down the hill with Palestine?

This train of thought carried America around again to the end of all her waking thoughts and troubled dreams: When the day of reckoning came, would she possess the strength of soul to refuse Ol' Uncle's gift of life? At best, he could only live a few years more. It was easy to imagine his pride, once the gallows trap had been sprung, and the gates of eternity had swung open to him. How joyously, yet with such deference, he would hasten into the celestial fields where Grandpa Ephraim and Father Radford, Brother William and Brother Tom awaited him! Soldiers all, they would bivouac in the open, around a campfire of stars, in some grove of asphodel beside the living waters of salvation. When they had made a place for him in their midst and were leaning forward with the light of loving expectation on their dear faces to hear the news from home, what lie could Ol' Uncle then tell to hide from them that she, their favorite young kinswoman, unlike them, had been afraid to die?

"You're certainly a picture, Miss Merry—standing there as if you'd swung a hoe all your life!"

The man's voice startled her into reality. She watched with distaste as he approached on foot around the icehouse hole. Having accustomed himself during twenty years of slave management to walk the fields, he led his glossy horse. She did not answer him until he was in the row beside her.

"What can I do for you, Mr. Cushman?"

"This is a bad business!"

"Sympathy would come better from you, sir, if you hadn't set your Damyankee friends on us."

"True, I've known Anthony Mudston all my life," the overseer chose his words carefully, as if unwilling to admit any involvement in this regrettable affair.

"So that's his name! Every army has its lice."

"Miss Merry, you wrong a zealous patriot and a rising politician. Among my new duties, I anticipate a very pleasant relationship with Mr. Mudston."

"What choice morsel have you raked out of our civic ashes for yourself, sir?"

"Haven't you heard the good news? I have been appointed the new postmaster of Charlotte Court House. Among my first acts was to sort out and deliver his mail to Mr. Mudston. It has been considerable, I can assure you, and is increasing. One day last week the young lieutenant of a cavalry outfit told me he'd left Mudston here the night before—to clear his own coat tails, no doubt, for Mudston has been missing for more than a week. Have you seen him, Miss Merry? Could foul play have befallen him here?"

"Foul play!" America repeated bitterly. Her eyes swept the ruined hilltop. "All around you is the evidence of foul play, Mr. Cushman. Now that you are a public servant," her accent on the word public was intentional, "I trust you will inform Mr. Stanton at Washington of this last outrage Mr. Mudston has perpetrated."

"How do you know it was his last? Is he dead?"

"It was the last outrage I saw him commit, sir. He had a squad of troops with him. Doubtless he rode north with them."

"Lookit those buzzards circling down. They'd light if we weren't here. Seems to me I smell something dead myself—over there," Cushman concluded, and turned towards the rubble of the house servants' quarters.

"De chimbly fell in on Spot an' her pups." Ol' Uncle spoke from behind America, although she had not seen his approach.

"What chimney, black man?"

"Dat front cabin chimbley, boss. You knows haow a houn'-dog is, she wouldn't leave 'em. An' hit doan' seem wuth heftin' dem big stones des' tuh bury her."

"I should say not! Not with all this work ahead!" agreed Cushman. He could not forget his former habit of never addressing a negro except in terms suggestive of the next duty urgently awaiting accomplishment. "Where're you living now, ma'am?"

"In the stillhouse down the hollow."

"Tut, that's no proper place for Miss Jincy! It's full of snakes and spiders, and she'll catch her death of cold. Years ago, when I first came to Charlotte County, your maw was the only person to speak to me as if I were a white man instead of a nigger. I was young then, sympathizing in my heart with the blacks, but with my head full of the notion all Virginians were fit to be President. It wasn't long, I tell you, before I found out niggers are born lazy and the Virginians—hump! There they were with libraries to make a man's mouth water, but they never opened a book! I found them opinionated to a man, and too hot-tempered to argue a question out reasonable. They ate too much, they drank too much, they sported with wenches. And all the time they were trying to pull the wool over their own and other people's eyes by sounding off in high-toned phrases how they were Quality, and everybody else was scum!"

He broke off, and spat. Having vented his long-accumulating spleen, he became his businesslike self again:

"Why don't you move your maw into town? I told my free-nigger Ajax, who's working for me at the post office for big wages now, a silver dollar every Saturday night"—Cushman interpolated for the ex-slaves' benefit—"I told Ajax I'd meet him here about mid-meridian. I sent him across the fields to see if he could find Mudston's horse. While I wait, I'll just locate that carrion—"

"You can't search Golden Hill without a warrant!"

Arrested by the note of alarm in the girl's voice, Cushman turned and gazed at her in mild surprise, before he started off, leading his horse briskly down the row towards the ruined slave quarters.

Hoe gripped in her hand, America ran after him. The earth was crumbly, the footing uneven. She stumbled, fell onto her outstretched palms and shouted at him from all fours, like a downed savage:

"Get off this hill, you Damyankee!"

The habit of a lifetime caused Cushman to close the garden gate, burned at the top hinge, after he had led his horse through it. America tugged in her turn, but the gate stuck. She was about to call out again, when she saw approaching around the parlor chimney, a weather-beaten Confederate soldier. He was perhaps thirty years old. Even in rags he was the handsomest man America had ever seen. He looked the way men in their secret hearts yearn to look, the way women imagine them. He appeared mature, yet young; experienced, yet without a trace of conceit. Eyes brown and secret dominated a high-bred, sensitive face. His dark hair and beard were uncut. He wore his scarecrow grey as if he were dressed to lead a cotillion, and the rags did little to conceal the power of his slender, campaign-toughened body. About him was the shine, the confidence of pure masculinity, as America had seen it in thoroughbred animals, but in no Confederate since Jeb Stuart and not since she herself had passed the gates of childhood.

"Who are you?" demanded Cushman.

"You wouldn't know if I told you," drawled the soldier,

with a gay wink at America. "And from what I overheard just now—no intention to eavesdrop, ma'am!—Miss Moncure doesn't care to know you further. Hadn't you better be going?"

"I'll be the judge of that," snapped Cushman. His annoyed glance lifted past the stranger's shoulder to something he saw beyond in the stable lane. "Good work, Ajax!" he called. "Where'd you locate him?"

"Daown by de swamp, boss."

They watched the negro approach with a limping, bridleless horse. A Union Army saddle and blankets were recognizable on his back.

"In a strange country, a cavalry horse returns to where he left his master," pronounced Cushman, and turned accusingly towards America. "I believe Mr. Mudston is still on this place, ma'am. You might as well tell me where you've hidden him, because I aim to find out."

As if she had not heard Cushman, America turned to the stranger and asked composedly:

"Who are you, sir? And how does it happen you know my name?"

"While you folks visit," interposed Cushman, "I'll just have a look around. Ajax, tie that horse and come give me a hand with those chimney stones."

"Don't you touch one of them, Mr. Cushman—or anything else in this yard!"

"Yank, that's a sharp hoe she's got. And as far as I'm concerned, General Johnston never surrendered," observed the Confederate. "What's been going on around here, anyway?"

"This man and his Damyankee friends burnt us out."

"Where's the family, now?"

"Why do you ask, sir?"

"I'm on my way West. My companion in arms used to live here and I stopped with him."

"Your— Where is he?"

"Sitting out front like the melancholy Jaques, mingling his tears with the rain water in yonder cracked fountain."

"Ephraim—Brother Ephraim!"

She picked up her muddy skirts, and started to run towards the front lawn. As if in response to her cry, a man appeared around the parlor foundations and came towards her. America stopped short, shocked that this gaunt and bearded giant could be the pink-faced youth who had run off four years ago to lie his resolute way into the First Army of Virginia. He spoke, and she ran forward again. Sinewy arms gripped her, held her to an iron chest. Beneath her ear a strong heart pounded as excitedly as her own. She looked up and saw above her Ephraim's unforgettable profile, inherited by one Collier in each generation since the first Ephraim had married a granddaughter of Pocahontas.

"Brother Ephraim!" she breathed, and let her taut body relax against this hard tower of strength.

"Merry, my dear! Let me look at you. Why, you're a grown woman now, and as pretty as ma, I do believe."

"Oh, Eph, we didn't dare to talk about your homecoming, for fear you'd never come! You're the only one left."

"I know. I got ma's Christmas letter. But tell me what's happened here. I thought at first I'd come to the wrong hill. Did Sherman's men do this?"

"Yes. They took our work mules—and our meat—and the silver two weeks after Appomattox. I'd hidden everything in the garden rows—"

"Didn't you realize that would be the first place they'd look?"

"I do, now! But I'll tell you the rest later, after you've made this Damyankee and his free nigger get off our hill."

Ephraim released her shoulders, and turned towards Ajax. His voice, tired with authority, deflated the black man's arrogance:

"Ajax, what was the last thing I told you, before I went to war?"

"Yassuh, boss, I's gwine!"

"Cushman, do I have to keep a pistol loaded for you, too? Sherman let us retain our sidearms, remember?"

"And Congress means to reprimand him for it! I'll go now, because I'm outnumbered; but mark my words, I'll be back with a squad of troops."

"And I'll blow every damn' one of you off this hill."

They watched Cushman mount his tall horse, and drop out of sight down the carriage road. After Ajax had followed, leading Mudston's lamed mount, America turned with a smile towards her brother:

"Aren't you going to present your friend, Brother Ephraim?"

"Sister Merry, this is your sixth cousin, Fant Annable, from Tuckahoe Ridge in Mason County, Kentucky."

They stood regarding each other with immediate attraction. The return of Ephraim, what lay under Pembroke's fallen chimney, ruined Golden Hill, Appomattox, her penniless present and even the hoped-for future shrank into triviality beside a new sensation which went tingling through her body and spread from the core of her being to the palms of her hands, to the high-arched insteps of her feet in leaky boots with newspaper wads against the soles.

" 'Scuse me, missy-ma'am," she heard Ol' Uncle at her elbow: "Woan' you tak Marse Eph an' dis gen'neman daown de hill naow, an' let Miz Jincy see de sun's done riz agin?"

By gay hints which brought a smile to Mrs. Moncure's lips and a sniff from Flora, Fant Annable angled an invitation to remain with his Virginia cousins until his letter requesting travel funds could penetrate the lifted blockade and be delivered into the hands of his wealthy, doting mother.

"I should think you'd walk home, if she loves you that much," Ephraim observed, inhospitably.

"The mistress at the Tuckahoe post office is as comic as a sheep," continued Fant, with a flash of white teeth at America. Immediately on arrival, he had appropriated one of Radford

Moncure's ivory-handled razors and daily wheedled Flora out of hot water and yucca root. To America, who could not remember when she had seen a man's chin, each shave made Fant appear delightfully boyish for one of his mature experiences. By a word dropped here and there he had built up the impression that he was used to good living, to leisure and travel, even to the danger that is sometimes welcomed as a counterirritant to boredom.

"What's her name?" America felt it only polite to carry on the conversation.

"Abigail MacGower. She's also the toll-mistress and neighborhood gossip. She's one of those raw-boned women who you know beats her youngsters with a pear switch as regularly as she washes behind their ears, and teaches them their catechism. She considers everyone who isn't a Scotch Presbyterian a heretic."

"What denominations are represented on Tuckahoe?"

"Campbellite—at Glade Springs church."

"You don't mean you're a follower of Alexander Campbell, that wolf in sheep's clothing?"

"Why, Arabia!"

"But ma, that's what Mr. Percy at Old Hundred called him."

"Lovie, do you mind if we don't discuss theology right now?" Fant addressed himself with mock anxiety to the earnest child. "When I was a little fellow, I got so stuffed with what Alexander Campbell was doing to the Baptist Fellowship I almost throw up every time I smell a hymn book, now. But let me say this for Glade Springs church! The two senior elders —Justinian Annable, my father, and Charles Moncure, your cousin down the pike—although they didn't see eye to eye about slavery, stood up there side by side every Sunday and held that community together through four years of war. 'We'll forget our daily differences at the Lord's Table,' they said. And they did."

"Very pretty sermon," jeered Ephraim.

"I just can't conceive a Moncure being an Abolitionist!" marveled America, and remembered afterwards that Fant's expression had changed.

America had heard all her life about her Kentucky cousins. Apparently there were two sets of them—Annables and Moncures. Before the war, Miss Jincy at Golden Hill had corresponded regularly with Cousin Margaret Collier Annable, at Timberlawn, on Tuckahoe Ridge. When this pleasant exchange of letters was ended in the gathering storm, America had assumed the blockade to have been the cause. Fant's remarks revealed why Father Radford Moncure had never cared to correspond with his distant relative, Charles Moncure, now known to be a Black Republican.

At supper that night Fant called in the mangy hound which had followed Ephraim from North Carolina, and set his Haviland plate on the floor before the half-starved animal, declaring with a wink at America:

"Have some bread and gravy, Sherman? I only do this, because it enrages Aunt Flora. Some day she's going to blow up like the Crater."

America was on the point of explaining that she and Flora were scraping the crib for themselves and the 'ninnies, not to mention stray mongrels. She saw just in time how easily Fant might misunderstand her words. She would rather bite off her tongue than make their Kentucky cousin feel he wasn't welcome to the little they had.

"I spoke to Cousin Homer Pettis in town today, ma," remarked Ephraim, watchful as an Indian in the shadow by the door. "He says he'll help me read law in his office on Court Street. I swapped several bags of Carolina bright-leaf for coffee at Mr. Trabue's. Gad, but prices are sky-high!"

"Is that what you've got in your pipe?" asked America, inhaling the smoke that floated back to them in blue streaks over Ephraim's shoulder. "Where did you get it?"

"Tell her, Fant."

"When the news came that General Lee was giving up at

Appomattox, we went through Durham Station on the double quick," chuckled the Kentuckian, as if the retreat of Johnston's ragged and starving Confederates was no more than so many boys playing run-sheep-run. "The town consisted of a railway depot, two stores and a tobacco factory where a retired farmer named Green chopped his favorite smokin' mixture. He squealed like a stuck pig when he saw us, but we filled our pockets and retreated on up the Hillsboro road. When Sherman's men came through the next day, they cleaned out our leavin's."

"Where did the—the surrender take place?"

"At the Bennett farmhouse about five miles beyond Durham. Sherman and Kilpatrick rode out with a flagbearer. General Johnston and Wade Hampton met them on the Hillsboro road. Sherman asked if General Johnston knew of any place handy where they could talk. Old Joe recalled the Bennett farmhouse he'd just passed a piece, and they went there. Ten days later, we threw down our rifles."

"What did they talk about all that time?" asked Arabia, raising solemn eyes from wiping baby Andorra's mouth.

"Sherman handed Ol' Joe his terms in ten minutes, but they were too generous. He had to revise them."

"Cousin Fant! Surely you don't expect us to believe that?"

"It's the Gospel truth, Cousin Jincy. When the Vindictives in Congress heard what they were, they made President Johnson come down on Sherman and stiffen 'em up. Sherman and Grant had gotten the same set of ideas from Mr. Lincoln, on one of his trips to the battlefield."

"Living in Kentucky has given you a false impression of Mr. Lincoln, Fant. He was the South's arch foe."

"He was her one remaining friend, Cousin Jincy. The South will have to go through dark days until they learn to let hard feelings die."

"Would you have us lick the hand that strikes us to our knees?"

"You'll never kneel to anyone, America Moncure. Not even

the Almighty. As far as I'm concerned"—Fant paused to tilt back in his Hepplewhite chair and stretch luxuriously—"all I want is peace and prosperity, with trade booming again and rich people traveling from place to place. May I sing you the first song I ever learned, Cousin Jincy?"

"If it's a proper one."

His eyes sardonic, his teeth ashine, he began to chant the two-part song, shouting the questions in a hearty wharfmaster's roar and replying through his cupped hands, as if the answers were being megaphoned by an officer on shipboard:

"Where are you from?
Redstone!

"What's your lading?
Millstones!

"What's your Captain's name?
Whitestone!

"Where are you bound?
Limestone!"

The childish song, or the troubadour who sang it, stirred memories in Palestine's sick brain. Since her illness, she had sat through family discussions as one who does not speak or comprehend the language used. The Moncures were surprised when she leaned toward Fant at the conclusion of his ditty and exclaimed with her rare smile:

"Well done, cousin! And all this time I thought you were a planter."

"Who—me, Teena? *Jamais de la vie!* I'm a river-boat man. When I turn farmer"—this with a swift glance at America, to make sure she was listening—"I'll ask you to marry me. And I couldn't wish a worse fate on a sweet young girl like you," he hastened to add, seeing distress come over Palestine's face like cloud shadows across a sunny hillside. The next moment, Palestine began to whimper:

"Ma, what's he saying? Don't make me marry him, ma! I don't want to marry anybody—I just want to stay here with you. Make him go away—I'm frightened."

Palestine stood in the middle of the cabin, wringing her hands and staring at Fant. While consternation gripped her listeners, she continued on a rising wave of hysteria which ended in screams:

"Go away, do you hear me? Go away—before Sister Merry kills us both!"

Mrs. Moncure arose. Grasping the stricken girl by the shoulders, she propelled her into the adjoining cabin. The others remained motionless, their backs to the closed cabin door, and listened. Within, the agonized wails subsided into a whimper which America found more embarrassing to endure. She felt Fant's gaze. Out of unshocked admiring eyes, he stared at her as if for the first time she really interested him.

"God, what a magpie I've been tonight! I've gabbled worse than Abigail MacGower!" Fant exclaimed. He arose casually. Snapping his fingers for Sherman to accompany him, he moved towards the doorway where Ephraim stood. When Fant did not glance back at America with the usual invitation in his eyes for her to step outside and flirt, America knew that he must have guessed her secret.

America lay wakeful the early part of that night. Thunder then clapped its hands in her ears. She awoke to see dawn in the loft, and to smell the rain. Dressing hurriedly, she let herself down the ladder and went to arouse Flora. Years ago, America had learned from her grandfather the secret of a good farm manager: Get in the lead of work to be done and the household must necessarily follow. On the way up the hill, she decided that even manslaughter must stand aside today for a tobacco season.

Three men, Arabia, baby Andorra and all the 'ninnies trailed her to the prepared ground. Since before breakfast, Ol' Uncle had been drawing plants. He had two tubfuls ready for them. America filled her apron, kicked off her shoes and stepped to the head of the first row, carefully laid out ten days ago in readiness for the life-giving rain. With a wooden peg, her right hand screwed a hole in the damp soil. Her left hand then dropped into it the crisp tobacco plant taken from her apron. She bent and with both hands pressed the muddy earth about roots and pale green stem. Rising, she took two steps along the row, bent and repeated the process with another plant. Step, stoop, make hole, drop and press the plant, rise; step, stoop, make hole, plant, rise—

By the time her first apronful of plants was used up, the muscles behind her knees, her back and her shoulders throbbed like a toothache. The constant changes in elevation kept the blood pounding against her eardrums. She knew if she stopped, her helpers would also stop. Even Ephraim's and Fant's campaign-hardened bodies tired, for the setting of tobacco calls into play muscles ordinarily little used. When the field was half planted, rain came to drench and refresh them. The 'ninnies' rags clung to their scrawny bodies, pot-bellied from malnutrition. The youngest ones retreated to the grape arbor in the orchard. Pembroke began to mutter aloud that work in the rain would bring on his rheumatism.

"Anyone who wants to stop can go down the hollow, and ask Flora to send dinner up in a pail," was America's only comment.

Seeing that she had no intention of stopping, the men worked on doggedly in the rows adjoining hers. The rain dissolved into a fine mist, the damp air gradually took on a luminous glow. She realized that the season would soon be over. When the sun burned through hot and bright, she would have to stop.

'Ninnies arrived with dinner. They stood about looking hopefully at her. America made no change in her rhythmic gait. Stoop, make hole, drop plant, press the earth around the tough green stem, rise; step, stoop, make hole, plant, rise—

Apron empty, hands clasped to the small of her back to

keep from crying out with the pain of straightening, she started to walk around the row end to the tubs for more plants. Ahead were only charred fence rails. She then observed that everyone had stopped work except herself. They awaited her beside the dinner cans.

"I'm too tired to cuss! Dammit, Merry, why couldn't you let us eat this rabbit grass while it was still hot?" scolded Ephraim, and forked more than his share of mustard greens onto his plate.

She did not answer. He glanced irritably in her direction, and saw on her clay-streaked face a look which shamed him. On the march he had seen men as grey with exhaustion as she was now, stepping along with that same far-away look in their eyes. She was still planting tobacco, he saw, with only her indomitable will to drive the dead muscles on. Many a time during retreat he had felt his own voice shout commands his ears were too weary to hear, his legs too tired to obey.

"Now I know what ma's niggers meant, when I used to hear 'em say at sundown they were too beat out to eat!" Fant complained cheerfully, and turned to offer America hog jowl and greens.

Thinking better of it, he heaped his own and her plate, then passed the can up to Pembroke who stood waiting to carry it over to where Ol' Uncle had sat his 'ninnies in a decorous circle. While he chewed tough corn bread and greens, Fant pretended not to notice that America was crying. He reached for the cup by the water jug, poured it almost full of juice from her plate and held it to her lips.

"Drink this. With good pot liquor inside you, you'll soon feel like a fighting cock again."

It was lukewarm and tasted like spring tonic. Over the cup, she smiled at him through tear-brimmed eyes.

Before thoughts of Fant began to push everything except the needs of her crop out of her mind, America had planned to bring Ol' Uncle up the hill some dark night, and with him lift the fallen chimney stones away and rebury Mudston's body in the swamp. Then Ol' Uncle slipped on a wet hillside rock, and lay helpless on a pallet near the cook hearth. Pembroke would, America realized, have the good butler's traditional distaste for soiling his hands. The June days were too long, the few moonless nights too short for America's puny strength to accomplish such a job alone. To start and not finish it might be fatal. Moreover, morning glories were covering the rubble. With Cushman probably spying on her day and night, was it wise at any time to disturb those concealing vines?

A new irresponsibility, a seeming blindness to her own danger, had taken possession of America. Instead of thinking of what she ought to do about Mudston, she found herself more acutely alive to nature's reawakening. Wide-eyed at dawn on her pallet beside Arabia and Andorra in the middle cabin loft, she listened to the voice of the stillhouse spring as it frolicked down its hillside steps. No longer it reminded her of slow tears dripping, dripping for Golden Hill and the Cause forever lost. As in childhood, she caught the flash of cardinals' wings among glossy rhododendron. She remembered the legend of dogwood as she studied the tracery of its branches too frail again to support a suffering Christ against the bright spring sky, or bent to touch the four crossed petals edged and centered with rusty red. A rabbit intent on its own business jumping along a path, pale sunlight slanting through young green leaves delighted her as before, yet with a new sadness, as if she too shared with every living thing this just discovered urge to expand, to bloom and to bear against the rush of old age and decay.

Caught in the magic of first love, America wondered why her family and Fant failed to see the extraordinary beauty of everything about them. That her tobacco seedlings should "show their ears," as Ol' Uncle described the two bud leaves that appeared on each plant above the red clay, seemed miraculous to her but natural to them. When Ephraim's chivalrous energy dissolved under the strengthening sun rays and he said he must read law with Cousin Homer Pettis in town, she was glad. His absence gave better opportunities for tête-à-têtes with Fant, when he returned from inquiring after his money order at Charlotte Court House.

"Your friend Cushman's getting too big for his breeches," Fant announced one afternoon and laid Grandpa Ephraim's squirreling-piece at the head of the row. "The Freedmen's Bureau opened its door and drew niggers like flies."

"Who's head of the Bureau?"

"Some Vindictive who rushed down from Washington after Mudston disappeared. His name's Matt Reid."

"He used to be the Bouldins' overseer."

"We bossed our own blacks on Tuckahoe. Now, we haven't ingrates like Cushman and Reid to turn against us."

"What's it like, Cousin Fant?"

"Tuckahoe? A long green ridge running southwest from the Ohio River—studded with red brick houses full of transplanted Virginians. The prettiest green ridge in the world, I think, and the richest! You'll like it, Miss Merry. And they'll like you."

He spoke as if some day she would see it with her own eyes. Glancing at him, she wondered if he had read her yearning, her secret hope that he might ask her to accompany him to Tuckahoe as his bride when his money order arrived. Only the press of immediate duties probably kept Cushman from returning to Golden Hill with a search warrant and, to enforce it, Yankee soldiers from the detachment quartered at near-by Lynchburg. Her best solution, America told herself as she drew fine dirt around a tobacco plant which had shot up like a 'teen-age boy, was for her to marry Fant. Provided she was safe with him in far-away Kentucky, what would it matter if Cushman eventually did sniff out old Sawbones? With her half across the continent, the negroes could and would convincingly disclaim all knowledge of how Mudston's body happened to be in Pembroke's cabin when the chimney fell. Out of the corner of her eye America saw the dog Sherman walking stiff-legged around the chimney stones. With Fant watching her, she dared not whistle the sniffing hound away.

"What're you expecting to see jump out of that rock pile?" demanded Fant. "Mudston's ghost?"

"Cousin Fant! I—I don't know what you're talking about."

"Oh, yes, you do! And besides, Cushman quizzed me in town this afternoon. Just as soon as he gets around to it, he means to make somebody produce his friend—or pay a plenty."

"You don't know anything!"

"True. But I've skated over thin ice too many times myself not to hear it crack under you."

"Then why don't you help me?"

"How can I, when you won't tell me what's worrying you?"

"I can't trust you—"

"That's complimentary! What about Eph, then? He's a born scrapper, if ever there was one."

She had long been considering the possibility of appealing to her brother for aid. To her, Eph still seemed the exasperating boy who had plagued her throughout childhood. Nearest in age and temperament, the two of them had always spatted. She told herself that it was hard now to realize that Eph was grown, that he was her only male protector left of the five Golden Hill men who had ridden away to war. Preferring Fant's help to Eph's, America decided that she could stand alone, on her own strength, until this rich handsome Kentuckian watching her with a quizzical expression in his chocolate brown eyes would see her need and snatch her out of Cushman's reach. She had already nursed her dark secret for weeks; surely she could carry it alone for a few more hours—or days?

"Eph talks, when he drinks," she evaded.

Trained in reading faces, Fant continued to look at her until he felt certain she had said all that she intended just now to tell him.

"Have it your own way—if you want to play your hand alone," he conceded. Turning towards the yard, he called back across his shoulder: "Hope you don't mind if I reshuffle those chimney stones?"

"Fant Annable, you come back here this minute!"

He continued on down the tobacco row. A long minute passed while America was admiring the free swing of his walk. Then she raced after him, and arrived at the cabin foundations to see him bend above where Sherman scratched with the energy of semistarvation.

"I'm your dark angel," Fant jeered in his sacrilegious habit of using Bible phrases to convey an opposite meaning. "I'm going to roll your stone away."

All she could do was stand there and watch. The reek of carrion pervaded the hilltop. Sherman dug and barked with increasing excitement. In spite of Fant's efforts to dislodge it, a heavy timber would not move. Sherman ran around to the other end of the charred beam, and began to scratch there. Fant followed and lifted away stones until the beam was partially exposed. Stooping, he gave an experimental lift, and Sherman wedged himself into the tunnellike aperture Fant had opened. Head and forepaws inside, Sherman arched his gaunt haunches, scratched, barked and scratched again. Apparently reaching his objective, he emitted a series of muffled staccato barks, then began to back out and pull, dragging his prize into Fant's nearer view. America heard Fant's shocked oath, then:

"Here, you brute, come out of there!"

Stooping, he seized Sherman by a hind leg and yanked him clear so forcibly that the hound fell into a yelping heap behind him. Fant shoved the beam into place again.

America fled towards the tobacco patch. She was chopping weeds in great agitation when she saw Fant approach down the row. When she could trust her voice to speak, she demanded:

"Haven't you any questions to ask?"

"Why didn't you bury him decently?"

"With neighbors and perhaps more soldiers due to arrive any minute? We dragged his body into Pembroke's cabin. It was on fire, and we thought the burning logs would consume him. Log houses usually burn for days. Instead, the chimney fell in. Then the wind must have changed, because the logs were only charred. Before I could think what to do next, Mr. Cushman came that same morning you did, remember? We don't dare touch anything now, for fear he might notice—"

"Who's 'we'?"

"Ol' Uncle and myself. Pembroke and Flora know, too."

"Now I understand what's the matter with your sister."

"He didn't hurt her, Fant Annable! I got there first."

"I can well believe that."

She ventured a sidelong glance at him. He was studying her with that peculiar expression she had observed on the night of Palestine's outburst, an expression half of appraisal, half frank admiration. As she gazed at him, his eyes seemed to spill over with warm amber light. Again she felt a pulse stir deep within her, as if it only awaited some move of his to overwhelm her.

"Dammit if you aren't my kind, after all!"

She saw his feet moving towards her, felt the grip of his hands on her shoulders. The hoe fell from her nerveless fingers.

"Merry, will you come away with me? With your spunk and high-toned ways—and my experience—we could make a killing everywhere we went. Will you come?"

"To Tuckahoe?"

"Hell, no! To Cincinnati and Natchez, to New Orleans and St. Augustine. Maybe even to San Francisco."

"I—I'd rather go to Tuckahoe."

"Maybe you would. I wouldn't."

"What did you mean when you mentioned something about our making a killing?"

"Don't worry, I shan't ask you to chop any more men's heads off! That sorrel top of yours, and the way you carry yourself, will attract them easy enough. You're smart. You'll learn fast."

"I'm not familiar with anything except running a planta

tion. Is it—is it your idea to be married here or at Timberlawn?"

"Who said anything about marriage? I'm talking business."

Here it was, the first dishonorable proposal that had ever come to her. To go away with him sounded the most natural thing in the world, and certainly the pleasantest. To hear him suggest it, Fant might have been asking that she accompany him to a clambake at the Oglethorpes' or in to town to call on Cousin Tan. Cavalier struggling against Calvinist within her, she tilted her head back to see his face, laughed as the delicious vista opened before her imagination, and then answered soberly:

"Fant, you know I can't travel with you except as your wife. Nice people wouldn't receive us."

"Tuckahoe's nice. And deadly dull. Who wants that?"

"I do."

"Beggars can't always be choosers," he warned, his golden pupils narrowing.

"What do you mean by that?"

"Nothing much," he answered carelessly, as if the whole business were not worth further talk, much less a loss of temper. "I just thought I'd offer you a chance to get away from old Sawbones. And Cushman. If you want to take it. You don't have to make up your mind, now."

Her face flamed. She had really thought he was joking. Who did he think she was, to come running like pore white trash the first moment he crooked his finger at her? There he stood in her tobacco row with that maddening expression of extreme masculine confidence on his handsome face, like the villain in a paper-backed novel astride a rose-back chair, with his fine eyes seemingly indifferent and his lips curved into just enough of a smile to show the crow's-feet of dissipation around the corners of his mouth. She'd like to slap him, she thought, her own temper blazing, she'd like to scratch that hateful expression off his mocking face. She made a sudden move towards him, then remembered just in time who she was.

"Of course you're joking," she answered coldly, feeling as she unclenched her fists where her neglected fingernails had cut into calloused palms. "There for a moment you frightened me. I actually thought you were speaking seriously."

"I never was more serious in my life!" He stooped for his gun. "Come on, Sherman. I'll pot you a rabbit for supper, since we won't let you have your Yankee."

She did not believe him until he began studiously to avoid her. He stopped coming to the tobacco patch of late afternoons. In the stillhouse he appeared to enjoy Palestine's company more than hers. Rising gallantly to offer her his chair, he would disappear for the night. America hardly thought of Cushman, so great had become this new anxiety of the heart, this aching premonition of impending loss. As she hung up her hoe in the woodshed one sunset, she heard Flora's voice and unconsciously stood to listen:

"I's obleeged tuh you foah wantin' tuh remembah me befoah you go, but I ain't got no use foah money naow'days."

"I don't see how you figure that," came Fant's amused reply.

"Libin' in a cabin lak dissa one, I ain't compelled tuh put on style lak we was back in de Big House."

"All right, auntie. If you won't take my money, you won't. We've your kind out in Kentucky, too."

"Den dat's de place foah dem—an' you."

In his new store clothes purchased that afternoon in Charlotte Court House, Fant had lost his familiar, returned-soldier look. He appeared a stranger to America, to them all. As she sat quietly with supper untouched before her, her mind told her pounding heart that she could have nothing further to say to a man who had asked America Collier Moncure to be his traveling companion, not his wife.

In Mrs. Moncure's pocket lay the generous roll of greenbacks—hated but sound Yankee currency—which Fant had tucked there in payment for the poor fare and uncomfortable lodging without which, he declared volubly, he might have starved to death while awaiting the arrival of his money order. Mrs. Moncure was raking her memory for one more cousin to be remembered to on Tuckahoe, when Fant declared reluctantly:

"I think I'd best be starting, now."

"Not tonight?" exclaimed America, caught off her guard.

"While the walking's cool. No, you mustn't any of you say good-bye. Don't you know it's bad luck to say good-bye?"

He had no baggage. Everyone except America arose and trooped to the door with him. She continued to sit motionless in her carved chair. Fant, first to surrender, suggested smoothly:

"Would you care to walk up the hill with me, Miss Merry? You and Eph?"

Her victory would be meaningless, America realized as she stepped up the path, unless he unlocked the silence which divided them. They reached the ruins of Golden Hill, silvery as the Parthenon under the high June moon. Ephraim melted Indianlike into the shadows. Below the garden, a mockingbird awoke and experimented on a single hushed note.

"You needn't be afraid of old Sawbones any longer," Fant announced, without preamble.

She stood and gazed at him.

"There's one Yank that Cushman will never locate, if he goes over this hill with a fine-tooth comb!" Fant was continuing. "Pembroke and I put him away for good. It wasn't a bad job for anyone used to burial-squad duty. We decided we wouldn't tell you where we buried him. It's better for you not to know."

She accepted this evident fact in silence. Some day, when this aching numbness left her, she would probably rejoice to know that she was free again from the long vigils in the blazing tobacco patch, from Anthony Mudston and Clarence Cushman, from the ordeal of court trial and the specter of Mrs. Surratt's gallows. Now, America could only consider her new life sentence, feel the guillotine of Fant's departure hanging above her.

"Aren't you going to thank me, sorrel top?"

"Some day I'll thank you, Fant Annable. Not tonight."

"Aren't you going to kiss me good-bye?"

"You don't want my kisses."

"My dear, you'll get along farther in this world if you'll let your lovers decide that."

Was he trying intentionally to provoke her into a quarrel? If she could hold herself above hot words with Flora and Palestine, certainly she could remain the lady with one so dear as Fant.

"Well, I must mosey along. When you get tired of being Princess Prim of Poverty Hill, come on out to Kentucky and I'll show you how to live."

Smiling at him, she answered in a brittle voice she hardly recognized as her own:

"Thank you. I'm sure I should enjoy seeing Kentucky. Some day I intend to go to New Orleans, too. And New York—and abroad. But not as a fly-by-night with you, Fant Annable!"

"As I said before, beggars can't be choosers."

"You may have found me barefooted in the tobacco patch, but I'll have you know I'm no beggar!"

"Must you take everything I say to yourself, my dear?"

"The only serious thing you've said to me, Fant Annable, was an insult. You know I'm in danger, because you would pry into my affairs. I—I killed a Yankee beast to save my sister. But that'll never make me a murderess in my own eyes—though it might in some people's—like Cushman's and a Yankee drumhead court-martial. But you can't have any real sympathy for me—or love," she made herself face the situation squarely, "to offer me escape under conditions I can't accept. And yet you've removed the evidence which might have sent me to the gallows. Why do you act like this, Fant? Are you merely kindhearted, or do you really care for me? Or are you just perverse?"

She realized, when he looked away without meeting her pleading eyes, that he was going to evade giving her a direct answer. What had been his background and his upbringing, that he so habitually refused to meet an issue face to face? Why can't you be honest with me, my dearest love, her heart was crying in protest against being left behind; what is it that really separates us? Twice you've referred to beggars. Even if you weren't the heir of rich Timberlawn, how rich you are in this world's goods compared to America Collier Moncure, now! And what do goods matter, when we both have youth and brains and the West before us?

"You're like all the rest of the women I've known," Fant complained, still refusing to meet her eyes. "You think the world's your private peach orchard, with money growing on trees for you to reach up and pluck. I know better. I know what it takes to buy good clothes—and steamboat fare—and to stake me in my business."

"What is your business, Fant? Tell me, for I know I can help you!"

"Isn't that what I asked you to do? Instead of coming along with me—for better or for worse—and helping earn your way as we go, you've climbed on a high moral horse, and acted as if you're the Queen of Sheba, instead of a penniless country girl with a murder warrant hanging over your head. Just because you've gotten by so far, doesn't mean you should crowd your luck."

"If I should come along with you, 'for better or for worse,'" America whispered, her face averted, "will you promise to marry me when we've earned our way?"

"I tell you, I'm not the marrying kind."

"And I tell you," she answered him with her indomitable spirit shining through her misery-dark eyes, "no one—not even the man I love—is ever going to drag me down from the ideal I've set for myself. Or from the high place I intend to win—in the proper world where I belong."

"For Christ's sake, stop talking as if you're still Miss America Moncure of Golden Hill!" his anger flashed at her. "Before the war, you Virginians could get away with acting like that, because you had niggers a plenty to wait on you. Now, you're like the rest of us pore white trash. You've got to go to work, if you want to keep on eating. What have you left but your grit, your brains and your good looks? Forget who you used to be, and come on out West where these three things count—and the pickings are easy. Before you could say Jack Robinson, we'd be rich!"

"And every decent door would be closed against me. No, I thank you."

"Merry, Merry," he cried, taking her by the shoulders and shaking her lightly, as if she were the Mary of the nursery rhyme. "Are you a prig—or still a child? Stop this ancestor worship, listen to me while there's still time. You can go anywhere—do anything—because you've got everything to go on. And don't you ever forget another Gospel truth: All doors open to those who knock with money enough in their hands."

"I—I couldn't face my own lost self-respect."

"When has self-respect buttered any turnips?" he turned off her dead seriousness lightly, and slipped his arms around her. "And, now, while you put what I've just said in your pipe and smoke it, I'm going to give you something else you'll never forget—something that'll make you mine as long as we both live—something that'll bring you after me to the ends of the world—for more. Because we two were meant for each other."

Before she could push him away, or call out to Ephraim, his lips were against hers. Thought and sensation surged to the union of their first kiss. Releasing her he shouted a ribald farewell to Ephraim and dropped out of sight into the well of the carriage road.

"That ought to teach you," observed Ephraim, emerging from the shadows, "that you can't play with tar without it sticking to your fingers."

The mockingbirds, she noticed in a vacuum of despair, had located each other. From hilltop to hollow and back again, they were singing follow-the-leader.

Chapter 3

Sunshine, wind and toil during midsummer weathered the bright edge of America's despair. Self-centered in spiritual turmoil, she took no count of what her tobacco crop might be costing. It became a welcome routine to engross her morning energies, to keep her plodding through the blazing noons, to send her too exhausted to think to her pallet every night.

Tobacco, after the plants have twice been hoed, becomes a finger crop. Before the July dews dried, America was stepping from plant to plant to snap off the terminal cluster of ivory blossoms wherever one broke like foam above a sea of waving green. Each discarded flower stalk wilting in the row reminded her of her own broken hopes. The sturdy weed then put out suckers at each leaf node and America twisted these off with fingers made nimble by practice on harp and piano. When dew mixed with tobacco gum soaked through her faded calico, and the midmorning sun dried it on her sensitive skin, the smart it caused went almost unnoticed compared to the remembered burn of Fant's mockery.

Topped and suckered, the plant poured its vital sap into the sixteen or eighteen leaves left on its stalk. Through August, these spread and thickened with nicotine cells which were capable also of absorbing the sweetening agents then in popular demand for chewing plug. America reflected deeply whether, by a similar excision of her love's tender growth, her own spirit might not thereby develop the tougher fibers of endurance, yield a sweeter sap of compassion for the household whom she had impoverished, whose present hardships she must alleviate.

By September, the tobacco was shoulder high to America. As she moved down the rows, her peanut-straw hat appeared to float unsupported on a choppy sea of leaves.

A distasteful phase was the constant search for worms. As the afternoon shadows lengthened, these hungry green pests, ranging from one-half inch to four inches in length, emerged from under the clods where they had found shelter from the noonday sun, crawled up the tobacco stalks and feasted all night on the dew-drenched leaves. In twenty-four hours a single worm often reduced a plant to a skeleton of lacy veins and stems. Even had she possessed money to purchase an insecticide, America would not have used it. On the Richmond tobacco breaks, buyers were quick to smell the poison on cured leaf, and scaled down their bids. Nothing remained but to go over the patch, tediously turning each broad leaf to locate any worm which might be clinging to its underside. America soon learned to swallow her squeamishness as she grasped the evil-looking head between thumb and forefinger, twisted it sideways, and flirted it away with green juice squirting and the bright cylindrical body curled over backwards. Ol' Uncle declared that it would take Virginia growers a good ten years to destroy the generations of tobacco worms hatched out and allowed to multiply undisturbed on the few neglected crops which had been grown during four years of civil war.

The blazing noons shortened, the September nights grew cool for sleep. Blue haze and long autumnal silences hung on the motionless air. Against the sky line, the woodlands were afire, and the crimsoned Virginia creeper ran like flame across the forest floor.

When her tobacco was yellow, America and Pembroke cut and sledded it down the hill to a barn below the stillhouse, the only tobacco barn left standing on three thousand acres of Collier land. The crop could hang there, she realized, only until it was cured. After that, if this sole asset was to be saved, it must be moved beyond reach of the pilfering hands of freed negroes who with the first cool nights came straggling back to the only hearth fires they had known.

Cook cabin and shed of the stillhouse overflowed. Queen Esther, Ol' Uncle's flighty granddaughter, brought home her five months' twins and abandoned them on Aunt Flora's knees. The sickly infants' incessant crying aggravated Mrs. Moncure's migraine.

Timber, sole freedman from Golden Hill to volunteer for the Union Army, returned from Georgetown. He made himself handy nursing Ol' Uncle until he was firmly established in the woodshed, then refused to work. The sight of him, arrogant in his tight blue Yankee coat, infuriated America. Twice she came around the corner of the stillhouse to find him stretched out as no slave would dare lie, his agate eyes watching the play of sunlight and shadow across Palestine's cameo face as the sick girl took the afternoon air on the bench outside the middle cabin door. The sting of America's tongue seemed rebuke enough the first time; at the second offense, she routed him like a rustic fury with her hoe handle. She had seen enough, however, to constrict her heart with dread.

She went no more alone to the tobacco patch. Taking Arabia ostensibly to pick up the turnips she dug between the rows, she found Timber gleaning tobacco flyings for his corncob. With the mild curiosity of an ox, he watched as America's blade turned out an appetizing root. Picking it up, he dusted its opal cheeks against his palm, ate it and helped himself to another.

"Timber, you can't eat my turnips unless you dig them."

He took the hoe America extended, and started to work with a chuckle:

"Seems kinda lak ol' times tuh be swingin' a hoe. Mistuh Reid, he say us cullud folks gwine git tuh vote. Den we-uns kin put you white folks tuh wuk foah us in de fiel'. Turn abaout's fair play, says Mistuh Reid."

"Give me back that hoe, Timber. You're cutting my turnips."

Between her and the huge black man, between her class and the changing order out of which the Yankees boasted they could raise a better South, lay only the thin shield of habitual command and obedience. "Funny abaout Spot an' her pups," Timber continued, gazing at the rubble of Pembroke's cabin. "Mistuh Cushman done offah me a silvah dollah tuh meet him up hyah at moonrise, an' lif' them stones offa her."

"Did you?"

"Yassum. But we didn't fin' Spot, er her pups. Nary a teensy-weensy lil bone. All dat was lef' was a little stink."

America stopped picking up turnips. If she were never to hear from Fant Annable again, she would always be in his debt for present security, if not for her life.

"Mistuh Cushman, he say each ob us darkies gwine git fohty acres an' a mule come Christmas. I chooses mah fohty acres right hyah," and his mighty arm in its tight sleeve encircled the top of Golden Hill.

"Sister Merry, how can you stand there and listen while Timber says such things?" demanded Arabia, almost dancing with rage.

"If every slave is to receive the forty acres he wants," America commented, thoughtfully, "you'll have to get your claim in early, Timber. Perhaps it might be a good idea for you to stay in town? Mr. Reid is more likely to hurry your claim along, if he sees you every day."

"Yassum. You's right abaout dat, Miz Merry. I'd bettah be gittin."

They watched him go loping off the hill. His coat pockets, filled with turnips, swayed to the gait of the born field slave, his bare heels kicked up puffs of dust as his weight settled momentarily on them. Her eyes round with wonder, Arabia turned to exclaim:

"America Moncure, I'm surprised at you!"

"You listen to me, missy. And don't you ever forget what I'm going to tell you"—America's voice was sharp with alarm.

—"Treat Timber and every other free nigger exactly the same as you did when he was a slave. Never raise your voice to him. Never let him make you angry. Do you understand? Otherwise, he'll think he's your equal."

"Even when he says outrageous things?"

"Pretend you didn't hear him. Now, help me get these turnips dug. The first thing tomorrow morning, I'm going to town and locate us a place to live."

One glance at his sister during breakfast convinced Ephraim that he had best escort her without argument to Charlotte Court House, even if it was market day. America insisted that Palestine accompany them. Pretending not to see the wives of tenantry who passed in wagons and on horseback, the Moncure girls stepped along the frost-laced ruts. Ephraim set them an infantryman's stride.

In the pike field of the Crenshaw plantation, several negroes were grubbing pine and oak scrub. Archie Crenshaw, who with Ephraim had run off to war in '61, had hitched his battle mare and an old white mule to a farm sled, and with them was hauling brush. Fretted by the unaccustomed work collar, the mare lunged and toppled over the insecure load. Crenshaw was preparing to reload the sled when he saw the Moncures approaching. To America's surprise, Archie ran to the nearest tree and hid behind its trunk.

"Can't say as I blame him," chuckled Ephraim. "I'd hate to have my sweetheart catch me at work in the field."

America checked an impulse to retort that the spectacle of a sister sweating in the tobacco patch all summer had left Ephraim unmoved. Tossing her head, she declared:

"He's not my sweetheart. And he never will be, if he's as puffed with false pride as that!"

"False or true, he would make you twice the husband Fant Annable would. Did that four-flusher tell you how we met? I caught up with him headed the wrong way at the battle of

Fort Stedman. 'What you running for, soldier?' I yelled, and started after him with my saber. 'Because I cayain't fly!' he shouted back. I had to ride him down to make him turn."

"Are you trying to imply he was a coward?"

"How does it sound to you? He's a drifter, to boot."

"Sister Merry, if you and Brother Ephraim keep on quarreling, I propose to march straight home," complained Palestine, and stood a charming picture of righteous protest in the road. "You know quarreling makes my head ache. I do believe I feel one coming on, now—"

"It's ma who has the headaches, Teena," America was compelled to abandon the field to Ephraim. "Don't you want to spend the day with Cousin Tan Carr? Maybe she'll let you look through her clothes press."

Ephraim left them at the locked butterfly gate of the Carr mansion, set in high-walled gardens opposite the courthouse. Pompey, shrugging into a mussed white coat, answered the tinkle of the ancient gate bell, and ran ahead of the young ladies to announce their arrival. Like a bedraggled hen, Cousin Tanis sat hunched over a smoking green-wood fire. Without waiting to greet her callers, the old woman demanded to know why countryfolk didn't keep their niggers where they belonged.

"If you'd stop feeding them, they'd have to come home and work," was America's unsympathetic rejoinder.

"Whenever I complain about the back kitchen being full, Pompey threatens to leave."

"I'd send him packing!"

"Then what's to keep this black rabble of Cushman's from stealing every teaspoon I own?"

"Cousin Tan, it might be a protection to you to have ma come in and spend the winter here."

"And fill the house with hotsy-totsy young ladies for Pompey to wait on?"

"Pembroke waited on you during the summers you spent at Golden Hill."

"You chit, how dare you speak to me like that? Palestine,

stop that sniveling, and tell me what's this I hear about you losing your wits?"

America arose with dignity.

"When you go downstreet, don't you dare pass under that filthy rag Cushman's had the impudence to hang above the post-office door!" fumed Cousin Tan, clicking her ill-fitting false teeth and glaring at her visitors. "How does he expect a Virginia lady to get her mail?"

At Palestine's elbow America walked upstreet past the clerk's office. Across the road was the courthouse, built from plans approved by the aging Thomas Jefferson. Here where Patrick Henry had debated with John Randolph the right of a sovereign state to oppose oppressive federal laws, America had imagined herself brought to trial for Mudston's life. Condemned murderers, she knew, were hanged in the jail yard behind the ancient courthouse oaks. Today, under the largest a group of idlers had gathered around some object of interest which their shabby backs concealed. Two gaunt horses cropped the shade-thinned courthouse grass. Near by lay pack harness and bags. On a tree limb rode a dilapidated saddle.

Downstreet, the market bell began to toll, calling buyers, sellers and the curious to trade. The crowd drifted away from the oak, to reveal a youth sitting cross-legged like a Turk on a cowhide under its low-hanging branches. On the cowhide were little mounds of finely chopped coin-gold tobacco. From each mound, with a short stick, the youth pushed different amounts of leaf into a pile growing between his flexed knees. Neatly arranged beyond one elbow were a dozen empty, home-sewn cotton bags. Beyond the other elbow were as many sacks, plumply stuffed.

His formula completed, the youth glanced up. In an era when fourteen-year-old boys went to war, America judged the lad to have reached perhaps eighteen. His face was long, with high cheekbones, an energetic nose and large ears thrust forward like blinders on a buggy bridle. Below a domed forehead, earnest hazel eyes were set wide apart. America had once asked her father why these Carolina mountain youths who occasionally drifted down to Charlotte Court House on market day wore the look of circuit riders. Smiling, Radford Moncure had replied that it was not piety or consecration which she had observed on their awed downy faces, but rather sheer wonder at this easier softer life of Charlotte County, theirs for the taking if they but knew it, after the rigors of mountain existence.

"I—I see you're mixing smoking tobacco," began America, annoyed to find herself at a loss for words before the interrogation of those clear eyes. "It occurs to me you might like to buy my leaf."

"How much you got, miss?"

"Three thousand pounds, perhaps. And it's good!"

"Is hit stripped? We couldn't use hit effen hit ain't stripped, and in sweet case."

"It's this year's crop. I raised it myself," America added, suddenly conscious that Palestine was waiting for her on the flagstones and that she was wasting good time in idle talk. "What kind is that you're using?"

"Car'liny bright-leaf, the best that grows 'round Durham Station."

"That's where my brother was mustered out—"

"Then he musta been with Johnston's Army."

"Were you in the Confederate Army? Did you see Sherman?"

"There's plenty good folks in No'th Car'liny didn't hold for Secession."

"Sister Merry!"

"Is she your sister?" asked the youth, gazing across the courthouse grass with the blank expression all males wore the first time they saw Palestine.

"Yes," America answered, unwilling to close the conversation before she had learned all she could about this novel way of marketing tobacco. Besides, Brother Ephraim might relish a few pipefuls of Carolina-bright more than coffee. "How much do you ask for your leaf?"

"A dime, ma'am."

He handed the sack up to her. Turning the tag over, she translated, then looked down at him with twinkling eyes:

"E Pluribus Optimum—best from many. Are you a Latin scholar?"

"Hell-damn, no! I took the first two words off a silver dollar I saw. A preacher thunk me up the rest. We wanted somepin easy, that folks ud know."

"What gave you the idea to fix up tobacco like this and peddle it?"

"Bruce Lord and his boys, Dan an' Jim. The Lords live not more'n a stone's throw from the family which adopted me. When Bruce came home from the war, he found a bulk of old leaf under fodder the Yankees missed. He and the boys chopped hit up, sweetened hit with sugar-tree sap and started peddlin'. Ever' grower in Durham County thinks his own smokin' mixture is the best. When he hear't how well the Lords was doin', Ol' Man Bledsoe said I better start aout for us."

"I wish I could think up something as clever, to make me some money for taxes."

He gazed at her. She realized that he was studying her critically, yet his eyes were too impersonal for her to take offense.

"We come through Lexington a while back," he volunteered at length. "Hit fair swarmed with broken-down gentry bringin' in their boys to Washington College. Iffen General Lee don't do nothin' else there, he's proved Virginians will always find money to edgicate their young uns."

"Do you think I could start a school here—a subscription school? I was graduated with high honors from Danville Female Seminary."

"When you figgered aout our tag so quick, I knowed right then you could be a schoolmarm. Ol' Man Bledsoe's al'ays at me to git more l'arnin. I told him hit might come in handy for preachers an' lawyers. Tradin's my pride!"

"But isn't money mighty scarce, now?"

"Times 'll git better. They al'ays have, ain't they? The West ain't a-goin' to stand still jest because we've had a war. An' when purses begin to fill agin, do you know who's goin' to profit the most? The trader who's looked ahead an' seen what the public wants an' who's got hit ready an' waitin' to hand!"

"Like your tobacco?"

"Yes, ma'am, like my terbacker. Or somepin else as takin' effen they don't fancy hit."

"Sister Merry, have you taken leave of your wits?" called Palestine, in a shrill voice of impatience. Pretty as a Watteau shepherdess, with her lovely face as empty, she gathered her skirts and came across the wet courtyard grass. "What do you mean, making a spectacle of yourself talking to poor white trash—to a peddler boy?"

"Teena, don't be silly!"

"I may be pore white trash to you an' her," declared the peddler, drawing his chin in so that his eyes, bright as a fox's under his domed forehead, burned up at Palestine. "But whar I come from, womenfolks has got somepin better to do than runnin' to town like hussies on market day, an' buttin' into talk before their opinion's sought."

"Did you hear what he called me, Sister Merry? Upon my word, I've never been so insulted in my life! Go summon Brother Ephraim to lesson this beggar."

"Go summon him yourself. He's at Cousin Homer's office," America shot a random bolt and was relieved to see Palestine turn away across the courthouse lawn.

It would never do to let her pass the Freedmen's Bureau in her present hoity-toity mood, America realized, but she wanted to talk further with this extraordinary youth. At once his quick intelligence had seen her own best capacities and had pointed out a profitable use she might make of them. A feeling of deep attraction to this peddler boy swept over her. Was it because they both dared face the future instead of the past? She wished he would remain in Charlotte County, so that she might know him better.

"What's your name?" she demanded.

"Tugger Blake."

"Tugger?"

"Zachary Taylor Blake's my real name. When I was a tad and wanted somepin, they say I kept on a-tuggin' till I got hit."

"Why don't you come out and see my brother sometime?" America continued pleasantly. "His name is Ephraim Moncure and we live in the log house below Golden Hill. The Yankees burned us out, but anyone will tell you where Golden Hill stood."

"I won't be comin' thisaway agin before spring," Tugger side-stepped the invitation. His face was hot with the anger Palestine's rudeness had whipped up, but he struggled to meet America's courtesy halfway: "If I meet up in travel with anybody wants some real good leaf, I'll send 'em to you."

"Thank you, Tugger Blake. When you come to see us in the spring, I'll be teaching subscription school."

"You'll git on well with hit, I'm sure, ma'am," the mountaineer answered her, and again bent over his piles of bright leaf.

With an elation she had not experienced since Fant's departure, America overtook Palestine and piloted her down Court Street. The two bright new flags hanging from the second-story windows of the post office and of the Freedmen's Bureau seemed an unbearable affront after four years' allegiance to the Stars and Bars. Old before the Revolution, the small brick building wherein a Pettis had practiced law since colonial days squatted on the stone sidewalk as if ashamed to be seen in such proximity to the Yankee flags. Cousin Homer, dragging the foot which had been sabered in the Mexican War, rushed to usher them into his private rear room.

"It's a pleasure to see you, girls! America, I trust Cousin Jincy realizes I would have been out long since to commiserate with her, had I a way to get there? With my affliction, walking is impossible. Mr. Cushman has offered to drive me out behind that spanking pair he bought in Philadelphia, but I realize a sheep-killing dog would be more welcome."

"Do you know any new riddles, Cousin Homer?" asked Palestine.

"Here is one that's been plaguing me. When Judge French handed it down, he said it's seldom solved. Rearrange these six letters to form the name of an article in common use."

"C-A-R-U-S-E," Palestine spelled off the slip of paper Cousin Homer handed her. Her smooth forehead clouded with thought, then cleared as she exclaimed gleefully, like a child: "I've solved it! How about you, Sister Merry?"

"Teena, you couldn't have, so quickly. Cousin Homer declares this is a puzzler."

"We have them every morning for breakfast," yawned Palestine. "While you slow-pokes put your heads together. I'm going upstairs and catch forty winks."

When Cousin Homer returned from making Palestine comfortable, he exclaimed admiringly:

"Gad, but she's quick! On the way upstairs, she told me the answer. And it's correct. This riddle, as nothing else could, has refuted the idle gossip I've been hearing about your sister, America. This is a profound relief to me, because—because some day I hope to make her my bride."

"Cousin Homer!" gasped America, and swallowed her surprise. How could she tell this middle-aged gallant that in all probability Palestine could never be any man's bride?

"I perceive by your expression that you consider me a poor life companion for one so richly endowed with beauty, wit and charm," Cousin Homer was continuing, mournfully. "True, I haven't had a paying client in three years. But I have struggled with the problem of my pecuniary deficiencies, America, I have struggled! And to ameliorate my penniless condition I have established new connections in a legal field where my efforts will, I feel confident, bear a rich harvest. In Missouri, to be exact. With new land opening up out West, there should be an abundance of remunerative title cases, in which branch of the law I am highly proficient, if I do say so myself."

"Cousin Homer, you don't mean you've really decided to go?"

"Of course I've decided! I'd go tomorrow if I didn't have these chambers on my hands. Living upstairs as I do, I hesitate to abandon the Pettis heirlooms."

"Cousin Homer, will you let us move in for the winter and take care of your things?"

"Merry, whatever could you do in town?"

"Open a subscription day school, sir. Virginians will deny themselves even bread to provide proper education for their children. Consider the enrollment at Washington College, over at Lexington."

"General Lee is the magnet there."

"The Collier–Moncure prestige will have a similar effect here."

"I do believe you've hit on an idea, America."

"May I bring in my tobacco crop and strip it here? Town niggers should be cheap and plentiful. If I leave it at Golden Hill, it will be stolen overnight."

He regarded her with respect, as he might have looked at an able colleague.

"Permit me to interpolate, America, that I share the admiration of all Charlotte County for the way in which you have risen to meet misfortune. With statesmanlike foresight and no sacrifice of your true womanliness, you have taken the reins of family management into your small but competent hands—more competent than your brother's, I'm compelled to admit. Ephraim will never make a lawyer."

"Fighting is the only thing he knows, Cousin Homer. He was defending the Confederacy with his life, when other boys were learning their sums."

She arose to summon Palestine. All summer she had nourished her hope on the faint possibility that Fant had written, but that Ephraim, recognizing the postmark, had destroyed the letter without mentioning it.

"Would you be kind enough to inquire for me at the post office, sir? That odious flag—"

"If you will deliver this letter to your sister," he bargained, producing it from his desk drawer. "As for the flag, since I bled for it in Mexico, I am not so opposed to walking under it as you ladies!"

While she waited, she looked about this musty apartment which in a few days would be hers. Clearer than the ancient paper ruffling the corners at ceiling and walls, more penetrating than the smell of law books, sealing wax and dead pipe smoke, she perceived life's sharp reversals. This time yesterday, she had been a frightened girl struggling in the field to defend her own from the approach of the beast. Today she sat safe in the promise of this tight roof over her own and her family's heads, with protection insured by the hateful flags on either side, and with the prospect ahead that she might become a self-supporting schoolmistress, whose value to Charlotte County would increase with her pupils. What had turned her desperate need into a promising future had been the farsighted suggestion of a peddler boy, a stray Carolina mountain youth whom she had never seen until an hour ago, and whom she feared she might never see again.

She must endeavor to develop, she told the America who watched from the inner tower of her mind, this faculty which the Tarheel possessed in such abundance, this habit of thinking a situation through to its logical conclusion, of using all the materials and facts at hand to reach a carefully selected goal.

"Sister Merry, have you guessed that riddle, yet?" called Palestine through the upstairs balustrade. "I vow I won't budge a step homeward until you solve it—or give up. Do you give up, Sister Merry?"

Throughout the family discussion which took place that night, America stubbornly maintained that she would rather teach other people's children in safety in town than continue to live like pore white trash on ruined Golden Hill.

"But you'd be little better than a governess!" wailed Mrs. Moncure, looking as if the end of her world had come. "Don't you remember how everybody looked down on poor Miss Armstrong?"

"Colliers do not leave the land," pronounced Ephraim. "Next spring, when you sell your crop, I'll hire a big force and raise a hundred acres of tobacco—"

"Like you did this summer?" cut in America, sharply. "We'll be lucky if my crop brings enough to pay taxes on Golden Hill's front fields. The rest will have to go."

"Sister Merry, I'd rather help you teach school than dig turnips—for Timber to eat," spoke up Arabia.

"Everybody better go to bed early and get a good night's rest," America gave warning, "because I'm going to start moving the first thing tomorrow morning."

Snorting his disgust, Ephraim stamped out of the cabin to go on a coon hunt. Arabia boosted Andorra up the ladder to the loft. Palestine, always disturbed by family arguments, had long since been led whimpering to bed. When they were alone, America produced Cousin Homer's letter to Palestine and demanded what should be done with it.

"This is one of the few occasions where it appears necessary to read another person's mail," Mrs. Moncure decided.

Drawing out the small-sized sheet of paper covered with copperplate penmanship, America held it up to the fire, and read:

Charlotte Court House, Va.
October 9th, '65.

Miss Palestine:

How difficult to approach a subject which may veil my life in darkness horrible!

Resolution has proved thus far to have no strength. When in your presence I fear to speak, lest expression disembogue eternal separation.

Should circumstances impel me from your cherished presence—to earn the wherewithal which would enable us never again to part—lonely would be the heart that now dwells embodied as your own. Yet reason tells me in tones like thunder that unless I go, never may I stay forever at your side. And so I go, soon to return. Were you older, I would entreat you to accompany me. I would demand the fixed sentiment, even though I realize your regard may prove only a brittle thread whereon I hang, a shred of mere affection which may snap and leave me naught but a mangled corpse of bleeding love.

I close to lose myself in sleep corporeal. My troubled brain will toss like foam on the billows of my agitated dreams, while my heavy heart drags like a slipping anchor.

Forever yours,
Homer Pettis

"When did poor Homer write this?" demanded Mrs. Moncure, trying not to smile. "Surely not while you waited?"

"He had it ready. And I think you're mean to make fun of him. It's an elegant, touching letter!"

"I'll have to put it away, now," sighed Miss Jincy. "We can't give it to Palestine in her present condition. Let's hope Homer thinks she's too coy to answer."

The next morning, while Ephraim went to a neighbor's to borrow a wagon and team to pull the Moncure possessions to town, America divided the stores of root vegetables, corn, squash, dried beans and winter fruit which Flora had already seriously diminished by sly generosity to her relatives. Hidden under fodder, America's tobacco crop went to town first and was rehung in Cousin Homer's servant quarters. Ephraim promised to sleep near it until the family arrived. After the last load of furniture had gone and the Moncure women were tying their bonnet strings, America stepped into the cook cabin to say good-bye.

Ol' Uncle lay on a fresh pallet before the fire. Around him swarmed the 'ninnies, in the background hovered negroes America had never seen before. Flora crouched on a hassock by the fire with a torn apron flung over head. At America's touch, Flora lifted her swollen face accusingly:

"You's no bettah dan a viper in mah boosum, 'deed you ain't! Look me in de eye, an' lemme hear you say you's leavin' us behin' foah fault."

"Flora, you know I've explained to you fifty times how it is," America tried to comfort her. "If we take you all to town with us, within a week we'll be in the same fix as the Arab who let the camel put his head inside the tent."

"Dar you goes agin, callin' me a pizzle-faced, bad smellin' circus animule!"

"Can't you reason with her, Ol' Uncle?"

"Let her be, missy-ma'am. She's grievin' kez she sees dat as a fambly we ain't no bettah naow den any yoder passel ob fiel' niggahs."

"As soon as I get my school started and we can afford to feed you again, I'll send for you, auntie. I swear I will!"

"Nome, you won't. You's a flinty-hea'hted drivin' woman, 'Mericy Moncyore! An' you's frowin' us uns aside lak an ol' shoe you's done wore aout."

America knelt on the hearthstones beside Ol' Uncle and took his hand. It was a bird's claw, and hot with fever. He didn't have long to live, America realized with a tightening of her throat.

"Good-bye, Ol' Uncle," she whispered. "I can't forgive myself for letting you talk me out of sending for Dr. Culp."

"All ol' niggahs come tuh de end ob de road, honey."

"And I'll never forget you offered to die for me."

"Dat ain't nuffin, eder. Lots ob good men gwine jump tuh do dat foah you."

"Now you're trying to make me feel like a belle, Ol' Uncle."

"You's gwine be dat, too. An' w'at's moah, you's gwine be rich an' famous."

"In Charlotte Court House—teaching school?"

"Nome, not in Charlotte Cayounty. Nobody ain't done no good hyahabaouts since we sta'hted plantin' des one stalk ob co'hn tuh de hill. I kin recollec' when youah Grandpap's paw could plant two stalks an' habe 'em grow. Maybe dey was a time when folkses could grow free stalks in Virginny, but dat time's done gone. Tak' good keer ob yerself an' ob youah maw an' pore Miss Teeny."

"And you do the same, Ol' Uncle. I'll be out Thanksgiving with a big meat dinner," America tried to cheer them from the cabin door. All she could see through the tears in her eyes was the bivouac of the dead, with eager Ol' Uncle limping forward to meet Grandpa Ephraim and Father Radford, Brother William and Brother Tom.

Dumb with misery, Flora stood in the cabin door, Pembroke in the littered yard, while the Moncures climbed up the path out of sight. Never again, they realized, would they bask in that affectionate privileged equality of slave with mistress which had distinguished the good Virginia house servant before the war. Now, they were just field niggers living in a cabin in a hollow.

Between the two hated flags, America marshaled her thirty-odd pupils on midafternoons, five days a week up Court Street. At the square, she felt it safe for them to make their separate ways home.

One grey December day in '65, when early twilight closed in with no reassuring suppertime smells of bacon and browning pone to humanize the approaching darkness, America found her homeward flight blocked by Clarence Cushman.

"Good evening, Miss Moncure," he greeted her, urbanely. "You may be interested to know I've prevailed on General Gregg at Lynchburg to open a formal investigation into Anthony Mudston's disappearance. Lieutenant Eppich will be subpoenaed from Gettysburg next spring—to testify."

Without answering, she looked him up and down. He was concealing something behind the skirts of the Prince Albert coat he now affected.

"Come, come, have you nothing to say?" Cushman demanded, testily. "Such an investigation may react to your advantage. But whatever its outcome, can't we be more neighborly? It don't seem hardly Christian for you and me to meet several times a day, like we do, and not speak."

"I would sooner neighbor with an Apache Indian!"

"My only idea in troubling you this evening, ma'am, was to do you a service. Here's a letter to your maw that's been waiting more'n a month to be claimed. Shall I send it back to Kentucky?"

"Oh, no—no, sir! I will take it, please. And thank you."

"You're welcome, I'm sure."

Her heart, these many months asleep or drugged by the constant demands of schoolroom and kitchen, leaped into America's throat and pounded there. Grasping the precious letter as if she feared it might jump away, she scudded home. In the hall she paused long enough to read the postmark. Mrs. Moncure sat knitting before the fire in Cousin Homer's rear office, now the family room. In the chimney corner, Palestine watched with the idle complacency of a huge China doll. Arabia was playing with Andorra on the hearth rug.

Lest her voice betray her agitation, America handed the letter without comment to her mother. At the eagle mirror, under pretext of removing her bonnet, America watched Mrs. Moncure open and glance through its contents before she announced pleasantly:

"It's from Cousin Margaret Annable, in Kentucky. She and Cousin Justinian wish to thank us for our hospitality to Fant last summer. Now, girls, wasn't that gentlemanly of him not to tell her he was a paying guest? She says they hope to get over to Charlotte Court House some day to meet the Virginia connection. Not knowing just when Cousin Justinian can manage a long trip, she thinks it would be nice if one of you girls came out to visit them on Tuckahoe Ridge."

"Ma, does she mean me? I couldn't leave the baby," Arabia decided, flatly.

"She says"—Mrs. Moncure consulted the letter—" 'whichever one of your older girls you can best spare.' "

How like Fant, America thought angrily, to take her pleasure out of the invitation by having Cousin Margaret include Palestine, when he knew only too well why Palestine could never make the trip!

"Too bad you're busy with your school, America."

"I intend to go."

"Daughter, whoever in the world would conduct your classes? You know how we depend on you for everything. You've always been so capable!"

"Mr. Cushman has talked General Gregg into holding a—a formal investigation into the death of some Damyankee," answered America, with a significant glance at drowsy Palestine.

"No! When?" whispered Mrs. Moncure.

"He said something about bringing Lieutenant Eppich down next spring to testify."

"Eppich?" yawned Palestine and then sat up suddenly, as if disturbed.

"What other news did you hear?" interposed Arabia, unconsciously dragging a red herring across the dim trail of Palestine's memory.

"This Kentucky trip might be just the change you need, America—after your close confinement in the schoolroom," Mrs. Moncure decided, with a pinched expression. "When could you start?"

"I won't have my tobacco money before spring—for railroad fare."

"Sister Merry, what'll we use for taxes on Golden Hill?" asked Arabia, lifting worried eyes from the hearth.

"Brother Eph will be furious if you go gallivanting—on the money he plans to spend," whimpered Palestine.

"Sister Merry, aren't you just dying to see Cousin Fant again?"

"What a silly question, Arabia! Of course, I'll enjoy the trip to Kentucky on the railroad cars. And meeting all our kin out there. You'll have to write Cousin Margaret it just doesn't suit now, ma," America concluded, trying to keep the fury out of her voice. What kind of a hussy did Fant Annable think she was, to come rushing half across the continent in the dead of winter, just because he crooked his little finger? "I couldn't think of leaving before May. . . . Upon my word, Teena, what's the matter with you now? Surely you don't want to go way out there by yourself, where you won't see ma for weeks and weeks?"

"Brother Ephraim will be crosser than you when he comes in," sniffled Palestine, and wiped away the tears which were rolling down her beautiful, emotionless face. "He always gets cross when you mention Cousin Fant. He'll make a scene. And you know scenes make my head ache. It's aching terribly, now—"

"I think I've indulged all the headaches this household will stand," pronounced Mrs. Moncure, with surprising firmness. "America, will you please fetch me your schoolbooks before you go to the cook cabin? I might as well take hold now, while I have you by my side," she concluded, with her rare smile of spiritual acceptance.

Chapter 4

On a sparkling morning in May, '66, America stood on the grimy wharf at Front Street, Cincinnati, and watched downstream for the packet *Magnolia* to appear out of green Kentucky hills. Day before yesterday, Ephraim had driven her to a Richmond and Danville train from Charlotte Court House. At Parkersburg at midnight she had been ferried across a confluence of rivers awesome as the Styx. Through a purgatory of acrid smoke, crying babies and ill-bred enemies, she had swayed in a coach across the rough Ohio country to Cincinnati. She spent the night lying fully clothed on an iron bed in a shabby hotel room, while a leaky gas jet sputtered and flared. She was afraid to turn it off, lest she asphyxiate herself or be overtaken in darkness by the perils which beset young women alone in a strange city. Breakfastless, homesick and dizzy, she now waited to embark on the final stage of her journey, the boat trip sixty miles upstream to Limestone, Kentucky.

"Travel, though broadening, fatigues one," volunteered another woman passenger. "Have you far to go, dearie?"

"The day trip only," America answered and turned with relief to watch the *Magnolia* approach.

"Surely I don't see you preparing to board this packet alone?" demanded the curious passenger.

The *Magnolia* bumped the wharf, obviating an answer, and the gangplank was run out. Other passengers disappeared into the ship's interior. America remained at the cargo-deck rail to make sure that her trunk came aboard among the heavy consignments of freight. Ordered confusion prevailed on deck and wharf. With profanity from the mates, grunts from the roustabouts, screechings of rollers and tinkling of bells, cargo went off and came aboard, the gangplank was lifted, the ropes cast away. Overhead, a silver whistle gave three elegant but penetrating whoops. Before she felt the boat's motion, America saw the accelerated rush of water beyond the rail. Midstream, the current caught the *Magnolia* as if she were a drift log to be rolled over and over, instead of the finest packet on the Cairo–Pittsburgh run. Like a swan arising, she steadied to the beat of her great stern wheel and floated upstream—

Upstream! America felt that she should be thinking of Fant and the tender joys of reunion. River and shore proved far too interesting. Wharves, red brick stores, tobacco warehouses and distilleries of Covington, Kentucky, flowed past as if on a moving theatrical backdrop. Cobblestone cross streets writhed slowly to the water's edge and stopped there like cautious eels refusing to leap. Congested downtown thoroughfares ran out into tree-lined avenues. Rows of brownstone houses and an occasional mansion aloof in its garden gave place to shanty-town cabins. One by one these shabby settlements dropped astern.

Upstream! Thrash as the *Magnolia* might to approach the bend ahead, the broad highway of the river, bounded on each side by the green hills and above by the blue sky, seemed to open its arms in welcome as the boat proceeded along the apparently ever widening yellow stream. To ease her eyes, America lowered them to the river's edge. Where the undergrowth had been cleared, plowed fields were laid off in anticipation of a tobacco season. Swells of the steamer's wake appeared to roll in over the pebbly beach, and to continue on up the hillside in black waves of velvety loam. Alternating the prospective tobacco patches and the bracken were cornfields alive with short green plumes. America squinted, counted five stalks to the hill, and was squinting to count again when warnings of impending disaster swept over her. If she fainted, would the passenger standing farther down the rail try to take advantage of her helplessness?

"Close your eyes, miss. Or look inside the packet," she heard a matter-of-fact voice declare from his direction. "To stare at the shore as steadily as you've been doing, would make a deckaneer sick."

She followed his suggestion. Relief was immediate.

"River traffic before the war was handled on the Kentucky side by white men—deckaneers, they called themselves," continued the voice down deck, as if she had asked for an explanation of the unfamiliar word. "Each town had its own band, usually Irish daredevils. Led by some jackanapes who could out-shout a river-boat mate, they contracted their price to load and unload before the packet touched wharf. They stood for no competition from local blacks, and formed a rowdy element in the river towns, though tradesmen were glad enough to take their silver on Saturday nights. Nowadays, whenever I pass, I expect to see them come swarming down the grade."

Before he finished his lecture, America had opened her eyes and was looking at him with interest. She saw a sober young man under twenty-five, smooth-shaven in an era when a beard was considered the outward mark of masculine virility. Blue as flax blossoming in ripe wheat, his eyes shone in a face weathered red and gold by sun and wind. The mark of the fields was on his stocky body, yet the ease with which he wore his good clothes proclaimed him no clodhopper. Solid as a boulder, he yet carried an air of pride and place, the look which she had come to associate with pioneering Virginians gone West and become Kentuckians—the "limestone look," America's father had called it, noting in the high cheekbones and tall frames of this new breed of Transylvania men the distillation of Kentucky's own blue limestone grass and clear cold limestone water.

"Now you're feeling yourself again, the purpose of my little homily has been accomplished," grinned the Kentuckian.

"You're very kind, I'm sure," America retreated into the formality the occasion warranted. "I'm an inexperienced traveler."

"Then you'd best engage a stateroom and lie down until you get used to the packet's motion."

"Thank you, I will. Good-day, sir."

As he did not answer, she grasped the handle of her satchel and walked towards the *Magnolia*'s interior. The Kentuckian made no move to help her with the carryall. She gained an impression that his eyes were following her as any good husbandman might observe conformation and gait of a young animal within his line of vision. A further thought struck her to wonder why so true-appearing a man should lack the gallantry every gentleman owes a lady in distress.

She found the *Magnolia*'s interior filled with miscellaneous freight, livestock in crates and on tether, a red farm wagon, a bar buggy and tobacco hogsheads. The crew rolled dice or nodded in the sun. A mulatto girl in uniform flirted with a sad-faced roustie picking chords on a banjo.

"Oh, stewardess!"

"Yassum? Kin I assist you tuh a stateroom an' git you a ticket,ma'ah? My name's Moselle—Elly foah sho'ht. I was named foah de packet w'at blowed up in midstream back in '37."

"Take my bag, Moselle."

"Yassum. Haow come you's trabblin alone, honey?"

Ignoring the maid's curiosity, an art in which she was well skilled, America followed through the purser's office. As she was passing a pair of amber glass doors, they swung open at a vigorous thrust from within and almost knocked America off her feet. A man in sporting clothes steadied her. His pouchy face was so close she could see his jaundiced eyes and bulbous nose crisscrossed with angry veins. On a sour whiskey breath he gushed apologies. America jerked herself free, and hurried without speaking towards Moselle and the handsome stairway leading upwards into the ladies' cabin. Although she had read that boats like the *Magnolia,* the *Bonanza* and the *Robert E. Lee* were floating palaces, she was unprepared for velvet carpets, full-length gilt mirrors, a piano, paintings and statuary. Several passengers in the cabin observed with interest America's progress to her stateroom door.

"Dat savigraous lady ovah dar," whispered the stewardess,

indicating the big-busted traveler who had accosted America on the Cincinnati wharf, "is uh famous temp'rance speakuh. How come you knows Mistuh Tom Haggerty, ma'am? Does you make dis trip offen?"

"If you mean that whiskey tippler who almost knocked me down, I never saw him before."

"He's a moughty fine gen'neman, I heahs de ladies say. He trabbels reg'lah from Pittsbu'gh tuh Cairo a-sellin' Ol' Limestone and Golden Stream."

"Spare me, Moselle! Here's the money for my ticket."

America moved across the tiny compartment. Should the *Magnolia* blow up, she could never squirm her reedlike hips through that narrow porthole. Across the water, the Kentucky shore floated downstream.

"De pussah done say dis heah bill am counte'fit."

Beyond Moselle's shoulders in the doorway, America gained an impression of other faces, some curious, the temperance leader's frankly disapproving.

"Give it to me!" cried America. "I'll go explain, myself."

As she ran downstairs, a dozen fears assailed America. She had heard tales of what the Yankees did to people who tried to pass counterfeit money. As she hurried to the purser's window, the whiskey salesman swept off his hat and smiled familiarly. These attentions so agitated America that, before she realized what she had done, she stepped into the line in front of a white-bearded gentleman in a rusty frock coat. When her turn came, she earnestly assured the purser she had intended no deception; indeed, she hadn't the faintest idea the bill was worthless.

"Country's flooded with the stuff!" the officer snorted with bluff good humor. "Where to, miss?"

"Limestone, Kentucky."

"Dollar'n twenty cents—two dollars more for a stateroom if you want it to yourself. Hurry up, ma'am, there's passengers behind you."

"I—I can't find my inside purse!" cried America, in an agony of alarm. "It was here just a moment ago."

"I've heard that story before. Step out o' line, till I sell these gents their tickets. Where to, Haggerty?"

"Limestone," spoke up the whiskey salesman. "What's the trouble? Has the little lady lost her money?"

"All I know is she's tryin' to pass counterfeit. Can't you see you're holdin' up the line?"

"Beg pardon, little lady," the salesman addressed America. "Can I be of any service?"

America looked from Haggerty's dissipated face back into her tumbled reticule. Ephraim said if you couldn't pay your fare on a railroad coach, the conductor blew the whistle, stopped the train and put you off on the tracks. Would the purser set her down on the next wharf, among the deckaneers? What could she do in a strange river town with no relatives or friends to meet her and only a counterfeit ten-dollar bill in her purse?

"Here, little lady," whispered the insistent voice of the salesman at her elbow, "I'll give you a good bill for your bad one."

Desperate with anxiety, America's eyes met the serene gaze of the old gentleman whose place she had preempted in the line.

"Look in your purse again, my dear," he blandly suggested. "Step to where the light is better—and you won't be troubled with whiskey slugs and river lice."

With trembling knees, too disturbed to hear the chuckles of other passengers, America moved away, and made a systematic search through the jumbled contents of her reticule. In the lowest corner was her billfold. Color flooded into her white face, mounted to her bright hair. Winking back tears, she smiled her thanks at her elderly champion, bought her ticket from the mollified purser and ran upstairs. Thrusting the coupons into the stewardess' hand, she slipped past her into the stateroom and locked the door. Where twenty minutes before she had felt so cramped, the room looked as welcome as home. Flinging herself into the lower berth, she buried her face in the pillow to stifle sobs of mingled humiliation and relief that shook her exhausted body. Spent by the violence of her emotion, she fell asleep. . . .

"Is you all right, honey?" called a voice which she mistook for Hattie's at Golden Hill, until Moselle thrust her head around the stateroom door. "You's been so still all day I was gittin afeart you mought be tooken sick. Ain't you gwine eat nuffin? De chef, he say he fry some mighty fine ribber cat foah suppah."

"Supper? Is it that late?"

"Hit's nigh onto six o'clock. An' we gits tuh Limestone at sebben."

"I'll bathe my face and come right out."

"Is you got ever'thing you needs? Bettah lemme bring you a tray ob good hot suppah?"

"You may go now, Moselle."

Emerging some minutes later, America was surprised by the cheerful sociability of the ladies' cabin. At the piano which apparently no one could play, stood a group of children. The elderly gentleman who had befriended America read a pamphlet under a prism chandelier. Near a table lamp, the temperance leader knit vigorously. America looked about for the dining salon.

"Good-evening," remarked the old gentleman, gazing at her with fatherly pleasure over the half-lenses of his copper spectacles. "You appear refreshed."

"Oh, yes, sir! I overslept."

"Young woman, did I hear the stewardess say you're bound for Limestone?" demanded the temperance leader.

"From your tone of voice, ma'am, I might think it brimstone."

"You saucy chit! Limestone, with its warehouses and distilleries, is the very center of the upriver whiskey trade. Haven't you seen that ogling liquor agent on this boat?"

America felt it wise not to answer this remark. The temperance leader stiffened into further disapproval. Could it be that this clear-eyed young woman with the high-bred face, shabby genteel clothes and general air of innocence was another river-boat hussy? There was one sure way to find out:

"Have you signed the pledge?"

At this question the old gentleman folded his spectacles into a worn purple velvet case, pocketed his leaflet, smiled on America and left the cabin.

"Please, miss, can you play the piano?" begged a childish voice at her elbow.

Turning, America looked down into the little girl's winsome face. Others at the piano beckoned. Wondering what to play for these Yankee children, America seated herself on the stool and began:

"In the gloaming, oh, my darling,
Think not bitterly of me—"

Her well-trained voice, soaring above the childish chorus, brought passengers out of their staterooms, in from the decks and the bar. Ladies and gentlemen gathered about the piano, until America found herself the center of a spirited group. The success of her music brought color to her cheeks, light to her eyes, dramatic feeling into her clear soprano voice. Transformed from the terrified country mouse of the morning, she drew all eyes including the bloodshot gaze of Tom Haggerty and the cool blue regard of the Kentuckian who had not offered to carry her satchel.

"Limestone!" shouted an officer's voice outside. "All ashore for Limestone, Kaintucky!"

America arose, excused herself from a regretful audience and hurried to her stateroom. Ignoring the obsequious attentions of the stewardess, for America felt she could not spare even a copper, she grasped her luggage and hurried downstairs to the cargo deck.

The Ohio, sweeping in two great bends out of a funnel of green hills, poured its broad flood past a narrow town which lay along the river's southern shore like a thirsty frontiersman stretched prone to drink at the water's edge. From midstream,

America could see warehouses, stores and brick houses facing the waterfront above the steep grade. In 1789, America recalled, the Virginia legislature had authorized the establishment of a receiving house for Kentucky tobacco at Limestone. Fourteen years later, the booming town had become the hemp center of the world and a famous stopover on Zane's Trace. This celebrated coach road carried travelers from Limestone to Lexington, Memphis, Florence, Alabama, and New Orleans. Crossing the Ohio River at Limestone, it ran northeast through Zanesville, Ohio, to Pittsburgh, Washington and New York.

Up from the river's edge at Limestone, the turnpike meandered past a market square, a white courthouse and jail, two churches and handsome brick houses set within open gardens. It then climbed through a gap in the hills to a plateau behind the four-streeted town. The sky, the glassy surface of the river broken by ripples as the *Magnolia* drifted in with paddles idle, and the steep bank were rosy with the afterglow of the sun. America scanned the approaching wharf float for Fant, but could not identify him there. He stood no doubt in the line of townsfolk silhouetted along the top of the grade to watch the *Magnolia* round in.

Overhead, the thin bell tinkled. Like a monster stirring in its sleep, the stern wheel turned, sent a surge of bright water shorewards, and lay still. In the hush that followed, a woman's voice came drifting sweetly down from the ladies' cabin, accompanied by the tinkle of the piano. A sense of the transitory quality of life, and of her own insignificance in it, overwhelmed America.

"All ashore for Limestone, Kaintucky!" shouted a red-faced deck mate. "Stand back, miss, till we get the cargo off."

The *Magnolia* edged the glistening piles, bumped the float. The gangplank came out, and a line of roustabouts began to trot down it with America's oval-topped trunk, with liquor cases and the considerable freight which the *Magnolia* always docked at Limestone. As she waited, America noticed a red calf of a breed which she could not identify, lying tethered to a deck support. The banjo-strumming roustabout approached the stanchion, untied the halter rope and tugged at the calf's head. The calf, its pink eyes rolling in a curly face, refused to get up.

"Blow in his ear!" shouted the mate, motioning to another roustabout to lend a hand.

When this attention failed to raise the calf, the mate stepped over and kicked it brutally. From several passengers came a murmur of protest. Gentler treatment got the calf on his feet. Once up, by well-placed kicks he scattered his tormentors and stood snorting with rage, blocking the gangplank.

"Game, ain't he?" hiccoughed Tom Haggerty at America's elbow. "He ain't scared to ride on a river boat no more'n you."

Turning her back, America watched the calf successfully resist the efforts of half-a-dozen men. Tiring of this war dance, the mate ordered him thrown and tied.

"All together, now, boys, heave him onto the wharf. Look out below!"

Shocked at such callous treatment, America watched the calf swing through the air and land with a sickening thud on the float. He lay still, the breath knocked out of him.

"Now, miss, it's your turn," joked the deck mate, and moved towards America.

As if she actually believed he might handle her with similar roughness, America scurried down the gangplank. She dared not look around to see if anyone besides Tom Haggerty had followed. The calf rolled wall-eyes of terror as she approached. She heard voices, one of them familiar, claiming freight. Clasping her reticule and with small head high, she stood waiting for Fant to appear out of the purple shadows of the grade.

Overhead, the little bell tinkled again. The *Magnolia*'s whistle set echoes bouncing against the Kentucky and Ohio shores.

"There's a respectable hotel up the bank, ma'am—the Lee House," declared the young man with the limestone look. "May I see you to it?"

"I hope to be met, sir."

"You'll be more comfortable waiting at the hotel. There's no charge."

"What about my trunk and satchel?"

"Look out for them with mine, will you, wharfmaster?"

"Aye, and thankee, sir," answered a dour Scot, catching the coin tossed. America's eyes widened. A silver dollar, in these times!

Under their feet, the float lifted to the surge of the *Magnolia*'s paddles. River, float and shore hung breathless in the spell of her departure, then were slapped into activity by her wake. Tom Haggerty's voice sounded truculent:

"Look here, Stone, no small-town rooster can crowd me off—"

"Tom, if I didn't know you're limber drunk, I'd knock you down. This young lady is my cousin—"

"Ho! Ho! I've heard that from Pittsburgh to Cairo!"

"This lady, sir—"

"Lady, *hic*? Then what's she doing traveling by herself at night?"

"Take that back, you drunken fool!"

From where he knelt above the calf and with tender hands was searching for broken bones, the Scotsman raised a warning voice:

"There'll be nae brawling on ma wharf, men."

"Take back all you've said, and apologize to my cousin!"

For a moment, America thought there was going to be violence. Blinking, Haggerty shifted his weight uneasily, and capitulated:

"Sorry, miss—*hic*!—I meant no harm."

"Now, let us pass."

Without offering her his arm, her protector started up the gravel bank. America scrambled to keep beside him. At the top, the crowd let them through. Her stolid Galahad, America decided, must be locally respected.

"Why, it's quite a town!" she gasped.

"You Virginians still expect to see a wilderness, don't you?"

"How did you know I'm a Virginian, sir?"

"It's my opinion you're America Collier Moncure, Fant Annable's intended. I'm your fifth cousin, Barton Stone Moncure."

"Cousin Stone! Then you must be Cousin Charles Moncure's son? And you live at Children's Chance, on the other end of Tuckahoe Ridge. Fant told me all about you. Why didn't you introduce yourself sooner?"

"You wouldn't have believed me. And if you did, you shouldn't have. Come on to the hotel, while I locate Fant."

They reached the Lee House, chaste and elegant. Stone guided America towards the ladies' parlor, excused himself and returned with the innkeeper's wife, a stylish creature with love curls bobbing on a lacquered forehead.

"Mrs. Lambeau, may I present Miss America Moncure, of Virginia?" Stone made the introductions. "Have you seen Fant hereabouts?"

"No—ah, no, not since midafternoon. He told me he was expecting you—languishing for you, Miss Moncure! He's very happy over your coming so far and on such a romantic errand."

"I'm only visiting—"

"Of course, modesty compels you to say that! All our young ladies of Limestone—and the whole county, I might say—are consumed with eagerness to meet you. You stole a march on Kentucky for sure, ma'am!"

America's polite protests were swept away by this torrent of words. Glancing with amusement towards Stone, America observed he had gone. Like a waterspout, Mrs. Lambeau turned her praises over him:

"You couldn't have met up with a steadier, more substantial young blade than Stone Moncure. A fine business fellow, too. And such a catch! The responsibility of running that big place his father left him last year may have sobered him a mite for his years. But I've heard few women complain because their husbands were too steady. Fancy you arriving on Tuckahoe with Fant Annable on your right arm and Stone Moncure on your left! Our local belles will scratch your eyes out, dearie, especially Miss Allilee Drake."

"She's my cousin, too," America tried dignity to stem this nonsense. Mrs. Lambeau was drawing a breath to continue when Stone returned. With a warning glance at the tavern hostess, which America did not miss, he began briskly:

"I've arranged to drive you out to Tuckahoe, ma'am. I go right past the Annable gates. They're hooking my saddle mare into a hired rig at Dalton's livery stable. I told my boy Jamie MacGower, who brought the mare to town, to drive down by the float and pick up our baggage."

"You're kindness itself, Cousin Stone."

"We'd best be starting. I hear Jamie outside."

Shouted "*Whoas*" and "*Stand still, lassie*!" informed them that Jamie MacGower was approaching with their vehicle. They left the parlor by the ladies' entrance. On the brick walk in front, the still curious stood about to watch Stone depart with his adventurous kinswoman. The Lee House, late promenaders, the wide store-lined streets were left behind as the mare drew them swiftly out of Limestone. Halfway up a long grade, with slender head tossing against the checkrein, she slowed into a walk.

"Oh, there's a white horse!" cried America, and leaned forward to peer into the gathering darkness of the curve below.

"Is it your sixtieth?"

"Cousin Stone, how did you know?"

"If it's your sixtieth white horse, go ahead and stamp it."

"They were very numerous in Ohio. I wondered if I should include them, considering that they were on the wrong side of the Mason and Dixon Line. I understand your father and Cousin Justinian Annable were the elders of Tuckahoe," she changed the subject.

"They kept Glade Springs church open during the war. Half dead on his feet, pa'd stand up there beside Mr. Justinian and listen to him pray by the hour for equality between blacks and whites. But aren't you forgetting something important? A white horse doesn't change color just because he happens to belong to a Yankee."

To please him, America executed the 'ninnies' immemorial rite of stamping the white horse by licking her right thumb, drawing it across her left palm and striking the palm with her fist. She then leaned sideways in the buggy and turned her twinkling eyes on him, declaring:

"That goes to show how little truth there is in darky superstitions. Do you know what they say will happen to a girl after she's stamped her sixtieth white horse?"

"The next man you look at, you'll marry."

"Yes, isn't that ridiculous? Because I'm looking at you."

"Any man who got the chance to marry you—even on sixty white horses—would be lucky."

If the road bank beyond the turning buggy wheels had spoken, she could not have been more surprised. Then the picture of herself arriving as a bride with the sixty white horses she had stamped, caused her to throw back her head and laugh. Out of a delicious new-found gaiety she teased him:

"Cousin Stone, how you talk! What do you know about me?"

"I know who you are and how you look. I saw you pick up that satchel this morning. I heard you sing. And I've watched you all evening, when you'd let me."

Such methods of rustic male appraisal silenced her more than the implied compliments. The plodding mare threw herself against the shoulder strap. In search of a less personal subject, America reworded a phrase of Stone's which had been echoing in her mind:

"Who did you say prayed by the hour for equality between blacks and whites?"

"Mr. Justinian Annable."

"Cousin Stone, how could that be? Fant fought for the Confederacy—"

"Did you ever hear of a Moncure being an Abolitionist?"

"That's what I couldn't understand. I—I can't believe Fant would intentionally deceive me."

"He probably realized he'd never get you out to Timberlawn any other way. Did he tell you about his running contraband?"

"Some of our best young men did that."

"Fant did it for the money, and to rile his pa. Fant's contrary-minded, like an old mule I've got. Pull him one way and he goes the other. Lumber was one of the few articles admitted to Kentucky through the blockade. Fant got a contract to deliver two-by-fours from Hillsborough, Ohio, to Lexington. His black men brought the lumber down to the wharf at Aberdeen, across from Limestone. There they put it on a shallow-water ferry Fant had reconditioned. The whole operation seemed small potatoes to the Union troops guarding the Ohio side, until word came through that contraband drugs, especially quinine and morphine—"

"The South will never forgive Lincoln for putting morphine on the contraband list."

"One day, while the soldiers were keeping a sharp lookout, Fant and his teamsters came down to the shore with a big load. A two-by-four slipped from a nigger's sweaty hand, and struck its end on a rock. Out came the plug and the powdered quinine inside. While the soldiers stared, Fant slipped into the water. The Yankees commandeered every boat in sight, but the river was so full of logs and drift nobody could see where he went. Cousin Margaret thought him drowned until Homer Drake was invalided home and said he'd seen Fant at the battle of Five Forks."

Absorbing as the tale had been, for nothing interested her as much as complimentary stories about Fant, America struggled to bring some order to her own tumultuous feelings. If Cousin Justinian was an Abolitionist, how could she live under the same roof with him, how could she accord him the respect and obedience due her father-in-law? Yet surely he would be easier to face than Colonel Gregg's military court of investigation, egged on by Clarence Cushman? As if he were reading her thoughts, Stone demanded:

"You've a reason—besides Fant—for wanting to stay out here in Kentucky, haven't you?"

"The reverses the war brought us, compel me to earn my own way," America pretended complete frankness. "And Cousin Margaret's expecting me; or at least, I wrote her I was coming. The letter may have miscarried."

"Kate Annable told Mrs. MacGower, and she told my sister Emarind when you were due. Knowing Fant, ma suggested I slip down to Cincinnati and see that you got on the right boat. I—I'd like to take you home with me, but ma's got sugar diabetes. Rindy's hands are full, with our slaves gone and what's left too old to turn off much work."

"What shall I do, sir? When Brother Tom was killed, I pledged myself never to set foot under a Yankee roof."

"You'd best forget hard feelings, now. Cousin Maggie's no Yankee, and Timberlawn belongs to her. It's been a cross, I can tell you, for her to put up with Mr. Justinian. Next to John G. Fee, and Cassius Clay, he's the Blackest Republican in Kentucky. Pa often asked him how he could talk Abolition in the parlor and fatten off Cousin Maggie's slaves in the field. As for me, I never could see the sense of getting so exercised over a passel of lazy niggers who were eating us out of house and home. They bred like rabbits, and yet no Christian liked to sell them individually. The luckiest thing that happened to us was when seventy of our slaves ran away in '59 to Felicity, Ohio. At the first snow-flurry they came home, and pa sold 'em downriver quick as scat. Mr. Lewis Robards drove 'em in one coffle to Natchez. I suffered most by their absence. I had to get along without them in the crop."

"Sir, do I understand you didn't go to war—an able-bodied man like you?"

"When I could raise two-dollar wheat for the Union Army?

And that's two dollars in gold, mind you, worth four in Confederate money! Well, for better or worse, here's Tuckahoe—and Timberlawn."

For several miles, they had been climbing a series of hills, the river rim. They rolled over the summit, and America saw spread before her the southeastern knob of an undulating plateau. Broad open fields silvery with moonlight sloped into shadow-black hollows, fields tented with hero-sized corn shocks, land rich-looking even in moonlight, young land judged by Virginia standards, although America knew Tuckahoe to have been settled seventy years ago. During the Civil War, Kentucky's early neutrality had saved her fields from the marching feet of armies. Her central location, within easy transportation by rail and waterway, gave her swift access to the expanding markets of Chicago, the booming West and the war-weary Atlantic without competition from the captive agricultural South. Down the Ohio River had come responsible, liberty-loving aliens—land hungry, eager to replace the freed slaves, to hire out until they could purchase for themselves some of this new limestone soil of Mason County, thumb of the Blue Grass thrust north to the Ohio River.

Farm-trained as she was, America recognized the visible signs of untouched virgin resources and of the rich way of life which follows the furrow of a lavish nature. On this eventful night so packed with anxiety, contradiction and disappointment, only Tuckahoe appeared as she had imagined it: the perennially filling cornucopia of lasting security. The long green ridge crisscrossed by slave-built stone fences and studded with handsome brick houses full of a hospitable and pleasure-loving gentry seemed more like home to America than Golden Hill, itself. For Golden Hill was gone, and with it the easy, pleasant, open-handed ways. Home now, America sensed, would have to be where she could find or create the nearest duplicate to the life she had known as a child. Here on Tuckahoe, at least, were the materials from which she could rear another Golden Hill.

America never forgot her first entry into the Annable home. It was as if the corrosive acid of Fant's shortcomings, together with newborn fear for her future, had etched its details into a memory hypersensitized by hunger and fatigue.

Stone drove into a dusty lane pale in the massed gloom of giant oaks. America saw at its farther end an impressive brick house, unpainted, with a small white Georgian double porch. Yellow lamplight from ground-floor windows streamed across a bright green lawn. A flagstone walk led from a doorway between lighted windows to a whitewashed stile, ghostly under funereal cedars. As Stone haltered his mare, the cedar boughs quickened with sleepy protests from guinea fowl and turkeys.

Some moments later, America found herself crossing the threshold into a large dining room. The spacious room was furnished with Kentucky-made copies of English mahogany. The uncovered floor had been scrubbed to a monotone. Around a lighted lamp on the cleared table sat four people, man and wife, a grown daughter, a lad of perhaps fourteen. All raised their heads and gazed at America with the same anxious intensity which she knew her own face must reflect.

The man could only be Mr. Justinian Annable. Tall, and nearing sixty, he loomed at the head of the table with blackclad arms outspread like the wings of a gigantic raven or South American bird of prey perched on the table's end. Lamplight threw the angles and hollows of his skull, with sinewy flesh stretched tightly across, into sharp relief. Above his beak of a nose burned a hostile fanatic's eyes. At his right hand sat a stylishly dressed young lady of doubtful years. In a long face, worried blue eyes habitually besought everybody not to make a scene. Large nervous hands continued to finger a page of the book from which she had been reading aloud, until the page was torn. The hands then became still, the knuckles gleamed white.

Across the table, the boy slouched low in his chair and stared, his mouth stupidly open. At the foot sat Margaret Collier Annable. Her smooth black hair, parted to show a line of pearly scalp, was drawn low in heavy folds over the lobes of her diamond-hung ears. Evidently a beauty in youth, she still possessed a warm fleshly charm, an essentially physical attraction of coal-black eyes, full red lips and fine bone contours, which revealed to America the source of Fant's spectacular comeliness.

"How do you do, my dear?" Mrs. Annable arose with an elegant rustle. "Mr. Annable, this is America."

"How do you do, sir?"

"Humph! I see you got here."

"And our daughter, Kate."

"What do you mean coming in at this time of the night with another man, even if he is your cousin? Where's Fant?"

"This is Edwin Dell, our younger son," Mrs. Annable's voice flowed on as if her husband had not spoken. "And how are you, Stone? It was kind of you to drive America out."

As Mrs. Annable finished speaking, America heard a sibilant hiss, as from a teakettle boiling under the floor. Startled, she looked at Mr. Annable, who demanded:

"Have you had supper?"

The bubbling sound arose again, this time unquestionably under the floor below her host.

"I dined on the *Magnolia,* thank you."

"That was extravagant of you," rebuked Mr. Justinian. From below came an echoing hiss.

"I—I beg your pardon, sir, but could there be fire in the foundation of this room?" America voiced her concern.

"That's Gander," declared Edwin Dell. "He always hisses after everything pa says."

"Mr. Annable has a feathered follower, my dear," Cousin Margaret hastened to explain, with her warm smile. "A young grey gander has become infatuated with him. So devoted is he that we took the house ventilators out to permit him freedom to follow Mr. Annable from room to room under the floors."

"He sleeps directly under pa's bed in the family room,"

Kate explained Gander's nocturnal habits. "Every time pa turns over, Gander turns, too."

"It's quite remarkable," began America.

"What's remarkable about it, missy? Some months ago I chanced to come upon him attacking a 'ninny. I kept knocking him down with my cane until he was quite ready to acknowledge me master," Mr. Annable concluded with unmistakable emphasis, and changed the subject. "Since you've supped, young lady, we will proceed to family prayers. Kate, ring for the niggers. Stone, will you stay? Good-night, then, and my respects to your ladies."

Although she wanted to extend her hand, America dared do no more than smile at Stone. He took his departure by the side door through which they had entered. America followed Kate into the adjoining room, where Mr. and Mrs. Annable evidently slept, and knelt before a slipper chair which seemed by tacit consent to be hers. Through the long devotionals, she tried to compose her thoughts. The dull ache of Fant's failure to meet her, together with his deception about Mr. Annable's political views, would heighten with time into acute misery, she knew, and into a proper sense of personal outrage. From whom, she angrily asked herself, could these Kentuckians have gained the impression that she had come out to marry Fant Annable unless from Fant, himself? She wondered if such boasting of amatory conquest was a general characteristic of male Kentuckians, such as profiteering on war wheat and selling repentant runaway slaves downriver.

As from a distance, she heard Mr. Annable asking God's blessing on the family and this stranger from an erring land whom they hoped to receive as a daughter into their midst. The long service ended, the family arose stiffly. Good-nights were said, and Kate showed America upstairs to her room. America looked around the spacious chamber. With its towering platform bed, swell-front chest of drawers, a Dolly Madison mirror over the fireplace and ornate Staffordshire vases on the mantel, it might have been her own room at Golden Hill. On the bedside stand was a Sheffield tray containing a glass of milk and three beaten biscuits laced with thin slices of country ham which she tried not to wolf. After she had undressed and bathed in hot water some unseen servant had provided, she stretched out on the corded bed and tried to formulate some plan acceptable to Cousin Margaret and to her own hurt pride. . . .

Sounds on the porch beyond her rear windows awakened America. Down the western sky, the setting moon hung low enough to throw a jaundiced glow into the bedchamber. America listened. Someone was being helped by a soft-voiced negro up the enclosed stairway from the lower porch.

"Dammit, I tell you—*hic!*—I had a reason to go to town!" Fant's drunken voice insisted beyond the window shutters. "Wassa reason I went to town, Uncle Cate?"

"Dat young lady from Virginny done arrive."

"Sorrel top! For Christ's sake—"

"Mistah Stone brung her aout. You's gwine wake youah paw iffen you mak so much racket, suh. An' you knows how he raise sand!"

"I—*hic!*" the voice gurgled off.

America heard the footsteps continue along the porch to a door down the L-shaped wing. The slippered footsteps returned, brought water and a broom, made swishing sounds, and retreated downstairs.

A tired America, with shadows under her misery-dark eyes, appeared for breakfast. Fortunately the meal was hurried and silent. An empty place remained at Mrs. Annable's right hand.

Morning had served only to bring America a heightened sense of being suspended between earth and air on the rediscovered instability of Fant's character. Why had he prevailed on his mother to invite her out to Kentucky, if he meant to treat her with drunken rudeness which would soon make her the laughingstock of Mason County?

The noonday meal at Timberlawn proved a Gargantuan feast. Everything that the garden, poultry yard, smokehouse and preserving pantry provided, was set forth. Fant failed to appear. An abstemious eater, Mr. Annable threw down his unfinished corn muffin, pierced America with his searching gaze and demanded without preamble:

"What's the condition of the freedmen in Virginia, missy?"

America told how the one-time slaves had gone skylarking to the towns, leaving on the plantations the very young, the old and the decrepit.

"And rightly so," nodded Mr. Annable. "They consumed their youthful strength serving you. Are no sweeping provisions being made to assist these unfortunate victims of social injustice into a proper place in civic and community life?"

"What provisions would you suggest, sir? Plantation owners certainly want to recover their fortunes in the shortest possible time. Naturally we urge our freed slaves to come home and gc to work. What other help have we? And how else may the negroes win a permanent place for themselves?"

"Interesting as this discussion is, I regret I must bring it to a close," declared Cousin Margaret firmly, rising from behind her coffee tray. "America, may I suggest a siesta? Our custom is to reassemble in the parlors about three o'clock. Doubtless your cousins up and down Tuckahoe will come to call on you this afternoon. And I want you to look your prettiest."

Timberlawn's double parlors, handsome as they were, could not hold a candle to Golden Hill. At a front window, Kate observed dust rolling up the pike. When its funnel stopped at the Timberlawn gates, she announced with satisfaction:

"I told you the Drakes would be the first."

Dapper little Doctor Taliaferro Drake, statuesque Cousin Theresa, and three younger girls, Minerva, Jane and Daphne, filed in. During the confusion of introductions, it was explained that Allilee was haltering the young pair. Before everyone was seated, she came rushing in with silks a-crackle and plumes anod, a slender girl restless as a humming bird. One look into Allilee's pretty discontented face, and America sensed the rivalry between them.

Seated decorously on a love seat before the fireplace, America became the object of discreet glances from the adult Drakes and of open curiosity from Minerva, Jane and Daphne. America felt her own heart harden towards her Kentucky connection. What could these happy, overfed people, complacent in their glistening new silks and linen, secure on their rich farms, untouched by death or the memory of violence, what could they know or care about life as it was being endured today on the major battlefield of a war which had brought them only profit?

As if he could read her thoughts, Doctor Taliaferro joined her on the other love seat and demanded to know about conditions in Charlotte County.

"There is absolutely nothing left," answered America. "We have no servants, no seeds, no tools, no implements, no teams, no cloth, no medicines, and but few able-bodied men to show us how to begin again. Our fields are grown up in oak scrub, our roofs are falling in. It is thirteen months since Appomattox. Yet when I left, few had adjusted themselves to that crushing blow, or to the new way of life it had brought."

"When primogeniture pushed my grandfather out of Virginia to fight the forest and the Indians," Doctor Taliaferro remarked, unexpectedly, "he felt himself badly used. Now, the shoe appears on the other foot. You'll find us Kentuckians changed, my dear. Living here on the middle ground, we have forgotten some of our old ways and taken on new ones which may seem mercenary to you."

"I've heard it said northern Kentuckians have picked up many of the best traits of their Ohio neighbors."

"That's a polite way to put it. Now tell me about the old folks I met on my last visit home. Cousin Jacova Collier, who read her Bible on her knees, how is she?"

"Grandma died fifteen years ago."

With one eye on Allilee's watchful face, America answered his questions. Hearing footfalls on the stair, she guessed by the quickened interest in Allilee's eyes that Fant must be coming. America was the only person who did not turn and gaze as he entered the room. She could not, because within her she felt the stirring of that deep unrest which awaited only some move of his to be quickened into ecstasy.

"Miss America Moncure of Golden Hill!" cried the buoyant remembered voice. "Welcome to Timberlawn! Ma told me only yesterday she had invited you out, else I could have shifted appointments to await you on the dock."

"Stone Moncure met me in Cincinnati, thank you. You're looking well, Cousin Fant."

"Never better, ma'am! Unless it was at your bounteous board on Golden Hill. Cousin Theresa, your servant, ma'am. Dr. Drake—young ladies—Allilee, my dear! Is it true the Doctor bought Golden Rod for you? Why wouldn't my Sunshine be the perfect match for her?"

With his back towards the others, Fant stood talking with Allilee, whose face brightly mirrored the animation of their tête-à-tête. Listen as she tried, America could not catch the drift of their conversation. If it were about horses, she knew she could hold her own here as on saddle leather. Politeness compelled her instead to listen to Doctor Drake:

"I was deeply distressed to hear of your father's passing. How did it happen?"

"He was at Richmond with President Davis through the autumn of '62," replied America. "After Brother Tom was killed at Gettysburg, father came home a broken man, and passed away before Christmas."

"And your brother William?"

"He was killed with General Stuart."

"And Ephraim?"

"He was spared to us. He's mother's mainstay, now."

"I expect Cousin Jincy has her hands full?" asked Cousin Theresa.

"Yes, ma'am," agreed America. Fant had doubtless told full particulars about the burning of Golden Hill.

In a moment of general silence, Allilee declared that she and Fant were going to the paddock. She returned alone in ten minutes and announced that Fant had commissioned her to convey his farewells, as he himself was overdue in Limestone. She ended with a glance at America which seemed to say: "See what comes when a fond mama tries to coerce her son's affections! He's wearied of you before you can exchange greetings."

Doctor Taliaferro and Cousin Theresa took their leave with hospitable promises. As if on the same string, Minerva, Jane, and Daphne curtsied and filed out. Allilee lingered to declare silkily:

"I trust you will enjoy your stay on Tuckahoe, Cousin America. We younger members have the merriest times at fish fries, moonlight rides and basket picnics in summer, in winter with oyster suppers and parlor charades. You'll not lack for what entertainment we can provide to make your visit agreeable, ma'am."

"I understand you are a famous horsewoman, Cousin Allilee. I would like to challenge your skill some day—on Sunshine."

"Do ladies ride stallions in Virginia, ma'am?"

"Since Sherman came through, we walk."

"Allilee, what's detaining you?" called Doctor Drake's impatient voice from outside. "You know this young team won't stand."

When Cousin Margaret and Kate reentered the hall, they found America standing in the front parlor doorway with an expression of unconcern on her heart-shaped face. Mrs. Annable's exasperation found immediate voice:

"Upon my word, America! I can't imagine what took Fant off to town like that."

"The same important business which detained him last night, I suspect. What a charming girl Allilee Drake is, Cousin Margaret—and such a beauty!"

"You should have seen her three years ago," declared Kate. "She's fading, now."

"I could see she's years your senior," America won Kate forever to her side.

"Allilee ought to be holding babies of her own, instead of those wild nags of her father's," smiled Mrs. Annable. "She delights to drive him on his professional errands. And now, Kate, you and I had better be making our own rounds. America, would you care to come with me while I gather up the eggs?"

"Every evening except tonight, ma'am. If you will excuse me, I will go upstairs. I haven't finished writing ma of my safe arrival, and your kind reception."

Mrs. Annable and Kate looked at her to see if she would mean what she had said. Unable to scale the wall of her reserve, yet won whole-heartedly to her side, they watched her shabby skirts swing out of sight around the landing balustrade.

"I could wring Fant's neck!" Kate whispered, fiercely. "Wouldn't you know he'd let the cat out of the bag? You can lead a horse to water, but—"

"Oh, dearie me!" sighed Mrs. Annable, the collapse of her intrigue heavy upon her. "And I had so hoped America's arrival might settle him down. Kate, you don't suppose it could have been that other Moncure girl he was attracted to, do you?"

"America's the one he described to Allilee. If you ask me, I think this girl's a thousand times too good for him."

"She's her mother's daughter," Mrs. Annable commented. "Tuckahoe is still too young to produce great ladies like Jincy Collier. This girl's prettier, but even she can't hold a candle to Miss Jincy for manners and charm."

"Where did you know her, ma?" Kate asked as she unlocked the door to the supply closet under the parlor stairs.

"At White Sulphur Springs, before I married Mr. Annable. I was a shy clumsy heiress from Kentucky, but she gave me the happiest summer of my life. And that's another reason why I mean to do all I can now to smooth America's path."

Fant did not return that night. Nor the next week. As the hot June days lengthened, America felt her position grow daily more intolerable. Humiliated beyond the acceptance of sympathy, she fitted herself into the feminine routine of Timberlawn as best she could. While Kate and Mrs. Annable were occupied with morning duties, America formed a habit of walking up the lane and across the pike to a promontory on the river rim which formed the southeastern knob of Tuckahoe. Through a gap she could see the Ohio, and beyond, the distant green hills of Pisgah, Promised Land to many a Kentucky slave. The water's quicksilver sheen was often fluted by a steamboat, which from America's height appeared like a black bug swimming ahead of its triangular wake. She learned to recognize the silver whistles of the *Bonanza,* the *Magnolia* and the *Evening Mail.* The freighters pushing barges on their noses had a masculine whoop. An incident of prewar days told her by Kate came often to her mind as she stood with the breeze stirring her skirts and gazed downriver into the distance which held the only person who could make this Abolition-poisoned Kentucky life bearable.

In 1858, going to the Severance administrator's sale in Georgetown to obtain an Alderney bull to inject new blood into his dairy herd, Mr. Annable had brought home instead a huge ugly-faced negro named Evan. An able worker, Evan refused to see the black girls who rolled eyes at him in the Annable slave quarters. Questions failed to penetrate his reserve until one day his mistress saw him listening to the *Magnolia*'s whistle downriver from Limestone. About to gather up her buggy reins, Mrs. Annable heard Evan whisper, as if to himself:

"Heah dat whistle? Dat whistle's gwine whar my Bet am gone."

"Your Bet, Evan? Who is she?"

"She war mah wife, mistis."

"But Mr. Annable told me you were put up single."

"Yassum, Ah war. When Miss 'Toinette got married, she

cry so hard foah Bet tuh go Souf wid her dat Marse Sev'rance say: 'Go on, Bet, and Ah'll send Ebe des as soon as de crop's in.' Foah Ah could git sta'hted, dat young hoss killt him. De boss-man executionah warn't gwine bother wid a dead man's promise tuh a nobody lak me."

"Executor, Evan. If Mr. Annable had known this, he wouldn't have bought you."

"Ain't Ah done mah wu'k willin', mistis?"

"Yes, but I won't have unhappy negroes about me."

"Marse Annable, he knowed. An' so did all dem folks up in de Bluegrass. Dat's why Ah come cheap. But me an' Bet, we war braced foah pa'htin' from de fust. We had de preacher w'at married us put in de lines: 'Till deaf or distance do us pa'ht!' "

"Listen to me, Evan! For what I say, I will do." Mrs. Annable had replied with more vehemence than was her custom in addressing a slave. "I will either buy your wife back for you here, or I will sell you downriver to her present owners, so you may be reunited. Which would you prefer?"

The slave, Kate said, had fallen on his knees in the dust beside the buggy wheel, blubbering and raising his clasped hands:

"Lemme go whar she's at, lemme go Souf tuh her! Gawd bless you, mistis, Gawd lif' up His face an' gib you peace."

"Your new master may put you into the cotton."

"Ah kin wu'k anywhar wid de best ob 'em. Bet, she mought have a chile she wouldn't want tuh leave."

Kate had ended the ordinary tale by describing how some weeks later, while Mr. Annable looked on in stony-faced silence, Evan had been locked into a coffle of runaway slaves Lewis Robards was making up for sale into the lower Mississippi. Carrying more than his share of chain, Evan had stepped joyously out of their lives with a hushed look on his flat face as if he expected to see Heaven instead of the cotton fields. Mr. Robards, on his return, counted eleven hundred dollars in gold and Miss Antoinette's executed receipt into Mrs. Annable's hand. "It was the only piece of business I ever saw ma transact," concluded Kate, "and from that day to this, I've never heard her or pa mention it to each other. Every year I take out that stack of gold from her writing-box and dust it off when I'm spring-cleaning, then lock it up again."

Hearing the *Magnolia* whistle downstream, America thought that to marry Fant Annable she must be braced for parting, as Evan and Bet had been. The woman who married Fant would have to take him on his own selfish terms, she realized, and remembered the look of unqualified surrender in Allilee Drake's unhappy green eyes.

America made it her custom to return from the knob by way of Sunshine's paddock and stud-stable below the yard fence. The bright bay stallion had been quick to make friends. He was always thirsty. America carried him a pail of water every morning from the back-kitchen cistern. While he drank with his muzzle deep-thrust into the wooden bucket and his shining agate eyes watching her every move, she gathered handfuls of grass from the lawn and piled them just beyond reach of the stallion's wet lips, until she could sit down and feed him at her leisure, the while she talked or sang to him in her softly slurred South Virginia accent.

"So that's the way you feel about Kentucky, missy?" she heard Mr. Annable trumpet above her one breathless July noon, to be echoed by Gander's hiss of approval.

"Were you never homesick?" she answered, glancing up with a disarming smile.

"Do I look like a schoolboy? What're you doing to that horse?"

"You see how he relishes a taste of green. He gets lonesome down here by himself all day."

"If he were mine, I'd have him altered tomorrow and put to some use. I told my son when he brought him here—he won him at cards!—that I wouldn't be responsible one day for his keep."

"So that's why the stableboys neglect him!"

"Do you think I'd let a valuable animal starve?"

"Oh, no, sir, not on a big rich place like this. I can see you're a fine farmer, Cousin Justinian," she added. Dusting off her hands, she rose to stand beside him, her eyes fixed on Gander lest the jealous bird nip. "I know, because I managed Golden Hill after my father's death."

"What could a chit like you raise?"

"Tobacco and corn, sir. I got thirteen cents a pound for my last year's tobacco crop."

"That did very well, I must admit."

He bestowed upon her his rare smile of approval, which broke through the harshness of his face to give America a glimpse of the charm he might have possessed as a young man, before fanaticism set his countenance into its present stern mask. Behind them Gander, tired after his morning's trek with his master across the fields, hissed and beat his wings with impatience to go on to the dining room where he knew shade, cool water and a plate of breakfast scraps awaited him under the floor boards.

"Come to the house, now," Mr. Annable concluded, thrusting with his cane at his satellite, "and ready yourself for dinner. Nobody's late to meals in this family."

Every weekday noon before he returned to the field, Uncle Cato hitched Bella into Mrs. Annable's buggy shafts and tied the mare to the cedar tree below the stile. If guests arrived early, she had to stand there unused, switching her tail and stamping flies until the men reappeared at sundown to lead her stablewards. Kate and America often succeeded in trotting her up and down Tuckahoe to return calls made on the Virginia visitor.

The ridge had been named Tuckahoe, America knew, because it was first settled entirely by eastern Virginians. Anyone living on or near the Tidewater was called a Tuckahoe by the jocular pioneers living in what subsequently became West Virginia and Kentucky. The word tuckahoe was of Indian origin, used to designate the tubers which grew on roots of aged oak trees. The Indians, Ol' Uncle said, ground them into meal and ate them, as they did chinquapin cakes. Even in Charlotte County, to be called a Tuckahoe was similar to being described as an old mossback.

On their first sight-seeing drive, Kate told America what she knew of Tuckahoe's settlement. The five thousand acres of ridge land had been issued by Patrick Henry in a land grant to Colonial Ephraim Collier for his services in the French and Indian wars. Preferring himself to remain in Virginia, Colonel Collier had built Golden Hill. His younger sons and daughters, with their wives and husbands, had migrated with slaves, livestock and domestic gear to claim the crescent-shaped plateau of cane and forest which the patent located for them on the southern shore of the Ohio River, between Lawrence, Glade Springs and Lee's creeks.

"That's a general idea of what happened," concluded Kate, slapping at Bella's rump with a line. "Of course the land's been divided and small parcels of it have occasionally come on to the market. But for the main, it's held by the grandchildren of the 'improvers' who occupied it in 1790."

Forming the spinal column of Tuckahoe was the limestone toll pike over which Bella now trotted with protesting gurgles from her fat insides. Tired of being mud-bound eight months of the year, Charles Moncure in 1845 built four miles of it from Sharon Crossing, on the river, past his Children's Chance to the MacGower post office and smithy at Tuckahoe's midpoint. He then presented his bill for twenty-eight hundred dollars to the Mason County fiscal court which tabled it indefinitely, but conferred a unanimous vote of thanks on its builder, and decreed that he and his might use the new road without toll for all time to come. The remaining miles past Timberlawn and on into Limestone, Mason County taxpayers were compelled to build at general expense because Justinian Annable wouldn't.

From Timberlawn the Annable place—as Margaret's inheritance was now called—rolled gently westward to a wooded glen out of which Glade Springs Creek slipped as unobtrusively as a garter snake to cut its way deeper at every mile through the river rim to the Ohio. Near the perpetual spring which formed its headwaters and gave it its name, stood Glade Springs church and school. America soon learned the facts and tradition which hung, like its curtains of Virginia creeper, about the church's walls.

In 1832, swayed by the eloquence of Alexander Campbell, recruits from the Baptist, Presbyterian and other denominations left their own communions to form a new Fellowship of Disciples, later designated as Christians. On Tuckahoe this reform group was led by Charles Moncure and Justinian Annable. While they were looking about for at least an upper room in which to meet, as had the Twelve, a survey of the Moncure, Drake and Annable land became necessary to settle an estate. As executors Charles Moncure, Dr. Taliaferro Drake and Justinian Annable set to work each with a surveyor and chainmen at their respective portions of the crescent. They met in Glade Springs glen, to find there a nine-acre plot which lay between the tracts each represented, beyond the points of call of the three groups of heirs.

"I will dedicate my claim in this plot to God," declared Justinian.

"Let us each bring his slaves," suggested Charles Moncure, "and raise God's House here, to be a light on Tuckahoe for all time to come."

"I'll give you a quitclaim to the land, but that's as far as I intend to go," declared Dr. Taliaferro, who was known to have read Tom Paine. "I can't abide the smell of brimstone that hangs about these country churches."

Access to church and school was had over the Cary trail, which sprang at right angles out of Tuckahoe turnpike, and meandered past the church's platform stile to the stately house of the rich and picturesque Ulysses Cary. From her talkative guide America learned why Letitia Bedford Cary was considered a local saint. One evening when Letitia sat nursing her firstborn, a son ten days old, Ulysses came stamping the snow off his boots into the firelit room with a bundle held awkwardly in his arms. Without explanation he extended it towards her. Her eyes, with quick maternal instinct, darted over its contours, and interrogated him blankly.

"It's my child—by Stella Barnes," he said. "I must have been drunk." As Letitia continued to stare at him over her own son, he went on: "She doesn't want it. Will you give it suck?"

She did not answer. He laid the bundle on her knees, and stumbled out of the house. Letitia put the new-born girl baby to her left breast, while Cary nursed the right. The foundling, Bess Cary, as she was called, grew to resemble her handsome father in everything except passion and pride.

"I don't know what I'd do without her," Lettie once confided in Kate's hearing to Mrs. Annable. "She gives me less trouble than any child I have."

Opposite Glade Springs stile was the fieldstone wall built by Major Argyle Chisholm "to keep the damn' Campbellite horses from pulling my fences down!" To give his thousand-acre farm west of the Cary place an outlet onto Tuckahoe turnpike, Major Chisholm had paid through his nose for the first parcel of Collier land to come onto the market. In the middle of an oak grove, the Major then built a twenty-room mansion surrounded by the finest boxwood in Mason County. No sooner was he well established than an elder brother died abroad and rumor had it that the slight, profane Scot had become a belted earl. When asked by Kate if he intended to return to Scotland and claim his heritage, Major Chisholm barked: "Do ye take me for a witless gowk? Gang hame an' starve? That's nae for me!"

At the halfway point of Tuckahoe turnpike squatted the tollhouse, smithy, postoffice and general store. One bar extended across Tuckahoe pike, another across the trail which led westwards to Minerva Ridge, which paralleled Tuckahoe.

One night in the spring of 1837, James MacGower, a Scotch-Irish journeyman blacksmith, had camped beneath the towering maple which marked Tuckahoe's future center. Aroused before moonrise by old Dr. Drake to replace the iron tire which his buggy wheel had thrown at the start of a race with the stork, MacGower set up his anvil, unswung his bellows, and went to work. Other customers followed. Prevailing on his first customer to sell him ten acres of Drake ground, MacGower established his smithy in a lean-to shed under the sugar tree, built a log house opposite it in the angle of the trails, sent for his family and became a neighborhood fixture. When Charles Moncure cast about in his mind's eye for a tollkeeper in 1845, MacGower and his sharp-eyed wife, Abigail, seemed placed at the sugar tree by a benign Providence which ordered all things well, and by the forelock.

"Mrs. MacGower is such a talker we'll never get away," whispered Kate. "Pretend you don't see her."

"And have her think me a stuck-up? How do you do, ma'am?" inquired America, and dropped the quarter Kate had provided into the palm of a rawboned Scotswoman who had stepped out onto the tollhouse porch.

"You'll be the Virginia lassie Fant Annable says will set the wor-rld afire! Aye, ye're bonnie tae see wi' chestnut-burr curls an' e'en beckonin' as sunshine on a distant loch."

"I've heard about you, too, Mrs. MacGower—how you scrub behind your children's ears with one hand and beat the catechism into them with the other."

"Fant Annable was verra kind tae speak sae weel o' me."

"Please raise the bar, Mrs. MacGower. We're overdue."

With a dour look at Kate, the toll-mistress opened the road to them. Some distance down the pike, Kate pointed out the Drake establishment, set in a hollow west of the turnpike. America was always to look upon it as the stronghold of Morgan le Fay. In search of a pleasanter sight, she turned her head and saw on the right beyond a fine open meadow a log house with four stalwart chimneys thrust against the eastern sky.

"That's the original Collier homestead, Foxden," declared Kate. "Grandpa Archibald built it."

"Who lives there, now?"

"Uncle Simmy Collier, ma's only brother. He's twice as old as she is, and rich as cream. He says he's going to leave Foxden to Fant, because Fant's the only one of ma's children with enough Collier spunk in him to stand up to pa."

Kate went on to describe the aged eccentric. After Emancipation, while former slave-owners in Mason County were trying to establish some system of land tenure whereby the freed negroes could work ground for one-half the crop and the landlord would furnish cabin, tools and team, Uncle Simmy gave his negroes each two suits of summer and winter clothes, ten dollars and his blessing to go North. When they returned, he drove them off with a buggy whip. Besides his saddle gelding, Uncle Simmy's only livestock were game chickens and a drove of hogs that fattened on his lush pasture in summer and pulled down his neighbors' fodder shocks in winter. Too frugal to return hospitality, Uncle Simmy accepted none. Fant once found him walking carefully around his stable lot looking for the nickel he had intended for the Sabbath collection plate. Nothing was ever lost, in Uncle Simmy's estimation, not even this nickel which was recovered by sundown. "How could I have spent the day more profitably?" he answered his spendthrift nephew's ridicule. When a fine colt of his leaped into the air and, falling, broke its neck, to Fant's sympathetic comment he answered: "Mind your business, boy! A man of property may expect losses."

"I'd take you to call, except he resents visitors," confessed Kate, peering nearsightedly up at the landmark. "It's really a wonderful old house. The upstairs rooms are sealed so tight with walnut planks Uncle Simmy stored wheat up there safe from rats. He sold it to the Union Army and hid the money in the cistern under the dog run. The niggers say you can taste gold in the water."

"Why does he call the place Foxden?"

"Because a vixen whelps under a cabin floor every spring. He says she's got more sense than any woman on Tuckahoe."

Beyond Uncle Simmy's fallow acres rose the red chimneys of the Walton place, the first brick house on Tuckahoe. From here Stone's mother, Clara Walton, had gone a bride to occupy Charles Moncure's cabin on the two-hundred-acre patrimony which his father Dabney had given him in 1834, when he became a man. Eight years later, Charles and Clara built Children's Chance.

"Cousin Clara's got sugar diabetes, now," Kate whispered, as if in the sickroom. "When she dies, Rindy—that's Stone's only sister Emarind—will marry Captain McCord, the high sheriff, and move onto the Walton farm which she'll heir. Stone will get the home place. And then he'll have to marry," she added with unconscious self-revelation. "There's Children's Chance, in that grove of black locusts. It has the prettiest approach on Tuckahoe."

Through massive gates and a stately avenue of landscaped green, America saw white columns rising in a double portico across the front of a green-shuttered red brick house. Kate, her face wistful, described how the county had wanted "to run Charles Moncure for the legislature, but he said he couldn't leave his flowers. On summer nights when there's a heavy dew and the wind's just right, you can smell his Confederate jasmine up at Timberlawn."

"When are we going to return Cousin Emarind's call?"

"We could today, except Stone won't be there. He and pa left before dawn to buy hogs at Mount Sterling. Of course Emarind will get her share of all this in addition to the old Walton place," Kate could not relinquish a subject evidently dear to her. "Even if Stone weren't so well-fixed, he'd be important. He's already handling tobacco, which takes him to Cincinnati to sell his purchase on the hogshead breaks. He'll need a capable wife to run things while he's away."

A reply was on America's tongue to say that the rising young business man of Tuckahoe had an odd way of choosing a mate—on sixty white horses—but she thought better of it. While Bella quickened her gait homewards, America gazed at Stone's future acres and wondered why destiny had bound her by more than love to Fant Annable, when Children's Chance might be hers if sixty white horses had anything to do with it.

Not much longer, however, was she to remain under Mr. Annable's hated Abolitionist roof. On her supper plate that evening, America found a letter addressed to her in her mother's handwriting. After he had finished his raspberries, Mr. Annable suggested that she read its contents aloud. Reluctantly America began. "Parents in default on their children's tuition fees," wrote Mrs. Moncure, "continue to send around eggs, milk and summer vegetables. Palestine has recovered sufficiently to give the Crenshaw girls piano lessons. A ragamuffin Tarheel youth, who calls himself Tugger Blake and claims to know you, has come to town peddling Durham smoking mixture. He has had the temerity to ask Palestine to go walking with him.

"To get her out in the air under safe escort," continued Miss Jincy's letter, "I let her go. The Union League has opened headquarters across the street. Truly, it is the most vicious of the many pseudo-humanitarian agencies foisted on us by Yankees who know nothing of our problems and little understand the excesses into which their new freedom and unaccustomed idleness has plunged our African population. The Union League"—America read on—"is said to begin its secret meetings in total darkness and with rites calculated to terrorize the childlike natures of our former slaves, removed as they are by but a few generations from the jungle. Lights are then brought in; inflammatory speeches are made by the League's members, who are drawn almost wholly from the lowest types of carpetbaggers and scalawags, and the negroes are given instructions in the use of the ballot against us. Those who remain loyal are threatened with dire punishments if they do not agree to vote as the League instructs them."

"Stop!" thundered Mr. Annable and smote the table with his fist so that the dishes jumped. "I will hear no such calumny against the high-principled organization to which I have given liberally both of leadership and means."

"Do you accuse my mother of falsifying the truth, sir?" asked America, her voice trembling.

"You chit, do you dare talk back to me at my own table?"

"Have I your permission to retire, sir?"

"You have not!"

With shaking hands, America endeavored to return the letter to its envelope. Mr. Annable motioned to the housemaid to place a lamp off the sideboard before him and clear the table. With a baleful glance at his family, he drew a religious pamphlet from his pocket and began to read.

Mrs. Annable and Kate, apparently accustomed to such scenes, sat with expressionless faces. On the mantelpiece the clock ticked away a half-hour, then prepared to strike eight o'clock. Under cover of its notes, Edwin Dell whispered:

"Ma, can I go?"

"Ask your father, son."

The boy, deciding not to risk it, turned resentful eyes onto America. From the kitchen came voices of the supping negroes. America's thoughts wandered to Fant. How many times had he been kept sitting through a childish ordeal like this? Looking up at her kinswoman, America found Mrs. Annable's wise tired eyes fixed upon her in an expression of compassion. Where truculence had failed, sympathy brought tears. Overflowing, they rolled down America's cheeks.

"Now that I see you properly repentant, I'll forgive you," Mr. Annable declared, stuffing his pamphlet into his pocket. "Kate, call in the niggers."

"Sir, I assure you—"

"Merry, for our sakes!" whispered Mrs. Annable and, rising, stood aside for her husband to precede her into the family room.

The weary family followed, knelt before their accustomed

chairs. Several negroes luckless enough not to have gone to their cabins, took their places in the dining room. Mr. Annable read a martial psalm, then launched into his euphuistic evening prayer, during which he recounted to the Lord every detail of his stewardship during the day.

"Vouchsafe, O God of Battles," Mr. Annable concluded, "to visit upon these unregenerate and impenitent traitors to our Union the full and bitter aftermath of defeat. Bend their stiff necks, O Lord; chasten their proud spirits and level them low in the dust of economic and civic humiliation—America Collier Moncure, where are you going?"

"To my chamber, sir."

"Come back this instant, and get down on your knees!"

"I claim the heritage of every Protestant Christian, to address my own prayers to a God of mercy and love. Good-night, all."

Before Mr. Annable could find suitable words to answer, America was on her way upstairs. Five minutes later, she climbed into bed. Listen as she might, she could hear no sound below. The big joyless house was still.

Early the next morning, dressed in her shabby black, with the streamers of her rusty traveling bonnet tied under her chin, America appeared on the front porch. Since dawn she had packed her belongings. She walked up the dew-drenched flagstones to meet Mr. Annable and Gander returning from their first supervisory trip to the stables. Her eyes on her host's black tie, loosely knotted because of midsummer heat, America began:

"I hope you will accept my apology for what you must consider a gross violation of your hospitality, sir. I was quite beside myself."

"You must know by now, ma'am, I am accustomed to respect from my household."

"You will no longer be troubled by my presence," America replied. Since only one course remained to her, she had accepted it and was anxious now to be on her way with as little commotion as possible. "Will you be so kind as to send my trunk to Limestone by the first stage, and say my devoirs to your wife?"

"What do you intend to do there?"

Because she had no course of action mapped out beyond leaving Timberlawn, America could not answer. Looking past him, she saw Sunshine walking along the paddock fence in anticipation of her approach. Here was one unfortunate in the Annable establishment, she thought, who would miss her.

"Don't you trade for credit on my good name!"

"You forget, sir, that while Fate has stripped me of all else, I still have my two hands," she answered him, trying to keep her voice steady. "In Limestone surely I can find one woman of Southern sympathies and Christian compassion who will take me into her kitchen to cook—or into the family room to instruct her children."

"I walked into Limestone thirty years ago with a pack of schoolbooks on my back. I was the only man on this end of Tuckahoe who owned a set of schoolbooks—and who had the knowledge to use them."

"Then in God's name, when you yourself were once as destitute as I am now, without a friend, not knowing which way to turn"—she cried, throwing back her head to keep the weak tears she despised from rolling down her cheeks—"in God's name, how can you be so cruel to me?"

Their eyes met in a long gaze that probed beyond anger and pride to an unspoken recognition of their mutual equality. Astonished by what she had seen, the girl was the first to look away in embarrassment. Above her she heard a tired old man offer terms of surrender:

"As yet, no pedagogue has been engaged for Glade Springs school. If you will go back to the house and compose yourself, I will secure the place for you."

"Why, sir! That is kind of you, especially when I know that Rebels are not welcome to you on Tuckahoe."

"Let Tuckahoe decide that. The intensity of my political

convictions has blinded me, I fear, to my manifest duty as a God-fearing man."

"Fant doesn't love me. I can see that, now."

"Fant doesn't love anybody or anything except his own evil ways!"

"I can't thank you enough, sir. I—"

"Tut, girl, don't cry. I was overhasty myself. Think no more of it. Go prepare yourself for breakfast. And get that infernal bonnet off your head before Margaret sees it, if you value my peace of mind!"

Chapter 5

Just before it joined the Charlotte Court House pike, Tom Cat Lane dipped with the rolling countryside. In this hollow, rain water had collected to form a mudhole of unknown depths. On either side red clay banks ran like open wounds. Jake, the wheel mule, took in these obstacles with a glance of his one good eye and stopped pulling. When Tom, the other mule, felt the traces slacken, he wilted in his harness. As the heavy wagon began to settle, Tugger Blake sat hunched on the wagon seat, his profanity for once exhausted. The leaden bowl of the sky, streaked with meager flame in the west above the ever present band of dark forest, pressed down as if heavy with more rain. It was March, 1867.

Because he must sell or barter or quit, Tugger had hit on the idea of working his outfit along the back roads. Ex-slaves, while they lacked silver, were said to possess an abundance of food distributed to them by the Freedmen's Bureau. Tugger had visited the Babylons of decaying great houses, the Shakerags and Scuffletowns where freed negroes had lived before Emancipation. These shabby settlements he found to be the gathering places of Africans on the march. They wanted his smoking tobacco for their corncobs as much as he wanted the extra United States Army rations they did not need. Under a top layer of fodder, his wagon was loaded with staple foods which Tugger hoped to sell to mountaineers on his way home, or exchange at Durham for ten times their weight in new-crop Carolina bright-leaf.

The rain fell steadily. The sweaty flanks of the mules steamed in the chilly night air. The team should be covered,

Tugger knew, but he sat motionless. Self-disgust mounted with his anxiety. If that old Jezebel of a black woman hadn't taken so tarnation long to make up her mind, he might even now be enjoying the drenched safety of the Charlotte Court House oaks. The subject of Tugger's successful trade had been the brooch of a set of seed-pearl and turquoise jewelry. Now he preferred not to think of what might, and often did happen on these Virginia back roads after nightfall.

His larger valuables Tugger kept buried in the cannister of mule feed between dashboard and wagon seat. Currency and jewelry were wrapped in rags and poked deep inside Jake's horse collar. Tugger dared not hide the brooch acquired this afternoon in the horse collar. The brooch might be the first thing some wench would ask for, should he be held up. With a mediocre assortment of other articles, he pocketed the brooch and vaulted up onto the right bank. Armful at a time, he began pulling the fodder off the top of his wagon to lighten it enough to get it through the mudhole and out onto the turnpike.

The ring of negro voices behind him made him pause with his hands on the ears of a sugar sack. A band of perhaps fifteen from Scuffletown bound for Charlotte Court House were coming down Tom Cat Lane. Tugger glanced around him for a fence rail, then realized the futility of trying to defend his wares. Besides, no white had a chance in a Virginia court these days against a nigger. In silence he watched the young bucks swarm over his belongings. He had always hated niggers, even the one sickly slave girl who had crept like a frightened bitch about the kitchen in far-away Durham.

Whiskey was what they wanted most. And then his small stock of smoking mixture, already sacked. After they had divided the tobacco amongst themselves, they began looking for his valuables. They threw his bedding and cooking utensils into the mud. With wasteful malice they slashed the sacks of Army rations for which Tugger had traded patiently from cabin door to cabin door. Sugar, pale as snow and as scarce in southern Virginia, flowed over the red clay bank. Rivulets of unroasted coffee beans ran out from slit sacks of *Arbuckle's Best* and were dammed by the mules' legs. When they tickled, the hoof came up with a sucking plop! The precious beans flowed into the cavity, and were ground out of sight when the hoof was replaced.

"Whar you keep youah spondulics, traduh?" demanded a powerful buck with a blue shine on his flat face, so black he was. "Gimme youah weasel, you heah?"

"Whar's dat purty blue breas' pin you done swap mah mammy aout ob, white boy?" demanded a skinny black girl with a purple bandanna around her head. She turned towards the giant who had demanded Tugger's purse: "Git dem back foah me, will you, Timbah?"

"Whar you hide youah pu'se, white boy? Is you totin' hit?" demanded the giant called Timber.

Another buck, Tugger noticed, was preparing to climb over the front wagon wheel. The cannister of cracked corn might be the next thing he would throw into the mud.

"Don't you push me too far, niggers!" Blake warned. "I got a pistol in my pocket I ain't afeart to use."

"Bantie rooster, is you scratchin' grabble at me?" mocked Timber.

Out of the corner of his eye Blake noticed that the buck had dropped off the front wagon wheel. On the bank, Timber was coming at Blake with hands open and outstretched, like a gorilla preparing to wrestle.

"Doan be a fool, white boy," called the skinny black girl. "W'at good is a pu'se tuh you daid?"

Before Timber's hands could reach him, Tugger stepped back. Out of his pockets he drew his fists clenched about his decoy assortment of valuables, among them the brooch and his snap purse. Timber snatched the loot, then struck Blake on the jaw. Reeling, Tugger felt his cheek laid open. Before Timber could examine his spoils, the black girls swarmed over him. Raising his paws above their heads, beyond reach of clutching fingers, he grumbled:

"Lookit dat, naow! You's knock dat purty breas' pin aout ob mah hand. Here, tak' dis trash. Dat breas' pin's de onliest thing Ah wants."

While the others fought over the lesser valuables, Timber bent to peer about in the trampled mud for the lost brooch. Twilight was upon them, swiftly deepening into night.

"Niggahs, w'at we foolin' round heah fo'?" called a tipsy bacchante, cakewalking along the opposite bank from where Tugger sprawled with his hand to his cut cheek. "We's got celebratin' tuh do."

"Come on, niggahs! Evuhbody grab an' git—"

"W'at foah should we tote, when we kin git a plenty in taown foah de axin'?"

"Oh, Mistah Reid, gimme somepin tuh eat," chanted the buck who had threatened the valuables in the cannister. "Gimme somepin tuh eat foah mah mammy!"

"Oh, Mistah Reid!" others took up the chorus, evidently a familiar one.

Hard-eyed, Tugger watched the hilarious band cavort down the lane and out onto the turnpike. The something warm trickling down the back of his hand he did not identify as his own blood. He was thinking too intensely. Other niggers would be coming along any minute now from Scuffletown. He'd better feed his mules the scattered fodder, Tugger decided, and collect his skillet and coffee pot while light remained to spot them. The sight of Jake and Tom eating, cheered him. With fodder in their bellies, a chance remained that they might pull the lightened wagon out onto the turnpike. As Tugger stepped back from loosening the check lines, he winced, hopped onto one foot and raised the other to see what had stung him. Hanging from the sole of his home-cobbled moccasin was the turquoise and seed-pearl brooch. Tugger pocketed it with a chuckle and pitched in methodically to salvage what he could of his spoiled rations.

Hoof beats down the turnpike caught his ear. Two horsemen were approaching. Niggers weren't the only ones who could steal. With considerable left to lose, Tugger watched anxiously as they approached the juncture of Tom Cat Lane. One of them rode like an Indian. They slowed gait, swung into the lane.

"Peddler, you've picked a poor place to open store," drawled Archie Crenshaw, splashing up to the mules' heads.

"Tugger Blake! Damned if you ain't stuck like a flea on a blanket!" chuckled Ephraim, and was out of his saddle onto the bank.

"I was lightenin' my load. I could 'a' gotten myself out if that damn' nigger and his droppin's hadn't come along twenty minutes too soon."

"Climb up on that wagon seat," Ephraim took command, "and let's hear you make love to those mules. Arch, tie one end of this rope onto the tongue end and the other over your saddle horn. Pull like hell when Tugger gives the word! I'll go around back and shove."

With good-natured profanity, shouts and grunts, men and animals broke the wagon free and moved it down the lane onto the turnpike. As he coiled the rope, Ephraim kept up a steady flow of half-jest mingled with gall:

"By moonrise, every buck nigger in Virginia will be limber drunk. Congress passed the Reconstruction Act today, Blake. I reckon you think you're in Virginia, the Old Dominion, the cradle of Washington, Jefferson and Marshall? Hell, Tarheel, you ain't! You're standing on U.S. Military District No. 1, that's where you are. And the Mother of Presidents is a conquered province tonight, dragging at the wheel of Yankee Rome."

Tugger made no reply. He had always believed in the sanctity of the Union.

"From now on," continued Ephraim, "instead of answering to God and a jury of peers, you'll continue to breathe, hold property and peddle your mixture at the whim of General John M. Schofield, U.S. Army, and General J. Irving Gregg, commanding the Lynchburg Division."

"President Johnson's veto-ed hit."

"The Vindictives passed it over his veto," Crenshaw grumbled. "Come on, Eph, if you expect to locate that nigger before he gets to town."

"I'll catch you," Ephraim reassured him and mounted. "Tugger, go to our house, and let ma fix up that cheek of yours. Tell her I say you're to sleep on the cook-cabin floor. Your wagon will be safe in the yard. Can you get your stuff reloaded by yourself?"

"I shore kin! And I'm beholden to you both," Tugger made sober acknowledgment. "You won't find me a quick forgitter."

Without waiting for Ephraim, the Moncure family and Blake had eaten in the cook cabin. When the dishes were washed and the fire banked, Mrs. Moncure took it for granted that Tugger would come sit with them "in the house." They dashed across the wet back yard to the porch and into Cousin Homer's rear office. Here eagle mirrors and the Monticello highboy caught the firelight richly as at Golden Hill. In due time, Arabia led Andorra off to bed. On the hearth, a green log smoldered and flared. Outside, the wind rattled a loose tin on the porch roof. Rain beat in squalls against the shuttered windowpanes.

Dry for the first time in several nights, Tugger sat with his legs sprawled to the fire. He had forgotten how pleasant a woman-cooked meal, a warm room and human society could be after his sodden nights in the wagon. He was a plumb fool to try to work these Virginia roads alone! A city was the proper place to live, nowadays. Country life was done for, since white folks had to work. What he needed was a scrapper like Ephraim to watch the wagon while he traded. Or else to get into something different, where a smart man could win singlehanded, by his wits. The city was the place for him, Tugger's thoughts came to the same old conclusion. He was wasting his talents on this traipsin' life.

In her slipper chair on the other side of the hearth, Mrs.

Moncure turned the heel of a stocking for Andorra. She had copy books to correct later on, but she must rest for a few minutes after supper. Before the war, she had considered the sound of rain on the roof soothing. During the winter campaigns she could not hear it without shivering vicariously for husband, father, and sons exposed in field headquarters or open bivouac. Now all but Ephraim were in their graves, and it sounded colder than ever. In her mind's eye, she saw rain-soaked Hollywood Cemetery at Richmond. Streams of cold water clear as tears ran down the headstones and soaked through the uncut grass. She saw rain welling up around lidless coffins wherein beloved bodies lay wrapped in their soldiers' capes with faces turned up to the rain, dear white faces and quiet folded hands unchanged by time because her love kept the memory of them firm-fleshed as at parting.

Palestine sat in the chimney corner. When the fire blazed, Tugger could see her lovely expressionless face. She seldom stirred. She made Tugger think of a huge China doll some giant's child had leaned in the chimney nook, and then forgotten. Tugger wondered if she would jump like an ordinary girl if he said "Boo!"

"I reckon I'll dream about country roads on dark rainy nights for the rest of my born days," he chuckled.

Sometimes it helped, Mrs. Moncure had discovered, to ease her own heartache by asking other people about their troubles.

"Tell me about yourself, Tugger," she suggested. "I know you come from Durham Station in North Carolina. Have you relatives there?"

"Nary a soul to call my kin," declared young Blake. "All I know's my name, and that hit's honest."

"Who raised you?"

"Old Man Bledsoe and his wife. They got us out of a Methodist Orphan Asylum. They said they aimed to give two deservin' young uns a Christian home, but they wanted cheap help."

"Whom do you mean by 'us'?"

"Mary Ellen Bledsoe. She's about my age, but she's no kin to me. I turned out so good the first year, the Bledsoes sent back to the asylum for a girl an' give her their name."

"Do you like her?" Palestine demanded. Tugger had hoped that she was listening. The room was too dark to see.

"She ain't much of a worker, miss. She come in handy, though, when Maw Bledsoe died."

Conversation languished. Tugger wanted to say more, but could think of little which might interest these elegant women. As near as he could judge, Palestine did nothing all day but sit around in silk dresses, and ask unexpected questions. Tugger watched her through half-closed eyelids. He had never seen a girl sit so still. Her knees were as tight together as if she were gripping the horns of a sidesaddle. The girls he knew sat with legs apart, as mammies sat when they wanted to have big laps. Tugger found himself wondering if so exquisite a creature as Palestine could share with ordinary girls the normal functions of life? How would it feel to touch such waxen flesh?

Yonder was the kind of girl an ambitious man ought to marry. Such a girl could keep pace beside him, might even step ahead and open closed doors. Mary Ellen was all right to cook a man's meals and wash his shirts, but she couldn't show her husband how to use his knife and fork, or tell him whom he ought to know. Back in Durham, Dan Lord was always looking ahead to the time when he'd be a millionaire. Dan wanted to do for tobacco what some Cleveland trader had done in the coal-oil business. If ever he got to be a millionaire in New York City, Tugger promised himself, he would come back to old Charlotte Court House off the railroad, and marry Palestine Moncure.

"What're you thinking about, peddler boy?"

Palestine's voice was thick with contentment. Drowsing in her chimney corner, she had felt Tugger's gaze and her curiosity had been stirred. Enough of her coquetry remained to make her invite men's eyes. Once she had their attention, panic seized her. Mistaking honest flight for further invitation, the normal man's reaction was to give chase. From experience Mrs. Moncure had learned to keep Palestine's admirers at arm's length. This Tarheel didn't count.

"I was thinkin' about somepin purty I picked up this evening," Tugger replied, and felt in his pocket. "Want tuh see hit?"

"Cousin Tan's long-lost brooch!" Palestine squealed with pleasure. "Look, ma, Cousin Tan's Persian brooch, that's been missing all these years. Where's the rest of the set, you thieving mountain boy?"

"I come by hit in fair trade from an old nigger woman out Scuffletown way."

"Some light-fingered house servant must have taken it years ago," Mrs. Moncure reassured him. "Palestine, hand it back to our guest."

"No-o—"

"It's his, Teena dear. Hand it back to him."

"She kin keep hit, since she's taken such a fancy to hit," Tugger was surprised to hear himself declare.

"It's a perfectly lovely present!" Palestine cried, looking from Tugger's embarrassed face to Mrs. Moncure's to see if such generosity could be accepted. Reading confirmation, she pinned the brooch onto her breast, pirouetted into the center of the room and swept young Blake a deep curtsey. As she rose, her radiant face grew pinched, her eyes dilated with terror. Her voice, at first a whisper, became shrill:

"Ma, I hear a horse outside—in the back yard! It sounds like the horses I hear in my sleep—Ma, is it the Yankees coming back?"

"Hush, Palestine. It's only your brother Ephraim."

"Why does he have to stay out so late at night?" whimpered Palestine, the brooch forgotten. "He never goes to bed when he should. I want to ride Whitefoot, but he's always too tired. Ma, don't let him in!"

The porch door was flung open. Through a shining curtain of rain drops they caught glimpses of Tugger's wagon standing in water in the grassless back yard, and beyond it the cook cabin with windows pink from the banked fire inside. The next moment the door was shut and Ephraim leaned against it. The family room, which until his entrance had seemed so secure, was not big enough now to hold his anxiety.

"Ma, where're the girls?" he began, his eyes on Palestine.

"Upstairs asleep. Why, son?"

"Take Teena up to bed and come right back. I've business to talk over with you."

"Ma, I won't be sent out of the room like a ninny!" Palestine rebelled with a pretty pout.

"Teena dear, don't you want to try on your new brooch with some of my earbobs?" Mrs. Moncure suggested. "You may go through my jewel case, if you wish."

Carrying the lamp, Mrs. Moncure led the way through the schoolroom and on upstairs.

"Do you want me to git, too?" demanded Tugger.

Ephraim looked at him. After all, the Tarheel was his invited guest. What difference could it make if he did hear the whole fantastic story? Blake must be resourceful, or he couldn't have kept his outfit going through these starvation years.

"Oh, no! Make yourself entirely comfortable."

"If you're in trouble with the law, I'd be proud to help," Tugger volunteered. "Before he got religion, Old Man Bledsoe was always dodgin' the Revenoors."

Too much a Virginian to admit any Tarheel could ever be of assistance, Ephraim received Tugger's offer in silence. The heat felt good on his cold back. What a damn' shame to exchange this pleasant room for a jail! Sister Merry had transformed Cousin Homer's moldy back office with Golden Hill heirlooms. Too bad Homer Pettis had gone West. As a trial lawyer, the old coot couldn't be beat.

Reentering, Mrs. Moncure approached Ephraim with an anxious question:

"Now, son. What is it?"

"I've got to get out of here—before Gregg's men arrest me."

"Ephraim, what have you done?"

"Nothing, dammit! For once in my life I'm innocent as a baby. But they'll hang me just the same."

"Tell me, son. Tell me so I can understand!"

"Sit down, then. And you, too, Blake," Ephraim tried to make his voice sound casual. "This afternoon, when I was out hunting in the big meadow below Golden Hill, that fool dog Sherman got the scent of something in the hollow. When I got there, dammit if he hadn't located half a man sticking out of the bank, where the spring freshets had washed away the dirt."

"Half a man?" echoed Mrs. Moncure. Her face went white.

"The rest of him was still buried in the bank. I couldn't leave a human skeleton sticking out for dogs to worry," continued Ephraim, "so I piled enough stones on it to keep away the varmints. When I'd finished, Sherman gave voice again. There in the bushes, watching me, was Timber."

"You mean that flat-faced big nigger?" demanded Tugger.

"That's him. I told him if he ever breathed a word about what he'd seen, I'd cut his gizzard out."

"You done wrong there," commented Tugger. "By sayin' that, you made him think you had something to do with hidin' the body. Why didn't you say it was an old family burying ground? Gawd knows thar's a plenty around these parts."

"I was so taken by surprise, I couldn't think of a thing to say," confessed Ephraim. "Besides, I never liked Timber when he belonged to us. He needs scarin' worse'n any nigger I know."

"Looks to me like you're the scared one," grunted Tugger. "What happened next?"

"On the way into town," Ephraim swallowed his impulse to resent Tugger's comment, "I began to see the fix I'm in. When Archie Crenshaw overtook me, I told him. Arch remembered Cushman had hired Timber two years ago to find out what he could about that missing carpetbagger, Mudston.

If I didn't shut Timber's mouth first, Arch said, he'd hot-foot it into town and tell Cushman. About then, we came on you stuck in the lane. When we got to Scuffletown, Timber wasn't there."

"I could 'a' told you that in the lane," declared Tugger. "Timber was the one took my weasel and cut my jaw."

"When we got to town, we spotted him in Cushman's office. By now he's probably told half the town I killed Mudston, and buried his body in that branch," concluded Ephraim, in deep dejection.

"Your sister America—" began Mrs. Moncure and could go no further. The truth might save Ephraim, but would accuse America. America was far away, but could be haled back to answer to a carpetbagger court which might drag the honor of the Moncure women in the dust. And after the verdict had been reached, with its dread possibility, who would believe that America had rescued Palestine in time? Who would want to marry a girl mentally unbalanced because she had almost been ravished?

"Ma, are you suggesting I go to Kentucky?" Ephraim considered. "I thought of that. By now Cushman 'll have men watching every road out of Charlotte Court House."

"You could come with me," spoke up Tugger. "I pulled in here after dark, I could pull out just as quiet. Nobody'd think to look in the bottom of my wagon."

"You mean you'd take my son south with you—so General Gregg's men can't find him?" demanded Mrs. Moncure, with hope in her voice.

"I'll take him to Durham Station, ma'am. We kin use a good man like Eph in the terbacker business."

"Tarheel, that's white of you!" cried Ephraim, his voice husky with relief. "When can we start?"

"As soon as we hook in the team."

"Crenshaw's downstreet on the lookout for soldiers heading this way," Ephraim declared, and began to look around the room for his things. "He'll hoot like an owl when he sees 'em coming."

"So you're one of them!" breathed Tugger, and looked at Ephraim with quickened respect. In Virginia, they called themselves by a highfalutin name—the Knights of the White Camellia.

"Tarheel, if that makes any difference to you," Ephraim flung back at him, "I'll stay here and face the music."

"Hell-damn, no! Politics butter no turnips for me. I peddle smokin' mixture. Once we git aout of town," Blake added, as an afterthought, "you might hoot to your friends to give us a hand over the mudholes."

"They'll see us safe to the border," chuckled Ephraim. "You'll have every soldier from Richmond to Knoxville smoking your weed, when they hear of this."

"Promise me one thing, Tugger Blake!" Mrs. Moncure cried out in agony.

"What is hit, ma'am?"

"Promise me you'll come back often, and bring me news of my son. He's all I have left—except my younger girls."

"I'll be right proud to do that," agreed Tugger, and glanced toward the chimney corner where Palestine had sat. "Effen I was you, ma'am, I wouldn't come out to see us off. Jest go on up to bed, as if nuthin' had happened. Across the street, Cushman will be watchin' your window to see the lamp go out."

Chapter 6

At Tuckahoe crossroads, the tollhouse crouched under the sugar tree as if seeking shade from the midafternoon heat. In lush August maturity the fields dropped away. Ahead, the turnpike lay deserted. Glum for once, Abigail MacGower scattered no conversational bait. Without reciting the speech she had rehearsed on her drive down the ridge, America plunged nervously into the object of her call. Mrs. MacGower grasped the tollbar with work-coarsened hands and demanded:

"Will ye get up at ma first call? After that, I'll throw water ower ye but once. Then oot ye gae! And ye'll hav' tae skim the milk an' churn the butter."

"I'll do that, gladly."

"An' tend the bairns?"

"When my dairy work is done."

"I'll tak' ye for one dollar the week. And I'll wash your shifts and petticoats with ma ain."

"That's very generous of you, ma'am."

"Dinna mak' me rue ma bargain!"

"Indeed I won't, Mrs. MacGower."

"So ye've decided tae be a schoolteacher instead o' a bride! Whaur's that braw Fant Annable?"

"I'm sure you know as much about him as I do," confessed America, and let the older woman see in her eyes the misery she felt. "Fant and I were never formally engaged."

Mrs. MacGower shut her lips on a sharp reply. Twenty-five years ago in Scotland, before MacGower came along, she had stood in this girl's shoes, asking only to be allowed to exchange work for honest bread.

"When can ye come?"

"As soon as you'll take me."

America moved the next day into the upstairs rear room of the tollhouse. The view at least was expansive. One of her dormer windows looked east across cultivated Annable acres, the other north towards Foxden on the river rim.

The thrifty Scotch household arose at four o'clock the year around. Breakfast was over at dawn. America then walked two miles, often marshaling her younger pupils before her up the ice-rutted turnpike. Arrived in Glade Springs, America opened the one-room brick schoolhouse, built a roaring fire in the cannon stove, swept the floor and sat down at her desk to plan the day's lessons. No kerosene was provided at the tollhouse for night work.

Forty-two pupils answered her opening bell. The Board of Deacons guaranteed her fifteen dollars a month to teach the three R's to her full enrollment. For higher education, she was permitted to collect as much as the parents of these advanced students would pay. To boys she offered Latin, American history and elementary algebra; to girls, American history and the Feminine Arts, which she defined as class instruction in oil painting and ornamental wreath fabrication. She wanted to include music and ballroom deportment, but as yet had mustered no pupils. Tuckahoe boasted only three pianos, and the Deacons frowned on dancing. When school matters were discussed, two outside members—Auld MacGower and Major Argyle Chisholm—sat with the Board. In '63, when Glade Springs school had been opened to admit deserving offspring of non-Disciples and of alien-born freeholders, Auld MacGower was invited to represent this group of parents. Major Chisholm attended as the one man in Mason County who had been to Oxford. He had only contempt for Campbellites. When meeting several of them on the street, his favorite challenge was: "If the devil should appear this very minute, which one of us would he take? Me, of course! He can get you Campbellites any time."

One morning in early December, a handsome boy of twelve, clad in cotton overalls, his knuckles cracked red from the cold, appeared before her desk. With a reckless gleam in his blue eyes, the lad offered to do the chores if America would undertake to teach him without tuition fees.

"The Board of Deacons will see you through reading, writing and arithmetic," America smiled at him.

"This here deal's got tuh be entirely between you 'n' me, ma'am! I kin read an' figgur some, but I want real larnin—enuff tuh go off somewhars an' read law. I aim tuh be high sheriff."

The titter that ran over the schoolroom should have been warning to America. Without heeding it, she leaned across her desk:

"I'll be happy to instruct you, since you're so ambitious to learn. What's your name?"

"John Willy Barnes."

With a sobering expression, America met the lad's defiant eyes. The young trader before her must be a son, legitimate or bastard, of the notorious Stella Malone who, with Jim Barnes, share-cropped on Lawrence Creek on the back of the Annable place.

"Take that empty desk over there by the door," she answered with outward serenity. "At noon I'll examine you and find out where you belong."

"Hit's a deal, ma'am! I'm shore proud you'll take me," John Willy declared, his face aglow.

Some days later Stone Moncure overtook America as she was walking home through the frosty December twilight. Dismounting, he walked along beside her leading his horse, a new white mare. As secretary of the Board of Deacons, he announced, it was his painful duty to convey to her their vote of censure because she had admitted John Willy to her school.

"John Willy is one of the brightest boys I have," America stood her ground.

"Don't you know who his mother is?"

"Every lady on Tuckahoe has felt it her duty to stop her buggy and whisper in my ear."

"And you still propose to admit him?"

"All the more reason to remove him from such a home. He's not corrupting the morals of my other pupils. He's clean and fair-spoken."

"One Board member claims you took him in because you're too lazy to build a fire," reported Stone, an amused gleam in his eyes.

"If John Willy never does another chore, I'll continue to instruct him, sir!"

"Another Board member maintains that, by admitting the son, we countenance the mother's way of life."

"Mr. Annable said that, didn't he?" America flung back. "Why doesn't he turn Jim Barnes off, instead of visiting Stella's sins on her innocent boy?"

"Because Jim's one of the best tobacco men in this county."

"And Stella's no laggard at pulling plants!" America matched his sardonic tone.

Throwing the bridle reins over his horse's head, Stone prepared to remount. From his saddle's height he gazed down at America's heart-shaped face. Those earnest eyes and the appeal of childish red lips above that firm chin never failed to stir him. Her cheeks were bright with color from her brisk walk up the hill, her shoulders were stiff with indignation. In the intelligent eyes upturned to him, Stone could read no consciousness of himself as an eligible young man on a high-stepping mare just bought to impress a Virginia girl who was rumored to know horseflesh.

"Don't you intend to apply for this school next fall?" he asked.

She gave him a glance of alarm, before exclaiming:

"Oh, yes, sir! But I couldn't turn away a boy as thirsty for knowledge as John Willy—just to please my Board." To soften what must appear stubbornness to him, she added: "That's a lovely mare you're riding, Cousin Stone."

"Do you like her? Then do me a favor. Take her and ride her back and forth to school. It worries me to have you walking these roads by yourself at sundown. I'll arrange with Auld MacGower for her keep."

"But I've been walking every day since school began!" She made light of his concern. In his eyes she must have seen something which made her think of sixty white horses, because she looked momentarily as if she might laugh out loud. He was on the point of laughing with her when her expression changed and checked him. She took refuge in formal speech: "You're very kind, I'm sure, but I couldn't think of accepting such an expensive gift. What would people say?"

"Aren't I your nearest male relative in Kentucky?"

"I mustn't detain you longer, sir," she dismissed him. "Good-night."

In the tollhouse that night, after the children had gone off to bed, America mustered courage to ask Auld MacGower about the vote of censure the Board had passed. He bluffly evaded giving her a direct answer:

"Ye forget, lassie, only six years ago Glade Springs school was opened tae the bairns o' a wor-rking mon like masel'. Whin I cam' doon th' Ohio, Mason County land was nae tae be had for ony price by puir Scots like us, or Irish frae th' potato famine, or th' Bavarians. This high-headed gentry didna need us then, they had their blacks. War gae'd us our-r toeholt. But this scum ye seek tae elevate, this imp o' Jezebel—"

"Mr. MacGower!"

"I told th' session ma tithe could gang fur the lad's schoolin'," MacGower answered, soberly. "An' when talk comes 'round tae your place nixt year, ye can count on Major Chisholm an' me nae tae tak' th' porringer oot o' your hand."

"Thank you, sir! How do you think Cousin Stone will vote?"

"Wha saw ye walkin' in th' gloamin' wi' Stone Moncure?" demanded Abigail, sharply. "Sic on-gaein's will link y'r name wi' Stella's on a dozen clackin' tongues!"

"Wist, Abbie, will ye scold th' lassie a' nicht? Gang tae bed, Americy. F'r a' his sober face an' solemn tongue, young Moncure will stand wi' Auld MacGower and th' Scots' laird at Charter Oak."

Spring came early to Mason County. On the eastern slopes of cleared land, where leaf mold was deep and the morning sunshine warm, plant beds bloomed with snowy canvas. The schoolhouse, cozy enough when winter rains were falling, grew stuffy to America. An impulse made her lock the door one gusty March afternoon, and set off down Glade Springs Creek. It was high time she reported John Willy's progress to Jim Barnes and Stella. There was a possibility they might insist on paying her a few hundred pounds of sweet-cased tobacco if John Willy did well in his final quiz. America was not willing to admit even to herself that she was frankly curious to see this notorious pair.

Cardinals flashed back and forth across the path ahead of her, as if to lure her away from nest sites they had chosen. She followed Glade Springs Creek to its confluence with Lawrence. Twelve miles upstream, civilization in the northwest had its taproot, she knew. One of America's first lessons in history had been to gather together for her advanced pupils the stirring facts of Mason County's settlement:

A hundred years ago the fabulous western land of Kaintuckee—easy of access down the Ohio and up the creeks, teeming with buffalo and wild turkeys, densely wooded or covered with lush canebrakes uninhabited and unclaimed by Indians—had sounded like the Land of Promise to Virginia planters struggling to make their tired red clay fields yield a living for themselves and their big families of slaves. " 'We didn't know then,' " she quoted her statesman-father, " 'that Kentucky was the Red Men's Middle Ground. They had fought over it so long that, for tribal preservation, they made it neutral territory, council and hunting grounds for all, but home to none. Thinking Kentucky unoccupied because we saw no Indian towns such as existed on the Ohio side of the river, like simpletons we rushed in when Boone and Kenton offered to show us the way.' "

In 1774 Simon Kenton, son of an Irish tenant farmer in Fauquier County, Virginia, had provisioned a dugout canoe and with Thomas Williams, a companion as venturesome as himself, started down the Ohio River. At Letart's Falls, they came upon a French trader established to barter with the "Indian Side" of the river. *Mais oui,* declared the trader, he had seen the Kentucky cane fields! The cane started a few miles back of a limestone creek which emptied into the river across a sandy point. Here Kenton might safely beach his canoe. The banks of the Ohio were then almost impenetrable with driftwood and vines, ideal ambush for Indians.

Kenton and Williams mistook the mouth of Cabin Creek for the limestone stream they were seeking, and went inland only to find no gap, plateau or cane. Wintering at the mouth of the Big Sandy, the following spring they again met the French trader, swapped their furs for ammunition and corn, and listened anew to his description of sky and shore line. This time Kenton so impressed the image on his mind that when he arrived at what today is Limestone, he recognized creek and point.

Leaving Williams to guard the canoe, Kenton set out to shoot game needed for food. A flock of turkeys led him along what he recognized as part of one of the oldest roads in America, a trace which buffalo had worn up the five-hundred-foot bluff. Every autumn, herds of these shaggy beasts drifted southward from the snow-swept plains of Ohio and Indiana, swam the Ohio River at Limestone where the double bend broke the current, and plodded up the bluff to crop bluegrass through the mild Kentucky winters and lick salt at Blue Lick Springs, sixty miles southwest of Limestone Point.

Toiling up the buffalo trace, Kenton saw spread before him canebrake and woodland as easily tillable as any land in the world. Overjoyed, he hurried down the hill to tell Williams, and they climbed to the edge of the cane. Near a fine gushing spring, headwaters of a creek they named Lawrence after the brother of George Washington, they pitched camp and cleared an acre. With what was left of the French trader's corn, they took planting possession for "as long as grass grows and water runs."

Later, Kenton and Williams wisely threw their lot in with that of other frontiersmen at Harrodsburg. Joining George Rogers Clark's expedition against the British forts in Illinois, they helped break British resistance in the Northwest.

In 1784, Edward and John Waller and George Lewis built a log blockhouse near the buffalo trace on the west side of Limestone Creek. Three years later, the Virginia legislature chartered the settlement as Limestone. Kenton, John May and Daniel Boone laid it off in half-acre lots, to be sold at public auction. With Limestone on the point and Kenton's Station four miles inland, this handful of settlers held the water gate of the Ohio River open against the Indians to hordes of homeseekers and land speculators—"improvers," they called themselves. Between 1790 and 1810, forty to fifty arks a day came floating downstream to the point. Passengers disembarked there and went by wagon train up to Kenton's Station and on over Smith's Road to Blue Licks, Lexington, Fort Bledsoe on the Tennessee, and on south.

Out of Kenton's Station grew Washington, which was established in 1786 as a town by the Virginia Legislature. Mason County, named for George Mason of Gunston Hall, was established in 1788, with Washington its county seat and the first post office west of the Alleghenies, the distributing point for mail throughout the Northwest Territory. Here also flourished the most celebrated female seminary in the West, presided over by Louisa Fitzherbert Keats, a relative of the great English poet, America had been proud to declare to her students, as if the presence over fifty years ago of this pioneering schoolmarm just six miles away dignified her own mean estate. When steamboats began to ply the Ohio, Washington's supremacy—

established by the wagoneers—vanished with them. Traffic, trade and population shifted back to Limestone.

Ahead, the wagon road forked. One branch led through a gap towards the Ohio River. The other plunged left into a now impassable ford and out beyond to curve around a steep hill. Above the ford, a narrow footbridge of planks swung too close for comfort over the torrent. Holding to the top strands of picket fence that sided it, America stepped dizzily across and followed the lane around the hill. On the slope above, two teams crawled in front of shining furrows like twin spiders drawing a glistening thread.

The wagon road ended in a muddy stable lot. Were the womenfolk who lived here too slovenly to lay down stepping-stones, or did they never go anywhere? America picked her way along a fence row towards the cabin. She had expected to see dirt, neglect, ragged children, even the chilly baby crying in the trash-littered yard, but not the fine horse tied in broad daylight where anyone could recognize him. Back in Virginia, poor white trash made jokes about country hussies whose lovers obligingly chopped supper kindling for them while their cuckold husbands toiled in the field.

At America's approach the sleek animal swung his quarters around, and neighed with impatience. The cabin door swung open and a tall slattern crossed the porch. Her tousled red hair was mingled with sufficient grey to give it a pinkish tone. She wore a cotton-print wrapper. Thin shanks and broad feet were bare.

"W'atta ye want?" she called.

"I came to speak to you about John Willy," America began timidly.

"W'at about 'im?"

"The Board allows me to collect a teaching fee from parents who feel they can pay."

"Nary a copper ye'll get from Barnes! Who asked ye to take John Willy? He'd better be out in the terbacker patch earnin' his kape."

"John Willy's a bright boy," America retreated. "I'll gladly teach him free."

"No son o' mine need pick up crumbs from the likes av you! Kape yer smilin' hypocritical face out av my business, do ye hear? An' yer meddlin' foot out av my lane!"

America beat a hasty flight across the barn lot. At the lane gate, America glanced back towards the cabin. The saddle-horse no longer circled at the woodpile. America picked her way down the muddy lane. Intent on avoiding puddles, she failed to see someone approaching until he was almost in front of her.

"Wal, miss?" he drawled.

"Oh, mercy me!" exclaimed America. Caught unawares, she stared. Everything about the man was cavernous. His hazel eyes were deep-sunken, his temples receded. A twist of fodder over his left shoulder held up singed overalls. He had been burning a late plant bed, and he reeked of wood smoke. Bony shins stuck through patched trousers, long muddy toes through broken home-cobbled shoes.

"Scairt you, didn't I?" jeered the tall farmer, laughing soundlessly. "I hear't Stella givin' you the rough side of her tongue. You must 'a' come on her unawares. That al'ays riles her."

"Are you John Willy's father?"

"Haow kin I tell, ma'am?"

"I—you know I didn't mean it that way! John Willy's a bright boy—a good boy, too. I'd think any man would be proud to claim him as a son. All I hoped in admitting him to my school was to help John Willy raise himself above—this," America finished weakly, with a gesture towards barn lot and cabin.

"Am I a-hinderin' 'im?" Barnes asked in his tired voice. "If John Willy kin pull himself up by his bootstraps, I won't put no weights in his shoes. You kin see I need him bad to plow. I ain't a-makin' him."

"We're both grateful to you for that, Mr. Barnes."

"I don't know fer shore yuh oughta be. But hit's a free country—they say! As fer me, I don't know nuthin' but the terbacker patch."

"You're a better father than I thought you were," she cried spontaneously. "You and I understand each other, Mr. Barnes. Good-day to you, sir."

"And tuh you, miss. Follow that cowpath up the hill an' you'll come out on Tuckahoe at Foxden, below the tollgate."

America started up the trail. The footing was uneven, at times precarious. It took her mind off her encounter with the Barneses. The wonder of John Willy—clean-spoken, fine-limbed, with an alert mind and boundless ambition—swept over her. It was a joy to be a teacher when she could set boys like John Willy firm on the path of self-improvement.

Foxden was where Cousin Simmy Collier lived. For months America had intended to go call on her aged kinsman. He had not come to church since her arrival on Tuckahoe. He had fallen and hurt himself, to what extent even his sister, Margaret Annable, could not learn. He was being tended, Mrs. Annable reported, by old Mahalee, the one ex-slave whom he had permitted to remain at Foxden.

The cowpath entered a fine growth of virgin timber, chiefly black walnut. Beyond the woodland, a crescent of meadow had been cleared up over the crest of Tuckahoe Ridge. Near the south tip was an empty tobacco barn, its doors propped open so that livestock could run in and out for winter shelter. Beyond the barn out on the windy river rim was a rectangular family burying ground enclosed by a fieldstone fence and studded with funereal cedars. On the highest point of the crescent, black against the setting sun, loomed Foxden. Three of its massive chimneys were dead. From the fourth spiraled a thin thread of smoke. Between America and the house were outbuildings, a stable and corncrib. In the front yard the twin blue ash trees which America had often admired from Tuckahoe turnpike pointed upward like the bishop's fingers raised in blessing.

As she crossed the meadow, America experienced a sense of profound well-being. She felt as if she had been here before, would return many times at sundown. A woman's voice calling *"Chickee, chick-ee-e!"* in an outbuilding might easily have been her own. America attributed this sense of familiarity, her feeling of soul's contentment, to Kate's remark on their first ride down the ridge. Cousin Simmy had said he meant to will Foxden to Fant because Fant was the only one of Margaret's children with enough Collier in him to stand up to Mr. Annable.

As she approached the house, America studied the ancient log structure with keen interest. It was built in the form of an H. Each side had been formed by erecting two twenty-foot log cabins together, making in all four spacious ground-floor rooms. Above each room must be a loft. The bar of the H was left open below to form a dog run; above was another loft connecting the left side of the house with the right under a common roof. The dog run, with well and sweep in its center, was paved with limestone flags which had been continued front and rear to make rough terraces. Used to the big frame mansions of Charlotte County, and with only a little of the Tidewater terrapin's preference for brick instead of wood, America decided that Foxden was a fine log house despite its age. Here she and Fant could be more than comfortable until Timberlawn was theirs. All that remained now for her to do was to make a good impression on Cousin Simmy.

America knocked on the whitewashed door. No answer came. Pulling the latchstring, she stepped inside. The room was bright with firelight. In a Sheraton armchair, the legs of which had been sawed off to bring it lower to the puncheon floor, an old man sat with his back to the room, his bushy hair spun silver above the carved chair top. Across his sharp knees hung an Indian shawl. Its intricate pattern glowed jewel-like in the light from the hearth. In the old man's hand, thin almost to transparency, was a South Sea pipe which he continued to smoke as if unaware of intrusion.

"I beg your pardon, sir, but may I come in? I'm cold," America spoke honestly.

"Come to the fire, then," pronounced a testy voice.

Without looking at her host, America stretched her chilled hands to the blaze. When she turned, she received the surprise of her Kentucky experience.

"Has the cat got your tongue, chit?"

"Sir, you could be my grandfather sitting there!" cried America. Like Ephraim Collier, Cousin Simmy had ice-blue eyes that twinkled under thick black brows. Spent though he was from long sickness, Cousin Simmy had the same formidable presence, still wore the born look of command.

"Then why haven't you come to see me sooner?" he barked.

"Do you think I'd have waited a day if I'd known?"

"You sound as if you set a heap of store by your grandpap," chuckled the old man. "It's been seventy years since I saw Ephraim Collier in Virginia, but we were the spittin' image of each other as boys. Anybody could tell you're a Collier, with that width between your eyes and the way you hold your head."

"Thank you, Cousin Simmy."

"Don't reach for bouquets where none's intended. You ain't half as purty as your ma."

"I've heard that all my life," she laughed.

"Do you like Tuckahoe?" he changed the subject.

"How could I when I'm little better than a servant here? And—"

"Finish your sentences, missy!"

She could not confess to this imperious old man that she had failed in the one consuming pursuit of her life.

"And Fant shows you no attention, eh? The trouble with Fant," confided Cousin Simmy, "is that he will try to live fifty years after his time. Hyenas 'n' bobcats, I've told him often enough the river-boat life went out with the railroads! Eh, but it was a fine, free life while it lasted. Maybe I'm to blame for filling his head full of mv talk when he was a lad."

"What did you do that Fant enjoys so much, sir?"

"I floated rafts of prime Mason County leaf downriver in hogsheads, Americy. Ten to a raft me an' my bravos floated 'em down the Ohio—and out onto the Mississippi—and on down to New Or-leens! There I cried 'em to the highest bidder on the Old Market wharves. When my business was done, we fought our way back on horseback over the Tennessee Trail. Many's the trip I brought seventy thousand gold dollars in those saddlebags in the corner. Sometimes I had commission lists long as your arm to fill. Trottin' stallions for the menfolks. Black enamel bracelets and diamond earbobs for the ladies. Once it was a Spanish jack that Squire Chisholm's pa had to have. That Balaam's ass cost six thousand dollars! An' he took to brayin' so continuous we had to tie up the critter's jaws, like a wench with the toothache, to keep the Injuns from hearing him. The Tennessee Trail warn't called the Bloody Way for nothin' in those days, missy!"

"What you say interests me enormously, Cousin Simmy. Fant said he was a river-boat man, but I hadn't realized that meant being a commission merchant."

"Ho! ho! You're a sly minx—"

"I beg your pardon, sir? Perhaps I don't entirely understand what Fant does on the river, nowadays. When I ask nobody seems to know, exactly. Won't you tell me?"

The ice-blue eyes shot a shrewd glance at her, then dropped to the bowl of the outlandish pipe.

"Hand me a coal, missy," Cousin Simmy ordered. When the pipe was drawing again, he grumbled: "From what Mahalee —she's the black woman who waits on me—hears from the niggers, Fant's mostly sparkin' that bold-eyed girl of Taliaferro Drake's, 'n' you do nothing to stop it. Haven't you any gumption?"

"What can I do, sir?" America demanded, stung by his scorn.

"Well, it's none o' my business if you choose to let a less

likely filly outpace you—just because you're too much of a lady to stretch your legs."

Here was frontiersman's talk for sure, for all it was expressed in the language of the trotting ring. An uninvited guest, America dared not resent it.

"I make it a rule, Americy," the crafty treble was continuing, "to keep my nose out of other people's affairs. I never advise; I just tell folks what they ought to do. Since I've been chair-fast, folks who'd never dare come around when I was well, swarmed in here with wine jelly and chicken broth. They'd come to inquire after my health, they'd say. But we both knew they'd come to see if anything could be done about the money they owed before I died and they had to pay. One of the first to arrive was Idy Belle Anderson, who owes me twenty-five hundred dollars."

"You mean the plump lady who leads the choir at the Limestone Christian Church?" asked America, feeling her face redden.

"She's the one. Have you ever heard her pray?"

"No, sir."

"She's one of the most savig'rous pray-ers in these parts And I'll admit she did herself proud over me. When she was wipin' her eyes ready to get up off her knees, I says: 'Idy Belle, that's the most beautiful prayer I ever heard. But it ain't worth twenty-five hundred dollars!' "

"That's really a funny story, Cousin Simmy," acknowledged America, with brittle laughter. "Why did you tell it to me?"

"I reckon you know why, from the way your eyes are shootin' darts at me."

"Good-bye, sir. Thank you for letting me warm my hands at your fire. You won't have the chance to tell me another story, Cousin Simmy."

"Maybe you haven't heard I don't like women?"

"I won't intrude again."

"To tell you the truth, Americy," confessed Cousin Simmy, with a direct look at her, and for the first time she saw the mortal weariness in his cold-blue eyes, "I don't like anybody around me, now. I'm an old man. And I'm tired. Young folks fill the house with their sayin's and doin's, their comin's and goin's, their spats and their makin's-up, till there just ain't any room left for me."

"I appreciate older people need rest and quiet. Good-bye, sir."

"Good-bye, missy. Be sure you shut the door behind you."

Outside, although the sky was a bowl of rosy reflection, the chill of night was in the air. As she hurried towards the pike, America realized that on both calls this afternoon she had received the welcome she deserved. She had gone in the hope of getting something extra, something she had not earned. For her trouble, she had been rebuked in words more direct than any she had ever heard before. Yet she felt exhilarated.

This afternoon, she told herself, she had seen passion and miserliness in the raw, naked as a babe at birth. Because both were of the essence of life, she had not been shocked; indeed, she had enjoyed the encounters. People like John Willy and Mr. Barnes, Stella and Cousin Simmy made the *politesse* of Golden Hill seem artificial, even stuffy. Here on Tuckahoe, as a penniless schoolteacher, was she actually beginning to live? Fant had promised her as much; indeed, far more. How could she, without eye-catching finery or a parlor in which to receive him or fine horses to ride and drive, draw Fant's attention away from Allilee? How could she, a nobody, outshine the belle of Tuckahoe whose every extravagant whim was indulged by her doting father?

As the end of the spring term drew closer, anxiety again overtook America. In guarded phrases Mrs. Moncure had written of Ephraim's hasty departure south with Tugger Blake. Led by Timber and Cushman, a detachment of Yankee soldiers the next day had exhumed Mudston's skeleton and taken it to Lynchburg, where a coroner's jury had pronounced death to have come from a blow on the back of the neck by a sharp instrument in the hands of a person unknown. "Among the Yankees, feeling runs high against your brother," wrote Mrs. Moncure. "I do not let Palestine out of my sight and hearing day or night. Her memory daily grows dimmer, but the sight of you might have the opposite effect. Much as I long to see you, America, do you feel it wise for you to come home for the summer recess?"

Behind a loose stone in the dairy house wall, America had hidden nearly seventy dollars, saved out of her teaching fees. While she was pondering the wisdom of spending boat fare to Cincinnati in the hope of locating a summer job, Mrs. MacGower proposed that America should stay on at the tollhouse after school closed and work out her board, sewing on the MacGower winter wardrobe. In her girlhood in Scotland, Abigail had learned to sew ahead of the calendar. Surely by fall the Board of Deacons would have decided whether or not they meant to offer America the Glade Springs school again?

"Folk gang up an' doon sae muckle in summertime I canna stitch a seam atween tollfares," Abigail complained, eying America thoughtfully. "Whin we finish th' woollies, we'll mak' ye a dress for the fair."

"I shouldn't spend the money. Suppose I don't get my school?"

"We'll choose a guid dark stuff ye can wear hame on th' steam cars. Frae th' fur-rst meenit I set een on ye, ma fingers hae fair itched tae fit your-r wee waistie."

America smiled affectionately at Mrs. MacGower. Fant had described the toll-mistress as resembling a molting turkey hen. Her nose was long, her eyes as sharp to notice a toll fare as a turkey to catch a grasshopper. Angular almost to gauntness, her big bones seemed to stick through the cheap salt-and-pepper calicos she wore. Under her horny Calvinistic exterior, she had the instincts of a pleasure-starved girl, and often surprised America by unexpected flashes of imagination and sympathy. Abigail's suggestion of a becoming new dress to wear to the fair kept America sewing happily through midsummer heat.

The Germantown Fair, announced on yellow cloth streamers tacked on fence rails and gateposts over five counties, was to meet as usual during the last week of August at its home grounds sixteen miles west of Limestone, on the Cincinnati pike. Started in 1852 by a colony of Bavarian immigrants, it had become the high point of Mason County's summer season. Even Fant Annable troubled to return to Tuckahoe for fair week.

In Auld MacGower's break-cart, Abigail and America drove to Limestone and selected as cool-looking, adequate for all seasons and cheap, a blue-green cotton poplin. Abigail then brought out the inspiration of her dressmaking zeal, a letter from the professional seamstress in Edinburgh who had taught her to sew. The letter contained a sketch and description of the new "round dress" which had superseded hoops in Paris and London, and was with rear fullness to lead the fashion trend towards the bustle. Abigail bemoaned the lack of a "fashion baby" to copy, as they had done in Scotland, "three shillin' twa copy the doll's dress in the shop, five shillin' twa tak' her hame owernicht." At her throat America planned to wear her grandmother Jacova's yellow topaz and onyx brooch, cunningly bordered with platted gold. To buy a hat, America led Mrs. MacGower into Miss Belt's shop, the best in Limestone. They chose a bonnet of blue-green straw and sat staring entranced while Miss Belt crowned it with a wreath of tiny artificial Gold of Ophir roses and tied it under America's right ear with short streamers of straw-colored velvet.

"Comb your curls into the fashionable new waterfall," advised Miss Belt. "To complete what sounds like a very modish costume, let me bring you a parasol, gloves and a beaded purse in the new mustard shades? It just happens I'm going to Cincinnati tomorrow."

America turned wistful eyes to Abigail, who answered tartly:

"Ye canna thraw siller aboot like a drunken sailor. Th' bonnet will be a', Miss Belt."

With nine general admissions to pay at the fair, the MacGower family could go but the one day, Friday, when the Saddle Sweepstakes was tied. Abigail, Jeannie and even America cooked all week before the great morning. After hectic bustlings about, America in her new finery took her seat on the rear springboard among four ecstatic MacGower children. Not until lunch baskets and jugs at their feet had been counted twice, would Abigail climb over the front wheel. Auld MacGower clucked to his team and the heavy-footed farm horses started off on their sixteen-mile walk to the fairgrounds. Jamie and the next MacGower boy, Kenneth, mounted on colts each had undertaken to break for the use of them, cavorted ahead.

Seldom away from the tollgate these days, America thoroughly enjoyed the drive down the valley pike. Iron weed bloomed to regal heights beside the road. In the fence corners goldenrod was beginning to feather. Tobacco, its broad leaves spread so that she could not see the dirt between the rows, was taking on a clear golden tint. The coolness of August nights lingered in the sparkling air.

About ten o'clock, the borrowed horses pulled them up onto the Cincinnati road. Here the dust hardly had time to settle before another fair-bound vehicle stirred it up again. Auld MacGower kept his slow team in the ditch, to make way for faster turnouts that flashed by and disappeared in clouds of powdered limestone. America tried at first to brush it off, then gave up the losing battle. On the front seat Abigail's best black bombazine was well protected by her Sunday linen duster. America had demurred against wearing the toll-mistress' ragged second best. When America was in despair for the freshness of her new outfit, Abigail turned around with a knowing smile and told America to pull the rejected duster out of the lunch basket at her feet.

A pair of high-stepping bays emerged from the dust clouds. On the narrow seat of the black tandem cart seemingly a featherweight behind them, Dr. Drake lolled in complete confidence of his daughter's skill at the reins. Allilee was gone before America could bow or even notice what she wore. In an open victoria, with two horses and Uncle Cato proud on the box, Cousin Margaret Annable and Kate clattered by. Until now, America had been too busy to notice that not one of her rich Kentucky connection had invited her to accompany them to the fair. At hunt breakfasts in Virginia, had they been so thoughtless, America asked herself. She then remembered how often the sallow face of Miss Armstrong, her own governess, had appeared at the schoolroom windows of Golden Hill to watch as she had cantered away.

Before they pulled in sight of the flag-decked fairgrounds, they realized its nearness from the wail of a calliope and the choking dust. The tiresome drive came to an end about eleven o'clock in a queue of nondescript vehicles waiting to approach the general admission gate. Handsomer equipages and horsemen trotted smartly in at another entrance marked: For Subscribers Only.

America looked around with keen interest at the grounds studded with fine trees. At long tables set up under giant beeches, gaily dressed ladies unpacked food, shook out tablecloths, laid silver and glass. White-aproned mammies turned freezers of sherbet, linen-coated black boys passed trays of silver julep cups to gathering clansmen. After one searching look for Fant, America did not turn her eyes that way again.

"Yonder's the amphitheatre," confided Anne Charlotte, pointing. It was a circular structure built around a quarter mile of open track. The cupola of the judges' stand in the center was visible from the outside. With shingled roof, whitewashed sides and red-painted trim, the amphitheatre reminded America of an enormous mushroom. Around its top circumference, protected by a hand rail and chicken wire, was a gallery known as the promenade. America, while sewing at the tollhouse, had imagined her sea-green skirts swirling beside Fant's polished boots along this most romantic of Mason County's courting galleries. Gazing at it now, she wondered if she would be asked to pace its rickety heights with anyone more exciting than Jamie MacGower. To the right of the amphitheatre stood Floral Hall, easily recognizable by two streams of women and girls jamming its entrance and exit.

"Miss Merry, wull ye get doon here an' tak' th' lassies through th' Hall?" asked Abigail, in some embarrassment. "That wad gi'e us time tae meet oor-r kin an' explain how we cam' tae tak' in a boarder."

"Why, of course, ma'am."

"Lassies, tak' Miss Merry's hand an' dinna let gae, dae ye hear? Gin ye get lost, come back to oor-r tree. We'll eat at twelve shar-rp."

At Floral Hall, they wedged themselves into the crowd that moved a step at a time forward on one side of the building and back on the other under a galaxy of prize quilts which hung from the rafters. Down the middle on tasseled easels or tacked to cardboards were exhibited hair and shell wreaths, watercolors, charcoal sketches and oil paintings. America was gratified to see that Beth Cary's large canvas "Hiawatha Presenting Minnehaha with a Deer," on which they had both toiled all winter, had won the blue ribbon in its class. She was wishing that they had made the sunset less ruddy, when she heard her name called. She looked up and saw Cousin Margaret Annable on the other side of the hall, through a gap between two easels.

"Merry, how pretty you look!" cried Mrs. Annable, speaking through the double chicken wire that protected the exhibits. "Believe me, my dear, I meant to write you a note asking you to drive over with us, didn't I, Kate? Kate—where are you?"

"I appreciate your thought, Cousin Maggie. Mrs. MacGower brought me."

"How are you, girls?"

"Very well, thank you, ma'am," chorused Jeannie and Anne Charlotte.

"Won't you show you forgive me, America, by joining us at dinner? We plan to sit down at twelve o'clock."

"I'd like to very much," answered America, truthfully. "But Mrs. MacGower is expecting guests."

"Fant's here. He came to show Sunshine in the Saddle Sweepstakes," interposed Kate, her long face appearing in the gap. Already Cousin Margaret had passed on out of sight.

"You'd get to eat in the grove," whispered Jeannie, with shining eyes.

"Go on, accept! We'll help maw," urged Anne Charlotte.

"I can't this year," answered America, firmly.

Released from Floral Hall, they saw that dinner was ready throughout the fairgrounds. For the first time in her life, America found herself on the wrong side of invisible barriers which separated the rich and the native-born from the alien and the poor. In the grove were plenty of simple folk enjoying themselves as heartily as the gentry. These women and girls wore cotton instead of silk; but like their men they bore themselves with a confidence which showed they belonged to Mason County as surely as a portion of Mason County's good brown earth belonged to them.

Not so the tenantry and the alien-born. The freed negroes and John Willy's kind who made up the share-cropping element of Mason County's population, dared not come to the fair for lunch. Hardier German, Scotch and Irish immigrants who had made the plunge, effaced themselves in diffident national groups in the less desirable picnic spots. To America, it seemed doubtful that these newcomers in their Old World Sunday best could ever be one people with the silk-clad gentry drinking juleps and the small landholders uptilting their jugs on practiced arms. Several recently arrived Bohemians mistaking the fair for a feast day, or because they had nothing better to wear, had come in the quaint peasant costume of their native villages, the women with bright scarves tied over their heads in happy ignorance that only slaves wore kerchiefs. When they realized their error, they appeared likely to die of embarrassment. Because of her new dress, her bearing and her high-born face, America felt herself to be as conspicuous as they. She hated her own caste consciousness which made her want to run away from present company and hide.

At the MacGower oak, flustered Abigail introduced the mouselike Scottish women to America. The cousins, too, had brought an overabundance of choice food which they had pooled with the contents of the MacGower baskets on red-checkered cloths spread upon the grass. Their menfolk, plainly dressed as they, all with weather-beaten faces, some with bodies dwarfed by undernourishment in childhood, had unhitched the teams and were feeding them. The farm wagons stood in a semicircle around the oak, so that their swaying tongues might be used for seats. About the wheels tumbled fat handsome children. Shy-eyed older girls watched babies asleep in the shade. Strapping youths matched their strength whenever any one, especially America, would look at them.

The patriarch of the clan, an old Scot with apple cheeks, asked a pious blessing. When America bent to serve him, he pulled her bonnet ribbons, the only expression of gaiety at the feast. After their men's ironstone platters had been heaped, the women seated themselves together with box tops on their knees. The men commented briefly on local politics, clan health and taxes. When they could eat no more, they scrapped their chicken bones over the fence into the weeds, laid cutlery and china near the baskets, and, smoking their pipes, strolled off to look over the prize livestock. The women broke into spirited conversation over one another's culinary triumphs. More homesick than she had ever been in her life, America sat apart so the Scottish women could enjoy themselves, and shooed flies off the sleeping babies. No one would let her help repack the food. By two o'clock, the baskets were in the wagons again.

Melodious strokes on a farm bell in the show ring announced the hour which America had been anticipating for weeks. From every direction spectators converged towards the amphitheatre. Mrs. MacGower marshaled her party into one of these human streams. From the red tunnel of an entrance way America gazed into the arena blazing with hot August sunshine. The judges' stand was full of laughing men and several bold horsewomen whom America did not know. Tiers of backless seats climbed the amphitheatre to the promenade.

"Here we are—Number 15," bustled Mrs. MacGower. Into the empty section the MacGowers flowed like water into a basin. "America, ye had best sit on th' bottom row. Then ye may rise without disturbin' folk."

America sat erect among the children and watched the choice seats fill with prominent county families. She located the Taliaferro Drakes by the flowerlike skirts of Cousin Theresa and her girls. Allilee was nowhere to be seen. Beyond the Drakes' section, Cousin Margaret held elderly court. Kate was looking unhappily about for Stone Moncure.

The bell by which the judges announced the different contests began to toll. Gilded, it hung over the double white gates which formed the only exit and entrance to the ring. A German band perspiring in their gaudy uniforms lugged shining instruments to the judges' stand, climbed the steps to the open loft and composed themselves with much mopping of wet red necks. In the grandstand, every entrance well was disgorging men who had hurried in from the stables and livestock pens to rejoin their families, as custom decreed, before the program began.

"Miss Merry, will ye promenade wi' me?"

America looked up into Jamie MacGower's embarrassed face. Much as she longed to be out of the dust of her present humble position, she realized that to accept Jamie's invitation would be to open the floodgate to a dozen other requests from the MacGower cousins, those red-necked swains who had expressed their admiration of her through their eyes and the way they grappled like young bulls before dinner. Feeling ashamed of herself, America smilingly answered:

"Will you excuse me, Jamie? I'm very tired."

"Ye did richt, lassie," Abigail bent to whisper. "In ma masterpiece, ye are nae for lads o' common folk."

From the band loft, flourishes on the French horn announced the entrance of Colonel Frazee, ringmaster, on a sedate walkin' horse. At the judges' stand, he took a yellow buggy whip from an attendant and cracked it at the gatekeeper to announce the first afternoon event open to contestants.

The program proceeded with spirit. Before she realized it, America was giving her full attention to the beautiful animals on parade. There was no racing. Competition centered in the appearance and performance of the horses themselves, the suitability of their rigs to the type of occasion specified in the program, and indirectly the skill of their handlers. America admitted to herself that not since childhood had she seen such exquisite horseflesh.

To feminine eyes the most exciting event on today's gala program was the Fancy Turnout ring. The band started to play Schubert's *Marche Militaire* with aplomb, the entrance bell tolled and a spider-wheeled new runabout drawn by high-stepping blacks entered at a spanking trot. Seen across the ring, the horses appeared to lift and replace their polished hoofs as if they trod on bubbles. One after another, five entries flashed in and took their moving places in the splendid circle.

"Miss Allilee likes to be late," whispered Jeannie, biting her nails.

To the tolling of the bell, which warned late entries that the gates were soon to close, Allilee entered. In a yellow organdy gown and garden hat with yellow and orange streamers, she resembled a crisp golden poppy atop her father's new tandem. Beside her, Fant Annable carried her long green gloves and purse in one hand, and with the other held a matching green parasol over her head. His face was flushed, his flashing smile too frequent, his bare head darkly handsome in the white afternoon glare. Golden Rod, Dr. Drake's unbeaten harness filly, was hooked into wheel position. Out in front high-stepped Sunshine.

The crowd welcomed the spectacular turnout with a roar and a following crackle of applause as Miss Drake sent her perfectly matched pair around the ring. Colonel Frazee snapped his whip to indicate that he wanted a quicker pace.

The seven entries whirled around the show ring in admirable unison. If one team got out of hand, if one vehicle lagged or shot ahead, the arena might be thrown into mortal confusion. Fant had laid aside gloves and purse, had furled the green parasol. Athough he still sat at ease, America could see that he was braced to take the lines in an emergency. The German bandmaster, moved by the exciting spectacle to signal for music, thought better of his inspiration and hastily silenced his players with outstretched palms.

"Walk your horses!" shouted Colonel Frazee.

As the equipages slowed, the ringmaster lined them up one by one in front of the judges' stand. Hostlers ran to loosen checkreins. Horses stretched aching necks and were allowed to breathe before their attendants coaxed them into the spraddled arch that is considered the proper stance for harness horses on display. With the confidence of a queen, Allilee swung in on signal. A judge with the coveted blue ribbon and embroidered purse of gold pieces was already walking towards her. With her hands full of line, she bent and caught the ribbon in her teeth. Fant received the purse with a laugh and a bow.

As winner, it became Allilee's privilege to drive twice around the arena as smartly as she could. Colonel Frazee ambled behind shouting her name, and the German band crashed into *I Dreamt I Dwelt in Marble Halls*. In complete dejection, America pretended to be fastening a shoe button both times the winners flashed by. She was caught unawares when a matter-of-fact-voice spoke close at hand:

"Miss Merry, will you promenade with me?"

Looking up, she saw Stone Moncure beaming stolidly down on her. With a bewitching smile, America took his extended arm and climbed the aisle to the courting gallery. Here two streams of gay young couples flowed happily in opposite directions. Her head high, her arm locked companionably in Stone's,

America swung along and chattered engagingly. Girls cast discreet or frankly curious glances at her new green frock, her trim bonnet and matching écru mitts and purse which Mrs. MacGower had tatted for her. Open admiration in the men's eyes, and the eagerness with which they raised their hats, were equally heartening. Stone had no more sense of rhythm than a boulder, but he could not resist her infectious gaiety and the lilting swing of her walk.

"If I was a flatterin' man, I'd say you look mighty pretty today," he rose to the occasion. "Something about you appears to attract all eyes."

"Perhaps it's my new frock, sir? Today's the first time you've seen me properly dressed."

"I'll never forget you at the *Magnolia*'s rail in that rusty alpaca and home-braided peanut straw!"

Was he poking fun at her? America retreated hastily:

"I was surprised to see Cousin Allilee wear such a frivolous hat into the ring. If it had blown off, it would have startled the horses behind her."

"Fant will pay dear for his play-acting!"

"How do you mean, Cousin Stone?"

"Sunshine 'll enter the Saddle Sweepstakes tired and with his mouth galled. Fant has declared to ride him, himself. He's overweight and heavy-handed when he's sober. You saw his condition?"

Too loyal to admit even to this good friend that the man she loved was intoxicated, America hung her head.

"Don't misunderstand my position, ma'am," Stone continued, watching her closely. "As far as I'm concerned Fant can drink himself into the gutter, and I'd gladly foot the bill. I'm riding Wild Man against him."

"Not that Hambletonian with the bad name who's won all the ribbons?"

"I bought him last night to have the pleasure of beating Fant Annable—in horseflesh, at least. Will you wear my ribbon, if I win?"

"I—look, there's Fant and Cousin Allilee over there by the steps!"

"America Moncure, the day's coming when you can't put me off for Fant Annable! I'll make you give me an answer."

"I'll give you the only possible one now, since you force me," answered America, her eyes darkening with storm signals. "When we first spoke of white horses, I thought you were joking. Now, knowing as you do that I love another, I can regard your attentions only as an insult. I bid you good-day, Cousin Stone."

"Come along, then, and worship your steamboat hero! I can wait till you grow up. Or until time opens your eyes."

"You choose a poor way to win my respect, by defaming your rival!"

Stone's jealousy, which had flared at sight of America's pleasure in seeing Fant, died as quickly.

"Miss Merry, I couldn't defame Fant Annable," he declared, honesty in his voice and smile. "It's Fant's boast he's broken every commandment and committed every sin in the decalogue. But I can't stand here spatting with you, when I'm overdue at the stables." Linking his arm through hers, he swept her along the gallery to where Fant and Allilee stood surrounded by a crowd of congratulatory friends.

"Howdye, schoolmarm!" Fant hailed her, and bowed in mock gallantry. "Ladies an' gen'nemen, I see I've made a slight mistake. Allow me to present you to Princess Prim of Poverty Hill."

"Fant, you're drunk!" Stone cut in sharply.

"If you were a gen'neman, Stone, you'd realize no other gen'neman is ever drunk."

"Cousin Allilee, let me congratulate you on your driving," America interrupted in her pleasant Virginia voice. "I thought it superb in that crowded ring. And you looked so charming!"

"Thank you, cousin. Let me return the compliment. That frock—it's very quaint," declared Miss Drake, her green eyes fixed with uncertainty on Abigail's masterpiece. After the fatiguing excitement of the arena, Allilee felt she was entitled to linger over the joys of victory, chief of which was to enjoy the discomfiture of this poor relation from Virginia who still walked and talked as if she were somebody.

"I'm glad you like it," America answered. "It's one of the new 'round dresses' that have taken London and Paris by storm. Mrs. MacGower received the pattern direct from Edinburgh."

"Indeed! I—" Miss Drake broke off to eye the dress again. Before America had finished speaking, Allilee and every other girl within hearing would gladly have ripped off her own hoops and thrown them at her favorite seamstress.

"There's the bell for the model ring," declared Stone. "The Sweepstake's next, Fant. Miss Merry, I'll leave you to talk feminine pleasantries with Allilee."

"I'll gladly come along with you, Cousin Stone," declared America. While she hurried to follow him down the promenade steps, she blinked back hasty tears. Fant had a perfect right to prefer Allilee's company to hers. But to remind her of her reduced fortune in front of all those strange faces was cruel—cruel!

"That was your chance to go sit with Cousin Theresa," Stone scolded when she caught up with him in the ground-floor aisle. "Now, I'll have to take you back to the MacGowers—unless you'd rather join Cousin Maggie and Kate?"

"You're thoughtful, Cousin Stone," America smiled at him through tear-brimmed eyes. "I'll go to the paddock and watch you mount."

"Ladies don't do that in Kentucky—without an escort."

"Surely I can walk from the stables back to the grandstand alone, when I came half across the continent by myself."

"I didn't approve of that, either. If you persist in pursuing Fant Annable to his stable door, I can't stop you," continued Stone, his voice hard with anger. "But let me warn you, ma'am, such bold action may cost you your school!"

"Are you threatening me, Cousin Stone?"

"Go where you please, and be damned to you both!" he raged, and strode away from her.

She stood marooned in the center of a large paddock. Low whitewashed stables ranged in U-shape around it; the open end gave access to the arena. Entirely womanless, the whole place teemed with activity. Negro boys walking blanketed horses around a center track to cool them off, stared curiously at America. From the ring, hostlers came leading the model horses hooked single to their show rigs. One by one they plodded wearily past America with cramped necks outstretched, the checkrein loosened, the vehicles empty and often with dangling reins. America was reminded of a scene backstage, when the actors pull off their wigs and the actresses start removing grease paint.

"Merry, w'atcha doin' back here by yourself?" challenged Fant's voice behind her.

Turning, she faced him. Her heart pounded so hard, her lips were so dry, she could only speak the truth in a voice too low for the stable boys to hear:

"I came to see you and Sunshine."

"We're honored, I'm shure," he jeered, taking her elbow and thrusting her along with him in his unsteady stride. "Soon as I'm mounted, I'll send you back to the grandshand with Unc' Cate."

"Fant, you can't ride in your condition."

"Dammit, don't rub it in!" he admitted with a sorry laugh. Stopping in front of his own stable, he took her by the elbows and turned her to face him squarely. At his touch, she felt the old tumult stir deep within her. "Listen to me, Merry—I'm in a bad fix! Up there on the prom'nade just now, I must'a' said some'pin to you—some'pin pretty rotten, 'cause you still look like I'd hit you. Whatever it was, forget it, will you? I'm so worried even liquor won't help me forget my troubles."

"It doesn't make any difference now what you said, Fant. Tell me, what's disturbed you so?"

"Ever' cent I could win, borrow or steal, I've bet on Sunshine to win the Saddle Sweepstakes. It looked so easy before Stone got hold of Wild Man."

"What if you do lose? Maybe then you'd have to come home and go to work like the rest of us."

"And marry you?" he mocked.

"Oh, Fant, would that be so hard?"

"Sorrel top, you're a thousand times too good for me!" he cried, and shook her gently by the grip he had on her elbows. "You're young—I'm old. Maybe not in years, but in the places I've been and the things I've done. You're ambitious—I'm lazy. You're sweet and honest—I'm—well, I'll go to jail tonight if Sunshine doesn't win."

"Fant, what have you done?"

"Not so loud, my dear. Last night at the Lee House I remember askin' Buck Lambeau to cash a check for me. I had run up quite a bill, an' I wanted some more cash to bet on Sunshine today, so I signed pa's name on that check."

"You don't mean you forged it?"

"Not so loud, I tell you! I—I jus' borrowed pa's credit for twenty-four hours till Sunshine can win. An' why shouldn't I, I'd like to know? Ma would give me a plenty now, if pa weren't so damn' stingy with her money! What right's he got pullin' the purse strings on me? Many's the time I've heard him boast he got off the boat at Limestone with only a pack o' schoolbooks on his back."

"Still I don't understand," insisted America.

"Buck Lambeau—he runs the Lee House—cashed the check out of his till last night because he wanted his own money an' he knew ma was worth the balance. This mornin' he took the check out to Timberlawn to collect. Ma, worse luck, had already started to the fair when he got there. Pa came in while Buck was decidin' what to do next, and snatched the check out of his hand. When he saw I'd borrowed his credit again, pa hit the ceiling and refused to honor it. If I don't make that check good before seven o'clock, Buck says he's goin' to turn it over to the high sheriff."

"Why don't you speak to your mother?"

"Haven't you seen pa sittin' up there beside her—with the buggy whip? Only thing I know that ud bring him to the fair would be the chance to lay it on me—in public."

"Oh, Fant!" she breathed, remembering the grim presence who had sat reading his religious pamphlet at the supper table while his family shifted uncomfortably on their chairs and watched the clock.

"So there's nothing left for this young Lochinvar to do but ride," grinned Fant, with a return of the old gay spirit which had characterized him at Golden Hill. "Will you bring me pressed chicken when I'm languishing in jail?"

"I'll ride Sunshine for you."

"You, Merry? Ho-ho, that is a joke! Unc' Cate, come out and listen to this one," Fant raised his voice to his stud-groom busy inside the stall. "Miss Merry here has just offered to ride Sunshine in the Saddle Sweepstakes!"

From the gloom of the stable's interior the white-wooled old negro emerged leading Sunshine. Bottle, his assistant, followed with pail, basin and sponge. They had been swabbing out Sunshine's cut mouth. The sun in their eyes made them blink momentarily. Then Sunshine fluttered his nostrils at America. Touched by this welcome from her one friend at Timberlawn, America went to the splendid animal and laid her cheek against the clean yellow satin of his neck.

"Unc' Cate, will you look at that?" marveled Fant.

"Dis hoss an' Miss Merry—dey's frien's, boss."

"Cate—you damned old rascal—you don't actually think she could ride him—and win?"

"I ain't nevah seed her on a hoss, boss, but she couldn't ride wussah'n you—lak you is naow," the stud-groom analysed the situation. "I ain't sayin' she could win agin Mistah Stone on Wil' Man. An' iffen she did win, I ain't sayin' de jedges gwine let you haul daown de pu'se an' aour winnin's in de bettin' ring."

"Eph used to claim you could outjump any fox-hunter on

the South Side," Fant declared, turning back to America. "As for the judges, they'll have to recognize you as my rider—if I notify the entry clerk before the ring is called. I'll run tell him now." Across his shoulder, he called back to America: "Get yourself ready, whatever you have to do, Merry! I'll be back with your entry card by the time you're mounted."

As she gazed at him, he ran across the paddock and disappeared into the nearest entrance of the grandstand. He hadn't stopped to give a thought to her safety or to her reputation! Not even in Charlotte County where a Collier could do almost anything, would she have dared enter a public show ring mounted on a stallion. Ladies never rode them in their home paddocks, much less exhibited them at a county fair. America turned her scared face towards the stud-groom, whispered through white lips:

"What do you think, Uncle Cate?"

"As fer as Sunshine goes, you kin han'le him, kez he's tooken a fancy tuh you. Wot dat Wild Man gwine do in de ring—er wot nice folks gwine say abaout you affawa'ds—is mo'ah dan I knows."

"Shall I wear my bonnet?"

"Effen you's done made up youah mind. Put youah gloves an' pu'se inside. Tie dem ribbons tight. Bottle, lay dat side-saddle on easy, an' den slap his hind-qua'-tahs wid youah rag, tuh git him used tuh sku'ts. Sunshine ain't nebbah carried a lady befo'."

The gate bell began to toll, calling all entries into the Saddle Sweepstakes. Three stables down the line, America saw a black horse come lunging out with three grooms swinging at his head. When Stone followed, she knew the outlaw must be Wild Man. America watched while they pulled him down with hobbles and held him until Stone was firmly seated. Capriciously accepting authority for the moment, Wild Man arched his neck against the curb and side-stepped like the devil in dancing pumps across the paddock towards the show ring.

"I fixed it up at the clerk's office!" cried Fant, returning breathless. "Merry, here's your entry card. Don't lose it, or they'll jump to disqualify you. I'm so relieved I've turned owl-sober! Black boy, haven't you got a bottle tucked away somewhere?"

"Ah's right busy naow, boss."

"Merry, you won't let yourself get hurt, will you? Are we crazy, both of us? Suppose those stallions get to fighting in there. You couldn't hold Sunshine a split second!"

That was precisely what America had been thinking, but she had no idea of admitting it.

"You's frettin' dis hoss, Mistah Fant," complained Uncle Cato. "You knows he doan like you nohaow. He's ready, miss."

"Give me your hand, Bottle."

With a spring, America was in the saddle, the first saddle leather she had touched in sixteen months. She was not worried about that. Born a horsewoman, always a horsewoman, her father used to say when she would come in winded with her brothers. Sunshine snorted and side-stepped at the unaccustomed featherweight and the sweep of her skirts against his ribs.

At the arena gate, Fant pressed close to her stirrup. The hands he reached up to squeeze hers in parting were unsteady. For once his brown eyes were honest, without mockery, as he whispered:

"Win this ring for me, Merry, and I'll do anything to please you. Anything, do you understand? That's a promise!"

Given his head, Sunshine pranced. The gate bell was clanging, the horses inside revolved like those on a merry-go-round. With voice and light hands, America steadied the stallion through the entrance well and on into the sharp sunshine of the arena.

Stunned silence from the grandstand greeted America's appearance in the ring. On her first trip around, she was too busy with Sunshine to hear the crowd's following chorus of *"Ah-h!"* And the whispered exclamations. From the betting gallery came a roar which trailed into distinguishable shouts:

"Switch me iffen hit ain't a lady rider!"

"Look at that red-headed girl on that yellow hoss!"

"Kin she ride?"

"I'll say she kin! Yippee fer the Tuckahoe schoolmarm!"

America quickly took stock of the ten other entries. With his usual placidity, Stone was battling Wild Man. A professional trainer was up on Ulysses Cary's Blue Stocking. Dr. Bacon, Limestone's leading physician, was giving a fine show on his well-mannered Sugar Pill. Seven other stallions were flashing around the circle at their best paces. Their riders, strangers to America, measured with sidelong glances as she was doing the competition each might expect and must overcome.

The red-numbered white posts of the grandstand were swinging dizzily past America with panels of blurred faces hung like quilts between them. America located the MacGower section. Jeannie's mouth hung open. Abigail's face was bright with pleasure. Auld MacGower's eyebrows were pulled down like a thundercloud. In the Annable section, Cousin Margaret gayly waved her handkerchief. Mr. Annable turned away his face. Kate stared, speechless. On the next time around, America located the Drake box. Dr. Taliaferro was grinning, Cousin Theresa hid her eyes as if she expected momentarily to see America killed, and Allilee was applauding Stone who across the ring had tamed Wild Man enough to lift him into his celebrated canter.

"Bring your horses in," called Colonel Frazee.

In a wide semicircle, they swung towards the judges' stand. Grooms leaped for the stallions' heads. Without a smile, one of the judges asked for America's entry ticket. She handed it coolly down to him. Seated with other Confederate veterans in the grandstand, was Major Argyle Chisholm. He, like Auld MacGower and Justinian Annable, had no nod and encouraging smile for her.

In pairs, the judges sent the riders out to match gait and speed. Out they danced to walk, trot, single-foot, rack and canter.

Glad to rest with Uncle Cato at the bit, America relaxed

her grip on the pummels and flexed her fingers cramped with holding Sunshine. She wished Fant would come into the ring, so that she could talk to him. If Stone Moncure would only smile at her, she would feel less friendless. He sat Wild Man not two horses distant. The angle of his bare head, turned studiously away so that she could see only the tight line of his jaw, banished any delusions America might have had that he meant to withdraw gallantly in her favor. Every line of his face and body indicated increasing control over Wild Man, bespoke a growing determination to win. America realized that Stone Moncure meant to outride her, to wear her down, to send her humiliated from the ring—if he could.

"Numbers Five and Seven!" Colonel Frazee called her out with Stone.

At a run beside the bit, Bottle started Sunshine. Behind her America saw the black stallion rear and strike with his forefeet as his grooms released the bit. America loosed Sunshine's reins, spoke affectionately as she signaled for a change of pace. Bowing his satin neck, throwing his hoofs, Sunshine trotted around the ring with mane flowing and tail plumelike behind him. Glad to be released from solitary confinement at Timberlawn, and apparently stimulated by the music and the yelling grandstands, Sunshine put into his performance all that his proud honest heart could give. Watching, the crowd began to realize that here before their eyes was an unusual exhibition of horsemanship, of unity and understanding between the slender girl so erect in the saddle and the magnificent stallion full of pride and vitality in every shining curve. With a throaty roar the betting gallery began to shout its preference:

"You Sunshine! Lookit that hoss an' lady ridah!"

"Tie hit on the red hoss, Jedge."

"Sunshine—you Sunshine!"

Out of the corner of her eye, America saw that Stone, on the black stallion, was coming up to pass her on the inside of the ring, between her and the judges' stand where the circumference was shorter. Speed was an important factor in judging gaits, she knew, provided the animal on exhibit did not break. The smallness of the arena and Sunshine's swift trot already had her dizzy. Grandstand and judges' box alike appeared a blur of hostile, tense faces swinging around her on a theatrical backdrop. As the closed entrance gates came by, she saw Fant sober above the pickets. What was she doing wrong, to make him look so anxious?

Stone and Wild Man were gaining. She owed them their chance to pass. With hands, voice and weight, she strained to keep Sunshine's head turned in towards the sloping wooden wall of the arena, so that he might not cut across in front of his oncoming competitor.

A snakelike black head shot forward, with yellow teeth bared. Wild Man had reached for Sunshine's neck just above the shoulders, a favorite grip of fighting stallions. America heard the sickening click of teeth, then Sunshine squealed and broke gait. Quicker than she could see, he freed himself, reared straight up and lashed out with his flailing forelegs. With the unnatural strength that had come to her once before in a desperate situation, she stood in her one stirrup and swung Sunshine into the amphitheatre wall. As from a distance, she heard his iron-shod hoofs strike hollowly on the scarred boards, saw terrified faces fall back behind the protective chicken wire. A moment later, Wild Man flashed by seemingly in a perfect demonstration of his fast trot. Ahead of her, Stone's back was straight as a cavalryman's.

"The black hoss wins!" called a strident voice from the betting gallery. "Tie it on Wild Man!"

"Sunshine broke—"

"Tie hit on the black hoss, Jedge!"

America brought the quivering Sunshine to a full stop. Her voice was audible to half the grandstand: "Steady, Sunshine!" With her handkerchief, she pressed his torn skin where blood was dripping brightly down to crimson the lather which reins and martingale had rubbed. Throwing the blood-stained linen towards the inside of the ring where the judges could not fail to see it, she gathered her reins and spoke as she might have done to a schoolroom of frightened children: "You're not hurt, Sunshine. Now, fellow, steady—hup, Sunshine!" With hands and knees, she lifted him into his gentle canter. Willing to forget his smarting neck, Sunshine went like a rocking-horse around the ring, fluttering his nostrils at each downstroke and rising again as if on springs. A sigh of relief, a ripple of applause like wind across a wheat field, arose from the hushed grandstand. In the music loft, the German band broke softly into *Carry Me Back to Old Virginny*. America straightened in her saddle to show that she appreciated the intended compliment.

"Ye're daein' fine, lassie!" called Major Chisholm from the judges' stand. He must have been concerned for her safety, America realized, for he relapsed into his native blur only when deeply moved.

"Dammit if I know who's purtiest—hoss or gal!" shouted an enthusiast from the Lewis County mountains.

"Rack your horses!" came Colonel Frazee's stentorian order.

Settled into his spectacular rack, for the artificial gait was his best, Sunshine began to inch on the snaffle to gain more rein. Wild Man was halfway around the ring ahead of him. America realized that if Sunshine could pass Wild Man without breaking gait, all else being equal, he would win the Sweepstakes on his better manners and disposition. In the same maneuver on the trot, Wild Man had been guilty of biting.

Suppose when the stallions were abreast, they turned on each other? What if Sunshine wanted his head only to get at Wild Man? America was already worn out by the unaccustomed half-hour of hard riding. How could she save herself if the stallions started to fight? Suppose her foot caught in the stirrup? She saw herself thrown, being trampled under the razor-sharp hoofs, her unconscious body exposed in the dust to the gaze of this thrill-thirsty and bet-maddened crowd. . . .

"Pass him, Sunshine!" yelled the betting gallery, horsemen all.

She felt Sunshine trying to steal rein with canny little jerks of his chin, so he could have his head to pass his opponent. Can't you see—now's the time? the stallion appeared to signal, the while his powerful body surged rhythmically forward like music beneath her.

> Dar's whar Ah labored so hard for Ol' Massa,
> Day after day, in the fields of yaller co'hn—

A rush of emotion swept over America, lifted her above imagined fears. Loosing the reins, she leaned forward in the saddle to give Sunshine all help she could. The grandstand saw her purpose, held its breath to watch. The band stopped playing.

"Yee-ee!" encouraged the betting gallery. "Now you've got him, miss! Come on—"

"Naow's yer time tuh pass dat black hoss!"

"Pass dat bitin' fightin' mean black hoss!"

Throwing his hoofs, Sunshine devoured the distance between himself and the hard-breathing Wild Man. The thought occurred to America to call out to Stone to keep his mount's head turned toward the arena wall, to give her at least the same sportsmanlike chance that she had given him. If she could not win without begging favors, she decided that she would have to lose.

"Now, Sunshine!" Her clear voice was audible over the ring, as she bent above the twitching golden ears: "Steady, boy! No biting! Keep going, Sunshine—steady, now!"

Abreast of each other, the two stallions went forward at top speed. America caught a glimpse of Stone's fiery face, with rivulets of sweat running down his cheekbones through the dust. What must she look like herself? Long since, it seemed years ago, she had felt her Leghorn bonnet fly off. The sweaty yellow velvet streamers under her chin held it flapping on her back, between her aching shoulderblades. Only the speed of their pace kept her bright curls out of her eyes. Her hands with the reins knotted around them were mottled white and red.

"Ye've got him, lassie!" she heard Auld MacGower roar like a bellows. "A mickle mair an' he's your-rs!"

Eyes forward like the sweet-tempered beast he was, blind to writhing black lips and narrow head fighting the curb to get leftwards at him, Sunshine gave his last burst of speed. In faultless gait, he pulled past his rival. Once around the ring, again past Auld MacGower's sunrise face—how long must they go on?

"Bring your horses in!"

Tossing his head to scatter flakes of foam, Sunshine let himself be guided into the center of the arena. As Fant came running to seize the bridle, America let the reins fall loose and gripped her pummels dizzily with swollen hands that pricked and burned. Smiling broadly, one of the judges held up the blue-ribbon rosette.

"Pin it on Sunshine's bridle, please!" she gasped. "Fant, you take the purse."

Around her she heard the grandstand shouting tremendous acclaim. Above her in the bandstand, the leader knocked with his baton on his rack. A moment later, the band began tenderly to play *Long, Long Ago*. Eyes on Sunshine's pricked ears, face expressionless lest she weep from joy and fatigue, America sent the champion around the arena wall while the grandstand roared and the gilded bell tolled the other entries out. As the German band played on, America's tired mind supplied the familiar lines:

> Now you are come, all my grief is removed,
> Let me forget that for long you have roved;
> Let me believe that you love as you loved,
> Long, long ago, long ago!

The words, more appropriate than the beaming bandmaster or the exuberant crowd could guess, brought tears brimming over her eyes, and to roll down her dusty cheeks. Chin up and slender spine stiff, she saw the exit gates through a blur and swung Sunshine towards them. Fant, Uncle Cato and Bottle ran to her side. Safe behind the scenes, spent horse and rider plodded wearily stablewards. For Sunshine there would be tender care, a full manger, rest. For her, in a world of cold reality, of outraged conventions, of jealousies and reduced fortune and the desperate need to earn her living, what was left for her?

Fant stretched up his arms to help her dismount. Hands on his shoulders, she smiled down at him and said tremulously:

"Fant, you've let me make a hussy of myself! I'll lose my school."

"You've won me a fortune, sweetheart!"

She slid down against his breast. His arms tightened about her, held her close. Against her weary flesh she could feel the quickening stroke of his heartbeat revivifying her, sending the tingle of awakening desire to the last spent terminals of fatigue-deadened nerves. Lips against her ear, Fant was whispering:

"Come help me spend it. Come away with me, lovie! We've just time to drive to Limestone an' catch the *Evening Mail.* Capt'n Fairchild will marry us on the bridge. Merry, darling, trust me this once, and say you'll come?"

"I—I haven't any trousseau—"

"I'll buy you every pretty in Natchez and New Orleans. While you wash your face and twist up your hair, I'll go collect our money and pay off Buck Lambeau. Unc' Cate, make the future Mrs. Fant Annable as comfortable as you can until I come back, do you hear?" Fant turned to address the grinning negroes. His confidence, his easy worldliness, had been restored. "Bottle, hook the young mares into the runabout. And don't forget to come for them tonight! I'll leave them at Dalton's livery stable."

"Yassuh, boss!"

"Lordy, Miss Merry, but you done rode lak a queen!" breathed Uncle Cato. "Step right dis way, ma'am."

Laughing and crying, America followed him into the stable. Never had she thought to ready herself for her wedding in a tack room, at an old negro's washbasin and before his bleary mirror. As she was replacing her bonnet, she heard Stone's voice outside asking for her. The look in her eyes when she appeared warned him that something momentous was afoot. He stiffened with anxiety as he spoke:

"Miss Merry, I want to apologize for my own and my horse s bad manners. We deserved to be beaten."

"Sunshine and I have both forgotten, sir," she answered truthfully.

"Won't you forget, too, what I said about your school? I was beside myself. I assure you, I'll do everything in my power to see that the Board awards it to you again!"

"That's kind of you, Cousin Stone. But I won't be needing a school this fall. I'm going to be married tonight."

He took the blow, if blow it was, in silence. She found herself clasping and unclasping her bruised palms, sore under the tatted mitts.

"Fant and I are going to be married on the *Evening Mail,*" she announced, gently.

"My dear, Fant Annable isn't fit to black your shoes," she heard Stone speak his mind over the ruin of his hopes. "He'll only break your heart. And drag your life down to the level of his own."

"What's that you're saying about me?" called Fant, approaching on a run with his hands and pockets full of winnings.

"I was just telling Cousin Stone, as one of the Board, that I won't be needing a school next fall," America smiled happily at both her swains.

"Is there anything else you wish to say to me, ma'am?" asked Stone, his voice stiffening. "Is there anything I can do to help you—as your nearest kinsman in Kentucky?"

"Will you please tell Mrs. MacGower where I've gone? I'll write her from Natchez or New Orleans. And thank her for her many kindnesses—she's been like a mother to me."

Aware only of blue eyes blazing out of a grey face lined with defeat, America allowed herself to be assisted into the high-wheeled runabout. Stone tucked the lap robe that Allilee had crocheted for Fant, about her dusty skirts. Taking the reins from Uncle Cato who stood holding them on the ground as Pembroke used to do, Fant leaped in and settled himself on the narrow seat. At a lift of the reins, the young mares lunged forward.

At the grandstand, the gilded bell was calling entries to the program's last event, the boys' riding match. As they turned onto the pike, America glanced behind her. Flag-decked fairgrounds and sky were bright with a ruddy sunset caused by the dust of vehicles already homeward bound. With Fant's fast team, they had ample time to get to Limestone and on the wharf well ahead of the crowd.

Chapter 7

On her honeymoon America threw herself into wholehearted enjoyment of Fant's way of life. As they traveled leisurely down the Mississippi, they found themselves always the handsomest, best-mannered couple on the packet boats which were struggling to reestablish regular schedules through a defeat-stunned South. If America saw shabbiness, if she realized that river travel already was outmoded by the iron horse, she kept her conclusions to herself.

Lighthearted Merry Annable promised mature America Moncure that when they reached New Orleans they would settle down. There Fant would doubtless occupy himself again with the substantial business—perhaps an export or cotton brokerage house—which had kept his purse lined with the gold necessary for trips home and betting indiscretions, far too frequent to suit America's inherent Presbyterianism. Surely he would settle down, now that he had a brilliant young wife to make a home for him and present him with a family? She imagined his house as located in the Vieux Carré, ornamented with iron-lace balconies, otherwise austere to the street but charming with a fountain in its inclosed rear garden. America felt complete confidence in her ability soon to make a model family man of her husband.

She much preferred anticipating the future to remembering the immediate past. She tried to excuse her undignified escapade at the fair and her runaway marriage on the *Evening Mail* by telling herself that any high-spirited girl in love would have done the same thing, after she had been cooped up for a dreary year in schoolroom and tollhouse, and had then been compelled to swallow the dust of Allilee's triumph in the Fancy Turn-out ring. Another reason, the more persuasive because it dealt with life's intangibles, had swayed America to cast her lot with Fant while the Sweepstakes bell was ringing. Even with slaves to do the hard work in Virginia, America had carried the burdens of agrarian life. Fant offered escape from this known into a mysterious land where money was easy, where leisure and gaiety were endless. How splendid must be his habitual environment if by comparison he considered Tuckahoe's lavish ways meager, how brilliant his friends if he found Taliaferro Drake, Letitia Cary, Stone Moncure and Major Chisholm rustic boors! New Orleans alone possessed a culture older than that of some of the river towns which had made the Creole city their market-place and had in turn brought back many of its ways, such as the fine iron-work which ornamented Limestone's houses and the cuisine which graced its tables.

Pondering life's way of returning much for nothing, of denying all to the individual who appears to deserve most, America remembered that in five short years she herself had lost land and an established position. Perhaps she might do better to explore Fant's hidden country, now he was willing to take her there as his wife, than to strive to reproduce in Kentucky another Golden Hill which in its turn might go up in flames as its original had done? A burned child fears even the tinder of another fire.

Tomorrow they would reach New Orleans! And tomorrow night Fant would probably introduce her to his friends, the cosmopolitan circle in which America considered herself well fitted by background, education and natural endowments to shine. On the way down, Fant had given her money generously. That she might be ready for her great occasions, America shopped with critical extravagance in Cincinnati, Louisville and Natchez. Quality in fabrics and style might not have trickled again into the far South. America smiled happily to realize that her sole worry was traditional with southern brides

—that a baby might come along before her trousseau had been properly displayed.

Arrived in New Orleans, Fant established her in an ornate suite at the St. Charles Hotel. America dared not show her disappointment that he had no threshold of his own across which to carry her, nor did she dare ask questions about his business connections. Fant's good humor was at low ebb. Of late he indulged himself frequently in moods which America did not consider becoming to an adult. He sulked, he was reckless, he was cross. America felt disloyal even to notice such character deficiencies in her husband. Her moments of enlightenment usually came of early mornings, between sleep and awakening, while consciousness emerged. She often turned in bed and gazed at Fant, while her mind tried to dissect his true character from his still impressive appearance. When he opened his eyes and smiled at her, her moment of clear perception was gone. She told herself that she loved her husband, as many a woman had done before her and especially in the South, not for his virtues but because as a lover he was completely satisfying to her. As yet, nothing more important than this thought-eclipsing, soul-shaking physical unity had come into her twenty years of life.

"Didn't I tell you we were made for each other?" he would smile into her eyes.

A month passed. No ladies left cards, and Fant took her to call on no one of importance. The women who lived at the hotel were hardly the type with whom she wished to form lasting friendships. In America's eyes, the only ladies there were Confederate widows compelled to stop overnight because they had no kinsfolk to visit. Fant took America out to dine often enough at Antoine's, but made little effort to shield her from the ogling of local dandies. On Sunday afternoons they rode the short-line railroad to Milneburg, on Lake Pontchartrain, for supper at the famous old Washington Hotel. America enjoyed these excursions enormously, for here she saw family groups of the old New Orleans aristocracy. Fant thought them dull.

New Year's Eve, America knew, was a time for open-handed hospitality. Surely the high-spirited ladies who had defied Beast Butler to his very teeth, would be at home over eggnog bowls, glass or even a China soup tureen if their plate was gone? America put on her handsomest gown, of creamy satin with écru velvet bows and real lace, and in her new stays literally panted for Fant's return. About nine o'clock that evening, when she was almost ready to faint from hungry disappointment, he rushed in and demanded five hundred dollars of the money he had given her.

"Lover, I haven't that much left."

"Now, that's carrying thrift too far," he laughed, admiring the swing of his Inverness cape in the mirrors. "I meant for you to salt it away. But not for keeps."

"Fant, you never said I wasn't to spend it," America tried to explain in a scared small voice. "I bought clothes—so I'd be ready to meet your friends."

"Merry, you couldn't," he whispered, his face wiped of all expression except panic. "Tell me you're joking. Such a joke would seem funnier, though, if you weren't scaring the living daylights out of me."

"But I did spend it! All but about ninety dollars. Oh, Fant, don't tell me you need it now to save your business?"

"My business? You little fool, you know I haven't any business!" he stormed at her. In his eyes, panic gave way to anger. His face, which had paled under the impact of her announcement, reddened with fury. He uttered a mirthless bark of laughter, then burst out: "God Almighty, what a joke on me! Here I give you every cent I can rake together, because I thought it would be safer with you than me! Why d'you think I've been taking you places like a sailor on shore leave, unless it was to get us both talked about so I could make a killing before Lent? From the way you fell in with my plans, I naturally supposed you saw what was up—while all the time you've been squandering my whole winter stake for silly clothes!"

"But you said you'd buy me a trousseau," she quavered, trying to smile.

"Of course I knew you'd need a few things—and I hated to say too much as long as it was Sweepstakes money you were spending. That was gone a month ago. What I've been giving you lately I've risked my own neck to win," he snorted, and looked her up and down. "That thing you've got on doesn't set you off half as well as the green one the turkey hen made for you."

"That's a street dress, this is for evening. Besides, Mrs. MacGower was a professional seamstress in Scotland, and we had an advance pattern to copy—"

"So you plunge right ahead making paupers of us both! I'd think you'd have remembered the barebone poverty you knew in Virginia—the rags I found you in—the starvation table you set at Golden Hill."

"Maybe that's why I was so extravagant. Oh, Fant, I've never had any of the pretty clothes or the gay times every girl longs for. In Virginia I was born too late for the good things of life. Naturally, when I got to Kentucky, I—I hoped you'd want to give them to me. Can't you try to understand?" she begged with tears of self-pity in her eyes. "Can't you make a few allowances for me?"

"You sniveling ninny! And you're the one I've been looking up to as so sensible and grown-up."

Because she knew herself to be at fault, she said nothing more. The tears that continued to run down her cheeks she wiped carefully away before they could spot the slipper satin of her white ball-gown. Her silent misery, instead of touching him to compassion, seemed to infuriate him further, as if he actually had been waiting for just such an opportunity to attack her and meant to press his advantage savagely, now that her defenses were down:

"For all your fine talk, you've run hog-wild with the first money you ever had—like Stella Barnes' girls and the rest of us pore white trash! Yet did I see you earning any of it—by suggesting a friendly little game to these carpetbaggers' women ripe for the plucking? Oh, no, not you! You're too high-toned."

"Fant, you know I've never approved of card games—for money."

"Where else d'you suppose I've gotten hold of money to buy you fine dresses—and let you guzzle at Antoine's—and sleep till noon under satin bedspreads—except in a card game for money?" he raged at her. "Don't think I haven't noticed how you turned your aristocratic nose up at these expensive rooms in this fine hotel, because you thought nothing but a private mansion on Royale Street was good enough for you! You're no different from the rest of the Virginia slugs I've met. You think ever'body else should fall down on their faces in front of you and slave for you the rest of their lives, just because you're from Virginia—" He broke off to listen to the French clock on the mantelpiece. It struck ten. Through the open doors of the balcony came sounds of happy crowds celebrating in the street below, to remind Fant that chairs were being drawn up to gaming tables, that new packs were being broken out and shuffled. "Give me that ninety dollars—all you've got left."

"You aren't going to gamble with it, are you, Fant?" she begged him across her shoulder, as she unlocked her bureau drawer. She was not considering the moral issues involved. All she could think of now was that steamboat fare for both of them to Cincinnati would cost at least ninety dollars.

"How else d'you think we'll eat tomorrow—or get out of this hotel? Are you willing to go down on your knees and scrub our way out?" he barked, snatching the purse she extended. At the hall door, he flung a parting challenge at her: "For two years you've purposely pulled the wool over your own eyes. Now they're opened, let's see what you can do to keep this family going."

Her tears dried at their source by the intensity of her own self-examination, America packed the white satin gown away in its papers, undressed, ate the last one of the apples Fant had brought upstairs some days ago in the hope of discouraging her from ordering expensive breakfast trays, and went to bed. Her wishful thinking, her ostrichlike refusal to see and accept self-evident facts, were now water under the bridge, she told herself, long since gone downstream with the substantial sums she had squandered. Looking at herself from Fant's point of view, she admitted that the brutal truths he had spoken were in part deserved. Instead of crying over them like the sniveling ninny he had called her, her problem was to analyse their present situation and Fant's character to see what should be the first practical step towards a successful reconstruction of their lives. New land, free western land, was open to people such as themselves, couples who hoped to turn their backs on failure and discouragement, a man and a woman who wanted to make a fresh start. The next decision was more difficult. Would Fant work in the field on the new land they might homestead? And if not there, where?

Wide-eyed on her lace-edged pillows, while the gas jets flared in the crystal chandeliers and gay crowds below her balcony celebrated the arrival of the new year, she lay staring into the hard future which stretched before her and the man she still loved . . .

She must have dozed, then awakened with a start. She heard a key in the lock, sat up in bed. The suite blazed with light. Somewhere a thin chime struck one—two—three—four. In the sitting room beyond, Fant was trying to close the hall door awkwardly with his foot. When he turned, she saw that he clasped his right hand, wrapped in a bloody handkerchief, with his left. He strode swiftly in to her.

"Get up and pack!" he whispered.

"Fant, your hand—"

"Never mind my hand. Get up and pack, I tell you!"

"I'll ring for a doctor."

"Merry, wake up and listen to me! We've less than ten minutes to get out of here. I've a cab I've paid to wait, and there's a produce boat going upriver in half an hour."

"But why must we leave in such a hurry—at dawn—like this?"

"My luck turned at Antoine's. I was down to my last ten dollars—but it turned! I was pushing it when out of a clear sky some drunken fool took a pot shot at me. Ever'body saw him do it. Ever'body said I have a perfect case of self-defense."

"Then why need we run away?"

"Because maybe there were others who saw—dammit, Merry, don't you realize the police try to make examples out of river-boat men like us? If you're coming with me, pack my things—and yours. I'm going downstairs now and bribe the night clerk to let me out of here. I'll send a nigger up in exactly ten minutes. If you aren't ready—here you stay."

America was out of bed before he finished speaking. She would have to dress on the boat, her stays took too long to lace. Dragging out her three new trunks, she tumbled her own and Fant's clothes into them without making any orderly effort to pack. Shoes and toilet articles went pell-mell into the two suitcases. In his good hand, Fant had taken his own hatbox, a shabby thing which he kept locked. When the sleepy porter appeared, America, in nightgown and wrapper, was lacing her shoes. Like a Simon Legree, she started him carrying the trunks downstairs. After the last one had gone, she threw her long Cobalt velvet party cloak over her boudoir finery and, hatless, staggered downstairs with a suitcase in each hand.

The coachman galloped his horse over the cobblestones and out onto the resounding pier. Fant must have bribed the captain beforehand to delay sailing. Leering at America, whom he mistook for an errant wife escaping with her paramour, the captain declared his boat wasn't fit to carry the likes of her. Indeed, its one cabin was crowded with sleeping farmers and fishermen. If America would go up into the bow, where the mate could look out for her from the bridge, he would take Fant aft and fix his hand.

Picking her way forward through shrimp husks, cabbage leaves and an occasional fish head, America stood and collected her thoughts. The humble little freighter pushed her dirty nose into a yielding wall of silver. As insistent as the thrash of her stern paddles, two questions beat in America's mind: Innocent, was Fant running away because with his past record he had no chance for acquittal before New Orleans' police and citizenry who wanted to clean up the river? Or was he really guilty of cheating, and therefore afraid to face other accusers who, like the man who had taken a shot at him, had actually seen him deal himself the extra cards necessary to win?

They were to spend the next two months running away from news that never came. Fant swore that he had been playing a straight game, that he could not have inflicted a mortal wound on his assailant. America dared not believe him.

Wrapped in her evening cloak, she sat uncomfortably through the bright winter day on the chair the captain had placed for her in the bow. With Fant's pistol hand in a sling, she feared to risk insult from the frankly curious passengers by asking them to vacate the cabin so that she could change her clothes. None of the crew, moreover, seemed willing to roust her trunks. Fant brought her food from wharf peddlers. In whispers they talked over their best course for the future. River travel, America insisted, must end tonight. Fant was too well known to risk the long trip upstream. Any boat large enough to go on through to Cincinnati must necessarily come from New Orleans with the latest police news.

At sundown, the produce boat tied up at Hahnville. No decent hotelkeeper would receive America in her nightgown, Fant declared. He took her, instead, to an upper front room of a river-front brothel. America was surprised to find how clean the room was, how well cooked the reasonable supper sent up on trays. She spent the first part of the night repacking their trunks. While Fant slept fitfully with his hand supported on a pillow, America racked her brain for a plan to get safely home to Tuckahoe.

Railroad service, she knew, had been reestablished between New Orleans and Canton, north of Jackson, Mississippi. The old coach road which ran through Limestone, she then recalled, had Jackson and New Orleans as its southern destinations. To think of the open road was to remember Tugger Blake peddling smoking mixture across Virginia and the Carolinas. Why couldn't she peddle her trousseau from town to town across Louisiana and Mississippi to the nearest railhead in Tennessee? Even at Vicksburg and Baton Rouge, America had found good clothes scarce. Surely in the provincial towns she could locate some carpetbagger's wife her size, who would pay enough for her unworn dresses to provide food and mule feed at least to the Kentucky state line?

When she proposed her plan to Fant the next morning, he shouted with laughter. Would she honestly rather do that than write his mother for funds? Tight-lipped, America bade him escort her while they located buckboard and a team of mules. Two mornings later, they lashed the new tarpaulin over their precious trunks and took to the road.

What Fant accepted as a lark proved a journey of despair to America. After several failures she realized that to make sales she and Fant must frequent the places where light women congregated. In these houses of shoddy pleasure, Fant by contrast shone as the handsomest, the gayest, the most courtly man present. Dressed in heavy mourning for a mythical dead mother, America's rôle was to tell a sad story of how they must sacrifice her trousseau to hurry home to her grief-stricken father. To haggle with half-dressed, half-drunk vulgarians while they pulled at her lovely dresses, sickened America to her innermost soul.

Her hands and thoughts were too full keeping the expedition rolling in the daytime for her to push a discussion of her future and Fant's when they should reach the Memphis railhead. With his arm still in a sling, she mapped their route, did the driving, curried and fed the mules at night and bedded them down. Her mind fixed resolutely on one objective, Tuckahoe, she only smiled when Fant mentioned other possible destinations for the two of them. To travel this wornout National Road in safety without a man would be impossible, she realized. To speak her true mind to her husband now might cause him to desert her. She came to prefer the clean quiet stalls where she drew the soreness out of the mules' feet with hot flaxseed poultices, to the roistering crowd in the bar, or even to her husband's company later upstairs. Like the weather, her manner towards Fant grew perceptibly cooler as they plodded north. She saw to it that the mules had a comfortable night's rest. Able to sleep in the daytime while she drove, Fant's ardor at night increased with characteristic perversity.

Early in March, they pulled into Memphis, southern terminal of the Memphis and Ohio Railroad which made connections with the "Ellen N." As at reunion with an old friend, America winked away tears of happy relief to see the engine with its huge bell-shaped smokestack chuffing in readiness to whisk them on to safety at Timberlawn. No sooner were they started than America began to dread their arrival, and wish for postponement at least until she could think up her next move. Thirty miles an hour towards public confession that her marriage was a failure is a dizzy speed to a disillusioned but stubborn bride. For two months America had been wishing the mules would hurry. Now, she almost hoped their wood-burner might begin to throw sparks enough to endanger the wooden coaches or the cotton in adjoining fields. Since the railroad was responsible for all such damage done, conductors were required to run their cars onto the nearest side track and leave them there while the engine went back to the nearest shop to repair the spark arrester. The fields were white with hoarfrost alone, and no smokestack trouble developed.

Arrived in due time at Cincinnati, Fant took America to the new Grand Hotel, where he was well known, it appeared. Before she could protest, she found herself alone in another two-room suite, this one handsomely furnished in red velvet hangings, marble-topped tables and full-length clothes presses with mirrors in both doors. From the chambermaid, America learned that her husband had entertained other ladies in these rooms before she and Fant were married, though none seemed to answer to Allilee Drake's description.

"Dese Miz' Annables warn't all de same pusson, eider!" sniffed the dusky gossip, flicking at the platform rocker with her dustcloth.

"Some women enjoy cards as much as men," America ignored the servant's pert implication. "My husband is very fond of card games."

Fant returned that evening full of enthusiasm for what he confidently called their shining future. He had always wanted to go to San Francisco, he declared, but could never screw up courage to manage the long sea voyage around the Horn, or the fever-infested trek across the Central American jungles. With the Union Pacific Railroad soon to be completed, they could ride out on the rails.

"Just a minute, Fant," America interposed, steadying her voice. "You and I have far more important subjects to discuss than any outlandish trip to San Francisco."

"I'd like to know what they can be? If you think I'm going into the dressmaking business here in Cincinnati, you're mightily mistaken. We'll mosey along to St. Louis. Haven't you an old family friend out there—Cousin Homer Pettis? While we're waiting for the railroad to be finished, he can introduce me around. The town's old enough to have a few substantial citizens by now—with sons who don't relish work any more than we do."

"When I married you," America plunged in, "I honestly had no idea you were a common river-boat gambler. I should have known, of course. Everyone else in Mason County knew but me. My love made me blind. And as you said, I wanted to stay blind."

"That's better!" Fant agreed hotly. "While you're calling a spade a spade, I'll lay my hand on the table too. I told you—in Virginia—I didn't want to marry you; I'm not the marrying kind. You knew I'd been drinking at the fair—I could have won on Sunshine as easy as you! Nothing would do you, you had to ride him—you had to show off—you had to marry me!"

"Fant, don't shout. If you think I—I took improper advantage of you when you were under the influence of alcohol, that I inveigled you into something against your will, that can be changed at once. You go your way, and I'll go mine."

"Lovie, that isn't what I want at all!" Fant met her cold rage with his flashing smile. "You're the side-partner I've been waiting for lo! these many years. Look at the way you pulled us out of that mess in New Orleans—it was a regular lark!"

"For you, maybe."

"For you, too. You think you're such a fine lady, but you've the soul of a Jew peddler. Seriously, you and I make an ideal pair. Don't you realize that? I wobble—you're firm. You're cautious—I'm a reckless fool. We'll make a killing anywhere the pickings are good! If you don't want to start in St. Louis, for fear Pettis might write home to your ma, we'll go on up to Council Bluffs."

"I won't go anywhere with you as long as you refuse to make an honest living—as long as you gamble."

"For Christ's sake!" He used the phrase she had come to recognize as the last thin filament of his fraying control. "What else can I do? For twenty years I've been waiting for pa to die, so I can come into Timberlawn and live like a gentleman. Pa's tough—he never takes a chance. And he's hogged ever' cent ma's got. What's left for me to do but mark time—and hope?"

"You might go to work."

"What could I do—for decent pay? I ran away to the river when I was fifteen—to get out from under pa's thumb. Here I am—almost thirty—able to write my name, and that's about all!" As if ashamed to confess further his limitations, he broke off and looked down at his hands, those wizard hands he knew could accomplish magic with a pack of cards in an open town like San Francisco. Lifting pleading eyes to America, he concluded: "You don't think I enjoy this hand-to-mouth existence, do you? Or that I don't realize it'll be hard going with the river maybe closed to me forever?"

"Fant, you're trying to live twenty years after your time. And only a fool goes on doing that," America spoke gently. His nostrils went white, she noticed, but she was determined to make her point. "What you think is romantic and daring—this traveling around living on your wits—is only shabby and old-fashioned. Gambling will still go on. It always has and it always will. But not on river boats. In Wall Street maybe, and not for penny ante. So why don't you stop trying to succeed where you're doomed to failure before you start, and come on back to Tuckahoe with me?"

"After they've killed the fatted calf for us there—what then?"

"Surely Cousin Margaret will set us up on some kind of a farm—when she sees you honestly mean to settle down and go to work. I'll run things till you catch on."

"Why not put me out in the kitchen to cook? Not on your tintype, my lady! This time you're coming along with me. And you're going to play the game my way—do you understand me?"

"Fant, I never expect to go another step with you as long as you continue to gamble. Nothing you can say or do will make me keep on being a party to your cheap way of life."

A man beside himself, America discovered, can present an uglier spectacle than an hysterical woman. After her husband's fury had exhausted itself against her silent resolution, she watched him pack his belongings. With the passing minutes, the wall of antagonism grew higher between them. At the door, Fant turned and met her bleak eyes.

"What do you intend to do?" he asked.

"I don't know."

"Are you going back to Virginia?"

"I honestly don't know."

Without saying good-bye, he set his things in the hall, stepped through and closed the door behind him.

As soon as she fully realized that Fant was not coming back,

America went downstairs to see the hotel manager, Mr. Judson. He said Mr. Annable occasionally left without paying his bill but always returned and settled in full. In the meantime, what were her plans? Could she raise sufficient funds to get home? America replied she would prefer to be employed, if the hotel could give her work. Eying her sharply, Mr. Judson declared a vacancy existed in the hotel hand laundry. The job paid five dollars a week and he could send her to a Mrs. O'Flarity who ran a decent boarding house in the warehouse district.

"She ought to ask you about four dollars a week for two meals and lodging," Mr. Judson concluded.

America accepted the place at once, and ended the interview with a formal expression of thanks. Her eyelids smarting with sleeplessness and unshed tears, she impressed upon the mystified desk clerks the vital importance to her that they give Mr. Annable her new address when he returned to the hotel. Then, like the sturdy Irish and German immigrant girls bent over tub and ironing board at her either side, she took her place on the treadmill of twelve hours' daily toil.

Through the single grimy window of her lodgings, she saw the brown Kentucky hills grow green with spring. Because it comforted her to watch their changing lights, and because she needed fresh air after six days of steam in the laundry, she walked down to the wharves on bright Sunday afternoons and stood leaning against the farthest piles. Occasionally she found a seat on the passenger benches occupied by lovers or strays as forlorn as herself. She seldom conversed with them. Sky, sunshine, brilliant clouds and yellow river swirling past the wharf offered her the one companionship her bruised spirit craved.

When the sun dropped low enough to shine directly into her eyes, she would turn and watch the yellow light throw the city into three-dimensional relief. Cincinnati might be Queen of the Ohio, but she had a beggar's pallor, America decided. What a poor place for free men and women to spend the swift precious hours of day! America thought of the clerks and millhands, artisans and domestics like herself confined within these grimy streets, bent over their insignificant tasks which to each were as vital as the bread and rest their jobs represented. For six days they slaved. Darkness alone freed them to hurry home to hall bedrooms or shacks where their children were doomed, like themselves, to spend their lives without daily feeling the spring of sod beneath their feet, or sharing the slow inquisitive friendships of bird and beast, or watching the vivid pageant of sunset and dawn across an open sky.

After the sun had dropped behind the Kentucky hills, America would turn her eyes again across the river to the substantial town of Covington. Recalling the good life she had lived with the MacGowers, she wondered if she were homesick for Tuckahoe. She had had no place and was not missed in the handsome brick houses that studded the ridge. Her yearning, she realized, was for the blue limestone fields dropping away from the tollhouse—meadows heavy with matted sod, cornfields tented with fodder shocks, tobacco patches green with rye—the strong brown earth itself over which the seasons tramped. With longing as acute as actual pain, her eyes ached for the windswept Kentucky horizons unblocked by buildings, and the blue Kentucky skies unclouded by smoke and perennially washed clean by the rain.

Climbing to her hall bedroom one twilight in March, 1869, she found Fant sitting on the top step awaiting her return. Hard times, he debonairly explained, were responsible for his shabby condition. Would she take him out to dinner?

America brought a pitcher of hot water from the kitchen. He bathed and shaved in her chipped bowl. He still carried his worn hatbox, as if no incongruity existed between present shabbiness and the top hat it must contain. America smiled at the improvidence in her husband's character which prompted him to keep the one most useless article he owned. When he was presentable, they went downstairs and America introduced him to her landlady. Like newlyweds, they ran from the dining room, odorous with cabbage and stale food. After a table-d'hôte on Fountain Square, they strolled homewards. The full moon put the street lamps to shame.

Fant's ragged clothes and the abashed look in his brown eyes melted America into a compassionate tenderness for this man whom she had vowed between clenched teeth never to love again. Love wiped her mind blank of resentment, fatigue, angry accusation. Reunited, she was willing to admit to herself how much she had missed her husband. Into their happiness had come a new tenderness born of mutual loneliness and need. In the garret room, while the moonlight streamed across them, Fant asked:

"Well, lovie, do you still think life's your private peach orchard?"

"It's the same as it always has been—since the war," she evaded. "Why do you ask?"

"I just wondered. Don't you ever get homesick for Virginia —or Tuckahoe?"

"Do you?" she challenged, hardening her heart towards him. If he were maneuvering for her to take him home to Tuckahoe and get him established there on a farm she would have to run, while he went gallivanting as soon as her work lined his pockets again, he was due for a rude awakening.

"I'll say one thing for Tuckahoe—people live forever there!" chuckled Fant. "Ten years ago I was sure Uncle Simmy would die any day and leave me Foxden. Now, I'm ready to bet uneven money he outlives me."

"He looked transparent as wax when I saw him."

"That's good news. If he ever does cash in, let's hope he hasn't tied Foxden up so I can't raise a nickel on it! When he was floating tobacco downriver to New Orleans, he thought grandpa ought to put Timberlawn up as security for him, as though there'd be anything left after Uncle Simmy's wild schemes! Nobody could locate him for grandpa's funeral, so ma stayed on at Timberlawn, although she should rightly have heired Foxden. Pa ran both farms with slave labor, and sent what they earned to Abolitionist societies."

"Lover, I never thought of it just that way before," commented America, surprise in her voice. "Maybe your father was sincere about Abolition, after all. He probably figured if he didn't work Cousin Maggie's slaves, some one else would. Why shouldn't he be their master—especially if he was kind to them, and could hasten their day of deliverance by contributing what they made to Abolition societies? No wonder he was stingy with you—and everybody else!"

"Listen to me for a change, will you?" smiled Fant. "I want to tell you about Uncle Simmy. He came home from California around the Horn in '46. Came home broke—can you beat that? —with gold lying around loose out there! Everybody twitted him so he turned hermit, and said he had no use for property. He refused to accept Timberlawn on a silver tray, and made ma swap title deeds with him. He soon got rich as cream, though, because he never spent anything. And Foxden's a fine farm."

"I only saw your Uncle Simmy once."

"It might have been better for us now if you'd cultivated him more. I used to talk to him by the hour about the river . . . Ho-hum!" yawned Fant. "Aren't you sleepy?"

When America awoke the next morning, he was gone.

Her first warning of pregnancy came from her throbbing breasts. Lye fumes rising from the tub as she mixed soapsuds never had seemed to bite into her nostrils with such acrid insistence. Twice she fainted during mid-July heat waves. On her return to work the morning after her second collapse, the forewoman insisted she report to Mr. Judson. He told her he was discharging her for her own good. She was not the first girl, Mr. Judson continued, to make a foolish marriage. Go home, he advised her, while she could still travel safely. Fighting back her tears, she thanked him for the week's pay which he extended and left the office.

That night, America canvassed all possible sources of aid. In Charlotte Court House, her mother was earning a bare existence for herself and the three younger Moncure girls in the schoolroom. Ephraim, still wanted in connection with Mudston's death, was in the North Carolina mountains, his address unknown, Mrs. Moncure had written. Her own best course of action—America looked reality in the face—was to return to Timberlawn and throw herself on the doubtful mercies of Mr. Justinian Annable. Once before, in her hour of acute need, he had befriended her.

A memory arose of Cousin Margaret, elegant in stiff black moire and summer muslins, her oval face framed in droopy coils of slick black hair, her long ears sparked by diamonds. America had sent her several shy letters but had received no answer. She thought she understood why. No Collier mother, and especially one as devoted to her black buck lamb as Cousin Margaret was to Fant, would soon forgive the girl who had bedazzled her son with cheap show-ring triumphs, and had consented to be married to him by a river-boat captain. Anticipating the reunion which must soon take place on the wharf at Limestone or in the Timberlawn parlors, America felt her father-in-law might be the easier parent to meet.

America made her plans. If she must return to Tuckahoe, she would go dressed in proper clothes, with her lips sealed and her head high. Behind the swinging dairy shelf in the MacGower springhouse were the seventy dollars she had saved from her year of school teaching. Until now, she could not bring herself to confess to Mrs. MacGower that Fant was not providing her with every luxury her heart desired. Tonight such wifely pride was submerged in maternal anxiety. America wrote the letter to Abigail, mailed it and went to bed.

An answer came in surprisingly short time. Out of folded tablet pages fell the expected postal money order. America settled back to enjoy the neighborhood news Mrs. MacGower had penned on both sides of three sheets. At the first sentence, the blood rushed to America's ears and pounded there. Mr. Simeon Collier had died in March and had entailed Foxden to Fant Annable's first-born, with America to serve as executrix and sole trustee without bond or accountancy until the legatee should attain his majority. In the event her first-born should die before reaching twenty-one, Foxden would pass to the second-born. Should America be found to have no living issue after thirty years of married life; or should she remarry without issue in the event of Fant's death; or should she attempt to raise money on or dispose of the property in any way to benefit her husband, Fant Annable, then title to Foxden would pass immediately to the Widows' and Orphans' Home at Louisville, Kentucky.

When she had twice read the great news, America lay back and tried to realize her changed position. The unborn child whose hidden spark of life she hardly dared acknowledge even to herself, because she knew no way she could afford to rear it, had suddenly become her most precious possession, the corner-stone to her astonishing good fortune, the living key which would unlock Tuckahoe to her. From a hotel laundress discharged because she could not get through the work expected of her, America found herself sole trustee and manager without bond of one of the best farms in the Blue Grass thumb of Kentucky, in Mason County famous for leaf which had repeatedly won first prizes in New Orleans and upriver for the past seventy-five years. At the thought that she was to become sole mistress of Foxden, with its eight log rooms and lofts furnished with Uncle Simmy's interesting accumulation of a life spent traveling God only knew where, she could hardly lie still long enough to map out plans for this splendid future.

Several mornings later, America walked upstreet and purchased an unobtrusive maternity dress outfit, her final preparation before leaving Cincinnati. Her letter written to Cousin Margaret had had ample time to be delivered. In it she had stated that she would arrive tomorrow night at Limestone on the *Evening Mail,* alone, in a delicate condition, almost penniless and in sore need of a kinswoman's advice.

So preoccupied was she on returning to her garret room that she stared several minutes before her mind accepted the evidence of her eyes. Fant lay asleep across her bed. Breathless from climbing three flights of steps, America could only stand and gaze at her husband. Unshaven, in rags, he appeared twenty pounds thinner. His eyes, when he awoke and sat up, had a hunted look.

"Where'd you get money to buy those clothes?" he demanded, staring back at her.

"I—" she began. How much would it be wise to tell him now? Fant thought himself Uncle Simmy's heir, he had expected for years to be master of Foxden.

"While you're thinking up a proper story, I'll go make myself presentable," he declared with an unpleasant laugh. Before she realized his intention, he snatched the purse out of her hand and clattered downstairs, calling over his shoulder: "I'll be back before dinner."

America sat down, weak-kneed with anger. She might in time overlook his failure to notice her pregnancy. Her new dress might be more concealing than she had thought it. Moreover, she had emerged from the dark stairway, she had startled him out of deep sleep. But now, if he should squander her teaching fees so that she would have to pawn her topaz and gold jewelry for their steamboat fare to Limestone, she would never forgive him.

Perhaps she had better not tell Fant about Uncle Simmy's will until tomorrow morning. It would serve him right; it would be proper punishment. America congratulated herself that she had paid her board bill this morning, and had asked her landlady as a parting favor to send supper up tonight on a tray.

Before her dinner arrived, Fant reappeared, jaunty in second-hand clothes and smelling of hair tonic. He found America in bed. His disappointed brown eyes noticed the strapped luggage, America's bonnet laid out as for a trip tomorrow. Feeling his way, he began to explain about the purse. He had been forced to borrow it so rudely, he vowed, because he couldn't endure to have her see him down-at-the-heel. Times were bad and getting worse. Money was tight, few could afford to travel on the new railroads. They were too fast, anyhow, for him to nourish in some sucker's mind the desire for a friendly little game accompanied by a few drinks. And she knew only too well why he didn't dare tackle the river boats where passengers had time to be sociable.

The more contrite Fant became, the firmer America's self-pity hardened into a stubborn resolve not to tell him yet that Foxden was to be theirs—for twenty-one years, at least. Let him worry as she had done! Had Fant told the simple truth—that he hadn't eaten in thirty hours—America would have forgiven him at once and they might have spent the night together in happy contemplation of their good fortune. Instead, she announced in white anger that she had been discharged from the laundry because she was sick. Even then he failed to guess about the baby. Looking sympathetic, he tried to take her pulse. She snatched away her hand, and went on to say she had written his mother at Timberlawn that she would arrive in Limestone tomorrow night on the *Evening Mail*. At mention of the packet, Fant's face grew grave. She ended, coldly:

"What are your plans?"

"Maybe you'll need me to look after you on the boat?" Fant suggested. "But what if I run into a warrant for that New Orleans scrape the minute we step up the gangplank?"

"Can't you think about anybody but yourself?" she wailed. "I'm sick, I tell you—I need help!"

"Lovie, what's come over you? You're a different person from the brave girl who pulled us out of that shooting mess in New Orleans," he tried to rally her. "Come on, Merry! Let's you and me go out to dinner and have some fun? Who knows when we'll be in Cincinnati together again?"

Such callous frivolity further infuriated her. Fant after two or three more attempts to pierce the high wall of silence in which she had encircled herself, left the room. He did not return until after midnight. America lay with her face to the wall. Her husband wasn't drunk because he didn't stumble in the darkness over the unfamiliar furniture. With considerate stealth he drew away the extra pillow, spread a blanket on the floor and stretched out there for the night. America's conscience kept whispering that she must pretend to wake up in a moment. She found herself almost wanting to call Fant over to her, to curl into the strong circle of his arms and announce the splendid news of Uncle Simmy's will. One minute more of the punishment he so richly deserved—one minute more—

She awoke with a start. The bedroom was hot with early morning sunshine. Regarding her thoughtfully, Fant stood dressed at the bedside. If she meant to catch that boat for Limestone, she'd have to hurry, he declared. He would go with her.

While she dressed, he outlined a brief campaign. From the expression in his eyes and his kindly patience, she realized that he had observed her condition. Their best chance not to be noticed until they were safely on the *Evening Mail* was to arrive at the last moment just before the gangplank was withdrawn. If a warrant awaited Fant on board, he could still dive into the river. America then would have to go on alone. Should minor trouble arise because he was known to be a gambler, America was to rush towards the purser's window where the passengers were congregated, and there pretend to faint. Few packet officers wanted to take the position before other passengers, of separating even a card-sharp from his swooning wife.

As America walked carefully down the cobblestones with Fant carrying his old hatbox and a black boy hurrying ahead with the other baggage, the beginnings of another heat wave pressed like a giant's sweaty palm over Cincinnati. Before they reached the wharf, the *Evening Mail* announced in two short blasts of her silver whistle that she was about to depart. America, her eyes on the resin oozing out under the hot morning sun rays, almost ran up the gangplank with Fant at her elbow. They were well inside when an authoritative voice challenged:

"Hold her, boys! Annable, you can't ride this boat."

"Just a minute, Mr. Johnson," Fant's voice was confident with relief.

"Get ashore, I tell you!"

"Mr. Johnson," protested Fant, stepping to the first officer's side to whisper audibly, "you can see for yourself my wife's—er, delicate condition. I am taking her home to Limestone. Surely you wouldn't ask her to make this long trip alone?"

All eyes turned on America. Feeling her face flame, she glanced down. In waves, the cargo deck rose to overwhelm her. She felt Mr. Johnson's and Fant's grip at her elbows. Reminding herself fiercely that she must not endanger her child's life by falling, she rallied her failing senses. Through the roar in her ears, she heard the gangplank come in, the *Evening Mail* whistle departure. Out of nowhere a negress' face materialized. Mr. Johnson's voice boomed:

"Stewardess, assist this lady to her stateroom."

"She can't climb those steps!" cut in Fant. "Doctor's orders, sir. Have you no staterooms on this level?"

"Escort your wife where you will, sir. You may purchase your tickets later."

"Thank you, kindly. Follow us with the baggage, boy. And be careful of that hatbox!"

"Yessuh, boss. Ah ain't hu'tin' nuffin."

Fant guided her down the passageway on the freight deck. Ahead of them, the stewardess was unlocking the door of a stateroom on the packet's shady side. America's nostrils were assailed by the ammonia-strong reek of latrines. Pulling away, she demanded a stateroom upstairs, one that opened off the ladies' cabin.

"Careful, now," Fant ignored her protest. "Sit down in the berth and hang your head between your knees. You'll feel better. Put that hatbox over there by the window, boy, then bring some ice water."

When the door had closed, America sprang up, exclaiming:

"Fant Annable, you shan't humiliate me like this! It isn't good for the baby to make me stay all day in this filthy hole."

From the broad glass partition, at which he was unscrewing the catches, he shot her an angry glance. Continuing his work, he flung her own words back at her across his shoulder:

"Can't you think of anyone but yourself? From the way you carry on, you might be the first woman who ever had a baby. These deck-level staterooms are the only ones where I could jump overboard if I have to. Just because we got by with Johnson doesn't mean I may not run into a U.S. marshal. You'll get plenty of fresh air. Don't touch my hatbox, you understand? And don't lock your door—even for a minute!"

"But, Fant—suppose somebody should try to come in?"

"Take a look at yourself in the glass, my dear. Anything else you want?"

Exasperated beyond speech, she could only gaze at him. She couldn't imagine a worse place or time to tell him about Uncle Simmy's will, but she must try:

"Fant, sit down and let me talk to you a minute."

"Sorry, lovie, but I'm in no mood for curtain lectures."

"This is important. I—I want to tell you something."

"If it's about the baby, I can see for myself—this morning. Last night, when you popped out of that dark staircase, honestly, Merry, I had no idea! Besides, I hadn't eaten for two days. You must have been madder than a wet hen all night, to keep back such news. When may we expect it?"

"Before Christmas. Fant, there's something else I feel I must tell you—"

"We haven't been living together lately, but I know you," he smiled at her, with a return of his rare tenderness. "I'm sorry now I asked you where you got the money for your new clothes—and this trip. I had just waked up. All I could think of was getting something to eat myself—and a shave—and clean clothes. I'm not asking you now, dearest. I love you. And I know you love me."

"Fant, you're just plain low down even to think such things!" she wailed. "I sent home to Abigail MacGower for my savings. That's how I came to hear about—"

"Lovie, you'll make yourself really sick, if you carry on so. Lie down now, and try to get a nap. I'll bring you a tray of good hot lunch. Do you want some coffee now?"

"No! I want to tell you—"

"Merry, you know as well as I do Johnson's watching for me like a hawk. If I don't hustle out there and buy our tickets—"

"Oh, go, and good riddance to you!"

"Now you sound like my high-headed girl again." He flashed his brilliant smile into the stateroom door at her and was gone.

America stepped to the transom and opened it. The pleasant morning breeze freshened the cabin. Outside, the water was a deep blue. America could hear the whisper of little waves slapping along the steamboat's flank. Under her feet she felt the throb of engine pistons, and from the stern the driving thrust forward of the packet's great paddle wheel. Men's voices talking in the near-by bar and occasional negro laughter were companionable sounds.

Bending into the lower berth, she stripped off coverlet and blanket, stuffed them into the upper berth and scrubbed her hands at the washbasin. Sheets and pillow cases were clean, she noticed thankfully. Removing her bonnet, she took off her new dress and shoes and lowered herself carefully onto the berth. She drew a tremulous sigh of relief. After their anxious wagon trip north, stopping only at saloons and brothels because they dared not show Fant's face to law-abiding people, they were apparently not wanted by the New Orleans police. After her hideous months in the Cincinnati laundry, with treadmill prospects of her future the hardest obstacle she had to overcome, Uncle Simmy's will had vindicated her rash elopement before all Mason County. With the man of her choice attentive at her side, she was returning in triumph to Tuckahoe, to Foxden, to home. More relaxed than she had been for a long, long time, she fell asleep.

In and out among the sand bars, following the drought-narrowed channel, the *Evening Mail* thrashed carefully upstream. The white-hot sun swung over the meridian and started down the coppery western sky. Beating across quicksilver water, it shone into America's eyes and awakened her. Wet with perspiration, she sat up. The stateroom was a hot-box. Flies buzzed over a covered tray of lunch which Fant must have left for her while she slept. She arose cramped, and gazed anxiously out the partition. The hamlet dropping downstream looked like Dover, one hour west of Limestone. If that was Dover, she must hurry to dress and locate Fant.

As she turned, her elbow brushed Fant's old hatbox. Her hand was on the lid when the habit bred in her through years of punctilious living on Golden Hill checked her. Why feel ashamed of herself for days to come merely to see a gambler's collection of old and new playing cards, poker chips and perhaps a pair of well-oiled dueling pistols?

She felt hungry enough to remove the napkin from the tray. Sight of fried river catfish and snap beans boiled black in greasy pot liquor took her appetite. She nibbled the stale corn bread, tasted the milk. A warning contraction of her stomach made her hasten her toilet. On the port, a cool breeze might be blowing down the great valley along the water, and she panted for it.

As she hurried along the passageway, she heard voices, one of them Fant's, in the bar. A latticework covered with dusty artificial pink roses and yellow honeysuckle had been erected to screen off this retreat for masculine sociability and to permit ventilation. America paused to hear more.

"Well, gen'nemen, that wash a friendly little game," Fant declared with evident satisfaction. He had been drinking, America realized. "Nobody was hurt much 'cept you, Buck, and you sure had it comin' after the way you tried to make trouble for me at the Germantown Fair. My turn today—your turn tomorrow! Now, gen'nemen, if you'll exchuse me, I'll go see how my wife's getting along. She isn't quite herself."

"Hurry on back to her then, you pimp," grumbled a whiskey-sodden voice.

Shocked beyond thought of personal dignity, America peeked under a faded green rose leaf into the bar. At a small table covered with cards and empty glasses all around, Fant stood facing her. On his right sat a tall lean mountaineer; on his left a plumpish man who looked as if he might be a small-town merchant. America could not see the face of the fourth man, hunched down into his chair opposite Fant. He must be Buck Lambeau, who kept the Lee House at Limestone and had threatened last August to turn her husband over to the high sheriff. What a pity that Buck Lambeau, of all people, should have been on this boat today!

"Buck, what wash that you just called me?" Fant asked, with an effort to understand on his flushed face.

"You heard me the firsh time—*hic!*" continued the drunken voice of the man named Buck. "Maybe tha's layin' it on a little shrong. But whassa diff'rence between a woman workin' for a man in bed or in the field? You al'ays were a lazy dog, Annable—an' too damn' lucky! Firsh, it's at cards. Now, you've got that good-lookin' Virginia girl to support you rest o' your worthless life."

"You leave my wife's name out of this, you hear? I don't want any trouble wi' you. We've had trouble enough, my wife an' me—"

"Tied purty tight to her apron strings a'ready, ain'tcha?" jeered Buck.

"Mister, do you know what he's tryin' to say?" Fant appealed to the man on his left. "Do me a favor an' tell us whish one is drunk."

"He's alludin' to Old Man Collier's will," answered the merchant. "Simmy Collier died five months back and left his good farm to your child—in your wife's keepin', provided she don't try to give you anything she kin make off hit."

"An' if that don't make you a pimp, I donno what does!" concluded Buck, triumphantly.

Through the latticework America saw her husband's face go crimson. Buck's hand came back to his hip pocket. Two shots shattered the silence and went reverberating through the packet's cavernous interior. Fant, his revolver smoking in his hand, stood staring down at Buck, who was sliding lower into his chair. In the dying man's limp fingers, America could see the corner of a handkerchief which he had started to pull out of his hip pocket when Fant mistook his harmless motion for intention to shoot.

A moment later, Fant came running down the narrow passageway towards her. He grasped her by the shoulders, jerked her up to look into her eyes.

"Merry, is it true?"

"Yes, Fant! That's what I tried to tell you this morning."

"God, woman, now I'm done for!" he gasped, and let her go. She collapsed against the latticework. He was running down the passageway, reached her stateroom.

As he dodged inside, men came rushing out of the bar. Mr. Johnson, the first officer, led with his revolver drawn. Like a pack of hounds in full cry, they surged past America down the passage and into her stateroom. All she could see were men's backs. She pulled herself up, ran down the passageway, clawed at their backs. All she could hear were men's excited voices inside:

"He jumped overboard!"

"Stop the boat—Annable jumped overboard."

"Don't shoot yet, sir. Wait till his head bobs up—"

"Shore, mister. Then you can pot him good!"

Somewhere above, a bell tinkled. The throb of the pistons ceased. On the bridge the captain must have stopped the engines, lest Fant's body be sucked into the thrashing wheel astern. From her stateroom came Mr. Johnson's bellow of rage:

'Let me out of here, men! I can't see a damn' thing down here—"

Johnson and his followers rushed past America. She ran after them through the purser's office, pulled herself one step at a time up the gilded stairs, panted through the ladies' cabin and out onto the deck. Passengers hung over the off-shore rail and pointed astern. Frantic with fear for Fant's life, America pulled at elbows and coats until a man looked impatiently around at her.

"What happened?" she gasped.

"Lady, ca'm daown. I wasn't in the bar, but I heard Annable shot a Limestone crony of his, another card-sharp. There was bad blood between 'em."

"Bridge ahoy!" bellowed Mr. Johnson's voice somewhere on deck amidships. "Trim your glasses on that black object in midstream—on the edge of the shadow, sir!"

Narrowed by drought, the river ran swift and deep around the sand bar opposite Limestone. In the late afternoon sunshine the water downstream sparkled blue on the Ohio side. From the Kentucky shore to midstream wavered lavender purple shadows of the steep Kentucky hills. Bobbing on the corrugated wake of the now motionless stern wheel was a black spot.

"That's him!" shouted somebody near America. "Damned if that ain't a purty shot—"

"Hit's aout of range."

"Log amidstream, Mr. Johnson!" came the ringing answer from the bridge.

"Shore, that ain't nuthin' but an old log," grunted a mountaineer at America's elbow. "I kin see the moss on hit myself—without no spy glass."

Mr. Johnson, his face red with exertion, appeared from the middle deck and bawled up at the bridge:

"It's no use, sir. He must have been sucked under by the wheel."

Over their heads the little bell tinkled musically, the great wheel surged ahead. America felt the motion like a blow to the pit of her stomach.

"Like as not we'll find what's left of him when we tie up at Limestone," Mr. Johnson complained disgustedly to the passengers. "And good riddance, too! All ashore for Limestone—"

As the knot of passengers melted away, America staggered forward and clung to the rail. Leaning as far out as she dared, she strained her eyes downstream.

"Lady, why ain't you gettin' off at Limestone?" Mr. Johnson's voice came seeking America.

Out of the ring of darkness closing around her, his angry red face approached. Their eyes met, then he gasped:

"Mrs. Fant Annable! Catch her, nigger—she's fainted dead away."

Lying motionless for two days in a darkened room of the Lee House at Limestone, America shut the door of her mind to every thought except the crisis on which her future hung. Her baby must be saved. When Dr. Thorpe announced that her husband's body had not yet been recovered, America realized that she was being summoned from drugged semiconsciousness back to a world of the quick and the dead. Did she feel strong enough, Dr. Thorpe concluded, to receive Mr. and Mrs. Annable?

They appeared in the doorway, two aging country parents dressed in funereal black. Disgrace had stripped them of the complacency which established wealth had given them. Without speaking, they came to the bedside. Bars of afternoon light slanting in through closed shutters revealed their faces grey with fatigue, pinched by despair.

"We've just come from Buck's funeral," whispered Cousin Margaret, on the verge of collapse as she sank onto the chair put forward by Nellie, the mulatto woman who was nursing America. "I declare, I don't know which unnerved me most: to see that coffin, or to have Flossie Lambeau nod to me like a Christian."

"She let them bring me here," America answered, as if it were yesterday she had parted from these two, as if love and new life and death did not lie in the twenty-three months between them. "While of course she hasn't been in to see me, the hotel servants have been most attentive. Doesn't this show she holds no hard feelings against us—as Fant's people?"

"It shows she aims to keep on running this sinkhole of iniquity!" barked Mr. Annable, his mouth twisted with the bitter effort of speech. "You might as well know the truth—Flossie Lambeau's sworn out a warrant for Fant. I asked her just now did she expect her murderous accusations to reach to river bottom—or hell?"

"Squire Annable, I'll have to ask you not to distress our patient," interposed Dr. Thorpe. "My idea in letting you see her was that you could set her mind at rest by answering any practical questions she might have about her immediate future. Emotional subjects had best be eschewed."

"We've come to take you home, Merry," Mrs. Annable tried to manage a hospitable smile. "We brought in the closed carriage so none of us would be stared at."

"I'm sorry you've had your trouble for nothing, ma'am," Dr. Thorpe answered. "Our patient had best not be moved tonight. Then I'd suggest she go to some place where she can be absolutely quiet."

"Yes, yes," agreed Mr. Annable. "Let me have five minutes alone with her now. Then we'll go."

"Five minutes, mind you! Come along, Nellie."

The door closed behind them. Mr. Annable turned his haggard face to America, to demand:

"Missy, is your husband dead or alive?"

"I don't honestly know, sir."

"Come, come! You can trust me."

"You know I'd tell you if I knew," declared America earnestly. "Here's what happened. I was so tired I slept all day. Fant had put me in a stateroom on the freight deck. They're the only ones with sliding windows big enough for a man to jump through, he said. When I woke, my cabin was a bake oven, so I started to go on deck for some fresh air. As I was passing the bar, I heard men's voices quarreling. Everybody seemed to have been drinking some. Buck called Fant an unspeakable name, then reached for his handkerchief in his hip pocket. Fant must have thought he was reaching for his gun."

"That's his defense," declared Mr. Annable. "Buck reached back for the gun in his hip pocket and Fant beat him to the draw—"

"It was his handkerchief, sir. I saw it."

"Tut, missy! Forget what you saw. You won't be subpoenaed. A wife can't testify against her husband."

"Everybody saw it," America declared. "Buck slumped into his chair and Fant came running down the passageway. He ran inside our stateroom and locked it. Then the men rushed past me. You know the rest."

"Do you expect me to believe such a tale?" demanded Mr. Annable, impatiently.

"I did see a log floating downstream, sir. Maybe he was clinging to the underside of that."

"I talked to the captain about that log," replied Mr. Annable. "He studied it himself for five minutes through his binoculars. It never turned or rolled—as logs do with people holding on to them. You can't throw us off the track with that log, missy."

"I've told you everything I know," sighed America, and closed her eyes.

"Then you must take me for a complete fool," accused Mr. Annable, his keen eyes searching America's face. "How do you expect me to believe a silly story like that, when you neither look nor act like a young woman who's just seen the husband she loved go to river's bottom? I don't know or care how much Fant may have abused you these two years. I do know you picked him as the man of your choice in Virginia—you followed him out here—you risked your good name and your livelihood to win him. You can't lie there now quiet as a China doll—without a tear in your eye—and make me believe you've changed your nature completely!"

"I am trying not to think about him any more than I can

help," whispered America, with closed eyes. "If I lose my baby, I'll have to go back to work in that laundry—"

"Time's up," declared Dr. Thorpe, appearing in the doorway with Nellie. "Well, have you solved this little lady's future?"

"We can make you very comfortable at Timberlawn," Cousin Margaret came into the breach.

"Tell me something about Foxden, please," America asked.

Mr. Annable must have realized that he could question her no further about Fant. He answered in a pleasanter tone:

"I've talked to Judge Stacy about that. Papers are being drawn up for your signature empowering me to act as your agent. I ran that farm for years—when Simmy was gallivanting here, there and everywhere. Nobody knows the ground better, or could farm it half as well as I can—and will."

"Is there a tenant living there now?" asked America, with deceptive mildness.

"Mahalee's there—like an old queen bee," smiled Cousin Margaret. "She's been the only woman around for so long she's rotten spoiled. It was all we could do to get an inventory for the court."

"If Judge Stacy will permit me—and as soon as Dr. Thorpe says I'm able to drive out—I'll take possession of Foxden," announced America.

Through the storm of protest which burst from Mr. Annable, America lay with lips resolutely closed and grey eyes calm. Now she knew from which parent Fant had inherited his talent for making a scene. Dr. Thorpe's protests at first went unnoticed, then he seized Mr. Annable and pushed him forcibly out of the sickroom.

Two hours later Cousin Margaret returned alone. The doctor wouldn't let her sit down, she announced, but she had two things she must say. She began in a strained voice:

"First, America, I want you to know I understand—and support you—in your courageous determination to go out and claim Foxden for Fant's child. Mr. Annable and I have just been talking to Judge Stacy. The court cannot qualify you as executrix until your son is born. I will stay here with you tonight and take you out to Foxden tomorrow. Mahalee and I will tend you there until your strength returns. I've already sent word to Cato to drive a good cow down the pike tonight, so you'll have fresh milk tomorrow. To raise a crop next spring, I'll give you my two best hands—Weed and Ben Shadrack—and furnish you with what money you may need until your tobacco is ready to sell. I have had a sum of gold laid away these many years—now I know what for. If it isn't enough, I'll call on Mr. Annable for more."

"What does he say to all this, ma'am?"

"For thirty-two years Mr. Annable has managed my substantial property. In this time I've never said yea or nay but once to anything he saw fit to do," declared Cousin Margaret, with old-fashioned formality. Then the reserve of years broke before a rush of maternal despair. Tears rolling down her cheeks, she burst into jerky confession: "Even when he cut Fant off without a cent—although I knew it would only drive Fant to further excesses—I held my peace, I respected him. On the street just now—when I told Mr. Annable I meant to befriend you—I had to remind him that Timberlawn belongs to me. Mr. Annable was beside himself—he scarcely noticed how people stared at us. Fortunately Judge Stacy was still in chambers when I got there. As Simmy's nearest of kin, I asked him to establish you at Foxden now, and he consented. Mr. Annable stood by throughout the interview and left me without a word when we reached the street."

"Someday our child will bless you, ma'am," America strove to quiet the panic in the good wife's eyes. "As for me, all I can say now is that the Lord has raised me up a helper."

" 'The Lord giveth and the Lord hath taken away,' " quavered Cousin Margaret. Through tears, the two women gazed at each other and then Margaret's bleak control broke. Her face crumpled like that of a little girl starting to cry. "Merry, can't you hold out a ray of hope to me?" she sobbed.

"I know he must have treated you shamefully, but don't lie there looking as if you're glad he's dead! He was my first baby, can't you understand now what that means? He was a wee, wee sweet thing, my black-eyed baby boy. And I love him so!"

"I loved him too, ma'am."

"Merry, you've got to tell me where you've hidden him! If you won't take pity on me as his mother, can't you trust me as his friend and yours, after what I've done to insure your future?"

"Cousin Maggie, I've told you everything that happened. There wasn't hardly a ripple on the water except for that log. Could Fant have clung to that log, or swum to shore without making a ripple? No matter how good a swimmer he was, he couldn't stay under water that long."

"You mean Fant actually was in the water?"

"Haven't I told you he jumped through the opened partition? A dozen men heard him splash. They tore the berths apart, and searched the packet from bow to stern before they docked at Limestone, Nellie said."

"Then he's drowned for sure," whispered Mrs. Annable, her eyes staring, the corners of her mouth drawn down like an old woman's. "Fant couldn't swim a stroke. All his life he's feared the water like a cat. He couldn't swim—and he wouldn't stay off the river."

Chapter 8

On a sand ridge above the Cape Fear River, the old port town of Wilmington, North Carolina, steamed during a late afternoon of August, 1869. Tugger sat on his carryall in the shade of an abandoned dock warehouse. He had come down to salt water hoping to introduce his smoking mixture into the waterfront saloons. Foreign sailors, said to be easy spenders, might have money for the tobacco Tarheels no longer seemed able to buy. Carpetbag and scalawag rule had slowed domestic trade to a standstill.

All afternoon at the main wharf a rusty hulled tramp freighter had loaded cotton bales. Liverpool was her home port, and above her name, the Union Jack hung limp as a rag in the calm before sundown. To seaward, the river glittered like a sheet of quicksilver.

Weariness born more of discouragement than fatigue engulfed Tugger. On each sales trip during the past six months, he had wrestled with the problem of dwindling sales. Tempted this afternoon to hire a rig, pick up a lively girl and drive down to Fort Fisher, Tugger had denied himself this pleasure because business was too slow. Yet he could not banish Fort Fisher from his mind. Tradin' was still his pride, but it never hurt a man to pick up a little education first-hand as he went along.

Although his thoughts seemed to lap aimlessly on the walls of his mind, as the tide lapped the dock piles beneath him, Tugger was spotting the liveliest of three waterfront saloons. Four men, a sailor and a girl in a white dress had gone into Kelly's Bowery, at the head of the main wharf. The girl must be new to the waterfront, because she carried her red hat like a country jake.

A breath of air came upstream like an invisible finger dipping into the water. The freighter's crew should be ashore any minute. Tugger wondered if Kelly kept his own bar. Whoever did would have to know how to use his fists to stay in business here. Now was as good a time as any to tackle him, Tugger decided. Grasping his carryall, he walked up the hot cobblestones and pushed through the saloon's sun-bleached glass doors.

After the white glare of the river, the cool interior seemed dark as a cave. The sweet-sour reek of rum told Tugger he'd come to the right place for sailors. As seen in the fly-specked mirror over the bar, the most conspicuous person in the saloon was himself in his new suit. Whenever the half-doors swung open, the mirror caught the glare from outside and flung it like subdued lightning into everybody's eyes. The mirror flashed twice while Tugger was getting his bearings. The girl in the white dress was sitting with her hat on a table in the far corner. Behind the bar an unhappy Irishman mixed drinks. He met Tugger's ingratiating smile with an authoritative gleam of ownership in watery blue eyes.

"Nuthin' this evenin', bub."

"No beer? Go on—spare me a small one!" joked Tugger. When it arrived, he turned his back on the free lunch, sipped the cool draught he wanted to gulp, and continued easily: "Nice place you have here, sir. Clean, too, and hardly a fly! Could I impose on your good will to let me try out a little experiment of mine?"

"My trade don't go for magicians an' parlor tricks."

"I'm being paid to find out which sells faster—Blake's *Fighting Cock* or Lord's *Bright Leaf*."

"Ye're backin' two losers, me bye. *Bull Durham* outsells thim both ten to wan."

"That's very interestin'," declared Tugger, visibly impressed. "If my boss would take your word for it, I could hire a rig and go see Fort Fisher. Were you here for the bombardment?"

"Do I look like a bloomin' hero? I come down in the rush three years ago. How I come to sink me life-savin's in this cesspool has me lyin' awake mornin's to figger out." There was no need to tell every clodhopper in from the hay that he'd lost the saloon, that now he was working for a smarter Yankee from New Bedford who had taken over the place. "Faith, bub, I'm so homesick for the Bowery," Kelly concluded, "I can't spit sthraight iny more!"

"Some day I aim to go to New York," declared Tugger and slid his coin across the bar. "You don't know anybody who'd let me count sales on their counter, do you?"

"Go wan, unpack yer stuff," the Irishman relented.

On the tobacco end of the bar, Tugger set out a dozen bags of *Fighting Cock* as if in battle array. Two years ago he had dropped *E Pluribus Optimum.* Eph had suggested this catchier name and symbol, a red cock crowing over a spiked antagonist, and had arranged for the expensive printing job through a comrade Knight in Richmond. With Kelly's eye on him, Tugger was forced to display an equal amount of Lord's *Bright Leaf* on the bar less advantageously than his own *Fighting Cock.* To advertise his rival's brand hurt when Tugger hadn't booked his own product into enough new outlets to pay expenses. Yet he could think of no better trick to get *Fighting Cock* into good saloons. When he got back to Durham, maybe he could talk Dan Lord into giving him something for the sales records he'd kept on Lord's *Bright Leaf,* although this too wouldn't make pleasant reading.

With his layout completed, Tugger swung his carryall under a table. Even with the new display, Kelly's tobacco stock was not impressive. Besides the three brands of smoking mixture, there was the usual line of chewing plug manufactured by the powerful Leonard & Morley Company, of St. Louis. A Frenchman in New Jersey named Pierre Longpré made good plug and snuff, but his brands were not represented here. The familiar Holt brands of snuff, produced in Louisville, Kentucky, and boxes of cheroots varying in price completed Kelly's stock. Apart from them in a corner lay perhaps twenty of some new-fangled product called *Turkish Fancies,* done up expensively in small boxes with the picture of a scantily clad female doing a scarf dance on the top.

"What're those things?" demanded Tugger, pointing.

"You mean them lady-killers?"

"What's the scarf dancer got inside?"

"You are green, ain't you, bub? I'm busy, now. An' besides, they ain't for sale."

Taking out his pencil and notebook, Tugger drifted down the bar ostensibly to keep tab on his own display. Outside, the sun had set, for a rosy glow instead of the glare came in with frequent swings of the half-doors. Tugger was maneuvering into position near the free lunch tray when Kelly warned:

"Lunch goes with hard liquor!"

"Any charge for usin' the lookin'-glass?" Tugger pleasantly acknowledged defeat.

"If you can stand it, the glass can."

Tugger surveyed himself thoughtfully. Association with Ephraim Moncure had taught him a lot, but still there was something missing. Eph knew, and Tugger felt he too had learned, the little things which make a hit with the ladies. Eph could spot the most important person in a roomful of people, Eph knew when a smile would save a fight, and prove twice as effective. It didn't seem to make much difference about Eph's grammar. Sometimes Eph said "ain't" and swore like a mule-skinner. Eph's voice had a quality in it that men with the same quality in their voices recognized no matter what Eph said. Try as he might to watch his own grammar and to copy Eph's inflections, Tugger just couldn't quite get it.

"Farm boy, ain'tcha, bub?" Kelly pronounced the verdict with sly malice. "Damned if I know how that Jew tailor upstreet tangles ever' one of you on his fly-paper! Caught you with his talk about that cloth being the best English worsted, just smuggled off a tramp by a British sailor, didn't he? Next time try somepin quiet. Folks won't notice you then—till you ketch onto city ways."

"Much obliged," murmured Tugger, biding his time.

"Kape the change."

The girl in the white dress was watching him. Tugger swung his shoulder so she couldn't catch his eye again in the mirror. He hadn't come in here to give offense to the Britisher paying for her drinks. Besides, he shouldn't fight anybody in his new suit. What was another girl to him, Tugger asked himself, after he had lived under the same roof with Mary Ellen Bledsoe for years? Mary Ellen's round face framed in plats of straight yellow hair came to his mind's eye. She wasn't bright, she worked just hard enough to keep ahead of the housework and nurse Old Man Bledsoe, bedridden with a broken hip, but she was female and honest. Almost every day when he was home for meals, she intentionally brushed his arm with hers whenever she put a plate or a cup of coffee before him. Yet would she let him walk up the hollow to the spring with her? No, I thank you! Because she wouldn't with him, Tugger sensed that she hadn't with Eph. Sometimes the panic in Mary Ellen's eyes, as she realized she was twenty and still unwed with two proper young bucks under the same roof, almost made Tugger bust out laughing right in her ordinary face. One of these days he'd come home and find Mary Ellen married to Eph. That would be all right, too, Tugger chuckled; for then he could leave Eph holding the bag while he lit out to the city, to a real town like Philadelphia or New York. A nobody like himself had no chance in Richmond or Baltimore. The thought of his changing places with Eph, he and Palestine living like lords in New York while Eph milked cows on the worn-out Durham farm, and emptied Old Man Bledsoe's bedpan, would be something to make a preacher laugh.

As the evening dragged on, fourteen men and two girls entered the saloon. Nine came directly to the bar, and looked over his display. Four asked for *Bull Durham*. five were chewers.

One bought a pack of Lord's *Bright Leaf*. Two youths, with a wink at each other, tried to steal a pack but hastily put it back when they saw Tugger bearing down on them. The Britisher left the girl in the white dress at her corner table, lurched to the bar, stuffed five packs of *Fighting Cock* inside his blouse, slammed down a queer-looking coin and staggered out. Beyond the swinging doors, he must have collided with someone about to enter the saloon. Tugger heard apologies, hic-coughing and a fine burst of marine profanity delivered in a crisp voice with a Cockney accent. A moment later, an undersized petty officer came in pert as a cock sparrow. Tugger watched while Kelly handed over to him all but one fly-specked sample of the *Turkish Fancies* with the scarf dancer on their box tops. With a shaking hand the officer opened a box and took out a white cylinder. Tugger thought it candy or opium until he saw the officer thump the cylinder on the bar to knock off a few flakes of what could only be chopped leaf, and then light the tube at the far end. While the officer was exhaling smoke with deep satisfaction, Tugger came closer with a question:

"Excuse me, sir, but what d'you call those things?"

"You mean this cigaroot, matie?"

"Cigaroot, eh? Do you really enjoy them as much as you appear?"

"Hye cawn't 'onestly sie Hye do," rejoined the Cockney, removing the smoking tube with a clerkish hand and gazing at it. "My Gov'nor learned to use the lidy-killers in the Crimea."

"Where's that?"

"Hye sie, matie, don't ye know? We fought a war there with the Roosians. My old man saw Roosian prisoners smokin' cigaroots in bed on each side of 'im at Scutari. Once 'e'd tried 'em, nothin' else would do. As a lad, thie were all Hye could lay me 'ands on, ye know."

"Do you have trouble getting them over here?"

"Hye'll sie Hye do! 'Ere's the only pub stocks 'em for me, eh, Kelly?"

"They look expensive," decided Tugger.

"Figgur hit for yerself, if a chappie smokes twenty-five or thirty a die like Hye do. Try one, why doncha?"

"Thirty a day? Why, man—" Tugger caught himself on the point of exclaiming: "That ud kill you!" Anyone could see the cock sparrow looked handy on his feet and stout as they came. From his soft hands and flat belly, he might be an assistant purser or supercargo, some one who did clerical work yet stooped down and raised up repeatedly. A man would have to have a heart of cast iron to smoke thirty pipefuls of *E Pluribus Optimum* a day, honest leaf though it was. What a gold mine those cigaroots might prove if he could get *Fighting Cock*'s mixture inside them! There couldn't be more'n half a teaspoon of tobacco in each cigaroot. And look how quickly they burned! Tugger thrust his hand into his pocket, pulled out his own product and offered it in his best sales manner:

"Accept a bag of Blake's *Fighting Cock,* sweet as a nut and twice as tasty! Try it out in your pipe when you get back aboard ship tonight."

"Thanks, matie," answered the Cockney, making no move to accept the sample. "The truth is, Hye cawn't touch the weed any way but this, now the 'abit's got me. So long, Kelly, till next trip. We're up-anchor when the tide turns."

"Sorry to see ye go, sor."

Tugger was slipping a piece of ham between buttered rye when the barman bore down on him with a truculent:

"What'll it be?"

"See that fly-specked box of cigaroots he didn't take?" indicated Tugger.

"Cigarettes, greenhorn! I've seen London swells just off the boats in New Yoik a-smokin' 'em."

"Cigarettes, then," Tugger repeated the strange word. "I'll take 'em. How much?"

"Fifty cents. I told ye before, free lunch goes only with hard liquor!"

Without relinquishing the sandwich in his right hand,

Tugger managed the transaction with his left. When the lady-killers were safely pocketed, he looked the Irishman in the eye. A good new idea always made Tugger feel cocky, almost cocky enough to fight.

"I could've bought two good whiskeys—an' five of the kind you pour—for the price of those stale cigarettes," he challenged.

"But ye didn't, see?"

"What kind of a barkeep are you, grudgin' me a bite of hawg an' rye?"

"Aw, go on, cheapskate!"

"Watch what you call me, you Irish baboon," warned Tugger, dangerously. When his mind was made up to something, he couldn't get into action quick enough—any kind of action. Cramming what was left of the sandwich into his mouth, he moved around the end of the bar.

In the mirror, Tugger could see that everyone in the saloon was watching him. The girl in the white dress had gotten up from her table as if she was worried. She wasn't used to saloon brawls, Tugger could tell from the way her knuckles had come up to her mouth.

"Now, go aisy, bub," soothed Kelly, retreating.

"Hell-damn, who d'you think you're calling bub?" roared Tugger. What if he did bust out the sleeves of this English checker-board that had him parboiled? He'd buy another suit, dark and rich-looking, before he tackled Dan Lord with his new idea.

"No offense intended, sor! Here, help yourself to all yez kin eat," the Irishman surrendered, and sent the tray of free lunch sliding across the bar. Turning his back so Tugger couldn't hit him, Kelly walked up to the tobacco case and bit himself off a generous quid.

In the mirror, Tugger saw the girl making her way towards the door. Somebody pulled at her white dress, but she stopped only to nod and smile. Tugger reached for his suitcase under the empty table, and began to repack. Sure enough, the girl had paused near the door to visit again.

"I'm much obliged to you for lettin' me conduct my little experiment in here," Tugger tried to make peace with Kelly.

"Git goin,' you!"

"Give me my change, then."

"Your change?" roared the startled Irishman. "Ye ain't bought nuthin' but a five-cent beer!"

"An' fifty cents' worth of cigarettes," Tugger corrected him. "How about the money that Britisher left for my five bags of *Fighting Cock?* I'll split fifty-fifty with you on them."

"Ye git aout av here before I bust yez with a bung-starter!"

Tugger liked to slip quietly into a place like this and breeze some big blow-hard along until he had to fight or back down. Fighting must come as natural to him as tradin', Tugger thanked his lucky stars. In a fight his heart beat faster, his eyes worked quicker, his mind stood by like a friend watching to call the first break in his opponent's guard.

"Irish," Tugger drawled. "I'm givin' you a cut ever' man in this room will say is more'n fair. Now, pass me over my two bits—and no counterfeit, mind you!—before I come around there and help myself."

He'd known all along the big grumbler wouldn't fight. Tugger pocketed his quarter, backed out of arm's reach and picked up his carryall. At the door, he paused to fling a parting insult at the defeated Kelly:

"Why don't you light the lamps and clean your mirror, bub? It's dark as a church in here. And twice as dull."

Outside, the harbor had sucked all the light from the faded sunset sky. Ahead of him the girl's white dress was a slow-moving mist. Catching up, Tugger grinned down at her:

"Howdye, sis! What's your name?"

"I—I'm sure that's no business of yours, sir!"

Only a newcomer to the docks would be ruffling her feathers like a little white hen, Tugger noted with satisfaction. In the afterglow reflected from the harbor her eyes were dark enough, her plump cheeks had down on them like the yellow fuzz on a peach.

"Now I know you're a country jake—from the way you talk, ma'am, not from how you look," declared Tugger, remembering in time one of the important little things he'd learned. "My name's Tugger—Jim Tugger—and I'm from the Piedmont. Ain't you goin' to be neighborly an' tell me your name?"

"Angelina—"

"Annie's enough for me. Comin' my way?"

"That depends."

"I've got to hop the night freight for Weldon. She'll stop at the first cotton gin outside town to bolt 'n' shackle some empties. Why don't you walk a piece with me?" Tugger suggested. "Maybe it ud be cooler up there near the woods. Come on—what d'you say?"

"Will you promise to be very good?"

"That's all I can afford right now!" laughed Tugger, and linked his arm companionably through hers. "Didn't you hear me offer to fight that Irish baboon for two bits? That's all I've got to show for an afternoon's hard work. Two bits an' an idea that's goin' to make somebody a millionaire."

"What's a millionaire, Mr. Tugger?" asked the country jake, walking close.

Tugger came out first from the sumac thicket. He'd wait for her on the railroad bank, he called. If he'd been alone, he would have changed then and there into the overalls he always carried to save his good clothes while riding the wood-burners. He could change later in the caboose, Tugger decided gallantly. Eph said you owed it to the girl who took you for a fine gentleman to stay dressed like one until you dropped out of her life.

Annie appeared shortly. She had twisted her hair onto the top of her head again, and was carrying her hat. It was too dark to see how she felt. When she raised his hand timidly to her cheek, it was flushed.

"Whar'd you say you lived, Mr. Tugger?" she asked, trying to hold on to her happiness.

"Richmond, ma'am."

"Oh! I—I thought you said the Piedmont. Effen hit war the Piedmont, maybe I'd git to see you agin sometime—when I go home."

"Then you must live on the East Tennessee and Virginia Railroad?" Tugger made conversation.

"Yes, siree! Paw, he used tuh call hit Eat Turnips an' Vinegar. Hit connects north with the old South Side Railroad, an' south with the East Tennessee an' Georgy—Eat Turnips an' Greens," Annie did her best to be entertaining.

"Mountain folks like to think up nicknames," commented Tugger. "A fellow I knew from Kentucky told me they had a short line named the Elizabethtown, Lexington an' Big Sandy. The pay-car, he said, always was two or three months late, so the hands called hit the 'Eat Little an' Be Satisfied.'"

"Ha! ha!" laughed Annie. "I reckon you never hear't tell of the Streakle Head Line?"

"You've got me there," admitted Tugger, listening. Overhead, the telegraph wire was singing the approach of Number Three down the curving track.

"Streakle Head's another name for the East Tennessee an' Georgy," explained Annie. "Georgy crackers go bareheaded most of the time, an' git their hair sunburned. Effen I ain't kerful I'll be a streakle-head myself."

"That's what caught my eye," declared Tugger. "You were bareheaded when you went into Kelly's place. I followed you in."

"Naow, Mr. Tugger, you know you come in tuh show off yer fine clothes!"

"Lookit that engine shootin' sparks. The wood-passer must be meetin' himself comin' and goin'."

"She needs all the head she kin make fer this grade. Paw worked on the railroad fer a spell. We lived right along side the track—"

"Well, Annie—good luck!"

"Ain't you goin' tuh kiss me goo'-bye, Mr. Tugger?"

"When I'll be back next week?" lied Tugger. He bent and kissed her bruised lips, no longer cool, then scrambled up the bank with his valise.

Annie, the memory of honest railroading upon her, hid in the sumac. Up the track labored the big-funneled engine. Tugger hated caboose jumping at night. Once too often with his heavy valise he'd try it in the dark and then he'd have to sell pencils on a street corner the rest of his life.

The new locomotive, made in England and already blowing like a grampus, pounded past Tugger. Wood tender and freight cars rattled by going at least twenty miles an hour. Tugger saw himself lying mangled under the clanking trucks. Up the track, a red lantern made a half-arc, and the train slowed down. As the front platform of the caboose drew alongside, Tugger swung his valise aboard and jumped for the rear platform rails. His feet struck the steps, he pulled himself up past a brakeman with an answering red lantern. Under his feet the platform shook as the trucks rolled over the siding frogs. Dammit if he wasn't through risking the only legs he'd ever have to save buying a railroad ticket! His knees still shaky, he pushed inside.

"Evening, Tugger," Conductor Stringfellow puffed out his squirrel cheeks without surprise. "I thought you'd be swingin' on presently. How's business?"

"Couldn't be worse," declared Tugger, and went forward to fetch his carryall off the front platform of the caboose. His *Fighting Cock* might be badly outsold by its competitors, but a sack of it all around was still worth a free ride up the North Carolina coast. The evening had turned out fine, thanks to the Cockney and Annie. Now, if he could manage a hearty supper! Except for the sandwich he'd pecked off Kelly's free lunch, Tugger hadn't eaten all day.

"Runnin' kinda light, ain't you, cap?" Tugger put out a feeler.

"We're picking up three empties twenty minutes ahead."

"How long you aim to lay over?"

"Ten minutes, I reckon. You ain't fixing to leave us so soon?"

"Not on your tintype!"

The crew went forward to set the hand brakes. Swinging off the caboose in due time, Tugger looked up and down the track. Five hundred yards back were several lighted cabins where a track crew lived. Tugger followed his nose to the rear of a whitewashed shack and peered through the window. A young mulatto woman was turning a pan of biscuits in the oven. At Tugger's knock on the opened door, she looked around startled and then smiled with pleasure at sight of his new suit. On top of the rickety stove sizzled a skilletful of country bacon.

"How'ye, gal! I'll give you a dime for that pan of biscuits an' side meat," Tugger offered.

"Den w'at's mah man tuh eat, boss?" she answered with the ingratiating whine niggers use when they want to bargain. "Dem's mighty fine clo's you's a-wearin', suh."

"You know that general storekeeper at the crossroads? He just put in a new line of Anti-Kink," Tugger tempted her, with one ear open for the bump of cars on the siding.

"How you know, boss?"

"I just stocked him. That's why I missed supper. The small-size bottle sells for a dime—and they won't last long. Make up your mind! I've got to catch Number Three."

"I ain't got no pan tuh spa'hr."

"Dump 'em in this paper sack. Here's your dime, and don't drink the stuff. If you do, it'll curl your hair in the opposite direction!"

Stuffing his mouth with the delicious food, Tugger ran towards the red eye of the caboose standing on the main track. Unless he could bolt the major portion of his supper and hide the rest in his pocket for breakfast, he'd have to share with the train crew. Conductor Stringfellow was returning with orders in one hand, and with his battered army canteen dripping in the other. Up ahead, the engineer whistled in the rear brakeman. Everybody swung aboard, and they were soon rolling.

"Seems to me I smell something mighty good," hinted Conductor Stringfellow, expectantly.

"Smells to me like fried meat soakin' into hot sody biscuits," spoke up Jennings, the older brakeman. George, a youngster who had railroaded up North, could only stare and wet his lips with his tongue.

"You must mean my box of lady-killers," declared Tugger and pulled it from his pocket. With his thumbnail, he broke the stamp and opened the expensive container. "Try one, all of you! They're called cigarettes and they come from Roosia. They're the latest thing, I've been told. The swells smoke 'em in London an' New York."

The diversion worked. Everybody but Tugger lighted up and sampled cigarette smoke as judiciously as if their verdict counted. Jennings was openly scornful. He, along with the other red-blooded men of the country, would take Leonard & Morley plug every time!

"What you going to do when the outdoor work's all done and you can't spit easy?" demanded Captain Stringfellow.

"Whatya mean—outdoor work?" asked Jennings.

"Wal, when we get the railroads built, f'instance."

"You don't think we're goin' to need more railroads than we've already got, do you?" demanded Tugger, surprised.

"Riding the steam cars is a habit that's hit the American people worse'n drink," pronounced Captain Stringfellow. "Damyankees al'ays had it. Us Johnnie Rebs got a taste during the war we'll never forget—the ladies while they were refugee-ing from city to city ahead of Sherman, and their menfolks in the Army. I ought to know—didn't I haul 'em myself? This here Union that's been forced on some of us is going to witness the biggest railroad-building jag the world has ever seen."

"Then I ought to go into the plug business, according to you," grinned Tugger, looking at his lady-killers.

"You cain't, 'cause you don't know plug leaf. And Leonard

'n' Morley wouldn't let you if you did," continued Captain Stringfellow. "The only chance you got selling these dodads is to wait till the railroads are built, like I told you. Then the men who built 'em will have to go inside to work—whar they can't spit free 'n' easy. This onhappy day ain't as far off as you might think. Ever' run I make to Atlanta 'n' Birmingham, I see more cotton mills an' steel foundries a-popping up."

"Once a chawer, al'ays a chawer," George agreed with Jennings, the senior brakeman.

"Son, I see you ain't married," the conductor commented, dryly. "Tugger, if you can coax the ladies into thinking these here cigarettes might banish the spittoon an' stop their menfolks from spitting on a clean hearth, your fortune's made."

Tugger folded himself into the front corner of the skipper's bench, and pretended to go to sleep. When the freight train swung around a curve, wood smoke and ashes filled the caboose. Tugger was used to discomfort, but could never feel quite safe on a train at night. Too much of the war spirit of git-through-or-bust-the-biler still clung to southern railroading. Tugger knew the difficulties the lines were facing. In the spring of '65, he had lain concealed in the bushes long enough to watch Sherman's men destroy track. By long practice they had reduced the job to a fine swift art. Twenty or more Yanks facing each other with crossbars thrust under the rails could exert enough pressure together to rip up a considerable section of track, which they laid on roaring fires kindled from crossties. Before the steel was red-hot, the spikes fell out of the burning wood. Two soldiers with tongs then grasped a rail at each end and ran with it against the nearest tree trunk, making another of Sherman's "hairpins." Before this rail could carry traffic again, it must go through the foundry. Trestles, culverts and bridges had been easier to destroy.

While the caboose humped itself over many a heat-warped rail slipped into the new track, Tugger sat on the end of his spine, with hands clasped around his knees, and gave serious thought to Old Stringie's remarks. How many railroads in the

South, mostly short lines locally owned by now disfranchised ex-Confederates, were running tonight? If one or two could be bought up cheap, a man stood to make a barrel of money. Folks who'd once lived along a railroad wouldn't want to do without it again, might even be willing to subscribe to a few loans to keep it going. How did a fellow get hold of a broken-down railroad? Stringie had advised the Richmond or Atlanta Stock Exchanges, but Tugger felt any Tarheel was whipped before he started in either of these high-toned towns. "No'th Car'liny, suh"—Eph liked to tease—"a valley of awkwardness between two mountains of pride!"

Whistling mournfully, the freight lumbered on through the night. Stringie snored on one bench, Jennings on the other. The young fellow George was having a time to keep awake and listen for signals from up front. Once before midnight, Tugger tossed him a cigarette, and lighted one himself. After his first lungful of smoke, he was sorry he had given away so many of them. If other Americans liked them as well as he and George did, plenty of pipe smokers—and especially those who were always leaving their pipe in their other coat—might be induced to change over. Why hadn't he asked that Britisher if he'd seen cigarettes being made?

Tugger examined his half-consumed lady-killer. It appeared to have been rolled and glued by hand. Supposing he started rolling cigarettes, how could he make Eph see to it that the black boys took proper pains? The Lords had the edge on him, because there were four of them—Old Man Lord, Joe, Martin and Dan. The old man did the buying, Joe and Martin the selling and Dan ran the factory, located at the Lord farm on the Hillsboro road outside Durham Station. Dan wanted to move into Durham, where help would be cheap and plentiful. The older Lords weren't willing to go so fast.

The thing for him to do, Tugger told himself, was to tie in with the Lords. Maybe he could make Dan see, from the figures he'd kept on *Bright Leaf,* that it would be just as easy to sell two brands of smokin' mixture as one. After a while, as soon as the new partnership was going good, they might put out some cigarettes? One thing sure, cigarettes would be fresh as morning-glories. "Morning Glories"—hell-damn, but that was a catchy name!

About three o'clock, Tugger arose to ease his cramped muscles. In search of fresh air, he stepped out onto the back platform. Far down the western sky, the waning moon threw a yellow light over landscape studded with small farms, cleared fields and black patches of woodland. Twice while he stood and gazed, they passed skeletons of plantation manors Sherman had gutted on his march north to encircle Raleigh. Around a curve a farmhouse came into lonely view. Its windows were bright with the activity of birth or death.

The thought struck Tugger that he himself was plenty old enough to be sitting up for the borning of a man-child he had sired. He wondered how it would feel to lie in a clean bed, to eat regular meals and to watch his young uns play in the sunshine. Such luxuries could come later, in abundance. Now, he and Palestine must wait until he had become a millionaire.

Ephraim slapped the account book shut and, moving to the office door, looked disinterestedly into the factory barn. At the benches Tugger had set up against either wall, sixteen black boys flailed leaf. Through the choking dust, sun rays slanted across the south side like shafts of light through the side windows of a cathedral. Pretending not to notice how the beat had quickened with his presence, Ephraim scuffed through the trash to the front entrance. The May sunshine outside was strong enough to make him blink.

From the doorway, Eph saw a dilapidated log stable, sheds and sagging double crib. A branch, fed by the mountain spring above, had carved a channel along one side of the barn lot. It was spanned by a footbridge into the yard. Hills encircling the meager farm establishment on its three upper sides made Ephraim feel imprisoned. He knew himself to be bound here by invisible ties stronger than these worn-out slopes.

Since Old Man Bledsoe had broken his hip by falling off the icy footbridge, nobody made a pretense at farming. His fields provided pasturage for Mary Ellen's cow and Ephraim's two good saddle horses. Unlike his sister America, who could not look at a farm without mentally dividing it into grain, hay and tobacco patches, Ephraim saw land first as horse pasture, then as covert for game and Yankees. Staring absently down the gap, Ephraim remembered this Carolina countryside quick with ragged grey troops. A pang for the free army life, for the gaiety of campfires and the swift hard impact of battle, lay heavy on his soul.

Ephraim realized that, in spite of his firm resolutions not to do so, he was watching the Bledsoe house. The two-story frame dwelling sat like a big weather-beaten packing box on a tiny island, for the branch flowed completely around it in flood. Since Old Man Bledsoe had broken his hip, his constant fear was that a flash flood back in the hills might wash him, bed and all, down through the gap. Three generations of Bledsoe women had tried to moor the house to its grassless yard with bridal wreath and sweet-shrub bushes. Not quite as fast as the bushes could grow, chickens picked away their tender sprouts and made dust wallows against their roots. During three springs Eph had watched Mary Ellen's buxom figure rush out the porchless kitchen door with apron flapping and shrill cries of *"Shoo! Shoo!"* In hot weather, interest waned on both sides.

His back to the black boys, Ephraim gave no indication he was aware that only half of them were carrying on the beat while the other half rested. Even if his trained ear hadn't picked up the reduced volume of sound, he would have known something was up by their heartier chant. Should Eph turn his cold eyes on them now, all would start flailing again as if General Forrest himself were after them. The day had passed when Eph had to draw K's idly in the dust behind a lazy boy's back to get more than an honest day's work out of him. Secretly Eph shared their opinion that "wu'k is a low-daown act."

Beside spring fever, Ephraim had another reason to watch

house and gap today. Tugger was overdue home. Eph was only waiting now for Tugger's return to light out himself for Knoxville. His travel orders from ol' Gits-Thar-Fustest Forrest had come through in the new name, Eph Radford, which he could never quite feel meant him. Once he was clear from slave-drivin' Tugger, Eph meant to locate a nice cool cave, hobble his horses close by in good pasture near a spring and sleep the clock around—for a solid week!—if he needed it.

Mary Ellen made a habit about midmorning of going to the spring five hundred yards above the house for fresh water in which to wash and start dinner vegetables. Ephraim watched the back door and worried how to tell her. He was no Fant Annable, to kiss and run away without a civil word of farewell.

Carrying her two buckets, Mary Ellen crossed the footbridge. Eph let her get well into the rhododendron thicket before he followed. She was expecting him, because she had left the shoulder-yoke at home. Women were like dogs and horses; even the mongrels sensed when you planned to go away and leave them.

"I thought you weren't comin' this mornin'," Mary Ellen smiled coyly at him, and pushed her clean sunbonnet back from straw-colored braids looped around her head for coolness. "Mebbe you better go back, with Tugger due any minute? He'd raise sand tuh git home an' find the niggers not workin'."

"They'll work better for a few lungfuls of fresh air," replied Eph. "I want to talk to you about my sister America, who married a rich planter's son out in Kentucky. She wants me to come visit her."

"Oh, Eph, you ain't a-goin'?"

"I'm tempted," he answered. "The only thing is, Merry and I don't get along any too well. When you oppose her, she never gives in. She's dynamite under pressure—explodes in all directions like the Crater at Petersburg."

"She sounds like a drivin' woman I recollect at the Methodist Home," declared Mary Ellen, kneeling on flat stones Eph had laid for her at the upper side of the spring. With her buckets filling in the basin, she turned her plump face invitingly up to him and challenged: "What do you do when you git cornered?"

"I ain't going to git cornered a second time," Ephraim replied. "I'll never forget the last two months of the war, when we were turning every which way to get out of Sherman's trap."

Disappointed, she sat back on her heels and silently considered his words. Streaked as she was with sunlight and shadow, she put him in mind of a young partridge hen frozen under cover while the hunter passes by. Desire came strong upon him to lean over and kiss her, to put his arms under hers and draw her to him in an embrace which he knew would end in complete mutual surrender. That she was willing, Eph had known now for more than a year. He reminded himself again that he was the last Ephraim Collier of Golden Hill, who could not betray the household which had befriended him. Mary Ellen sensed his change of mood. Slapping her hands on her thighs, she thought aloud:

"Maybe hit's the war makes you so puny still. I was meanin' tuh cook up another mess o' rhubarb an' mustard greens today."

"For my sake, don't!" pleaded Eph, voluble with relief now that the moment of temptation was past. He bent into the spring for the buckets. "With every mess of them I eat, I feel more like a twitchy-nosed rabbit."

She looked around at him with a queer expression, as if she wanted to say something uncomplimentary but had thought better of it. She hadn't given up hope yet, Ephraim chuckled inwardly, and followed her down the path sloshing water at every step. As they came out of the rhododendron thicket, the unexpected silence caught their attention sharply.

"Hit's Tugger come home!" wailed Mary Ellen. "Gimme my buckets. You git back tuh the barn quick as scat—"

"Hold on, Mary Ellen—it's only a grower with another load of leaf," Eph sized up the situation.

"Git back tuh work, you lazy niggers!" she shouted, her voice breaking hysterically with relief. Picking up a tobacco stick, she started towards them. With easy laughter that bordered on insolence, for they knew she dared not strike them, the black boys parted around the wagon and drifted towards the factory door. Ephraim took several steps towards them and they broke for cover like sheep at sight of a killer dog. The rhythm of the flails rose at once and continued in a staccato beat that would have satisfied even Tugger.

Mary Ellen, her shoulders pulled down by the water buckets, went on alone to the house. Ephraim studied the grower with the load of tobacco. He was short for a Tarheel, with reddish beard and the eyes of a trader.

"Whar you keep yer co'hn, mister?"

"You're taking a lot for granted, stranger," drawled Ephraim. "I'm not Tugger Blake—and you're not feeding your team at his expense. Who are you, and what're you here for?"

"My name's Monteith, Jim Monteith," declared the grower. "I was comin' across Powder Crick jest now when my left hin' wheel slipped into that big mudhole. When my team couldn't pull hit aout, I had tuh unload on the bank. Workin' by m'self an' all, I got this here fine load of terbacker a mite mussed up."

"Take it home, then, and sort it out," ordered Ephraim, turning to go back to the barn.

"Jest wait another minute, will you, mister?" pleaded Monteith, looking anxious. "I got a land note tuh meet tonight before sundown. I could take this load home an' sort hit like you say, but you know I'd miss today's leaf sales at Durham an' I'd stand tuh lose my farm. Tugger's place bein' the handiest an' he havin' done me favors a plenty, I jist thought I'd pull on up here an' offer you all this load mebbe a cent er two cheaper all around. How 'bout hit—is hit a trade?"

"How do I know, when I haven't seen the stuff?"

"Look at hit, yerself," urged Monteith, hauling down the tarpaulin to reveal sweet-cased tobacco of excellent quality. "Effen hit warn't so mussed up, wouldn't that be a purty sight?"

"Tugger isn't home now," declared Ephraim. "You can

leave your load in the scales shed yonder. I'll give you corn for your team and you can come back tomorrow. I don't buy tobacco."

"But you could in a pinch, mister. I got tuh meet that land note by sundown, like I tol' you," pleaded Monteith.

"What did you have in mind to ask for it?"

The price Monteith named struck Ephraim as surprisingly low. Tugger was always at him to show more real interest in the business, to assume responsibility of a full-fledged partner. Eph started trading in a disinterested fashion and beat the grower down a cent and a half more, to what Monteith declared was the bottom dollar of his land note.

"Pull your load in," Ephraim accepted the price in the local phrase. This purchase would be his swan song, would convince Tugger that he, Ephraim Moncure, could spot a bargain and drive a trade as well as any Tarheel tobacco peddler.

Thoroughly pleased with himself, Ephraim unlocked the scales shed and watched Monteith drive in. After the horses had been fed, Eph good-naturedly went to work with Monteith to straighten out the tumbled load. Each type was sorted in piles around Tugger's new platform scales. The leaf had been taken off the sticks, an unusual procedure, and weighed much heavier than Eph had expected. He added up the columns of weight by type and was about to write out the check when he heard somebody coming. Looking up, he saw Tugger approaching.

"Well, Monteith"—Tugger spoke in the tight voice Ephraim had learned to dread—"I see you beat me here, after all. You've had your trouble for nothin'."

"Wait a minute now, Tugger!" interposed Ephraim. "I bought this load—at a good price."

"Did you pull the load, Eph?"

"No-o, but I've hefted most of it. And it's fine heavy leaf."

"Hit's heavy, all right. But I ain't buyin' wet sand. Except for the honest layer he spread on top, Monteith's tied every hand of this load with wet sand an' gravel to make it weigh heavy," explained Tugger, his eyes black with anger, his voice contemptuous. He picked up a bundle of leaf, tore off the butt wrapper. "Monteith, when they ran you off the floor at Durham, who told you I wasn't coming straight home? Did you see me start out to the Lord place?"

"Sand er no sand, yer man accepted my terbacker an' we agreed on a price," declared Monteith, his sly eyes narrowing. "Go on, mister, write me aout my check."

"You knew as true as you're standin' there I'd never let a fool like Eph buy tobacco!" snorted Tugger, and flung the loaded hand of leaf at the Virginian's feet. "Start reloadin' your wagon. I'll give you just one hour to pull out of here before we turn your stuff into the crick. I'm goin' to the house now. Comin', Eph?"

They watched Tugger swing down the barn lot. He made a fine confident figure. After he had crossed the footbridge, Monteith turned on Ephraim, and blustered:

"Naow, by Gawd, I'm a-goin' tuh whup you good!"

Ephraim had been standing with the envelope on which he had figured weights in his hand. Crushing it in his fist, he raised a face of such cold fury toward Monteith that the grower fell back abashed. Flinging away the crumpled envelope, Ephraim reached for an armful of the dishonest tobacco, tossed it onto the wagon and reached for another. Monteith vaulted over the wheel onto the wagon floor and began to lay them down straight. They worked in silence for a time, then Monteith grunted affably:

"Soljer, ain't yuh? How come you tuh be sech a good worker, an' know so little abaout terbacker?"

"Save your breath to get this leaf loaded."

When the tarpaulin was spread over the top of the load and lashed down, Ephraim stood back to watch Monteith hook in his team. As he climbed onto the driver's seat, Monteith spat uncomfortably close to Eph's feet, and drawled:

"Leastways, I got a good feed fur my team. Git up, Charlie!"

When he reached the house, Ephraim could hear Tugger in the dining room discussing him loudly with Old Man Bledsoe in the bedchamber. Ephraim went upstairs. In his garret he piled his belongings on the quilt his mother had tucked around him under the straw of Tugger's wagon bed over two years ago, and knotted its ends. Was it possible that after thirty months in the tobacco business, which he had hated from the start, he was leaving the Bledsoe house empty-handed, with only his silver-backed military brushes, his razors, a toothbrush, the blood-stained New Testament Jeb Stuart had given him and half a dozen pieces of shabby clothing to tie into the old quilt, less indeed than he had brought? Remembering his moments of temptation at the spring, Eph congratulated himself that he was leaving nothing more vital than a scheming girl's disappointment. With the quilt bumping his knees, he ran downstairs and into the dining room.

Tugger took in the meaning of Eph's bundle, swallowed and began to negotiate:

"Eph, I didn't mean what I said on the scales. Set daown an' eat your dinner."

"That's all right, Tugger," the Virginian answered, controlling his voice carefully. "Which of my two riding horses would you rather keep?"

"Ridin' hosses? What ud I want with a hoss when I ride the railroads all the time?"

"Eph, are you really goin' to Kaintuck like you said?" interposed Mary Ellen.

"Yes. And then to California."

"There's more gold to be had in a year selling Car'liny bright-leaf than all the dust you could pan out of a California crick the rest of your life!" exploded Tugger. "Hell-damn, Eph, I've said I'm sorry for what I called you at the scales. Hit's because you could be such a help to me, if you only would, makes me go off the handle! There's nobody like you in all Car'liny for gittin' work out of niggers."

"Tugger, I came to say good-bye, not to have words with you."

"Eph, listen to the proposition I've got tuh make tuh you," pleaded Tugger. "Only this morning I saw the Lords an' what d'you reckon? Dan's a-goin' tuh take us into partnership—that is, he's willin' tuh take me. An' you kin come along."

"You go by yourself this time, Tugger," smiled Ephraim. "But don't you think for a moment I'll ever forget what you did for me back in Charlotte Court House. Or that I won't always be grateful—"

"Wait 'll I finish, can't you?" interrupted Tugger. "Dan's an' my idee was we'd team up on our two brands an' mebbe put aout a new line. We could do the sellin' while you run the factory."

"Count me out on that right now."

"But you ain't hyeard the fancy salary we're willin' tuh pay you—twelve dollars a week! I know you think you've come aout the little end of the horn here—with no wages an' all. But honest-tuh Gawd, Eph, the way you run araound nights you ain't been worth much tuh me."

"That'll do, son," interposed Ephraim, and stood up. Throughout his lean six feet two inches, he was all Indian now, the seasoned fighter who in council has learned to speak quietly: "If I hadn't ridden nights, you couldn't have peddled smokin' mixture in the daytime. You and this whole backwoods state would be stuck deeper in the mud of carpetbag corruption and niggers running wild than I found you in Tom Cat Lane. Tugger, you and I have come to the parting of the ways. I'm done with the tobacco business forever."

"You think you kin go on soldierin'—jist because you like hit an' hit's the only business you know," Tugger tried to reason with the angry Virginian. "Times are changin', Eph. We're in for a spell of buyin' an' sellin' the like of which this country ain't never seen. Dan Lord feels the same as I do—that thar ain't never been sech a chance for traders. Come on in with us!" In a humbler tone, he began anew: "Tell you what let's do, Eph. You come along with me tuh the Lords—until we git well started thar an' I show 'em what I'm worth. Then you kin ease out."

"No, Tugger. I'll take the bay horse. He's the better of the two, but you say you don't need a good horse any more—and I do. Will you shake hands? All I want to hear you say now is that our slate's clean. Come on—what about it?"

Tugger slowly reached up his hand and acknowledged with a sorry grin:

"You don't owe me nuthin', Eph. An' I ain't got any hard feelin' agin you."

"Thanks for that!" cried the Virginian, his face bright with relief. About him already was the joy of the happy traveler soon to take the high road again.

"I'll git yer dinner naow," whispered Mary Ellen, from the depths.

"I wouldn't think of troubling you, ma'am. Step in and see if Mr. Bledsoe is ready to say good-bye, will you, please?"

"Come right on in, you traipsin' Johnnie Reb!" called Old Man Bledsoe, who could hear well enough when the occasion demanded. "Pick me up a chromo or two from the places whar you're goin', will yuh?"

Mary Ellen followed Eph out of the dining room. Tugger sat by the littered table, but the confidence which had shone from him at the scales shed was gone. There wasn't anything left for him to do but to slip out quietly some night and go to New York. Until he learned how to buy a railroad, Mary Ellen would have to shift for herself and for the old man.

Chapter 9

During her first four months at Foxden, America felt herself to be living a dual life. Her thin face white against her widow's weeds, the red gold of her hair dulled by pregnancy, she presented a calm exterior to her servants, to her solicitous kin and to the many callers who turned their horses' heads into the lane. Only at night, and then not often, did she let herself think about Fant. Dr. Thorpe had impressed on her the danger of prolonged and uncontrolled weeping. She permitted herself few tears to wash away her anguish.

Ever present in the back of her consciousness, like the genie caught in Aladdin's lamp and only waiting to be recognized before it ballooned into hysteria as overwhelming, was the sense of her own blood guilt. If Fant had known beforehand about Uncle Simmy's will, might not he then have remained his usual cautious self? No man could help being upset to hear that the legacy he has anticipated all his life has been left instead to his wife, with forfeiture the penalty if she permits him to lay so much as a finger on it. Suppose the sharp edge of her husband's chagrin had been blunted the night before on her, as it should have been, could Buck Lambeau have taken Fant so completely by surprise? Disappointed of his hoped-for inheritance, blind with fury at her, Fant had misinterpreted Buck's innocent reach for his handkerchief to mop his streaming face, had lost his head and had fired the shots which subsequently lost two lives—Buck's and his own. So she reasoned and pronounced judgment against herself.

In the retrospect of her grief, America's year of married life began to appear in a different light. Fant's flashing smile arose to haunt her. She reproached herself with a dozen cruel slights, with a hundred omissions of the loving sympathy a good wife owes her husband. When he had taken her to his favorite places—months spent over a washtub had taught her how choice these places had been!—she had shown disappointment because they were no finer, because the suite in the St. Charles Hotel had not been a Creole mansion. Sums of money he had obtained by his wits—she remembered how he had once barked: "Maybe you think it's easy to separate the men who gamble on river boats these days from their wallets? The suckers ride the railroads"—this money he had risked his all to obtain and had entrusted to her to put away against their desperate future need, she had squandered buying a wardrobe a princess might envy. Where had she expected to wear it, she now asked herself. Fant's gaiety, which she with secret superiority had called light-headedness—could that have been the gallant courage of a high heart which refuses to admit overwhelming odds? The wonder was that Fant had dared step foot on a boat, with the ever present threat there that sooner or later he might have to jump overboard. Although she had swum at Virginia Beach since she could stand up in the breakers, she herself had been afraid the *Magnolia* would explode.

Hardest of all for her was to lie alone at night in Uncle Simmy's huge bed. Had ever two people found deeper joy in each other's love than she and Fant? When she could no longer face the realization that never again might she lie in her husband's arms safe from her soul's loneliness and fear of the outside world, she would turn over and sob into her pillow. When she began to see herself swimming to the river's bottom in search of Fant lying there wax-white and still, she would light her bedside candle, get up shivering and take one of the sleeping tablets Dr. Thorpe had prescribed. The next morning found her sitting down to her seven o'clock breakfast paler than usual, with shadows deeper under her bleak but all-seeing eyes.

America's first task at Foxden was to put her house in order.

While they were being driven out to Tuckahoe, Cousin Margaret had told America how Mahalee had established herself there. As a young slave, Mahalee belonged to Squire Walton, the older brother of Stone Moncure's mother. The squire's wife—"a high-tempered woman herself," declared Cousin Margaret—used to beat Mahalee until the lower end of Tuckahoe often rang with the abused negress' cries. When Brother Simmy returned from California with his head stuffed with expansive western ideas, he must have said something that encouraged Mahalee to seek sanctuary at Foxden. Every time Squire Walton went there to recover his chattel, Mahalee managed to give him the slip. Even the sheriff couldn't return her to her rightful owners, though the entire ridge knew she was keeping house for Brother Simmy."

"So Mahalee's the vixen at Foxden!" smiled America, gazing at its chimneys massive against the eastern sky.

"She's the sly, whiney kind," concluded Cousin Margaret. "Squire Walton never thought she was vicious, else he wouldn't have tried to get her back. You'll have a time straightening her out, though."

As if the house were really hers, Mahalee met the two Mrs. Annables at the front door and shadowed them resentfully through their first inspection. More flies are caught by sugar than with vinegar, America told herself, and set out to win Mahalee's loyalty. When she wanted to supervise the cleaning of the big old rooms, Mahalee had to work among her fowls. Furniture which America and Weed spent the morning in rearranging, Mahalee sneaked back into their former places while America was taking her afternoon nap. Trained to patience with old family pensioners, America tried flexibility until she realized it was being mistaken for weakness.

"Mahalee," she began, while Weed ate his dinner within earshot, "I want you to put a figure on your fowls—give or take."

"I thought you'd come 'raound in time tuh payin' me foah all dez aigs you's been lettin' Weed guzzle—lak they was saour apples on somebody else's trees."

"I've kept track of them. I'll pay you the going price, Mahalee, but of course I can't continue to buy eggs and chickens from you—especially when you've been feeding them out of my cribs. Besides, I need the chicken house for my own fowls. Mrs. Annable at Timberlawn says twenty-five cents would be a big price for mixed poultry like yours. Some of the chicks aren't feathered out yet, but I'll give you a quarter apiece all around. Or would you prefer to move them off Foxden?"

"Whar'd I move 'em tuh?"

"That's your responsibility, Mahalee. You have a daughter over on the Minerva Pike."

"You knows Cap'n Doggett ain't gwine let no hired han's mothah-in-law keep two hunnerd chickens on his fa'm."

"Then maybe you'd like to sell them to Mrs. MacGower?"

"Dat furringer? She's close as de skin ob youh teef."

"Find someone else then, Mahalee. I want my henhouses by Saturday night," answered America, gently.

"Seems to me you's talkin' mighty big—foah a pore relation w'at's gwine bear a daid chil' an' be set aout on de pike come Chris'mas!"

Looking at the old woman, America remembered a phrase of Aunt Flora's. Mahalee was so angry she was "spittin' green" at the very thought of being dispossessed.

"That's a harsh thing to say against Mr. Fant's child," she answered, impersonally. "You must be terribly worried about your own future, to say anything so unchristian. I don't want to turn you off Foxden, where you've lived so long, but you must see my position, too. You're the only servant I can afford—"

"Huh!"

"You're the only servant I can afford," America repeated, firmly. "And if you stay here, you'll have to do the work I lay out for you. Your wages will be two dollars a week—just what Mrs. Annable pays Aunt Henrietta at Timberlawn, with four field hands and that big family to cook for. Do you want to accept the place I'm offering—or would you prefer to go live with your daughter?"

"I'll go visit wid her till come Chris'mas, when de high shur-uff turns you aout intuh de snow!"

"I'm not turning you out, Mahalee. You probably feel disappointed Mr. Collier didn't remember you in his will. For years here you've made a good thing out of your fowls and butter money. Probably he thought that was reward enough. After all, he fed and clothed you," America pointed out. While Weed sat eavesdropping at the cook-cabin table to repeat the other side of the story, she didn't intend to let Mahalee go cackling up and down the ridge that she'd been robbed by Colliers.

"Hit's a miracle dat pore chil' doan' shrivel up daid ob pison gall inside you!"

"Don't you know better than to talk like that to a woman in my condition?" America took the last word with steady eyes. "If my baby and I were to die of natural causes after you'd talked like that, people would think you'd poisoned us. And then you'd hang, no matter how innocent you were. Let me know by Friday milking time what you've decided to do."

Mahalee stayed, and did her work well.

After this object lesson, America led Weed out into the crescent-shaped meadow at the rear of Foxden on the windy river rim. He wanted to plow the sod for tobacco ground, but she demurred. They'd get neither good weight nor bright color unless they cleared forest land enriched by leaf mould. After they had stepped off ten acres of the south woodland and he had agreed to fell the big trees and grub out the underbrush, they selected forty acres of corn ground in the front pike meadow. This handsome piece of land needed plowing. Foxtail had begun to wave its telltale plumes here and there over the heavy sod. Before he started the grubbing, America concluded, Weed was to finish cleaning all the yards and barns, scrape the ponds and turn over ground on the front lawn for her flower garden, so that the sod could freeze, thaw and rot during the winter.

Weed accepted the heavy schedule as a matter of course.

So powerful was he that hard work meant nothing to him. As long as he received his five dollars a week every Saturday evening, could sit down three times a day to an enormous hot meal, was allowed off midday Sunday and wasn't skimped on feed and pasturage for his raw-boned gelding or on table scraps for his big white English bull dog, he was happy. To show her appreciation of his willingness to go ahead by himself under petticoat rule, America asked:

"Weed, how would you like to take care of Sunshine?"

"By doggie, I plumb forgot tuh gib you a message from de boss-man! Dat fust night I come hyah, Mistuh Annable he say tuh tell you he doan' in-tend tuh feed dat Sunshine no mo'," grinned Weed, shamelessly.

"Fix a place for him today, then go get him. Perhaps you'd better explain to Mr. Annable why I didn't send for him sooner."

"Yassum, but he unnerstan' how easy I forgits. He was al'ays sayin' he meant tuh whup me good fer it."

"Did Mr. Annable whip his people for fault, Weed?"

"Lawsee, ma'am, he warn't half ez hard on us as he was on pore Mistah Fant!"

Sitting on her front flagstones of afternoons, America watched Tuckahoe change from August's maturity to October's harvest. Where was Brother Ephraim? He had left North Carolina in August, Mrs. Moncure had written, and should come riding down the ridge almost any day to see her before he continued on out West to fight Indians. November rains extinguished the autumn foliage, quenched the running fire of sumac in the forests and dissolved the blue haze that hung in the gaps. Weed and Mahalee worked hard the evening before the first black frost to save what they could of the tomatoes, butter beans and late snaps in the garden.

As her crisis neared, America's surface calm appeared more noticeable. To feminine Tuckahoe flocking to call on the beautiful bereft widow, her uncomplaining courage became a neighborhood wonder. Across the tollhouse counter Abigail

MacGower did full conversational justice to the virtues of her one-time boarder, virtues which she had recognized long ahead of everybody else, she claimed.

Alone in Uncle Simmy's four-poster at night, with the flame from the backlog throwing familiar furniture into distorted outlines, too uncomfortable to sleep more than two or three hours at a time, now denied Dr. Thorpe's sedatives, afraid to get up and walk off her soul's misery lest she catch the lung fever all expectant mothers of her era feared worse than labor pains, America was compelled to reach back into the well-springs of her Collier and Moncure heritage for what intellectual reassurance, what spiritual strength, she could muster to carry herself along to the hour of her deliverance. Recently in dreams she kept seeing her mother's war-saddened face bending above her. And once, as her arms went out hungrily towards the dear thin shoulders, America awoke to find herself crying like a child afraid of the dark. Where was Brother Ephraim? Useless as most men are on such occasions, America found herself pinning her hopes on Eph being close at hand to help her through her approaching maternity.

Christmas Eve dawned with leaden skies and a piercing wind from the northeast. After the noon meal, America went to stand at the front window and wonder what everybody might be doing in Charlotte Court House. Across her shoulder, she called:

"You'd better hurry with those dishes, Mahalee. It's beginning to snow."

"I's hurryin'. Is you shore Miss Maggie's a-comin' tuh see you dis ebenin'? Looks tuh me lak dat baby's fixin' tuh come."

"Go and string popcorn for those grandchildren of yours. You needn't come back tomorrow. I want you to enjoy your holiday with your family."

"Yassum. I 'spects dissa one will be mah las'. Is you got a plenty fiahwood?"

"I told Weed to fill all the boxes before he left, and give Sunshine an extra feed."

The house, when she was alone in it, seemed to cool by the minute. Going to the woodbox in the front room to build up the fire there, America found only about a dozen chunks of split oak. If Weed had forgotten to do one of his chores before leaving, he had probably forgotten them all. The kitchen hearth was bare except for the great backlog smoldering in the stone fireplace. Stepping carefully out into the dog run, America found the woodbox along the house wall empty, too. Snowflakes dry and light as goose down scudded across the flagstones before the cruel wind.

From his paddock, Sunshine saw America and nickered. Weed must have overlooked him, too, in his eagerness to get limber-drunk in Dulcy's cabin. America dared not try to negotiate the slippery stepping-stones to the stable. If she felt better by supper, she would carry the stallion half a bucket of warm corn mash, which would have to satisfy him until Weed came in the morning to milk.

Telling herself that she felt unduly frightened because she was alone, America reentered the house and transferred the wood from the front-room box into the cook room, where she piled it on the hearth. If she froze to death in the blizzard which was whipping past her windows, it would not be because she had failed to do everything in her power to keep warm. Fed one stick at a time to keep it burning, the backlog ought to last until tomorrow morning.

Unaccustomed exercise heightened her feeling of general physical unease. The kitchen hearth was the warmest place in the cabin. Perhaps she had better lie down on it for a few minutes, she decided, before she began stuffing window frames and door cracks to keep out the snow. Dragging in quilts from the front-room bed, she spread them down on the stones, lowered herself carefully and pulled the top quilt over her.

Some hours later, when she awoke and tried to rise, pain seemed to cut her in half. Telling herself that the stab meant nothing, that she was only scared, she lay waiting for another. It came, and then a third, and a fourth. Competent plantation mistress that she had been on Golden Hill, childbirth then seemed a routine thing when some black woman was experiencing it. If Cousin Margaret did not arrive as expected this afternoon, America told herself she would prefer to undergo the ordeal alone rather than have Mahalee her sole attendant. In a vengeful desire to dispossess her while she was helpless, Mahalee might strangle the new-born heir to Foxden and later claim the baby had strangled during birth.

During the murky afternoon, pain ebbed and flowed. At each wave, it seemed to carry America closer to the breakers of agony through which she realized she must fight her solitary way to safety for herself and the child on whom her future depended. With teeth locked so tight her jaws ached, she managed to push two oak chunks against the backlog, and creep closer among the ashes towards the blessed warmth they gave. Of what use now the dainty nightgowns and bed jacket laid by with lavender in the clothes-press drawers? In work-day woolens Weed would find her tomorrow morning frozen stiff as any roadside wench whom labor had overtaken before she could crawl home to her mammy's cabin.

As the flames fell, the room grew dark with twilight. Outside, the snow descended in a still white blanket. In Charlotte County during the last year of the war, a "pore white" girl had died unaided and alone in childbirth in a fireless cabin. Where was Cousin Margaret? America listened for the chimes of the clock. Once she thought she heard Sunshine neighing for his supper. With sickening finality, she realized that Cousin Margaret was not likely to come now before tomorrow morning. She had been here yesterday. America's one hope now was a forlorn one, that Brother Ephraim might arrive for a surprise holiday visit. Once before in her acute need, when Cushman was bending to lift the fallen chimney stones, Brother Eph had appeared.

Damp with sweat, shivering from pain and the encroaching chill, America gnawed at her grimy knuckles to keep from screaming, and endured as best she could. She realized that she ought to be praying for her soul's peace. All that she could think of was when the next tide of pain would come, and how to battle it through to relief.

Her conviction grew that someone was in the room with her, some woman who screamed in a high-pitched voice and called for Fant. From where she twisted on the pallet, she saw the wind thrusting at the outside door. Another push like that, and the bar would give to admit the storm. She looked again and realized with inexpressible relief that she must have died, because the door was opening. There stood Fant in fine clothes, as she had seen him when his luck was running high.

"Fant!" shrieked the other woman. "Do something for me! Do something. You've got to help me!"

A wet cheek and cool lips were laid against her own. Under the snowy shoulders she gripped with hands like talons was Fant's dear familiar flesh. The room, which had seemed strange as the grave, swung slowly into its normal forms again. That other voice, which had shrieked and raved, quieted until all America could hear was her own hysterical sobbing, and Fant's reassuring whisper:

"Lovie, you're going to be all right! You're not alone any longer, my brave girl. Where's ma—what does she mean leaving you by yourself like this? Has she gone for Dr. Drake?"

"You mustn't go for Dr. Drake! There's a warrant out for you for murder, Fant. You mustn't go to Limestone—or step a foot outside Foxden! I know what to do—if you'll only stay here, where it's safe, and help me."

"Of course I'll help you, sweetheart. The first thing is to get you off this draughty hearth and into a clean, warm bed. I'll build up a big fire in the other room."

"There's no wood."

"I hid behind a woodpile five minutes ago," he laughed, and heaped around the backlog the oak chunks she had planned to make last the night. "When we burn that up we'll begin on the walnut grove."

"Fant, how did you save yourself on the *Evening Mail?*"

"Ask me no secrets, and I'll tell you no lies! When did you get my message?"

"What message?"

"The one I sent you last fall—by a shanty-boat man named Sims. He's a friend of Jim Barnes. Anchors off the mouth of Lawrence Creek every fall."

"Old man Sims never got this far downstream. His body was found tangled in his trot-lines above Portsmouth. Where did you meet up with him?"

"In Pittsburgh. October, as I recall. I've done well—Yankees ain't as smart as I thought they were. Tell me, lovie, about yourself. Why aren't you at Timberlawn—did pa drive you out again?"

"Everybody's been kindness itself. I—I'm living here because I like it better—because I want to get a crop started. Oh, Fant," whispered America, gazing at her husband with her heart in her eyes, "I've nearly died of remorse!"

"You, sorrel top? That doesn't sound like you. Why?"

"For not telling you that night in Cincinnati—about Uncle Simmy's will."

He stood in the center of the floor with his coat off, rolling up his sleeves. All he said was:

"I had it coming to me, I reckon. Now, I'm going after that firewood."

The baby, a boy, was born after midnight. Fant bathed him, laid him in the cradle which America had prepared, and cooked a hearty breakfast. Awakening America to urge her to share the breakfast with him, he counted five notes which the clock was striking.

"Listen, Merry, it'll be dawn in another hour. And I've got to get out of here. How can I send word to ma to come down and take care of you and young Fant?"

"Weed will come some time during the morning to milk. As soon as he sobers up, he'll remember he didn't fill the woodbox. Or feed Sunshine."

"You'll be the wonder of Tuckahoe when they see you've

had a baby all by yourself—and even washed up the breakfast dishes afterwards!"

"I'll never tell anybody the truth. You may count on that."

"If you ever do, I'm a goner, sure!"

She could hardly hold her cup of coffee, for drowsiness. As he loosened her fingers about it, she was sound asleep. When he awakened her again, the room was grey with dawn on the snow. Fant put a pillow under her head. For the first time she observed him clearly. His suit was of fine broadcloth. The greatcoat into which he was shrugging was warm and expensive-looking. His luck had changed, he told her gravely. He had money again, half of which he had hidden for her in the bottom of her sewing basket. Could she remember that, in her sewing basket? He would have to go now, he repeated, but he would wait in the walnut grove until he saw Weed return.

"Fant, will you write me?"

"Too risky, sweetheart. Abigail MacGower smells every letter. She's got a nose like a pointer dog."

"When'll you be back?"

"In the spring, when you and baby Fant can travel. Then we'll go west to San Francisco. You'll like it out there, lovie. They say it's just your kind of country—big and free. If you'll come with me I'll turn over a complete new leaf. With you and young Fant to work for, I'll even get a job—a good job!"

"It's good here at Foxden," she murmured drowsily.

"You know I can't stay here, lovie. There's a warrant out for me. You told me so yourself. I'd be taking my life in my hands to come back here again."

"Fant, you've got to come back next summer! Suppose this baby should die?"

"Is that all you want me for now, to secure you the succession to Foxden? Six hours ago, you were singing a different tune."

Behind his teasing was laughter, Fant's irrepressible laughter that kindled his warm brown eyes and overflowed in his brilliant, flashing smile. If she had not felt so sore and sleepy,

America would have laughed, too. As from a distance, she heard him talking about farming. No woman could raise a crop with niggers what they were since Emancipation. If she didn't believe him, consider the fix in which he'd found her, with the livestock untended and scarcely a stick of wood in the house. Moreover, why struggle along on a penny whistle like Foxden, when fortunes were being made in mining stocks out in California? The West was the place to go now to get rich, declared Fant.

"Money comes easiest out of good land—close to steady settled markets," she heard herself sleepily quoting her statesman-father. "And when everything else goes, you can still live off the land."

"You incurable clodhopper!" Fant's laughter rang above her. "Take care of yourself and young Fant. I'll be back this spring."

She carried the hard pressure of his lips and the pleasant smell of soap, which he had just used in shaving, with her into deep dreamless sleep.

Chapter 10

Like any other country jake coming to New York to make his fortune, Tugger Blake stood in the bow of the Jersey ferry and searched Manhattan's low brown sky line for Trinity Church spire. Across the rubbish-littered water he recognized the Battery's blunt nose fringed with steamboat piers. Miles of closely built city blocks stretched up the island to run out into rag-pickers' shanties on the rocks above marginal swamps lapped by Hudson River tides.

Watching the West Street slip draw closer, Tugger found himself sweating like a mule. Uncomfortable as he was in his Wilmington suit, he dared not take off his coat. Inside its lining he had sewn what he could salvage from his tobacco business, nineteen hundred dollars. In like fashion, Dan Lord used to boast on quiet evenings in Durham, he had stitched his railroad ticket and wallet secure from thieving fingers in the pretty-girl saloons and panel houses of the Bowery.

After the ferry had bumped into her wharf, Tugger started up the Cortlandt Street grade. Several times he had to sidestep to prevent being knocked down by teams heaving the day's first load up the cobblestones. At Broadway he put his suitcase down on his toes, so no one could filch it without his feeling its loss, and gazed at the tumultuous stream of life sweeping down to the financial district. Matched pairs of clean-legged Hambletonians fretted at the reins held by their gentlemen owners seated in spidery driving traps, with a groom hunched over in the compartment behind the high single seat. A shining black wagon bounced three feet into the air when its red wheels hit a dried mudhole, but the sporting gentleman at the ribbons gave his pearl-colored topper a pat, laughed at the friend he was dangerously passing and was whisked out of Tugger's sight by wild young bays. Child beggars in rags swarmed everywhere. Like brown flycatchers they would poise on the curb, then dart into the thick of traffic. When it seemed to Tugger they were doomed to destruction, back to the curb they would dart in safety. Dan Lord said the police called them street rats after their rodent counterparts that made New York's city dumps unsafe at night for a toddler, for a cat or for dogs except in packs.

After a mug of coffee and Yankee fried dough, Tugger swung down Broadway. Pine—Wall—Exchange Place ran the street names. The morning sunshine slanted between old chimneys, shone on mellowed brick residences converted into brokers' and insurance company offices. Tugger stared curiously at the Custom House on Wall Street. He identified the Stock Exchange from Dan Lord's description. In its handsome new building erected in '65 and extending through the block to New Street, it was impressive enough, Tugger admitted. At its doors he asked a big Irishman in a special officer's uniform what a smart boy like himself could do to earn a living in Wall Street.

"Ye could be a pad-shover."

"What's that, sir?"

"Iv'ry brokerage house on the sthra't swarms wi' thim. They wait outside bounds till the broker's man on the Exchange floor gives them the latest prices stocks are sellin' at. Thin the pad-shovers run like hell shoutin' these prices into half a dozen offices av the broker's clients. Importhant operators have their own byes."

"How about a job taking care of horses?"

"They's two byes an' a nigger askin' to bed down with iv'ry horse on Manhattan—for a bowl av hot oats in the mornin'."

"Where's a good bank?"

"W'at's wrong wi' the Farmers and Drovers across the sthra't? All the swells go there."

Tugger leaned against a lamppost near the curb and watched the bank's uniformed watchmen admit a thin trickle of clerks. Opulent-looking older men proud of their mutton-chop whiskers came bowling down the narrow street, stepped out of their handsome rigs and ran briskly up the steps of adjoining business houses. When the bank's doors were opened, Tugger was among the first to enter. Putting his suitcase on the floor out of the general traffic, he sat on it, removed his coat and with his knife began to unrip hundred-dollar bills from its lining. He had not removed half-a-dozen before he found himself the center of a ring of men as curious as the yokels who used to watch him blend smokin' mixture under the Charlotte Court House oaks. Looking up with his contagious smile, Tugger met the intent gaze of a pair of keen black eyes. They belonged to a dark-bearded dwarf of a man in his early thirties. From the respectful way others stood aside for him, Tugger guessed he must be a somebody. He was followed by a fancy dresser in a maroon Admiral's coat festooned with gold buttons, braid, epaulets and tasseled cords. The fancy dresser puffed his drooping walrus mustache in jocular speech:

"Lookit him sweatin' like a mule, Jay! I'll bet he ain't had that coat off since he left the sticks. How much you reckon he's quilted away in there?"

"Want to bet, gentlemen?" Tugger challenged with a flash of white teeth. "If you do, I'll hold on till you get your bets placed."

"Where you from, you spunkie?" asked the dark-bearded dwarf called Jay.

"No'th Car'liny, sir."

"In those imported English togs?" jeered the fancy dresser. "Where'd you get 'em, son? They're the real thing."

"A Jew tailor talked me into 'em on the Wilmington waterfront—said the cloth was smuggled in," grinned Tugger, completely at ease. The only thing wrong with his suit had been that it was too good for Tarheels to appreciate. "Place your bets, gentlemen!"

"I've a hundred says he's got a thousand on him, Jay," drawled the fancy dresser.

"Any Tarheel smart enough to carry his dough-ray-me in English tweeds—and bring it here to unload—wouldn't bother with a measly thousand, Jim," commented the man named Jay, staring thoughtfully. Under those keen black eyes, Tugger felt his scalp tighten in a way it had when he found himself in the presence of a whip-smart trader, somebody like Dan Lord, but never Eph Moncure. "He's got nearer two thousand."

"Done!" agreed Jim. "You say he's got closer to two thousand—I say he hasn't half that much."

"Any more bets, gents?" laughed Tugger.

Men had come in from the street. They stood pulling at one another's elbows to see what was going on. The dwarf named Jay drew out a worn snap purse, dragged a thin roll out of it and like a Vermont storekeeper peeled off and threw to the floor two fifty-dollar bills. The fancy dresser tossed down a hundred off a roll that would have choked a horse. Tugger ripped his own money loose and stuffed it into his shirt front. When the job was done, he drew it out bill by bill, smoothed and counted it, reading:

"Twelve hundred — thirteen — fourteen — fifteen — sixteen —seventeen—"

"You win, Jay!"

Stooping, the winner gathered up his bills. "You can have that un," he indicated the last fifty, as if money didn't interest him as much as the element of chance.

"Hell—damn—why, thankee, sir!" gasped Tugger.

As quickly as they had gathered, the onlookers dispersed. Tugger found himself alone again under the envious eye of the special officer. That big Irish foot was moving towards him, the next second might see it planted on his yellowback. Tugger snatched up the bill and grinned at the officer's complaint:

"So that's yer game—passin' yersilf off as a country jake to sell Mr. Gould a bet instid av a gold brick?"

"You don't mean that was Jay Gould?"

"Mike, here's a rich wan for you," the special officer called to his assistant at the door. "Here's a con man sets up his act to catch Misther Gould's eye—and thin tries to make me think he don't know Misther Gould an' Misther Fisk after he's worked thim for a touch! Hey, you, come back!"

When Tugger reached the street, he found Mr. Gould already seated and Mr. Fisk climbing into the back of a driving wagon.

"Mr. Gould—sir!" panted Tugger, rushing up to the wheel. "Lemme be your pad-shover, will you? I've come all the way from Durham, No'th Car'liny, to work for you—I'll begin emptyin' wastebaskets an' sweepin' out the store."

"We don't trade in money just that way," smiled the one-time salesman for Jordan & Marsh, Boston merchants. "Unfortunately I'm not in need of office help right now. How about you, Jim?"

"Don't this young fellow kinda remind you of yourself when you first hit New York? He does me," confessed Jubilee Jim and turned friendly eyes on Tugger. "Seems like the ol' Erie payroll could stand one more good pad-shover. Drop around to see me at the Erie offices on Twenty-third Street, son. I'll fix it up."

Thus began Tugger's association with the lords of Erie. His daytime duties consisted mainly of foot work between the Stock Exchange and the brokerage house of Smith, Gould & Martin on Wall Street, that narrow residential eddy deserted when fashion moved uptown to Washington and Gramercy squares. Wall Street's houses crowded almost to the flagstone sidewalks. Decorative stone eyebrows over Dutch windows gave their narrow fronts a thin-nosed, supercilious look. Steep iron steps leaped areaways to permit entrance into second-story doors. Ancient lampposts converted to burn gas lighted the rough cobbled pavement. Near the home of the Dupont Gunpowder Company, a clipper ship mast topped with three transverse arms carried a bundle of the new ticker-tape wires and strung them into Wall Street's more progressive brokerage offices. Telephones were not to arrive until 1878. At the head of Wall, across Broad and New streets and Broadway, arose Trinity Church spire, an admonishing finger raised out of the expiring piousness the neighborhood had once known.

After the Stock Exchange had closed, Tugger usually received an envelope marked private from Gould to deliver to Fisk at the Erie Railroad offices located forty blocks uptown in Fisk's Grand Opera House on Twenty-third Street and Eighth Avenue. On the way Tugger often saw New York's finest horseflesh on parade. Handsomely dressed ladies sat erect on the back seats of open victorias with two liveried coachmen on the box and a high-stepping pair out front. Their tiny parasols seemed to poise like butterflies between their faces and the westering sun as they chattered brightly to husbands or fathers seated beside them on dove-colored cushions. Cabs and a rare closed carriage drawn by sedate dobbins found themselves crowded to the curb by the faster-moving vehicles in Broadway's midcurrent. To think that some day soon he too might be weaving his flashing steppers in and out of this glittering stream, with Palestine Moncure Blake riding like a queen beside him, made Tugger almost giddy.

Recalling the moribund calm of Virginia and Carolina villages at sunset, Tugger decided New York was the most alive town he had ever been in. Here was America's biggest marketplace for wits, shrewdness, vice, dishonesty, beauty, brutality and farsightedness. Here on Manhattan were crowded nearly a million souls from every outlandish foreign shore, their hundred different tongues mingled into the one boisterous voice of the nation's biggest city, their thousand smells tickling Tugger's country-accustomed nose. Here was no room for the rambling gait of dusty lanes, no time for the long-winded opinions of cracker-barrel prophets, no quiet noons for the sleepy and inert, no long twilights for the half-dead. Get on about your business, Manhattan's very air seemed to whisper even at nightfall. Get on about your business of making a million dollars in the quickest possible time; and if you've accomplished that, get on about the pleasures of spending it. Get a move on, Tugger Blake—hump yourself! Because New York hasn't time to receive even the open-mouthed adoration of country jakes like you.

In the outer offices of Smith, Gould & Martin, near the door leading into Gould's private sanctum, stood a heel-scarred bench on which the pad-shovers sat to await assignment. Anxious to swing by Gould's coat tails safely through his first breath-taking dip into the stock market, Tugger concentrated fiercely on overhearing everything he could that might come through or under Gould's private office door. Only an indistinct murmur of voices, punctuated occasionally by Jim Fisk's bray of laughter, or a thump of Jay Gould's tight fist for emphasis, rewarded Tugger's eavesdropping. Nor would Henderson, the veteran pad-shover, pass out any tips.

"Cut your own wisdom teeth, Tug," was his callous answer to Tugger's hints.

By the spring of '70, Tugger had picked up enough information to realize that something was due in Erie. A burly newcomer Stephen Maddon the previous summer had picked up several hundred thousand dollars in Erie which Fisk and Gould felt rightfully belonged to them. Forming a three-way pool with Maddon, the lords of Erie soon had the gullible newcomer taking the lead in another buying movement. As the price began to climb, Fisk and Gould began artfully to unload.

From the loose talk around the office and because he realized that he must sometime take the first cold plunge, at the start of the operation Tugger had bought at the Coal Hole, a near-by bucket-shop, as much Erie as he could get on a narrow margin of fifteen hundred dollars cash. Tugger realized that he couldn't survive a prolonged soft market. Erie must go up, or his hoarded nickels would be drained away with Maddon's half-million.

Everything went well for the first three days of the pool. Maddon then grew suspicious and stopped his buying orders.

Erie sagged. Tugger agonized whether to sell and forego future profits, or hold and maybe lose his all.

"Maddon smells a rat," Henderson whispered on the pad-shovers' bench. "He'll come rampaging in here tomorrow morning to blow off steam. You mark my words."

Early the next morning a message arrived from Maddon asking for a noon conference in Gould's office, a conference which might last a considerable length of time. When Gould appeared about eleven o'clock, he called Henderson into his private office. Reappearing, Henderson announced that he was going for an early lunch and left the office. Half an hour later, Tugger's fears sky-rocketted when he saw Maddon enter and stride truculently into Gould's sanctum.

"You snake-in-the-grass!" Maddon roared. "Damned if I don't think you and Jim are unloadin' on me——"

"Steve, the market's made you jumpy as a horse with pin-worms," Tugger overheard Gould chuckle, as the door was closing. "You know I wouldn't let Jim pull a dirty trick like that on a partner of mine."

"I know you won't today!" shouted Maddon. "Because I'm goin' to keep you right here—so I can watch you—until my brokers find out where this Erie stock's a-comin' from. I just gave them orders to buy up all that comes onto the exchange. This afternoon we'll see just how well the market's supplied with it—while you're off the floor!" concluded Maddon, and locked the door on the inside.

His lunch hour forgotten, Tugger sat squirming on the pad-shovers' bench. Caution urged him to sell while he could; cupidity advised him to hold on for the last sweet top dollar. Henderson returned, tried the handle of the locked inner office door and called to his employer that he had the latest market quotations.

"Shove 'em under the door!" shouted Maddon, from inside.

Henderson obeyed, curled up on the pad-shovers' bench and whispered to Tugger:

"Erie's gone up another three points."

Within the private office, conversation became excited.

"You damn' cry-baby, let me out of here!" Gould's voice reached the listeners on the bench, as he pounded on his desk to give vent to natural exasperation. "I want my lunch! And I've got a dozen better things to do than sit cooped up here all afternoon."

Yawning, Henderson uncoiled himself, drifted out, returned in a short time and shoved another market report under the locked door.

"Erie's still soaring," he winked at Tugger.

The early afternoon wore on. Conversation behind Gould's closed door several times reached name-calling and desk-pounding heights. Henderson several times drifted out and returned. Eighteen minutes before the market closed, the senior pad-shover could not resist boasting that he had surely earned his pay today, and a fat bonus besides!

"What have you done I haven't?" growled Tugger, biting a fingernail, his eyes on the clock. "The boss hasn't given an order all day."

"You mean you think he hasn't," scoffed Henderson. "Every time he pounded on that desk in there, I went out and shoved another thousand shares of Erie onto the market."

"You don't mean Gould's been selling all this time Maddon's had him locked up?"

"The boss gave me his written orders this morning—to deliver one every time I heard him pound on his desk. Maddon tipped off his own hand when he asked for a long appointment, without interruptions. Hey, where you going, Tug?"

By running himself breathless, Tugger managed to unload his few hundred shares of Erie before the stock market closed at three o'clock. Adding up his profits at the Farmers and Drovers Bank the next day, Tugger found his risky turn had yielded him almost five thousand dollars profit. Re-depositing his original fifteen hundred, he added to it half his Erie winnings. The other half he took to another bank as a future operations fund. During his next twenty years of trading, he never failed to divide his winnings into halves, one of which he added to his untouchable nest egg. Nor did he ever forget the then current philosophy of Wall Street stock market transactions, expressed with ferocious exuberance in verses which rumor whispered Jim Fisk had written to describe Jay Gould's relationship with Uncle Dan Drew:

> The tarantula jumped on the centipede's back
> And chortled with ghoulish glee:
> I'll poison the murderous son-of-a-gun;
> If I don't, he'll poison me!

As his purse and his confidence expanded, Tugger began to feel more at home in New York's varied night life. Often, by the time he had reached the Erie offices, Jubilee Jim was looking around for boon companions. Tugger was asked to go along, first to learn the ropes, as Jim put it, and then as guide to lesser politicos or visitors whom Fisk wished to honor with his box at the Opera House and later with supper at Josie's down the block. Tugger soon learned to make himself as agreeable to the Elegant Oakey Hall as to Josie's girls, and never poached, blabbed or slopped over. Nobody seemed to think he ought to lay out hard cash for a room downtown, when Josie's mansion was always open to Jim's satellites and friends.

In time, masculine taste as robust even as Tugger's began to grow restless after seeing Josie's girls enact "The Twelve Temptations" five nights a week on the stage and elsewhere. Like a conscientious bird dog Tugger worked over first one thicket and then another of Manhattan's varied night life. He began with the pretty-girl saloons in the Bowery. Here the waitresses wore aprons over pink tights to distinguish them from hired singers and dancers who wore no aprons. Tugger breezed through the concert saloons, lager gardens and panel cribs, then turned his attention to Manhattan's own unique sport, rat fights. Betting centered on the length of time it took a terrier to kill his given quota of rats. Thirty to forty minutes was the time required by an average dog to work through a classic of one hundred rats, but champion dogs often accounted for their hundred in twenty-five minutes or under. Every Bowery bucko, every rising politician yearned to develop a champion ratter. To his inquiries about the sport's future, Tugger was relieved to hear that the city's thirteen open garbage dumps located in the Hudson and East River marshes seemed capable of supplying an endless stream of rats. His favorite rat-pit referee was a pleasant Scot named Sandy MacGuffogg.

Feeling that he had gained at least a beginner's knowledge of rat baiting, Tugger bought a promising puppy, christened him Tarheel with champagne at one of Jim's parties, and paid well for his schooling. When the trainer pronounced Tarheel ready for his first public match, Sandy arranged a ten-rat bout before kindly betters. Kneeling at the pit edge in a crowded Bowery saloon, Tugger felt his own heart pound as excitedly as that of the young dog in his arms.

"Counters, are ye ready?" called Sandy.

"Yes, sir," answered the two enumerators.

"Let in the rats!" shouted Sandy.

The rat catcher, thrusting his cage over the metal flange of the pit, opened the wire door. Ten particularly vicious-looking rats, Tugger thought, jumped down into the pit.

"How many, sir?' boomed Sandy.

"Ten rats!" shouted the first enumerator.

"And ye, sir?"

"Ten rats it is!" agreed the second enumerator.

"The count is correct—ten rats!" confirmed Sandy and looked at his stop-watch to mark the required five minutes. "Let the rats tak' their ease. Any objections to any beastie, men?"

One better thought he detected a limp in the left hind leg of one rat. This weakling was removed, and a grizzled warrior put in his place. All the rats began running around the bottom of the pit, as if they sensed their five minutes of grace was drawing to a close. A rawboned rat charged the polished pit wall. Tugger unconsciously put him down as a terror.

"Ready!" Sandy warned Tugger to lean over the pit with Tarheel in his arms. "One—two—three—drop!"

At the last command, Tugger tossed his dog to an empty spot on the pit floor. Hardly had Tarheel's pads touched, before the rats were on him. The wall climber fastened his teeth in Tarheel's left cheek. Ignoring him, the terrier went to work killing one rat after another as methodically as a veteran. Before Tugger could realize it, the bout was over. Someone opened a panel in the pit wall, and shoved him inside. Without a trace of after-fight faintness—the exhaustion which often follows the effects of rat bite—Tarheel leaped into Tugger's arms and ecstatically licked his master's sweaty face. Tugger held him high, and thought of the yellowbacks the happy little dog had won him. The friendly audience cheered to the echo. Thus was born another champion. After Tugger had placed Tarheel in his basket and straightened up, for the first time he saw his hands were bloody.

That night, unmindful of the danger of lockjaw infection from rat bite, Tugger slept with the bandaged Tarheel on the bed beside him. The dog's fever flared, but Tugger kept his head cooled with towels wrung out in ice water, and soothed him during nightmares when Tarheel dreamed himself again in the rat pit. Tugger fought Tarheel for twenty-one months, until the dog's ears were tattered and his game heart weakened by the toxin of countless rats' teeth. At the end of a hundred-rat classic, Tarheel fell over in a dead faint, and never regained consciousness. When the trainers and veterinarians could think of nothing more to do, they handed Tarheel's limp white body over to his owner.

It was a mild October night, without a moon. The smell of burning leaves hung over Union Square. Carrying the dead dog in his arms as he had so often cradled the living, Tugger started walking. He reached Fifth Avenue and turned uptown without noticing what he did. The avenue was empty except for a hansom cab that slowed hoping for a fare, then quickened step and disappeared to gayer haunts. Jaws clenched, eyes unseeing, Tugger strode on past handsome mansions, the Brick Church. When the sidewalk ran out, he realized he had reached the reservoir, on the southwest corner of Fifth Avenue and Forty-second Street.

Through the starlight he swung on, Tarheel a featherweight in his arms. In his shock-numbed mind, an unrealized purpose was taking shape. Farm boy himself, Tugger had decided that even a city-bred dog might want to lie beneath green trees, under sweet-smelling sod. After the flaring circle of ringside gas jets, the reek of segar smoke, the whiskey-hoarse shouts of sportsmen, the stench of rats, Tarheel should sleep well in Central Park.

"W'at th'ell do ye think ye're doin'?" challenged a rough Irish voice. "So it's buryin' a baby ye are, is it?"

From his knees, where he had been scooping back moist earth with his hands, Tugger raised his eyes, his fighting jaw to the policeman.

"I'm burying Tarheel," he said.

"A foine tale that, when Tarheel's hangin' up anither record tonight! Wait till I sthrike a light—"

"I'm buryin' Tarheel, I tell you."

"Mary defend us, if it isn't Himself!"

"If you think"— began Tugger, his breath coming hard —"I'm goin' to let—some damn' ragpicker—dry Tarheel's bones on a stinkin' garbage dump—"

"Begorra, begorra! It's a sad night for all who loved the clane hard fighter he was," grieved the big Irishman. "May he rhest in peace, the darlin'! Many's the five- an' ten-spot bets he wan for me—"

"Shut up, will you?"

"Shore, an' I know how bad ye faal, Misther Blake," sympathized the officer. "Now ye just set back before ye spile your han's. I know where the work squad kapes their shovels. I'll have iv'rything ready an' nice in half a minute, sorr."

Tugger never attended another rat fight, nor owned another dog.

Chapter 11

With the secret knowledge that Fant was alive, with his son in her arms to insure Foxden to them both and with Tuckahoe's affectionate approval warm as April sunshine wherever she turned, America faced the crop year of '70 with joy in her heart. Every day she told herself she had been born and by choice would die a farmer.

The routine of country life, which must be energetically well ordered to prosper, filled her waking hours with activity she knew, and sent her to bed tired enough for deep slumber. With a hungry child to awaken her. America rose at five. Mahalee had breakfast ready by six. America worked in the dairy until it was time to bathe young Fant and put him to sleep in his covered crib. She then worked in her poultry yards. An hour of gardening followed in the flower borders America was developing along the new yard fence. The ladies of Tuckahoe had given her a good start by presenting her with roots or bulbs of their own favorite plants. Before noon, America bathed and put on a fresh dress, nursed the baby and herself dined like a lady at the Sheraton drop-leaf table near the family-room window. After a nap for them both, she carried baby Fant out to the fields to observe the black men's progress.

Had Fant been at Foxden, what could he have done with himself all day? He was unused to hard physical labor. Like Archie Crenshaw who had hidden behind a tree rather than be seen clearing his own land, Fant probably considered work beneath his dignity. He lacked the precise agricultural knowledge to make his supervision acceptable to field hands as competent as Weed and Ben Shadrack. Because he was never tired, he had always been bored by Timberlawn's rest hours and half-holidays. Yet the law of every prospering farm is that each creature it feeds, except the very young, must exchange for bounties received some needed service of hand or brain, of labor or leadership. What had Fant to give?

America wisely let Weed take the leadership in the field. Early one blustering March afternoon America fought the wind out onto the ridge path to where her hands were dragging grubs off her future tobacco patch. Against the bluing spring sky she could count three spirals of plant-bed smoke rising on Tuckahoe. Weed had four plant beds ready to burn, he had told her at noon.

"What're we going to do for good tobacco seed?" America asked. "In Virginia we used to scatter the seed in corn meal onto the cooled ashes—one teaspoonful of seed to each hundred feet—and spread the cotton on the bed at once. How do you do it here?"

"Des de same," agreed Weed. "When we's ready, seed 'll show up."

Before her on the plowed strip of sod the black men had piled split logs, saplings and brushwood from the cleared land. Ben Shadrack had brought out a hod of live coals from Mahalee's dinner fire. Stepping along the plant bed's upper end, where the high wind would fan the flames down its length, Ben sprinkled embers off his hearth shovel into prepared tinder. With a rustle, then the crackle of a dozen tiny red fists clutching for dry leaves, the fire caught and mounted into a clear sheet of flame. As a child clinging to her grandfather's saddle pummel in Virginia, America had thrilled to this first spring ritual of the tobacco patch, this burnt offering intended to kill insect life in the turned sod of the plant bed but symbolic also of the farm's high hopes for a prime crop. Now, America clasped her first-born in her arms and felt the same lift of heart the daughters of Miriam must have known to see the holy fire called down by Elijah confound the false prophets of Baal.

"Give us peace and a plentiful harvest, O Jehovah!" She

found herself breathing the prayer Ephraim Collier nad prayed for Golden Hill.

When she stepped back from the heat, America saw Stone Moncure standing behind her. In one hand he held his bridle rein, in the other something shrouded with last year's weathered plant-bed gauze. They smiled at each other, then looked back at the mounting flames.

"To see the first plant bed catch always makes me feel solemn," Stone remarked, at length. "To save me, I can't help thinking of the Children of Israel."

"Cousin Stone! I was thinking the same thing. Maybe it's the unaccustomed spectacle of fire in an open field—"

"Pa used to think it before me," Stone refused to rationalize, and chucked baby Fant under the chin. "And so will you, young feller, if you're a real dirt farmer like your ma. Here's a present for you, Miss Merry."

"Tobacco seed! Now I understand why Weed's been acting so mysterious. It's a stalk of your famous White Burley, isn't it? I hear it's worth its weight in gold. Tell me about it."

"Now you're playing on my weakness," grinned Stone, whose fondness for lecturing on tobacco seed strains was well known in Mason County. Plant the right seed, he preached to his string of growers, and your crop is half sold. "Did you ever hear how White Burley got started? Folks around here were mostly growing a heavy dark red burley, which we thought was an improvement on the Blue Pryor pa sowed in the 'forties. In '64 a farmer named George Webb near Higginsport, Ohio, secured some seed called 'Little Burley,' of the Maryland instead of the Virginia type. When he came to set out his plants, he found a few which were of a peculiar white or yellow color. Taking them for diseased or dwarfed, he pulled them up. Next year, being scarce of seed, he again sowed what was left of the Little Burley, and again found the freak white plants which excited his and his neighbors' curiosity. In '65 Webb set out about a thousand plants which caused so much talk I rode across the river to see the patch. Then and there I gave Webb a ten-dollar gold piece to turn me out three good stalks of his new type, and to sack them against insect stings and bees mixin' the pollen. Around Higginsport about twenty thousand pounds were raised. It cured into a thin leaf with a smooth kid-glove finish, a leaf that colored well and produced the pounds. Two hogsheads of it sold for a high price on the Cincinnati breaks. When those hogsheads took first and second premiums for cutting tobacco at the St. Louis Fair in '67, and brought fifty-eight dollars a hundred, growers just never would stop talking."

"I can understand that," laughed America, who had considered herself lucky to average thirteen dollars in '66. "What happened to the rest of that first crop?"

"It took third prize at the Cincinnati Tobacco Fair, and sold for thirty-four dollars per hundred."

"And you gave me a stalk of that seed?"

"I actually had to keep a man with a shotgun sitting guard over my tobacco patch all last summer. I took the night watches myself, but not before thieves had stolen my earlier seed stalks. Funny how an otherwise honest farmer, who goes to church on Sundays, will walk through his neighbor's tobacco patch, break off the best stalk his neighbor has carefully sacked, slip it under his coat and never acknowledge it even to his own conscience!" laughed Stone, extending the stalk. Through the tobacco cotton America could see the terminal cluster of dark brown pods clenched like little fists to keep safe the hundreds of tiny seed each pod contained.

"Thank you, Cousin Stone! Are you sure you can spare it?"

"I turned out an acre of seed plants—to help my neighbors along. There's no string tied to it, except I hope you'll let me have the last bid on your crop next fall."

Impressed by his neighborly good will, which also showed farsighted business acumen, America looked at the giver instead of his gift. Against the sunburn already spread over his high cheekbones and bare forehead, Stone's eyes appeared startlingly blue. Before the declaration in those eyes America blushed. Clearer than words, they assured her confidently that he waited now only for a decent period of mourning to elapse before he meant to claim for his bride this Virginia cousin whom he had loved from first sight. The next baby America Moncure would be shifting in her arms, would be his.

"Let me take him," smiled Stone.

"He's not used to strangers," she answered. Imagine Fant Annable offering to carry anybody else's baby!

"All young things like me—because they know I like them. You can hold my horse. Here comes Weed after his tobacco seed."

Out of the plant-bed smoke Weed emerged. He had been rolling the burning logs inch by inch down the bed's length. Already his rubber boots were seared, his trouser legs flaked with ash.

"Ain't no need your standin' 'round hyah no mo', ma'am," declared Weed, taking the stalk as carefully as if it had been alabaster. "We's gwine be half de night burnin' an' rollin' dis bed."

Man and baby, woman and the quiet horse strolled towards Foxden. It was late afternoon and the boisterous March wind had blown itself out before sunset. From the wagon tracks curving along the crest of the river rim, Tuckahoe dropped away on all sides. Below them to the east lay the wide Ohio valley with the great river spreading in flood like a yellow lake across its rich bottom lands. To the west across Tuckahoe turnpike America could see the Drake hillsides covered with blossoming patches of dogwood and redbud, as if Cousin Theresa had laid out her pastel quilts to sun. The air was full of the melody of running water. Treble notes sounded close at hand where busy little rivulets dropped over limestone ledges; deep-throated thunder boomed from the far side of the Drake hills where Lee's Creek rushed riverwards. "Ain't you nevah hear't de voice ob Lee's Crick when hit's vexed?" Weed had described this distant roar. From thicket and meadow arose the lush wet smell of burgeoning life, the smell that makes farmers' palms itch for the jerk of plow handles between them. On a warm slope America's lambs had lined up to play leap-the-hollow. When they stood almost nose to nose, as on a starter's signal they sprang high into the air, raced down the slope, soared across a rill and landed on the green sod opposite, shook themselves, flung their legs in all directions, and bounced up the other grade to repeat the gay maneuver coming back.

"The grass is rising," announced Stone, in the hushed voice he always used to describe this perennial miracle of his woodland pastures.

" 'He maketh me to lie down in green pastures,' " quoted America. Was it only a year ago she had stood hopeless on a grimy Cincinnati wharf to watch the Kentucky hills turn green across the swirling Ohio? " 'He leadeth me beside the still waters. He restoreth my soul.' "

"David's the only man could write about nature to satisfy me," commented Stone. "I used to have something else in common with him, too. We both coveted another man's wife. But that's over now for me, praise God! This time next year you and I will be walking our own fields."

She gave him a quick look, then lowered her head.

"Tell me you'll marry me, America—before snow flies?"

"You were the first man I met on Kentucky soil, Cousin Stone—my first friend," she answered, thinking that she must not let any man except her husband make love to her. "Let's go on being friends, can't we?"

"But you're free now—except for a lot of silly conventions women make."

"Promise me you'll stay my friend?"

Gazing at her, he sensed her darkly prophetic mood. A man's man, he had had and wanted little experience with women. Yet the quicksilver changes in mood which often rippled across America's mind fascinated him. Stone was reminded of climbing a hill pasture to its crest and coming on a sunlit sheet of pond water sparkling in a lively breeze. Clouds would then pass across the sun, the breeze would die, the waters darken—

"I'll promise," he agreed. "I'm no schoolboy. I can wait."

Under canvas on the edge of the walnut grove, the tobacco seedlings showed first as pin points of green, then as dimes, quarters and fifty-cent pieces strewn thickly over the ashy plant bed. Wireworms crawling under the sun-warmed cotton at night menaced the plants. America bought arsenic at Mrs. MacGower's counter, mixed it in corn meal and gave it to Weed to dust over the four precious plant beds. Like gorillas squatting on a plank above the green mosaic, the black men weeded the beds with the patience good farmers muster for every phase of this finger crop. A dry spell followed. Of afternoons, America scanned the heavens for rain clouds, while Ben Shadrack hauled out pond water in two barrels mounted on the farm sled, and Weed sprinkled the growing plants. Dry weather was what they needed now, if it didn't last too long. Dry weather makes good root systems.

Between each step of the vital plant-bed routine, Weed and Ben Shadrack had been carrying on other phases of farm work during their fourteen-hour day. The corn was planted and up, the vegetable garden made, the tobacco ground dragged, combed with an A-harrow and laid off to await a tobacco season. Listening happily to rain on the roof when she awoke for the baby's feeding, America led the household at dawn out the ridge to the tobacco patch through blessed white fog. In his crib baby Fant rode on the farm sled like the son of any other tobacco-grower whose mother's nimble fingers are needed to draw plants. Even old Mahalee, her rheumatism forgotten, stepped briskly along to do her part.

When the heave of tobacco setting was over, Tuckahoe farmers settled back to catch their breath. Wheat began to yellow, the corn was thinned and plowed for the third time. In the tobacco patch, the transplanted seedlings showed their ears like rows of inquisitive rabbits. Noons grew whitely hot, afternoons lengthened. Baby Fant began to fret and America weaned him. Twilights were long and late. Foxden's family room seemed a stuffy cage wherein America could not sleep. The July night sky, as she gazed up at it from the front flagstones late one evening, was luminous with stars so close she felt that she had only to reach her hand to touch them. From the walnut grove out on the river rim, a mockingbird whistled a familiar melody:

> Tell—me—the—tales—
> That—to me—were—so dear,

She sat up, galvanized. No mockingbird could whistle like that! She stood, walked to the yard gate and listened again, the words forming on her lips:

> Now—you—are—come,
> All—my—grief—is removed;

Without a thought for her young son sleeping alone in the house, for Mahalee who might be watching from the cook-room step, for Ben Shadrack snoring on a cot in the tack room or Weed roaming the fields, America picked up her skirts, ran across the stable lot and out along the dusty wagon road towards the walnut grove. Fant came forward to the shadow's edge. Then they were in each other's arms, laughing and crying for joy of reunion . . .

America overslept next morning. Weed's voice booming into the family room awakened her:

"Whar's Miz Merry? Mahalee, you tell her foah me we's got tuh post a man wid a gun in aour terbacker patch."

Startled, America drew on her dressing sack, tiptoed over to the cook-room door and opened it another inch. At their breakfast table sat Weed and Ben Shadrack. On the hearth Mahalee was frying in two skillets the half-dozen eggs each hand was allowed for breakfast. Claws on hips, Mahalee sat back on her heels to toss a scornful answer to the huge black man whose appetite she never ceased actively to resent:

"Who you hootin' at naow, night owl?"

"Des 'fore dawn, when I was a-comin' up de holler, I seed

a man crossin' aour terbacker patch," declared Weed, buttering the five soda biscuits left in the pan and quartering them with his knife. "When I fust seed him, dar was a gal wid him—"

"You's a fine one tuh go 'roun' spyin' on young fo'ks, you is!" jibed Ben Shadrack, content to wait for the second pan of biscuit.

"Young folks' doin's ain't nuffin tuh me—so long as dey stay aout ob my terbacker patch," declared Weed. "I mos'est had dat varmint! I was a-layin' foah him wid a rail I grabbed off de fence. He musta smelt me, 'kez instid ob comin' on daown de path, he lit aout across de p'int."

"Didn't you light aftah him?" asked Ben.

"Shore I did, but he war gone cleaner 'n a whistle."

"What'd he look lak?"

"I ain't got cat-eyes—tuh see in de dark."

America leaned against the doorframe. Relief was so great that the sweat which had started on her forehead felt cold. As she turned to dress, she noticed that baby Fant in his crib had been screaming for attention until his face was purple. She picked him up and, while soothing him, thought of his father. By now Fant should be well below Augusta on the shanty-boat carrying him downstream.

When nature is fruitful, that which is planted must grow and come to harvest. Topped and suckered, the tobacco turned pale gold, was cut after dinner, was leaned six plants on a stick thrust into the earth to wilt under the yellowing afternoon sun, and hung to cure in the big barn out on the river rim. Black frost laid low the suckers on the cut stalks, rimed the corn shocks, sent America's pin-feathered white chickens for shelter to the coal house from which they emerged grimy as stevedores. With Foxden's harvest laid by, America realized she couldn't hope much longer to conceal her second pregnancy from Tuckahoe's already curious eyes.

"Dar ain't no call foah you tuh come traipsin' aout hyah befoah de rain," Weed declared without looking at her, disapproval in his voice. "Me 'n' Ben, we kin drag in dis shirt tail ob rye."

"I want you to feel I'm interested," answered America. She had been nerving herself to face her servants' judgment. Good negroes liked to feel they were working for the best people in the community. "Where do you think we'd better plan to put tobacco next year?"

"I won't be wukkin' foah you next year, Miz Merry. I's quittin' come Thanksgivin'."

She received this catastrophic news in silence, and considered its consequences. Who would know when to touch the crop? Ben Shadrack was a willing worker, but he lacked the experience which makes for crop judgment—if he stayed.

"And Ben, too?" she asked.

"I dunno abaout Ben," Weed evaded. "We's wukked togeder so long he mos'ly follers whar I goes."

"Would you care to tell me why you're quitting?"

"It's Dulcy," Weed confessed, made uncomfortable by the look on America's pinched face. "She's agin mah wukkin' hyah. I tol' her she ain't got no call tuh frow stones, but she keeps on a-talkin'."

"I see," answered America steadily, although her cheeks flamed at this indirect condemnation by Tuckahoe's dusky Delilah. "Will you stay through hog killing?"

"Effen you needs me, ma'am."

"You know I need you. Thank you for telling me, Weed."

"Yassum."

Watching a brood sow carry straws one late November sunset, a barnyard prediction of colder weather in the air, America at supper that night told her household to prepare to butcher early next morning, should the sow's prognostication come true. Cool weather held through sausage grinding and lard making. As she faced this final process, America found herself so tired she could scarcely stand. With sly malice, Mahalee told how in slavery days pregnant Big Mandy had been overtaken by a dizzy spell while tending the lard kettle, and had fallen into it. The fire which resulted had consumed everything within a fifty-yard radius. Charles Moncure, Mandy's owner and the father of Stone, piously buried the kettle and the ashes surrounding it, with proper religious ceremony.

"Effen Mandy warn't sech a big ha'nt, some nigger on Tuckahoe would 'a' had dat kittle dug up y'ars ago," Mahalee concluded, and waved her thick-waisted young mistress away.

The next week Stone came, he said, to look at her tobacco. Throwing Cousin Simmy's worn Paisley over her head, America followed him out to the ridge barn. The walnut trees were brown against a sullen sky, their fingered yellow leaves piled in hollows or whirling ahead of her along the wagon tracks. A memory of that March afternoon when she and Stone had stood to watch the lambs overwhelmed America. How could she hope to conceal her condition from Stone? Those searching blue eyes had been trained by years of observation to detect the first signs of gestation in his barnyard beasts.

"The light's getting bad, ma'am," he commented, as he took the pole away from propping the barn door shut. "Would you rather I'd come back next week?"

"The November rains are here," she answered. Next week, she would look worse. "I'd rather you'd make a bid now, please."

She watched him swing onto the nearest tier pole and climb up into the barn to inspect the hanging crop. His trained eye automatically judged color, texture, the length and breadth of the leaf, its quality and the preponderance of each type. When he was on the ground again, he figured in his little book and offered her a price "all around," which included all types at the same figure per pound. To her timid inquiry as to how he had arrived at this figure, he showed her the rough poundage estimates of each type and quality which he had jotted in his notebook, a method by which he could calculate his average with less actual margin of speculation than at first seemed apparent. These notes at the same time gave him serviceable memoranda for future reference when the stripped crop was delivered to him the following January, he explained.

"You don't mean you expect me to deliver it stripped—at that price?" asked America, shocked into bluntness.

"I'm afraid that's the only way I can receive it, ma'am. It's all I can manage to feed hands to strip my own crop, since Rindy's moved to town."

"But it's your fine seed!"

"I've made full allowance for that. Last week in Cynthiana I talked to Tom Coyle, one of the biggest handlers in the Blue Grass. He feels as I do. We're in for hard times."

"Cousin Stone, times couldn't be harder than during these last eight years!"

"The North and the West don't know what hard times are, ma'am. We're still paying for the war, and two-dollar wheat, and building all these railroads we'll never use," Stone answered her volubly, as if relieved to have an impersonal subject to discuss. "If you don't believe me, ask any other tobacco man you see. It's our business to try and figure ahead what farm prices will be eight months from now."

"My father used to say tobacco prices always followed cotton—"

"True. But cotton can't stay where it's been any more than cows can live in trees. Supposing I go around now contracting your leaf for three cents more than it'll be worth to me in January, you'll expect to be paid what we agreed on when you deliver your crop, won't you? Supposing the market keeps on going down, by June when I get your leaf on the hogshead breaks, this three cent loss will have dropped to five. Then what happens? The warehouse men in Cincinnati take Children's Chance, which stands as security for the money they advanced me to make this purchase—and I'm broke! I'd have to start life all over again share-cropping on another man's hillsides."

"Well," said America, looking wistfully up at the fragrant yellow leaf, "if that's the best you can do—"

"Would you rather I'd send another handler around to make an offer?"

"He wouldn't offer as much as you have, I'm afraid."

"I know he wouldn't! Then we understand each other, ma'am. You'll throw in the trash free, of course?"

"If that's customary."

"With my men. I must be going, now. I've two more crops to look at today, and the air feels like snow," Stone continued, again voluble as he saw that she had something else to say to him. "I never buy tobacco when there's snow on the ground. You can't tell a thing about its true color in snow light," he concluded, his face hardening as he watched her step ahead of him towards the door.

"Stone," she challenged him. She could not let her first friend go like this. Yet what could she say to dissolve the hurt in his eyes?

"Yes, ma'am?"

"Is this all you have to say to me?"

"You're the one to explain, I'm thinking!"

America turned her head to hide a rush of tears. Emotionally unstable, she realized that she must choose every word she spoke with the greatest care. As the wife of a man wanted dead or alive for murder and as the expectant mother of his child, a child which must remain nameless for the present, she must not let anything—self-pity, friendship or even compassion for another's suffering—turn her from the hard road of wifely duty which she saw stretching ahead of her, a road which on Tuckahoe could lead to but one forlorn destination. Complete ostracism, she had long since decided, was preferable to living with her own conscience betrayed, with Fant's blood forever on her soul.

"America, look at me!" Stone's voice was harsh. "Tell me—what I see with my own eyes—can't be true! Has Fant Annable come home again? Is your husband alive?"

"How could he be?" she answered, her face averted like the dull slut she must make him think she had become.

She heard him draw in a long breath, and exhale it without speech. In front of them, beyond the open barn door, the rain began to fall in big drops like tears.

"America Moncure—if Fant is dead—there must be some other reason—for what appears," Stone began again with the patience of a mind in firm control over emotion. "Let's you and me see if we can't figure it out sensibly, as Christian folk should. People are like horses and dogs and birds. They don't change overnight. Or go completely back on their blood lines. You couldn't any more do what you appear to have done—what Allilee Drake says you've done—that I could, unless I was drunk. God knows you've had enough to make any woman break under the strain of these last years! And maybe women break differently from men. Men go out and get drunk. So I'm going to judge you—"

"Why judge me at all, sir?"

"Let me finish! I'm going to give you the benefit of the same standard by which men judge men. I'm going to believe you were drunk."

Outside the rain fell like a curtain of tears. Nothing she had previously met on Tuckahoe had prepared her for this chivalrous tolerance. On Tuckahoe, as in Virginia, a woman without virtue must remain an outcast, so that youth may recognize sin by the price it costs the sinner. America was opening her lips to thank him when Stone's careful voice continued:

"Since the niggers first started whispering about you, I've been trying to figure out what's best for the four of us. You're my fifth cousin. You used to bear my name. I'm your only male relative across the mountains. I'm not saying part of me wouldn't be glad if I'd never laid eyes on you—glad if you'd leave Tuckahoe forever, so I could get a proper night's sleep! But I can't. And if you left Tuckahoe, you'd lose Foxden for your boy."

He paused to give her a chance to defend herself, if she had any defense to make. She could think of nothing to say, nothing to do to divert his painful logic from moving to whatever conclusion it had reached. His eyes bleak as glacier ice, Stone went on stoically:

"Now, the only way out I can figure is—is to ask you to

marry me. If you marry me right away, maybe folks will think we just couldn't wait—till your year of mourning was out. With my name to protect you—and your child—maybe in time folks'll forgive you—and forget. God knows I'll try! Letitia Cary has made a big success of that girl Ulysses had by Stella Barnes. There are two things I can promise you: I won't abuse these children of other men you bring under my roof. And I'll give the three of you a good home in the hard times ahead—something you can't have here at Foxden with every decent hand raised against you."

She lifted her head and looked at him. Too angry to want to meet her brimming eyes, he glanced away. His face for a moment appeared as if his control might break. Before she realized, she thought aloud:

"Now I know what people mean when they call you a Christian gentleman."

"Christianity hasn't anything to do with it—or us," declared the unhappy voice above her. "My misfortune is that I loved you the first minute I laid eyes on you—and I can't seem to stop. The truth is, I want you any way I can get you—even if the church turns us both out. Oh, we'll be turned out, I warrant you for that! Justinian Annable's never really forgiven you for liking Fant. And now we'll give him just the proper example he's been looking for to scare the young folks into behaving themselves. But after he's gone, folks 'll forget—and the church 'll need my tithe again."

"I don't care half as much what the church thinks about me—as what you think, Stone."

"Even if we're never reinstated, I'll jump to marry you, America. And by God, I'll keep you straight if I have to break every bone in your body to do it! It all comes from this newfangled freedom for women. You started it when you came gallivanting out here by yourself. Living on the loose a year with Fant Annable finished the job—until you seem to have forgotten who you are, and what's expected of you!"

She realized she couldn't go on standing here like a schoolgirl rejoicing in this Galahad come to rescue her. For her, from the road down which she must travel alone, there could be no rescue, no helping hand over the rough places, not even a backward glance. How did a shallow woman act in a situation like this? What would Palestine have said?

"You don't paint a very attractive picture of married life, I must confess," she began, with an attempt at a sniff. "If you talk like this before we're married, what might you do afterwards?"

"Merry!"

"Oh, I'm not thinking just of myself. I'm thinking of my children. A fine chance they'd have, paupers on your charity! And what about Foxden?"

"Children's Chance is worth ten times this rough little farm!"

"Yes, but you've signed Children's Chance as security for your annual tobacco purchase. You just said yourself you might lose it if tobacco prices drop too low next year. Here at Foxden I've got bread and meat for myself and my babies as long as I'll work—and can pay taxes. You know I'm a good manager. You've said half a dozen times I'm the best woman farmer you ever saw—a natural born dirt farmer."

"Then you honestly don't care—what you do—or what people say about you?"

"One thing I did learn with Fant Annable!" she flared at him. "Words butter no turnips."

She heard him breathing quickly, saw through sidelong averted eyes how his hands had clenched until the weather-tanned knuckles gleamed white.

"If anybody had said you'd answer me like that, I wouldn't have believed them. Now I know. I've heard with my own ears," he pronounced judgment. "You are mercenary—and shameless—and vile."

She could not believe that Stone Moncure was standing there saying such things to her. What other innocent woman had ever been so cruelly maligned? Throwing back her head, she answered with spirit, out of the fire struck by his insults:

"In spite of bitter words—and hard looks—I mean to stay on here—to keep on working for my children—as Penelope kept on weaving year after year."

"Don't think you can drag the wool over my eyes by comparing yourself to some storybook heroine—unless it's Jezebel!"

"Stone Moncure, you've said enough."

"I have, indeed. Rest assured I'll never trouble you again, ma'am."

"But—but you'll take my tobacco?"

"I bought your crop this year, but it's the last I'll ever buy from you. Since I started handling tobacco, I've made it my rule to let nothing—neither hell nor high water—interfere with my receiving in January the leaf I contracted the previous October. Your crop won't be the exception that proves my rule. And now, good-day to you."

"Cousin Stone—"

"You're no cousin of mine."

"As you choose, sir. But there's no occasion for you to go rushing out into the rain."

"Rain's what I need—rain's clean!"

She leaned against the barn doorway and watched him go splashing along the flooded wagon tracks towards the house. Bare-headed, he seemed to melt under the silvery darts. A wild impulse seized America to follow him, to plunge into the cold downpour. Should she slip and fall, should she lose her unborn child and herself lie at death's door, then surely she might gasp Fant's secret to clear her name for her young son's sake?

The wave of self-pity ebbed. Nothing that Stone or anyone else could say, had altered the facts or could change her situation. "For better—for worse—till death do us part," she had accepted a contract she intended to keep. Compared to that Cincinnati hand laundry where she had toiled for mere subsistence, here at Foxden she was rich! Sooner or later, her course of action would be vindicated.

She sat down on the wagon tongue to wait for the rain to slacken.

On Thanksgiving Eve, America paid off Weed and Ben Shadrack with the last of the money Fant had left her on his July visit. From now until she received her tobacco money in January, the Foxden household would have to live on the credit America had built up on Abigail MacGower's books in exchange for butter and eggs. When none of her servants appeared Friday morning, America did the barnyard chores, turned her livestock to grass and considered her problem over a cup of coffee and cold biscuit eaten in the quiet cook cabin. When Mahalee came back for her wages, America decided, she could take her clothes and go for good.

Shouldering baby Fant, she walked up the pike to the tollhouse. Abigail was tight-lipped until America asked her to dispatch a note to Limestone's leading veterinarian asking him to come out to Foxden and geld Sunshine. In her present condition, she couldn't carry water and feed twice daily to the stallion in the absence of stable hands.

"Wha'll strip oot your-r leaf?"

"Will you tell anyone who comes along looking for work I need good strippers?"

"Wha's tae dae your-r chores?"

"I can sell my sheep. I'll milk and feed as long as I can. By spring I'll surely be able to hire hands—and a more loyal cook than Mahalee. Stone Moncure says hard times are coming, so there ought to be plenty of niggers who want work."

"They'll nae work at Foxden."

"They won't if you won't tell them," agreed America, looking steadily at the Scotswoman. "Would you prefer to have me tack up a notice on the Foxden pike gatepost?"

"So every tramp wha passes by may ken ye want a man? Lassie, lassie, were ye moon-struck, sae tae shame yersel' an' y'r innocent bairn nae six months after Judge Stacy confirmed ye as agent f'r Foxden? Weighin' th' tussle ye had wi' th' wean in your-r arms, I wust ye'd thocht twice afore plungin yersel' in the same fix all ower again!"

America remembered that moonless July night, when Fant's whistle had wooed her out to the walnut grove. In his arms she had lain laughing at the stars close above her husband's shoulders, stars which she remarked had rushed together like scandal-mongering old women to peer over the treetops into the dark well of their happiness. Dropping her eyes, America listened meekly while Mrs. MacGower pronounced judgment:

"Land's guid. An' 'tis fine tae be mistress at y'r-r ain hearth-stane. But nae at th' price ye've paid, ma lass! If 'twas your aim tae mak' siccar o' Foxden by lyin' in the hedge wi' th' fur-rst passer-by, then God hae peety on your ignorance! The land gaes tae Fant's issue, nae tae your mistakes."

"Is this what the ridge is saying about me?"

"Aye. An' mair. Wi' ma ain twa ears I heard Allilee Drake tell Kate Annable ye hae hit on the yin way tae pleasure yersel' an' at th' same time keep Foxden. The way ye rode at the Fair showed how shameless ye are, says oor-r fine Miss Allilee! Bein' ower fond o' drivin', ye noo can haun'le th' lines yersel', wear th' trews an' lift up y'r-r skirts whene'er th' mood tae wanton turns ye deef tae decency."

Moving from counter to open door, America looked across green winter rye fields to the Drake chimneys, Morgan le Fay's stronghold.

"What do you think, Mrs. MacGower?" she asked tonelessly.

"I dinna ken whit tae think, lassie! Auld MacGower agrees ye hae chosen th' yin way tae cheat the auld man's will. He vowed if he catches me sayin' mair than yea an' nae tae ye across ma counter, he'll belt me blue—he wha hasna said a sharp speech tae me since we left Edinburgh!"

"Then this will be the last time I'll trouble you, ma'am," America tried to smile at the distressed toll-mistress, who looked more than ever like a turkey hen with tears rolling down her long face.

"Ma bairnie, tell me 'tis naught but a bad dream!"

"I wish I could, ma'am."

Trudging homewards, America realized that Cousin Margaret hadn't sent a black boy in a buggy to drive her to church for more than a month. In the turmoil of her own thoughts, and the confusion of losing her servants when she felt so wretched herself, divine worship had slipped from her mind. Now she found herself longing for it. Weed had left his break-cart in the barn, and the work gear for one of the four mules ought to fit Sunshine.

When Sunshine could travel, America hooked him into the cart one Sunday morning, and with baby Fant in her arms drove up the pike. As she pulled into the queue of vehicles awaiting their turn to approach the church stile, she saw it was crowded with ladies who clutched their skirts and exchanged greetings in high-pitched voices.

Ulysses Alcorn assisted her out, and offered to hitch her horse. After thanking him, America swung around to find the stile empty. As though they were late instead of early, the ladies were scurrying churchwards. With a pounding heart America walked carefully up the flagstones and entered at the women's door. She had planned to march to her customary place beside Cousin Margaret in the Annable pew, but her courage failed. Slipping into a rear aisle seat, she busied herself with making baby Fant comfortable on the cushion beside her. Fortunately he was asleep. Had he been screaming with temper, their entrance could not have attracted more attention. With bent head, America told herself she had been a fool to come. When she dared raise her eyes, she met only the curious stares of unmannerly tenant children.

In groups the men entered the left side of the church and found customary places. Uncle Cato, colored deacon, led his flock on respectful feet up the double inside stairs to the gallery. Across its rail pious blacks might blink directly into three chandeliers, each lighted with fourteen kerosene lamps set in tiny mirrors and hung with crystal prisms to dazzle the eye with a promise of spiritual glories awaiting the faithful beyond

Jordan. Today was not "preaching Sunday." For reasons of economy necessary to both congregations, the Reverend Gillespie's stipend and services were shared by the Glade Springs and Germantown churches. As senior elder, Justinian Annable did the honors to a gentleman of military bearing whom he seated in the carved chair reserved for visiting clergymen on the right of the pulpit. When her father-in-law turned to lead worship, America was shocked to see how he had aged.

From among the choir facing the congregation, Allilee Drake arose in a new beaver tippet, and ran an introductory trill for Kate Annable at the hand organ to approve. Cousin Edwin Dell joined with his budding tenor. All three smiled complacently to each other and eyed Mr. Annable. At his signal the congregation, rising, began to sing the first hymn:

"Love divine, all loves excelling,
  Joy of heaven, to earth come down,
Fix in us Thy humble dwelling,
  All Thy faithful mercies crown!"

In her rear aisle pew America held her head up and tried to sing. The familiar words at first brought deep consolation to her own trembling heart. Allilee Drake might have chosen this particular hymn purposely to embarrass her, but America hadn't expected Kate Annable to follow Allilee's malicious lead. As both choir leaders sang with more than necessary emphasis "all loves excelling," "pure unbounded love Thou art," "take away the love of sinning," they glanced significantly towards America. Several young girls, following the direction of their eyes, looked around at America and tittered. Outwardly impervious to any situation the hymn might be creating, the elders sang on, although Stone Moncure's face had turned dull red. After the Scripture lesson and announcements, Mr. Annable declared the congregation fortunate to have as their guest today a very lion of the Disciples' faith, Professor Joe Dave Langston, pupil of Alexander Campbell at Bethany College, world traveler, educator and beloved fighting-chaplain of Kentucky's famous Orphans' Brigade.

Slender as a rapier blade, with a domelike head and piercing blue eyes, Professor Joe Dave mounted the high walnut pulpit. Below it was spread the Lord's Table; on either side were handsome amber Bohemian windows with jewellike borders of emerald, blue and ruby glass through which the light suffused in such brilliance that his head and shoulders appeared in silhouette. Unable to see his face for the rosy splendor on his either side, she felt in his voice the quality of a disembodied spirit.

It was the most cultivated voice America had heard in Kentucky. Professor Joe Dave, she knew, had been educated at Princeton and abroad to succeed to his father's diplomatic triumphs in South America and Europe. After a trip around the world, he had met Alexander Campbell and been so shaken by the experience that he had embraced the Disciples' ministry, instead. His text, he announced, was the somewhat threadbare I Corinthians 13, which he would endeavor to interpret anew in the light of recent archeological discoveries unearthed in Palestine, and according to his own interpretation of the Greek original phrases.

During the next half hour, America found her starved mind fed by his scholarship. Her soul, harassed by a hundred worries and faced with a situation too desperate even to guess its outcome, slipped into the cool waters of spiritual love which the soldier-divine dared preach. His cultivated tones flowed on. Her soul in her eyes, America listened and felt the first peace of mind she had known since that July evening months ago when Fant's arms had drawn her into her present plight.

" 'And now abideth faith, hope, love, these three,' " rang the reassuring voice from the aura of splendor surrounding the pulpit, " 'but the greatest of these is love.' "

As the thrilling tones ceased, silence held the congregation. A sigh from the negroes in the gallery, the rustle of taffeta petticoats and a series of creaks followed as the men shifted themselves on the benches. Stone Moncure arose, walked to the communion table and said with simple feeling:

"Words of mine, dearly beloved, can add nothing to the inspiring message which we have just heard. May it open the minds and hearts of any here present to the love of Jesus Christ," he continued, in his father's formula, "so that they will come forward and confess their faith in Him who died for us, as we gather about His Table—"

"Brother Stone!"

The challenge came from Mr. Annable, on the other side of the pulpit. In his Sunday black, he moved forward like a raven about to alight on the communion table. Where was Gander, wondered America.

"Distressed as I am to air the unclean garments of this church before Brother Langston," Mr. Annable began, "I feel that I would be deaf to his lofty message, and a traitor to my own conscience, if I allow one who appears to be living in sin of the blackest dye to approach the Lord's Table unchallenged, unrebuked and unrepentant, and enjoy the Christian fellowship of Glade Springs church."

Among the congregation were some who sat as if galvanized to their pews. Guilty hearts lifted in terror to dry throats. How had the old fox found them out? Who had betrayed them? Where had their furtive, carefully laid plans gone awry? Without at first suspecting that he might be talking about her, America looked at three or four necks reddening within her field of view and felt sorry for their owners. Down the ages, why had Christians felt themselves called upon to judge and punish? Christ Himself had had only words of loving compassion for sinners:

"Go, and sin no more."

"That this sinner has come into my family by wedlock in no way lessens my responsibility as senior elder of this flock, and my duty as a God-fearing man," the stentorian voice was continuing, "America Moncure Annable!"

That was her name—America Moncure Annable. A sea of

faces, several of them shiny with sweat, had turned and were staring at her.

"America Moncure Annable!" repeated the voice of human judgment. "Come forward and show good cause why you should not be expelled from this congregation for living in widowed adultery."

She felt the color flood her face. Anger, the soul-sustaining rage of the unjustly accused, brought her to her feet, her head high and flung back to utter the rush of words which her mind checked just in time. What could she say that would not set cruel tongues wagging still faster? "I am innocent," her lips might proclaim, but who would believe her? The one irrefutable evidence would be Fant's body; he had sworn that no man should take him alive. For better—for worse—I pledge thee my troth. . . .

"What have you to say, America Moncure?" thundered the voice of her father-in-law.

"Nothing."

Aware of faces, some pitying, the majority shocked, a few openly lustful, America bent and gathered baby Fant onto her left arm. Half turned in their pews to watch her, the congregation sat so still that the creak of the door sounded harsh and loud as she opened it, stepped outside and closed it behind her.

At the fence row where Sunshine was hitched, she fumbled with one hand to untie the stoutly knotted halter. Snow had fallen, and she hesitated to lay baby Fant in it in order to use both hands. Behind her, someone was approaching. The hope that Stone had dared follow her out both agitated and soothed her churning emotions. She raised her head to protest and saw Professor Joe Dave looking searchingly at her from the last of the flagstones.

"Let me hold your baby," he suggested, with urbanity. "As I am not a member of this congregation, my absence during a—a disciplinary vote—is entirely suitable."

"I was a fool to come!" she burst out. "I should have known better, but I missed—I missed—"

"'The everlasting arms?'" he quoted with Christ's own smile in his sapphire-blue eyes. "Give me your baby, my dear."

Too moved to speak, America surrendered Fant with trembling hands, untied Sunshine, backed him out into the lane and climbed into the cart. When she was seated and had a firm grip on the reins, Professor Joe Dave laid the child in her lap, and stepped clear.

"Thank you, sir." America tried to make proper acknowledgment.

"May I come to see you, ma'am?"

"Not if you mean to pry into my affairs!" she blurted, too upset to realize how her words might sound. "I've had all of Mr. Annable's kind of religion I can stand for the present."

"No one but an innocent woman would have entered the lion's den as you just did," declared Professor Joe Dave in his wise cultivated voice. "And that means Fant Annable is alive. Next time I'm on Tuckahoe I shall give myself the pleasure of calling on you. By that time you may care to tell me how you managed his escape—realizing as you must that the lips of God's servants are sealed. No? Then perhaps we may have a quiet game of chess. Did your father ever tell you that I once played chess with him—as well as a youth's hero worship would permit?"

"Oh, sir, it's well he's dead. He's spared seeing what's happened to his daughter today!" she wailed, and mustered her wits to try and deny the terrifying truth he had deduced. "As to your guess about the—the paternity of my expected child—please let's not discuss that!"

"As you will, my dear. Time—and simple biology—will tell. And now, *au revoir*."

The problem remained as to how she was to get her tobacco stripped. Mrs. MacGower could send her few day laborers because those who lived on Tuckahoe were occupied with their own crops when weather permitted the handling of leaf. Caps in hand, two German youths appeared one late afternoon at

Foxden's door to beg shelter from an approaching storm. They explained they were on their way to Cincinnati to live with an uncle making violins for Rudolph Wurlitzer, and had stepped off the *Morning Mail* at Limestone to walk the seventeen miles to Dover to see the country.

"I'll take you in if you'll help me take down my tobacco," America bargained.

"But ve are tired, now!" laughed the one called Wilhelm.

"How long vill it take?" asked Hans, the soberer fellow.

"Four hours. Then I'll fry you young chickens and old ham for your supper—and send you along tomorrow morning with all the breakfast you can eat."

"Fry us the chickens and ham, now," drawled Hans. "We can pay. And bring us beer—*bitte, schnell!*"

"If you won't work, you see the way to the pike," answered America. "I have no beer, but I can offer you buttermilk—or elderberry wine."

"Save the wine to wash down those chickens," laughed Wilhelm. "Who knows, Hans, ve might find goot ham here—yah?"

"It's better than your Westphalian hams," America urged. "I've eaten both."

"Ho! ho!" they mocked her. "Where's that buttermilk?"

India shawl over her head, America led them out to the ridge barn. They had never handled a tobacco stick before, and both were particular about splinters in their hands until America tossed them Weed's old cotton work-gloves. Sizing up her helpers, America realized she could not hope to take more than a thousand sticks down tonight, in the time for which she had bargained. She dared not stretch up herself, or bend over the bulk to lay the sticks down. Hers were the middle hands that received the stick from Wilhelm on the tier pole and passed it along to Hans at the bulk. The tobacco was of prime quality, weighing perhaps six pounds to the stick, which in itself weighed a pound. To keep the youths' thoughts off the heavy toil, America questioned them about their travels, their impressions of New York City, what they intended to do in Cincinnati. They hoped for employment in the Wurlitzer plant, they said.

"When times get hard, come back and help me raise tobacco," proposed America, almost nauseated with fatigue.

"*Nein,* you vork too hard!" laughed Wilhelm.

"Can you sing?" she challenged them. Song, she realized, would carry her through the next half-hour.

When the barn bent was cleared, she told them where to get fodder and how to place it over and around the rectangle of leaf laid down on hickory tobacco sticks. In the bulk the leaf would continue to "case"—to absorb moisture from the air—until it was pliable enough to strip from the stalk, sort into different types and grades and tie into bundles for market. Tier rails were laid on top of the bulk to hold the fodder down and the job was done until strippers appeared. America turned to pick up baby Fant.

"Give him to me, *meine gute Frau,*" spoke the observant Hans. "You have yet chickens to cook."

In the family room, the youths bathed before her roaring fire, fell across the bed and slept until she called them for supper. Drinking elderberry wine in quantity, they soon made the cabin rafters ring with their songs. Trying not to think how far their lusty young voices carried, America did not spoil their fun. At midnight they staggered to the bed and she let them sleep until the pale December sunlight fell across the breakfast table.

"Ve should pay you, Frau Annable!" Wilhelm called back from the yard gate.

"*Auf Wiedersehen!*" promised Hans.

With leaf in the bulk ready to strip, no strippers appeared. On Christmas Eve, America put baby Fant to bed and went into the cook cabin to read the Nativity story. The sentences seemed barren compared to memories of last year, when her husband had pushed into the cold room to save her and their son. Twice now, Fant Annable had saved her from mortal peril. She sat down in Uncle Simmy's mutilated Sheraton chair to await Fant's arrival. . . .

She awakened cramped with cold. At any moment she might have toppled onto the floor like a bag of meal, she realized. The last thing she could afford now, was a miscarriage. As she tiptoed into the front room, her numb legs buckled and she caught at a chair to keep from falling. Rubbing circulation back into her legs, she saw by the mantel clock that it was after three o'clock. If Fant came before Christmas dawn, he would have to find his wife asleep. . . .

Mrs. Justinian Annable called Christmas afternoon with toys, a handsome beaver topcoat and a matching cap for baby Fant. They tried it on, admired the fit.

"America," Cousin Margaret began in a troubled voice, "I want you to let me take this child back to Timberlawn with me."

"Cousin Maggie!" gasped America, and snatched baby Fant off the older woman's lap.

"Before he would let me have a horse to drive down, Mr. Annable made me promise to ask you," Cousin Margaret continued.

"Oh, now I understand—"

"I would have asked it on my own volition. Foxden is no suitable place in which to rear a child—if you intend to keep on carousing at all hours of the night, America."

"Cousin Maggie, I was afraid you'd hear about that," America hastened to explain, with her direct eyes fixed pleadingly on her kinswoman's face. "Mrs. MacGower sent me two German boys—nice, clean boys. I made a bargain with them—if they'd take down my leaf, I'd give them a good hot supper and a bed for the night. Can't you see I had to bulk down some of my leaf while the season lasted, if I'm to get it stripped in time to pay my taxes next March? The boys wanted beer with their dinner, so I gave them a jug of Mahalee's old elderberry wine. They did sing, I will admit, but that's as far as it went, I assure you. Don't you believe me, ma'am?"

"I don't know what to believe, America. Your lips say one thing, your—your appearance another."

Silence settled between them. Gazing at the green silk velvet of her mother-in-law's skirts, America had a moment of inner rebellion against slaving in rags to protect this rich woman's son. Was Fant's safety worth her own increasing humiliation and exhaustion? More important, how much longer could she wage this losing battle against the community, her neglected fields, starvation itself?

"I had hoped to pay you back the five hundred dollars I owe you out of this year's crop," America's voice hardened with pride. "Cousin Stone offered me only four cents all around for it, stripped. There will be little left after I hire hands to strip it, and pay my taxes."

"You need feel under no obligation ever to repay me," replied Mrs. Annable, coldly.

"But I want to, ma'am!"

"I do not care to take your money."

America felt the color mount her thin cheeks. With hands that trembled, she took from the fretting baby the expensive beaver coat and cap, the cost of which might have gone one-quarter of the way to pay Foxden's taxes, and laid them among the rustling papers of their box.

"America, I have brought you a present," Mrs. Annable began again, in a low voice which she kept steady by a strong effort of will. "It is not the kind of Christmas present I ever thought to bring my daughter-in-law—and you of all persons—but I mean it for your own good. Yet now I—I actually hesitate to give it to you—"

"Until today, you've never given me anything but loving kindness—and unfailing help, Cousin Maggie."

Reaching into her black moire reticule, Mrs. Annable drew out a small ladies' revolver and laid it on the near-by table. A box of cartridges followed. Shocked into immobility, America sat staring at them. Could Margaret Collier Annable be reminding her of the code of the Tidewater—that the wages of sin for an erring gentlewoman must be death by her own hand?

America's whirling thoughts clarified slowly around the one central source of her endurance and strength. She had committed no wrong. As long as sanity was left to her, Professor Joe Dave had told her yesterday on his holiday visit, she must remember this one outstanding fact. And when her strength of mind was spent, she must fall back on her faith. Because she herself was guiltless, she could walk through the valley of the shadow, and fear no evil. The Lord defends His own.

"I brought this weapon—because I'm afraid you won't be safe much longer from the black men—if you continue to carouse with every young tramp off the road," Margaret Annable with difficulty managed to finish what she had come to say.

The silence of irreconcilable hurt, mutually shared, settled between them. Mrs. Annable was the first to break it, in a voice verging on tears:

"One mistake I could forgive! You're young and passionate and lonely. But you brazenly keep on! How you can sit down and write your lady mother, I fail to comprehend!"

"Have you written her about—about what you call my mistakes?" asked America, carefully.

"What do you take me for? You were once my dead son's wife—although you seem to have forgotten it!"

"Thank you for not writing her."

"Now that I've warned you, it will be best for us both if I do not return."

"As you will, ma'am."

Thinking over this conversation Christmas night, America wished she had said nothing about her vital need for help to get her leaf stripped to deliver. She might as well have kept her pride, for all the help Cousin Margaret had offered! In their strained parting, America had forgotten to put the beaver jacket into Mrs. Annable's buggy. If America took it to town, would the Limestone merchant who had sold it to Mrs. Annable give her the money back or credit it for necessities? America decided to keep the useless gift—and her pride.

Her thoughts turned towards her other assets. If she tried to sell her four mules, two heifers, two sows and Sunshine, she could not hope to pitch a crop next spring, or have dairy products and smoked meat to feed hands to work it. Uncle Simmy's valuable curios weren't hers to sell. She had three fine stalks of White Burley seed hanging behind her best dress under lock and key in her clothes press. One she needed for next year's crop; another for the following spring, should the season fail entirely next summer. How could she sell the third when Stone was giving them away to his growers on Tuckahoe? America had turned out fifty of the five-foot plants, but one by one as they ripened, thieves had carried them off in the field. She understood now why some farmers raised their tobacco seed plants in their wives' flower beds!

Through powdery snow the next morning, America trudged out to the ridge barn to take stock of her critical situation. After she had built a roaring fire in the stripping-room stove, she carried a bundle of her bulked tobacco in from the main barn and laid it on the stripping table. Giving a few experimental tugs, she was surprised to see how soon her hand filled with flyings. She resolved to go back to the house, bring baby Fant out here where he would be safe from accident, and see how far she could get towards stripping the crop herself.

On the brisk walk, she recalled the stripping rooms at Golden Hill. Standing all day before a long table facing the even north light necessary to uniform grading, the competent black men and youths had told jokes, spat and chewed, while before them the plants of cured tobacco seemed to move like living things from hand to hand until each set of deft fingers had stripped off its particular grade of leaf. The stalk would then fall graceless onto a mounting pile at the farther end of the house.

America could not recall when she had learned the different grades of Virginia leaf. Surely Kentucky burley couldn't differ much? The papery "flyings" grow closest to the ground. Next to them come the "trash," so-called because with the flyings they were unmarketable. Many growers left these valueless grades unstripped on the stalk, to be thrown out to fertilize potato patches or on ridges where the earth had been galled. More generous masters before the Civil War had rationed them weekly to slaves to smoke in corncobs, share and share alike to men and women.

Growing above the chaffy trash, the "lugs" and "bright leaf," yellow in color, with an oily resilient stretch when pulled, had given Mason County tobacco fame on the New Orleans breaks. This bright leaf was in brisk demand for cigar filler and chewing-plug wrappers, and commanded good prices whereever it was offered. Above the long "bright" grew the heavy "reds," the thick gummy leaf capable of absorbing the maximum amount of licorice, molasses, saccharine and maple sugar which popular taste then demanded in chewing plugs. In the seventies, "cherry-red" grades were bringing the highest price on the stalk, because they, too, were used for plug wrapper. Above the reds are the "tips" and "green," which like the chaffy lower grades, were not considered worth prizing and hauling to market.

As the tobacco plant fell before the first stripper, with his right hand he had jerked off the flyings and tossed the plant along to his neighbor who was stripping trash. Down the table went the plant, losing lugs, bright leaf, red and tips at each handling. Each stripper made two grades of his type, one before him on the table, the other clutched in his left hand. When a bundle of leaves classed for length and color felt comfortably full in his palm, he leveled the stems and tied them tighty together with a matching leaf jerked out from the "hand." The bundle was then set astride a tobacco stick thrust horizontally between table apron and top, so that each stripper stood in a stall-like space between partially filled sticks. As soon as he had fourteen hands on his stick, he announced it full. The foreman then offered him an empty stick, took the stickful of leaf and carried it into the tobacco barn, where he rehung it among its own type already stripped, "to sweat into summer case," when it would be prized down into hogsheads and marketed.

Optimistic by necessity, America placed baby Fant to play with his new toys by the stove, and laid a dozen tobacco plants down the length of the table. First she pulled off the flyings. They did not make a hand, but she laid them together over by the door, and stripped off the trash into another pile. By the time she reached the red, the leaves were almost dried in the warm air of the room. She realized she could not afford such wastage. To strip the dozen plants must have taken her half an hour, and uncounted steps. Five thousand plants to the acre—ten acres added up to fifty thousand plants—fifty thousand plants to strip before March the first!

By midmorning, even America had to admit she could not strip her crop alone. Her eyes were too blurred by exhaustion to grade the different colors of each type of leaf. Her head pounded, her back ached like a dying tooth nerve, her ankles were swelling.

At spirit's ebb, she saw a man and three youths coming up the hill through the frozen tobacco stalks. As she reached for her new revolver, she recognized Old Man Barnes, John Willy and the twins, Elmer and Ollie. Entering, Barnes unwound the burlap sacking about his head and announced he had come to strip out her crop. They had finished their own the previous afternoon, John Willy volunteered, and added that the law he was reading in return for janitor's service and foot-work in Judge May's office could wait another month. Ignoring the tears which were making furrows down America's dusty cheeks, Barnes took command:

"You set over thar by the stove and tie leaves."

While his sons went for armfuls of leaf, Barnes stuck tobacco sticks into stalls, spat onto the cannon stove which answered with a vicious hiss, and declared unexpectedly:

"Seems tuh me you'd do best tuh stop these waggin' tongues

by hintin' who's yer man. Sooner 'r later, the high shuriff's bound tuh ketch him, anyhaow."

"Mr. Barnes!"

"I knowed that wouldn't set easy in yer craw. But Stella 'lowed I'd better say hit—fer yer own good."

"How did you all know?"

"Ain't nobody comes up this holler Stella don't see, iffen he's young an' good-lookin'!" jeered Old Man Barnes. "He didn't show up Christmas, did he?"

America could only stare.

"The shanty-boat man who brought Mr. Fant upriver last year, tied to our dock this morning," explained John Willy, entering from the main barn.

"Will he tell Sheriff McCord?"

"Not even a shanty-boat man ud turn informer!" declared Elmer, the talkative twin, returning with his arms full of tobacco. Dumping it onto the head of the table, he delivered himself of an important message: "Maw says tell you she'd 'a' come up an' tied leaves too, iffen the neighbors wouldn't gab so. They're jawin' their heads off naow, she says. But she'll come 'n' stay when you're lyin' in with your young un."

"Thank you all," America declared, humbly.

"Us pore folks has got tuh stand together," pronounced Elmer, swiping at his runny nose with his coatsleeve while his fingers stripped flyings like a veteran, "because the Quality I've seed ain't got no more notion of pore folks' troubles than a hawg's got religion."

"You're the only friends I've got."

"Yessum, we're the only friends you've got naow," agreed John Willy.

During an early February thaw of '71, America drove her wagon top-heavy with stripped leaf down the stately avenue of Children's Chance. Behind her Elmer Barnes followed on his father's wagon loaded with the rest of the Foxden crop. As they took their places in line with two other loaded wagons,

America felt an inner glow, a sense of abundance, until she sobered to second thought: Here inadequately protected from a fine drizzle of rain stood the result of three entire families' unremitting toil for fourteen months. To the manufacturers who would eventually receive it, the leaf on each wagon meant so many thousand pounds of good or medium or common air-cured burley. To her, as to the other families which had grown these crops, the leaf meant subsistence and the vital balance between debt and getting along, the mortgage foreclosed or education and prosperity.

At his big warehouse in the stable lot Stone Moncure was driving his men to get the waiting loads inside before the threatened rain. When her turn came, Stone gave America a tight-lipped nod and grasped the wagon tongue himself to help run it onto the platform scales. Little was said as the sticks of fine yellow leaf were handed down. Grower and handler wrote the weights of each type onto the back of an envelope, added up totals, subtracted the weight of the empty wagon, computed the net price.

"I get seven hundred and sixty-three dollars and eighty-four cents," declared Stone, looking directly at America for the first time. "How do you figure it?"

"The same way."

He wrote the check, tore it out and handed it to her. Between them lay his pledge never to buy another crop of her leaf. She took the slip of paper, folded and slipped it into the snap purse which she returned to her dress pocket. Now that her first Kentucky crop was sold, she felt curiously let down—a tired woman seven months' along with a nameless child. Stone had sent a hand to the stable for her team. They watched Vach hook in the four young mules, drive the wagon through the west doors and disappear on it around the side of the warehouse. America and Stone walked under rows of stripped leaf hung by type in separate parts of the warehouse. The air was fragrant with a hundred thousand pounds of White Burley in high case. Vach had the wagon waiting outside.

Feeling herself the object of disapproving masculine eyes, America climbed over her front wheel. Stone was chivalrous enough to step to the lead mule's bit, lest the mules try to bolt before she was seated. The master of Children's Chance had not asked her to dry her feet before she started up the pike. Nor did he bid her farewell, as he had done the growers ahead of her, with his cheery: "See you next fall! If you aren't satisfied with your seed, drop around in a few weeks and I'll see what I can do to spare you a teaspoon of mine."

"Good-bye, sir," America hazarded, looking down from the wagon seat at the man who had forsworn kinship with her.

"Good-bye, ma'am," he answered, and raised cold eyes briefly to America's unhappy face.

When she reached Foxden, Old Man Barnes and the taciturn twin, Ollie, had a load of stalks on the sled ready to scatter onto the vegetable garden for fertilizer.

"Only way I kin see you've got a chance tuh raise a crop this spring," commenced Barnes, "is fer me tuh send you a passel of white boys. What niggers ain't honin' tuh run off tuh Dayton, won't work fer you."

"I know," admitted America.

"Up in the mountains, they's plenty of stout lads too biggitty tuh go on workin' fer their paws, but too young tuh rent aout as full-time han's," continued Barnes, his shrewd eyes twinkling. "Fer a piece of money ever' Saturday night—an' the promise of maybe fifty dollars if they stick till you deliver your crop—they'd jump tuh hike their chairs to yer cook-room table—an' roll up in yer quilts at night. O' course, ol' hens ud cackle up an' daown the ridge, but I honestly don't see how else you're goin' to raise a crop."

Fant's failure to appear at Christmas convinced her that she could not look to him for the money necessary to keep the farm, no matter how nearly self-contained. Although Foxden produced its own meat, vegetables and dairy products, and America could trade butter and eggs across Mrs. MacGower's counter for staple groceries and coal oil, cash must be raised to pay taxes and buy shoes, clothes and drugs. Burley was the surest money crop. At Golden Hill, America had tasted the salt of her own sweat, had experienced personally all she cared to learn about women working in the field. To raise ten acres of tobacco without masculine aid lay beyond the powers of an Amazon, much less the slip of a girl she was, with more drive than muscle and to be delivered of her second child at the height of the spring plowing. The care of her two babies would keep her closely confined to Foxden all summer. Why shouldn't she wash, make beds, cook, churn and raise poultry for three or four boys whose combined man power ought to replace that of Weed and Ben Shadrack in the tobacco patch?

"Your plan sounds reasonable to me, Mr. Barnes," she commented, thoughtfully.

"Then I'll slip daown the hill an' tell Stella tuh pass the word araound you'll take four boys. You mustn't caount on the same boys stayin' steady, you understan'. You'll al'ays have four boys, though."

"Whom will I pay the fifty dollars to when I sell the crop?"

"Tuh the one you made the trade with fust this spring."

"It sounds rather indefinite to me. But if you say it'll work—" America gave uncertain consent.

"Hit's the onliest way I know will work," declared Barnes, spitting for emphasis. "You're a prime cook. An' you got the knack of talkin' easy tuh men-folks."

Spring work at Foxden was well along when America gave birth to a girl whom she named Virginia Sue after her mother. While America lay abed, Stella managed the farm in her able but careless way. On the afternoon of her intended departure, Stella volunteered to send her oldest girl up the hill to do the washing and carry pails until America's full strength returned.

"Katie Cath'rine's a willin' worker," promised Stella. "Hit'll do her good tuh see haow nice folks live."

"That's an interesting name," commented America, sitting

up in Uncle Simmy's chair. "How does it happen you gave your girls two names each?"

"I figger two purty names is abaout all a share-cropper's gal has got tuh start life with. You teach Katie Cath'rine haow tuh cook good, you hear? The boys used tuh tell me this spring hit war yer sour-milk-'n'-sody biscuit kept 'em in the grub patch."

"But suppose Katie Cath'rine falls in love with one of them?" America looked ahead.

"That's a main reason I'm a-sendin' her," Stella confessed. "She's ripe. An' I'd rather her fust would be some boy who'll hanker tuh stay with her, instead of one of the ol' buzzards who light on my woodpile."

America considered Stella's phrase. As the seasons marched across the fields, a girl ripened, was plucked without ado from the parental branch by the nearest man who could reach her, and in time herself bore fruit. When America put her mind's eye down to earth as Stella's phrase suggested, the convolutions of romantic courtship such as she had dreamed about on moonlight nights at her open window at Danville Female Seminary, seemed more unseemly than Stella's way of marrying off her good girls by placing them in proximity to clean boys who would be swayed by youthful idealism enough to want to do the right thing by them.

Like cumulus clouds which cast thin shadows, the anxieties of summer passed lightly over Foxden and its maturing crops. White morning mists of late September turned to black frosts. With the corn half shucked, Welburn, America's lead boy, came to her one morning when she had her hands in salt-rising bread dough, and announced his intention to take Katie Catherine home to his folks in Rowan County "while she kin travel easy, withaout no risk tuh aour young un a-comin'."

To deck out this unannounced bride who had bent uncomplainingly over the Foxden washtubs all summer, America bought pretty woolen yardage in Limestone and offered to pay Abigail MacGower to make it up into a coat and dress for

Katie Catherine. Several fittings were achieved in secrecy at the tollhouse, and the happy young couple slipped away. Swinging two baskets of eggs across the counter in first payment for the sewing fee, America was shocked to observe Abigail's left eye poulticed with linseed mash.

"Auld MacGower found out, didn't he?" she whispered.

"Aye," nodded the toll-mistress, reaching down under the counter for one of her own baskets into which to transfer the eggs.

"Mrs. MacGower, I'm so sorry! It's all my fault—I shouldn't have urged you."

"MacGower has his ain dark shed tae hide in. Braw smith though he be, th' mon's nae born can lay me across his knee!" declared Abigail, her sound eye snapping fire like an old eagle's. "Say nae mair aboot it, lass."

"What am I going to do about selling my tobacco?" America changed the subject. "Last year Stone Moncure said he never expected to buy another crop from me."

"Every morning I see him coming up the pike seated sideways in yon fine buggy o' his—those fast black mares steppin' oot in front," agreed Abigail, and spread her practiced claws around five eggs each to start counting them.

"Why doesn't he send some other handler around to look at my tobacco?"

"Stone Moncure's nae that kind o' a Chreestian. Wheesht, noo, while I coont your-r eggs."

"But couldn't you pass the word around I've a prime crop to sell?"

"Nae ither haun'ler wad invade Stone Moncure's hame district—withoot he consents," explained Abigail, making a mark in her book for each ten eggs transferred from America's basket to her own. "Dae ye want me tae cheat ye? Your-r tongue gaes like a wag on th' wa'!"

"Why couldn't I learn to handle my crop myself?" America demanded, with a note of excitement in her persuasive Virginia voice. "Mr. Barnes said he'd show me how to prize it down into hogsheads. Aren't the Cincinnati tobacco auctions free? Couldn't I take my hogsheads downriver and sell them myself next June?"

"Are ye daft?" exclaimed Abigail, losing her egg count completely. "No woman e'er spent half a day on a Cincinnati warehouse floor—an' kep' her guid name!"

America smiled.

"Wist, gir-rl, ye see? Ye'll al'ays be ma bonnie guid lass."

"Thank you, ma'am. What would I need to leaf and prize my crop?"

"A prizing screw—a fair set o' scales—an' a dozen poplar hogsheads," Mrs. MacGower declared, laying her work-gnarled hands on top of America's second basketful of eggs.

"Where would I get them?"

"Wi' times sae dour, mony's th' tobacco speculator wull gae broke come summer. Watch th' *Limestone Eagle* tae see their bankruptcy sales. MacGower gaes tae them a'—he wull bid in scales an' screw for ye."

"I don't see what makes you think that," commented America, looking at Mrs. MacGower's battered face.

"Whit brocht him tae his knees was whin I asked did he aim tae starve y'r innocent bairns tae mak' a public spectacle o' ye," declared the toll-mistress. "While he thocht that ower, I clipped him a clout on the lug he'll nae forget."

On a mild May night of '71, with the moonlight bright beyond the wide-flung doors of the ridge barn and slanting in through open shutters, America and her helpers took down her second crop of leaf and bulked it under fodder, to keep it clean and moist. The stripped tobacco was well into "the sweat," the fermentation or chemical change which brought it into sweet case in readiness for prizing down into hogsheads.

"Not one planter in a dozen can sweet case tobacco properly," America had often heard her grandfather declare at Golden Hill. "They let it get too high after it starts into the sweat. So when they take it down and pile it into the bulk, of course it rots—funks, the buyers call it. Once leaf begins to case, the process goes right on in the bulk."

The next morning, Old Man Barnes appeared at the ridge barn to show America how to leaf and prize burley tobacco. America had a table placed near the open doors. While she and Ollie stood by to watch—her other hands were weeding plant beds—Barnes made a first and second choice by hands of each stickful of tobacco Elmer laid before him on the table. When he had thus graded a considerable amount, Barnes told Elmer to climb into the nearest of two hogsheads. Father handed son the graded leaf, with instructions how to place it inside the hogshead. When four layers had been laid down, Elmer climbed out. Barnes and America then turned the one-ton circular prizing screw onto the leaf tight enough to press but not to bruise it. Auld MacGower had bought the equipment and installed the prizing-screw on the one condition he need not look at the lass he "had loved like ma ain girl-l, but wha has shamed us a'. I canna ca' mysel' a Chreestian tae starve her bairns, or ha'e that screw fa' doon on guid lads wur-rkin' for a start in life."

While one hogshead was being pressed, Barnes and Elmer continued to sort and pack another. When each was filled and prized to weigh exactly a thousand pounds, the head was fitted and nailed onto it. The type of leaf and America's stencil of ownership were painted conspicuously onto the hogshead's sides and it was rolled aside to await shipment.

While his experienced fingers leafed automatically, Barnes impressed on America that her future success as a handler would depend on her absolute accuracy of eye and hand while she was packing tobacco. The keystone of the hogshead trade lay in the uniformity of the entire thousand pounds of leaf in each hogshead with the samples which buyers would pull from its outside edge on the Cincinnati auctions. A favorite trick of the prizing trade was "nesting," in which dishonest handlers filled the center of a hogshead with leaf inferior to that packed around its edges. Another sharp practice was to tuck pebbles into the tie leaves of each hand to give false weight. No handler ever prospered by such methods, explained Barnes, because the manufacturers discovered the hoax when the hogshead was unpacked at the factory, and levied reclamation fees back through the warehouse against the dishonest packer.

"Wuss'n that, the buyers 'll jest walk araound yer hawgshead in the sales line," declared Ollie.

"In all the y'ars he's been a-handlin' aour terbacker, paw ain't niver yit had tuh pay a single reclamation fee, have you, paw?" boasted Elmer.

"I hope I can say as much twenty years from now," America answered, and beckoned to Ollie to lay a stick of stripped leaf on the table before her.

America's first eleven hogsheads of prized leaf went downstream with a thousand eastern Kentucky hogs squealing in pens around them on the *Bonanza*'s freight deck. Because of the stench which arose from the swine, America could not stay long at the rail on the passenger deck above to watch Limestone drop astern. Could it be only three years ago she had stood in this lavender evening light to watch for a hunted dark head to bob up on the river's swelling breast?

In the ladies' cabin, America found the hog drovers almost as offensive as their charges. These twenty men and boys had been on the turnpike with their accumulating drove of hogs for a fortnight. With but one more push between them and Cincinnati's packing houses, where half a million swine were slaughtered yearly, the mountain men were smelly, dirty, limber tired, and silly drunk after sleeping on the roadside. America had hoped to avoid the extravagance of a stateroom, but found herself the object of bold glances and barnyard jokes. Had she been accosted in like manner on her first packet ride in '66, America couldn't have closed her eyes all night. Locking her stateroom door, she laughed to remember Fant's challenge to come out to Kentucky and learn to live. In four short years she had taught school, eloped, been a fugitive as she thought from justice, toiled in a city laundry, inherited the management of a fine farm, been outlawed from church and the society of her peers, borne two children without medical attention and was now on her way to match her wits against those of shrewd professional buyers on the Cincinnati hogshead market.

Being Tuckahoe's scarlet woman had one advantage, she told herself as she laid her twenty-cent peanut straw with lime-green ribbons in the empty upper berth and unbuttoned her white dotted Swiss. On her rare public appearances, she no longer felt obliged to don the weeds of a widowed lady and wrap herself in a flowing black veil stuffy as a shroud. Except for her wedding ring and topaz brooch, she was dressed as might have been any simple country girl going to the city to locate work as a domestic. Years ago she had ceased to notice in her mirror the beauty of contour and coloring which now made observant men pause in the street to look twice at her heart-shaped face.

The stewardess called her at five o'clock the next morning. America ate her box breakfast on the *Bonanza*'s windward deck and watched the smokestacks and warehouses of Porkopolis, until recently the nation's largest inland city, loom out of the morning haze. In Cincinnati in summer there never seemed enough air astir at night to cool the cobblestones and brick buildings before the afternoon sun pelted them again with heat rays from the brassy western sky. After the *Bonanza* was made fast to her dock, the hogs took their own gait down the gangplank, across the wharf and up the grade. By the time they reached their slaughter pens, every hurrying citizen whose path they had blocked wished them already dead.

While decks and wharf were being hosed down, America picked her way ashore, and engaged draymen to haul her hogsheads the two blocks to the Growers warehouse. Her heart pounding, she hustled upstreet after her last cylinder of leaf. In Richmond, only the wrong kind of women occasionally tried to intrude themselves on the leaf markets, and usually received short shrift there. Yet if a woman is compelled by economic necessity to grow tobacco, why should she leave its sale to a middleman? She had never been one to let an outsider skim the cream off the full crock she had herself milked from her own heifer! Leaf handlers put too high a valuation on their services—particular work, to be sure, but easy by comparison to the drudgery of the tobacco patch. If by her sober conduct on the hogshead breaks today she could pioneer as a lady handler, she felt that her economic future was secured.

In the office of the Growers Sales and Warehouse Company, clerks were donning green eye-shades and black alpaca sleeve protectors after doffing celluloid cuffs. America knew that to get her leaf on today's sale, her hogsheads must be rolled into the auction line before ten o'clock. Losing patience, she challenged the nearest clerk:

"You, there! Stop your primping and come wait on me. I'd like to speak to the president, please."

"Ain't you heard he lives in the White House, miss?" drawled the clerk, with a wink at his fellow workers.

"Whom do I see about a consignment of leaf?" she asked an older man unlocking the drawers of the cashier's booth.

"I'm sorry, miss, but our house rules bar ladies from the auction floor. Where's your leaf?" he added, as an afterthought.

Exasperated, America turned away. Ahead were double swinging doors marked: TO THE SALES.

"Wait a minute, miss—you can't go in there!" the cashier called after her.

America found herself on the reverberating auction floor. The huge cool warehouse, fragrant with a fifty-year procession of sweet-cased leaf, was single-storied. Row after row of skylights honeycombed the whitewashed roof, and shed a diffused brilliance over thousands of hogsheads. Most of them stood cheek by jowl around the sides of the building. In the cleared center, where the light fell most evenly, a row of hogsheads had been spaced under overhead tracks along which ran hoisting gear to lift the container off the leaf. This was the sales line, America knew. Sight of the clean poplar hogsheads, which appeared to waddle down the long spaces like fat soldiers, the squeal of handtruck wheels under their load as hogsheads were being trundled into place, the good-natured profanity of the floor boss as he harried his men, and the pungent blend of new wood and aging leaf, awakened in America a tingling delight. Now she knew what her grandfather had meant when he said: "Speculating in tobacco—once it gets into a man's blood—goes to his head like strong drink."

On the right side of the warehouse was the receiving deck and driveway. There America recognized her draymen lined up awaiting her appearance. Any minute the cashier might come after her, she realized. Dodging like a white mouse down a lane of hogsheads, she reached the receiving deck and confronted an Irish giant, who demanded:

"Is this yer husband's shipment, ma'am? Whin's he showin' up?"

"I'm consigning this leaf, sir."

"Sorry, lady, but house rules—"

"The hogsheads are here, now," America answered with confidence. "While I pay off these teamsters, I'd appreciate it if you'll get my leaf onto today's sales. I want to go home this afternoon."

"Home's the place for yez, all right!" agreed the foreman. "Where's yer weigh bill?"

"My what?"

"Yer weigh bill. I can't wheel your hogsheads into line without a weigh bill."

"Those young men in the front office were too busy admiring themselves to give me one," America tried to look appealing. "Can't you help me out—with the time so short, Mr.—er—"

"Terry's me name, ma'am."

"Thank you, Mr. Terry. I'm a widow—with two babies waiting for me at home on Tuckahoe Ridge in Mason County, Kentucky."

"Tuckahoe is it ye're from, ma'am?" marveled the Irishman, raising his black eyebrows. "Now don't try to tell me this is some o' that fine White Burley ye've grown all by yerself?"

"Yes—and prized it, too."

"Go wan!"

"This is my box of samples, Mr. Terry," America tried to talk down the mounting derision in the foreman's voice. "Open it for me at once, please."

"Ye'll hev to see Mr. Meiers, ma'am."

"Where is he?"

"In the social room—jollyin' the buyers."

"Where is that?"

"The second door over yander."

"While I speak to him, you get my hogsheads into the line!" America called back in the tone which made even old Mahalee jump. "This is a public sales floor—and if I miss the market today, I'll hold you responsible."

Composing herself, America approached the door Terry had indicated and opened it, to confront perhaps fifty pairs of startled masculine eyes. About thirty of the men were buyers, who in dress and manner resembled the church officers they were on Sunday mornings. Each had inherited or built up a prosperous plug or snuff or cheroot business with its own brands, factory and retail outlets usually as far distant from Cincinnati as delivery wagons could trot in a week. The rest of the buyers were salaried agents of million-dollar companies like Leonard & Morley of St. Louis, Pierre de Longpré of New Jersey and the Holt Snuff Works of Louisville. Promoted from former jobs as salesmen, some of them still affected the flamboyant clothes, loud voices, flashy jewelry and livery stable humor which "commercial tourists" as a class seemed to feel they must sport to attract attention and secure orders. America's quick eye noted a clean-shaven Englishman, doubtless buying for Ogden's of Liverpool. The rest of the group seemed to be young men-about-town gathered to catch the opening leaf prices, as they might stand around outside the Stock Exchange or loll in a central enginehouse to hear local news or the latest water-closet joke.

"Well, miss!" a blustering voice challenged America. "You seem to have wandered into the wrong door. This is a tobacco auction."

America saw bearing down on her a short fat man in his early sixties. His florid color and the pretentiousness of his jewelry revealed a lingering appetite for the good things of life.

"Are you Mr. Meiers?" America began, earnestly, "I've consigned eleven hogsheads of tobacco here, but your clerks won't answer my civil questions. And your foreman wants a weigh bill before he'll have my hogsheads wheeled onto the floor."

"Dearie, d'you know the difference between trash and a lug?" interrupted a bored young dandy in riding clothes seated on the table swinging a glossy leg.

"Nothing trashy here, eh, boys?" declared his companion, ogling America.

"Now, if you'd said 'hug,' Tom—" a third continued the jest.

"Young gentlemen, where are your manners?" demanded an important little man, emerging from a group by the side board. Like the Englishman, he was dressed in immaculate China silk and wore a Jamaica straw hat. Even his cane, an ebony-mounted narwhal tusk, matched his ivory-colored summer suit. He must be the dean of the buyers, America decided, from the respectful manner in which the younger men made way for him.

"Mr. Meiers, we're losing precious time," she took advantage of the ensuing silence. "I've come from Tuckahoe and I must get my crop on today's market, so I can catch the afternoon boat home."

"If you're from Tuckahoe, why ain't Stone Moncure handling your leaf?" demanded Meiers, who mistook truculence for executive ability.

"We—we couldn't trade, sir."

"Who did handle it, miss?" spoke up the pink-cheeked Englishman.

"I did, sir—with expert instruction from an old tobacco hand," America answered.

Frowning at America in a fatherly manner, the dean of the buyers took charge:

"I think, my dear, you'd best run along home and leave men's work to men. To handle tobacco takes years of practice—and recognized integrity. By prizing your own crop, you may hope to pick up a few more pennies for yourself. But, I assure you, ma'am, it won't pay you in the long run. This is a business house," he continued, emphasizing his points by thumps of his narwhal tusk on the floor, "governed by rules we've adopted for the good of all concerned, manufacturers, growers, handlers and warehousemen alike. All of us have a mutual stake in its success. The majority of us are sober family men who've elected me their spokesman. We can't have venturesome country girls coming in here to make eyes at our young buyers—"

"Sir, I assure you—"

"No offense meant, my girl! We all make mistakes. The quickest way you can prove your intentions were good, that you simply wandered into the wrong pew—"

"Ha! ha!" laughed the booted dandy called Tom.

"Mind your manners, Tom Gary—or I'll bar you off this floor."

"Excuse me, Mr. Piper."

"As I was saying," continued Piper, raising his cane to emphasize his next point, "all you have to do now is wait outside in the office till Stone Moncure arrives. He'll take your crop off the floor, allowing you for your labor and boat-fare, and see you safely down to the wharf."

"Say, fellows, I just heard a good one on Mason County," Tom Gary interposed. "A crowd of us fellows were talking last night to the Cincinnati chief of police. He said whenever a new gambler or chippie shows up in town, he can find out their names just by asking who left Limestone the night before."

"Tom, what's turned you so sudden against the pasture where you were dropped?" challenged a hearty voice near the window.

In the laughter which followed, America saw a fat man in his thirties push closer. Dragging one foot, he supported himself on a gold-headed cane. From his drooping walrus mustaches and the flamboyance of his clothes, he appeared to be a follower of the nationally admired Jim Fisk.

"What d'you mean by that, Morris?" bristled the dandy, dismounting from the table.

"No offense, my boy. Everybody knows your granddad made the fortune you're running through in record time out of a brothel-saloon—beg your pardon, ma'am—on Limestone's Front Street and the upriver whiskey trade," Morris announced urbanely, before turning to introduce himself to America. "My name's Morris—Henry Morris, from Portsmouth, Ohio. I roll cheroots—*Ohio Belle*'s my brand. Now, if you'll permit me to escort you to some spot more fittin' for a lady—"

"If you weren't a cripple, I'd demand satisfaction, Morris!" blustered Tom Gary.

"What have I said that ain't the gospel truth?" Morris pretended surprise. "You must have a hangover, son. Kelly, can't you give our young friend here a hair of the dog that nipped him?" Morris called to the dapper Irishman who stood at the sideboard.

"Thank you, Mr. Morris," America disengaged her arm from her champion's moist grip. "Unfortunately, as a widow I find my own and my children's livelihood depends on my remaining here. Mr. Meiers, this is a public auction floor. By your permit you are required to let any person in good faith offer tobacco here for sale."

"Of course you may offer it, ma'am!" agreed Mr. Meiers,

with mock deference. "You may offer it from now till doomsday, eh, Piper?"

"Boys, there's the bell!" declared Kelly, the house auctioneer, and left the social room.

To secure choice places around Kelly in the sales line, the buyers flocked after him. Slower because of his foot, Morris reached the door and then remembered he had offered to help America. Eyeing her uncertainly, he found himself hoping that she wasn't going to ask him to "pin-hook" her leaf, to buy it at the curb sight unseen. Last week he had been caught by a sweet-faced front for a nested crop. But this woman looked different, really fine, all silk and a yard wide.

"I reckon I could pin-hook your crop," he was surprised to hear himself offer.

"You wouldn't know what you're buying," America answered him, soberly. "And, besides, Mr. Piper might say that had been my object all along."

"You don't talk like a country girl, ma'am," Morris breathed his relief.

"I'm a Virginian. Maybe that's why I understand tobacco culture so well. Kentuckians brought it down the Ohio with them from Virginia, you know. But hadn't you better go now, Mr. Morris? The sale's started."

"When you make up your mind what you want to do, send a boy, and I'll come help you," Morris called back.

Outside on the warehouse floor the farm bell had ceased to toll. This bell was a relic of the days when its summons had been needed to call general commission men from their offices out onto the New Orleans wharves when hogsheads of Kentucky leaf were to be offered at public auction. America followed Morris' retreating back across the floor. Kelly's singsong, as he cried the day's first hogshead, came to her from the far end of the line. Looking for her own stencil, America was relieved to see her hogsheads sitting where Terry to play safe had trundled them into the line. The thought of waiting in defeat on the office bench under the eyes of pimply-faced clerks until Stone Moncure came reluctantly to her rescue, seemed unendurable. At her wits' end, America sat down on her type case to think what to do next.

Down the sales line she heard the rattle of block and tackle, saw an empty container rise off its cylinder of leaf, heard Kelly's sales chant end in a staccato: "Sold to Mr. Piper for Leonard & Morley!" While the hogshead was dropped down over the purchased leaf, the sales line moved one unit closer to her crop. America knew she ought to be thinking up something more clever than merely to sit here like patience on a monument. What else could she do but wait and hope that at the last minute Mr. Piper might relent? The buyers were within half a dozen hogsheads of America's first offering when she heard the office doors swing behind her.

"Oh, Moncure! Here's a lady waitin' for you," called someone from the sales line.

Glancing across her shoulder, America met Stone's startled gaze. The comfortable white linens he wore contrasted sharply with his weather-beaten skin and blue eyes.

"Yep, Stone. Here's a ewe lamb strayed from your fold," declared Meiers, with a belated effort at fatherliness. "Buy her leaf, man—and let her go home where she belongs."

Stone looked at America, wet his lips and answered carefully:

"Mrs. Annable and I can't trade."

"You can't trade—God A'mighty, Moncure—if you didn't want her leaf, why couldn't you have sent another handler to look at it?" burst out Henry Morris.

"I have no reason to believe she needs any help from me, Henry."

"But, Stone! She says she's a widow woman—with babies to feed—"

"That's true," agreed the Tuckahoe handler and walked towards the sales group, "but don't let me keep you gentlemen from picking up some good White Burley. It's my seed—that much I will claim."

"I say, you know, it may be funked—or nested," the British buyer took fright.

"You'll pull it, won't you, Mr. Hill?" Stone refuted the first objection in a reasonable voice. "As for nesting, I don't think you need be afraid of that. These hogsheads were packed under the direction of a competent handler."

"Who?" demanded Henry Morris.

"Old Jim Barnes."

"Old Jim Barnes! So she's one of that crowd, eh, Moncure?" exclaimed Tom Gary. "What a fool that makes you out, Henry! Next time you will play Lancelot, you'd best find out what kind of a Guinevere you're defending."

"Is this a tobacco auction—or a literary sewing-circle?" demanded Piper, severely. "Stone, I don't see any of your hogsheads. I came down myself this morning because I heard you were putting some of that Tuckahoe leaf of yours on the floor."

"I'm sorry, gentlemen," Stone washed his hands of this whole troublesome business. "I'm catching the noon boat upriver. Good-day, all."

In surprised silence, the buyers watched his stocky figure walk across the floor and disappear through the swinging office doors.

"Go on with the sale, Meiers," snapped Piper

Hogshead by hogshead, they approached America's offerings. She had been watching the big warehouse clock. They should be able to dispose of five or six of her hogsheads before noon, she judged by the amount of time it had previously taken them to buy one unit of leaf. The crowd of buyers, clerks and laden sample boys began to swarm around her first hogshead. Hatchet and chisel in hand, Terry approached and stood watching Meiers' face for the nod which would start him knocking in the container's head.

"Well, gentlemen," declared Mr. Piper, giving the floor a vigorous thump with his tusk. "I'm going to dinner. See you tomorrow morning."

"Sale's adjourned," declared Meiers.

Stunned by such discrimination, America kept her seat on the type case until most of the men had left the floor. She then hurried to the receiving deck, looked hastily around to make sure she wasn't observed, and jumped down into the driveway. Peering around its opened front door, she saw Tom Gary and a friend on the street waiting probably for her to emerge from the office door. When she turned into the driveway, Henry Morris was stepping out of the cab he had instructed to pull up at the rear.

"Lady-bird, get in!" he invited, expansively. "Driver—the new Grand Hotel."

She accepted his assistance onto the musty cushions. To refuse to have luncheon with him was provincial, she felt. Moreover, she was hungry. In her purse she had less than three dollars and her return ticket to Limestone. After he had ordered and eaten with a gourmet's relish, Morris pushed back from the snowy linen and beamed on her.

"Now, dearie, tell me about yourself," he ordered. "What're your plans?"

"Before my husband was killed, I used to work here in the hotel laundry. They sent me to a boarding house kept by a Mrs. O'Flarity down on the river. I'll go spend the night with her."

Such frankness startled him, she could see. He looked hastily around in hope the waiter hadn't heard. He had apparently been expecting her to say she was Mrs. Astor, in disguise.

"As for my tobacco," she continued, "I don't see anything to do but wait here till they buy it."

"Don't hold your breath, ma'am! Piper's blackballed that crop sure as shootin'. Didn't I hear you say something about young uns waitin' for you out on Tuckahoe? Take my advice and when you get home, ask Stone Moncure to help you out."

"I'll work downstairs in the laundry first!"

Across the table, his eyes were fixed on her mouth. Behind his good-natured face she could see his mind work. He was quite evidently looking for romantic adventure; yet he no doubt dreaded involvement with anyone who might load him with family responsibilities. Probably he had a wife and children of his own up at Portsmouth. *Eh bien,* he had been kind to her, and rescued her from Tom Gary, had bought her a good dinner. Laying her napkin aside, she smiled at him across the crystal and silver condiment stand, and said:

"It's been a long time since I've enjoyed such a delicious meal, Mr. Morris. My husband liked good living. He used to take me to places like this."

"Don't mention it, Mrs. Anderson."

"My name is Annable, Mrs. Fant Annable."

"Not the river-boat gambler who shot—who was—"

"Yes. The river-boat gambler who was caught astern three years ago by the *Evening Mail.*"

"Well, well, if it ain't a small world!" beamed Morris, looking as pleased as if she were the President's wife sitting opposite him. "To think you're Mrs. Fant Annable—and me talking to you just like you was ordinary folks. When I was sewing my own wild oats, I used to think Fant Annable was just about all a man oughta be. Handsomest feller I ever saw, bar none! Being here with you like this only goes to show I ain't lost my eye, don't it? I can still pick the winners. Waiter, bring my check," he called. When his change came, he heaved himself up, gained his balance with the aid of cane and chair and ended what in spite of his words and expression he must have inwardly considered a compromising acquaintanceship: "I've just time to catch the boat for Portsmouth, but Kelly 'll keep me posted on what happens to your crop. If it don't sell right soon, maybe I can help you out," he strove visibly to be gallant. "And now, can't I drop you off at that boarding house on my way down to the wharf?"

On arrival at this shabby establishment, America saw that nothing there had changed for the better. Mrs. O'Flarity apparently did not believe America when she said she had a thousand dollars' worth of prized leaf on the Growers floor to sell the first thing tomorrow morning. Yes, she had a vacancy, the second floor front which would be eight dollars a week—in advance. No, she couldn't afford to accept three dollars on account, especially when America had practically no luggage. To accommodate a former guest, however, she would take that topaz brooch as security for the other five dollars. America wearily unpinned and dropped it into Mrs. O'Flarity's calloused palm.

For four days through record heat America sat forlornly at the head of her unwanted crop which now stood by itself in the middle of the warehouse floor. The sales line had been moved to stand under another hoisting track. If she abandoned the auction now, America realized she would never again be admitted to any sales floor. Word as to her identity had passed among clerks and sample boys. "She's the widow of Fant Annable—you remember him?" she heard them whisper. She must be the laughingstock of the Cincinnati breaks, to judge from the number of men who came to stare at her. Even to the well intentioned, she had nothing to say. She laundered her dotted Swiss at night and in Mrs. O'Flarity's best bed lay awake to wonder how soon she might be living with her babies in a garret room again, another city slave chained for life to her washtubs in this grimy sprawl of packing houses, iron mills and wagon shops. For without cash in hand on March first, Foxden would in time go under the sheriff's hammer to the highest bidder on the Limestone courthouse steps.

The warehouse, America knew, closed Friday afternoon till Monday morning. When the buyers had gone, Meiers himself came waddling down a lane of hogsheads to speak to her:

"I'll pin-hook your crop—to get you off my floor!" he wheezed, desperately.

"That wouldn't help me next year," she answered in her courteous Virginia voice. "To keep my farm I must raise tobacco every year—and sell it."

"Lord deliver me from a stubborn female!"

The following Monday morning, America arose early and left the boarding house before breakfast to avoid seeing Mrs.

O'Flarity, who might ask her for another week's rent in advance. As sales did not start before ten o'clock, she walked down to the wharf in search of a breeze. Here where on Sundays she used to sit to watch the Kentucky hills, she found an empty bench in the shelter built for passengers awaiting packets. What, she asked herself despondently, was the use of hoping there would ever be any real security for her in this world of reverses? Here she sat worse off now than before, because now she had two babies to feed. How was Stella getting along with them at Foxden, she worried. Virginia Sue was subject to colic; and before he went to sleep, young Fant liked to have his small back rubbed. She had been teaching him to lisp "I'm a wee, wee sweet thing," as his father had done before him. By now he'd probably forgotten it.

Like a fat swan, the *Bonanza* came 'round the bend upstream, whistled elegantly and in a surprisingly short time bumped the dock on which America sat. If she carried another consignment of hogs, America would have to move across the blazing-hot wharf in search of other shade. No porkers came crowding down the gangplank, however, and she turned her eyes away to rest them from the glitter of morning sunshine on the *Bonanza*'s new coat of white paint.

"Well, well, if you ain't the veree little lady we're a-lookin' for!" boomed a familiar voice behind her. "Mrs. Annable, let me present you to Mr. Dinwiddie, ma'am—U. S. Marshal Dinwiddie, of the Federal District Court."

She blinked up into Henry Morris' jovial face. Beside him stood a keen-eyed man with a look of action about him. America's first thought was for Fant, whose waking hours must be spent dodging these lean runners of the law. She felt her throat tighten, tried to speak naturally through dry lips:

"If you're after my husband, sir, he's been dead for years—"

"Priss the Piper is the man we're gunning for today, ma'am," chuckled Morris. "Sure you've got the papers in order, marshal? 'Cause if you ain't—and there's any slip-up to this, I'll never live it down."

"I've got the papers all right," smiled Dinwiddie. "This is the easiest part of my job."

"But I don't understand—" began America.

"We'll explain on the way to the breaks," declared Morris, and gayly took her arm. "Seein's how I want to go on buying leaf, it might be wiser if I don't appear, eh, Dinwiddie? If he finds out I've had a finger in this, Priss the Piper might bid every hogshead I try to buy clean out of my reach—until he breaks me. I'll just go on into the social room and lay low for the time being."

As she crossed the Growers floor with the U.S. marshal at her side, America was relieved to see that her hogsheads had not been removed. Dinwiddie touched the clerks and sample boys on the shoulder and they fell back, opening a way to the circle of buyers grouped around Kelly. America had time to return the polite nod of the British buyer, to observe that Stone was still sulking at home in his tent, before Dinwiddie began pleasantly:

"Sorry to stop your sale, gentlemen. Which of you is John Augustus Meiers?"

"I am, sir."

"I've a paper to serve on you, Mr. Meiers. It's from Judge Anderson, of the Federal District Court, on complaint of one America Moncure Annable, Trustee for Fant Annable, Jr., infant-in-arms," the marshal continued, producing the order and consulting it. "Complainant—this lady here—demands to know why you shouldn't have your license revoked for refusing to have her tobacco cried at public sale on your floor, Mr. Meiers. The market's falling, she complains, and you're detaining her here in Cincinnati when she's needed at home—by said infant-in-arms."

"Hell 'n' blazes—" began Meiers, and swallowed.

"Damned if she ain't out-foxed you, Piper," laughed Tom Gary. "Ho! ho! ho!"

"Jove, but this is ripping—good as a play, y'know," chuckled Hill, the buyer for Ogdens.

"How about it, Meiers?" Dinwiddie continued, thrusting the court order into the warehouseman's hand. Turning to the buyers, he volunteered an opinion in the easy confidence of men who serve the federal government and therefore need not worry themselves about putting their foot into a local squabble: "Seems to me the easiest way out of this would be for some of you men to buy this lady's leaf—"

"I'll bid on it!" Morris raised his hearty voice from the rear.

"Count me in," grinned the Englishman.

"How about it, Mr. Meiers?" Dinwiddie's voice was impersonal.

"Kelly, cry her crop," the warehouseman surrendered.

"Mr. Meiers, I'm surprised at you," began Piper, his face crimson.

"Come, come, sir! Surely you don't expect me to lose my permit—and maybe go to jail—just to enforce a bunch of house rules you fellows have made?" Meiers tried to reason with the important Leonard & Morley buyer. "I'm here to sell hogshead tobacco, Mr. Piper—I ain't looking for any trouble from anybody."

After an outraged glance at America, and a vicious jab at the nearest basket of leaf with his narwhal tusk, Piper strode off the floor. Nobody dared laugh until the office doors had swung behind his self-important back. A babel then burst out as everyone surged after Kelly, who was striding towards America's hogsheads. America felt herself steadied by someone's arm.

"Let me help you up on this sample case," suggested Dinwiddie.

From this height, America could see the ring of laughing men make way to admit Terry with two of his men. At a nod from Kelly, the foreman knocked off the hoops while a helper came pulling on the overhead track the block-and-tackle which held the grappling hooks.

"Up she goes, Terry," the auctioneer gave the word.

Terry struck the hook points into America's hogshead,

tightened them into a firm hold and nodded to his men to raise the container off the leaf.

"Here she stands, men—sweet as a nut and twice as tasty!" cried Kelly, as the hogshead rose slowly and the mellow fragrance of the leaf pervaded the air. "How much am I bid for this sound hogshead of prime burley tobacco? It's your favorite type, Mr. Hill—cherry-red. It's chewing plug like this—an' good Jamaica rum—that's made Britannia rule the waves! Where shall we break it for ye, sir?"

The custom of "breaking" the leaf, so the buyers might pull out sample hands to examine, was as old as the hogshead auctions. More than a hundred years ago in New Orleans, it had given the levee warehouses of the Old City their distinctive name of "tobacco breaks." When the tobacco trade moved upstream to Louisville and Cincinnati, custom and name followed.

"Here—and here," the Englishman touched with his walking stick the smooth cylinder of tobacco left standing on the floor.

Terry struck expertly into the cylinder with his prizing iron. His helpers, seizing the other end of the bar, threw their powerful backs into the considerable task of parting and lifting the top of the cylinder long enough for the buyers to pull out a hand or two of the leaf. Easing the tobacco down again, they "broke" it in the second place Hill had indicated.

"Taste it! Smell it! Stretch it!" Kelly settled to the serious business of selling the hogshead. "There it is, the genooine kid-glove finish! What am I bid, gentlemen, what am I bid?"

"House starts it at twelve cents!" cried Meiers, who now felt called upon to show his good sportsmanship.

"Thankee, sir. Twelve cents—re, re, re—twelve cents—"

"Twelve and a-half!" shouted Morris.

"Thankee, Henry. Twelve an' a-half cents—re, re, re—thirteen cents? Mr. Akin. Thirteen cents—re, re, re," chanted Kelly, filling the pauses with his singsong and swallowing when he could postpone the function no longer. His eyes darted from one buyer's face to another, as he continued: "Thirteen an' a-half cents—fourteen cents? Thankee, Mr. Hill. Look at this good red leaf, gentlemen—sweet as sugar, and ready to jump right into the plug. Are you going to let Ogden's have it for fourteen cents? Mr. Akin"—Kelly addressed the senior buyer for the powerful New Jersey company—"P'erre Longpré can use good red burley like this. Fourteen cents, gentlemen—re, re, re—fourteen an' a-half! Do I hear fifteen cents, Mr. Chris? Fifteen cents, men, I've got fifteen and a-half cents— Do I hear sixteen? Sixteen an' a-half, Mr. Akin! Seventeen, Mr. Hill! Are you all finished, gentlemen? Seventeen cents—sold to Mr. Hill, of Ogden's, for seventeen cents! Step this way, gentlemen!" He moved quickly forward to the next hogshead, continuing in the same breath: "And now, who wants to break this fine hogshead"—his eye caught the stencil—"of bright leaf?"

As the group moved to the next sale, Hill's clerk and the house bookkeeper jotted in their ledgers vital information about the hogshead which had just been sold. Hill's sample boy bundled with wire the hands of leaf the buyers had pulled, and tossed them onto the replaced container top for anyone interested to examine before they were carried away on Mr. Hill's leaving the floor.

"Sounds to me like you got a right good sale, ma'am," Dinwiddie smiled at America from the hogshead on which he stood. "Here's Morris, so I'll be going, now."

Several of the buyers, among them Hill, came over to ask her if she was satisfied with her sale. Beaming with pride, Morris stood at her elbow and winked at such colleagues as were known not to be in Piper's camp.

"Cheerio!" grinned the British buyer. "See you next year."

In the office, where the staff was affability itself, Morris guided America through the details of floor charges and reclamation deposits. In a hack, with a twelve-hundred-dollar check and sixty-five dollars in cash in her purse, America turned to thank her benefactor. Morris asked rather pleadingly if he might not be of further service to her before she left Cincinnati. Reluctant to hurt his feelings, she looked down at her work-roughened hands. His eyes on her mouth, which was both invitation and warning, he seemed on the point of taking her in his arms. Something in her quiet face must have checked him.

"Believe me, I'm grateful to you, Henry!" she declared, her eyes bright with emotion. "I'll send you a check for your court costs and expenses. Will you try to understand—if I go right home now? I've just time to pick up my things at Mrs. O'Flarity's and catch the noon boat for Limestone."

Chapter 12

"A politician in coming forward," Tugger Blake once heard Boss Tweed remark, "takes things as they are."

As hard times and the Tweed Ring took New York in what seemed an ever tightening grip, Tugger sensed the hardening pulse of popular revolt, the quickening public demand for honest reform. Sleeping cheek by jowl with politicians at Josie's, Tugger knew how rotten city government was. Through his Wall Street pad-shoving, he had learned that nothing mattered with America's financial overlords except to win. Disgusted by flamboyance, sick to nausea with vice, Tugger sat down one morning in Smith, Gould & Martin's, and wrote three letters.

The first was to Palestine. In it Tugger told her that he loved her and hoped soon to have enough money to propose marriage. He was working, and getting along as well as could be expected, considering how hard the times were everywhere. He had been in New York long enough now to recognize Mrs. William Backhouse Astor driving around Washington Square in her carriage. She couldn't hold a candle to Palestine for looks or bearing, Tugger concluded.

His second letter was to Mary Ellen Bledsoe. He was sorry he had run off without saying good-bye, but if he hadn't gone on the spur of the moment, he would never have had the nerve. How was Old Man Bledsoe? Were they still living on the farm? What were the Lords doing, and had anybody in Durham begun to roll cigarettes? If times were as hard there as in New York, she and the Old Man could probably use a little money, so he was enclosing a check for fifty dollars. Maybe he could scratch up some more in a month or two, provided she'd write and tell him the news.

His third letter was addressed to Dan Lord. The advice Dan had given him about keeping his coat buttoned up tight had worked slick as a whistle. He had a fine position as Jay Gould's private secretary, Tugger declared on Gould's engraved letter paper. It wasn't so much the pay as the opportunities connected with his job which were reaping him a golden harvest. If Dan needed a good man to smooth out a rough spot in New York or especially Washington, please remember Tugger was his friend and knew the tobacco business. Being so close to Gould, Tugger had met many swells in high places. Suppose the revenue tax on manufactured tobacco should go higher, for example, Tugger felt sure he could explain to the proper authorities in Washington how hard such a tax was on Carolina tobacco growers, when it was passed on to them by manufacturers just able to make ends meet. In other words, if the tobacco manufacturers didn't have to pay the government such a high revenue tax, they could offer the farmer more for his leaf. President Grant had surrounded himself with practical businessmen who understood these questions, who realized that money talks and that the farm vote is important in a Presidential election year.

As a postscript, Tugger asked Dan if he had started rolling cigarettes. When he did, how about Tugger locating him a little fresh capital to get him off to a flying start? Mr. Gould was always looking around for promising young businesses in which to invest.

Mary Ellen alone answered.

After the farm had gone for taxes, she wrote, she had moved Paw Bledsoe to town. She hadn't minded, because things were livelier in Durham; but paw was heartbroken and blamed the loss of his land on Tugger. A little money sure would come in handy from time to time, because she only made four dollars a week at the Bull Durham plant. The Lords had moved their tobacco business to town, too, where nigger help was plentiful and cheap. Bruce Lord had told paw they'd sold over one hundred thousand pounds of Lord's *Bright Leaf* last year alone. Of course paw hadn't believed him. Paw said Bruce only told him to make him feel like a pauper. Times were awful hard in Durham—everywhere in North Carolina—Mary Ellen complained. Tugger's old friend, Conductor Stringfellow, had stopped in to ask about him. "Tell Tugger now's the time to buy that railroad he's been a-hankering for," Mary Ellen concluded.

Tugger had given the offices of Smith, Gould & Martin as his only address. Alone there, for he often slept on the pad-shovers' bench these days, Tugger read Mary Ellen's letter twice. It was Christmas Day of '71. Everybody else was at home eating big turkey dinners. Those who couldn't afford to eat turkey, could get drunk on whiskey, to be had at ten cents a quart, or "swipes," free in as large quantities as an early bird could drink in return for sweeping out saloons or helping draymen with their beer casks. If Tarheel were alive, Tugger knew, he wouldn't feel so lonesome. He had a good mind to go take one of the four-horse stages up Fifth Avenue and have a talk with Tarheel, but experience had taught him that such trips did little to dissolve the hard knot of loneliness lying like indigestion in the pit of his stomach.

Why not go on up to Josie's, he asked himself, and get drunk with the crowd? Even Josie's was changed. Josie had thrown Jubilee Jim over for a swell named Stokes, who was making a good thing out of something connected with coal oil over in Brooklyn. Tugger pigeon-holed coal oil with tobacco in his mind. He must remember these simple recurring daily needs of every American family, and worm himself into several of them while they were still young. Dan hadn't answered his letter about putting political pressure on Congress to lighten the revenue tax on tobacco products. Tugger hadn't expected his suggestion to bear fruit overnight. Dan didn't do business that way. And maybe the time wasn't ripe?

Tugger had learned much and, with his innate country shrewdness, business instinct and quickness to grasp the significance in his immediate Wall Street world, had matured rapidly. He found here a wider and more lucrative field for his old trading talents—"Tradin's my pride!"—which expanded with his boundless self-assurance. By following Gould only on the market turns which he fully understood, Tugger had salted away in the Farmers and Drovers Bank enough money to buy himself a seat on the New York Stock Exchange. All he was waiting for was a bargain, and to save a nest egg to use on the proud day he should walk up to the board room and be admitted by obsequious guards onto the floor. Thinking of the hard times which he considered overdue, from conditions he had seen all over New York, Tugger began to wonder if Jay Gould was losing his snap. Like Boss Tweed in City Hall and Jim Fisk with Josie, Gould seemed to think Wall Street would keep on dancing to his tune every time he snapped his fingers. Where were his eyes, couldn't he read? Word by word and line by line, like the drawings burnt with acid into waxed plates which the swells called "etchings," Horace Greeley's editorials in the *Tribune* and Tom Nast's cartoons in the *Times* were eating into the callous conscience of New York's nine hundred thousand honest burghers.

With his course of action mapped out, only two questions remained to trouble Tugger. Both represented problems in timing:

When would the acid of reform touch the quick of New York's conscience? Before that could happen, Tugger knew he must find some way to cut himself loose from Fisk, a hard thing to accomplish in Manhattan where the Americus Club, or Big Six, with a fierce Bengal Tiger's head as its emblem, had set a fashion for loyalty.

And, second, when would the panic, so long overdue, break? Before that happened, Tugger knew he must get himself on the short side of the market, even if he had to stop trailing Jay Gould and begin to follow his own hunches.

Two bullets fired from Edward Stokes' revolver at dusk of January 6, 1872, solved Tugger's first problem. Following Jim Fisk to the Grand Central Hotel, Tugger had arrived in time to see Stokes on the landing fire point-blank at Jubilee Jim, who was ascending the stairs to the ladies' parlor. Stokes' first bullet crashed into Fisk's abdomen, the second tore through his left arm. From the minute Tugger eased his benefactor to the floor and gently uncovered the gaping belly wound, he knew Fisk was a goner. Jubilee Jim prided himself on his toughness. It took him eighteen hours to die, a fact which also played into Tugger's hands.

After he had helped the gasping lord of Erie upstairs and onto a bed, Tugger backed away as if to make room for the doctors. Once out of notice, he sprinted over to Josie's, stuffed his every belonging into his bags, and hurried away with them without waiting even to call a cab. This shooting would smell to high heaven, Tugger realized; and he wanted no taint of it hanging on his clothes when the reform reporters arrived to go over Josie's house. Even cabbies have long memories when there's a five-spot or a tenner to be had for recalling whom they hauled from Josie's the day of the shooting. Blocks away, Tugger set his luggage down before the most respectable mansion he could see, and whistled up a hansom. Throwing his bags inside, he told the driver to take him to the toniest rooming house he knew on Washington Square. As the crowbait went clopping across Fourteenth Street, Tugger grinned to realize he had carried over one piece of wisdom from his rat-baiting days: He knew when to leave a sinking ship.

The failure of Jay Cooke & Company, the Gibraltar of conservative banking in Philadelphia which had financed the government's 7–30's and the Northern Pacific Railroad, solved Tugger's other problem and precipitated the panic of '73. Word of Jay Cooke's impending crash came privately to Gould early on the morning of September 18th, but he refused at first to believe the appalling news. Not so Tugger Blake. By the time Gould had made out his sale slips, his favorite pad-shover was nowhere to be found. Tugger at the moment was hanging on the ropes out of bounds listening for confirmation of his own sales orders. By 12:15 P.M. when a clerk stepped out of the Cooke offices in Philadelphia to post the notice of suspended payment, Tugger was well on the short side of the unsuspecting New York market.

During the avalanche, he made his first real killing. Year by year as bankruptcies increased until the panic reached its crest with over ten thousand business houses failing in '78, the one-man firm of Zachary Taylor Blake, 48 Wall Street, climbed steadily but cautiously upward over the financial corpses of the fallen. From the three most talked-about, the three most powerful and certainly the three most hated men in New York, Tugger had received lessons in high finance which were to serve him even better than they, when his turn came to raid the unprotected chicken coops of Wall Street.

From Boss Tweed, Tugger learned to break into its separate classes the sucker public whom he wished to influence. After he had probed for the tender spot of each group and had turned up animosities often brought over from the Old Country, Boss Tweed by stabbing under cover at these weaknesses had set one group against the other. Then while class fought class, he ran off with the bacon. Tugger modified this technique into an uncanny sense of forewarning, of calamity ahead, which less observant men called "Tugger Blake's ability to smell panic a-coming." Tugger knew his sixth sense by its truer name—an abiding respect for the power of American public opinion when aroused. Only a fool lies down in front of a moving steam roller, and stays there.

From Jim Fisk, Tugger learned to connect names with faces, to single out the shy but important man in the crowd and play up to him, to use laughter to cover up fear, to spend money like water if the ground to be cultivated is parched, to pretend to have no enemies, to be hail fellow well met to all. Tugger now needed no tutoring in how to wear clothes and jolly the ladies. His high-buttoned, single breasted English jackets made by

Gould's own tailor set off his farm-hardened figure to perfection. He brushed his hair slickly back from the lean face so concentrated on money-making that he still wore the look which America on her first sight of him had mistaken for the consecration of a mountaineer circuit rider. No smart young fellow as observant as Tugger could have aped Eph Moncure for a year without picking up many of the Virginia aristocrat's quiet voice inflections and distinguished manners. Tugger often chose two shaves a day in preference to three meals. His cheeks seemed always to shine smoothly blue, his nails were clean, his skin smelled of the best lilac-scented shaving lotion.

From Jay Gould, Tugger learned to think directly, never to allow his affable tongue to betray even an inkling of his plans, to hit ruthlessly and to kill without compunction. So alike were they in their secret thought processes that neither felt entirely comfortable in the other's presence. Both had been raised on a farm, both had built up defense mechanisms to cover a hidden sense of personal inferiority. Gould was ashamed of his family's reduced position in Roxbury, New York; Tugger wondered to his dying day if he himself were a bastard. Neither had gone to war, had troubled to be patriotic; both preferred to regard the nation's struggle for unity rather as a lucky opportunity for traders. Both had been born with the feeling that they would never have quite enough time to make all the money each was sure he would need. Both gave an unswerving allegiance to one rule alone—

> The good old rule, the simple plan,
> That they should take who have the power,
> And they should keep who can!

When Tugger returned to North Carolina to attend Paw Bledsoe's funeral, he found Durham changed from a railroad stop of less than a few hundred inhabitants into a pleasant elm-shaded manufacturing town of five thousand. To the one-time peddler boy, nothing except the encircling hills looked natural and as he had remembered. Yet to Zachary Taylor Blake, of Wall Street, no young industrial city he had seen looked half so promising.

Bruce Lord, Sons & Company were building their big brick factory on Main Street. The Bull Durham plant already covered two blocks. Both companies had begun to roll cigarettes in '81 under the direction of J. M. and David Seigel, who had learned the closely guarded secret of the Russian government monopoly in Kovno and had practiced it in London and New York. Now, they were teaching the trick to more and more quick-fingered black boys in Durham. Mary Ellen Bledsoe, promoted to assistant bookkeeper at the "Bull" plant, was eager to tell Tugger all the tobacco news which she knew.

What the infant cigarette business needed most, declared Mary Ellen, was a cigarette-rolling machine which would work. For years inventors had been trying to perfect one. The William S. Kennedy Company, of Rochester, controlled the Allison machine; the Goodloe Company in Brooklyn, the Emory patents. Amber & Gaines, most powerful of Richmond leaf manufacturers, were said to be experimenting, as were the Lords, with the erratic machines invented by James Bonsack. The Bonsack machine differed in principle from its rivals. When fed chopped leaf and paper in continuous rolls, the Bonsack machine compressed, glued and cut cigarettes into desired lengths in one complicated operation untouched by the human hand. On the two Bonsack machines placed on a royalty basis in the Lord plant Dan was known to be working night and day with William O'Brien, a former Bonsack mechanic whom Dan had coaxed onto his own payroll when O'Brien came down to install the Bonsack machines.

Was Mr. Blackwell, astute owner of the Bull Durham plant, using Bonsacks too, asked Tugger. Mr. Blackwell, admitted Mary Ellen, would give his eyeteeth for one which would work at least as well as Dan's pair spat out cigarettes. Black boys who could roll twenty-five hundred cigarettes daily on Thursday and Friday, caroused so over the week end you couldn't get half that production off their shaky fingers Monday and Tuesday, until they had sobered up. And if you docked them, they went whistling over to the rival plant.

On the drive back to town from the cemetery, Tugger mentally reviewed his own efforts to horn into the cigarette business with Dan Lord. Although he had been busy establishing himself in Wall Street—he had bought one of the forty "new" seats offered in '79 when the New York Stock Exchange raised its membership to eleven hundred—Tugger had gone out of his way to put the Lords under obligation to him. Dan had accepted all the help Tugger could give in the concerted drive being made on Congress by tobacco manufacturers, distributors and growers to lower the revenue tax of one dollar and seventy-five cents a thousand on cigarettes. When Tugger hinted to be let in on the ground floor with, say, a few thousand shares of Lord stock, Dan looked him straight in the eye and dispelled any hopes Tugger might previously have entertained about applying the Wall Street sprinkling-pot to this sprouting Durham cigarette bed. Ownership of Bruce Lord, Sons & Company was divided into five equal parts, Dan said. He and his brothers, Joe and Martin, each owned three and their father the fourth part. Tugger did not need to be told that the fifth part was held by Jim Waters, formerly of Baltimore, treasurer of the firm and as loyal as a pit bull.

When they reached town, although it was almost twilight of the shortening October day, Tugger strolled around to the Lord offices. Dan fortunately wasn't in, and so Tugger asked Old Man Lord if he wasn't getting mighty tired, at his age, of worrying about the tobacco business. Nope, Bruce answered with a gleam in his shrewd eyes; and if he was, it wouldn't do any good with Dan planning next year to open a branch factory in New York City. He'd be needed bad here in Durham to keep costs down, Bruce concluded. Take, for instance, this tricky little box Dan had patented to hold the Lord cigarettes. Two boxes they really were, one big enough for the other to slide inside. They were strong as iron, and cheap as dirt to make. Dan had thought so well of them his first order had been for fifty thousand.

The longer he stayed in Durham now, Tugger realized, the worse he was overplaying his hand. His best chance to buy into the Lord firm now would be to wait until Dan overextended himself financially in New York, on Tugger's own home ground.

That night Tugger took Mary Ellen to the new Durham Hotel for supper. Perhaps the kindest way to let her know he didn't need her as a listening post any longer, with Dan coming to New York, would be for him to have Palestine send her a little note or a newspaper clipping while they were on their honeymoon. After he had disengaged himself from Mary Ellen's plump arms at her boarding-house door, Tugger boarded the late train for Richmond, and swung off early the next morning at Drake's Branch, Virginia. There the station agent agreed to keep his grip safe until he returned that afternoon. Hiring a rig, Tugger stepped into the rear seat, lit a puro and told the impressed black boy to drive him over to Charlotte Court House.

The wheels of the surrey rolled in dust two inches thick, dust which Tugger recognized as the summer disguise of his old enemy, red clay mud. It filmed the asters and Queen Anne's lace growing on roadside banks Tugger had cause to remember. Maple leaves were beginning to color, the pines shone slickly green among yellowing oak scrub. They passed mile after mile of second growth timber which Tugger had first seen waist high in fields cultivated for two centuries until four short years of war had started their return to wilderness.

"Can't you make those nags step along a little faster, George?" suggested Tugger, thinking of what he had to do this morning. While Palestine dressed, he could go get the license and locate a preacher.

"Mah name's Bob, suh," declared the boy, stinging his horses' rumps with a broken peach twig.

In time they neared Charlotte Court House. Off the railroad, the once prosperous county seat had fallen into decay. Tugger's rig, with the nags trotting briskly towards the livery stable they apparently knew, was the only moving object at the sun-dappled crossroads. The handsome old brick houses, Tugger remembered, sat back in their gardens like mellowed belles turned spinsters who no longer care because life has passed them by. Tugger looked at them with metropolitan appreciation of their fine Georgian simplicity. What wouldn't he give to have that old Carr house on his new corner lot on Fifth Avenue at Sixty-fourth Street? Age in a good house, like generations of breeding in a person, was something which could not be duplicated in raw new materials, yet was recognizable at a glance by those few who themselves possessed both.

"Drive on to the livery stable, George," instructed Tugger. "Give the horses a good feed of oats 'n' hay, and be ready to leave about noon."

"Mah name's Bob, suh. Whar'll I git you?"

"I'll come to the stable," Tugger evaded the negro's curiosity. "Let me out in front of the courthouse."

Nothing had changed. Here were the same spreading oaks, the mossy stone horse trough, the stone stiles at the four corners of the public square, the ancient jail, the classic red brick courthouse with its bell hanging between white columns in line with the carved front doors. Childish cries from the direction of Court Street announced to Tugger the approach of Palestine with school children whom she was taking for a walk during the morning recess. As he waited for them, Tugger looked critically at Palestine. She was still slender, with tiny waist and long graceful limbs. Her white skin was waxy smooth, curls black as onyx framed her cameo face. Being much with children, she had picked up their directness in speech and gaze. Time apparently didn't exist for Palestine. Even under the bright newfangled "electric" light he had seen in the Menlo Park laboratory of Thomas Edison, Tugger felt that Palestine could still hold her own! She saw him, paused delicately as if on an impulse of flight, and came along upstreet after her youngsters, several of whom knew Tugger from previous visits. They crowded around him hoping for sweets, but too polite to ask.

"Golly, I forgot all about candy!" exclaimed Tugger. "While I speak to your mother, Teena, why don't you take this fifty-cent piece and go buy them some?"

"Please, Miss Teeny—please!" begged the children.

"There isn't time—during recess," demurred Palestine.

"You go buy the candy," urged Tugger, tucking the coin into her palm, "and wait for me on our bench by the horse trough. That'll give you time to eat your share in peace." He touched lightly on her weakness for sweets.

"If I do, will you children promise to go right back to the schoolroom without me?"

"Yes, Miss Teeny!"

"You won't be long either, will you, Tugger?"

"I should say not!" he laughed, thinking of all they had to do to catch that Richmond train from Drake's Branch.

The children raced off to register their selection first at the candy store. Palestine hurried after them. Swinging down Court Street, Tugger noted with satisfaction that the Freedmen's Bureau was closed, its twenty-year frolic for spoilsmen ended. Even the niggers must have been compelled to go back to work, because only an old hound drowsed in the sunshine before the shabby post office.

Composing himself, Tugger pulled the bell cord below the faded sign: MRS. MONCURE'S SELECT SCHOOL. Inside he heard a muted voice call someone; then noisy feet came clattering. The mulatto girl who opened the door was new to Tugger. At sight of his subdued splendor, her jaw dropped.

"Is Mrs. Moncure at home?" he inquired in his best voice, for the benefit of one tired listener. "Will you ask, please, if I may speak with her alone for a few moments—on a most important matter?"

"Yassuh."

Through the half-opened doorway, Tugger could catch a glimpse into the rear room. Turning his back like a gentleman, he waited until he heard taffeta rustling, and Mrs. Moncure's pleasant voice:

"Why, Tugger! This is a surprise—a pleasant surprise, I may add. Won't you step in where it's cooler?"

He followed her through the battered schoolroom to the rear apartment which had looked so fine to a mountain lad just rescued from the mud of Tom Cat Lane. By Gad, his youthful appraisal hadn't gone far wrong! Those gilt mirrors, that spinet and highboy were as good as anything he'd seen on Washington Square. Because he was honestly anxious to transplant this room, and everything it contained, to his future mansion on Fifth Avenue, he found himself sweating like a mule in that low-down habit he couldn't outgrow when some object involving his deeper ambitions was at stake.

"What is it you want to say to me, Tugger?"

He wet his lips carefully.

"Now that you've become such a man of affairs, I won't take up your valuable time," she reminded him gently that her own brief minutes of relaxation were flying.

"Mrs. Moncure, I've come to ask you for Palestine's hand in marriage," Tugger heard his voice utter the often-rehearsed words. "When I met her up the street just now, I suggested she should wait for me under the courthouse oaks—so I could speak to you first, ma'am."

"I appreciate your consideration, Tugger. Unfortunately—"

"Don't say you need her here in your school!" he blurted out, himself again. "Since Arabia married that boy from the Meadows of Dan, and Andorra went to keep house for Miss Tanis Carr, I know you and Teena have had your hands full, Mrs. Moncure, I've—I've been as lonely in my early life as you might find yourself here, if I took Palestine away from you. My hope is that you'll close this musty old school, and come live with us in New York. I never knew my own mother. And I swear I'll be as good, if not a better son to you than Eph!"

"Tugger, that's sweet of you."

"Oh, don't think I won't be doing myself a good turn into

the bargain, ma'am. When she gets to New York, Teena will have all she can do to catch onto city ways and at the same time run the big house I plan to build on Fifth Avenue, the way I want it run. You could be a big help to Teena, livin' in the clouds as she does most of the time—and to me too, ma'am. I own a seat now on the New York Stock Exchange. With another Wall Street man, I'm consolidating several broken-down southern railroads into a trunk system which should pay handsome dividends all around. I've just come from making arrangements in Durham to get in on the ground floor of the cigarette business. To you and Palestine, I can promise ease, luxury, happiness—a steam yacht as big as Commodore Vanderbilt's *North Star*—everything your hearts could want—all that you lost at Golden Hill and more!" he finished, without adding that he lacked only what they themselves would bring him, an invitation to the Patriarch Balls and acceptance by the best people of Tugger Blake as Palestine Moncure's husband.

With each glittering inducement he had dangled before her, Mrs. Moncure had barely nodded her head with that shining look on her face worn by those who have sat in high places, been reduced, and yearn to regain their lost estate. Her eyes reminded Tugger of Tarheel's, when he used to tease the little dog to sit up for a piece of meat. The thought of Tarheel always melted Tugger's heart, made him want to put his arms around somebody. He and this overworked shabby old gentlewoman knew, as no young person like Palestine could ever know, how rough the going had been. He felt his heart go out in a rush of affectionate sympathy towards Mrs. Moncure. He and his mother-in-law would be the exception to the jokes, he and Mrs. Moncure would be friends.

"The only thing I regret now," Tugger hurried on, "is that I can't stop over long enough for you to arrange the big wedding every girl wants—and should have, I admit." He saw a look he couldn't fathom come across her eyes. Mistaking it for offense at his haste, he tried to dissolve it by further explanation: "It's this tobacco deal I'm on. The only way I can handle it is to buy up all the stock secretly, you understand—on Wall Street. You know how quick we traders have to move sometimes, don't you, ma'am?"

"I remember how you used to say 'Tradin's my pride!'" Mrs. Moncure answered in a shaky voice. Looking down, she gathered her resolution as if in her two hands before she spoke again, firmly: "Tugger, you paint a rosy picture for your fortunate bride—and her equally fortunate mother. How attractive it sounds to me, who have had no man of my blood to guide or help me for nearly twenty years, you will have to imagine for yourself."

"Then you accept—for Palestine?"

"First, I want to thank you for your kindness to us both—for your tender thought of me in my need—and for the honor you have done my girl."

"Good! Now that's settled—"

"You must hear me out, Tugger. I thank you, but I must reject your suit for Palestine's hand."

"You reject it? Why, ma'am—" he gulped, too surprised to say more.

"I am compelled to reject it," Mrs. Moncure continued in a strained voice. "Palestine will not make you the wife you deserve, Tugger. Put her out of your heart—for your own sake look elsewhere, I beg you! Surely in New York there must be a hundred girls far prettier and more sensible than Teena, girls who'll jump to grace your fine house and present you with strong-minded children."

"Mrs. Moncure, let me see if I understand you," Tugger began with deceptive calm. "You mean—after all these years I've courted Palestine, I'm not to have her—just because of your pride? Just because she's a blue-blood—and I'm a nobody from No'th Car'liny?"

'Tugger, of course not!" Mrs. Moncure raised shocked eyes to his face, eyes he could see were honest until they clouded over with a secret knowledge of something she would not tell, something he must find out if he were ever again to hold up his head.

"Is it something you know about me, ma'am? If you're concealing something disgraceful about my birth—tell me what it is! I've combed the records at the asylum. I was left there by honest folks. My parents were simple, honest married folks!"

"Tugger, I'm sure they were," her voice comforted him, but her eyes showed no intention of telling what she knew lay between him and her daughter. "Can't you see it's Palestine who's lacking—not you?"

"What's the matter with her? She looks healthy enough—and young."

"It isn't her health or her age."

"Then what is it? Come, come, ma'am, this is no time to be delicate! I've told you all I know about myself. I've said everything I can think of to promise you and Palestine protection and happiness. Maybe you feel I ain't said enough about love? Set your mind at rest, ma'am; I know I can make Teena happy! Surely by now you realize I've loved her all these years? Since the day I laid eyes on her, I've had nobody else in mind for my wife except her. It's just that experience has taught me to be a good provider first," he ended with more confidence, encouraged by the look on Mrs. Moncure's face to believe he was playing his trump card, that he was representing himself to be exactly the type of son-in-law who would appeal most to her character and, to judge from appearances around here, her genuine need. Hell-damn, he'd shown more concern for grabby Mary Ellen and malingering Paw Bledsoe, who'd adopted him only because he needed a strong willing kid handy to do chores, than Eph had shown for this half-sick, grief-stricken old mother of his who until the war had never had to raise even a finger for herself!

"Mr. Blake, we're only prolonging unnecessarily a scene which is painful to us both," Mrs. Moncure dismissed him. Sorry as she felt for this nice enough man before her, Palestine was her daughter, her flesh and blood. Palestine's honor was her honor, the honor of all Moncure women, and therefore not to be discussed with any man, gentleman or parvenu, who while maudlin with disappointment might whisper in his cups truth told of events long past, of reason blotted out by terror in the cataclysm of war.

"It's just your damn' stiff-necked Virginia pride!" blurted Tugger, his voice thickening with fury. "That's all stands between our marryin'—you an' your pride! You'd rather starve to death—and make Palestine starve with you—than give her to a nobody like me."

The children were stampeding into the next room. Recess was over, he had to go.

"Good-bye, Tugger," Mrs. Moncure whispered. She was so overcome by a fresh realization of Palestine's tragic lot, and by the weight of the years ahead for her, she had to cling to the front door to support herself. "Some day you'll thank me for what I've done—when you've forgotten my poor girl in the happiness you deserve."

Almost blind with anger, he strode up the street towards the courthouse. "He travels fastest who travels alone!" he tried to tell himself. Moreover, any woman as far behind the times as Mrs. Moncure had shown herself to be, could never fall into step with New York ways, would set him wild the first week under his roof, no matter how large the new house might be. On the stone bench under the oak tree, with her faded summer hat lying beside her, Palestine sat guzzling cheap store candy. Tugger realized he mustn't touch her, his hands shook so with rage. He sat down and tried to compose himself, while Palestine chattered brightly:

"Oh, Tugger, guess my new riddle! I've been saving it up for you, and it's very good. When I wrote it to Cousin Homer Pettis out in Kansas City—he's prospering there in the mule business, although when he went out, he said he meant to practice law. Not much difference between a lawyer and a mule, Cousin Tan says, but she must have meant a jackass, I reckon. She's felt that way about lawyers ever since she lost her case with that carpetbagger. What was I talking about, Tugger?"

"Your new riddle—"

"Of course! What three words in the English language—what three words only, mind you—begin with *d-w*?"

"Dwarf," answered Tugger, thinking intently of something else. There were other ways of catching a fine bird than by bulging into the front door of its owner and asking to buy it! If he couldn't out-smart one shabby old widow woman in Charlotte Court House, he'd better close up shop on Wall Street.

"That's right," admitted Palestine, with an upward inflection of respect in her silky voice, a glint of blue eyes through smoky lashes. This strange look Palestine occasionally gave him excited Tugger more than the most practiced wiles used by sirens at Josie's or in the palaces of pleasure on Fourteenth Street where shadow-dancing was the latest fad to stir the senses. "Dwarf is right," Palestine was continuing. "Guess again, Tugger."

"How about dwell?"

"Oh, you're just too smart—or have you heard this one before? I don't see how you do it!"

"Go down the alphabet. Palestine, honey, listen carefully while I talk to you about something important. Will you run away with me? I just asked your maw for your hand, but she refused."

"Lots of boys have asked for my hand," boasted Palestine. "But you haven't guessed the last word, Tugger. Maybe you'll fall down on the last word—"

"Stop jumping from important things back to your silly riddles!" Tugger's inner fires flashed as when the door of a boiler carrying a full head of steam is momentarily opened. At this juncture, he warned himself, he could not afford to show impatience towards this strangely provocative girl whom he wanted to hold in his arms more than he had wanted anything except money since Tarheel died. To frighten her now would spoil everything. After they were married, there would be plenty of time to change her airy mannerisms, her flighty way of speech, the habit her undisciplined mind had of playing around a subject instead of focusing straight on the point. His tone casual, he began again: "Teena, how'd you like to drive over to Drake's Branch with me? My rig's down at the livery stable, and I've got to be moseying along."

"You know ma won't let me go buggy-riding with boys," objected Palestine. "Besides, how'd I get home?"

"You wouldn't. Have you forgotten my promise to take you to Richmond some day?"

"But ma can't leave her classes, now."

"Yes, but why should that spoil our fun? After we get to Richmond, I'll buy you the prettiest white satin dress and take you to the best hotel in town!"

"Tugger, you'd buy me a white satin dress?"

"Yes, and dozens of everyday ones."

"And a string of pearls?"

"Ropes of pearls!"

"And—and a pair of diamond earbobs?"

"Yep," he courted, tongue in cheek, "with a diamond tiara and dog-collar to match. I'll give you a mansion on Fifth Avenue—and a yacht as big as the *North Star*—and a Wagner Palace car—until your shabby memories of Charlotte Court House dwindle away into luxury and pleasure."

"Tugger, that's the word! Dwindle's the word—"

"Of course it is. Why not let me guess your other riddles while we're driving over to Drake's Branch?"

"Ma won't like it—"

"I'll answer to her."

"You will? Then I'll go! Only when we get to Richmond, you won't forget your promise to buy me everything I want?"

"I won't forget."

"On your word of honor—as a gentleman?"

"On my word of honor," he pledged with sobering voice,

his eyes grim. This wasn't the way he had dreamed of winning his bride. Long ago he had learned, however, that half a loaf is better than no bread. What really mattered now was to get Palestine Moncure into his arms as his wife. He arose, extended his two hands.

"Shall we start?" he smiled down at her. "We've a long way to go together, my dear."

Chapter 13

With the birth of her second daughter America's ostracism at Foxden became complete. Across the toll-house counter Mrs. MacGower reached for her eggs in tight-lipped silence. Even sewing-machine agents dared not be seen turning their horses' heads into the Foxden lane. Cut off from her own kind, too self-respecting to enjoy the low pleasures of such tenantry as would associate with her, America yearly grew more self-contained, better able to live within her own physical and spiritual resources.

During her first months in Kentucky, America had longed to revisit Charlotte County, to see her mother and the girls, to match wits with Brother Ephraim, even to call on selfish Cousin Tan living alone in the big Carr house facing the sun-dappled crossroads. After her daughters were born, America tried to hole into Foxden in the hope that Tuckahoe's repudiation of her might not be carried back to Virginia by letter or breath of scandal. Like an ostrich with its head in the sand, America refused to contemplate the only event which could reinstate her on Tuckahoe, Fant's capture there. The possibility that her husband might go West and be shot or disappear leaving no ripple of identity to clear his wife's name and establish the paternity of his daughters, had not yet come to haunt America's brief hours of introspection. With the fierce strength of those who have no other alternative except to hold on or go under, America made herself believe that in some miraculous way which would also be safe for Fant, her hermit years would some day end, her loyalty would be rewarded, her reputation restored. And in the meantime, until this miracle occurred, she and her children had best lie low and let the storm blow over their discredited heads.

Daring to live such a gamble, America was also too realistic in her mental approach to life not to realize the considerable odds against her. Ephraim might show up any day, evaluate the situation after a few words with the right people whom he could always spot with uncanny accuracy, and then engage her in a family scene belligerent enough to put Palestine to bed with a headache, had she been present. Fortunately Brother Ephraim failed to appear on Tuckahoe. He had drifted from Tennessee on down into Texas and the wild Arizona country, Mrs. Moncure wrote. She often mentioned incidents, or enclosed newspaper clippings that showed Eph was making quite a name for himself out there as a law-enforcement officer. Following America's generous example, Eph occasionally sent his mother a postal money order which was a big help over financial humps such as Arabia's wedding and putting a new roof on Cousin Homer's house. When her mother indignantly wrote that Tugger Blake had persuaded poor foolish Palestine to run off with him in spite of her own best efforts to discourage his suit "by every means short of telling the truth, which was none of his business," America felt her heart lift with something deeper than profound relief. At last money, and lots of it, had come back into the Collier-Moncure connection! And what's even better, America congratulated herself, we have in the family a man who is able and more than willing to face the future instead of the past. . . .

Second only in importance to the great day when she would be restored to her proper place among her peers on Tuckahoe, the problem of her children's education loomed larger and larger on America's mental horizon. She had been able to teach young Fant and Virginia Sue their three R's during the midmornings, while she peeled potatoes or shelled peas for dinner. When her second daughter grew too big and restless for the three of them to sleep in Uncle Simmy's bed, with Fant in the trundle beneath, America realized she must make some changes in Foxden to accommodate her expanding household. Taking the profits of a crop of leaf which out-sold itself, America had the log walls of Foxden's unused right wing weather-boarded and painted outside, plastered and papered within. The big square front room she furnished as a parlor, its mate in the rear as a schoolroom. The lofts above were ceiled, and a flight of steps was built up to them from the dog run. In these upper chambers America placed beds and chairs for her four field hands. While they were at it, so she excused the considerable expenditure, the carpenters made a bedchamber for her daughters out of the loft above her own family room, and another for young Fant above the cook room, with a curving inside stairway to replace the ladder her mountain lads had been glad to ascend for years.

"I don't know what you want a parlor for," grumbled young Fant, when America set him to washing the new windows.

"When they grow up, your sisters will need a place in which to receive their beaux," America answered.

"Who'd come to see them, I'd like to know? Stella's crowd wouldn't know what to do with 'emselves in a parlor!"

"The day will come"—America took time to turn around on her stepladder to look levelly at her son—"when the best people in Mason County will hitch their buggies in our lane all the way to the pike."

"Huh! Not till we're dead—or the sheriff sells us out!"

When he learned that the schoolroom had been equipped principally for him, young Fant was even more outspoken in his disapproval. He had no intention of spending his evenings poring over dull books, when the other fellows were having fun down the hill at Stella's, where roosters were fought and moonshine was drunk in quantity, America knew. Not the least of her worries these days was her tall stoop-shouldered son. Failing to realize that the lad's bent posture was a physical expression of his intense inferiority complex, America kept at him constantly to stand up straight. Young Fant had an alert mind, but America never succeeded in interesting him in his studies. Before her eyes, in spite of her best efforts to prevent it, young Fant was developing into a sullen unkempt image of his father, who had always met the disapproval of his peers with gay defiance and had managed to keep himself a little more presentable than his circumstances warranted. Conviction crystallized in America's mind that young Fant would never be a man until he cut himself loose from what he must secretly consider her disgraceful apron strings, until he mustered courage to run away from Tuckahoe where, like an Ishmaelite, he found all men's hands turned against him and seemed instinctively to turn his hand against all men, and especially against his own mother.

America's pride and "second pair of hands," as she made grateful acknowledgment, was Virginia Sue. From her grandmother, Margaret Annable, the child had inherited her sunny, lovable disposition and dark beauty; from Mrs. Moncure, a strong-fibered spiritual acceptance of whatever fate held in store for her. Romantic as a moonless June night, Virginia Sue's cheerful temperament won her the nickname of High Jinks. Her good mind kept pace in the schoolroom with her tomboy's body in poultry yard, orchard and field. All she asked of Foxden's hermit life was for America to tell her Homeric legends or hero stories of Greek and Norse mythology at night, and provide colts to gentle in fair weather. Her favorite poem was

> Are you ready for your steeplechase,
> Lorraine, Lorraine Loree?

and she never quite lost her secret hope that some day she herself might duplicate America's triumph in the Germantown Fair ring.

"It beats all," sniffed Emarind McCord, when she heard the *rat-tat-tat* of flying hoofs approaching down the pike, "the colts that woman lets her wild girl ride. Like mother, like daughter—"

"Like Brünnehilde, I'd say!" chuckled Captain McCord, and in spite of his rheumatism considered it worth the effort to hobble to the window to watch Virginia Sue clatter past on one of Sunshine's spirited grandsons.

America's youngest child Nickettai—so named in nostalgic memory of the Indian chief who had first recognized her own stoutness of heart—was high-tempered, aggressive and given even as a toddler to dramatic flights of fancy which always took her away from her home and mother. To discourage her tantrums America several times threw cold water over the hysterical child and hurried on about her own exacting schedule. After such encounters she often felt Nicke watching her with a hard glint in her hazel eyes, as light shines through a yellow diamond. Loving clothes and Uncle Simmy's curios carefully displayed in the parlor for the edification of guests who never came, Nicke pored over the drawings of metropolitan ladies in the marked copies of *Harper's Weekly* which Professor Joe Dave rarely failed to send America from Lexington, where he was president of the Agricultural and Mechanical College.

If life at Foxden had quickened and was expanding with the years, changes also came to Tuckahoe Ridge. Having walked through the matrimonial forest too infatuated with Fant Annable and memories of him to pick up another stick, crooked or straight, Allilee Drake filled her empty days teaching at Glade Springs school. Had Allilee been willing to admit what she called "the young whelps at Foxden" to her classes, America would not have sent her children there, even for the satisfaction of counting their tuition into Miss Drake's aging palm.

Following the birth of America's third child, Stone Moncure had closed Children's Chance and gone to live in Georgetown, where he rented a warehouse and spent his time handling quantities of prime Scott County leaf. Small growers on Tuckahoe, when unaccompanied by their wives, often stopped their buggies beside America as she trudged to and from the tollhouse with her egg baskets, and suggested that she come look at their leaf with an eye towards buying it. Much as she would have liked to handle half a dozen good little crops with her own, America always refused. Tongues would wag faster than ever if she went around farmers' barns contracting their tobacco. Moreover, Foxden was not hers to put up as security for the cash necessary to make such a purchase.

"Miss Merry, guess what's happened to your old friend Professor Joe Dave?" John Willy burst into her cook cabin one evening to announce. "He's going to be the next superintendent of public instruction of the Commonwealth of Kentucky!"

"You mean he won the nomination?" America smiled at her former favorite pupil, now a law clerk in Judge May's office in Limestone and just returned, she knew, from the State Democratic Convention at Frankfort.

"Ain't that all he needs in this state, ma'am?" retorted John Willy, his clear eyes shining. "Let's see if I can recall how Colonel Billy Breckinridge nominated him," continued young Barnes, and assumed an orator's pose in the middle of the cook-cabin floor. "When Colonel Billy came a-limpin' down the aisle, we knew we were to be honored with the silver side of his tongue, as Judge Stacy put it. 'Soldiers all,' Colonel Billy began, and there wasn't a hiccough in the whole hall, 'I call before your minds the blood-soaked fields of Shiloh. The crest of combat has swept by, leaving in its wake agony and death. As the smoke pall lifts, I see a tall ministerial figure leading the cohorts of mercy out to salve the wounds of partisan strife. His eagle eye sweeps the field of carnage, he pauses here and there to offer the last comforts of religion alike to friend and foe.

" 'When I overtook this spiritual Moses of the battlefield,' " John Willy continued to quote Colonel Breckinridge, " 'I found him kneeling beside the body of a dead Yankee soldier praying for his departed soul. I observed him unobserved. I saw him close the foeman's staring eyes, compose his powder-stained hands. Bending lower, he must have seen something that shocked him into action, for he sat down, pulled off his own boots and put his much needed socks on the cold feet of that dead Yankee—lest the women who were to receive his body should learn their beloved had died for a country which had not even furnished him with adequate covering for his blood-stained feet! Who, I ask you, veterans, could be so magnanimous—so compassionate—so lofty in concept and so tenderly practical in execution—that all his scholastic and spiritual attainments now rise and shout his preeminent fitness for this outstanding position as mentor and guide of our youth—who, I ask you, but our valiant comrade-in-prayer, Chaplain Joe Dave Langston of the Orphans' Brigade, whose name I now give you as the next superintendent of public instruction of the Commonwealth of Kentucky.' "

"You're quite an orator yourself, John Willy," applauded America. "I'm delighted to hear Professor Joe Dave's services as an educator have been recognized and will become state wide—although I'm afraid Tuckahoe will see less of him."

His new public duties kept Professor Joe Dave at Frankfort except for the Christmas holidays. He and his wife, Orleana Chisholm Langston, then brought their five handsome children home to visit her father, Major Alastair Chisholm, at Charter Oak on the hill west of Glade Springs church.

An account of other eloquence came to America at Foxden. When posters up and down Tuckahoe turnpike announced that John B. Gough, famous temperance lecturer, would speak at Glade Springs schoolhouse, America's children begged so hard to be allowed to go sit unseen among the churchyard tombstones to hear him that she consented in spite of instinctive misgivings. On their return, young Fant blurted out disgustedly:

"Well, Nicke disgraced us—like I said she would when you told us to take her."

"What happened, High Jinks?"

"Let me tell—let me tell!" cried Nicke, jumping up and down. "Ma, you said yourself I tell a story better'n anybody in this house."

"What happened, Jinks?"

"I'll have to tell you Mr. Gough's speech, to show how Nicke butted in," began Virginia Sue. "When he got up to talk, everybody inside was so still they must have heard the twit-twats and jar-bugs in the trees near us. Mr. Gough talked a while about Demon Rum and the saloon evil. Then he told about a workman who had nine children and a sick wife who took in washing. This workman had to go past a saloon every Saturday night after he'd gotten his pay envelope. Next door was a butcher's shop, but the workman always went into the saloon first and came out with only a dime left—just enough to buy a mess of pig's liver for his family's supper. One night who should he meet coming towards him down the street but the saloonkeeper's wife, all dressed up in silks and a taffeta petticoat. Seeing her so fine, the workman stepped into the gutter to let her by, and asked himself: 'What's the matter with me—that my wife has to take in washing and my children must eat pig's liver for supper?' 'Whiskey—whiskey!' rustled the fine silk skirts of the saloonkeeper's wife. 'Whiskey—whiskey!' they went on down the street."

"The next Saturday—" interrupted Nicke.

"Let High Jinks finish, please," America cut her short.

"The next Saturday when the workman entered the butcher shop," continued Virginia Sue, lifting grateful eyes to her mother's face, "there stood the butcher with the pig's liver all wrapped up and waiting. 'No more pig's liver for me and mine!' cried the workman, slapping his unopened pay envelope down on the counter and knocking the pig's liver off into the sawdust. 'From now on, my wife's going to wear silks and taffeta, too. Give me a dollar's worth of round steak—'cause I'm going to take the pledge!' And that's where Nicke butted in."

"You don't mean she interrupted Mr. Gough?" demanded America, her face whitening.

"She certainly did!" barked young Fant. "Before I knew what she was up to, she ran lickety-split across the yard and into the schoolhouse door yellin' she wanted to take the pledge, too."

"What did Mr. Gough—what did everybody do?" asked America, bracing herself.

"She broke up the meeting. Ever'body started talkin' so fast about you—and us—Mr. Gough couldn't get started again," repeated young Fant.

"Nicke, what possessed you to do such an unmannerly, impolite thing?" America turned towards her youngest. "Haven't I told you a dozen times we aren't wanted on Tuckahoe—"

"It's you they don't want—not me!" cried Nicke, her head thrown back, her eyes like yellow diamonds. "When I said I wanted to sign the pledge, Miss Allilee Drake objected. Miss Kate Annable answered, Christian folks oughtn't to visit the sins of the mother on the head of an innocent child like me."

"Nicke, aren't you ashamed?" rebuked Virginia Sue.

"No, I'm not!" Nicke screamed, jumping up and down again in the beginnings of a tantrum. "I'm sick an' tired of being buried alive on this hateful old farm—with no day-spendings—or fish fries—or Sunday school to go to like other little girls! The darkies say ma has her good times a plenty—why shouldn't we?"

Nobody answered her, until America found her voice. Trying to keep it steady, as she spoke she made herself meet Virginia Sue's troubled eyes:

"Will you see that Nicke goes to bed, Jinks? I—I'd rather not come upstairs tonight, if you don't mind. Don't worry about me, children," her lips with their deep hurt attempted a smile to reassure her older daughter, "I'm just going for a little walk—out to the walnut grove and back."

"D'you want me to go with you?" offered Fant.

"No, thank you, son."

Several weeks later, America was awakened by pebbles thrown onto her bed through the open window. Although he had not been home for over a year, America awoke at her husband's signal, stealthily carried the stepladder into the dog run, placed it under the opening into the garret between Foxden's double wings, and climbed aloft. In a few minutes, when the coast looked entirely clear, Fant came out of the bridal wreath bushes near her window, made a dash for the dog run, climbed into the loft and drew the ladder up after him. In each other's arms, husband and wife felt themselves safe if they scarcely moved, if they spoke in the softest whispers, if they parted several hours before dawn. Fant stayed hidden in the garret for three days and nights, urging America to leave Foxden and accompany him to Chicago, where he declared good jobs were plentiful.

"What about the children?" she whispered in a tight voice of opposition.

"Oh, ma 'll jump to take care of them!"

"You're not seriously asking me to give up young Fant's heritage?"

"What's Foxden but some old hillsides that yield you the hardest kind of a living?" he whispered, savagely. "When pa dies, you can run Timberlawn for the rest of your life. I need you, now! To tell you the truth, I can't seem to make a go of anything without you. I'm ridden by a thousand devils—of loneliness, I reckon. Sometimes I get so discouraged I feel like jumping into the river—if I wasn't afraid the God of Abram, Isaac and Jacob would make me a Wandering Jew for all eternity!"

Self-pity in others had always left her cold. Her first duty now was to her children. Hard as it was, Fant had brought this fly-by-night existence upon himself on the *Evening Mail,* by preferring the company of card-sharps to that of his sick wife. Water seeks its own level, America told herself; people do what they want most to do and choose their way of life, their friends, to mirror themselves. What a fool she would be to try to live with Fant again even for a few months! When she came home pregnant again to Tuckahoe, Justinian Annable would be in possession as trustee of Foxden, Cousin Margaret would have the children at Timberlawn.

"Under a new name in Chicago," Fant mistook her silence for a melting mood, "with your push and my gift of gab we'd get along fast. Then you could slip back here some night and get the children. Probably we'd have to be satisfied at first with less than we once hoped for, but at least we'd be together. And when pa dies, I'll be a rich man. Then all five of us could come home in triumph! Wouldn't you like that?"

She could not remind him that the warrant out for his arrest on a murder charge would not be affected by Justinian Annable's death.

"Remember how well we did on that wagon trip north?" Fant continued gayly. "Whenever I think of you soaking those mules' sore feet in flaxseed mash—when you'd counted on being Queen of Comus—I have to laugh right out loud!"

In spite of herself, she smiled.

"Those two months with you were the happiest of my life," he sighed.

"Because I did all the work?" she started to ask, and bit her lip. Before the war, Southern heiresses often married handsome young gentlemen who couldn't make a go of anything except fox hunting, drinking and begetting handsome children. Their wives' able plantation management covered up their deficiencies and provided a fine living for everyone. So it might have been for Fant and herself here at Foxden now, as Uncle Simmy had tried to insure it in his will, and on a more lavish scale later at Timberlawn, if Fant hadn't lost his head years ago on the *Evening Mail* and shot an unarmed man. For his moment of panic and her own stubbornness in not preparing her husband for the news of Cousin Simmy's legacy, both of them now seemed doomed to live the forlorn life of fugitive and hermit.

"Tell me, lovie—weren't you happy, too?" Fant insisted.

America had often caught herself wishing she had kept a diary of her trip across the Far South at that historic time as her father undoubtedly would have done. She hated to admit even to herself that she had felt too resentful against life and Fant to raise her mind above the trivial hardships of the journey, to lift her eyes from her mules' hoofs to the countryside through which they plodded.

"How could I be happy in low dives—with ruffians and whores?" she bridled.

"They seemed a light-hearted lot to me—after the blood and hate of the war," Fant tried to vindicate his vulgar taste. "Certainly those carpetbaggers' wenches bought your finery with an open hand."

"Oh, Fant, must we talk about them—when we have so many more important matters to discuss?"

"As for instance what?"

"Young Fant's future. He ought to go off to military school where he can associate with gentlemen's sons instead of these rough mountain boys I take in to raise a crop. Of course I'm teaching him myself, but I'm just not able—with my other work—to prepare him properly for Washington and Lee or the University of Virginia."

"My dear, spare yourself—and him—the pain of being refused."

"Refused what?"

"Admission to any school attended by gentlemen's sons."

She thought over his words. During her rare childhood illnesses she had been terrified by a fever dream, always the same dream—that she lay in an open field with a great boulder on her chest which she could hold off only by almost superhuman exertion. When her aching forearms were about to buckle and let the boulder's crushing weight on her heart, she found herself being gently awakened. Now, the future reminded her of this fever dream, except that no one awakened her. Laying her cheek against her husband's, she whispered:

"Lover, what's to become of us all?"

"I don't know," his voice was heavy with despair. "I've suggested the only way out I can see, but Foxden and the children mean more to you than I do."

"It's city life that terrifies me—and the thought I'll have to go to work in another laundry."

"Haven't I told you I'll work my arms to the bone for you?"

"Yes, but—"

"You don't trust me, eh? God, woman, you only gave me one chance—those few months on our honeymoon! Can't you see I'm different now—I'm a changed man? You've got to help me now, or I'll go under sure as fate."

Dawn was in the garret, its walls were emerging out of the darkness. Seen in this wan light, the face beside her—which America had once thought so handsome—appeared to have broken down into tired eyes, pouchy cheeks, a dissipated mouth drooping into a week-old black beard mottled with grey. Who could entrust three children's future to the owner of this face, who could take their trusting hands and lead them away from plenty to follow this defeated stranger into poverty and shame?

"Don't you slave here from dawn to dark?" Fant had strength enough to charge once more against the stonewall of her resolution. "Could anything in Chicago be worse than this hell you're living here on Tuckahoe—and making our innocent children live with you—because you're such a clodhopper you're afraid to leave the land?"

"Hush, Fant—before you wake somebody!" she turned aside his bitter thrust. "Even if what you say is true, I agree with Grandpa Ephraim that it's better to be your own master on a dunghill than the king's favorite slave in a palace."

That night April swept in on a freak blizzard that soon whitened the plowed fields. A full moon behind storm clouds made the familiar landscape look enchanted. When America took Fant his supper after her household was asleep, she found him impatient to leave. The falling snow, he said, would cover his tracks. She gave him two hundred dollars she had withdrawn for this purpose from the Farmers Bank in Limestone, and insisted on accompanying him as far as the point. After he had kissed her good-bye, she watched the snow drop its rhythmic curtain of white around his descending figure. Huge clinging snowflakes melted on her flushed cheeks into her tears. Scrambling homeward, she despised herself for putting security ahead of love. Where was the high-hearted schoolgirl, America Moncure, who had leaned from her window to breathe Emerson's "Give All for Love" on the moonlit spring air of a world of easy abundance?

Pushed to the back of her mind by problems closer home, was America's concern for Palestine. A dozen questions of delicate conjugal relationships, the answers to which Mrs. Moncure would have been too much of a lady to put down in black and white on tablet paper had she known them, arose to intrigue America's mind, to pique her curiosity. How could a man of Tugger's direct mental processes endure for a month, let alone a lifetime, Teena's silly chatter? Had the Tarheel become a gentleman in the process of acquiring a seat on the New York Stock Exchange? Had he really married Palestine—and, if not, where was she?

"You keep asking me about Teena," Mrs. Moncure finally answered America's written questions. "After the disgraceful way her husband filched her off like a pair of candlesticks from the sideboard, I haven't seen fit to answer his peace overtures or to accept him as a son-in-law. I must confess, America, that the school taxes my strength now to the utmost. How much longer I can keep going, I don't honestly know. If I bring Andorra home now, Cousin Tan will certainly cut her out of her will, as she almost daily threatens. Andorra's situation reminds me a little of Isaac's. As soon as she completes seven years of servitude—in her case for a dot instead of a bride—Cousin Tan's longevity adds another seven. Could you spare me Virginia Sue? She must be almost sixteen by now, and should see something of the world. Though Charlotte Court House is far from gay, she will enjoy the young Carringtons, Bouldins and Crenshaws."

Much as America hated the thought of being separated from High Jinks, Mrs. Moncure's suggestion impressed her as wise. Joe, one of Foxden's mountain youths, after polishing his plate with his last half-biscuit, began to sit overlong at the supper table to stare at Virginia Sue, the while he absent-mindedly rubbed the dark fuzz sprouting on his upper lip with a soil-roughened forefinger. High Jinks fortunately had no use for boys of any age. America bought her a creditable wardrobe in Cincinnati, impressed on her that "we Annables never discuss our family affairs," and with a smile close to the tears behind it, saw her off at Limestone on the new Chesapeake & Ohio sleeper train to Richmond where Andorra was to meet her.

Some weeks later, in June of '85, America received a letter on handsome stationery engraved 860 Fifth Avenue, New York. Opening it, she was astonished to read:

Merry, dear—

Come help me. I need you—you saved me once before.

I can't manage the servants—they keep me locked up in my rooms. I was sick and had twins—the boy is named Junior, the girl Sally. Nurse says it spoils them to let me play with them—and I mustn't go places for fear I'll meet the wrong people. I had to mail this letter on the sly.

Come help me put nurse and the servants in their place. Tugger won't take me anywhere any more, and leaves me by myself weeks and months at a time.

Your abused sister,
Palestine

The next afternoon young Fant drove America into Limestone to catch the Friday evening boat for Cincinnati. Although she could have gone down on the new railroad completed in '76, America chose to start her trip on the familiar *Bonanza* which, she declared, was safer, cheaper and less apt to frighten country women's buggy horses. Aware of how people were staring at them, mother and son stood apart on the wharf and in low tones discussed the last important details before departure:

"Maybe you can keep Nicke at home by pretending you two are young foxes—and I'm the old vixen gone to catch you a big fat goose."

"Maw, the things you say! Folks 'll hear you."

"To show you're embarrassed never eases an embarrassing situation, son. In fact, it has the opposite effect. There—hear the *Bonanza* whistling around the bend?"

"Wisht I was goin' with you!"

"I wish you were, too."

They gazed upstream. America wondered if her son was experiencing her own youthful illusion that the Ohio was a broad highway bounded on each side by hills and above by the sky. The silver road this evening seemed to open its arms to draw them away from the known anxieties of Foxden to the possibilities of a richer, happier life beyond the darkening hills. America put her arm around young Fant's shoulder and tried to comfort him:

"You've had a hard time, son. When you come into Cousin Simmy's will, if you feel you'd prefer city life—which has always stifled me—I'll do everything I can to help you get established there."

"But I want to paddle my own canoe! By myself. Without you or anybody else tagging after me. And please don't pet me in public, maw. It fair sets me wild."

"I'm sorry, son."

Around the nearer curve of the river the *Bonanza* came into view. To America the packet boats no longer seemed like silver swans strung with golden beads of light. The *Magnolia*, her back broken by an explosion in midstream in '68, lay rusting in the mud at the bottom of the river. Her sisters, the once bright *Morning Mail* and *Evening Mail* and the *Bonanza,* appeared what they now were, dingy inland packets kept on schedule by shrinking consignments of hogshead tobacco and hill-country swine bound for Cincinnati, which was also feeling the competition of speedier railroads and their booming terminus, Chicago. All that seemed left of the gracious leisurely days of packet travel were the silver whistles on the aging stern-wheelers.

The *Bonanza*'s melodious whoop caught America's throat in a grip of memories. How could she tell this sulky faced young man who no longer wanted her near him, that sixteen summers ago in this same lavender evening light by sheer force of will she had shut the door of her mind to grief and shame, that his unborn heart might continue to beat under her ribs, and that he might grow to claim the rich farm legacy he now despised?

"Good-bye, son," she smiled at him.

"Goo'bye, maw," he answered, still not looking at her.

From the freight deck, America watched her son climb the grade and disappear in the direction of Dalton's livery stable. The *Bonanza,* with no hogs to load, was midstream by the time America composed herself on deck to enjoy the afterglow. What was the use, she asked herself wearily, of crying over spilt milk? She would take what consolation she could from the thought that she was only thirty-eight years old—and didn't look that, even in this hastily purchased navy blue silk which was at least genteel, if not becoming. What Frenchman had said no woman reached her prime before she was forty?

At the Union Depot in Cincinnati the next forenoon, she took a train for New York. She found the through day coach to New York as comfortable as anyone could desire, with a clean pillow and folding table furnished free on which to eat her box-lunch meals. What must the Wagner Palace sleeping cars and the gilded diner be like, she wondered, and gazed wistfully up at them while she stretched her cramped legs in the various stations where her train stopped. Sleeping cars could not be flagrantly immoral, her common sense told her, because at twilight Sunday she heard hymns being sung in the end car. The accompanying tinkle of a piano put her in mind of her first boat ride up the Ohio, when Stone Moncure had stood sunburned in the ladies' cabin door of the *Magnolia* to listen to her play for Yankee children

> In the gloaming, oh, my darling,
> Think not bitterly of me!

As she walked up the resounding wooden platform to her own car, America decided that conditions of travel change. Only the human heart remains frightened and alone.

Arrived in Hoboken, America took the ferry across the Hudson River and as directed walked six blocks across Twenty-third Street to Sixth Avenue. Sight of a little engine puffing along with several cars swaying dizzily behind it on tracks laid on high wooden stilts was the first of Manhattan's wonders which America viewed in shining-eyed delight. An Irish policeman told her the best way she could get to her destination was to walk another block east and wait there for one of the four-horse public coaches, which would take her right past Number 860 Fifth Avenue. On their way up the handsome thoroughfare, America gazed at endless brownstone fronts and at a bubblelike Château de Blois mansion at Fifty-second Street which they passed. Midmorning, it was still too early for fashionables to be out. Grasping her telescope, America arose at the fare-collector's signal and stepped off the coach, which immediately rumbled away.

Across Fifth Avenue was the welcome green of Central Park, with the five-year-old mass of the Metropolitan Museum of Art looming ten blocks north. Facing her on the corner arose Number 860, its robust Georgian simplicity as familiar to America as an old friend's face. The three-storied residence, of red brick with green shutters and white woodwork, only recently had been finished. On scaffolding, a workman was putting a last white coat on a carved cornice. In adjoining vacant lots cows and goats grazed. At the rear of the mansion, America saw treetops of a newly planted garden enclosed by a serpentine brick wall. Gazing at the wall's undulating waves, America realized why Number 860 looked so familiar. How clever of Palestine to copy the old Carr house in faraway Charlotte!

Feeling much heartened, America lugged her carryall up the slippery portico steps and rang the polished eagle door-pull. A husky Irish manservant wearing a butcher's apron opened the door. Behind him America caught a glimpse of packing cases half opened, and the dull shine of a Waterford chandelier hanging in the stately white hall.

"Is Mrs. Blake at home?" America asked, and stepped forward to escape the glare of June sunshine on the mansion's marble steps. As against an iron bar, she collided with the manservant's upraised arm.

"No housemaids needed here yit, miss—"

"Mind your manners, sir!" America interposed, sharply. "I'm Mrs. Fant Annable—Mrs. Blake's sister from Kentucky."

"How could that be now, whin herself is out there a-visitin'?" inquired the manservant, with an impertinent rise in his voice.

"What's going on here, Denis?" inquired a haughty voice from within.

Glancing across the footman's shoulder, America saw an English butler bearing down on them. The habitual backward tilt of his head was so supercilious she found herself gazing at his well-shaved jowls rather than into his expressionless face. Relieved to be met by someone in authority, America reintroduced herself.

"Sorry, ma'am, you must 'ave the wrong number," the butler dismissed her, politely. "Denis, carry the lydy's luggage down to the coach."

On a park bench opposite her destination, America consulted Palestine's letter again to see if she could have misread the address. There it stood up expensively under her thumb—860 Fifth Avenue, New York. A hansom cab, its driver's eye caught by her valise, bore down on her out of the quickening pre-luncheon traffic.

"Could you take me to Tugger Blake's office in Wall Street?" America threw economy to the winds.

"I could thot, mum!"

At a handsome new building which appeared to have settled down by mistake in a shabby old residential street, America followed her cabbie into a marble lobby, and paid him surprisingly little for her long ride. The forbidding scowl of a jackanapes in brass buttons did not deter her from bringing her suitcase into his gilded cage, which she recognized as one of the new contrivances *Harper's Weekly* had pictured and described as a lift. After soaring three stories, she stepped out into a large room furnished like a rich men's club, and was met by a young man with watch-dog eyes. In the lapel of his skin-tight morning jacket was a chestnut bell, also described by *Harper's Weekly* as a pseudo-elegant device its wearer could ring rather than laugh at a twice-heard joke. The young man made a bored pretense of taking America's name, disappeared somewhere and returned to regret that Mr. Blake had gone to Jerome Park for the afternoon. Brushing past him, America approached the door from which he had just emerged, opened it, stepped inside and closed it gently behind her.

She found herself in a huge cool room heavily curtained against the hot noon sun. An ornate Italian marble mantel extended across one side of the wall. On the floor lay a pink and silver Persian rug. The chatter of a ticker drew her eyes to the silhouette of a man seated behind a flat-topped Italian table desk which might have graced the Vatican. The ivory China silk suit he wore accentuated his mature bulk. In those thick shoulders, that strong bull neck, the sleek head, there was nothing to remind America of a lank mountain youth with a circuit-rider's face who had sat on a cowhide blending

Carolina bright leaf under the Charlotte Court House oaks. Because his back was square to the slit of sunlight streaming through a narrow opening between brocaded curtains, America could not see his face.

"Tugger Blake?" she asked, recognizing this strong man as immediately as he recognized her.

Across his Kermanshah rug, Tugger Blake frowned at this latest interruption. Even in his private office, it seemed he couldn't escape domestic worries! This woman, his thoughts sped back twenty years, had something to do with his first meeting with Palestine. Could it have been twenty years ago he had glanced up from his smokin' mixture and advised this girl to leave the tobacco patch for a schoolroom? She evidently hadn't taken his advice, he noticed with grim inner amusement, because no woman could sit twenty years behind a desk and still have those hips! His new secretary, Thompson, had said a rube was outside asking to see him, but Tommy-boy had slipped up this time, for sure. In spite of the tacky outfit she wore, everything about this woman proclaimed she was both nob and swell. Tugger had met smart women a plenty, and had married a beauty without wits; but something about this woman leaning against his mahogany door made his breath catch in his throat. Since he used to pick up buckeyes in the North Carolina woods, he hadn't seen color as rich and glossy as her hair. That warm red mouth, resolute yet tender, had drunk fearlessly of many experiences, he saw, and was tasting none of the lingering bitterness of regret which soured life for him today. The sea-grey eyes met and held his own. Here before him, Tugger realized with a stirring of the pulse in his wrists, was one soul who feared nothing—not even the loneliness which comes to those who win to the heights.

"You've come a long way from your cowhide, Tugger Blake," began a liquid Eastern Virginia voice, with the magic inflections which he had seen open mansions to Eph Moncure but never to himself. "So have I, else I shouldn't have entered so intrusively just now."

Tugger arose and seated his guest. Years ago he had discovered that sometimes a natural movement, like pulling out a chair or lighting a puro, would give him the few invaluable seconds he needed to collect his thoughts or organize a defense. Just as he never allowed a scrap of paper or a pencil to litter his desk when he was operating a pool—lest in his nervousness he make some telltale mark which might betray his plans to his Wall Street foes—so now he wiped his face bare of expression, kept speech down to a minimum of words. At his right hand the ticker was spitting tape, but the information it gave seemed unimportant compared to the battle he saw gathering in the eyes of this great lady opposite him.

"I remember you, now," he temporized. "You're my wife's sister—from Kentucky."

"I'm glad you still acknowledge her as your wife. That, in itself, takes courage and loyalty."

"What's that you're saying, ma'am?"

"You might have sent her home at once—when you found out her condition."

In storybooks, Tugger had read about characters who sometimes established an immediate understanding, a sympathy of mind and spirit so complete that their thoughts ran side by side as on parallel steel tracks at express speed in perfect rhythm, only occasionally aware of the strong ties underneath which held them together to make such unity possible. In eight short sentences, he and this woman had wiped out twenty years, and reestablished friendship rare as it was complete. Gazing at her, Tugger felt his resentment against the whole Moncure tribe, against all Virginia aristocrats, melt away.

"It was my own fault," he confessed, unexpectedly. "Your mother refused her consent—I thought because I'm pore white trash compared to you folks. So I made Palestine run off with me."

"And ma has written you nothing further?"

"What is there to write—except that I've married an idiot!"

"Tugger, Palestine isn't an idiot," the earnest voice was saying across the table. "You need have no such fear for the sanity of your twins."

He winced visibly. Because it was not his nature to be hurt without striking back, he burst out:

"How can you say that, when you haven't seen her in twenty years? She's crazy as a loon, I tell you, because she shrieks like a—a fiend if I come near her. And damned if I can figure out why! For months I lay awake nights trying to think up new things to give her, new ways to make her like me—without success."

He stopped speaking and braced himself to hear her ask how, then, had Palestine borne him twins. At his elbow, the ticker began chattering like a scared guinea hen until she reaches roadside cover. Silence then hung in the dim room. Venturing a shamed glance upwards, Tugger saw that his visitor was not looking at him. Instead, she traced a pattern on the old mahogany between them with a finger in a home-tatted glove. The expression on her face put him in mind of a traveler who on returning at last to familiar childhood scenes cannot decide whether or not it is wise to peer too deep into the well of the past.

"Tugger, listen carefully to me, because I'm going to tell you something I never expected to tell a living soul—something which even now might cost me my life," America began, leaning across the desk and speaking earnestly. "The night Golden Hill was burned, Teena wouldn't believe that carpet-bagger, Mudston, would come back with his Yankees as he threatened. She went to bed and was half asleep when I dragged her downstairs—and across the lawn just before they arrived. After they'd fired the parlors, she remembered her new green dress. By now, I expect you know how much pretty clothes mean to her? Before we realized what she meant to do, she ran out into the open to save her things. Mudston—that carpetbagger—fell on her."

"You don't mean he raped her?"

"No, Tugger, no! I got there first. I killed him—with a corn knife. The blood—and the firelight—and Mudston's body were too much for Teena. But I'm sure her mind's not affected seriously enough to make any difference with the twins—because I've talked the situation over with a famous teacher in Kentucky, a man who has studied psychology in Paris and Vienna."

"But—but why didn't your mother tell me this when I asked for Teena's hand?"

"And incriminate me, Tugger? Why should ma tell a comparative stranger like you that one of her girls had had such a terrible experience—and that another had saved her by—by manslaughter? Wasn't it better for ma simply to reject your suit and hope you'd accept her decision with good grace? If I'd been in ma's shoes," America looked courageously towards the day when she must not let the shadow across her own life spoil the future of some fine young man who might love High Jinks or Nicke, "I think now I'd do just as ma did two years ago—in a kindly way, of course."

"Oh, she was kind enough," he remembered, in a dazed voice. "She said Teena wouldn't make me the good wife I deserved—that there must be a hundred girls in New York who'd jump to grace my fine house, and bear me strong-minded children."

"Tugger Blake, stop thinking or talking about your children! Palestine had a bad shock, I will admit, but there's never been any insanity on either side of our family. I know Teena, I tell you! She's like my younger girl, Nicke. Both use tantrums to get their own way—to attract attention to themselves. I'll bring her around in short order, I promise you that. And I'll set your house to rights, so your impudent servants don't turn people who can be of inestimable help to you, out into the street."

Tugger sat staring at his visitor. He knew his mouth was open, that at any moment the tidal wave of relief which had welled up inside him would overflow his eyes and run down his cheeks. What was the use of his trying to conceal from this superb woman the flood of relief, of hope which she had brought him? He felt like the small boy who has run a gantlet of darkness into a safe lighted room where the family are seated around a cheerful fire telling jokes and eating popcorn. He wanted to put his head down and cry, he wanted to reach out and touch this woman across the desk. Pulling his handkerchief from his pocket, he wiped his eyes, blew his nose like a foghorn and grinned.

"Well, Sister Merry!" he made proper acknowledgment. "You can see for yourself you've given me a new lease on life—you've made a new man out of me. Hell-damn, how come I got so scared, d'you know?"

"Teena on a high horse is enough to scare any man, Tugger."

Feeling like Cinderella, America went methodically to work to establish the House of Blake on firm domestic and social foundations. At any moment the clock might strike midnight, the shabby crown princess of Golden Hill might stand revealed as the vixen of Foxden. In her downfall, America realized, she might carry the social futures of Junior and Sally Blake, of Virginia Sue and Nicke Annable. Tugger, she felt, didn't count. Hadn't he boasted years ago: "Tradin's my pride?" Always a good gambler, America accepted the odds. If she stayed unobtrusively in the background, the chances that anyone from Tuckahoe Turnpike would meet her on upper Fifth Avenue were slight. Dr. Drake had died, and Cousin Theresa was a poor farmer. Allilee now taught school for a more practical reason than to escape boredom.

America's first move in setting Number 860 Fifth Avenue in order was to persuade Mrs. Moncure to accept Tugger as a son-in-law. When this was accomplished by several exchanges of letters, America commissioned Mrs. Moncure to engage a staff of servants in Charlotte County who would agree to go to New York and produce at Number 860 an atmosphere similar to Golden Hill's prewar elegance. When Aunt Flora, Pembroke and fourteen younger house servants, gardeners and hostlers arrived at Newark, the bandannas of the women and the respectful cap-bobbings of the men attracted the attention of a young lady reporter sent from New York to interview an incoming notable. Coached by Mrs. Moncure that "us Moncyore-Blakes nevah discuss our fambly affa'hs," the negroes smilingly repeated this formula which in time found its way into Manhattan's crustiest evening journal. Tugger bought three copies, and in the privacy of his office washroom read them over and over with delight. With even less fanfare a steady stream of heirloom silver, china and English furniture began to trickle in from wherever in Virginia Mrs. Moncure could purchase choice pieces from war-impoverished relatives or friends.

In straightening out Palestine, America experimented with methods which had proven successful with Nicke. She slept in the same bed with the mental invalid and studied her night and day. Croquet in the serpentine-walled garden, America insisted, was safer for the present than to accompany Tugger while he tooled his high-steppers around Central Park. Aunt Flora was authorized to do any necessary water-throwing which, when reported to her, America declared undignified displays of childishness on both their parts. Palestine was given the run of the house, but not for one moment were her whereabouts unknown to watchful eyes. When Tugger stayed downtown, America and Palestine supped alone in the stately Adam dining room. If Palestine threw silver or became petulant, Pembroke carried her up frugal trays until the irritable mood passed. After six tempestuous weeks for all concerned—the first three of which Tugger wisely spent at Saratoga—Palestine began to understand what was expected of her. Once she realized that tantrums brought only bread and milk for supper, and that she could not run screaming out of Number 860, she adopted a puppylike anxiety to please which everyone found endearing.

"Isn't there a Savannah beau here in New York who's a great friend of Mrs. William Astor?" America asked Tugger one evening. "His aunts, the Telfairs, used to bring him to visit at Golden Hill. His name's McAllister—"

"Not Ward McAllister?"

"Yes. He was named after his uncle Sam Ward, the gifted conversationalist. Do you know Ward?"

"No, but I'd give my left arm to!" laughed Tugger, drawing a long breath. "Ward McAllister makes out the list of guests Mrs. Astor invites to her annual ball. 'And why are there only four hundred people in fashionable New York society?' " Tugger mimicked McAllister's Savannah accent. " 'If you go outside that number, you strike people who are either not at ease in a ballroom, or else make other people not at ease. See the point?' The real reason, of course," snorted Tugger, "is that 350 Fifth Avenue only holds four hundred—at a tight squeeze."

"Ward would be delighted, I'm sure, to secure a card—if it would entertain you to go, Tugger," she answered, demurely.

In mid-August, America dropped a note to McAllister. Would he care to revive youthful memories by bringing Mrs. McAllister around some afternoon for tea? Palestine—did Ward remember little Teena?—had married Tugger Blake. She, America, was visiting them from Kentucky, where she had been widowed some years ago and now lived in the country. Time, she found, served only to draw old friends closer. America would expect the McAllisters after four o'clock any day next week.

The Savannah dandy—who later advised "if you see a fossil of a man shabbily dressed, relying solely on his pedigree dating back to time immemorial, who has the aspirations of a duke and the fortunes of a footman, do not cut him; it is better to cross the street and avoid meeting him"—replied that his ladies were in Newport, but he himself would come the next afternoon. Over Madeira and transparent pudding, the equals of which he vowed he hadn't tasted since his visits to Golden Hill, McAllister evaluated America's chances of crashing Mr. and Mrs. Tugger Blake into Manhattan's *haut monde.* While McAllister talked, America sipped her wine and thought how certain details of her own past, as furnished by Allilee Drake, might sound when whispered behind scandalized fans of Newport fashionables sheared by Tugger Blake in Wall Street. She had heard the ice crack under her before, America silenced her caution. Nothing ventured, nothing better than the hard bed of some liquor-drinking, rooster-fighting Kentucky mountaineer could be won for High Jinks and Nicke Annable.

Since her own credentials were impeccable, McAllister continued, his eyes grown searching, all that need be considered now was the social peak desired, and whether the ladder had best be gold, silver or Colonial pewter. Was America aware that "in New York a fortune of a million is respectable poverty?" Perhaps it might be well for the House of Moncure-Married-beneath-Itself-to-Blake to continue to appear as Virginia-Carolina nobs? Certainly Number 860 was more nobby than swell, opined the *arbiter elegantiarium,* lifting his eyes appreciatively to the Waterford chandeliers. If America could coax Tugger to register his racing cracks as from the Tarbaby instead of the Tarheel Stables, who would know whether he himself came from North or South Carolina? After all, South Carolina had produced Rutledges, Calhouns, General Wade Hampton and the St. Cecilia Balls.

Nobs are born to their position, McAllister continued his lesson, but "society is carried on by the swells, the nobs looking quietly on and accepting the position, feeling they are there by divine right. But they do not make fashionable society or carry it on. A nob can be a swell if he chooses; that is, if he will spend the money, but for his social existence this is unnecessary. A nob is like a poet—*nascitur non fit.* Not so a swell—he creates himself!"

America found it difficult not to smile at all this pretense.

She felt like saying that both nobs and swells were essentially just plain snobs, unlovely examples of New York's social caste. She knew at the bottom of her heart that her good common sense and her appreciation of fundamental values in human character would make it possible for her to rise above these vanities, and that she could extract from them what she coveted for the good of her children.

The climb was slow but steady. When America felt she could do no more for the present in New York, she and Tugger went to Charlotte Court House and prevailed on Mrs. Moncure to close her school there and return to New York with her son-in-law. On her way west, America took Virginia Sue as far as Staunton and entered her at the Virginia Female Institute, presided over by a childhood friend of Mrs. Moncure's, Flora Cooke Stuart. When America reached Foxden, she was pleased to see that Fant had gotten in the crops in fairly good order. Nicke's summer of freedom had gone to her head to such an extent America found her unmanageable. On her next trip to New York, America took Nicke by way of Staunton and left her there with Virginia Sue and Mrs. Stuart. Both girls' vacations were spent in New York at the Blake establishment.

Throughout the spring of '88, America kept reminding herself that her son would in two years be a man and would come into his inheritance. What could she do to insure her own and her girls' future against the day when young Fant would bring his wife home to be mistress of Foxden, a wife whom he could choose only from among Stella's girls or their kind? America had not heard from her husband for years. Was their parting in that April blizzard to have been their last? With the necessity looming ahead that she must soon give up her stewardship of Foxden, America pitched her crop and in July hurried to New York in the hope of turning up something remunerative there. Several nights after her arrival, while the Moncure women sat in the rear garden, America was pleasantly surprised to hear Pembroke announce that Tugger had come home and craved her company in the library. When she reached the ornate room filled with the elaborate Italian decoration and furniture which had overflowed into Tugger's Wall Street offices, America found her brother-in-law seated in his shirt sleeves at his desk, feet up, a dead segar in his mouth, the evening paper wrathfully crumpled into a ball and thrown into the middle of the rug.

"The funny men are taking another crack at me, Sister Merry," he snorted. "Between Mister Dooley and Pulitzer, New York journalism has certainly gone to pot!"

"What's really worrying you, Tugger?" smiled America, pulling a chair closer towards the open front windows in search of a breeze across the park from the river.

"This damn' cigarette war!"

"Tell me about it, why don't you? Business interests me."

"That's another reason I say you're one woman in a thousand," grumbled Tugger and launched into an account of the industry's latest battle.

By perfecting the Bonsack machines, Dan Lord had cut the manufacturing cost of cigarettes from eighty cents to thirty cents a thousand. At the same time, Dan had invented the sliding box in which to pack his product cheaply yet without risk of breakage. By joint pressure from everyone interested in tobacco, Congress in March of '83 had lowered the revenue tax to fifty cents a thousand. The tax cut took effect on May 1, 1883; but on the previous January 1, the Lords announced that orders received from jobbers would be filled immediately at five cents per box instead of the then universal price of ten cents, provided three-fourths of the goods ordered might be delivered after the reduced revenue tax went into effect. With the cheapest, tightest rolled and best boxed cigarette on the market, the Lords sold thirty million cigarettes in the first nine months of '83. The next spring Dan came to New York and opened a cigarette factory on Rivington Street. By day he ran the plant, at night he sold its output.

"I used to see Dan walking along Fourteenth Street counting discarded cigarette boxes to find out what type of cigarette was the most popular," declared Tugger, "so he could push his own similar brand on the neighborhood merchants. Dan boasts he knows the names of more wooden Indians in Manhattan than Tammany does Irishmen! Another favorite trick of his is to place several dozen boxes of his cigarettes in a shop for a day's trial, and then make a demand for them himself by sending bootblacks and bellhops from half a dozen near-by hotels and barbershops to buy them back. When he shows up at sundown to see how his brands have sold, of course he lands a first order. And don't you believe his big tips don't make those bellhops remember *Morning Glories* when a real customer sends 'em out for coffin tacks! Yet all this time Dan's been sleeping in a hall bedroom in the Bowery, and eating at hash-houses and free lunch counters in saloons. He's the lad taught me how to save railroad fare by jumping freights."

"Yet you're generous, now," America smiled at Tugger, hoping he'd retaliate with the long deferred suggestion that she submit her own bill for services rendered.

"In this town you have to spend money to make it," Tugger ignored the bait. "If I've heard Dan say that once, I've heard him say it a dozen times. To save money isn't enough. To do anything worthwhile here, you have to spend a lot of it."

There he was, harping again on his pet hope that America would soon give an entertainment which would eclipse Alva Vanderbilt's fancy dress ball. Ward said she wasn't yet ready for fireworks. And America realized she couldn't have society editors writing back to Kentucky to place Mrs. Tugger Blake's sister and co-hostess, Mrs. Fant Annable.

"Weddings are the only really appropriate time to splurge," she evaded.

"Hell-damn, do we have to wait till the twins are grown?"

"There's nothing quite so impressive as a double wedding. Can't you just see Sally and a younger sister—"

"You know that's out of the question."

"How about my Nicke? She's not much older than Sally."

"I've been wondering how long your little Nicke would stay hidden in the woodpile!"

"Why shouldn't I hope you'll give my fatherless girls a chance?" she challenged. No use to complain she had worked here for nothing, not even her transportation back and forth from Kentucky, to this curiously tight-fisted and open-handed man who had all his household expenditures taken care of by his Wall Street bookkeepers! America now regretted that she had introduced this subject obviously before the time was ripe. She tried to backwater in generalities: "Southern families feel more responsibility to help place each others' young people in life, I believe, than Northerners do. But that's a long time ahead for us, isn't it? Just now, my chief worry is whether prized tobacco will bring enough in June for me to send my girls back to Mrs. Stuart's boarding school next fall."

"Isn't she the widow of the immortal Jeb?"

"Yes."

"Is this a touch, Sister Merry?" asked Tugger, reaching for his pocketbook.

"Fiddlesticks, no! You make me tired."

Opening his wallet, Tugger took out something folded small, laid it on the table out of America's sight, and returned the wallet to his pocket the while he continued talking, his eyes sardonic:

"I hope it isn't, because you're not your mother's daughter if you mention anything as vulgar as money. When I used to call on Teena, I thought I'd improve my chances if I told your maw how well I was getting along. D'you know what she said?"

"I was brought up on it," smiled America, light-headed at the possibility that Tugger might have lain on the table a thousand-dollar bill to pay for her girls' schooling next year. "Ma said: 'No lady—' "

" 'Or gentleman—' " Tugger took his cue.

" 'No lady or gentleman ever mentions money in the parlor!' " they chorused like children. Now that he was enjoying his little joke—to keep her guessing a while before he handed over the thousand-dollar bill—America suggested amiably: "Go on with your story about Dan Lord. I asked you who else manufactures cigarettes in this country."

"There are four going concerns," Tugger took up the story of the cigarette war. "The largest is Amber & Gaines, of Richmond."

"Their factory is 'way downtown—in the burnt-over district," nodded America. "My young Fant buys their cigarettes to get the lady in tights they put inside each box. She always startles me, because she's not the company you'd expect Major Gaines to keep. He's a gentleman of the old school, if there ever was one!"

"D'you know him?"

"Better than I know you, Brother Tugger. Why?"

"Oh, nothing in particular. Amber & Gaines installed the Bonsack machines in '87. The Frank S. Kingsley Tobacco Company, with offices here and in Richmond, puts out a good cigarette. William S. Kennedy, of Rochester and Oxford, North Carolina, have another. Kennedy controls the Allison patents. The Goodloe people here in Brooklyn use the Emory machine."

"One Richmond—two New York—and two North Carolina firms with New York branches all putting out machine-rolled cigarettes," summarized America. "What's next?"

"I'm still trying to horn into the Lord firm, which manufactures nearly half of this country's yearly production of almost a billion cigarettes. They're a closed family organization, and if I don't get in there soon, Dan will have 'em busted higher'n a kite. National advertising, as he calls it, may be a good idea to start the ball rolling, but he's carried it too far!"

"I pass his billboards all the way from the Hudson to the Ohio," agreed America.

"And on out to San Francisco, if you'd go that far! Last year Dan spent twice as much in advertising as his entire net profit. Of course the other four have to follow suit. Lookit this thing—" Tugger stopped sputtering, reached around to the table and, instead of the thousand-dollar bill, produced a small booklet perhaps an inch wide by three inches long.

She had to duck her head to hide her disappointment. It was *A Short History of General J. E. B. Stuart.* On the inside of the rear cover were alphabetically listed fifty names of other generals whose biographies were to be had in the Lord Small Booklet Series. A modest line credited the handsome little volume to "Lord's Cigarettes."

"It's very well done," America admitted, grudgingly.

"They're too well done!" blustered Tugger. "You ought to see the *President Series* he's planning—and the *Prize Fighters*—and the *Famous Actresses.* Fancy booklets and billboards ain't all, either. Dan actually put a ladder-back chair, with his brands painted on each slat, in every tobacconist's shop in the U.S.A.!"

"I'll bless him if he'll put a few on the Cincinnati tobacco breaks."

"The Lords' advertising costs have run about twenty per cent of their gross sales!" snorted Tugger. "And, of course, the other cigarette manufacturers have to play follow-the-leader. Now, if I could talk the Big Five who're left into some sort of an armistice before it's too late—"

"Why can't you?"

"Last year when the tobacco manufacturers were making out the list for their annual dinner, one of them suggested Dan's name be included. 'We don't consider him a manufacturer,' said another. 'He'll go broke before the year's out.' When I told Dan, he snorted: 'I don't talk—I work.' Maybe it's just as well Dan didn't go to the dinner, though. Old Richmond—in the person of Majuh Gaines himself, suh!—might 'a' had a stroke if he'd been asked to sit down with upstart Durham."

"I'll bet I could talk Major Gaines into some kind of a cigarette armistice," America thought aloud.

"You ninny, this is Wall Street—not a pink tea!"

"We could start with a quiet little dinner party here at home," she continued, as if Tugger hadn't spoken. "We'd ask the presidents of the other three cigarette companies— two are here in New York and Rochester isn't far away."

"Would you have Dan Lord?"

"Not yet. We'd bag some star attraction like—like Pierre de Longpré, who's just home from Paris. Pierre being in the plug business, your cigarette men wouldn't be so apt to shy off. Once we'd mellowed them up on Aunt Flora's cooking and your '48 Claret—"

"They'll think I'm a cheap-skate if you serve anything except champagne!"

"You leave that to me," America answered. "After dinner when the ladies—and Pierre, who likes to sing tenor—gather around the piano, you can drag your victims in here and devour them singly—or in a group."

"If you have ladies present, won't you have to include Teena?"

"We've got to start including her some time, you gallant man! Could anything be easier for her than a quiet little dinner party at home?"

"D'you honestly think it will work?"

"Tugger Blake, for a man who's supposed to be the saber-toothed tiger of Wall Street, you have the social spunk of a yellow kitten! Of course it'll work."

She watched Tugger summon courage to ask his next question:

"What d'you expect to get out of all this, Sister Merry?"

"I'll name my fee, later."

"Oh no, I'm not buying a pig in a poke!"

"Run your own dinner party, then."

"If you want me to help your girls make suitable marriages," he surrendered, "I've meant to do that all along."

"Thanks for telling me. I'll remember that—and ask for something else," America took advantage of him. A self-made brute like Tugger, she knew now, would never have any real respect for a woman until she scorched him well with his own fire. To out-trade the trader who made tradin' his pride offered no mean challenge to the only woman-handler on the Cincinnati hogshead breaks.

"You'll never get Pierre de Longpré under this roof," chuckled Tugger, rising to follow her out of the library. Side by side, they looked through each other's eyes towards their common goal. "Pierre's hated my guts ever since my Mountain Laurel left his Highboy at the turn of the Withers Stake last May."

"You leave Pierre to me, Tugger. Is it a deal?"

"It's a deal, sorrel top."

He had never called her that before. The phrase brought back a hundred memories of Fant Annable. Seeing America's expression soften, Tugger reached on an impulse for what he saw mirrored in her face, for a kind of love about which he knew nothing. All he got for his greediness was a stinging slap across the cheek, and America's voice declaring coldly:

"Now you've spoiled everything, Tugger—including your cigarette deal."

"Dammit, Sister Merry, it's your own fault! That's the first time I ever saw you look like you've got a heart inside of you —instead of a stone. No wonder it went to my head."

"Good-night, sir. Tomorrow I'll engage you a housekeeper."

"I tell you I'm sorry, ma'am. I—I don't know what came over me."

"I'll accept your apology—if you never let it happen again."

"Hell, no! You're the most valuable man I've got working for me," he tried to turn the whole bad business off with a grin. Hand to cheek, he watched her sweep out of the library.

Half-closing her eyes, America studied herself in relation to the Blake drawing room. Against its white woodwork, soaring eagle mirrors, gilt furniture with flesh-tone Aubusson tapestry, the floral Italian ceiling gathering into two great drops of dew in the Waterford chandeliers, her black lace dress appeared right for a late August evening. She wore her glossy hair piled high. Her only ornaments were Palestine's pearls and a huge fan of pearl colored ostrich feathers. From the chair where he perched watching her and the French mantel clock, Tugger exclaimed nervously:

"Golly, suppose they don't come?"

"Ward McAllister will come," America smiled. "He believes a dinner invitation, once accepted, becomes a sacred obligation. If you die before the dinner takes place, he says, your executors must attend."

"Mr. and Mrs. John Clarkson—Mr. Thomas Goggin!" announced Pembroke.

Clarkson, with iron-grey side-burns and a churchwarden manner, was the portly president of the Goodloe Tobacco Company of Brooklyn. Tom Goggin had been taken into the firm to secure the patents on the cigarette-rolling machine he had developed in his blacksmith shop near Danville, Virginia. Mrs. Clarkson was rushing the season in a gold brocade ball gown which looked hotter than a suit of gilded armor. By the time America had greeted them, Pembroke announced Mr. and Mrs. Dudley Marshall, from Rochester. Marshall was a courteous middle-aged man thin to the point of emaciation from worry over the cigarette war. Mrs. Marshall appeared to the parlor born in an écru mull dress with bracelet and brooch of what must be an important family set of emeralds. A Miss Kennedy, she had brought to Marshall as her dot the William S. Kennedy Tobacco Company, to the preservation of which he was now apparently sacrificing his digestion. A responsible man—America made a mental note.

"How kind of you to come down in the heat!" she greeted them, appreciatively. After the smoke of battle cleared, she and Mrs. Marshall would be friends.

"Mr. and Mrs. Franklin Kingsley!" Pembroke announced with aplomb.

This short wiry president of the Kingsley Tobacco Company looked like a Scotch Tom Thumb in tails, by the side of his fat overdressed wife. Heartened to see Mrs. Clarkson shining like a mountain of gold across the room, after introductions Mrs. Kingsley barged over and added her diamonds to the already dazzling pile. In the hall the tall Chippendale clock began to strike.

"Tugger, you must remember to set back that runaway clock!" declared America, cozily. "Ward never was late in his life."

"Mr. Ward McAllister—Mr. Pierre de Longpré!" proclaimed Pembroke and disappeared, indicating that the party was complete. Where was the hostess, America caught the look of puzzled inquiry in Mrs. Marshall's eyes. America had sent out the notes of invitation in Palestine's name.

Pierre de Longpré, scion of plug barons resident in New York since 1750, shot one glance at the double treasure heaps on the love seats, blinked and, like one of his young thoroughbreds at the starter's flag, appeared as if he might bolt. His rolling eye lighted on America, his desperate expression brightened and he made for her. America handled introductions with easy informality and watched the circular stairway leading from the hall to the upper regions of the mansion. Seating themselves, the guests began to talk to the person nearest them until they found their attention drawn to the twins' nurse hurrying down the stairs into the front hall. Fräulein rustled starchily to America's side, spoke a few excited words in German, and rustled out.

"Tugger, I'm distressed to tell you Teena can't come down—it's another of her frightful headaches!" declared America, and turned in apologetic explanation to the others: "My sister hurried up from Virginia Beach especially for tonight, but the heat of the city has evidently been too much for her. What a Spartan you are, Mrs. Marshall! Oh, Pembroke, please remove my place from the table. Mrs. Blake is indisposed," America interrupted herself as the butler swung open the doors leading into the vast white dining room. With America's plate removed, the Dresden place cards were all wrong.

"If you'd sing, we could play musical chairs," laughed America, and reshuffled everyone into the permanent places she had been memorizing for two weeks. "After dinner, will you sing *White Wings* for us?" she continued to De Longpré, at her right.

Under the mellow glow of candles burning on sideboard and serving tables, dinner progressed. Over the table hung the great crystal chandelier Tugger had imported from Warwick Castle. At any moment the guests expected to see it burst into vision-shattering brilliance equal to that which Mr. Clarkson associated with Gabriel's horn on the day of judgment. How, thought Mrs. Kingsley, could anybody own such magnificence, and resist showing it off?

The cuisine which Aunt Flora had been rehearsing for days was quite unpretentious, even simple for an era which the visiting Earl of Rosebery had described by saying: "You Americans have made a mistake. Your emblematic bird should have been a canvas-back, not an eagle!" Instead of terrapin, Pembroke's assistants placed before each guest crayfish delicately browned in butter and lemon juice. Instead of game and joints there appeared squab stuffed with tender green corn. Sauterne to the shell fish, Pontet Canet to the bird and Monopole to the dessert promised no headaches for tomorrow or hemorrhage to Mr. Marshall's catarrh of the stomach. With the salad course Pembroke himself offered paper-thin slices of hot Smithfield ham, while Clay followed with Camembert cheese, and Earle with water crackers. Crème de Menthe sherbet and ladyfingers completed the short repast which Ward so far forgot himself as to pronounce perfect. Above their heads the Warwick Castle chandelier burst into lightninglike glory, somewhere an organist struck the opening challenge of Beethoven's noble *Fifth*.

"Ladies, shall we have our coffee in the music room?" suggested America, rising. "Mr. de Longpré, you promised to sing *White Wings* for us, remember? Ward, would you prefer to smoke with the men in the library—or show Mrs. Marshall the Golden Hill fans?"

After the coffee tray had been removed, America took her place at the piano. With the diffident pleasure of a man who really likes to sing, De Longpré leaned against the concert grand, nodded to America and began:

"Sail home, as straight as an arrow
My yacht shoots along on the crest of the sea;"

When he reached the chorus of the popular song, he raised his arms to indicate that the ladies were to sing with him. They accepted; Mrs. Clarkson in a cracked high soprano, Mrs. Kingsley off key:

"White wings, they never grow weary,
They carry me cheerily over the sea;
Night comes! I long for my dearie,
I'll spread out my white wings
And sail home to thee!"

Across the room McAllister was showing Mrs. Marshall heirlooms which Mrs. Moncure had sent north to add authentic background to the Blake ménage. Ward and Mrs. Marshall dutifully applauded the rendition of the song, then returned to their obviously more congenial objects of interest. At the piano America began to play *Sur le Pont d'Avignon,* and Pierre enthusiastically took up the melody. Side by side on a comfortable couch Mrs. Clarkson and Mrs. Kingsley, finding themselves unfamiliar with both air and words of the folksong, began to whisper about the effects of summer heat on their baby grandchildren, then realized that this might appear discourteous to Pierre and America and seized the ensuing moments as opportune for snatching forty winks of sleep.

"You must have been mystified to receive my note offering to sell you Pony Express, Mr. de Longpré," murmured America, her fingers wandering into the *Moonlight Sonata.*

"Frankly, Mrs. Annable, I was."

"With Mrs. de Longpré at Newport—and your house closed," continued America, spacing her phrases to the rippling melody, "I could think of no better time or place—to discuss the matter—than here tonight."

"Blake at home is a different man from Blake in the Street or on the track!" agreed Pierre, his eyes hardening. "What makes you think he'd consider selling Pony Express to me?"

"How can he sell what isn't his, sir?"

"You mean the horse is yours?"

"Let's not waste precious time in trivialities, Mr. de Longpré. Tugger will be here with the others any moment now—and you know it wouldn't do to let him hear me trying to sell Pony Express to you!"

"I—I admit our track rivalry is keen, ma'am," laughed Pierre.

"Are you prepared tonight to make me an offer?"

He took her fan, unfurled it and began to trail the pearly banners back and forth in time with the *Sonata,* the while he bent to whisper:

"How much d'you want for him?"

"As you doubtless know, Tugger has two horses entered for the Withers Stakes—the Pony and Greased Lightning. He seems to favor Lightning—"

"You mean he says he does!"

"That will be settled next spring when the Withers is run. For the Pony, I'd fixed my mind on something around—say, ten thousand dollars."

"Then he's bowed a tendon—or met with some other accident!"

"I guarantee him sound of wind and limb. With this ten thousand, which I realize is absurdly low, go other considerations more valuable to me than money," laughed America, and played in crescendo.

"What, for instance?"

"Assuming we could agree, where could I meet you to conclude the sale?"

The ends of the fan recorded his momentary surprise, then swept smoothly on as he answered:

"Could you come to my office?"

"Mr. de Longpré!"

"I beg your pardon, ma'am. Let's see, are you going to the Roosevelt dinner next Friday?"

"As I remarked before, we are comparative strangers in New York. Unfortunately we know few congenial residents here," declared America, and looked directly at De Longpré whose wife, if she would, could open doors in Manhattan as aristocratic as and certainly livelier than the iron grilles of Ward's exalted patroness at 350 Fifth Avenue.

"I grasp your meaning, ma'am," Pierre answered in the tight voice of a trader who discovers that what he took to be a bargain, may prove the most expensive nag in his stable.

"There's another condition," America whispered. "I can't give you the transfer papers on Pony Express before next May."

"But the Withers Stake is run on May thirty-first!"

"You will have the papers, executed, on May thirtieth—if you and Mrs. de Longpré care to make proper arrangements for me to deliver them to you. And now after you have heard all of my terms"—America's voice lightly stressed the last phrase —"perhaps you would prefer to drop the entire matter?"

"Are you sure I've heard them all, Mrs. Annable?"

"Quite sure."

"Then it's a deal at ten thousand—including other considerations."

"It's a deal," smiled America, and continued: "As a sop to Cerberus, could you throw in membership for Tugger in the Coaching Club? I didn't make this one of the terms because I'm aware one member—even one as influential as yourself—isn't always able to sway an entire board of governors. Of course, we both appreciate the need for the most complete secrecy."

"Dammit, ma'am, I'm only too anxious to place my bets under the rose!"

"And I to preserve peace in the Blake family as long as I can."

"Until Mrs. de Longpré can call, I shall be consumed with curiosity to know what manner of person Mrs. Blake may be. Does she resemble her sister?"

"You'll see—in good time."

"One more detail. What about the Pony's training?"

"Tugger will attend to that."

"Why, you sly minx!"

"Wouldn't that be better than changing handlers now—or asking the Pony to go through training with another stable-mate when he's so attached to Greased Lightning? I've heard everybody say the Pony and Lightning are the most promising entries for the Withers Stakes, yet what fun is there in backing two horses in the same stable? In the last analysis, aren't we running them—and betting—chiefly for fun? If between the three of us we can arrange things so that the best horse sets a record, does it make so much difference which one of us accomplishes the trick? The race track isn't Wall Street, you know."

"Merry, what's become of that stunning collection of Sioux wampum and war bonnets your father had?" called McAllister from across the music room.

"They went up with Golden Hill, Ward."

After the last guest had gone, Tugger came striding like a conqueror back into the music room where America was snuffing out candles. No need to ask him, she saw, how his part of the plan had worked.

"Sister Merry, we put it over!" he cried, rubbing his hands together exuberantly. "When I put the idea up to them that they stop this silly fighting and all come in under the one big top on equal terms—according to their capitalization and assets, y'understand—the three of them almost choked with relief. And when Kingsley began to trade, I knew I had 'em. Now, the next thing is for you to hustle down to Richmond to see Major Gaines—while I bring Dan around. Come on into the library, and let's celebrate! I've ordered up another bottle of Monopole."

"Not me, Tugger, I'm going to bed."

"But I want to settle with you now, while I'm feeling big-hearted."

"This room ought to contain your generosity even better than the library," she answered dryly.

"You seem to be expecting a plenty, Mrs. Annable."

"Let's hear what you've got to offer."

"Well, Sister Merry, how about that set of Holbein etchings old Markoffson let me have?"

"You mean 'The Dance of Death'? Not interested in etchings."

"Well, how about those pearls you're wearing?"

"They're Teena's."

As she spoke, she snuffed the last of the candles. The vast room, with its soaring organ pipes, lay in semidarkness except where light streamed in from the hall. There Pembroke was putting out the candles in the Adam sconces, there the tall Chippendale clock which the third Ephraim Collier had brought in his own sailing packet from England began to strike midnight. One—two—three—four sounded the full throaty notes, striking for her the end of all this dear familiar beauty. It might as well come now as later, she wearily decided. Tugger himself had spoiled it by reaching for what belonged to Fant Annable. In the hubbub which Tugger would raise over having to part with his pet horse, in the estrangement which would inevitably follow, the look she had seen too frequently of late in her brother-in-law's eyes would dissolve into anger.

"Very well then—if you insist," she answered, "I'll take Pony Express."

"W-what's that you said?"

"I said I'll take Pony Express."

Even in the dim room she could see the light of victory fade from his eyes, the boyish grin from his lips. He swallowed. Glancing down, she noticed that his hands had balled instinctively into fists to meet the first impact of shock which her choice had brought him.

"Sister Merry, you wouldn't do that to me?"

"I would. And I do."

"But you know how long I've been grooming the Pony for the Withers Stakes—I even bred him out of that War Dance mare by Texas Ranger!"

"You've been telling me Greased Lightning was the better horse."

"That's just teacup talk for you to spread! Greasy hasn't a chance—"

"Then must you win the Withers every year? The way you've been hogging the good stakes will soon break up racing."

"Sister Merry, take this house—"

"No, thank you! I want to see how it feels to watch my silks win. What shall my colors be? The Keene Stable is white with blue spots, isn't it?"

"I'll buy you a farm in Virginia—I'll fix up one of those tumble-down places on the James for you and your maw."

"Shylock, you'll be offering me Sally next. The Pony's my price."

"You're the Shylock, you blood-sucking viper I've nourished in my bosom. I won't do it!" he roared.

"Then you go see Major Gaines in Richmond," she called across her shoulder as she started up the steps into the hall.

Had it not been for her struggle with Tugger over Pony Express, the winter of '88 through '89 would have been the gayest of America's life. On her first October at home, America was overjoyed to see the chestnut high-steppers and claret milady of Mrs. Pierre de Longpré approach Tugger's door. Its owner, a tiny woman of great distinction, paid America the dubious compliment of sending in cards, and then following personally to see what manner of women her husband had asked her to sponsor.

"Pembroke, tell Mrs. Blake we have guests," America gave

the fateful order that Palestine be brought in to meet her first New Yorker of importance. How Teena might act lay on the lap of the gods. "Since the birth of her twins, my poor sister has had to conserve her strength, both mental and physical," America continued. "To Tugger's and my deep concern, all that seems to interest her now is the nursery."

Behind her studied smile, Mrs. de Longpré gave assent that she had received America's honest warning that all was not well with Mrs. Blake's mind. Nothing short of the most violent *dementia praecox,* both women knew, would keep this horse trade from going through to its agreed finish. Palestine, followed by Fräulein and the twins who went decorously on upstairs, came in bright as an autumn leaf. America had been coaching her for this hurdle which seemed simple compared to the rewards offered. Palestine sat down in a low chair, fixed her lovely eyes on Mrs. de Longpré's Paris toilette, answered yes and no in the proper places and in other respects appeared spellbound. Even the most reluctant social dragon could not fail to be flattered by such schoolgirl adulation.

January of '89 saw the next milestone passed. Thanks to Ward, cards arrived inviting Mr. and Mrs. Zachary Blake and Mrs. Fant Annable to attend the Patriarch Ball. To subject Palestine to the excitement of night lights, gaping crowds and perhaps fireworks seemed unwise. America sat on the side lines talking genealogy with Murray Hill mothers while Tugger danced with their unpopular daughters. At one o'clock the Blake carriage was called.

On the way home Tugger gave tangible evidence he appreciated the progress America had made, by announcing that he had trebled Palestine's dress allowance and would be disappointed if America did not spend at least half of it on her own wardrobe. Now that they were really being invited out this winter, continued Tugger, eying America from his corner of the closed carriage, was the house amply staffed? And when did America intend to carpet their sidewalk for a ball?

"The next important thing on our schedule is my trip to

Richmond—after you give me the Pony's transfer papers," declared America. "If you want me to bring the Major around, you'd better hurry because I must go home soon to burn plant beds."

"Hell-damn, Sister Merry, how much do you make a year on that farm?"

"Over two thousand dollars."

"I'll give you ten thousand—and your clothes—to stay here with Palestine."

"That's really generous of you, Tugger," America tried to pretend the old friendliness existed between them, "but to carry out the conditions of Cousin Simmy's will—and win Foxden for young Fant—I must stay there at least six months of the year."

"Is the will a life sentence?"

To tell Tugger that young Fant would come into his inheritance next Christmas didn't match with his mother's strategy. Closing her eyes as if too tired for further discussion, America had the last word:

"You make over those transfer papers—if you want me to talk to Major Gaines."

April of '89 saw the spring campaigns of the cigarette war well launched. Sign painters fanned out over the entire nation, splashing the names of Lord products on tenement house walls, billboards, sides of barns and even country rail fences. In Richmond, the Amber & Gaines Tobacco Company "stuck to tradition," reported the *New York Sun*, "putting in each package of cigarettes a bright picture of a lady in tights. It was a spectacular fight—a battle of tights and paint brushes. . . ." By May 10, Tugger realized he could not let a mere horse stand longer between the impending death struggle and anything he might do to effect an armistice. The afternoon after he handed America legal title to Pony Express she was on her way to Richmond. She had her own reasons now for wanting to close this deal.

Taking an open cab at the Richmond station, America sat

back to enjoy the ride to the "Court end" of town. For her, childhood memories clung about the fine Georgian houses with iron-grille balconies on Franklin Street. Here more than on upper Fifth Avenue a Moncure was at home. Her destination, the Gaines residence, was within a block of the Brockenbrough mansion which had been the White House of the Confederacy. Gabriella Gaines Harvie welcomed her ecstatically.

Yes, the Major was in the library. Why didn't America run in and speak to him? For her sake if not for the good of his own grandchildren, America begged the peppery old president of the Amber & Gaines Tobacco Company wouldn't he at least talk to Dan Lord? The Major knew, America hurried on, that Gabbie here and Clayt up the James couldn't earn an honest living if the Lords put the family out of the cheroot, plug and cigarette business. What if Old Richmond might have to bend its stiff neck enough to sit at the same directors' table with upstarts from Durham, North Carolina? Hadn't Palestine Moncure married Tugger Blake, also a Tarheel? There were compensations, as Gabriella may have noticed if she chanced to read an account of the Patriarch Ball. In 1779, which was exactly one hundred and ten years ago, Williamsburg had given way to Richmond as the capital of Virginia. Who was Major Gaines to block the present national swing of big business to New York, while at the same time he deprived Gabbie and Clayt, war-crippled as he was, of becoming multimillionaires?

"You tell Dan Lord he hasn't got money—and can't borrow enough—to buy me out, do you hear, Americy Moncyore?" shouted the Major in a voice which could be heard way downtown.

"You tell him yourself, sir," she laughed, and arose to accompany Gabriella upstairs to take off her hat.

"All right, missy—I will. Send that young squirt down here—and I will!"

"Major, is that a promise—by Marse Robert?" answered America, winking at Gabriella.

"That's a promise by Marse Robert, John Marshall, Tom Jefferson and the Great Horn Spoon, ma'am!"

When America arrived home in New York, on her desk she found a large thick envelope containing an invitation from the Pierre de Longprés for dinner on the evening of May thirtieth at Delmonico's in honor of Mr. and Mrs. Zachary Taylor Blake. The mere presence of the big square card gave mute evidence that Pierre de Longpré had peeked into the transfer books of the New York Jockey Club, although both the breeder and the new owner of Pony Express had requested that the utmost secrecy veil their recent transaction. The next fact to penetrate America's whirling thoughts was that on this momentous occasion Palestine would have to appear.

As fate happily would have it, Tugger found himself too engrossed in cajoling Dan Lord to keep his end of the appointment with Major Gaines, to think much about the Withers Stakes or his one entry, Greased Lightning. The historic name-calling between Old Richmond and New Durham was set for May twenty-eight. Tugger got home just in time to dress for the social triumph of the House of Blake. With Palestine looking like a Maréchal Niel rose in pale yellow and emeralds, America dazzling in white slipper satin, and Tugger travel-weary in faultless tails, they were driven down Fifth Avenue towards Delmonico's on Fourteenth Street.

"How did you and Dan get along with the Major?" asked America.

"He blew like a harpooned whale and sounded," reported Tugger, too tired to think of anything except what lay immediately before and behind him. "We'll bring him alongside in time."

"I'm glad of that. Teena, if you don't behave tonight, none of us will ever be asked out again," whispered America as their carriage swung in under the porte cochère. "Never mind the crowds. They've only come to see the pretty clothes."

"They don't bother me," Palestine preened herself. "I like people to look at me when I'm dressed up."

Entering the restaurant, they found Mr. and Mrs. de Longpré awaiting them in one of the larger reception rooms. In due time seventy of Manhattan's fashionables arrived. After everyone had survived the receiving line, they stood about expectantly. From far away sounded a silvan horn which grew louder until a huntsman in green tights and jerkin swung unexpectedly off the balcony and beckoned the guests to follow him.

"Why, it's Robin Hood!" Palestine gasped, and with childish delight took her host's arm.

America drew a Mr. Beauregard; Tugger, Mrs. de Longpré. The Merrie Men hurried ahead and pulled out chairs. No one noticed them, in astonishment over what awaited the dinner procession when it reached the large ballroom overlooking Fifth Avenue. Walls and ceiling were decorated to resemble the Forest of Arden. A long extended oval table, with just enough space for waiters to pass around it, filled the historic old apartment. In the table's center was a miniature woodland glen. Guests could look under the trees across the table at each other. On a pond in the center swam black swans from Prospect Park in Brooklyn. The forest floor was a mat of spring flowers—violets, trailing arbutus, ladies' slippers, azalea, dogwood and rhododendron—in compliment to the guests of honor. In rustic cages overhead, song birds filled the ballroom with melody.

A three-hour repast such as King John himself never tasted was then served. Seventy-pound Columbia River salmon appeared whole on planks lavishly garnished. Peacocks with their tails outspread collapsed to reveal dozens of toothsome squab. Lambs roasted whole were carried in on a long spit by Robin Adair and Little John, who paraded around the table demanding to know which cut each guest preferred. When a four-foot pastry was trundled in on a wagon, and Friar Tuck carved it with his sword, by this time the bedazzled guests were expecting the four and twenty blackbirds which flew out. Claret, Burgundies, Madeira, Monopole, and good brown ale flowed like water. There was so much to look at, conversation seemed unnecessary. Pierre de Longpré devoted himself to Palestine. On his left America wondered if he had forgotten the purpose of the party. On Teena's right sat Ward McAllister.

"Oh, Mr. de Longpré!" cried Teena in a moment of silence. Down the long curve of the table people stopped talking to gauge the conversational powers of Mrs. Tugger Blake, obviously a beauty but rumored none too bright. "What's the difference between you and that swan?"

"My dear lady, I haven't an idea!" laughed Pierre, while America held her breath. "Were we both ugly ducklings?"

"When we hear a swan sing, we're sorry—because we're afraid it will never sing again," declared Palestine, pleased as a precocious child to be the center of attention.

"And with me—are you afraid I will?" Pierre carried on with good sportsmanship.

"That's where the difference comes in," flashed Palestine, with a triumphant glance at America. "We hope you will."

"Bravo, Mrs. Blake!" someone shouted down the table.

"Oh, I know lots of dandy riddles," Palestine called back. "Here's one my big brother asked me when I lived in the South: What is it that is all black—has eighteen ears—and catches flies?"

A murmur ran around the table. "All black . . . eighteen ears . . ." America guessed that Tugger at his hostess' right must be wilting his collar into a limp rag.

"Do you all give up?" demanded Palestine. "A nigger baseball team!"

"That's one of your best, Teena," America interposed, firmly. "It's Ward's turn now to tell one."

As conversation began again, America bent to recover her napkin which had slipped off her stiff white satin lap.

"Have you dropped something, Mrs. Annable?" asked De Longpré, courteously. Reaching down, his hand encountered more than the linen's folds. In a moment the exchange of napkins—and title to Pony Express—had been effected.

"Won't you autograph my menu, Mr. de Longpré?" asked America and handed him the handsome scroll of birch bark. Enclosed within it was a scrap of paper on which she had written at home: "Tomorrow please put my ten thousand on the Pony's nose—to win."

Around the table gold pencils came out, scrolls were unfurled. In the general zeal to exchange menus, Pierre managed to pocket the transfer papers, and the note.

"How do you know you can trust me?" he smiled at America.

"I recognize a sporting gentleman when I see one," she murmured. The attentive Mr. Beauregard on her left immediately appropriated the remark to himself:

"That's kind of you to say, ma'am," he declared, looking immensely pleased. "My little string is nothing compared to Pete's and Mr. Blake's. Do you enjoy seeing the ponies run, Mrs. Annable? Do you place a little bet now and then, yourself?"

"Oh, no, sir," answered America, knowing that Pierre was listening. "I'm a country mouse—how would I know where to find an honest bookmaker?"

Pierre de Longpré sprang to his feet, his champagne glass held high:

"Ladies and gentlemen!" he cried, the undercurrent of excitement in his voice catching every ear. "May I propose a toast? To the country girls of Virginia—from Pocahontas and Evelyn Byrd to Palestine and America Moncure—who have come to London Town and taken our hearts by storm!"

Around the table arose spontaneous applause which caused Palestine to lean forward and exclaim in the subsequent lull:

"You see, Sister Merry—they really do like us! And if they like us, they'll ask us out again, won't they?"

In the uproar which followed, the majestic black swans in the middle of the pond trod water, flapped their wings and hissed. Far away, through an open window behind her, America heard the clock in a tower on Madison Square begin to strike twelve.

America arose early the next morning to do her last-minute packing. The white ball dress, restuffed with papers, was returned to its elegant Worth box, tied up and addressed to herself on Tuckahoe. After the family had left for the races, Pembroke would send it by express. America's two trunks had gone yesterday to Newark, there to await rechecking on to Cincinnati. America had even written young Fant what boat to meet at Limestone.

After she had snapped shut her traveling bag, which Pembroke had instructions to conceal among the picnic baskets, America realized that nothing remained for her to do now except to take a last look around Number 860. Walking pensively through the beautiful rooms which she more than anyone else had created, America wondered why fate had decreed that her own stay here, as at Golden Hill, must be so short. Beyond this afternoon, for herself she saw only an old log house on the crest of a windy ridge in Coventry.

This mood of premature nostalgia held over on the drive out to Jerome Park, Leonard Jerome's sumptuous race track in Westchester, New York. Since none of the fashionable hostesses having picnics had included the Blakes on their guest list —preferring to discuss Palestine's debut at the De Longpré dinner among themselves before openly falling into line— Tugger had insisted on making a family affair of the Blake outing. While the twins napped under some shady oak, he and Teena and America would drop over to the track and see their horses win and place in the Withers Stakes.

A holiday crowd gathered from across the park to see them off in Tugger's new English tallyho with six matched blacks out front. Running underneath was a brace of Dalmatian coach dogs. Petulant from loss of sleep, Palestine climbed irritably inside and was soon drowsing with her head on Aunt Flora's ample shoulder. On the rear top seat sat the coachmen and two tigers in the Blake livery of laurel green. Fräulein sat in the middle tier, with Sally and Junior vocal in joyous anticipation on her either side. America was to tool the spirited six through Central Park, it had been previously agreed, lest some untoward accident mar the happy occasion. Once in Harlem Lane, Tugger felt sufficient confidence to take over the reins.

Aware that the crowd mistook her for Mrs. Blake, America chatted with an assumed gaiety she did not feel. A smart linen duster protected her Worth taffeta creation of Stuart hunting-plaid with green velvet piping, a voluminous veil tied on her Scotch cap which dripped pheasant feathers over her right ear. With only two occasions to dress for—last night's dinner and today's triumphant appearance on the turf—America had felt Tugger could afford the best for her. Equally impressive in London tweeds reminiscent of the Wilmington waterfront, he gave her a hand up into the driver's seat.

Through Central Park, with hoodlums running alongside and catcalling to the twins, America tooled the fresh sextet smartly into Harlem Lane. There they found many fashionables exercising resplendent horseflesh in tandems, stanhopes, phaetons, dennet gigs, dogcarts and sulkies. Tugger almost burst with pride to see his spectacular turnout, presumably his dashing wife and his handsome children the object of all eyes. America made such a fetching picture, he declared, he wouldn't think of taking over the ribbons.

"Only to 162nd Street, then," she agreed. "You've got to get in practice for the Coaching Club's autumn meet."

"Why, milady?"

"You'll be a member by fall—or next spring at the latest."

"I will, like the old lady kept hotel," he grumbled.

"How's that?"

"Like hell!"

"Really, Tugger, you're very witty sometimes," she applauded, swinging over to let one of the younger Vanderbilts by in a light wagon drawn by 1:06 trotters. "Just you keep on being yourself—in moderation, of course!—and you'll turn out a brilliant success. By the way, I didn't see you take off your hat to Mrs. Vanderbilt. They just passed us with those trotters."

"I've never met the young lady."

"That's immaterial, now we belong. Besides, aren't we all one big fellowship of horse-loving sportsmen? It's the same on shipboard. Like recognizes like and may nod, but not intrude."

"Yes, teacher. What did you think of the party last night?"

"I suspect it will go down in fashionable New York history."

"As the most expensive dinner ever given? I'll bet so, too! The *World* this morning says it cost a cool ten thousand, if a dime. Think of that, Sister Merry—that's nearly one hundred and fifty dollars a plate."

"Mrs. de Longpré paid Teena a deft compliment in having the theme of the party something she could really enjoy," America chose to comment pleasantly, although she wondered what her father would have said to see live swans demoralizing the noble art of dining.

"Our little Teena came through with flying colors, didn't she? Better than some I could mention! You never slop over, do you, Sister Merry?"

"I'm a lady, I hope. If you'd like to hear it, I'll quote you one of father's favorite passages from Juvenal on that subject."

"Here's where I get brushed up on the classics!"

" 'The click of the castanets, songs too corrupt for harlots' lips, and all the ingenuities of pruriency,' " America began, with mock seriousness, " 'may well be left to those whose floors of Spartan marble are slippery with wine—the wine that they spit out. As to such we make allowance for their rank; but gambling is scandalous, adultery no less is scandalous for middle-class folk. When your rich men do such things, we only style them gay and smart.' "

"Naow, ain't that somepin?" drawled Tugger.

America looked at the rolling green fields, the pleasant farmhouses and apple orchards past bloom in bright new leafage, the clear blue sky heaped with cumulus clouds. It was fortunate she liked the country, America told herself, because in a few hours she would be on her way there for the rest of her life.

"That toast of Pete's struck me as pretty smart, too," Tugger commented more seriously. "Dan Lord made a similar remark just the other day. 'The best men,' Dan said, 'come from the backwoods churches. The country boy can come to town and soon learn all the town boy knows; but the town boy never can get all that the country boy has had.' And that remark goes for you, too, Sister Merry."

"Thank you, Brother Tugger—"

"Keep the change."

A lesson in tooling followed. When that was over, Palestine began to call hungrily for lunch. Two hours were consumed in selecting a proper tree in a meadow empty of bulls, stallions and snakes, in spreading, eating and then repacking the lunch baskets which were as lavish as the other appointments of Tugger's imported vehicle. The twins were then coaxed to lie down and nap in Fräulein's care, with one of the tigers left on guard. The horses were hooked in, Aunt Flora was shoved inside, and Teena boosted up on top of the tallyho. Tugger and America climbed aboard and they were off to the races. Watching her breast watch suspended by a bejeweled ribbon pin, which had been Tugger's Christmas present, America killed time by complaining about the middle span's bits, then about the lead horses picking up stones. When they arrived at the track, the second race was run, the bugle sounding for the Withers Stakes.

"Hurry up with your primping!" Tugger fumed, while his ladies removed linen dusters and veils. "I'll see you and Teena to the grandstand. Then I must get over to the paddock."

"Tugger Blake, you'll come right along into the box with us!" commanded America. "Today of all days, you know you ought to stay and speak to people—to our new friends."

"But I've got some last minute instructions to give. And I want to see if the Pony's in order—for you."

"Yesterday—while you were in Richmond—I gave all the last minute instructions the Pony 'll need," declared America, feeling like a thief in the night. "Besides this is my race. And I want it run my way—not yours."

"Now, wait a minute, lady. You forget Greasy's at least going to start."

"What else could you tell your rider that he doesn't already know? You've declared Greasy to win—and that's all there is to it."

"You mean you don't want me to instruct him to pull the race for you, ma'am?"

"Oh, Tugger, behave yourself—or people will hear you! How about you, Teena, honey—are you all right? You look just lovely. And your nose isn't sunburned one bit. Aunt Flora, you can sit here in the coach, and I'll bring her back in half an hour."

"Yassum, Miz 'Mericy."

When the Blakes and America entered the grandstand, well-bred excitement rippled across the section of boxes. Men swept off their caps, lorgnettes came up, Clarissa de Longpré waved gayly from her box. There was no denying it, the quality of today's greeting was different. Prodigal as it had been, the De Longpré dinner was not enough, America knew, to thaw out crusty old-timers like the Jays, the Newbolds, the James Gordon Bennetts. Only a supreme act of good sportsmanship could accomplish that.

Six three-year-olds, America noticed, were bouncing out onto the track behind the sedate lead pony. In the commotion of getting Palestine advantageously seated, they had filed past the Blake box before Tugger could look up. Pierre de Longpré's Voyageur led in first place with the Pony crowding his heels. Tugger's Greased Lightning stepped springily along in third. The Thomas Puryear entry Peanuts followed with one of Senator Hearst's cracks from California in fifth place. Mr. Astor's Father Knickerbocker brought up the rear. From the board America could see that the overnight transfer in ownership had raised the Pony's odds to 4 to 1. Greasy was now lead ing in betting favor.

"Hell-damn, Sister Merry, at this distance your silks look exactly like Pete's!" swore Tugger, straining his eyes. "Where're my field glasses?"

"Oh, Tugger, I forgot—and left them on the pier table at home!"

"Well, it's your horse race—not mine," Tugger resigned himself. "Lemme have my card. How does it look to see your name in print above a winner like the Pony?"

"Didn't you buy a card, Tugger?"

"Sister Merry, what's come over you? You asked me to stay with Teena, while you ran over to get the cards," cried Tugger, mildly exasperated.

"I—I must have met somebody. Please don't scold me now, Tugger," America begged for time. In another moment surely the starter's flag would come down. "I'm so excited I don't know what I'm doing! Aren't you excited, Teena?"

"My head aches, I want to go home," whimpered Palestine.

"Oh, Teena, dear, not when Tugger's having such a good time!"

"My good time ended when you claimed your pound of horseflesh, you female Shylock!" Tugger grumbled good-naturedly and settled himself to see what he could above the birds' nests and cock feathers of ladies' hats in front of him.

"They're off!" roared the crowd.

Father Knickerbocker was left at the post. The California crack took the lead around the first turn, but the De Longpré entries overhauled him in the outfield.

"Come on, you Pony!" shouted a man in the next box. "Blake, you sure slipped when you let go that Pony Express."

"It's all in the family," answered Tugger, and beamed affectionately on his sister-in-law.

With every cent she had in the world out there on the Pony's nose, America knew she ought to be watching the race. She could not resist sidelong glances at Tugger. There he sat, the big-handed Tarheel, happy to concede her racing honors today for the social triumphs she had brought him last night.

"Pony—Pony Express!" shrieked the crowd as the field swept into the stretch. The Pony had the lead, but Greased Lightning was coming up fast.

"Tugger, I hope you've got a bet on Greasy?" asked America, dumfounded by the thought of what might happen if the Pony should lose.

"Of course I have—a whopping big bet!" laughed Tugger. Cupping his hands to his mouth, he bawled in a voice the twins probably heard three miles away: "Greasy—you Greasy! Come on in, you hear me?"

"Pony—Pony Express!" rocked the grandstand.

"The Pony wins—"

A moment later, the big bay thoroughbred, his legs moving with the precision of automatic scissors, swept past the finish line in the De Longpré silks. One length behind came his tiring stablemate, Greased Lightning, with the California crack third.

"Hey, wait a minute—there's been a mistake!" began Tugger, blinking. "Merry, how'd Pete's rider get up on your horse?"

"Hush, Tugger! Yes, Teena, we'll take you to the coach—yes, right away," America attempted to divert him.

"Let go of me, Merry—while there's still time to explain to the judges!" cried Tugger, and flung off her detaining arm. "You take Teena to the coach—I'm going to the judges' stand."

"Tugger Blake, you stay right here—unless you want to make yourself the laughingstock of New York!" America hissed at him.

"W-what's that you're saying?"

"Sit down quietly and I'll explain. I sold the Pony to Pierre de Longpré."

"You did what?"

"I sold the Pony to Mr. de Longpré while you were in Richmond," repeated America, and made herself meet Tugger's eyes. "I had him transferred yesterday—"

"You mean you sold my Pony—that I bred in Texas for this one race—behind my back—to my track rival? For how much, ma'am?"

"Ten thousand—Tugger, let go my arm! You're hurting me. And people are staring—"

"If they weren't I believe I'd kill you, America Moncure! Of all the cheap shoddy tricks—and on top of it, to throw the Pony away for one-fifth of what he's worth!" Tugger whispered, savagely.

"I tell you, I want to go home," whimpered Palestine, looking first at her husband and then at her sister and gnawing her gloved knuckles in mounting fear of the anger which she saw on both their faces.

"Tugger, listen to me—because the twins' future in New York depends on how you act during the next half hour," gasped America, leaning towards him. "For seven years you've hogged the track. I saw a chance to let you do a sporting thing gracefully—in my name—to sell the Pony to Pierre for almost nothing—and—and other considerations—"

"What, you female Judas?"

"You saw last night."

"Well, I'll be damned!"

"Tugger, do be still—and control yourself," America implored. "Don't you see what a fine thing you've done—or rather, I've made you do? The Pony and Greased Lightning ran a great race—a close race—and that's all that really counts."

"Oh, Mrs. Annable!" shouted a familiar voice from below. Three steps at a time Pierre de Longpré came bounding up the stairs, rushed into the box. "I'm off to the judges' stand, Mrs. Annable—where'll I see you later?"

"I'm leaving for Kentucky in ten minutes, Mr. de Longpré," America tried to smile as he took her two hands and pumped them ecstatically.

"Where'll I send your check?"

"To Tuckahoe Ridge in Mason County. Can you remember that?"

"Will I ever forget it?" bubbled De Longpré, making a note on an envelope. Turning to his rival, he gripped Tugger's hand, shook it and exclaimed: "Today for me—tomorrow for you, sir. That's the true spirit of racing, as Colonel Jay was just saying about you, Tugger. That's the spirit that used to make the old match races in Kentucky great before the war, Mr. Newbolt says. Mrs. Blake," he turned to Palestine, "now don't you and Tugger run away, because Clarissa and I are counting on you for the Coaching Club supper tonight, you hear? We want to try your new tallyho, so don't disappoint us—or we'll have to walk. Tugger, you won't spoil my brief hour of triumph by not coming, will you? And now, dear lady"—he took America's hand, and kissed it—"*au revoir!*"

Three steps at a time, Pierre went bounding down the stairs and was swallowed into the crowd which surged towards the judges' stand to see the Pony weigh in. Drawing a long breath, America turned to meet the judgment in her brother-in-law's eyes.

"What was that he said—about a check?"

"I told him last night to put my ten thousand on the Pony's nose to win."

"You mean you made a killing like that—and never let me in on it?"

"Oh, Tugger, can't you see that would have spoiled the whole thing?" America wailed.

"No, I can't—you ungrateful, disloyal—"

"Don't you start calling me names, you big Tarheel!" she flared dangerously at him. "Maybe I have lost you a few bets you can afford a thousand times over—and your pet horse. But I've given you something a million times more valuable. In spite of your social climbing—and your occasional bad manners—and your greedy grabbing in Wall Street, I've made you do the generous—the sporting—the gentlemanly thing for once in your life. Instead of calling me names, you ought to get down on your marrow bones and thank the Lord you've got the Moncures—and Pony Express—to get you into polite society!"

"Sister Merry, you certainly do look pretty when you're mad clean through—just like that French girl with the peaked cap," giggled Palestine, refreshed by this spectacle of her betters making a scene as childish as any of her own.

"And now that I've done all I can for you Blakes," cried America, her voice breaking, "I'm going home to my tobacco patch—and to the only way of life I ever really cared two pins about—"

"Shucks, Sister Merry, forget what I just said and come along to the party—"

"I can't," quavered America, feeling desperately sorry for herself. "My being there would take the edge off Pierre's triumph—and maybe steal your thunder—"

"Who cares a damn about that?"

"No, I can't risk it. I can't have all those society reporters writing me up—"

"I'd like to know why not?"

"It might get back to Tuckahoe--to my creditors there I'm on Easy Street now, of course. But I'd better go on home—before anything happens I might regret all my life."

"Sister Merry, don't tell me your past is catching up with you?"

"Fiddlesticks, Tugger! Teena, I'm going back to Kentucky now, but ma will keep you company. And as soon as school's out, my girls will come spend the summer with you and Sally. Good-bye, Tugger. I'll take Teena to the coach—"

"Good-bye, you country jake! Have you all the money you need?"

"Maybe you'd better let me have a ten dollar bill for the extra cabfare, if you don't mind? No, don't give me your roll—ten dollars will be quite sufficient, thank you."

"Sister Merry, you are a card," he pronounced slowly, with no ridicule in his voice and eyes. "Some day I simply won't be able to stand you any longer. And when that time comes, you'll see me put my head down on my desk—and bawl like a schoolboy."

"When that time comes," she smiled at him through tears as much of farewell as of self-pity, "I won't be here to see you."

"Uh-huh," he grunted in negation, "your kind don't die young."

When she had delivered Teena to Aunt Flora, donned duster and veil and taken her traveling bag from the tiger's reluctant hand, America turned quickly away into the crowd to avoid a teary farewell with Palestine. After all, what was the use in squandering good money on a cab back to New York, when the stagecoaches made the trip every hour on racing days? Ducking her head so that none of her fine friends could recognize her, America pushed her way through the crowd to the line of waiting vehicles. Thus she left the *haut monde* as she had entered it, in a public conveyance.

Chapter 14

ON HER RETURN, America found Tuckahoe knee-deep in June. Unspotted by weeds, the bluegrass in heavy seed swayed to every passing breeze. Horses fat again after the heavy spring plowing, stood head to tail with chums in the shade. Woodland pastures were lively with lambs and foals at play. Every pond had its several ruminating cattle. Overhead in a cobalt sky thunderclouds trailed pastel shadows across the sunny ridge meadows, the wooded hillsides, the deep little valleys laced by silver streams to the quiet blue Ohio.

To America, Foxden appeared like a scene of a Homeric legend beloved in childhood, laid aside and now reopened in maturity. The admonishing fingers of the twin ash trees, the bold thrust of limestone chimneys against the eastern horizon rested her eyes accustomed to the overornamentation of New York houses. Clove-scented garden pinks, shafts of blue delphinium, snowdrifts of white peonies along her front-yard fences moved her more deeply than had Jay Gould's conservatory of prize-winning orchids. The basic law of farm life—"by the sweat of thy brow shalt thou eat bread"—soothed America's spirit stretched taut by New York's daily reach for more millions than anyone could spend, more clothes in a season than one could wear out in a decade, more food than a giant could digest and more invitations than there were hours of the day to enjoy them. Had she been a lazy woman by nature, she might have missed the expensive ease of Number 860 Fifth Avenue. Instead, she felt safe, relaxed and free at Foxden. New-found contentment gave her perspective. Like the priestess in a Greek frieze she saw herself a central figure pacing with Homeric simplicity through the quiet summer days.

She found much to do in house, poultry yard and farm. Elizabeth Jane Sims, one of Stella's married girls, come home after the wire fence which her husband had been helping stretch had let go and disemboweled him, had kept house carelessly for young Fant and the youths who had drifted in and out during America's absence. Fant had plants enough for only six acres of tobacco, and had put in less than ten acres of corn. When America suggested that they drive into Limestone to see Judge Stacy, her son vehemently declared himself sick and tired of farming; he was going away. He had only stayed on to keep things from going to rack and ruin while she was away. Checking an impulse to answer that Fant could now better appreciate the years of lonely effort she herself had expended to secure his inheritance for him, America offered to send him fifty dollars a month for living expenses, which he could regard as rent for Foxden, if he so chose. From her own experience on a trip she had taken through the Far South, America continued, she had discovered that one often fails to see the distant mountains when one is hungrily searching the roadside for berries. Moreover, she had won a considerable sum on a Westchester horse race and could now afford it. Eying his mother's embroidered pique morning dress which had looked austere in New York beside Teena's lacy elegance, young Fant declined her offer, and left with his gun and his dog.

Within the week came a frantic letter from Virginia Sue at Charlotte Court House. Instead of going directly to New York with Nicke after the Virginia Female Institute had closed, High Jinks had prevailed upon her sister to accompany her to Cousin Homer's old house on Court Street. Bayard Langston, third son of Professor Joe Dave and Orleana Chisholm Langston, was railroading at the Bristol division headquarters of the merged Eat Turnips, Vinegar and Greens. Bayard had two weeks vacation the end of June. He and High

Jinks had planned to meet in Charlotte Court House and there be married. Finding Cousin Homer's house practically stripped of furniture, continued Virginia Sue's letter, she and Nicke were staying with Aunt Andorra at the Carr house. Too senile to realize what she was doing, Cousin Tan had generously agreed to have the wedding in her big double parlors. Wouldn't America go break the news to Professor Joe Dave and Cousin Orleana in Frankfort, and then catch the next train herself to Charlotte Court House? If America could induce Mrs. Moncure to run down from New York for the ceremony, the away-from-home wedding would look more natural. "You understand, ma," asked Virginia Sue in a pathetic little postscript, "why I can't be married at Foxden? And where am I going to get a white dress?"

Thankful that she had brought her two Worth creations home in almost pristine freshness, America wired High Jinks she would arrive with a wedding gown as soon as steam could bring her. In Frankfort, America bought a bridal veil and then hurried over to the Capital to break the news to Professor Joe Dave. Cousin Orleana, whom America had never met, took to her bed on hearing it, but Professor Joe Dave saw America off on her train and promised to follow in three days to marry the children himself. Mrs. Moncure and Tugger rushed down from New York, Tugger en route to Durham on business in connection with Dan Lord's pending cigarette merger. Like mother, like daughter, thought America, seeing High Jinks stand up in the Worth ivory satin gown which had witnessed her own triumph at the De Longpré dinner. Marry in haste, and be happy ever after? How her own knees, exhausted from gripping the saddle pommels on Sunshine in the Germantown Fair ring, had quivered when she stood up twenty-two years ago on the bridge of the *Evening Mail*! "For better, for worse . . . I plight thee my troth." Where was Fant these long years since he had melted into that April snowstorm? Any other man but Fant Annable would have induced some stranger to address an envelope to carry his letter past Abigail

MacGower's watch-dog eyes, or would have sent a message by a shanty-boat man. After Bayard and High Jinks, in America's Scotch coaching-outfit, had driven off through a storm of rice, Tugger with his arm around Nicke turned to America and proposed:

"This young lady's promised to come spend the summer with Sally. Your maw's needed to look after Teena. With your boy run off to see the world—and High Jinks married—what's the use of your going back to those wornout hillsides? You'll just naturally have to come along home to New York with the rest of us. What d'you say?"

"I say you're the most hospitable man I ever met, Tugger Blake, and that's a fact!" laughed America.

"Tarheels are nothing if not family men," grinned Tugger, with the poaching look in his eye America did not like. "Then you'll come?"

"You youngsters are too much for me. I'm going home—and rest."

Back on Tuckahoe, Foxden seemed all hers again, as on that breathless July morning in '69 when Cousin Margaret had first driven America out to claim her unborn son's inheritance. With the short crops young Fant had pitched, she engaged only one mountain youth to help her tend it. Appreciating that Foxden might look to them as Tugger's mansion did to Nicke, America sent a note down to Stella suggesting that she send one of her unmarried girls up to spend the summer. Anna Claire arrived that afternoon.

White July noons cooled into dewy August nights. Katydids rattled their miniature drums in the blue ash trees after supper. The illusion that she herself was a young bride awaiting the birth of her first child tightened its hold on America's consciousness. After the mountain lad had gone to bed, and Anna Claire sat quiet as tenant girls often sit to wonder what life has in store for them, America found herself listening to every mockingbird that poured its gushing torrent of song onto the balmy night air. Where was Fant Annable, and when would he whistle again from the edge of the walnut grove out on the river rim. . . .

One mid-August morning, while she spread out to dry on the schoolroom floor the dried bunch beans she had pulled out of her garden rows, America heard a negro's voice excitedly calling her name.

"Uncle Cate! What's happened?" she demanded, stepping into the dog run.

"Ain't you hear't, Miz Merry?" gasped the old coachman from Timberlawn. "De Boss Man, he done fell aout ob de big barn whar he was housin' terbacker an' bust he hip. He's got infernal inj'ries bad."

"When did it happen?"

"Yistiddy mo'hnin'. You bettuh hurry, ma'am. He's been a-callin' foah you all day an' Miz Maggie's plumb deestracted."

When America entered the family room at Timberlawn, she found Justinian Annable lying with closed eyes deep-sunken in a grey shocked face. Instinctively she looked towards the window sill half expecting to see Gander, dead these many years, roosting there. In a slipper chair by the bedside, Cousin Margaret managed to smile wanly at America before her agonized gaze returned to her husband. On the hearth, his back to the roaring fire at which Kate was bravely heating bricks—an act which warned America the end was near—young Doctor Gillespie from Limestone stood watching his patient. Against the wall were ranged Edwin Dell, Cousin Theresa and Allilee, Emarind and Captain McCord and Stone Moncure who must have hurried over from Georgetown on hearing of the accident.

"You called for me, Cousin Justinian?" America broke the heavy silence which had greeted her entrance.

"Let me see—your baby," gasped the weak voice from the pillows.

"Nicke's living in New York now—with my sister. She's a big girl now, sir," answered America.

"So she is," whispered the weak voice. "Maggie, send

these friends out—and go yourself—if you will, please. I must speak to America alone."

Everyone else filed solemnly out of the overheated room.

"They've gone, sir."

The crêpey eyelids furled. Behind the feverish glitter in Mr. Annable's eyes, America watched the once-powerful mind gather strength to focus on a question:

"Where's Fant?"

"Why, sir—I don't know," America turned her astonishment into the simplest answer she could make.

"Can you reach him—in time?"

"I haven't seen or heard from him for years. He may be dead, for all I know. Cousin Justinian, how long have you realized Fant wasn't drowned?"

"Since I first saw that black-eyed girl of yours."

"Then why haven't you spoken out for me on Tuckahoe?"

Mortally tired, the grey eyelids were rolling down again. Lest the feeble flame of consciousness go down with them, she hurried on:

"You've been my loudest accuser, Mr. Annable. How could you, when you've known all along I loved only your son?"

"I loved him, too—in my own way."

"But had you no regard for truth or justice, sir?"

The eyelids rolled up in a last flare of Mr. Annable's one-time spirit, as he answered:

"Your shoulders are broad, America. And now, you'll have to excuse me. Call them back. And stay yourself—if you find it in your heart—to forgive me."

"I'll stay, sir," she managed to whisper.

The death watch lasted three hours. Backed against the wall by herself, America divided her attention between the ashen face on the pillow and Cousin Margaret fighting for composure as she held her husband's hand. Through the open door, America could see the double parlors filling with relatives and friends. The women sat straight and motionless, the men stood in their Sunday best with hats held formally against their left forearms. Beyond the open windows of the family room, in respectful sorrowing procession, moved a line of bareheaded negroes, the ex-slaves whom Justinian Annable had worked in the field while he sent the proceeds of their toil to Abolitionist societies. The golden noon wore on, to the drumming of locusts and an occasional solo of bird in the meadow and wheels on the pike.

"Pull up the shade—will you, Kate?" whispered the grey lips on the pillow. " 'Oh, Messer Sun, my brother most of all!' "

"What's that you're saying, Mr. Annable?" Cousin Margaret besought.

As the sunlight flooded the room, America heard faintly: "Every day since I came a man—I've watched the sun rise, Maggie. Just now I feared—it might be cloudy. The Lord has willed—I see—to let His servant depart in peace."

"Pa, don't talk like that!" cried Edwin Dell, his voice breaking.

"My knees are cold," gasped the weakening voice.

"I'll be right there, pa!" called Kate, rising from the hearth with a flannel-wrapped brick in either hand.

"Thankee, daughter. I'm obliged—but take them away."

Pouring whiskey into a tumbler, Dr. Gillespie presented it to the dying lips.

"What's this?"

"Whiskey, sir."

"Take it away—"

"It will ease your pain."

"All my life—I've lived to meet my Maker. What makes you think—I'd dull my soul—with whiskey, now?"

"It shall be as you wish, sir," Dr. Gillespie answered respectfully, the scientist in him for once stilled before the miracle of Christian faith.

Whenever Abigail MacGower looked across the fields towards Foxden. her heart hardened with unwifely rebellion against Auld MacGower. Let them who would be pious. As for herself on this fine Indian summer afternoon in November of '89, she would prefer a heart-warming talk with America about the ways of the great in New York. Although Tuckahoe turnpike had been declared free in '87, habit brought Abigail to the edge of the tollhouse porch, where she sat basking in the sun like a turtle before hibernation. Occasionally she snapped at passers-by.

Before sundown, when Abigail was thinking she must go feed the chickens, a tall unknown, his bare head streaked with grey, came down the pike on a footsore but exceptionally fine walkin' mare. Stopping her like a cavalry officer, by knee pressure instead of with the reins, he bowed politely and inquired if Mrs. MacGower had seen—

"You're th' hameliest mon I e'er hae seen!"

"That's my Injun blood," he replied, no whit disturbed. "I'd appreciate it if you'd direct me to where America Moncure Annable lives."

"Ye should be ashamed tae look an honest woman in th' face, ye wi' your bold questions!"

"What's bold in asking where my Virginia cousin lives?"

"Y'r cousin? They'd a' say that, nae doot! When fur-rst ye spoke sae courteous, I thocht ye might be th' bairns' father come tae claim your leavin's. I see noo 'tis nae likely, for th' lassies are bonnie."

"If you'd talk Greek, I'd understand you better, ma'am," Ephraim lied to uphold the family honor. This noon in Limestone, when he had tried to learn a few facts about America from a merchant or two and the jailer, he had been met with this same gush of slander—if slander it was.

"If ye maun gae there, it's th' fur-rst auld loghoose on th' richt half a mile doon th' pike."

"Thank you, ma'am. Good-evening to you."

Ephraim, one with his horse as only a man can be who has spent most of his waking hours in the saddle, continued on down the pike. Law enforcement officer that he'd been for twenty years, he approached meeting the outcast of Tuckahoe with a mixture of eagerness and dread. What was that old Greek story pa used to tell about a brother and sister who after years of separation met under tragic circumstances in a strange land? To avenge the murder of his father Agamemnon and cleanse the honor of his house, Orestes had had to kill his adulterous mother, Clytemnestra. Fleeing the civilized world with the Furies at his heels, Orestes with his faithful friend Pylades had reached outlandish Tauris, where strangers were sacrified to Diana by an alien priestess whom he recognized as his own sister, Iphigenia, snatched up by the maiden goddess and set down in Tauris to work out the complex designs of fate.

Like his footsore mare, like Orestes and friend Pylades, Ephraim felt he had come a long way. And to what end? Ephraim asked himself if it was to be his last bleak duty as a professional hunter to cleanse the Moncure honor befouled by his favorite sister? If the stories he had heard in Limestone were true, stories in part confirmed by that old turkey hen roosting on the tollhouse porch, then Sister Merry could no longer be America Moncure, but some bitter-hearted modern Iphigenia who lured inexperienced lads strayed down from the mountains into her Foxden to destroy their souls, as Orestes' sister had laid the knife of pagan sacrifice to shipwrecked sailors' throats on that far-away Taurian shore.

Thick dust in the Foxden lane muted his horse's hoofs. While he slipped his bridle rein over a paling Ephraim saw evidence of the green fingers of a Moncure woman in the flowers blooming along Foxden's yard fences. Through the dog run of the interesting double log house, he saw a girl seated on a rear step working freshly churned butter. As he approached, Ephraim noticed that she had mouse-colored braids, thick wrists and ankles and that she sat with legs apart as no grown Moncure girl ever sat.

"*Chickee—chickee!*" called a woman's voice somewhere

below the vegetable garden, a voice which turned time a quarter-century back for Ephraim. Lest he startle this servant girl of America's, he scraped his boot on a flagstone.

"Oh, my goodness," gasped Anna Claire, almost dropping her crock. "What a start you gave me!"

"I'm sorry, Miss Annable—"

"I'm Anna Claire Barnes, sir."

"Do you live here, Miss Barnes?"

"Well," began the girl, and hung her head shyly over her work again.

"Where may I find Mrs. Fant Annable, Miss Barnes?"

"That's her—a-feedin' the chickens. Jest you go on along by the garden thar."

As Ephraim started down the path, he realized that he hadn't had a worse job in the Cimarron. Beyond the frost-blackened rows, in a chicken yard with hens, guinea fowl and ducks gobbling corn about her feet, stood a slender woman with sunset light on her hair. The straight flat back was half turned to him, but Ephraim recognized the long fine body, the unforgettable lift of pointed chin, the hair glossy as buck-eyes. As a bad dream fades at awakening, Ephraim's fore-bodings vanished. All he saw before him was the dear companion of his boyhood, the flower of the Golden Hill flock.

"Sister Merry!" he called, and began to run towards her.

"Ephraim!"

Dropping her pan of corn, America met him in the darkness of the henhouse. The strength of their mutual embrace left them breathless. Laughing like children, they pulled each other out into the light and stared.

"Damned if you ain't a good-lookin' woman, Sister Merry! I used to think Teena had the edge on you—but not now."

"And you, Eph!" she gasped, tucking in curls knocked down by their tumultuous greeting. "Now I know why Cap'n John Smith called Powhatan a kingly savage."

"From what I hear in Limestone, you're the savage,"

Ephraim decided to get unpleasant subjects over with before they settled down for a grand old talk-fest. "What's this I hear about you being a—a roadside harlot?"

"Now, Eph, must you start calling me names the first minute we meet?"

"Yes, isn't it silly?" he answered, with the whole picture clear at last before his eyes. "Where're your children?"

"Young Fant's out seeing the world. High Jinks married last June. And my baby Nickettai—remember that old chief who called me 'pretty little thing'?—Nicke's spending the winter with ma and Teena in New York."

"I'm sorry to hear that," Ephraim plunged grimly on. "As soon as I see your children, I'll know I'm right in assuming that Fant Annable's still alive."

He watched the warm color drain from her face, leaving a pinched expression around her nose. That was the look women wore in mortal stress, the look which came across the faces of men dying unmasked on the gallows or from gunshot wounds. Used to serving death sentences alike on the weak and on the strong, Ephraim's heart warmed to this display of his sister's stout heart. That old Redskin had called the trick, all right.

"The next time Fant Annable sneaks in here to beget another nameless brat for you to raise," Ephraim faced up slowly to his duty, "I'm afraid I'll have to catch him, my dear, and turn him over for trial."

"Eph Moncure, what nonsense are you talking? Ma wrote you years ago how Fant was drowned on the *Evening Mail.*"

"Sister Merry, you may have succeeded in pulling the wool over the eyes of these dull country burghers—and even that fat high sheriff, Swillevant, in Limestone. But don't try your little tricks on me," Ephraim declared, watching her. "I've cut my teeth on real outlaws like Billy the Kid. I'm hard to fool."

"Then, sir, I think you'd better march right on back to Texas!"

"Naturally you'd feel that way," he answered, sadly. "That's why I thought we'd better talk this thing out now—before I eat your salt."

"You see the way to the pike."

"Ain't life hell, Sister Merry?" Ephraim complained. "Honestly, I hoped I was through being a human blood-hound—that I could come here to rest—and be near you and ma. I even hoped you'd introduce me to some easy-going Kentucky heiress who ud want to marry me—and keep on running her own farm while I go off to Confederate reunions. Instead, I find you still mired to your eyebrows in Fant Annable's rottenness. Damned if I didn't make the mistake of my life not to saber that yellow-livered pup when I had the chance!"

"Now that you've had your say, it's my turn," declared America. "Let me tell you right here and now, Eph Moncure—"

"Shu-ush, Sister Merry! You're talking to Eph Radford, now. I'm still wanted in Charlotte Court House for the murder of some old Sawbones I found half-buried down our hollow. I had to skip out quick in Blake's wagon the night after Timber saw me rebury that body. Timber was hand and glove with Cushman, who'd sworn to make somebody pay for killing a Yankee friend of his."

"I'll tell you now what ma couldn't say then—and didn't dare write in a letter—for fear of incriminating me. That dead Yankee's name was Mudston and he brought out those troopers who burned Golden Hill. When Mudston tried to rape Teena I got there first with a corn knife."

"So it was you who killed him! Now I begin to see what's wrong with Teena—"

"Nothing's wrong with Teena!" America's temper blazed at this oft-repeated statement of a condition which could and must be met only by vigorous denial. Eph was as slow-witted as Tugger had been, in seeing that no good would ever come of admitting Palestine's bird brains had been inadequate to meet the strains of war. "Do you think I'd stand around like a 'ninny at a time like that?" America resumed her narrative. "While the others hustled Teena on down the hill, Ol' Uncle and I pulled Mudston's body into Pembroke's cabin, thinking it would burn. The chimney fell in, the wind changed and—well, you saw Cushman smelling around the day you came home. Fant noticed right off what you were too selfish and blind to see. Fant saved my neck by reburying Mudston in the hollow."

"Pity he couldn't have made a better job while he was at it!" snorted Ephraim. "Because of his bungling, I had to drop my name—and can't go back to old Charlotte."

"You aren't missing anything. Nobody—not even a railroad—goes to Charlotte Court House, now."

"Well, Sister Merry, you've solved the two great mysteries of my life," drawled Ephraim. "The first was about old Sawbones. The second is why you felt you had to stick to shoddy all these years."

"I loved Fant Annable."

"You may have loved your own idea of Fant rushing to your rescue, and are too stubborn now to admit your marriage was a mistake. You weren't exactly cold to being the future mistress of Timberlawn, either. It's a handsome place, I admit. And you haven't done badly for yourself right here," conceded Ephraim, raising his eyes to Foxden and beyond it to fields green-furred with winter rye. "My real opinion is that you're one of these drivin' women who don't need men—except occasionally—and so you've been content to go along sacrificing your reputation to having your own way. Damned if I'm not sorry I came back! What business is it of mine if you wear skirts and breeches too—and drag 'em both in the mud—so long as I don't know it? Now I'm here, it's my bounden duty to catch Fant Annable and haul him into a Limestone courtroom—where he'll have to tell the whole world he's the father of your children."

"I tell you, Fant's been rotting on the river bottom for more than twenty years!"

"Oh, no, he hasn't. You couldn't speak that way about the husband of your bosom if he were, my dear."

"You're crazy, Ephraim Moncure—"

"I'm plain Eph Radford, now. Be so kind as to keep my little secret—since it saved your precious neck! And now I've had enough of you and Fant Annable for one day," confessed Ephraim, wearily. "I'm going to walk back to Limestone because my mare's too lame to carry me, and I'm going to hire out as a deputy to Sheriff Swillevant."

"What makes you think he'd take you?"

"For your information, Eph Radford's a name known wherever men ride far and draw quick. There ain't a sheriff on either side of the Mississippi wouldn't jump to get me as his deputy."

"How do you know I—I won't inform on you?"

"For the same reason I knew Fant Annable was still alive," he flung back at her across his shoulder, then turned to have the final word in somber compliment: "You couldn't be an informer any more than you could be a whore."

Sheriff Swillevant must have engaged Ephraim, because America met him on the pike the next week riding to serve papers on some tax delinquent. Before the winter was out, handsome Bethenia Doggett fell into Eph Radford's arms like a sun-sweetened peach when the branch is tapped gently with a rake. Rich old Captain Doggett, confined to his wheel chair since the battle of Kenesaw Mountain, would not hear of his only daughter leaving home; and so Ephraim moved his horses, gear and guns into the Doggett's pleasant country seat outside Dover village, nine miles down the river from Limestone. Accustomed to the direction of his farms from his wheel chair, Mr. Doggett continued it. Ephraim, who had always preferred soldiering to work, let his willingness to represent local veterans at Confederate reunions be known. His whispered war and Klan record and his known fame as a Texas Ranger, his unquenchable gaiety and his striking appearance made Eph an eye-arresting figure among the defeat-saddened cripples for whom the pleasantest thing life now held was to attend conventions and there relive over frosted mint juleps their high martial experience.

Disciplined since childhood in the penny-pinching school of war and farm economy, America felt extravagant in subscribing to the *New York Times* and the *World.* When the newspapers arrived, however, she turned first to the financial pages, then browsed through the society columns. She used sections containing items on fashion trends and New York department store advertisements to line egg baskets she pushed every Friday noon across Abigail MacGower's counter. These subtle seeds of friendliness bore two fruits. Within six months Abigail and America were speaking again. And a marked improvement in style was soon evident in the dresses which came out from under Mrs. MacGower's gifted needle.

Alone at Foxden before the family-room fire, America in February of '90 read in her New York papers announcement that a cigarette combine had been formed. Chartered on January 31 as a New Jersey corporation, the General Tobacco Company was made up of the five major combatants of the bitter cigarette war, and was capitalized at twenty-five million. All assets, trade brands, patents and good-will of the five companies were thrown into a common pool. Dan Lord became the first president of General Tobacco, with Clayton Gaines of Richmond second in command. America was also pleased to read that Dudley Marshall, who had sacrificed his digestion to preserve his wife's patrimony, was secretary; that the alert Aberdeen terrier, Frank Kingsley, was treasurer.

"My object in forming the General Tobacco Company," Dan Lord declared in an interview, "is to get an organization . . . of people who will be of assistance in conducting the business. And then besides, I expect to make a profit out of it, because you can handle to better advantage a large business than a small one."

America laid down the financial page and gazed into the

fire. Tugger Blake's name did not appear anywhere in either paper's account of the historic transaction. Had Dan Lord succeeded in giving Tugger the cold shoulder again?

Within the same month, a local tobacco problem presented itself to America. Her stewardship of Foxden had expired, yet young Fant's whereabouts were unknown to her. Should she hire hands, clear ground and burn plant beds in the event he might return and want to raise a crop? When she appeared before Judge Stacy, he advised her to let the farm lie fallow. Tobacco impoverishes even limestone soil to such an extent that good husbandry ordains that leaf be grown not oftener than once in seven years on the same plot of ground. Thus, every tobacco crop grown for America's self-support might be construed, declared Judge Stacy, as having diminished to some extent the value of young Fant's legacy. The opposite view, however, was held concerning the occupancy of a house. Foxden would be safer if America continued to live there until its lawful owner returned, than if she moved out and left it to the mercy of wind, rain, mischievous boys, thieves and itinerants.

As she left the courtroom, America met the sympathetic gaze of a few men honestly sorry for her because she was forbidden to raise the one money crop which kept Mason County farmers' heads above water. Personally, she felt relieved. Judge Stacy's opinion freed her from another ten months over a hot cook stove. Thanks to Pony Express, for the first time in her life she need not worry about money. High Jinks was married, Tugger Blake met Nicke's expenses in New York. Walking from the Limestone courthouse to the Farmers Bank, America knew she was the smartest-dressed woman in town in Teena's discarded but scarcely worn *trotteur* of hunter's green broadcloth and Alaska seal. When she had presented Pierre de Longpré's check for forty-eight thousand dollars for collection, eyebrows at the Farmers Bank and elsewhere had gone up. Word that it was actually good, further scandalized the United Daughters of the Confederacy and church sewing-circles. America's reputation as a big city Jezebel soared into five figures—"and her own, a devilish fine one!" declared Limestone rakes, as if they knew more about the one-time hermit of Foxden than they would care to confess to their wives.

Judge Stacy had said nothing about the six acres of tobacco raised on Foxden in the crop year of '89. When it came into sweet case in May of '90, America began to prize it into hogsheads. She was methodically grading lugs one bright May morning when a man's voice called out in German:

"Put off is not given up, Frau Annable."

"Why, Hans Claussen!" she recognized the more responsible of the two Bavarian youths who had taken down her leaf in return for a night's lodging years ago. "You said you'd come back."

"*Ja,* I come vor dat job you promised."

"Too bad! This is the first year since '69 I'm not pitching a crop."

"Den ve talk. Go on mit your vork," he answered, moving towards the leafing table with her. She unconsciously began again to sort the tobacco before her. Unaware that he was watching her, she asked:

"And that Wilhelm, who drank up my elderberry wine. Where is he?"

"Still vorking for papa Wurlitzer in Zinzinnati. I can do dat goot as you."

"Do what?"

"Vot you do."

"You mean leaf tobacco? Hans, it takes years to train a man's eye to recognize and class different grades of tobacco."

"Maybe zo. But not zo long as it takes to match vood for violins."

Impressed, she looked up with an unvoiced question.

"*Ja,* zince I vas zo high in de Old Country, I match violin vood," declared Hans. "Now I quit. I find a house on dis green ridge—four months of year I vork for you, *nicht wahr*?"

"But I haven't enough tobacco to keep you busy for four months, Hans. And besides, Judge Stacy won't let me grow a crop this summer," she temporized.

"I see goot crops growing here—dare—ev'rywhere. People say you are a rich voman, Frau Annable. In Zinzinnati I vatch how quick tobacco spec-culators grow vat pocketbooks, und vatter here," he chuckled, slapping his own thick middle.

"Get behind this table, and let's see what you can do," was her laconic answer.

America's purchase that summer numbered only nine crops, less than a hundred thousand pounds of leaf. On the momentum of the "expanding eighties," she sold it well. Her profits in '92 were less, but her quantity larger. By then, she had become a familiar figure flashing up and down Mason County's white limestone roads in her expensive bar buggy drawn by fast bay mares. Tuckahoe gentry, especially the ladies, looked the other way when she met or passed them on the turnpike. Because she never tried sharp practices on her tenant-growers, and because she seemed willing to give them a slight edge in every trade, confident that she could make up these few dollars so vital to them by Hans' meticulous handling and low overhead, she gradually became known as "the pore man's friend."

Throughout Mason County, the practice lingered among some growers to deliver crops in sweet case. A favorite trick of unscrupulous speculators was to throw aside armfuls of good leaf with the false pronouncement: "It's funked!" Such a one was "Bully" Miljohn. With his long walrus mustache, fine clothes, and roaring buffoon's voice, Bully often succeeded in intimidating backwoods farmers into accepting whatever reduced price he then chose to offer for the alleged sour leaf which he had thrown out.

"Gabe, those Mason County growers are a mighty techious lot," Miljohn was said to have complained to another sharp trader, Gabriel Pettigrew. "I had throwed out nigh onto a thousand pounds of as sweet leaf as you ud want to put in vour mouth, when damned if that hillybilly didn't pull a gun and order me to put that funked leaf right back onto the scales!"

"You didn't let him get away with a bluff like that, did you, Bully?"

"Shore I did. There's plenty of suckers left in the Blue Grass. Besides, how was I to know he was bluffing? I aim to enjoy my four thousand acres that I've racked all over this state to accumulate."

After fifteen months of silence, young Fant wrote from Breathitt County that he had married a mountain girl named Effie Mae Cox. They were living with her folks, the letter continued. Young Fant had no idea of returning to claim his inheritance until his father's name was cleared and he could hold his head up among decent folks. In the meantime, Effie Mae was expecting again, and they needed money. Could America send him the landlord's share of any income she might have derived from Foxden since the farm had come to him? If she hadn't raised a crop, what about house rent? He hated to ask her, but he needed cash.

America asked Judge Stacy in chambers what he would consider a fair rental for the Foxden house and pasturage sufficient for her reduced livestock. Each month for as long as she could afford it, she sent her son the twenty dollars a month which the court had advised.

In '93 the "rich man's panic" swept across the nation. Everywhere little business collapsed. Farmers of the South and Middle West owed eastern banks two billion dollars in mortgages. Tobacco, paralleling four-cent cotton, sank to all-time lows. Corn was offered at ten cents a bushel, with no buyers. Yet in her New York dailies, America had read how the year had opened with one hundred per cent dividends and consolidations of vast industrial empires. Fortunately, she had sold her purchase early in June. The losses which Stone Moncure sustained in August became the talk of the Cincinnati hogshead market. Instead of cutting down his purchase or lying low as America did until the storm had spent itself, Stone tried to keep afloat by trebling his volume. In later years, America attributed her financial caution to the fact that she had to spend hard coin, not credit based on warehouse loans secured by a rich farm like Children's Chance. When her money was gone, her purchase was necessarily completed.

At this critical juncture, the Supreme Court handed down the first of three epochal decisions which seemed to strike to the heart of the farmer's and laborer's despair. The first was rendered in January '95, when the high tribunal dismissed the government's suit against the E. C. Knight Company, which had united many eastern refineries into the Sugar Trust. The decision was discussed around the stove of every crossroad's store in the nation, including Auld MacGower's on Tuckahoe. At the counter, America half turned to listen:

"Olney, the Attorney General," Stone was explaining, "based his case on the theory of monopolistic manufacture of sugar within Pennsylvania, instead of on price-fixing and monopolistic selling across state lines. Is it any wonder he lost?"

"Be that unlawful same as bigamy, squire?" demanded one of the illiterate Ruggles men.

"Cleveland evidently feels the Sherman Act is of little value, but he's mistaken," declared Dr. Gillespie, warming his shins while Auld MacGower shod his mare. "A courageous President, with public opinion behind him, could put teeth into it that would tear the trusts to pieces, and give the little fellow a chance."

On May 20, the Supreme Court handed down its decision outlawing the income tax, previously laid on the affluent to bring in government revenue and at the same time to help reconcile the farm and laboring classes to the rising prices which they had to pay for American factory-made products under high tariff protection. Seven days later came the Eugene V. Debs ruling, the bitter aftermath of the Chicago Pullman strikes.

Around the boot-scarred table in the social room of the Growers Sales and Warehouse Company, discussion waxed hot.

"Freedom of speech—the right av the working man to protest his wrongs—has been outlawed," snorted Kelly, the auctioneer. "I didn't believe it wad iver come in this country. I've lived too long."

"You don't think we're going to take this sitting down, do you?" roared Henry Morris. "Wait—wait until us Democrats meet next July to nominate our candidate for the greatest Presidential struggle this country has ever seen! Then we'll fix Cleveland and the bloated capitalists!"

"An appeal to your electorate would indeed appear the next step," spoke up the Ogden's buyer.

"That's our one hope, now," America agreed, and was surprised a moment later to hear herself quoting her father. "That, and the fact that the fighting Anglo-Saxon stock from which we Americans—like you British—have come, has never yet permitted itself to be ground down to the level of a peasantry."

Everyone turned and looked at her, as at a Cassandra, until the sales bell called them out onto the floor.

When she received her newspapers describing the Democratic National Convention held in Chicago in July of '96, America spread them out on the cook-cabin table at Foxden, and read them all. The outstanding speech of the Convention, which had won its maker the Democratic nomination for President, had been made by a young Senator from Nebraska named William Jennings Bryan. The farms, declared Bryan, were the basis of American prosperity, but the petitions of the common people had been mocked, so that the issues of 1776 and the new contest for national independence in 1896 were the same. "Having behind us," Bryan challenged, "the producing masses of the nation and the world, the laboring interests and the toilers everywhere, we will answer their demand for a gold standard by saying to them: 'You shall not press down upon the brow of labor this crown of thorns—you shall not crucify mankind upon a cross of gold!' "

Though the significant words made her nerves tingle, America laid the newspaper down and tried to translate them into terms of her neighbors' business situation. If Bryan were elected on November 3, to satisfy the debtor and laboring classes which put him into the White House he would immediately legislate his free-silver plank into law making the American dollar worth fifty cents. Knowing this, Stone Moncure was trying to hold his hogsheads off the breaks until after election, when he hoped to pay his warehouse debts with two new inflated silver dollars for every deflated gold dollar he now owned. Augustus Meiers and the other warehousemen who had advanced Stone cash to make his huge seasonal purchase, were pushing Stone to sell; first, because they needed cash to protect other investments caught out in the free-silver blizzard and, second, because by a squeeze play when leaf prices were at rock bottom, they hoped to foreclose on Children's Chance, which secured Stone's warehouse loan.

On August 26, the Cincinnati and Limestone papers carried in heavy leaded type: STONE MONCURE ASSIGNS! A week later, Abigail told America that Stone had talked the court into giving him sixty days in which to try to effect a settlement with his creditors. For three mornings, America saw the familiar weather-beaten buggy with Stone seated sideways in it behind his fast trotters spinning briskly up the pike. Lying wakeful at night, she heard them clattering wearily homewards. Was Stone finding his Mason County neighbors as hard-hearted, she wondered, as she knew them to be? On the fourth day Stone must have stayed home. That night America dreamt that she was married to him, and that both were reduced to share-cropping for Justinian Annable on the back hillside farm where Jim Barnes and Stella lived.

Arising at five o'clock the next morning, America saddled thirty-two-year-old Sunshine and walked him down to Children's Chance. Hans had told her the evening before that volunteers from the neighborhood planned to meet there this morning and house Stone's crop, an early one now wasting in the patch for its grower's lack of money to hire help. As she rode on out to the field, Stone came to meet her with the hurried stride of a man still under a desperate strain. His sun-scorched face was fresh-shaven. He wore a clean but rough-dried shirt and overalls instead of his habitual plantation linens. America knew he had dismissed his house servants and was himself cooking for Weed and Ben Shadrack, who refused to leave him. Worry had cost him thirty pounds' loss of weight, America judged. The pleasure which her coming evidently gave him, made her fumble with shaking hands for the check she had written out at Foxden and folded into her pocket. Extending it, she began hesitantly, not daring to meet the blue eyes raised towards her:

"Stone, I wish you'd take this check—and regard it as a loan until you're on your feet again."

"Why, Merry—it's for twenty thousand dollars!"

"It's half my capital. I won it on Pony Express, a race horse my brother-in-law gave me in New York. Because I didn't know any honest bookmakers, Pierre de Longpré placed my bet—and wrote the check for my winnings."

"You don't have to explain that to me, America. I don't need your money—"

"I was afraid you'd feel that way," she answered tonelessly, and leaned forward for her bridle rein which had slipped to Sunshine's ears when he reached down for a mouthful of clover. So on this barren ridge she wasn't to have the privilege of helping a one-time friend and kinsman? Well, she had endured his scorn before in the tobacco barn out on the windy ridge rim at Foxden; she could meet it again until she could leave this field where a dozen men, black and white, stood staring curiously at her. This ought to be a lesson to her; would she never learn that everybody here on Tuckahoe meant always to take her at her worst apparent value?

"The miracle is, I don't need it," she heard Stone's voice declare. "My neighbors have saved me."

She gasped and stared down into the wondering blue eyes.

"Yes, they actually saved me!" Stone was whispering. "I—I didn't know there was that much Christian kindness left in this whole money-mad nation, let alone Mason County. When I'm an old man, I'll look back and remember—like pictures hung on a gallery wall—my meetings with my creditors. They've been the greatest experience of my life—these meetings—and you bringing me this check this morning—and my neighbors coming in to help me house my tobacco."

Behind her eyes, was the sudden sting of unshed tears.

"What happened, Stone?"

"When I went down to Cincinnati last week—it seems a year ago—I was a crazy man. I purposely left my gun at home, because— There they sat around that table, fat city slugs who couldn't do a day's work in the tobacco patch if their lives depended on it! I asked them for time, I told them my notes weren't due till next January. Meiers cut in, and said they had my hogsheads on their floor. I owed them the money, and they meant to start selling in the morning. When I reminded them my purchase wouldn't pay out, that fox-faced treasurer said my land was good for the deficit. Then I lost my head. If they so much as laid a hand on my hogsheads, I said I'd kill them. Who was I but a damn' Rebel from across the river, asked an old Yankee colonel. Another one said I might kill several of them, but not the whole board. All they had to do, Meiers put in, was to notify the Cincinnati police to lock me up for a wild-talking hillbilly—and let me out when my purchase was sold."

"So that's why you assigned!" breathed America.

"In the nick o' time, too," Stone agreed. "Kelly was ready to cry my first hogshead when the marshal appeared, sealed my purchase and ordered it back into storage. That afternoon we prevailed on the court to grant me sixty days to try and effect a settlement. What was the use, I asked, of dumping my land and my leaf on the worst market this country has ever seen? Even if Bryan isn't elected—"

"He won't be," interposed America, thinking of Wall Street full of creditors like Tugger Blake.

"I don't think so either—now," smiled Stone, ruefully. "Suppose Bryan does go down, we argued to the judge, when the Republicans come in they'll put prices up again, won't they? They always have. Why wouldn't it be better for all concerned to let me wait and sell my leaf then—and work the balance of my debt out of Children's Chance, even if it does take me the rest of my life?"

"You don't mean your creditors have agreed to let you keep your land?"

"Yes, I do! Sol Liebman, that old Shylock who walked into Limestone forty years ago with a pack on his back, said men had come running to borrow money from him for years, but I was the first broke man who'd ever come myself to see what was to be done about paying it back. I'd been a good handler, he said. I'd brought prosperity into Mason County whenever there was any to bring. He agreed to sign my settlement papers and then he told me to get down off my horse and come on in to dinner. Aunt Molly Spradlin—"

"The rich old woman who keeps marrying young hus-hands?"

"Aunt Molly said my interest money had built her barns and fences. She agreed to sign my paper. So did Auld MacGower. And Mr. Trayem, the Limestone grocer. And Mose Dalton, the livery-stable man—and the directors of the Farmers Bank. Everybody, even you," he beamed at her, tears behind his smiling blue eyes, "wants to give me another chance—to help me on my feet again."

"I wouldn't have believed it," began America, gathering up her reins.

"Neither would I—of hard-fisted farmers," confessed Stone and began carefully to tear her check into fragments. When the last undecipherable scrap of paper had fluttered down the wind, he looked up again into her eyes and declared serenely, without embarrassment or any attempt to confuse his meaning: "I'll keep your kindness in my heart. Now, I'd better get back to work—to save my crop for you all."

On November 3 the Republicans and Gold-Democrats swept McKinley into the Presidency. The sharp squeeze for money at once eased. "Maybe I haven't made a killing!" exulted Tugger to America, and went on to write her of Dan Lord's plans to launch a second tobacco war, this time into the rich plug trade.

Common and preferred stock of the General Tobacco Company had first been listed in May of '95 on the New York Stock Exchange. The year after the cigarette combine had been organized, it had paid a ten per cent dividend on its common stock. In '91 through '94, the dividend rate had been increased to twelve per cent. In December of '95, General Tobacco announced that no dividend would be paid, and immediately led all tobacco stocks downward on the New York Stock Exchange. Bears, hoping that this suspension of dividends indicated a crack they might widen in Dan Lord's defenses, made a strong drive against the combine's securities. Small investors were sheared, often of life savings, in the falling market. "We insiders are being charged as usual," Tugger wrote America, "with trying to clean out the little fellows, and buy in all the outstanding shares of General Tobacco at our own figure."

"Well, aren't you?" countered America, in her next letter.

"Dan needs cash," Tugger answered in January of '96 and went on to explain how the cigarette trust was buying into the plug trade. Years ago, he and Dan had found it unprofitable to handle only one specialty, cigarettes. Moreover, the reformers were making such a hullabaloo about paper-wrapped coffin nails that General Tobacco's board thought it wise to buy one St. Louis and three New York firms manufacturing established brands of all-tobacco cigarettes. Once started, wasn't it the most natural thing in the world for Dan to add half a dozen old-line plug manufacturers in Louisville and Baltimore to give his salesmen plug brands to peddle along with the paper-wrapped and all-tobacco cigarettes?

"Yes, but it's the way you're doing it," countered America. "On the Cincinnati breaks they're saying that when you bought out the Whitaker cheroot and segar business in Richmond, you made Phil Whitaker sell the exclusive use of his name, and agree to become an employe of General Tobacco and not to engage for twenty years in any other form or organization of the tobacco business. What do you call it when you crowd a man to the wall and then force him to work for you and nobody else—to sell out to you lock, stock and barrel on your terms or go broke? You may call it high finance, but to me it sounds like a new kind of brigandage. If you weren't in Wall Street and so rich that nobody dares criticise you, you would be accused of acting like old-fashioned highway robbers."

Before Tugger answered this outburst, America saw in her New York dailies that the General Tobacco Company had purchased the Pierre de Longpré Company of New Jersey, important producers of plug and snuff. For the approaching "plug war" which everybody saw was now inevitable, three pioneer plug companies of St. Louis lined up to battle the expanding cigarette trust. Leonard & Morley, whose Mr. Piper was still dean of the Cincinnati breaks, was the most powerful, with the Grummond and the White companies close seconds. Behind these "Big Three," hundreds of local independents, like Henry Morris with little businesses scattered in towns along the Ohio River close to the hogshead breaks of Cincinnati and Louisville, hurried forward to hurl their pebbles at the Tarheel giant. These foot soldiers of the plug war, many of whose names Dan Lord never even knew, foresaw that if the captains of the plug trade went down, he could pick them off in his own good time, or sweep them under in national advertising and price-cutting, as he had done the small fry in the cigarette war.

Grummond & Company fired the first price-cutting salvo by reducing its popular *Toddy* to fourteen cents a plug. General Tobacco answered by reducing its *Battle Axe* to thirteen cents. Leonard & Morley, rumored to possess cash reserves comparable with General Tobacco's, brought out its special formula *Gray Goose* at twelve cents. And while Dan Lord was experimenting for a mix to equal *Gray Goose* in quality and flavor, the White Company brought out a spectacular new plug, *Champagne Dry,* which swept the country.

"How good are you at spying, you incurable bushwhacker?" Tugger wrote America early in March of '97. "If you'll disguise yourself, hop over to the White factory in St. Louis and get me the formula for their *Champagne Dry,* I'll give you ten thousand dough-ray-me's, and the finest wedding for Nicke that money can buy. Be careful, though, if you try it, because the White people aren't standing for any nonsense in their plant these days. You'll probably have a better chance to carry off the bacon if you darken your skin with walnut juice to get into the stemmery, than if you try to push past the guards all leaf manufacturers throw around their laboratories these days. You'll have to step lively, because Dan has big schemes ripening. You need feel no qualms of conscience about spying for that formula, because it was stolen from Dan by buying over his chemist, Anderson, whom he had carried on his pay roll for years to develop a good plug formula. After you've got the formula, come on over to New York and meet your future son-in-law." In a postscript, Tugger added: "Incidentally, what did you do with that money you won on Pony Express? Now's the time to buy General Tobacco, before the news gets touted around Dan means to make it the carryall for his new plug line-up."

If Tugger Blake thought she was going to go spying around among factory hands after trade secrets, thought America, tossing the letter aside, he was mightily mistaken. Probably the only way she could get through the plant gate would be to stain her skin with walnut juice and tie her hair in a bandanna! Tugger's suggestion about purchasing General Tobacco stock before it climbed higher with each announcement of new plug concerns added to its assets, impressed her as advice well worth consideration. Thirty or forty thousand dollars put into General Tobacco common now might yield her more profits in a month than she could make prizing leaf in ten years. The money was lying idle in two banks in Cincinnati and one in Limestone, bringing in nothing.

On the point of going downriver to locate a reliable broker, America received a letter from Cousin Homer Pettis, in St. Louis. After some euphuistic paragraphs about family health, Cousin Homer got down to brass tacks and gave the reason for his letter. Last week he had received a telephone call at his home from "a man named Walter Fox who claims to be a friend of yours, America. He's here in St. Louis at the Good Samaritan Hospital, he said, and begged me to write you to come see him at once, as he was critically ill. If you couldn't come, would you please send him a hundred dollars, Fox asked. As this is a common device of unscrupulous persons to get money under false pretenses," continued Cousin Homer's letter, "before communicating with you I decided to drive around to the hospital first and have a look at the fellow. I found him in a lung-fever ward feeling very sorry for himself. He reminded me of somebody I used to know back in old Charlotte, but to save me, America, I can't remember where or how. He seemed so worried about money matters I let the poor chap have fifty dollars. When he first called, I thought he might be your brother Ephraim in trouble and traveling under an assumed name, but he wasn't. This man is middle-aged, with dark eyes and greyish hair. Do you know him? If not, let me caution you against communicating with him, as I assure you this is an old game employed by sharpers to get gullible widows with good farms enmeshed in their toils."

Before she had finished reading Cousin Homer's copper-plate script, America realized that Walter Fox must be Fant Annable. Hoping to flag her attention, her husband would have chosen just such a name. How now could she give Ephraim the slip, and prevent herself from being recognized when she arrived in St. Louis? When she had delivered Cousin Homer's letter to America, Abigail had commented on its St. Louis postmark and had probably mentioned it also to Bethenia Radford. Eph often used his wife as a pump to bring up Tuckahoe gossip. If it wasn't convenient for Eph himself to follow his sister, all he need do was to wire his fellow hounds of the law in St. Louis to watch out for America Moncure Annable when she arrived at Cousin Homer's, and see if her long-wanted husband didn't himself show up in time. The quicker she got the jump on Eph, after dragging a red herring across her own trail, the better!

America's active mind took under consideration her next difficulty. Assuming that she were safely in St. Louis, what if the police, shadowing Homer Pettis at Eph's request, should see her cousin recognize her on the street? To avoid such a calamity she must frequent the places where a man of Cousin Homer's substance would rarely go—the riverfront, the slums, Darkytown. What was it that Tugger had suggested, about disguising herself with walnut juice to get into the White stemmery? Why not stain her skin yellow, put on a Creole costume and try for a job in the White factory while Fant was recovering at the hospital? Who would be the wiser if Walter Fox in a public ward had as an occasional visitor a yellow-skinned factory hand? He wouldn't be the first white man who found a touch of the tar barrel sometimes sticks closer than family or fair-weather friends. And while she was looking after her husband, perhaps she could also pick up that information Tugger wanted, something about the formula for a rival plug called *Champagne Dry*. . . .

While she planned her campaign, America sat on the floor of the corncrib knocking hulls off several bushels of unshucked walnuts she had spread there last fall to dry. Sweeping the hulls into two feed baskets, she carried them to the house and put them to soak in warm water in a washtub. Boiling the solution down, she poured it into two whiskey bottles the boys had left, put on her oldest clothes and packed a shabby bag. After locking Foxden, she opened the poultry-house doors, turned the calves into the cow pasture and started down the hill. She was going to Chicago where Bayard had moved his family, she told Stella, to officiate at the birth of High Jink's second baby. If the Barnes connection would kindly keep their eyes on Foxden for a few weeks, she would feel relieved about the safety of its belongings. America then walked down the C. & O. track and caught the five o'clock accommodation train at South Ripley.

Arrived in Cincinnati that night, she studied the financial pages of the *Enquirer* in the Grand Hotel lobby, then retired. In a reputable broker's office the next morning she placed an order to buy General Tobacco common on a forty-point margin, made out checks for thirty-five thousand dollars to pay for it, and asked the curious customer's man to hold her receipts until she called for them. From the broker's office, America hurried to a theatrical costumer's, bought a shabby Creole outfit and carried it back to the hotel. While she paid her bill, she mentioned for the benefit of possible listeners that she was going to Chicago on the noon train to visit her daughter. At the Union Depot, she bought a day-coach ticket and disappeared into the white women's restroom. She emerged half an hour later in the Creole's outfit, her head tied in a spotted bandanna, her skin so brown from the walnut stain she had applied that a train announcer pointed to the Jim Crow sign on the adjoining restroom door.

"I'm from Martinique," declared America in slovenly English. "I don't un'nerstan' you, suh."

Within an hour, she stood at the cargo-deck rail of a grimy freight boat threshing down the Ohio. For several days America lived the life Fant had preferred to Tuckahoe's sun-drenched plenty. Her pretense of speaking only French protected her from intrusion. Moreover, the Ohio River had been the thoroughfare during the past twenty years for too many Scandinavian and eastern European immigrants hurrying towards free western land for crew or passengers to notice particularly one morose Frenchwoman past her prime.

In St. Louis she went at once to the Good Samaritan Hospital and asked for Walter Fox. Eying her suspiciously, the clerk at the information desk said that Mr. Fox was no longer there. Something in America's desperate anxiety moved him to send her to talk with Thompkins, the male nurse of the tubercular ward where Walter Fox had stayed less than a week.

"We had him for observation," declared Thompkins, a grey rind of a man gaunt from answering sick bells, turning patients and emptying bedpans. "When the diagnosis come through it was lung fever, all right. Fox nearly had a fit. To try an' keep him down—he was in pore shape generally—Doc didn't tell him he was still in the early stages. Fox thought he was goin' to die that night, from the way he fretted. To ca'm him down, I let him get to a telyphone an' call a relative. There, gal, was whar I got off the track, whar I sized him up dead wrong."

"Whatya mean, suh?"

"His telyphone call brought around an old party next morning who threw Fox into chills 'n' fever. They talked maybe half an hour, until Walter coughed so hard I hadda put the old gentleman out."

"Did—did he leave his name?"

"Not to me, he didn't. That night the fever made Walter talk wild—about wantin' to jump into the river to get away from somepin which was all the time a-follerin him."

"You don't mean he wanted to commit suicide?"

"That's the way he talked. I wisht you'd gotten here two days earlier. Fox skipped that night."

"You mean he walked out of the hospital?"

"Yep! Without leavin' a trace."

"Ain't you some notion whar he went, boss?" pleaded America, dropping her eyes for fear he see the despair in them, in the hope that he might think her what she appeared.

"I ain't got any real reason tuh say this, you understand," announced Thompkins, picking up his medicine tray. "I'm guessin' like the next un, but it's my private opinion that rich old party recognized Fox as—as somebody wanted by the law, and Fox lit out while the goin' was good. It's an old story with us, gal. Hospitals is mostly whar they catch these shabby birds o' passage when they get old and sick."

Carrying her bag, America walked down the hospital steps. Somewhere in this smoky city Fant lay hidden, coughing, desperate. With only Cousin Homer's fifty dollars between him and starvation, he wouldn't last long. How could she find him before death touched him first on the shoulder, how did a woman go about finding her beloved in a city of half a million strangers, when she dare not go to the police or to a family friend for help?

Walking down the street, in her preoccupation America collided with an elderly man. He must have seen the trouble in her eyes, because instead of swearing at her he accepted her profuse apologies and went about his business. If he had happened to be Cousin Homer, she realized, her goose might have been cooked. Slouching up to a policeman, she asked where the White factory was located, and in time found it fenced and guarded like a penitentiary. Two brawny policemen at a locked gate marked "Colored Help Only" laughed and motioned her on her way when she asked for work. Too upset to think further, she crossed the street, sat down on the opposite curb and tried to figure out what she had best do next to locate Fant.

Through the open windows of what must be the stemmery came negro voices singing spirituals. Change of time and tempo soon announced that the workers inside were thinking about more earthly matters:

"I haven't cooked a 'possum—Lord!
For such a long, long time,
It seems to me I've lost somehow
De very chune an' rhyme.

"De times is changed, an' we ain't got
De consolations which
We're 'bleeged to have if we would cook
De 'possum sweet and rich.

"De cabin an' de big fireplace
Dey neither one is lef'—
With fires so good de 'possum would
Almos' jes' cook hisse'f."

At twelve o'clock the factory buildings disgorged negroes of all ages, seemingly entire colored families including a patriarch with white mutton-chop whiskers and a three-hundred-pound old mammy who bore herself as if she were of real importance. Most of the negroes ate their lunches in family groups within the fenced inclosure. A few bucks and wenches jollied the gatemen to let them out for a glass of beer. Acting silly, they came across the street and entered the saloon behind America. When one of them intentionally or by accident touched the Creole woman's bundle with his foot, America was too dispirited to resent it. At closing time the old mammy lumbered over and stood looking down at America before she demanded:

"White woman, w'at's de mattuh wid you?"

"My man's sick—and I can't find him," answered America, too tired and discouraged to care now that her disguise had fooled nobody but herself.

"Does he wuk hyah?"

"I don't know. I doubt it, though, because when he left the hospital they said he was too sick tuh work anywhere."

"Whar'd he go?"

"I don't know, auntie. I honestly don't know."

Up and down the street negroes happy to be released from work called and flirted with each other, family groups started home.

"Chil', you cayain't des' sit hyah all night," declared the old negress, gently. "Is you broke?"

"Not quite, thank you."

"Den iffen I wus you, I w'udn't give up hope so easy. Effen I wus you, I'd go on daown de street tuh whar I'll take you—an' rent a decent room an' eat a hot suppah—an' git a good night's sleep. Den in de mo'hnin' ever'thing's gwine look brightuh, honey."

"Maybe you're right," America tried to smile her thanks.

"Cou'se I's right! Ol' Mandy's allays right. Den I'd git me a good job wukkin' hyah. 'Cause soonah uh latuh ev'ah nigger on de river comes in an' goes aout ob dem gates yondah. Dem dat doan' come deyselves Mandy hears abaout!"

"I wouldn't be surprised but what you're right, auntie," agreed America. One place would do as well as another to wait in, she decided. To find Fant now would be sheer luck, like sticking your finger on the needle in the haystack.

"Git up den, an' come on. Tumorra mo'hnin' I'll speak foah you tuh Mistah Malone, aour white boss-man. Kin you stem?"

" 'Course I can, but I mostly graded at home. Havana or burley, it's all one an' the same thing to me," America hazarded the boast, knowing that St. Louis plug factories saw precious little of the expensive Cuban segar-leaf. "Have you been workin' here long enough for those gate men to—to take your word for a stranger?"

"I's been wukkin' yeah nigh ontuh fifty years, chil'. An' I's mighty perticular who I stands foah. Me an' mah chillun an' mah gran-chillun all wuks at de same table in de stem'ry. I knowed you was folks when you nevah even raised youah haid at dem fresh young niggahs."

The stemmery, with its spirituals rising like the leaf dust through cathedral rays of spring sunshine, closed by day over

America's turbaned head. With hand and eye trained through years of stripping burley, she had little trouble to keep ahead of the work placed before her on the grading table. At night she frequented the wharves and docks where she thought Fant might go. In her fourth-class boarding house, she scanned the personal columns and police news of St. Louis' morning and evening papers. One warm May night she was shocked to read a brief account of the probable suicide of a man who was seen that morning to jump into the river. Although his body was not recovered, identity had been established by his shabby coat left on the freight wharf from which he was seen to jump. In the coat pockets were found a bottle of cough medicine and prescriptions made out to Walter Fox. Police investigation revealed that such a man, in the early stages of lung fever, had recently left the Good Samaritan Hospital against the orders of physicians there.

America laid aside her paper and started to walk to escape her grief, her conviction that for her, life and hope were at an end. Without money or friends, and probably despairing that she had ever received his message from Cousin Homer, Fant had given up his pathetic struggle. Behind her pity for him came the realization that with her husband actually drowned this time, and his body not recovered, for her there could never be the long hoped-for day of vindication on Tuckahoe, of reinstatement there among her peers. Before she noticed the direction which her footsteps downhill had carried her, she was at the river. Beyond the wharf piles the Mississippi flowed majestically southward under a spring moon three-quarters full. Thirty years ago, as now, America told herself, she had stood in agony to scan the river's silvery breast for a beloved dark head . . .

When in time her grief permitted her to look around the stemmery, America learned that the aim of the manufacturer was to make a plug out of varying ingredients which would have a uniform characteristic taste, and which would keep sweet under all conditions of weather and storage. Thus, the formula of *Champagne Dry* was not a scrap of paper to be stolen from the chief chemist's desk. Every carload of burley changed the set-up, made necessary a slightly different amount of brown sugar or bay rum or licorice which was weighed and added to the "soup" in which the stemmed leaf lay to absorb these flavoring agents before it moved on to be pressed into plugs, encased in a fine scrap of wrapper, and packed in tinfoil for shipment. Far more important, she learned, than the varying amounts of each ingredient was the degree of heat to which each ingredient must be subjected individually or in a mixture before they flowed through separate pipes to blend into the "soup."

By June, America had recovered herself sufficiently to think about going home to Tuckahoe. All she had left to do now in St. Louis was to pick up the *Champagne Dry* formula Tugger wanted, and buy a ticket to Cincinnati.

Without noticing how she had won to such a place of confidence, America realized that she had the run of the factory. Every morning she carried the time-sheet of the stemmery to Mr. Malone's office for Mandy. The only room barred to her and to other trusted hands was the laboratory where chemists set the controls which regulated the secret flow of raw ingredients into mixing vats in the adjoining "soup" kitchen. To this locked laboratory door America went often with samples of leaf which indicated some change in type predominant enough to make her errand seem plausible. Anderson was the name of the chief chemist, the pompous originator of the *Champagne Dry* formula. Robert Eames, a homesick young Californian, was his first assistant.

One July morning, when heat and humidity made the city gasp, America with her arms piled high with leaf found the laboratory door propped ajar for coolness. Through it she heard Eames' earnest voice:

"Just listen to it once, won't you, sir? Tobacco—one hundred pounds; sugar—five pounds; licorice—two and one-half pounds; rum—two and one-half; and here's the secret, sir, California prune juice—two and one-half pounds!"

Prune juice! thought America. Was it prune juice in *Champagne Dry* which Tugger had mistaken for Albemarle apple-jack which in its turn had soured Dan Lord's experimental blends?

"Eames, I tell you it won't work!" pronounced Anderson.

"But it did, sir!" contradicted young Eames. "Last March —fourteen months ago—I cooked up a batch in my room. I took the prune juice up to two hundred twenty-two Fahrenheit by itself. And you can see how sweet the plug still is—it hasn't even mildewed."

"Only fool's luck, my boy, only fool's luck!" snorted Anderson's almost resentful tones. "Who ever heard of making plug tobacco without glycerine? You know *Champagne Dry* owes half its popularity to that five pounds of glycerine we dump into every hundred-pound batch."

Below her, someone had entered the corridor leading from the mixing-room to the circular iron stairway which gave access by an iron balcony into the laboratory. Not daring to look down, America pretended to knock on the laboratory door. Inside, Eames' voice was speaking with the desperate anxiety of ambitious youth in collision with prejudiced conservatism:

"But prune juice gives the same smoothness. And think how much cheaper it is!"

"You're wasting your time, boy—and mine. I believe in young fellers being ambitious—that's how I got my start—but you've gone off half cocked."

In a moment whoever was coming up the stairs would catch her eavesdropping. America swayed, dropped her armful of leaf, and crumpled against the laboratory door. Flannery, the mixing-room foreman, was immediately at her side.

"I knocked—and waited," gasped America, rolling her eyes backward. "It was so hot—and nobody came."

Back at her leafing table, she wrote down the conversation

she had overheard on the back of a reclamation blank. The prune juice formula, she realized on second thought, must be an experimental one Eames was urging the chief chemist to try. America had been in the factory long enough to realize that no formula is of much value without the temperature figures of the re-dry rooms which put the stemmed leaf into uniform case, and of the different "soup" pots. There were a dozen ways to cook these ingredients separately or together, and then to introduce the cased leaf into them.

At noon, America felt so shaken she went across the street for a glass of beer. Emerging, she saw a commercial photographer taking snapshots of the younger negroes. To have a picture of herself might be useful in after years, when she could summon courage to tell her children how their father had died. Who would believe the fantastic story, only too true, even if she had a photograph of herself in this ridiculous garb to show that she had actually been in St. Louis?

"Smile this time, can't you?" demanded the photographer, as he took a second picture. "You look like you've just come from a fun'ral."

The two prints the photographer handed her showed a pensive beauty with haunted eyes above a smiling mouth, wrists and ears hung with gypsy gauds, hair concealed in a polka-dot bandanna, her calico dress unbuttoned at the throat because of midsummer heat.

In her hall bedroom that night, America wrote Tugger the conversation she had overheard between the two chemists, and enclosed her notes on the prune juice formula. "The next time you hear Dan Lord say he needs a good young chemist," she continued, "why don't you recommend this lad, Robert Eames, to him? And don't tell ma where I am because I'm going home next pay day."

Before she sealed the envelope, an impulse prompted America to send Tugger one of her new photographs, the smiling one. Across its back she scribbled: "Whose wild honey is this?" and enclosed it in the envelope. She had been surprised lately by the resiliency of her spirits. Once before, she had believed with her mind, but not her heart, that Fant Annable was dead. And in her hour of greatest need he had come back to her safe and well.

On her way to the laboratory several days later, she found the door of the "soup" room open. From a loose pipe joint a dark liquid was dripping into a pool on the floor. The coast seemed clear, the temptation too great for America to resist. On the heat gauges, the mercury registered two hundred and nineteen Fahrenheit. She knelt to dip her handkerchief into the puddle—

"This time I've caught ye red-handed!" boomed Flannery's voice behind her.

She tried to stuff the handkerchief into her skirt pocket, to dodge away from him and run. Flannery was too quick. With one hand he caught at her calico skirts, ripping through the much-washed fabric in an attempt to snatch the sticky handkerchief out of her pocket, while with the other hand he grasped her arm. Plain-clothes men came running. She gazed down in consternation at her exposed white knee.

"So it's a damn' spy ye are!" breathed Flannery, staring with the others. "I thought as much when I caught yez listenin' outside the laberatory!"

Without answering, she jerked away and ran for the blending-room door. A plain-clothes man got there first with a drawn revolver. America ducked behind a "soup" vat and then found herself cornered. With the strength which had come to her once before in a crisis, she tried to fight them off. Her fingernails were bloody, she noticed, as she picked herself up from the corner where Flannery's open-handed blows had knocked her. Her nose was bleeding, her ears rang. The special policemen charged, and handcuffed her wrists behind her back.

She spent the next hour refusing to answer the questions of several worried men in the general manager's office, and was then hustled two blocks to the precinct police station.

"I'm no more a spy than you are, captain!" she denied Flannery's charges before a middle-aged sergeant. "Send one of your men over to the stemmery to ask Mandy. Ever'body knows her, she'll bear out my story."

"Let's hear it first," suggested the sergeant.

"I come from Loueyville, Kentucky," America declared. "Last February, I received a message from my—my man to meet him here in St. Louey. I hustled right over and got a job to wait for him. A week ago—you recollect how hot it was, suh?—I keeled over on the balcony with an armful of leaf I'd carried up to show the chemists. Mistah Flann'ry has been layin' tuh have me fired ever since."

"I caught her eavesdroppin', Eddie!" interposed Flannery.

"Ev'rybody's eavesdroppin' over at the plant," refuted America, wearily. "Honest, suh, the bosses are so spy-sceirt they jump if a stem drops."

"Now let's hear your side," suggested the sergeant to Flan nery and shifted his quid as if he'd heard the foreman tell spy stories before.

"I told you how I caught her listenin' the other day at the lab door," growled Flannery. "So this mornin', just to prove I'm right, I unscrews a pipe joint and lets some 'lasses drip. Shore nuf, here she comes, thinks it's the 'soup,' an' tries to get a sample by soakin' her handkerchief in it—"

"I slipped, I tell you!" America sharply denied.

"Then why didn't ye hand me your handkerchief nice 'n' ladylike, when I asked ye for it?" roared Flannery. "Instead, Eddie, she runs like an alley cat. My plain duty was to get back that sample she hid in her pocket, now wasn't it, Eddie? I reached for it—an' we all saw she was a spy. Lookit her knee! If that knee don't show she's a spy come to steal our trade secrets, I'll eat my hat."

"Then you'd better start, you big baboon!" America blazed at him, "because the only thing my knee shows is that I've been bathing in the river every spare minute I could get away from the plant. Cap'n—gentlemen," she appealed to the listening policemen, "as family men, I ask you if it isn't just a heavy sunburn you see on my arms and legs and face? Naturally my skin would stay white under my bathing bloomers."

Behind the blotter the police sergeant raised his hand to his mouth. Several of the listening officers smiled, one guffawed.

"My advice to you, ma'am," interposed the sergeant, "is to forget all about the White Company, and get on back to Kentucky where you belong."

"Not without my back pay!" America protested, shrill again. "And I won't set foot in that factory without an officer to protect me from these hoodlums."

"What about it, Flannery?" asked the sergeant. "I can't lock this woman up when you see for yourself her story holds water. D'you want us to keep her here while we recheck it by that old woman she mentioned in the stemmery?"

"I want you to get her out of this state before sundown!" snorted Flannery, turning away in disgust.

"Go along with her, Tim. Before you take her across the river, call in here. By then I'll have heard from Headquarters if it's all right to let her go."

Wild Honey plug was General Tobacco's trade answer to *Champagne Dry*. The nation's billboards, walls, fence rails, magazines and Sunday supplements bloomed with pictures of America laughing in her Creole outfit, her teeth ashine against a clear gold skin. Having adopted part of her idea, America felt sure that Tugger had gone whole hog by using the prune juice formula to manufacture *Wild Honey,* especially since it undersold all competitors for a dime. Home again at Foxden, she wrote Tugger demanding her ten thousand dollars reward, and to know if Dan Lord had properly recompensed the Eames lad by giving him a good job.

"Dan outfoxed me again," Tugger took his own time to reply. "I thought we had a gentlemen's agreement, but he's gone to hole with your bacon. However, I'm cooking up something fancy of my own and, if it succeeds, I'll personally see that you get your ten thousand—if and when revenue reports show *Wild Honey*'s sales have run ahead of *Champagne Dry*. Nicke's changed her mind about her beau, but I'll take home the next smart young fellow who shows up on the horizon. We're expecting you here Christmas—to hire somebody to take the management of Teena and this big house off your maw's shoulders. Your maw hasn't been well lately, and the girls are always gadding. Besides, I want to see you, myself."

While she was in New York, America took special pains to ask Tugger about the future of General Tobacco common. She couldn't help worrying about it, since most of her eggs were in this one basket. Tugger and her financial sheets told her that Dan Lord was buying up every plug manufacturer he could bring to his terms, and putting their factories and trade brands into the cigarette trust's general pool. America, like other mothers with boys away from home, kept wondering if young Fant might have run off to the Spanish-American War.

Returning to Foxden in April of '98, she put out a vegetable garden and began to think of selling enough of her General Tobacco stock this summer to finance a small leaf purchase. Before she began to ride the circuit of her growers' barns, in late September she went to Cincinnati. To her considerable alarm, on arrival at her broker's office she found that General Tobacco had fallen until she had only eleven points of safety left to her margin. Dreading to take the substantial loss which any sale would now involve, she wired Tugger for advice and registered at the Grand Hotel to await his answer. The next morning, before it came, General Tobacco broke thirty points on the New York Stock Exchange.

"That wipes me out," America smiled wryly to the customer's man.

The Growers warehouse seemed to be as good a place as anywhere to go to lick her wounds. She was listening to the dull bidding when Henry Morris burst onto the floor waving a newspaper and shouting wildly:

"Dan Lord's formed a plug trust, boys—we're dead cocks, now!"

Kelly stopped the sales for lack of buyers. Everyone rushed to gather around Morris and his newspaper. There the announcement stood in ink still smeary from the press: Half a dozen leading plug manufacturers were to be consolidated into the Inter-Ocean Plug Company, of which Dan Lord was to be the president. Instead of General Tobacco being the carryall, as America with the rest of the sucker public had assumed, the cigarette trust announced that it would transfer its factories and trade to Inter-Ocean. No wonder General Tobacco had crashed thirty points when news of the separate plug set-up leaked out! Riding a bear market, Tugger had probably raked in more millions including her insignificant thirty-five thousand.

One of the first companies to be transferred by General Tobacco to Inter-Ocean Plug was the White concern ot St. Louis, secretly bought by Dan Lord early in September of '98. One by one that autumn, while the nation added up losses and gains following the Spanish-American War, the Lord interests quietly acquired plug manufacturing plants in Kentucky, Ohio and Virginia. In St. Louis the Grummond Company came "under the big top" for three and a half millions. When the plug trust was incorporated in December of '98 for seventy-five millions, Leonard & Morley alone stood out in angry defiance. One important smokin' mixture firm, the pioneer Bull Durham, which had successfully resisted Dan's efforts to buy it, and one large cigarette manufacturer, the National Cigarette and Tobacco Company, stood with the St. Louis plug giant against the trusts. When Tugger Blake with four Wall Street associates offered to buy them out, all three accepted and went into Blake's new combine, the United Leaf Syndicate. Aware of his own considerable nuisance value, Tugger then opened guerilla warfare on Dan Lord's plug and cigarette combines. This time Dan Lord did not choose to fight. General Tobacco absorbed the assets of the United Leaf

Syndicate, which was then dissolved, and paid Tugger and his allies in new stock worth thirty-five millions. A "melon"—the largest cut to date in Wall Street's lush patch—consisting of a hundred per cent cash dividend on its old common, was declared to General Tobacco's stockholders, in addition to its annual routine dividend of eight per cent. Director's chairs were also placed for Tugger and two of his allies at General Tobacco's table, at last bringing Blake in on the ground floor.

"Didn't I tell you to hold onto General Tobacco—that it ud pay out rich as soon as I was in position to twist Dan's tail?" crowed Tugger in a letter written in March of '99. To America's confession of loss, he answered callously: "Ain't you the young lady who called me a short sport because I cried over losing a horse race? I was fond of the Pony, while you loved only your money bags. A first rule of Wall Street is never to hold grudges, Sister Merry. In the morning we cut each other's throats, grin at each other at lunch and are thick as thieves hatching something new by sundown. Playing the game means more to us now than the stakes, we say. And I might add—like hell, it does! I reckon you'll have to come on back to New York—like I've been begging you for years. Nicke's got another beau, Steve Holt. He's one of Dan's bright young men and ought to be able to handle Nicke, who puts on more airs than the Duchess of Marlborough. Sally's picked herself a polo player, Mitchell Ayres. Come forget your troubles planning that double wedding we talked about years ago, remember? Here's your big chance—I want to splurge!"

After the wedding, America asked herself, what would there be left for her in New York except to become a pensioner on Tugger's bounty? She decided she would prefer to raise another crop.

"Lass, hae ye gone daft?" panted Abigail, her breath spent from running across the thawed fields. "Plowin'—at your'r age?"

"What else can I do?" asked America, wiping the sweat off her forehead with her bare arm. She couldn't tell Abigail that for the first time on Tuckahoe she felt that she had no future other than the shamed drudgery of the fields which now confronted her. "Farm hands all seem to have gone to town. And Wall Street's cleaned me out."

"Ye speak tae the neb noo," sighed Abigail, her long face anxious. "Auld MacGower says Dan Lord will clean us a' oot."

"He's like Pharaoh of old," answered America, stung to rebellion by weariness and a sense of frustration which seemed to meet her every way she turned these days. "He's sitting on the top of a business pyramid which Henry Morris says will crush the life out of the little fellows. God pity us all if Dan Lord ever turns on the growers."

"In his ain guid time he wull, says MacGower."

"He better not!" flashed America, and remembered her childhood dream of lying in a field with a boulder crushing the breath out of her body.

"Wull ye win whaur-r braw men hae lost?"

"Not by myself!" laughed America, and clucked to her old mules. As they started, with America bent forward to engage the plow point in the sod, she called back to Abigail: "When you get home, tell Auld MacGower to take a look at the Kentucky state seal on the new bank calendar. We're still a commonwealth of tobacco growers—don't you forget that!"

Chapter 15

In August of '99, Mrs. Moncure's letters failed to arrive at the Tuckahoe post office. A wire from Tugger then informed America that her mother's summer cold had developed into pneumonia. Would America come to New York at once and bring her cousin, Eph Radford? Frantic with concern, America left Bethenia to locate Eph, and herself took the next train to New York. Eph had attended a Confederate reunion at Dallas and after adjournment had gone to visit boon companions living on ranches in the Pan-Handle. By the time Bethenia's telegrams located him, Mrs. Moncure had faced death with the same smile of spiritual acceptance with which she had met postwar poverty and Fifth Avenue splendor. Not daring to return to Charlotte County for the funeral, although Tugger Blake promised by wire to have that old charge quashed before he arrived, Ephraim ate his heart out alone in a Texas hotel room, while the glittering Blake ménage on a special train rolled into Richmond and escorted the body of one more Confederate widow whose heart had really ceased to beat in '64, to rest beside a statesman of the Lost Cause in Hollywood Cemetery.

Nor was Palestine among the Moncure family circle of mourners. Despondency had overwhelmed her periodically in recent years to such an extent that her physician, Dr. Cantrill, had been compelled to prescribe closer confinement and constant expert care. Tugger had accordingly engaged a Miss Vosburgh, trained in Viennese methods of looking after the mentally sick, to take care of Palestine and run his Fifth Avenue and Long Island establishments. Teena's empty days revolved around childish pleasures such as food, new dresses which she wore once and "kept nice" for the parties she never attended, and riddles, guessing games and elaborate mechanical toys.

After the funeral, America took Aunt Flora to Charlotte Court House "in an avalanche," as the old black woman boasted, and made her as comfortable as possible in Cousin Homer's house on Court Street with two young negroes to wait on them. Flora's days were numbered by cancer. While she waited for the ex-slave to die, America packed what could be spared from daily use of the remaining heirlooms she herself had saved from Golden Hill. Before she had completed the nostalgic job, Homer Pettis' body was brought from St. Louis by a seedy Vermonter, his partner in the mule business. When Cousin Homer's will was read, it was seen that he had left his fortune to Palestine.

"Her as has, gits!" grunted Aunt Flora, when told that Miss Teena would come into two hundred thousand dollars in addition to her dower claim on Tugger's millions.

"Ain't it the truth?" echoed America, reduced to slang by the thought of how far such a legacy would have gone to secure her own uncertain future.

Three weeks later America was at 860 Fifth Avenue, going over household problems with Miss Vosburgh. When told they could have a quiet wedding now but otherwise must wait until a period of mourning had elapsed for their grandmother, Nicke and Sally chose to wait. On her second day at Tugger's rococo Victorian mansion at Glen Cove, her host took the morning off to show America his stables and gardens. Winded, both paused to rest in the thin October sunlight on the lowest terrace.

"Tugger, that double row of Georgia pines is the finest thing about this whole place," interposed America. "How'd you have sense enough to leave them standing?"

"Tarheels like pines. Besides, when Dan told me how much it cost to carve up his flat New Jersey estate into hills and ravines—so it ud look like Durham, No'th Car'lina—I figured myself lucky to have a little natural scenery thrown in," chuckled Tugger.

"It's lovely," mused America, narrowing her eyes to imagine how she would light the noble approach.

"Postponing the wedding suits me fine," declared Tugger, his thoughts paralleling hers in the congenial way their minds worked. "I've sent Junior out to Louisville to try and earn his salt, and I don't want him coming back here till he does. Besides, I'm up to my ears in Dan's 'snuff war.' We're set to launch the General Snuff Company next March—as a carryall for the drive we'll make to corner the snuff business."

"Do you expect much of a fight?" asked America, carefully.

"A fight? Ha! ha!"

"Don't forget every Goliath has his David."

"Why, there're only two groups can stand up to us," snorted Tugger. "One is the Atlantic Snuff Company which—would you believe it?—actually had the gall to gather a flock of little snuff makers in Virginia, Delaware and Tennessee under its wing. The other is the George W. Holt crowd who own a whole town over at Holtville, New Jersey."

"Aren't you afraid the government will call a halt to you, Tugger?"

"What's the government got to do with us fellows in Wall Street?"

"Don't say the government, then—say the people," answered America with spirit. "If I were one of these snuff manufacturers you're crowding to the wall, I'd go to court—I'd invoke the Sherman law against you."

"Law suits are an old story to us. In May of '96, some disgruntled stockholders tried it in the New Jersey courts, but the suit was dismissed the next March."

"I suppose you'll start in on segars as soon as you've finished mopping up the snuff makers?"

"Surest thing you know!"

"Will Dan Lord be president of all four trusts?"

"Who else can handle 'em half so well? And won't they make him a fancy turnout?" exclaimed Tugger, enthusiastically. "That reminds me of the day we drove the children to Jerome Park, remember? Golly, but you looked a picture settin' up there beside me! Everything about you was tiptop—that green plaid silk dress—those game feathers on your hat—the way you spoke to ever'body whether you knew 'em or not. Looking back, I don't think I've had a prouder—or happier morning in my whole life."

"That's kind of you to say, Tugger."

"I mean it! Just to prove it, I'll pay for all the new duds you'll go buy yourself," he concluded, without looking at her.

She knew her sprigged muslin which had done well enough for Foxden afternoons, didn't fit into a Glen Cove morning. Clothes were changing with everything else in New York, America had noticed. Instead of material and cut being of prime importance, suitability to the occasion or the sport seemed to be the criterion, nowadays. She appreciated Tugger's finesse in making known to her that she looked tacky. Fifteen years ago, he would have called her a hayseed.

"Will you go get yourself some glad rags—and charge 'em to me?"

"What would I do with a Worth dress in the tobacco patch?"

"Sister Merry, you can't go back to that damn' log house! Nicke's told me how inconvenient it is. With your maw gone, who'll run these two big places of mine—and keep an eye on the young folks—and cheer up Teena?"

"Miss Vosburgh is very capable. What else did Nicke tell you?"

"She said some petty-fogging old judge down there won't let you grow tobacco because it might impoverish your boy's land."

"My good friend Judge Stacy died, so I put out a crop on the assumption it's only fair to let me raise enough to pay taxes," answered America, meeting her brother-in-law's eyes.

Wild Honey was outselling *Champagne Dry* two to one, yet Tugger had said nothing about paying her the ten thousand dollars and expenses he owed her on that St. Louis trip. After this morning's talk, he couldn't hedge by pretending he didn't know she needed the money. It was remarkable, she decided, how young Tugger looked. The only signs of age she saw in him were his greying temples, a slight thickening of his powerful figure and a certain shortness of temper, a tendency to bully which might come from the vast power his millions gave him or from rising blood pressure due to the high living he enjoyed, if the stories Nicke tried to tell her were true.

"Now I must go pack," she declared, rising from the marble bench.

"Sister Merry, once before I warned you! Some day you're going to try my patience too far."

"Barking dogs never bite," she smiled back without coquetry at him as she started up the steps of the seven landscaped terraces.

Nicke's and Sally's double wedding was set for the third Saturday in August of 1900. By mail, Tugger gave America a free hand to plan it. Her one condition was that she be allowed to keep the general decorative theme a complete surprise to everyone, including the principals. Her mail became so heavy that Abigail MacGower kept a special egg basket in the post-office booth to contain it. In addition to the detail of asking for bids and placing orders, America supervised the farm work of two mountain boys she had engaged, cooked and kept house for them and for herself.

After supper one mid-July night, when she sat alone in the front yard at Foxden watching the strip of fire fade along the western horizon, she heard the sound of farm-sled runners and horses' hoofs striking rocks in the barnyard lane.

"Miss Merry?" called a voice from the dog run.

"Yes? Oh, it's you, John Willy. Sit down."

"Where're the boys, Miss Merry?"

"They said at supper they were going over to the blacksmith shop to pitch horseshoes."

"Come around back, ma'am."

John Willy's tone brought her quickly through the dog run. One of the Barnes' crowbait teams hitched to a farm sled was approaching the yard gate. Elmer, the talkative twin, drove. Ollie and Old Jim Barnes walked beside the sled. On it lay a long shape wrapped in quilts to the unforgettable face.

"Fant! Oh, my dear—"

While America hovered frantically over her husband, John Willy opened the gate, the sled runners slid across the grassy yard and came to a stop near the flagstones.

"Fant, answer me— Mr. Barnes, why doesn't he answer me?" asked America, on her knees beside her husband, her hands gripping his thin shoulders. Near the death-mask face lay what appeared to be the butt end of a mossy log.

"He's got lung fever, ma'am," replied Old Jim. "Stella says she kin smell hit on him. An' bein' in the river ain't done him no good. We better git him inside."

"What's that piece of log doing on the sled?"

"Look at hit. Damned if ever I saw hits equal."

"Why, it's his old silk hat!"

"And a heap more."

With shaking fingers, America examined the water-soaked headgear. Its ancient beaver exterior had been covered with a thatch of moss. Inside was a helmetlike framework of bamboo and leather, the ends of which extended down to fit the wearer's throat like a garrote. The framework could be buckled on with trustworthy straps.

"Ain't that a clever contrapshun tuh keep his head above water?" Old Jim was continuing. "He didn't need tuh know haow tuh swim, with that thing on. An' nobody ud waste good powder 'n' lead on an ol' log a-floatin' daownstream."

"Where did you find him?" whispered America, and saw in her mind's eye the Ohio bisected by sunshine and the purple shadow of the Kentucky hills. In midstream a mossy log bobbed serenely away on the channel current . . .

"He was caught in our trot-lines when we rowed aout this evenin'," declared Elmer, throwing his reins on the ground. "We thought he was dead, but paw rolled him over a barr'l an' he come to. He's so puny the trip up the hill must 'a' been too much for him. If hit warn't so rough, we cudda hauled him up on the wagon. He coughs fit tuh bust."

"He must have jumped off an empty coal boat, rather than risk riding on the train," John Willy concluded. "He told maw he'd been waiting all summer for the river to warm so the shock wouldn't kill him. Where shall we take him, Miss Merry?"

"Into the parlor."

While America ran to the cook room for keys and matches, the Barnes men drove the sled into the dog run and stopped at the front room of Foxden's right wing. Opening the door, America pulled down the chimney stuffing and lighted the fire laid in the great limestone fireplace. The Barnes men lowered Fant onto America's cabbage-rose carpet and began carefully to take off his wet clothes. America closed the inside shutters, brought towels and a blanket and hurried back across the dog run to make coffee. She returned to see firelight warm on her husband's emaciated body which Barnes was propping up to the blaze.

"Heat 'll bring him to quicker'n anything else," diagnosed Barnes. "Set the coffee pot daown whar hit 'll keep warm. What you aimin' tuh do wi' him, ma'am? He ain't fitten tuh travel."

"I'll hide him here till he gets stronger."

"Whar'll he sleep?"

"Boys, would you please bring in the trundle from under my bed?"

Glad to be given something to do, John Willy and Ollie clattered out.

"Maw says she'll board yer hands for you," volunteered

Elmer. "Want me tuh step over tuh the store an' fetch 'em home with me tonight? I kin git 'em plenty drunk."

"That might be best—for the present," America dismissed the relatively unimportant.

"He's comin' to," pronounced Old Jim.

"Oh, Fant, darling—what has happened to you?" cried America, on her knees beside him.

"Hello, lovie—don't kiss me or you'll catch lung fever," croaked Fant. "Is that coffee?"

They watched him take the cup in shaking hands and raise it to his bloodless lips. He had the long transparent hands of the consumptive, America noticed, and remembered how she had thrilled to the touch of those trembling fingers, once so swift and sure, which could handle a deck of cards or a revolver as most men handle a hoe or a pen.

"God, that's good!" sighed Fant, and surrendered the half-emptied cup. A paroxysm of coughing seized him and doubled his body. His lean ribs heaved, the cords stood out like ropes in his gaunt neck. His face turned crimson with labor. They stood helplessly by and watched until the convulsion passed.

"I heard you talking just now—about hands," began Fant, whispering so as to use as little breath as possible. "Have you got a crop?"

"Five acres of tobacco. And a hillside of corn," answered America.

"You'll have—to leave it," continued Fant, lifting his eyes bright with fever to her anxious face. "Turn your help off quick as you can. We ought to get out of here tomorrow night—at the latest."

Tomorrow night America had planned to take the through train to New York. Wetting her lips with a dry tongue, she asked gently:

"Where do you want to go, Fant?"

"To California," he gasped. "The doctor says I've got to go West—fast. You, Barnes, your job's to locate a shanty-boat man who'll take us. You better start looking tonight. Come back with the sled tomorrow night. We'll be ready to start."

"You ain't fitten tuh travel."

"Are you my doctor?" Fant answered with a flare of his old spirit, "—or do you want to see me hang?"

"Fant, lover, nobody would hold a sick man on an old charge like that!" America tried to soothe him. "For all we know, it may be outlawed by now."

"Not while I've been out-of-state so long," contradicted her husband, and fixed his enormous brown eyes on Old Jim's face. "Barnes—are you going to help me or not?"

"All right, all right, Mr. Fant. You know I'm yer friend or you'd have been a goner years ago. Well, ma'am," Barnes added, exchanging a meaningful glance with America above the sick man's head, "I'll jest slip up here tomorrow morning an' tell you have I located somebody. Help me git a nightshirt on him, John Willy, then we'll go on daown the hill. We'll let the boys tend tuh the rest of this business. Hit'll look more natchal."

The trundle bed was in the corner. America made and rolled it up to the fire. Although the July night was mild, her husband's teeth were chattering when she drew the blankets to his chin. She realized that she ought to get him something nourishing to eat, but she had a question she must ask first:

"Fant, were you in St. Louis last summer?"

"You mean when I sent you that message through Cousin Homer?"

"Then Walter Fox actually was you? My dear, if you only knew the heartache you caused me! I reached the Good Samaritan Hospital two days after you'd left, your ward attendant said. Why didn't you leave some word, some clue I could follow?"

"And have Pettis put the police on my trail?" barked Fant, his skin grey against the white sheet in the firelight. "I'd talked once or twice with the old codger in Charlotte Court House, when Eph was pretendin' to read law in his office.

Pettis recognized my face at the hospital, but couldn't recall my name or where he'd seen me. That's why he gave me those fifty bucks; he realized I was some family connection of his. So all I could do was skip out the next morning, before he had time to sleep on it—and remember who I was."

"Did you leave your coat on that freight wharf to make Cousin Homer and the hospital attendants think you'd committed suicide?"

"You don't think I jumped into that cold river for my health, do you?"

"I'm surprised you telephoned Cousin Homer in the first place—"

"I thought I was going to die or I wouldn't have!" he burst out impatiently. "It was only pure consideration for you and your brats made me do it. I realized you'd all have an easier time if old Pettis could bring the *corpus delicti* back to Tuckahoe for the gossips to drool over!"

He had talked enough, she could see. Stirring the logs so they would burn out before Abigail might notice sparks issuing from the seldom used parlor chimney and come across the ridge path to investigate, America replaced the poker and asked cheerfully what Fant could eat for his supper.

"The doctor said raw eggs—and whole milk—and rare beef steaks."

In the cook room, America built a fire in the coal stove, made soda biscuit and set them aside to wait for the oven to heat. From the dairy shelf she brought cottage cheese left from supper, night's milk and freshly salted butter. While the biscuit baked, she beat three eggs into a nog with whiskey from a pint of Golden Stream which she had kept for emergencies. Her thoughts, like the eggbeater in her hands, whirled around the decision she must make:

If she took Fant to California tomorrow night, who would supervise Nicke's and Sally's wedding? Her plans were so original Tugger and Miss Vosburgh would never have the courage to go through with them. Should they bungle the affair, or give up beforehand, Nicke would probably never forgive her. And more important, Tugger would doubtless seize on her desertion at this crucial moment as ample excuse never to pay her the ten thousand due on their *Champagne Dry* agreement, ten thousand which in her hand would insure proper care for Fant and a new start for them both in California.

When the biscuits were brown, America arranged the food on a floral tray come to her from the distribution of Golden Hill heirlooms, carried it into the parlor and placed it on a stool near the trundle bed. Kneeling, she fed Fant so that he could keep his shoulders covered. With the necessity to decide their future strong upon her, America began persuasively:

"Lover, I know you mustn't talk, but has the thought struck you we might go to New York?"

His fever-bright eyes questioned her.

"Tugger Blake, whom Teena married, is very powerful there," America hurried on. "He'd know doctors who could prescribe the latest treatment for lung fever. And Tugger has a beautiful place in the country where you could recuperate."

"Where?"

"At Glen Cove, on the Sound."

"At the seashore? I'd be dead in a month, the doctors said."

"I hadn't thought about the sea air," acknowledged America, sitting back on her haunches. "I've heard Asheville recommended highly for sufferers from lung fever," she ventured again, stirring what was left of the eggnog. "How would you like to try it for—say, six weeks? Then you would have enough strength to tackle that long trip west."

"Asheville would be a perfect stop-off, if it were on the way," agreed Fant.

"What about money? Have you given any thought as to how we'd live in California?"

"Stella says you're a rich woman," he answered, pouting his lips for her to wipe the eggnog froth away. He was clean-shaven, America noticed, but did not stop to wonder how he had managed it as a stowaway on a coal barge.

"I did well enough for several years speculating in tobacco," she admitted. "Then the Lords got a strangle hold on the plug business, and burley prices have been going down ever since—"

"You don't mean you're broke?"

"That's why I'm raising a crop this year. Without it, I couldn't pay taxes next March."

"So we're two of a kind after all, eh?" he barked hoarsely at her. "My life has been a failure, I admit. But I was counting on you to make a better showing, lovie. In St. Louis—when I was in the hospital I'd lie and read—or just think about you and me. Looking back over our lives—it seemed to me you had about everything it takes to make a woman successful—courage, beauty, ambition, drive."

The thought surged into her mind to exclaim: "And see how you've made me hide my talents under a bushel here at Foxden—because you wouldn't grow up and face your responsibilities as a family man!" She did not say it. She hoped life had lessoned them both enough so that neither of them would say things now which might stand between them in their last brief moments together.

"Have I done so badly?" she asked in a low tone. "With every man's hand raised against me—I've supported myself decently and raised three children. To shield you, I've let Mason County think I'm another Stella Barnes, although I've never looked at any other man except you, Fant Annable. And don't think I haven't had chances during these thirty years the world has thought me a widow!"

"I can see now I've been a rotten husband—and father," he sighed. "Luck was always against me. And in the bottom of my heart I figured if you really loved me—if you needed me and wanted me around—you'd come with me the next time. That's why I kept risking my neck to come back here—to put you once more to the test. But you were always too busy having another baby—or farming. That made me desperate—to think I'd figured wrong on you again—as on everything else in life."

She could not pause to comfort him. The impact of his words upon her own self-respect had been too overpowering. Here in kindlier speech than Ephraim and Abigail MacGower had used, was their same accusation: That she was by nature more the oak than the ivy, more Martha than Mary. Such an accusation, she felt in a flood of tempestuous rebellion, was unjust—cruel—wrong! How could she have stuck by Fant all these years, she justified herself, if she hadn't been at heart a deeply loving woman? For every moment of ecstasy she and Fant had enjoyed, she had paid with year after year of loneliness, one restless night of desire piling up with the next against the wall of her iron control, her will to keep the faith with her own womanhood: "For better, for worse, I plight thee my troth. . . ." Was this the accomplishment of a cold-hearted woman? And there had been other ties to hold her to Foxden, ties less strong than these tendons of the soul, but none the less ties of flesh and blood, of bread and butter and milk.

"I had the children to consider," she whispered, raising her eyes brimming with tears from the mortal hurt he had dealt her image of America Moncure. "You know how terrified I've always been of city life—of being broke and sick the way I was in Cincinnati when I worked in that hand laundry. Maybe because everybody in Virginia nearly starved to death during the last year of the war, I've always had the fear of starvation hanging over me—and the children."

"Ma would have jumped to take care of the children—as she'll jump to raise you the money we'll need tomorrow—and while we're in California." Fant sighed, sorry that he had brought tears to America's eyes yet secretly heartened that she still cared enough about him to cry at anything he could say. A scene was the last thing he wanted tonight, he told himself; the doctor, after Cousin Homer had left, had been very definite in his instructions about avoiding emotional scenes. "By the way, what has become of those precious children of ours? I don't see them around—or are they ashamed to speak to their old dead fish of a father?"

Now, America realized, was the time to tell him about Nicke's approaching wedding, and her central part in it. Yet after what he had just said, how could she mention anything as material as a society wedding, or even the ten thousand apparently tied to it? Time, she knew, was of the very essence in treating cases of lung fever. Don't tell him tonight about Nicke's wedding plans, whispered the clear small voice of her soul; wait till tomorrow, sleep on it. If it has been a mistake to put your children and Foxden above the absentee love you have kept alive thirty years for a tramp of a husband, then don't make that same mistake again. But if to be a drivin' woman hasn't been a mistake, then wait—wait! Anything may happen before that shanty-boat man throws off his shorelines tomorrow night.

"Come now—are you afraid to tell me?"

"Oh, yes, the children," she answered, in a shaky voice. "Young Fant married a mountain girl in Breathitt County and lives there with her folks. They have four youngsters—three boys and a girl. I pay them twenty dollars a month house rent here on Foxden."

"You mean that young squirt actually has the gall to charge you twenty dollars to go on living in this old sieve—after all you've sacrificed to hold it for him?"

"He's not like you and me, Fant. He's moody, and holds grudges. Living by ourselves as we've had to do—because I couldn't explain to people you were the girls' father—made young Fant like Ishmael—and Nicke hard as steel. Virginia Sue—High Jinks, we call her—is true blue, the flower of our flock. I realize now she escaped embitterment because at sixteen she fell in love with Bayard Langston."

"Did he marry her?"

"Wonder of wonders, yes. They have two girls—and live in a Chicago suburb."

"No! And me thinking last winter I might die any night alone in a Halsted Street flop house—and my own daughter not an hour away!"

"Fant, darling, why didn't you write? Why didn't you ever let me know I—I meant more to you than just a night with a woman in a walnut grove?"

"I married you, didn't I? But let's not get emotional, lovie. The doctors all say if I get emotional I'll cough my lungs right up into my hands—or words to that effect. Go on about the children."

"Nicke's our youngest—the girl you've never seen. She's a freak of nature—like that April snowstorm in which you went away. She lives with my sister Teena in New York."

"The one old Sawbones scared out of her wits?"

"There never was anything the matter with Teena's mind that Tugger Blake's millions couldn't cure," America went on, realistically. "Tugger and Teena have twins. Nicke makes an ideal companion for their Sally, the girl twin. Of our three children, Nicke's the one who'll go to the top. She's inherited my good looks but none of our saving weaknesses—such as your fellow-feeling for the cornered and my sense of honor which has kept me faithful to you. But all this is water under the bridge now, isn't it, lover? And you need sleep," she concluded, rising stiffly with the tray. "If I brought you another eggnog, could you drink it later?"

"Sleep 'll do more for me now than eggnog. God, Merry, but I'm glad to be safe home with you! You're so g-good to me—" His voice trailed off into a sob. Catching her hand, he pressed it to his hot lips. Feeling his tears, she dropped on her knees to comfort him:

"Fant, lover, don't cry—"

"Stay away, or you'll catch it, too. Merry, will you—show me—how to die?"

"Oh, my darling! You're not going to die," she cried, and laid her cool cheek against his burning one. "Everybody says it's wonderful in California—yellow sand and purple mountains and—and glossy orange trees. Think what fun I'll have learning to farm a new way—while you lie in the sun and watch. Every once in a while Eph says it does him good just to see me work—"

"Your brother Eph? Is he out here?"

"Yes. He's a deputy—with a big reputation."

"I saw him once. In the Ozarks. I'd have touched him for a ten-spot, but Eph was always a stickler for law 'n' order—and always broke."

"He means to bring you to trial, to make you acknowledge in a courtroom you're the father of my girls," she could not resist saying. "But now you must get some sleep. You haven't coughed once during all this time we've been talking. Doesn't that show you're getting better already?"

"That's so. Oh, lovie, you're so strong and cheerful! I feel like a scared 'ninny who's safe home at last with his mammy."

"Nothing will ever separate us again," she made her decision.

Chores next morning took on a different aspect as America realized that she might be doing them for the last time. Walking along the ridge to the tobacco patch, she found her hands sprawled under a tree sleeping off the effects of last night's liquor. Without awakening them, she returned to the house, fed and bathed Fant and started dinner. At noon she suggested to her shame-faced youths that they stay down at Stella's until they learned how to behave themselves. After they had gone back to sucker tobacco, John Willy appeared over the hill to report that Sandy, a shanty-boat man, would take Fant and America to Kansas City for a hundred dollars a piece in advance, all expenses to be paid by them.

"I don't know where we can do better," America agreed, reluctantly. "How much will he need to lay in a supply of groceries?"

"Better let me buy and keep them till you get on the boat," decided John Willy. "Fifty dollars' worth ought to get you to Cairo."

"I'll write a check," answered America, thankful she still

had a few hundred dollars left in the Farmers Bank. She must hurry if she was going to see Cousin Margaret and get to town herself before the bank closed. "When can we start?"

"Tomorrow night."

"Fant will be disappointed, but I'm glad," she sighed, relaxing.

After John Willy had dropped down the hill again, America went into the parlor to tell her husband the news. He became so concerned over the delay that he brought on a violent fit of coughing. Tucked under the trundle were towels bearing telltale stains. America took them out of the room when he quieted, and put them to soak in a basin behind the stove.

She could not dismiss from her mind what those rusty stains might portend. If Fant's malady were advanced to such a stage, what good could the hard expensive trip to California do him? Nothing could be worse for a consumptive than to live for days concealed in the damp cabin of a shanty-boat drifting down the Ohio. August nights were famous for their heavy dews. River fogs were frequent, typhoid often epidemic. If he reached Kansas City alive, they would do well. Another month of easy travel by train should put them somewhere in the Indian Territory, that graveyard of many consumptives hurrying hopefully towards the promised land of California. Fant's death in some outlandish border town would be hard; but a telegram to Ephraim would bring him hurrying to escort them home at last to Tuckahoe. By then the wedding would be over, the House of Blake probably closed to America Moncure Annable, free for the first time in thirty-three years.

But how much better, she thought, if Fant Annable could for once face up to reality! Under a death warrant more grim and far more immediate than any which Sheriff Swillevant or Ephraim could serve on him now, how much braver, finer for all concerned—and especially for himself—if he could only muster courage to stand and face his accusers in this last supreme test which life would present!

To focus her mind on less distressing thoughts, and because

time was short at best, America began to pack. Against a list of what they would need most on the shanty-boat, she checked off woolen blankets brought out of cedar chests, an antiquated suit and overcoat of Cousin Simmy's kept in a cotton bag hung from a garret rafter, drugs, cooking utensils, her own clothes. The revolver and shells Cousin Margaret had given her were lying in the top drawer of the Chinese cabinet in the parlor. When she went in to try these coats on Fant, she must get them out and pack them in her valise. Who could tell when some river rat, seeing her practically defenseless with a dying husband on a shanty-boat, might not try to attack her? Picking up the coats, she entered the parlor, dropped them on the trundle bed and laid out the pistol and shells while she remembered them. Helping Fant into the suit coat, she was surprised to hear herself say:

"Fant, have you thought how damp and unhealthy that shanty-boat will be?"

"Of course I have. But you know how conspicuous a sick man is on a train."

"You could stay home. Who'd drag anybody as sick as you into court?"

"Didn't you just say your brother Eph was circling around like a buzzard—to do just that?"

"If I were you, I'd prefer to die like a man in my own bed—rather than get stuck on some malarial sand bar. The river's low in August, it's full of sewage."

"You didn't talk that way in Virginia, when the noose was tightening around your neck!"

"I've been waiting to hear you say that," she answered quietly, in a strained voice. "Of course I'll take you anywhere you want to go. My only consideration now is what's best for you."

"California's best for me!" he shouted at her. "For Christ's sake stop offering objections—and go fix that coat."

Alone in the family room, she found her hands too unsteady to sew. She laid the coat aside while she composed herself. It could wait till tonight. She thought of writing to Nicke and Tugger, but realized that too had best be done later. Food was the most pressing consideration now; she'd better prepare plenty while she still had a good coal range on which to cook. She would bake bread and make several transparent pies. Fant liked them, and they were very nourishing. She would churn, put down eggs in brine, lay out preserves and jellies for packing into something easy to carry. Chocolate was good for invalids, she would stir up a big chocolate cake . . .

She could not have her cake this time, and eat it, too. Clear before her at last lay her first duty—to her husband.

Through the pleasant midsummer nights, Tuckahoe turnpike supported a traffic of which Abigail MacGower knew little. Up and down its four-mile length young negroes frolicked, white boys roamed like hounds. Ambrosia, daughter of Cousin Theresa's cook, scratched her lean flanks against the Drake pike gate, and flirted skillfully with her town beau, cocksure Archie Rice, who had sneaked a horse from Dalton's livery stable and was urging Ambrosia to ride double with him back to town.

"Miz' Allilee ud fotch me home quicker'n scat," Ambrosia objected. "An' mammy'd war me daown tuh de bone."

"Ain't I done tol' you I'll tak you tuh Dayton?"

"Nigger, show me steam-car fare!"

Confronted by this realistic obstacle, they both sighed and gazed unhappily at the pale ribbon of turnpike bisecting the moonlit fields.

"Lookit dat light a-bu'nin' at Foxden," observed Ambrosia. "Hit bu'ned las' night, too. Miz Allilee say so at breakfust."

"Mebbe somebody's sick up dar."

"Dat's what Mistis say, an' axe hadn't somebody bettah walk ovah an' inquiah. Miz Allilee, she toss her haid an' say dat's de lastest place any nice woman orter go. Miz Jane, she say no wunner Miz Allilee look lak a witch dis mo'hnin' effen she will set up all night a-stewin' bile tuh spit at a widow-woman who's lonesome and has done made a mistake. 'A litter ob mistakes, doan you mean, Jane?' axes Miz Allilee, nasty-sweet, an' jumps up from de table."

"I wish love was moah ketchin' araound hyar," Archie declared, gazing at the yellow gleam on the hill. "D'you reckon Miz Annable's bein' as mean tuh her man as you is tuh me, honey?"

"Le's go see!"

Fleeter than Archie, Ambrosia reached Foxden ahead of him and paused for breath. Above them, the old log house slumbered, except one front room on the right from which the lamplight streamed. The young negroes stepped around the beam of yellow light slanting across the yard, and approached the shuttered window.

"You look. I's scairt ob dat woman," Ambrosia whispered.

"Miz Merry's packin' clo'es intuh two telescopes," reported Archie.

"Whose clo'es?"

"Looks lak she's fixin' tuh take a trip wid a gem'man frien'. Who you reckon he is?"

"I see can'le light in de pa'lor."

They raised themselves over the parlor window sill and squinted through the closed inside shutters. Bob-dog then came rushing from the stable and they took to their heels. Satisfied with himself, the terrier stood barking at the yard-gate lane until a door opened at Foxden. A woman's figure stood silhouetted in the light, then Bob-dog trotted past her into the house and the door was closed. As they hurried down the lane, the negroes looked back to see the lamp wink out.

"Golly-moses!" breathed Ambrosia, leaning against the rail fence. "Do's you reckon she's kep' some pore white man hidden in dat pa'luh all dese y'ars des' tuh carry on wid him?"

"I wondah if I knows who am dat sick man," mused Archie, thinking hard. "I's got hit! Honey-lamb, will you promise tuh meet me at de Limestone depot tomorrah in time tuh ketch de F. F. V. foah Cincinnati?"

"Niggah, quit talkin' foolish an' tell me who you 'specks dat white man is—"

"I ain't talkin' foolish, an' I's already done tol' you. Dat man's Mistah Fant Annable des' as shore as you's bo'hn yaller!"

"Mistah Fant—her husban'?"

"Shore. I ain't nevah seed him, but dat ain't gwine keep me from swearin' tuh de high shuriff dat's him all right—an' claimin' mah reeward."

"Black boy, you wudn't do dat?"

"I'd do a heap moah'n dat tuh git us two tuh Dayton."

About nine o'clock the next morning, America was fixing Fant's breakfast tray when she heard Bob-dog barking. Removing her apron, she hurried through the family room to unlock the front door. At the front-yard gate, Allilee Drake was tying her horse. Love has its own telepathy, thought America, and walked down the flagstones to meet her unexpected caller.

"Good-morning—Cousin Merry," began Allilee.

"Good-morning, Allilee," America answered. How could she ever have called this thin-chested, bitter-mouthed spinster Morgan le Fay?

"Ma saw your light and—and sent me over to inquire if you were ill," Allilee continued, with a quick look at Foxden's shuttered windows.

"Will you thank Cousin Theresa and tell her I'm in excellent health? I trust you are all well?" America responded, realizing that the conversation sounded like that of two neighbor children who have quarreled. What did Allilee really want?

"Are you—is everything all right over here?" Allilee began again. The desperate glances she was sending towards the house reminded America of the way in which imprisoned chimney swifts darted this way and that seeking escape.

"Nothing has changed in the past thirty years," America's voice hardened. "While I don't mean to be discourteous to a guest, your concern seems belated, to say the least."

"Merry, don't stand there wasting precious time—time which might save Fant's life!"

Their eyes met while America asked:

"What have you come to tell me, Allilee?"

"This morning—ten minutes ago"—Allilee's words tumbled out fast enough now—"I caught our housemaid Brozie in my linen chest—fixing to steal my embroidered vests. I was upset about—about the light I'd seen burning up here at Foxden—so I whipped her good. She broke down and confessed she was planning to run off with Archie Rice as soon as the sheriff's office opens this morning—"

"Allilee, is this another of your efforts to trap me?"

"Can't you see I'm trying to save Fant's life? If it were you the high sheriff wanted, I'd gladly see you hang!" Allilee almost spat the desperate words at her.

Down the pike a buggy with two horses came trotting briskly. Only men on urgent business drove two horses these days . . .

"You'll have to excuse me," whispered America, staring at the buggy to see if it was slowing down for the Foxden gate.

"Merry, what can I do?" gasped Allilee, watching the buggy turn into the Foxden lane.

"Bring your horse around to the back-yard gate!"

"Shall I change the sidesaddle?"

"No. Do as I tell you, quick!"

America ran to the family room, caught up Cousin Simmy's suit she had mended, raced with it across the dog run and aroused her sleeping husband:

"Fant! Archie Rice has informed on you! The sheriff's coming up the lane—"

"Go 'way and let me sleep, Merry—"

"Fant, wake up! A nigger boy has informed on you."

He sat up quicker than she would have believed he had the strength to do. His face seemed all dark eyes and white skin stretched drum tight across his gaunt cheekbones. He stared blankly at her, his fever-chapped lips whispering:

"Merry, what'll I do?"

"Oh lover, it's not too late to stand and face it like a man! No court would try anybody as sick as you—"

"Woman, are you crazy? Get me my clothes and a gun!"

"Here's the suit I fixed. Don't take a gun! Nobody'll shoot a sick man if they see you haven't got a gun."

"Look out the window! Tell me what you see?"

While she hurried to the front window, he stood up in his trousers, fastened them and stepped over to the Chinese cabinet shelf on which lay the revolver and shells given America by his mother. Before she could look around, he had pocketed them and was back in a chair reaching for his shoes.

"The sheriff's getting out of his buggy at the yard gate," whispered America. Thank God Allilee had led her horse around to the back-yard gate!

"God, can't you help me on with this coat?" gasped Fant, struggling into it. She sprang across the room, steadied him to his feet, pulled on the coat.

"Allilee's holding her horse for you at the back gate," she whispered. "Take my arm. I'll help you mount—"

"I never could ride. Shall I wait for you on the shanty-boat?"

"Pick me up tomorrow night on the Growers Warehouse dock in Cincinnati," she decided, giving him her purse.

At the schoolroom door, the coast looked clear. Allilee's horse stood with hanging bridle reins cropping the grass along the fence. Allilee must have gone through the dog run to intercept the sheriff at the front door.

"Now's my chance—I'm going to make a run for it," whispered Fant, loosening his grip on her shoulder.

"Fant, throw away that gun!"

She saw him reach the yard gate, jerk it open. Startled, Allilee's horse threw up its head, stepped on its own bridle rein and tried to shy backwards. Fant reached the corncrib. Under it, America saw his legs running unsteadily towards the field gate. His next shelter was the tobacco barn out on the river rim. Below lay the walnut grove—safety—escape.

"Good morning, sheriff," America heard Allilee's voice

around the front of the house. "What brings you out so early, sir?"

"It's no use, ladies," boomed Swillevant. "I knew he'd try to make a run for the river, so I posted my men all around that back field. Eph Radford's waitin' for him out in that ridge barn."

"Fant, stay away from the ridge barn!" screamed America, running after her husband. She reached the barn-lot gate Fant had left open, was halfway through it when a deputy stepped in front of her, a deputy who had intentionally let Fant pass. "Eph's hiding in the ridge barn," she screamed again, before the deputy could get his hand across her mouth.

Fant must have heard, because he dropped into a grassy dip in the middle of the field. From the opened doors of the barn, Ephraim stepped out with his shotgun across his arm, the muzzle pointed downwards. As unconcerned as if he were going squirrel-hunting, he came sauntering along the ridge path between Fant and escape.

"Get out of my way, Eph—or I'll blow you to hell!" called Fant, and turned his head in time to see another deputy crawling towards him from the walnut grove. A wisp of smoke curled from Fant's revolver, the slower sound of the explosion shattered the midmorning calm and set echoes bounding backwards and forwards against the Ohio and Kentucky shores. Squinting, America saw that Fant's shot had stopped the deputy. He moved once, then lay still.

Fant jumped up and started running towards the river rim.

"Company—halt!" shouted Ephraim.

"Eph, you damn' fool," cried Fant and paused long enough to present a target.

Half a dozen rifles cracked simultaneously from the near-by woods. Fant's knees sagged. To America, wrenching free from the deputy's grasp and running towards her husband, Fant seemed to melt to earth with surprising slowness. Ephraim reached him before the dark head touched the sod. When America arrived, the two men were smiling at each other as if time had turned back thirty-five years, and they were together again at Fort Stedman.

"It's not so bad after all, eh—soldier?" Eph was saying.

"Not half so bad—as fear," gasped Fant. "Tell Merry—"

"Fant, lover!" cried Merry in agony, dropping on her knees to take her husband's hand.

"Lovie, goo'bye—"

From three sides men's legs and one woman's skirts came running. The July sun shone hot, a grasshopper jumped off a stem of red clover. A green field in midsummer, thought America, laying down her husband's hand, is a lovely place to die . . .

After they had carried Fant into the parlor and laid him on the haircloth sofa, America went into the family room, put on a black dress and sat down to receive callers. Ephraim, she knew, would stay at the front door. A deputy had already driven the hysterical Allilee home in his buggy with her saddled horse trotting along behind, swinging its head first right and then left to escape the dust. Sheriff Swillevant promised when he reached town to notify the undertaker and to send America's telegrams to High Jinks and to Professor Joe Dave. America had been adamant in refusing to notify Nicke and young Fant that their father would be buried tomorrow afternoon.

She stood in the family room where her husband had helped her deliver her first-born and watched her neighbors pass, their faces like masterpieces hung on a moving gallery wall. She had thought these moments of reunion after thirty years of separation, these broken sentences, silent handclasps and honest tears rolling down wrinkled cheeks would be balm to her bruised spirit. Instead, all she could think of was her husband's terror, all she could see was not their repentant faces but Fant's knees melting like butter into that bluegrass field under the blazing midsummer sun . . .

The next to arrive after Abigail MacGower was Margaret Annable, a frail old woman leaning on the arm of a rawboned spinster who must be Kate. Cousin Margaret had been crying, but her face was like a cloud the other side of which is lighted by the sunset.

"Oh, Merry," she gasped. "If only Mr. Annable had known—"

"He did know. That's what we talked about—just before he died," answered America. "He said he'd known ever since he saw my oldest girl."

"But pa was your loudest accuser," blurted Kate, in her frank way.

"He did it so people wouldn't suspect," answered America, steadily. "When I asked him how he could persecute me so, when he knew I had loved only Fant, he answered: 'I loved him too—in my own way.' "

"Oh, my blessed girl!" sobbed Cousin Margaret. "By telling me that, you've eased the bitterness of a lifetime off my heart. What else did Mr. Annable say?"

"He said my shoulders were broad."

"Sister Merry, I hope you'll try to forgive me," stated Kate, blinking behind her thick glasses. " 'There's none so blind—' "

"Wouldn't you like to see Fant?" America interposed gently, and showed them to the door. "He's in the parlor."

Of them all, Auld MacGower came nearest to shattering her iron control. Grasping America by the shoulders with his great blacksmith's hands, he rumbled deep in his throat:

"Lassie, ye hae fought a guid fight—ye hae run your-r course—ye hae kept th' faith!"

Twenty people must have volunteered to sit up with the corpse. America could hear them tiptoeing through the dog run at intervals all night. By midmorning a hundred more had come with their hands full, as if by their presence and their gifts of garden flowers or a choice dish of food covered by a snowy napkin they would salve their consciences of past unkindliness, and by paying respect to the dead do tardy honor to his widow. Never at any Mason County funeral had Weed and Ben Shadrack, come from Children's Chance to put up horses and run buggies out of the way for new arrivals, counted so many cakes of every size and description, roasted fowls, cold boiled hams, crocks of potato and chicken salad, custards and floating island, tipsy and transparent puddings, beaten biscuit, deviled eggs and cheese. Covered with new plant-bed cotton to keep off the flies, there the viands stood on a long table under the twin ash trees for any hungry person, white or black, to come and help himself.

"Makes me think ol' time o' plenty is back agin," whispered Ben Shadrack, pushing broken slices of cake into Weed's cupped paws before both hurried to stable more horses.

At four o'clock that afternoon, when Professor Joe Dave escorted America from the family room to the parlor, everybody realized the services were going to begin. America's face was unveiled. Behind her came High Jinks and Bayard, both slightly embarrassed. A chair was set forward for the widow. Professor Joe Dave took his place at the head of the closed casket covered by a Confederate flag. Opening his Bible, Professor Joe Dave began to read in his deep, moving, cultivated voice:

" 'And when they were come to the place which is called Calvary, there they crucified him, and the malefactors, one on the right hand, and the other on the left. . . .

" 'And one of the malefactors which were hanged, railed on him, saying, If thou be Christ, save thyself and us. But the other answering rebuked him, saying, Dost not thou fear God, seeing thou art in the same condemnation? And we justly; for we receive the due reward of our deeds: but this man hath done nothing amiss.

" 'And he said unto Jesus, Lord, remember me when thou comest into thy kingdom.

" 'And Jesus said unto him, Verily I say unto thee, Today shalt thou be with me in paradise. . . .' "

The procession serpentined out to the old Collier burying ground beyond the ridge barn. The ancient rectangle of ground enclosed by its slave-built limestone wall could not hold the crowd. The family ranged themselves around the open grave. The delegation of Veterans in their uniforms of Confederate grey approached carrying the coffin and placed it on the upturned sod.

" 'I am the resurrection and the life, saith the Lord,' " proclaimed Professor Joe Dave in a ringing voice. " 'He that believeth in me, though he were dead, yet shall he live . . .' "

As the casket was being lowered out of sight, Ephraim stepped to the head of the grave. With an uncertain look at his sister, he produced a battered bugle from under his Confederate cape, raised it to his lips and began to blow taps.

"Go to sleep!" sounded the silvery notes, as they had soared over the filling graves for generations of America's menfolk. "Go—to—sleep—" the river echoes tossed the soldier's requiem back against the sounding-board of the hills.

As Professor Joe Dave was escorting America housewards again, two self-important young negroes went skipping past them in a hurry to start home before the crowd.

"Ain't dis been a great day foah Miz Merry?" asked the young buck.

"Hit shore has," agreed his wench, a high yaller girl who giggled across her shoulder as if she wanted to be overheard. "I jes' bet she done put dat lamp a-purpose in de winder—so's we couldn't help comin' tuh see who dat was."

"You damn' stupid niggers!" exploded Professor Joe Dave, forgetting himself. "Mind your manners—and your tongues."

America, with the supreme effort of her life, held herself erect and quiet until convention permitted her to be alone, to go to bed. Lying with her face smothered into her pillow, she did not see Professor Joe Dave give Fmarind the sleeping tablet he had secured from Doctor Gillespie. When Emarind urged it upon her, she gulped it down with a swallow of water and buried her face again. After spraying the room with cologne, Emarind tiptoed out. Professor Joe Dave composed himself in Simmy Collier's mutilated Sheraton chair on the cold hearth, and prepared to wait until America should need spiritual comfort. During his watch, he wondered anew if timing were not the decisive factor of an individual's life, as it was of success on battlefields such as Waterloo and Gettysburg. Why did those young nigger Iscariots have to do their blabbing at just the one moment when they were within earshot of the one person in that entire field whom their malicious talk could hurt?

Before midnight, hearing America sobbing again into her pillow, Professor Joe Dave asked Emarind to leave the room for a few minutes while he spoke to the widow. Alone, he approached the bedside with the night candle held so that its flickering light illuminated his dome-shaped forehead, his distinguished face and snowy hair.

"What is it, my child?" he asked.

"Professor Joe Dave! You stayed?" gasped America.

"I wanted to see you get some rest."

"There'll never be any rest for me as long as Fant lies out there alone."

"We all have to die, America. Those deputies' guns were kinder than his malady would have been."

"I—I know that."

"Then why do you distress yourself needlessly? Try to get some sleep."

"Professor Joe Dave, I've sinned against love! Without realizing what I did—I betrayed my own husband when he trusted me! Two nights ago—the night before he was shot—"

"Listen to me, America," declared the compassionate voice above her. "Whatever transpired while Fant rested here before his death, let that remain forever a secret between you and him."

"That lamp Archie saw—"

"Like the good wife beyond price, you kept the lamp of your love and faith burning for Fant throughout these difficult years," Professor Joe Dave interrupted her, resolutely.

"But you don't understand, sir! I—I was worried about taking Fant West instead of my going East as I'd planned. Although I'd made up my mind to go to California, I couldn't sleep—so I stayed up to sew. I didn't think about that lamp—that informers might see it."

"Some time in our lives—to some degree—we are all unwittingly the tools or the victims of unscrupulous persons," he interposed, again. "When that happens, we can only go on living as bravely and as honestly as we can. This is what we mean when we say our characters—our souls—have come of age, America. This is the cross of secret grief each one of us must carry alone along our hidden way of sorrow. Fant's way was easier, shorter. It lay across that field under the gunfire he feared, the accusers he could never bring himself to face. From what I've been told, I truly believe his soul reached maturity only as he died—when he confessed to Eph Radford that death was easier to bear than fear. So you see, my dear," he smiled at her, "you mustn't grieve for him any more. Would you hold him back from his soul's growth, America?"

"No, sir—"

"Death came to him after a long life—in the guise of an old friend as on the battlefield," whispered Professor Joe Dave, thinking of his own boys in the Orphans' Brigade, called so young to die. " 'After life's fitful fever, he sleeps well.' And you, my dear. You should carry with you through the years to come, the sustaining thought that you have given—and given unsparingly—the three supremely great things of life—love and service and sacrifice, each of these in your hands enriching and enlarging the other, as you have ministered so unselfishly through these long bitter years to the welfare of your husband and your children. And now, will you try to rest again—or shall I call Rindy back into the room with us?"

"Please go get some sleep yourself," she smiled at him. "I'll be all right now."

Several days later, after she had made arrangements with Jim Barnes to take over her crop, America turned the key in the Foxden back door. Lugging her shabby bag, she started out across the meadow to walk down the hill towards a train which would carry her to New York. Pausing in midfield, she looked across the pasture to the Collier burying ground enclosed in its fieldstone wall with its lone cedar pointing skywards. For a moment she gazed dry-eyed at the yellow scar of Fant's fresh grave, then turned and trudged on over the river rim. For the first time in her life, she appeared small and old.

At Glen Cove, America found herself living a dual life. The Martha in her made out engraver's lists, went over menus with Tugger's French chef, checked furniture and servants' liveries with Pembroke, entered the donors' cards into proper books while Sally and Nicke *oh'*ed and *ah'*ed over lavish gifts, hurried into New York with her excited girls to make swift, sure suggestions to dressmakers on breath-taking creations for the three of them, rushed back to Glen Cove, spent hours consulting with an architect, a zoologist and Tugger's chief gardener about the decorations for the outdoor wedding, and wired Ephraim to come give away Nicke "in your full-dress Confederate uniform." America's inner self, like Mary of old, sat grieving beside a closed grave in a private burying ground . . .

Late afternoon before the wedding she waved Tugger and the bridal party off to a neighbor's for a shore picnic, and herself drove to the Glen Cove station to meet Ephraim.

"Why didn't you let me know earlier?" smiled Ephraim, hoping indirectly to bring out the reason why Sister Merry hadn't included his wife and the children in this rare treat.

"I couldn't bring myself to—to forgive you any sooner," America confessed. "And besides, you and I will be all the country jakes Nicke wants around here tomorrow."

"There's nothing countrified about you in that dress. All you need is a good night's sleep—"

The cob stole rein with canny little jerks of his chin. To be driving a high-spirited horse along a country lane in the summer twilight with Sister Merry thoughtful beside him took

Ephraim back to the days when as a boy he had been allowed to pick her up after some children's day-spending in old Charlotte.

"How're you going to introduce me?"

"As my brother Ephraim. The reporters already have it right."

"You don't mean I'm to be Eph Moncure?"

"Tugger succeeded last week in having that old charge against you quashed. It was just a suspicion anyhow—in some musty old reports in Washington which have been conveniently lost, he said. Tugger's good at that sort of thing."

"Has Tugger forgiven me for refusing to go on doing his drudgery for him?"

"I don't know," answered America. "He took the young folks over to a neighbor's so I could get carpenters started on the house. Here are the lodge gates," she announced, as she used to warn him as a boy-driver that it was time to draw rein. "Tomorrow the wedding guests will leave their carriages here, and walk to the house between that double row of pine trees. See the sheds I've built for their fancy horseflesh? Of course, all this will be hidden under evergreen boughs. One of the finest string quartets in New York will play old-fashioned songs in that Temple of Love—to put the guests in a nostalgic frame of mind—and make them forget they have to walk in their best shoes. This isn't to be any ordinary orchid wedding," concluded America, watching Eph's face as they swung around the last curve under the Georgia pines.

"Damned if that house doesn't look exactly the way I remember Golden Hill!" swore Ephraim, staring.

"It is Golden Hill," America smiled.

"But you said at the station Tugger had bought this place—"

"It's a false front. It's Golden Hill against the most God-awful mess of nigger-rich-pore-white-trash wooden gingerbread anybody ever saw."

"I wouldn't have missed this for the world!" breathed

Ephraim. "Do you remember how the moonlight used to sift down through the trees? And the way the mockingbirds sang follow-the-leader?"

"You'll hear them tomorrow night," promised America, steadying her voice to say the thing for which she had been gathering resolution all day. "And of course, Eph, nobody here knows anything about—about Fant's death."

"I'll be the last man to breathe it to a living soul, my dear."

"I knew I could count on you to help me through this wedding," quavered America, blinking away her tears. "And now would you like to freshen up before supper, while I talk to the gardener? Don't change. I haven't time. Here's Pembroke. He'll take good care of you—won't you, Pem?"

"Welcome home, Marse Eph—welcome home!" beamed the ex-slave, coming down the stone steps to meet the last Ephraim Collier of Golden Hill.

With her brother out of the way, America hurried to the fernery, where Dr. Jensen, the zoologist, had based his mysterious activities. America saw at a glance that his breeding cages had been moved out, one under each of the Georgia pines. All day the Blake buckboards had picked up ventilated tin drums at the railroad station. Dr. Jensen had felt it wise to stagger shipments so that, if accident befell one consignment—if the baggage car should get too hot or too drafty—another dozen drums might come safely through on the next express.

Finding the fernery empty, America ran over to the avenue of pines. Here Hans, the head gardener, and Dr. Jensen were bending over a tray of home-raised spiders when America approached. Behind them waited a corps of assistants with ladders, paint brushes and buckets of pine tar.

"I hope you're right about our natives acting as leaders," declared America, bending to look at the insects Dr. Jensen had hatched from cocoons. "If none of them will budge, what then?"

"We'll give 'em a snort of cyanide spray—sweep 'em up—and you'll have to use your powder dry," smiled the young scientist, starting up a stepladder Hans had adjusted against the tree trunk.

"Are you sure they're hungry enough?" demanded America, anxiously.

"They're as hungry as I dare let them get—and still leave 'em with strength enough to work. Hans, hand me up that box—and my feather. You there—with the pine tar," called Dr. Jensen to a helper, "paint your ring of tar around the trunk of this tree just below where I'm sitting. Mind it's above where guests might get their fingers sticky if they investigate. Mrs. Annable, here we go!"

With a feather, he began to coax spiders out of the box and up the main stem of the tree. A few ran perversely down, encountered the encircling belt of tar, turned and scurried upwards again out of sight in search of supper.

"It's going to work, ma'am!" called Dr. Jensen, rubbing his hands gleefully. "Arachnids never failed me yet."

"I'm afraid you've an all night job on your hands putting them in every tree," sighed America, wiping the perspiration from her forehead. The suggestion of the pine-tar belt had been her own. Had everyone of them escaped down the tree boles into the grass without first doing their stint, she hated to think what Tugger might say when presented the bill for a hundred thousand Mississippi bayou spiders, not to mention the ones Dr. Jensen had raised in the greenhouse.

America had left strict instructions at the stable that all vehicles, even Mr. Blake's, were to use the rear road until after the wedding tomorrow. She and Ephraim sat reminiscing on the south terrace until Tugger and the young people came home.

"Why, Eph! You lop-eared, rabbit-shootin', nigger-scarin' ol' hound!" Tugger welcomed his former business associate with true mountaineer hospitality.

Too tired to sleep, America lay wide-eyed in her French bed. Outside in the moonlight how many of her tiny decorators were hard at work for her? How many were loafing or felt travel-sick? How many had escaped, how many were being gobbled up by hawks, owls, snakes, even the polecats she had been hunting off the estate? Did grasshoppers eat spiders, she wondered drowsily. That big brown hopper which had jumped off the blade of red clover while Fant lay dying in the field looked as if he could handle at least six. To keep her thoughts off Fant, because Nicke's mother mustn't appear a hag to-morrow, America began counting spiders running up a tree trunk . . .

She awoke at two o'clock, and enumerated on her two hands the duties she must attend to the first thing this morning. Running out of fingers, she remembered Fant's hands clutching that cup of coffee on the Foxden hearth. Fant had so loved romantic display. What a pity he could not be here to play his part in the bridal pageant as a dashing father! Instead, she saw him lying with his consumptive's hands crossed over his racked breast, feverish eyes closed, bloodless lips no longer a thin blue line of resolution taxed beyond the puny strength of his body and spirit, that spirit broken in childhood by Justinian Annable. "Spare the rod, and spoil the child"—crush him, humiliate him, turn his sweetness to gall—until the only response he can make to life's problems is to turn his back and run away before he even begins to fight!

Grief, like a wave of physical pain, surged over America. Oh, Fant, my darling—my black-eyed baby boy! Wasn't it Cousin Margaret who, while grieving for you in '69, had repeated your baby prattle: "I'm a wee, wee sweet thing!"

You must control yourself, commanded America's intellect. Shut the door of your mind to Fant lying dead under sun-baked yellow clods out on the river rim. Today you are hostess for the House of Blake. Today you and Nicke stand before New York's elect as two human links between your proud past and the future. Behind you stands a procession of country gentlemen turned soldier or statesman, each with a drivin' woman at his side. Ahead of Nicke stretches a line of factory managers and office executives, with whatever kind of woman the new indoor city life may breed. Nicke, in spite of her bad manners and her acquisitiveness, is only what you have made her by blood and by precept. Be the strong link in the chain today! Tomorrow and for the dreary years to come, you may lead your own life at last. Then indeed you may weep for pity of the defeated boy who never grew up, you may long for the lover's arms which will never hold you again, for the laughing eyes which never again will brim over with warm brown light for you . . .

Morning was in the ornate guest room when America awoke. Springing out of bed, she ran barefooted to the window. Below her the avenue of pines marched two by two holding out their arms hung with fairy lace. From almost all of the lower limbs shone silvery cobwebs dripping with dew.

America was dressed in five minutes and whirling the dial of the library safe to unlock it. Inside lay fat sausages bearing the stamp of the United States Assay Office. Dr. Jensen, Hans and trusted assistants carried out the gold and silver dust, America relocked the safe and tiptoed after them. Shaking silver into a bellows, Hans blew the powdered metal onto the nearest cobweb, fixing the spider like a nugget in its center. When the sun struck the web, America hoped the dew would dry and leave the web a scrap of silver lace stiff enough to handle. On the handsomest of the webs Dr. Jensen blew gold dust. Hollow-eyed assistants picked up bellows, filed past America's table where she sat measuring out the precious dust, and started to work on stepladders. Within the hour, before the sun had looked over the treetops, every cobweb had its gold or silver varnish.

Tugger and the young people did not come downstairs until Pembroke rang the chimes for luncheon. America and Ephraim stood near by to watch their faces. The shining pines drew Tugger to them like a magnet. He then turned, and for the first time saw the changed façade of his house.

"Sister Merry, you certainly take the cake!" was all he could say.

"What gave you the idea?" asked Mitchell Ayres, thrusting an inquisitive forefinger through a hardened golden web.

"No handling, please!—before the ceremony," cautioned America. "While Dr. Jensen was doing research on a certain species of Chinese spider now running wild across the bayous of the Far South, he stumbled across the account of this gold and silver wedding, as it was called. A Mississippi planter—and he must have been a very wealthy man, Tugger—wanted to give his twin girls the most beautiful and the most expensive wedding ever held in this country. So he had the spiders brought over from China—in a clipper ship around the Horn."

"Did these spiders come from China, too?" marveled Sally.

"Only from New Orleans."

"How many got away?" demanded the practical Steve.

"Enough to make the Long Island farmers bless Tugger till the end of his days. Spiders are great assets around any garden for destroying insect pests," America informed her city-bred young people.

The day, seemingly begun with magic, moved with stately speed towards sunset, the appointed hour for eight hundred invited guests to arrive. In the kitchens, Pinard was preparing supper for a thousand. Below the rose gardens and in the Temple of Love, musicians alternated in playing the plantation songs of Stephen Foster and other favorites such as *Moonlight and Roses* and *Backward, Turn Backward, Oh Time, In Your Flight.* When the haunting melody of *Long, Long Ago* drifted in to America supervising the adjustment of the brides' veils upstairs, while Palestine looked on, munching chocolates from a five-pound box in her lap, America felt momentarily as if she might faint. Miss Vosburgh revived her competently with smelling salts.

Before five o'clock guests walked down the avenue of cobwebs towards the front terraces. In sea-foam hoops with a silver lace parasol held between her eyes and the setting sun, America floated out on the arm of a personable somebody named Dan, and took her place near the smilax-wreathed altar set on the front grass before the Golden Hill façade. At her nod, Mr. Damrosch led his orchestra into the measured beat of the *Lohengrin* march. From the croquet court came Mitchell Ayres and Junior, who was serving as his best man, from the rose garden Steve Holt and his roommate. The young men ranged themselves on the right of the altar, looked expectantly towards the mansion.

Impressive in his stiff red silk vestments, Bishop Potter came down the stone steps to the altar. He was followed by Tugger with Sally on his arm. Behind them came Nicke and Ephraim in his own distinguished grey, the rippling Confederate cape thrown back to show its yellow lining. Both brides wore identical hoop-skirt dresses of white slipper satin, with long rose-pointe veils imported from Brussels to begin in this country another hundred years as family heirlooms.

" 'We are gathered together in the sight of God and man,' " began the Bishop.

As she stood to watch, the handsome picture blurred before America's eyes. Oh, Fant my dearest, you should be standing there in Ephraim's gold and grey! Missing our loved ones, thought America, we weep in self-pity of our own emptiness of heart. Rather should we weep in pity of the dead, who lose the beauty of earth at twilight, the warmth of hand clasping hand, the smile of dear eyes plunging deep into the beloved's, the touch of vibrant shoulders, the electric smoothness of satin skin . . .

" 'Whom God hath joined together, let no man put asunder!' " admonished the Bishop, and wrapped his gold-embroidered stole signifying the Yoke of Christ around Nicke's and Steve's joined hands.

Cold steel can separate, America remembered. Deputies lying hidden in summer woods are men. And the grave, dug so deep the wild soil shows in yellow clods, can put asunder forever . . .

The long reception line swung into place; the congratulations, felicitations and kissing began. As the twilight deepened, artificial lighting effects worked out by the stage manager of the Metropolitan Opera House came on in rainbow beauty. While the wedding guests supped on Aunt Flora's triumphs Pinard's chefs had learned to cook, Bert Green and his troupe entertained with songs and tap dancing. Moderns again, in dusters, motoring veils and caps, the bridal couples pecked feminine relatives' cheeks, gripped outstretched masculine hands, climbed into the Oldsmobile roadsters Tugger had given each groom for a wedding present, and outdistanced their rice-throwing friends. After the *chuff-chuff* of the auto cars had died away in the distance, Tugger and America stood on the terrace to receive the farewells of their guests. The same phrases kept recurring:

"Those trees are still the loveliest sight I ever saw!" declared Mrs. Dudley Marshall, in the Kennedy emeralds. "And so characteristic of you, America."

"What a triumph!" raved Pierre de Longpré. "What beauty!"

"Tugger, your Midas touch has done it again," Ward McAllister conferred the accolade on their host, although everybody realized that America standing haggard-eyed beside him really deserved it.

When even the laggards had gone, the three of them walked painfully towards the Georgian front porch. Here they sank in exhaustion. Removing his shoes, Ephraim complained:

"My feet stood two years of Stonewall's forced marches better than tonight!"

"How'll I write the checks for this shindig?" grumbled Tugger, nursing his cramped right hand.

They sat and watched the waiters pick up the last fallen spoons, crawl under the tables for crumpled napkins. At the end of the cobweb lane, the electricians had begun to disconnect the individually lighted trees. One by one they winked out. As America's eyes accustomed themselves to the comparative darkness, she decided the avenue looked lovelier in natural than in synthetic moonlight, more as if she were seeing it through a cool mist of tears. Behind the iron stag at the edge of the rhododendron hollow, one of the mechanical mockingbirds began to sing.

"Somebody's forgotten to disconnect the circuit," sighed America, preparing to rise.

"Eph, can't you take care of it?" suggested Tugger, urbanely.

"Delighted," grinned Ephraim. "Just like old times."

Tugger did not turn to look at America until the shadows had swallowed the tall Confederate. She sat leaning against one of the porch columns, a woman of fifty-three with the figure of a girl. Neither of those two simpering brides could hold a candle to her for looks, Tugger decided. She's like a full-blown rose, lovelier in maturity than any close-fisted bud could ever be. Or a perfect statue, he changed his comparison. Experience, the unerring sculptor, had chiseled those resolute lines of mouth and jaw, had buffed the ivory planes of forehead and cheekbones, had rounded the childish upper lip with tenderness, had filled those steady grey eyes, now closed, with the wisdom and calm of maturity. Only a woman satisfied with life, a woman secure in her own resources, decided Tugger in a moment of panic, could sit so still, with hands relaxed, palms upward in her sea-foam lap. What had he to offer such a woman except money and position? America Moncure had had position since some black nurse first laid her in her cradle. Money—money meant ease, freedom, leisure to enjoy the good things of this good old world.

"Well, Sister Merry, you did yourself—and all of us—proud!" Tugger began.

"I'm glad you're satisfied, Tugger," she smiled, turning her head towards him without lifting it from the pillar. "Let me warn you—while the glow is still on those trees—to brace yourself for what they cost."

"Oh, that's all right! It isn't the actual bills that'll hurt most. It's for what the New York tax collectors will reassess my real estate when they read about this shindig. It's gotten so a man can't spend his own hard-earned dollars the way he wants to any more. This country's going to the dogs—what with talk about reviving the income tax—and coal miners able to paralyze industry with strikes—and demagogues stirring up class hatred Americans never thought of until politicians took to soapboxes to create jobs for themselves."

There are no job seekers or stump speakers on Tuckahoe tonight, thought America. Yet Hans Claussen is lying awake wondering if tobacco prices this fall will cover the yearly interest and installment payment due on his land note. And what about the county gentry, whose boys have left their patrimonies for fatter city jobs? Stone Moncure is up to his eyebrows in debt. Allilee Drake pays Cousin Theresa's taxes with her schoolroom stipend and wonders how soon she will be replaced by a younger, better-educated teacher. Major Chisholm, pocketing his pride and his unpaid bills, has posted another of his hundred-acre meadows for sale. Kate Annable is burning expensive kerosene oil to compare mail-order catalogue prices with those of local merchants, in the hope of saving a few cents on clothes, household replacements and farm machinery. Timberlawn quite frankly now is running on Cousin Margaret's cash reserves Justinian Annable salted away for his widow in the Farmers Bank in Limestone. What if, overloaded with farm paper, the bank should go to the wall? It would carry half of Mason County with it in its downfall, among other losers Fant Annable's widow with her three-hundred-dollar cash balance.

"Sister Merry, are you listening to me?"

"I—I beg your pardon, Tugger. What was it you said? Something about the country going to the dogs, wasn't it?"

"That was five minutes back. I've been telling you what I thought might be best for Teena," repeated Tugger, with a patience unusual to him. "Have you any ideas on the subject?"

"Can't we take this up in the morning?"

"It's tomorrow now. And I've got to be in town by noon," he pressed her. To avoid the confusion, Tugger always left early the morning after a party.

"All I've noticed is that Teena's getting worse," America stated in a flat voice of exhaustion. Sick people—mentally and physically—selfish girls and grabby men! When was she herself going to rest, to get a few hours' sleep? For the past month—ever since she had heard the scrape of sled runners on the barn-lot stones—she had been driving herself beyond her strength, beyond human endurance. How much longer could it last?

" 'Her condition is steadily deteriorating' is the way Doctor Cantrill puts it," continued Tugger. "Nicke, little simpleton, thought I hadn't realized—or that Miss Vosburgh, to save her own job, wouldn't tell me. Miss Vosburgh has had three strong-arm nurses upstairs for a week—to keep things on an even keel tonight—but of course you know all this."

"Go on, Tugger."

"Sister Merry, if I asked you a—a simple favor, would you grant it?"

"That depends—"

"Will you hear me out without interrupting—or flying off the handle?"

"Why, of course!"

"Remember, you promised," grinned Tugger, and took a long breath before he continued, his eyes on the avenue of precious frosted trees: "During these years a blind woman—and you're far from that, America—could have seen how it's been with Teena and me. I haven't complained, because I made my bed—and it was up to me to lie in it."

"You married Teena for social position and children, Tugger."

"You're right—as usual, Sister Merry. John Barleycorn helped me get the twins—and you did the rest. Both these undertakings required time and patience. The twins are grown, now. Their playtime's over. After tonight, it'll be up to them to show the kind of stuff they're made of—and this goes for Nicke, too. Don't you agree?"

"Yes, Tugger."

"Now, let's get back to Teena. Doctor Cantrill feels she

will do better under more careful supervision—where she can't bully the servants or loot the ice chest in the middle of the night."

"Is Teena up to that, again? I'm surprised at Miss Vosburgh."

"No woman can work twenty-four hours a day every day for years—and stay alive. Take a look at yourself in the mirror, if you don't believe me. To make a long story short, Miss Vosburgh is quitting—as soon as I can make other arrangements. She's going back to Vienna."

"I can well understand that," agreed America. "What are your plans?"

"Here's where I want you to listen to me with an open mind," Tugger declared, wetting his lips. "For several years I've been investigating the laws of different states concerning the insane. My signature alone isn't enough to commit Teena here in New York—I'd need yours, and maybe Eph's, too. Here's what I had in mind: Suppose you take Teena out West—she'll go anywhere with you without making a fuss that might get into the papers. You'd put her into the finest private asylum out there money can buy. Then you'd come back here, and keep things going at Number 860 for as long as might be needed to get the proper medical reports from that asylum. Nicke and Steve could visit you. What could be more natural than my sister-in-law running things here as usual? Then as soon as everything was all set, I'd quietly sue for divorce—on grounds of Teena's mental condition—in some state where I own a home and plenty of property—like Tennessee or Georgia which are tied up tight with my railroads. What local judge could stand out against the state's biggest taxpayer, especially when the law's all on my side? I might if necessary even get the state legislature to help me out."

"Few men, I'm afraid, would have stood by Teena as long as you have, Tugger," sighed America. Fant—oh, Fant, my darling! The years I gladly gave to you—the precious years of youth, now gone forever.

"Well, that's the set-up, then," exclaimed Tugger, and rubbed his hands briskly in the habit he had when well pleased. "It'll be months before the back-stairs grapevine gets the news around New York that Teena's even gone. By then, I'll have my divorce proceedings half through—and I'll be damn' careful to stay out of sight when I do come back to New York. Before we know it, America, you and I'll be walking across the gangplank of my yacht, the *Buccaneer*—as Sally and Mitch will walk next week!"

The fog of despair between her and her surroundings cleared, as if blown away by zero winds. In a sharp cold voice, she stated carefully:

"I—I don't believe I understood you, Tugger. Will you please say that again?"

"I thought that ud make you sit up and take notice," he chuckled. "For thirty-five years—ever since I glanced up from my old cowhide under the Charlotte Court House oaks—I've been in love with you, America Moncure. Only with a boy's calf judgment, I thought it was Teena's pretty face I'd fallen for—instead of your courage and grit. But don't you think for one minute—just because I happen to mention your fightin' qualities first—I ain't noticed how well you've kept yourself, what a good looker you'd still be with some rest and the proper clothes. As I told you once before, you were the damn' finest-looking woman ever tooled a four-in-hand out Harlem Lane!"

She looked at him standing two steps below her on the imitation flagstones. The Bond Street perfection of his tails, the urbane confidence shining from his face, the sheer brute power born of habitually successful elimination of all opposition did not blind her to a realization of what he had said. Here before her stood the man who for years had been friend and clansman, a man whom she had trusted and served like a brother; yet who had just proposed that she enter into a relationship with him which might well daunt a hardened criminal's fancy woman.

"Tugger Blake, are you crazy?" she whispered.

"I'm crazy about you!" he declared, in his muted voice of passion. "But don't look like that. I can wait. Haven't I waited fifteen years—to get you the only way I could keep you the rest of my life, and still enjoy the things we've both worked so hard to win? Come on—answer me properly, Sister Merry. Give me a great big sisterly kiss to seal our bargain, eh?"

"I've lived a precarious life, Tugger Blake," America answered, trying to steady herself. "I've taken risks. Coming of age as I did during the war—and afterwards—I've had to. But deep in my conscience I've known the end justified the means. And as somebody once said of me, my lot has been—service and sacrifice. But now—what you just said—"

"I reckon my proposition makes it all seem worth while?" Tugger exulted. "You and I are cut off the same bolt of cloth. We're tough—we can stand wear and tear. And if we stretch a little now and then, we can snap back. But we're both getting on in life. You're tired and broke. And I'm lonesome. All these years—ever since a terrier I had named Tarheel died—I've been the damn' lonesomest devil in all New York City. How many women a man may have doesn't make any difference. It's what's inside—that gnawing emptiness that nothing can fill—no matter what I eat—or where I sleep—or how many more millions I squeeze out of suckers in Wall Street. Ain't it been the same with you, now, honest, America?"

"You didn't let me finish," she answered, icy cold. "I started to say I'd lived a precarious life. But not even on the hogshead breaks—where no decent woman ever went before me as a tobacco handler—have I been so grossly insulted, so foully besmirched as by you, Tugger Blake—by what you just proposed to me—that I help you put away my poor sick sister so we could enjoy ourselves—and your millions!"

"Hell-damn, what's wrong about that—if we fix up everything nice and quiet and easy, so folks won't smell a rat?"

"Tugger—Tugger Blake! Have you had your way so long in Wall Street you can't tell black from white?" she asked. her voice a ringing bell. "Have you turned color-blind to all sense of moral decency? Have you forgotten the sin of David?"

"The sin of David?" he repeated, the blood rushing to his face. He stood glaring up at her, his big hands twitching. "You're a fine one to preach to me, you country Jezebel—after you've made a practice for years of lying up with every tramp who came past Foxden!"

"Tugger Blake, you know that's not the truth."

"I only know what your nameless brat has told me!"

So Nicke had betrayed her for a few pieces of silver—to be able to stay on at Number 860 Fifth Avenue—to escape being sent home to Foxden? To what purpose, America asked herself, dropping down on the nearest step, had she slaved in cook cabin and field to raise two such children as Nicke and young Fant? High Jinks—lovely loving High Jinks was all she had left—High Jinks, and to be free to tell the truth at last:

"Because we'll probably never see each other again, Tugger—I would like to tell you something which should clear up any misunderstanding you may have had about me," America began in her dead-tired voice. "Fant Annable wasn't drowned in '69—as everybody thought. With a murder warrant out against him, naturally we had to be very careful about seeing each other. I shielded him all I could. And even the shanty-boat men won't turn informers. So with the river just behind Foxden, Fant did get back occasionally to—to see me."

"You don't mean Fant Annable was Nicke's father?"

"Fant was the father of both my girls."

"God, Sister Merry, I've blundered again—when all I wanted was to take care of you the rest of our lives—to share my money with you—to have you by my side!"

"Let me finish, please," continued America. "A month ago Fant Annable came home—dying of consumption. He asked me to take him to California. A doctor at a Chicago clinic had told him that the mild California climate was his only chance. As usual, he was broke. And much too weak to attempt such a long trip alone. I hid him at Foxden for two nights, while a friend was locating a shanty-boat man to float us down the river—and I was trying to decide whether to be a good wife and take him West, or to come on East and go through with Nicke's and Sally's wedding."

"How could we have had it without you?" asked Tugger stupidly, looking at the moonlit avenue of cobwebs. "None of us knew your plans."

"I realized that. While I was deciding, a black girl and her bucko spied on us, and turned informer. Poor dying Fant tried to make a run for it, but Ephraim—"

"Not your brother Eph?"

"Eph probably didn't tell you he's a famous Texas Ranger? Not being able to go back to Charlotte Court House on account of that old charge, he naturally came to Tuckahoe to see me. One look, and he immediately guessed the truth. Because he loved me, he believed in me—he knew I couldn't be what I seemed," she explained, meeting Tugger's eyes with a crooked little smile that haunted him the rest of his life. "That night Eph walked back to Limestone and hired out as a deputy sheriff because he considered it his duty to catch Fant—to take him into court where he'd have to admit he was the father of my girls."

"And in high time, I'd say," snorted Tugger. "So Eph took it on himself to avenge the family honor, eh? How come, then, you were so keen to have him here for the wedding? I know if he ever got a shot at Fant Annable, he wouldn't miss!"

"Eph didn't kill Fant," America continued. "Even if he had, I could have found it in my heart to forgive him—because he was doing the right thing. And besides, all my life I've known nothing but bloodshed and struggle. But to go on: The high sheriff put his men in the woods around the back field which Fant had to cross to get over the river rim. Eph was waiting for him in a tobacco barn. When Fant—tried to make a run for it—Eph called out for him to halt—just as he used to do when Fant was serving under him in the war. Being a soldier, Fant automatically stopped long enough for other deputies hidden in the woods—to draw a bead on him. They shot him down—like a sheep-killing dog!"

"Sister Merry, you should have told me," whispered Tugger, in a voice he had not used since he walked up Fifth Avenue with dead Tarheel in his arms.

"And spoil Sally's and Nicke's wedding? Sally's never been anything but kind and affectionate to me. Why should I let the tragedy that's shadowed my life cross her happiest day?"

"I don't see how you went through with it—I declare I don't!"

"I can do anything life calls on me to do," she concluded tonelessly, and arose from the step. "Now, I'm going home—to Tuckahoe."

"To Fant's grave, I'll bet," Tugger said with new insight into how America must be feeling, had felt during these past hectic weeks under his roof. "Well, Sister Merry, all I can say is that I'm sorry. And that I hope you'll find it in your heart—someday—to forgive me."

"I could forgive you for reaching, Tugger—all greedy boys reach," she smiled that crooked smile at him again, "but not for believing the worst of me—or that I was so bad I could be partner to the worst in you."

"They're hard words you're saying, America Moncure," he gulped. "Can't you make any allowance for me? Remember, I got my facts—what any reasonable man would accept for the facts—from Nicke, from your own daughter."

"Nicke doesn't count."

There was no use arguing any more tonight, he saw. As long as Teena was alive—and Doctor Cantrill said he had known similar cases to live with good care to be eighty years old—Tugger realized he would not see America again. He looked at her hungrily, trying to impress her image on his mind for the barren times ahead. With a sense of rising loss, a sense almost of panic, he realized that he didn't have even a single picture of America, except that fool *Wild Honey* poster, as a memento of her dear and characterful face.

"When are you planning to leave?" he asked, swallowing.

"I'd prefer to go now—as soon as I can change. There's the stable clock striking one. We could catch the milk train."

"Do you have to be—so cruel?"

"Why, Tugger! It isn't a case of being cruel," she said in her normal voice, and unconsciously laid her hand on his forearm as she might have tried to comfort a stranger, anybody, in such evident distress. "It's just that I feel I'd sleep better on the train—in town—anywhere but here under the same roof with you and Teena. And I have just got to have some sleep."

Turning, she started up the stairs. On the top step, she turned, spoke down to him with the ghost of her pleasant smile:

"You could do this for me—if you'd be so kind? You could ring for a carriage to take us to the station. And tell Brother Eph to pack—that I'll be ready in half an hour."

"America, is that all you're going to say to me?" he cried, in agony.

"Tugger, my dear," she spoke looking down across her shoulder, "you mustn't feel so badly. We're two different kinds of people, that's all. What else can we do—except go our different ways?"

As America and Ephraim approached Foxden in the buggy he had hired, she saw a man cutting her tobacco green in the Foxden pike field. A nine-year-old boy was driving her team and wagon loaded with tobacco sticks along the head of the rows. Another lad's head moved along the lush rows dropping sticks.

"Young Fant's come home," America anticipated the worst. Where now could she go to earn her daily bread?

"He's heard about his father," commented Ephraim, handing America the reins before he swung over the wheel to open the Foxden gate. "Want me to go tell him he's cutting that tobacco too green? Even I know that."

"From now on," America resolved, aloud, "he'll have to paddle his own canoe."

Although young Fant must have seen her in the buggy, he did not stop work to come to the house and greet her. When they reached the yard fence, Ephraim swung down her old Gladstone, for she had brought none of her wedding finery home with her and had traveled in the simplest of her new dresses. Two dirty babies digging at the roots of her early-flowering chrysanthemums looked up and stared as she walked past them into the trash-littered yard. Somewhere in the rear, strange dogs began to bark. The next moment a pack of mongrels rushed them.

"They look like good coon dogs," diagnosed Ephraim. "Down, you Rover—down, boys!"

Recognizing a fellow hunter, the mangy pack yelped and jumped around Ephraim. Attracted by the commotion, a black-haired mountain girl appeared, wiping sudsy hands on her ragged calico skirts. Her eyes were gentian blue, her face in spite of overwork and too frequent child-bearing was still beautiful.

"You're Effie May, aren't you?" America greeted her daughter-in-law. "I'm Fant's mother. And this is my brother, Ephraim Radford Moncure."

"I'm right proud tuh meet you folks," declared Effie May. "We been expectin' you any day, ma'am."

"When did you come down from Breathitt County?" asked America.

"The day after that talkin' Barnes boy brought us word of the shootin'. Won't you folks take cheres, an' sit a spell?" Effie May urged them, with shy mountain hospitality. "Fant, he'll be in to dinner in a little while. He's worked himself into a plumb swivet about that patch o' terbacker."

"It's too green to cut yet," America said, before she realized it.

"I done told him that a'ready, ma'am," agreed Effie May, "but you know haow he is."

"Look here, Sister Merry, I wish you'd come on home with me!" declared Ephraim, unexpectedly. "Beth and the Cap'n would be mighty glad to see you. There's that big empty cabin in the yard—all furnished with Doggett heirlooms—ready and waiting for you to move in and take a good long rest. How about it?"

"Thank you, Eph," America smiled her appreciation. "But I'll stay here—until I see young Fant."

"Will you promise to come then—after you've seen him?"

"I won't leave Tuckahoe without letting you know, Eph. And now, you'd better be starting for home yourself—or you'll be late for dinner," she dismissed him, affectionately.

"Miz Annable—?"

"Effie May, you'd make me feel much happier if you'd call me America—or ma."

"Yes, ma'am. I jest want tuh say—before he comes in—I hope you'll stay on here with us."

"Effie May, you don't want an old woman like me around the house."

"Why, Miz Annable! You shouldn't say that, when you're younger lookin' than I am. That's a mighty purty dress you're a-wearing."

"Do you like it, Effie May? Then I'll give it to you," America answered, the icy hand that had gripped her heart relaxing a little. "The color's too bright for me—the way I feel."

"Yes, ma'am. I expect you feel mighty porely," Effie May sympathized. "He says you ought 'a' told folks how things was y'ars ago. But I say tuh you—before he gits here—I think you done just right! Ever' woman's got tuh stand by her man through thick 'n' thin, I say."

"By 'him' do you mean my son, Effie May?"

"Yes, ma'am. He never liked tuh hear me speak his name aout full—on account of his pappy, I reckon," explained Effie May. "An' naow I'll fetch you that chere, so's you kin set in the dog run whar thar's a breeze, an' rest."

"I wouldn't think of it, my dear," declared America, thanking God in her heart for this girl and High Jinks. "You're washing today, aren't you? I'll get dinner."

"Hit's most ready, ma'am. You jest set daown thar fer a spell an' lemme look at you. You're so purty, ma'am. An' ever'body says you're so good."

When he came in to noon-day dinner, America found young Fant unchanged. The meal, poorly cooked by America's standards, was not a happy one. Her four grandchildren stared at America. She could not persuade Effie May to take her proper place at the foot of the table. Confronted by Ishmael's taciturnity, America felt like a chatterbox. No mention was made of his appropriation of her growing tobacco until he pushed back his chair to return to the field.

"I reckon—since you've carried the crop this far—you feel you've got a claim on it?" he asked.

"You're cutting it green, Fant," she answered, without looking up.

"That ain't what I asked you."

"No, son. I make no claim on anything here at Foxden."

"When the crop's sold, I'll give you a piece o' money—for what you've laid aout to get it along this far. And o' course you'll have your bed and board here with us," he added, trying to smile as if he were glad to see her.

"Thank you," she answered, without returning the smile.

That afternoon, when she hoped Effie May wasn't looking, America slipped away from the noisy dogs and dirty babies and walked along the ridge path past the tobacco barn to the Collier burying ground. Fant's grave was still bare, baked pale in the summer sun. She sat down cross-legged on the near-by grass and looked forlornly about her at the clods, the field-stone wall, the cedar tree, the hazy September sky strewn with wisps of clouds like an old woman's greying hair.

"Fant, darling," she whispered, her lips quivering. "Now I know how you felt. Now I know what it is to be old—and homeless—and unwanted."

The next moment she was weeping stormily, her arms outflung on the drought-seared grass, her sob-racked body pressed downwards against the hard dry earth . . .

When her emotion had spent itself, she lay listening to the myriad sounds of an early September afternoon in the country. One of her work mules must be grazing near by, because she heard unshod hoofs walking along the path towards the burial ground. Mules were curious, they liked to see what people did. After a while she turned over, gazed straight upwards into the sky. It would soon be time for her to drive in the cows. They probably hadn't been half-milked since she left over a month ago—

"Oh!" she gasped, and found herself gazing into the flax-blue eyes, the sun-reddened face of Stone Moncure sitting on the burying ground wall. "Cousin Stone! I didn't hear you come up. How long have you been sitting there?"

"Since 1866," he smiled at her.

"How—how did you know I was home?" she asked, wondering if she had heard him correctly. What a sight she must look in this old calico work dress, with hair tousled and eyes swollen from weeping!

"I bribed Mrs. MacGower to send word to me the minute she found out you were home," grinned Stone, not moving from the wall. "She must have recognized you walking out the ridge, because she certainly kept her promise. America, when will you marry me?"

"Marry you?" she echoed, foolishly.

"Yes, my dear," he said, intensely serious. "You haven't sixty white horses—and Children's Chance is loaded with debt. But you know I've loved you since the moment I first laid eyes on you at the *Magnolia*'s rail."

Chapter 16

In the sunshine of Tuckahoe's belated approval, America's year of mourning seemed to pass more quickly than had a single month of Coventry. For the first time in her adult life, she dared turn her inner thoughts from the problem of Fant's, her own and her children's future and took a more objective point of view.

She first tried to teach Effie May how to keep house easily, so that she might have additional time to rest and to be with her children. Until she saw that she was doing more harm than good, America then endeavored to show her son how to farm. With difficulty America had carried young Fant through the equivalent of a common school education. Absence of companionship with well-mannered youths on Tuckahoe, and of strong paternal authority after he had grown too large for America to enforce her orders with a pear switch, had developed in young Fant a lack of self-discipline which had increased during the years he had spent in Breathitt County, the years after he had left her roof. His disposition, never sunny, became more and more morose as he found himself swamped with problems of Foxden's management, problems and toil which had seemed simple and light when he had watched America plow resolutely through them. By the time the two of them, backing and jerking like an ill-matched team, had set out an average small-farmer's crop, young Fant so resented America's presence at Foxden that she preferred to stay as much out of his sight as possible in her side of the log house, the parlor and the old schoolroom. Her heart often ached for submissive weary young Effie May. Knowing her son's temperament, and the uncomplaining loyalty of mountain wives to their husbands, America interfered in no way, and only occasionally counted the weeks before she could transfer her trunks, books, Golden Hill heirlooms and the few choice gifts received from the Blakes and their New York friends to Children's Chance.

Before her winter fire, America enjoyed her leisure. She read one local and three metropolitan newspapers. Stone, on his weekly calls, often demanded to know how she could put up with the Louisville *Courier-Journal,* edited by the brilliant Marse Henry Watterson whom America defended as "perhaps the last of the great American journalists." The paper had once been the Bible of Kentucky farmers, but Stone now looked back with bitterness to the time when Marse Henry had sided with the Gold Bugs against the Silverites in the Bryan-Palmer-and-Buckner fight. Thereafter, the *Courier-Journal* was regarded by Stone and his neighbors as an organ of Wall Street, and therefore an enemy of the American farmer.

In her New York dailies America followed the organization of the holding companies—"those great strong boxes!" Thomas Fortune Ryan had called them. The drive on northwestern railroad stocks resulted on May 9, 1901, in a stock market crash amounting to a major national catastrophe. Out of the debacle Dan Lord and Tugger Blake apparently arose stronger than ever, with Dan in the driver's seat of the four-in-hand Tobacco Trust—cigarette, plug, segar, and snuff. The Lord interests had already invaded the British market by buying Ogden's of Liverpool as a springboard, and in 1901 aggressively fought a fifth "tobacco war"—this time to control British and world trade.

When an armistice was finally negotiated, British tobacco merchants agreed to confine their trade solely to the British Isles, the Lord interests their activities entirely to their home country. To develop and handle Empire and world trade, a baby Hercules in world trusts—the British-American Tobacco

Company—was created, with the Lord group owning two-thirds of its initial capital stock. Dan's personal spoils of victory were reported at seven million dollars. One clause in the peace terms caused America to lay down her financial page and stare thoughtfully. The new set-up provided that all Yankee-grown raw leaf destined for the new world trust should be purchased in the United States solely by Dan Lord's agents. Wouldn't this clause, America asked herself, banish the pleasant-spoken English, Dutch and other foreign buyers from the Cincinnati breaks? Their bids on many a hogshead of hers had lifted its final sales price out of loss into profit.

In late September of 1901, after the tobacco crop was housed, America and Stone stood up in the Foxden parlor to take their marriage vows before Professor Joe Dave. The old log house and lawns were crowded with guests come to wish Tuckahoe's two most brilliant citizens happiness. Seeing young Fant's eyes fixed thoughtfully on the lane crowded with horse-drawn vehicles, America took care not to let her own expression show that she too remembered her prophecy made in his boyhood. There had been more buggies in the lane for Fant's funeral. Indeed, they had then overflowed into the adjoining fields. America still felt that her son's and Nicke's disloyalty to her had not entitled them to see their father's hunted face in his coffin.

During the lavish wedding supper which America had engaged Abigail to prepare and bring over from the tollhouse, Nicke and Steve arrived dramatically in their Oldsmobile. They had been delayed by blow-outs, spark plug trouble and scary teams, they declared, but if the bridal couple dared risk it, they wanted to attempt to drive them to their Limestone train. Someone suggested a race, with a handicap for the auto-car. Stone's black mares took one look at the Oldsmobile and won a 2:10 trot up the hills to outdistance the chugging monster.

After several days at White Sulphur Springs, the honey-mooners visited Arabia now happily married to a Virginia farmer living at the crossroads called the Meadows of Dan. Their host walked Stone tired below the Pinnacles of Dan to show the Kentuckian his fat cattle grazing on "second generation" bluegrass pasture which shone like green velvet winter and summer due to heavy precipitation caused by altitude. America and Stone then continued leisurely on to Charlotte Court House, where they found Andorra mistress at last of handsome Carr House. At the ripe age of ninety-eight Cousin Tanis had relinquished her tenacious hold on life and her possessions. Andorra had at once married her grey-haired childhood sweetheart, Stephen Crenshaw, perennial clerk of Charlotte County. America found the classic courthouse drowsing in the golden October shade of its ancient oaks. The sun-dappled crossroads boasted a new memorial statue to Charlotte's brave boys in grey. The age-mellowed Georgian town houses and the handsome frame and brick country manors set among enormous virgin oaks out of sight off the forest-bordered red clay roads, impressed America as even lovelier than she had nostalgically remembered them. The Carringtons, Bouldins, Mortons, Bruces and Reads entertained the handsome Kentucky couple at Gravel Hill, Do Well, Ville Vue and other Charlotte County landmarks, and were kind enough to declare America hadn't changed a bit since she had reigned a belle among them during Civil War days.

"How," whispered Stone when good manners permitted, "do farmers make a living here? Look at those puny corn stalks growing one to a hill!"

Home on Tuckahoe, America reported the high point of her trip to Ephraim:

"When I didn't burst into tears to see Stone startle a deer out of the fountain at Golden Hill, I realized I was weaned away for good from old Charlotte. From now on, Kentucky and Children's Chance will be home to me."

Stone's temperament, she also realized, was responsible for her more serene acceptance of life. Without looking forward to worry or backward to regret, Stone met what each day had to offer with placid amiability. His good humor, she saw, was an outward manifestation of power—physical, mental and spiritual. Confident that he himself was any man's equal, he tacitly accepted everybody as his. From her second husband America dared not hope for the ecstasy which Fant Annable had brought her, which she had at first felt was worth the misery of her hermit years. To her surprise, she found Stone's quieter devotion more satisfying. The current of their complete congeniality ran deeper. Both knew that they had left behind them the headwaters of love, the chattering brooks, cascades and perilous narrows. Ahead lay only the broad smooth channel of the river nearing the sea.

"You're the bookkeeper, now," grinned Stone on the second morning after their arrival home, and tossed her his desk keys. "It'll be up to you to make a better showing than I have done."

From the double portico of her domestic kingdom, from Children's Chance set in old gardens at the end of its stately avenue of black locusts, America took stock of her new world. According to the Golden Hill formula, she and Stone had every ingredient except children for happiness—love, a pleasant home, the affectionate regard of the community and rich fields. Stone's land was, however, still encumbered with a debt which a farmer as energetic as her husband and a manager as able as herself should be able to pay off in six or seven years, provided leaf prices maintained traditional levels.

The ingredients were there, she saw, but where was the money? America and Stone worked as neither had worked in their youth, from dawn till dark. To see Children's Chance fall into decay because they couldn't afford to hire carpenters to repair it made them conscious of their own shortcomings as stewards. Scant satisfaction remained to Stone in being called "Squire" by ragged stay-at-homes, when the new title of national approval had become "big city millionaire." And how can any farmer pay off a thirty-thousand-dollar debt at ten per cent annual interest with the sale of seven-cent leaf? Even in slave days, ten-cent tobacco was considered the balancing point between profit and loss.

"The general market average for burley last year was six and a half cents to the grower," sighed Stone, taking stock of his situation in mid-January of 1903. "I suppose we ought to be thankful if we can pay taxes, interest, and the local tradesmen."

"I remember hearing father say the tobacco market struck bottom in 1847 with six-cent leaf—at the glut of slave labor," commented America. "He called me his 'hard-times baby,' because I was born that year."

Stone put his elbows on the table, cupped his face in his hands and grinned at her:

"I'll bet you were a cute baby."

"I—" she was continuing her former train of thought, then realized that he wanted to play. Touching his cheek with her hand, she continued, still serious. "I've been wondering for some time now if we wouldn't do better share-cropping Children's Chance."

Startled, he looked his silent protest at her.

"I know it's considered poor farming—and it will ultimately impoverish your land," she admitted. "But with share-croppers, we wouldn't be put to the certain expense of boarding high-priced hands on a falling leaf market. Yet you'd be sure at least of receiving your landlord's half of the tobacco and corn which your tenants would raise—at no labor cost to you."

"I'd like nothing better than to get Hans Claussen on this place," Stone warmed to the idea, "especially since he's going to lose the Bierbower farm this March. Those tow-headed boys of his are workers."

"Poor Hans picked a bad time for buying land," sighed America.

"Yes, and Jamie MacGower is making the same mistake," prophesied Stone gloomily, standing up to slap his pockets for his pipe. "Did I tell you Mrs. MacGower has sold the smithy and her store—to help Jamie on his first payment? She's going to live with them on the Bierbower place."

"Abigail hasn't been the same woman since Auld MacGower was killed in that reaper," sighed America, reaching for the lamp. Everything about the tollhouse probably reminded Abigail of life-long associations with the stalwart old Scot. "Then you'll keep Weed for another year? By hiring day labor from town during tobacco setting and housing time, couldn't you two fill the barns here at Children's Chance?"

"And make you cook for a black man? No, I thank you, my lady."

"I don't mind cooking for Weed, if I had a girl to make his bed and do the washing," America thought, aloud. "I could manage her wages, and run the table, out of my egg and butter money," added America, thinking of the three hundred dollars she still had in the Farmers Bank, and of the ten thousand Tugger Blake owed her. She would never get that now, she realized; but at least she had had the wisdom a week before Nicke's wedding to accept Teena's offer of two big trunkfuls of old clothes. The fabrics were beautiful. With them, and with the illustrations of department store ads in the *New York Times,* Mrs. MacGower could keep America the best-dressed woman on Tuckahoe.

"You're a captain," Stone smiled his appreciation.

"Careful of the lamp!" she cautioned, moving closer within the circle of his arm.

Thus did Children's Chance pass from owner operation to the less tender, unhusbandly hands of tenants. That week Stone and Weed began felling hard wood and hauling it while the ground was still frozen, to the sites of its future use, one near the big tobacco barn on the upper end of Stone's farm opposite Foxden, the other below Children's Chance on Lee's Creek opposite the Bierbower farm. A Lewis County mountaineer moved his portable sawmill onto each site, and in return for half the oak and all the burl walnut, which he shipped to Grand Rapids for furniture veneer, cut and stacked the lumber to dry under the warming February sun. On March first, Hans Claussen made way for the MacGowers by moving his family and gear across the pike into Stone's tobacco barn. A German-American friend of Claussen's, Gus Schraedlich, took possession of the barn opposite Foxden. Their crops kept both families too busy to complain against the tent roof Stone provided till midsummer. When their womenfolk grew tired of the inconveniences of camp life, Hans and Gus would point to the stacks of drying lumber, and plod away about their own business. In the August lull Stone advertised burgoo and prizes for a double housewarming, and had both tenant dwellings completed with outbuildings in a week of neighborhood hilarity.

Anna, Gus Schraedlich's wife, tipped Stone's tobacco scales above three hundred pounds. Every summer weekday noon, Gus lingered behind to hitch up the phaeton buggy for her, hoist her into it, and trudge up to the pike gate to open it. With the regularity of a fine Bavarian clock, he left his crop just before sundown to open the gate again to admit her after an afternoon of visiting among the many German families who were share-cropping or already owned small freeholds in Mason County. Yet Gus was a tireless driver of his strapping sons and daughters in the field. All corn was cut and shocked at night under the autumn moon, when the dew limbered the dried leaves, so that no blade of fodder would be lost. "Let me see your hands," was Gus's favorite challenge to laborers seeking seasonal employment during threshing or tobacco-housing time. "*Nein*, too soft! You see de vay to de pike."

"If one ear of corn remains after Gus has divided the crop," laughed Stone, "he'll break that ear, and throw half into his wagon and half into mine."

In June of 1904, America accompanied Stone to Cincinnati when he took his hogsheads downriver to offer them on the Growers floor. Arrived at the reverberating warehouse on the river front, the Moncures found the social room deserted. Dusty file cases of the defunct Meiers regime occupied the space where in the prosperous eighties buyers and growers had toasted one another on the hospitality of the house. In the dingy office they were informed that Dan Kelly had succeeded Meiers as manager. With a fine burst of old-time cordiality, Dan welcomed and showed them to the auction line, where a spiritless young auctioneer named Calvert was crying a sale to eight or nine hot tired buyers. Only five of them, sharp-eyed strangers to America, were bidding.

"Who are they?" asked Stone's eyes.

"Dan Lord's supply department heads," whispered Kelly, leading the Moncures out of earshot. "They ain't actually bidding against each other, as you might think they are. Every morning in New York, Dan Lord's hirelings set the price for the day's burley average and wire it to these men and his other set of buyers on the Louisville breaks—only he calls this price his requirements. Then his boys here go through the motions of an auction—to keep you country yokels fooled."

"I can't believe that!" Stone answered, indignantly. "Ever since tobacco culture came west from Virginia in 1790, leaf's been sold at auction."

"That's why Dan hasn't changed the system. Get over there into the line, and see if you can hear any competitive bids."

"I—I don't know these men."

"Stanley, the tall chap, is the cigarette buyer—and boss on this floor. Watch him take out the trash and flyings. The little man who looks like his stomach hurts is Jim Patten. He used to own his own company back in New Jersey. Now he's buying lugs and bright leaf for the General Cigar Company, which closed him out. You know Ben Piper, the old fellow in the torn coat."

"That—that can't be Mr. Piper, Leonard & Morley's head buyer?" gasped America, remembering the dean of the buyers who had led the boycott against her at her first appearance on the Cincinnati market.

"The plug war aged him. Besides, he's got family trouble and has to hold his job. So he's buying filler and wrapper for

Inter-Ocean Plug. You remember Chris Walker and the Harvey boys? Chris went broke last year, but he likes to put in his time down here. The Harvey boys are buying for General Snuff. Watch 'em take what's left in the line."

"No wonder the bottom's dropped out of the market!" sighed Stone, and remembered the swift, spirited bidding of the hundreds of small manufacturers which in the eighties had given the hogshead trade its resiliency and profit for all concerned.

"What's Tom Coyle doing here?" demanded Stone, noticing a debonair young man who had swung across the floor into the sales line. His father, Matt Coyle, of Cynthiana, was said to be the last big handler left in the Blue Grass.

"He's undertaken to ginger the market," explained Kelly.

The coarse phrase, which referred to a practice of the horse-show ring, caused America to stiffen and reply with dignity:

"I don't understand you."

"For a dollar a hogshead, Tom's willing to bid up your leaf as high as he dares."

"What if he gets stuck with it?" jeered Stone, disbelieving.

"He's always paid for it so far, although the way he juggles his assets reminds me of a seal balancing balls on his nose," grinned Kelly. "When Tom gets stuck with, say, a hundred thousand pounds of leaf, he hops over to New York and sells it personally to Dan Lord, who likes his gall. But young Tom can't keep his balls in the air much longer, because Dan's about reached the mopping-up stage. Want to engage him to ginger your leaf, Stone? Lemme call him over—"

"I'll go broke first!" declared Stone in quick anger, and turned away towards the office doors.

"What does he think he is now, the butt-headed farmer!" Kelly whispered anxiously to America. "You talk him into it, Miss Merry. He can't afford to be proud—any more than the rest of us."

"You sound worried, Dan."

"Why shouldn't I be? The hogshead breaks are doomed,

you mark my words. Didn't Tugger Blake intimate as much, when he dedicated that big receiving warehouse General Tobacco has just built over at Bowling Green for dark fired leaf? He said General Tobacco was establishing this depot in the hope growers would bring in their types and sell their crops stripped—in winter case—direct to Dan Lord instead of to some broken-down old speculator to funk in the handling. Dan Lord could prize it in quantity cheaper for all concerned. And by cutting out the speculator's profits, he thought there ought to be more money in this new system for the growers."

"I think he meant stockholders—those seven millionaires in New York who own and control the Tobacco Trust," sniffed America, and hurried after Stone.

That night, the Grand Hotel dining room looked only half as large as America remembered it. Feeling like honeymooners, although they knew they presented the appearance of elderly country gentry come to town on a spree, Stone and America ate a dollar dinner inferior to the daily summer menu at Children's Chance. The waiter was pouring their coffee when Henry Morris appeared in the doorway. As he came weaving over to their table, America noticed that his sporty clothes were shabby, his once good-natured face liquor-flushed.

"Now, ain't you two a sight for sore eyes!" Henry boomed, jocosely. "Kelly just told me in the bar you'd gotten hitched—*hic!* You're a lucky dog, Stone. She wouldn't have me."

"Thank you, Henry," smiled Stone, rising to shake hands.

"Sit down, won't you, and join us in a cup of black coffee?" America invited, torn between old loyalties and her pledge of the W.C.T.U.

"Don't mind if I do," accepted Henry, expansively. "Waiter, you know what I drink—Golden Stream."

From adjoining tables came feminine glances of sharp disapproval against hard liquor being served in the ladies' dining room. America pretended not to notice, and studied her first friend on the hogshead breaks. Henry's bombast, she decided, served only to heighten rather than disguise his general appearance of defeat. His red eyes, whiskey voice and short breath proclaimed the chronic alcoholic.

"When did you close down, Henry?" Stone was asking.

"Last year—*hic*!" gasped Morris, and took another swallow. "You know yourself it just ain't possible to make plug tobacco without licorice paste—no more'n you can pack it without tinfoil."

"Tell us what happened," prompted America.

"Winter of '99," began Morris, "the General Tobacco Company got control of John Conley & Sons. After that, I couldn't get tinfoil out of 'em for love nor money. Luckily I'd laid in a supply cheap from Johnson Tinfoil and Metal, of St. Louis. When that was gone, I couldn't get any more. Conley had bought Johnson out, too, but how was I to know that? Johnson keeps right on in business under their old trade name, damn their eyes, but when I send 'em my order, I find out they aren't taking any orders now except from the trust."

"You mean they're filling Dan Lord's orders first?"

"Well, ain't that the same thing—as far as I'm concerned?" demanded Morris, belligerently.

"I'm afraid it is," agreed America. "Waiter, you may take this bottle. Go on, Henry. You were going to tell us about licorice paste."

"Last May, Inter-Ocean Plug bought out MacAndrews & Forbes, biggest producers of licorice paste in this country," continued Henry, looking regretfully after the bottle of whiskey departing on the waiter's tray. "We didn't know it then, but Dan Lord and Tugger Blake planned to use MacAndrews & Forbes as a basket to hold all the little licorice makers they could buy up."

"You mean form a licorice trust?" asked America.

"Sure, like they hogged the cigarette, plug, segar and snuff trades," agreed Henry. "I heard Inter-Ocean got two-thirds of the new licorice trust's stock by offering to place its own whopping big orders for licorice paste with them, but o' course no outsiders could prove that—*hic!* All I know is that the new

MacAndrews crowd began to pull all the little licorice makers in under their big top, they called it. The next thing I found out was that paste makers who wouldn't go to MacAndrews & Forbes were being swallowed up by the National Licorice, of Connecticut. Then the National and MacAndrews must have agreed between 'em not to sell paste to anybody except the Tobacco Trust, because I ain't heard of a single delivery they've made recently to independents in this district! Who else makes licorice? French frogs grind the root abroad, but how'm I to get their stuff in over these Black Republican tariff walls at a price I can afford to pay? So I just had to quit, although it purt'nigh killed me to close down the plant paw ran and grandpaw started."

"It seems pretty much the same story with all you small fry, Henry," sympathized Stone.

"Tinfoil and licorice paste ain't all, either," wailed Henry, gulping down the last of his Golden Stream. "Next thing I knew, I couldn't get cigar boxes. Dan Lord has bought out the Mengel Box Company. The last straw was cotton bags. Honest to God, now, would you think a man who's climbed as high as Dan Lord has on bankrupts' shoulders—or Tugger Blake who's gotten so nigger rich he sprinkles gold dust over a double mile of forest pine trees at his girls' wedding—would bother about hoggin' all the cotton bags in this country—so's I can't buy any to hold my shirt tail full of smokin' mixture? Well, they did! They bought up the Golden Belt Manufacturing Company. And cased leaf rots the bottoms out of paper sacks!" Henry shouted, thumping on the table so that the silverware jumped.

"How's your health—with all these worries?" asked America. If Henry could be switched off his trade grievances, perhaps he might quiet down.

"Never felt better, or had a bigger appetite!" declared Morris. "My doc' did caution me last year to watch out for my heart, though—and to avoid excitement."

"What're you doing, now?" put in Stone.

"Just looking around—for another opening."

"Why don't you try to get a job soliciting for the Growers warehouse?" America suggested the last hope of bankrupt speculators. "Stone would be glad to put in a word for you with Kelly, wouldn't you Stone?—as if that were needed!"

"Suppose I meet you on the breaks tomorrow morning—to talk it over?" agreed Morris, struggling to his feet as America rose to leave the dining room. The waiter had just placed Stone's change on a tray before him. Eying the new bills, Henry whispered hoarsely: "Rather take a whuppin' than mention it, Stone—but could you lemme have that fiver till the bank opens tomorrow?"

"Of course, ol' man."

That night America lay wakeful beside her sleeping husband. For her, the Grand Hotel was full of memories. America congratulated herself that she had told few details of her former life to anyone on Tuckahoe. A wave of popular disapproval, it now appeared, had surged across the country following what some New York journals called "the Blake girls' Lucullan wedding feast." Who would have thought it could reach Henry Morris' ears while he was sinking under the icy waters of trade extinction? America remembered the opinion of a clergyman printed after one of Newport's lavish fetes, that "such an affair draws attention to the growing gulf which separates the rich and the poor, and serves needlessly to increase the discontent of the latter. It is hardly to the point to talk of setting money into circulation." Heavy on America's conscience lay her own sense of personal responsibility for fiddling while Rome burned. Being her father's daughter, why hadn't she realized that decent men and women were starving on city streets for want of jobs, and the families of hard-working farmers were being dispossessed, while she had lain awake nights worrying whether spiders could spin enough webs to use up all her gold and silver dust?

The next morning America coaxed Stone to start for the Growers warehouse early enough to engage Tom Coyle to ginger their hogsheads in the sales line. The thermometer hanging in the shade outside the office entrance already registered eighty-eight. Today would be a scorcher, thought America, and hoped she and Stone could catch the five o'clock train to cooler, airier Tuckahoe.

The buyers now met at a flag stuck into the hogshead where the bidding had stopped yesterday. The tolling of the traditional bell had been discontinued, because Jim Patten had complained that it got on his dyspeptic nerves. Seeing Tom Coyle nowhere, America surmised that ten o'clock must be too early for him to appear without professional engagement. Five buyers, Dan Lord's supply executives, stood around young Calvert. But where were the British and the Dutch buyers? And where were the independents? The half-dozen remaining in business in Cincinnati, explained Kelly in a whisper, didn't dare put in an appearance before afternoon. When Dan Lord's men had filled their requirements, the local manufacturers might come forward shabby and watchful as street sparrows to pick up their crumbs.

At a nod from Kelly, young Calvert wiped the sweat from around his already wilted collar, declared the sale open and asked Stanley, the cigarette buyer, where he wished Terry to break the first of Stone's hogsheads.

"Anywhere," Stanley replied indifferently. Turning, he glanced down the line to estimate how soon they could run through the day's offerings, and so get away to a cooler place.

Stone set his teeth and watched the crew strike in the hooks. If Stanley thought this warehouse was hot, let him try suckering tobacco under an August sun! As the container rose, the fragrance of Stone's bright leaf pervaded the sales floor.

"Smells funked to me," Stanley doomed the hogshead.

"It's sound," Ben Piper came to Stone's rescue, without looking at the Kentuckian.

"D'ye hear that, sound as a dollar and twice as tasty!" the auctioneer began. "What am I bid for this fine hogshead of prime bright, gentlemen—re, re, re, what am I bid for this cream o' the crop?"

"Seven cents," Kelly started it.

"Seven cents! House starts it at seven cents. Let me hear your bids, gentlemen—re, re, re—seven cents."

"That's too high for funked leaf," Stanley accused, looking hard at Piper. "Besides, how d'you know it isn't nested?"

"I've been selling on this floor for forty years, and I've never yet had to pay a reclamation fee!" Stone burst out angrily.

At his indignant words, the buyers turned and looked at him. Patten's whispered inquiry as to Stone's identity, and Kelly's supporting answer, were audible to everyone.

"We'll never get anywhere if we're constantly interrupted," Patten complained.

By stubborn boosting, Kelly managed to get the price up to nine and three-quarter cents, where it was knocked off to Piper for Inter-Ocean Plug. Fifteen years ago plug wrapper of this type would have brought twenty cents. Heart-sick, Stone turned away. At this rate, his crop would not pay interest on his debts.

As acute as his deep personal disappointment was the hurt to his pride, and to his sense of proper trade procedure. Over a hundred years ago on the New Orleans breaks, grades and price levels for tobacco had been established and maintained throughout the succeeding years of trade, even after the hogshead centers had moved upriver to Louisville and Cincinnati. Who were these New Jersey upstarts, who couldn't tell funked leaf from sound, to come here and upset the sound business practices of a century? To hear them bid, a tobacco man might think they were trying to level out all grades to one price, so that they could buy leaf like hay! And when they did that, they rang the knell of conscientious handling, of careful, scrupulous leafing and stripping. For even dogged Jamie MacGower and Hans Claussen would get discouraged, to see their expertly stripped leaf knocked off for the same price as leaf which had been tied without regard for different grades of color or size.

The sales line had moved to Stone's third hogshead when a commotion occurred at the front doors. Hoping for Tom Coyle, America swung around and saw Henry Morris limping across the floor. Henry had obtained more liquor and was in an ugly mood, America observed with a sinking heart. The suspicious bulge in his right hip pocket might be that of a whiskey flask.

"Good-morning, gentlemen!" Henry called out with old-time joviality. "Fine morning to buy leaf. The heat brings out the stretch and fragrance. Hello, Kelly, you old owl! What've you got that's choice today? I'm working up an order for some rich old parties across the pond, and I'm needin' the best."

"If you'll step into the office with me, I'll go over the weigh bills and we can order out something special," Kelly tried to coax him from the sales line. Kelly, too, had seen the bulge in Henry's hip pocket.

"Wha's the matter with Stone's crop, here?" Henry objected, catching sight of the familiar stencil on the hogshead nearest him. "Fine fellow, Stone. Game cock, too! You don't see him taking his troubles lying down. Only man I know ever backed Meiers an' his money-lenders off his land—"

"Is that a gun or a whiskey flask in his pocket?" America whispered to Kelly.

"You high-headed Kentuckians usually carry both, don't you?" answered the floor manager, sourly.

"We're busy men, Kelly," Patten broke in.

"Continue the sale, Calvert."

"How much am I bid for this hogshead of cherry red, sirs? It's plug wrapper, gentlemen, if ever I saw any. Six cents, Mr. Piper? Thank you, sir. Six cents—re, re, re—six cents—"

"Twelve, to start it!" roared Henry, and thumped the floor with his gold-headed cane, which had escaped the pawnshop only because with his club foot Henry needed it.

Exasperation visible on his face, Patten exchanged glances

with his colleagues, then challenged Henry's right to a place in the line. Calvert appealed to Kelly.

"Accept the bid," snapped the manager, and added urbanely: "Mr. Morris has been purchasing leaf on our floor for thirty years, gentlemen."

With an incredulous lift of straw-colored eyebrows, Patten appealed to Stanley. The hogshead under consideration was out of his bailiwick, his shrug of indifference proclaimed. As it was plug wrapper, let Ben Piper do the job.

"Go ahead, Piper," instructed Stanley, as if deferring the first bid to the senior buyer. Stone had heard tales of how Dan Lord's men occasionally ran a hogshead to fantastic heights, to lift it out of the reach of some independent whom they wished to crowd off the market. If this was what Stanley's curt phrase had meant, everyone might be in for trouble. Henry was plainly in no mood this morning for horseplay.

"Twelve cents, gentlemen. I am bid twelve cents for this good hogshead of cherry red—re, re, re—twelve cents," droned the auctioneer, "do I hear twelve and a-quarter, Mr. Piper? It's plug wrapper, sir, just the type Inter-Ocean needs—re, re, re, twelve cents—"

"Fourteen," barked Ben Piper, thinking fast. Henry Morris was through. Anyone could see that. But if Howard Stanley wrote in to New York that Ben Piper wouldn't follow instructions when the time was ripe to eliminate a warehouse nuisance, Ben Piper would be through, too, in the next mail.

"Fifteen!" answered Henry, truculently.

"Sixteen—"

"Twenty!" roared Henry.

"Twenty-five," whispered Piper.

"Sold!" interposed Kelly, firmly, "sold to Mr. Piper for Inter-Ocean Plug at twenty-five cents—"

"Looky here, Kelly, you can't do that to me!" bellowed Henry, turning furiously on the manager. "This is still a public auction, ain't it? You never even took my last bid."

"Come along, men, let's get out of here." Stanley rallied

his forces. "When you're ready to conduct leaf sales in an orderly manner, Mr. Kelly, without letting every half-drunken tramp off the street slow us up, we'll return."

"You say that again, you smart Alec from New Jersey!"

"Henry, that's no way to speak to Mr. Stanley," Piper apparently forgot he was no longer dean of the Cincinnati breaks. "He shouldn't have called you a tramp, I admit. But you know you can't take this hogshead off the floor at any price—"

"Don't you come bootlicking around me, you Judas Iscariot!" Henry whirled on him. "If it hadn't been for you sending word you'd take care of me, I'd have stocked Dan Lord's brands years ago, and been sittin' purty, now. And look at you, you turncoat!"

"I—I've a sick wife to support, Henry."

"How d'you think I feel? You and Leonard & Morley sold your friends down the river like a passel of stinkin' niggers. And when we tell you how we feel, you snivel and hide behind your wife's bustle!"

"Henry, you don't mean that."

"Don't I? Well, how about this?"

America could never understand how a man, in the heat of liquor and rage, could draw and fire so quickly. As the shots struck him, Piper's expression showed disbelief, then surprise and momentary anguish. He crumpled against the cylinder of cherry red. Shocked into inaction, everybody watched death sponge the anxiety and fatigue off his tired, lined face. Stone was the first to move, to catch the dying man's head as he slumped to the floor.

"Tell my wife Betsy—she mustn't be long," whispered Piper, and sighed like a worn-out old plow horse.

"He's dead, gentlemen," announced Stone, looking up with his blue eyes darkening, his jaw set.

"Sale's adjourned!" Kelly took command. "Stone, d'you want to get Morris out of here—across the river? I've got to notify the police."

"You may inform the sheriff I'll be waiting for him at Stone's country place on Tuckahoe," Henry pronounced grandly, as if he were the challenged on a field of honor.

"You'll hang for this," Stanley said, grey-white and looking as if he might at any moment vomit.

"There's not a jury in Cincinnati but what'll acquit me!" Henry took refuge in bravado. "This used to be a tobacco town. Men know what I've suffered—what we've all suffered at the hands of hogs like Dan Lord and—and—"

He could not malign the dead, nor look at the relaxed figure whose lifeblood had spread brightly over the twenty-five-cent cherry wrapper. Stone, with the freak associations that come to men in crises, remembered how lush and fine those gummy top leaves had spread themselves in the tobacco patch and how Gus Schraedlich had saved out sample hands when stripping to boast of their quality. Who would enjoy them, now?

"I—I must 'a' been crazy with the heat," faltered Henry, pulling at his collar. "I didn't mean to do it. He was the best friend I had."

Stumbling nearer, he leaned across the cylinder of leaf now red with Piper's blood, to gaze down at his handiwork.

"Ben Piper was the first man to give me credit following the Panic of '73," Morris continued in a hoarse whisper. Suddenly dropping his revolver, he gripped at his left armpit with his right hand, then fell over heavily on his face. Everyone stared until Stone, remembering what Henry had said at the dinner table last night, knelt and gently turned Henry's face into the suffused radiance falling from the whitewashed skylights.

"Gentlemen, his heart—" began Stone, feeling for the beat and finding none, "his heart—once so kind—has been his executioner."

"Sales adjourned!" repeated Kelly, and dropped beside Stone to close the now serene eyes of old Ben Piper.

On the kitchen wall at Children's Chance, close at hand where she could mark the dozens of eggs and pounds of butter she delivered twice a week to a produce house in Limestone, and the dates on which she had set her hens, America had hung a calendar issued by the Farmers Bank. For several years this calendar had shown the seal of the Commonwealth of Kentucky. America looked often at the figures of two men clasping hands with the motto beneath, "United We Stand, Divided We Fall," before she realized that here might be a solution to the burley growers' problem of economic survival.

Unlike Jason of old, she had no dragon's teeth to sow in Stone's pastures, teeth which would sprout into warriors fully armed to fight the Tobacco Trust. The denizens of Mason County's fields she grouped roughly into four classes—the impoverished gentry like Stone Moncure, the Annables, Major Chisholm, Ulysses Cary, and Captain Doggett; the smaller freeholders, either native or born of German, Scotch or Irish immigrant parents such as Jamie MacGower and Hans Claussen; share-croppers ranging from Gus Schraedlich to Stella and Jim Barnes; and the dwindling negro population, now composed largely of ex-slaves too old to join the general exodus of young blacks to the Ohio Valley cities or to Chicago.

The gentry and the farsighted freeholders, America decided, could be counted on to fight Dan Lord to the death. What about the share-croppers? On her trips to Limestone, America began to study them. Mute and clumsy, they stood about on the street corners, to be covertly jeered at by mill hands, grocery clerks and even proprietors in the old market town. Put these clodhoppers in their fields, thought America, or on tier rails of their landlord's tobacco barns, and they could outwork or outbargain these town bar-flies and merchants who held their noses with one hand, while with the other they reached for the rustic's coin in trade. What was it that made a farmer and his wife shrivel up inside at the very thought of ridicule from a small-town merchant?

An incident which occurred in front of Griggs' grocery store disturbed America, jealous as she was for all country folk. Rather than sit in the livery-stable waiting room which reeked of near-by toilets, America strolled riverwards. Here on the bank, Stone had told her, coffles of slaves bound for the Cotton Kingdom used to bathe their sore feet in the tawny flood. Here red carpets had been spread from wharf to the Lee House to welcome General Lafayette, James Madison, Daniel Webster and Henry Clay. Here today lay the railroad which had superseded the white and gold packet boats of America's young womanhood. Facing track and river was Griggs' grocery store, in front of which old Griggs was haggling with a country woman over several burlap sacks.

"But fifty cents a bushel ain't enough," objected the country woman unhappily, her comical hat askew. "There's a heap of work in growing and shelling all these butter beans."

"That's all they're worth to me," replied the grocer. Turning, he picked up the bag as if absent-minded, and carried it into the store.

America watched with discreet eyes while the country woman took out a market list and calculated. Anxious to learn the middleman's spread, America called a town 'ninny playing on the ties, gave him a dollar and told him to run buy her a peck of dried butter beans at Griggs' store. The boy returned in a few minutes with the beans and some silver.

"How much did he want for them?" asked America, loudly enough for the country woman to hear.

"Dey's sixty-five cents a peck, but dey's extra fine big ones, he say."

"Take them up to Dalton's livery stable, and have them put in Mr. Moncure's buggy. Then come tell me when he's ready to leave town."

"Yassum."

The boy trotted upstreet. The grocer came out to the curb again, and inquired of the country woman selling beans:

"Well, lady, have you made up your mind?"

"Fifty cents isn't a fair price, when you're charging sixty-five for the identical beans—"

"I take all the risk, don't I? Do you want to sell 'em, or don't you? Make up your mind," snapped Griggs.

"I—I guess I'll have to let you have them."

"It's about time! I'd say maybe there's three bushel in those sacks—"

"Aren't you even going to measure them?"

"Listen, ma'am! I've got good cash customers, town folks, waitin' inside. All you country people think we've got to do is stand on the street corner and gab like you do," snorted Griggs. Snatching her market list, he hurried inside to fill it in trade due on the bean transaction. America turned in disgust, and was starting up the street when she heard a timid cough behind her.

"I beg your pardon, ma'am," began the country woman, "but could I sell you some butter beans? We've got plenty more out at home."

"I just bought a peck so you'd hear what he was charging retail for them," declared America, bluntly. "Don't you know there are four pecks in a bushel? He's making two dollars and ten cents a bushel off you—and you let him! If you can't figure any better than that, send some other member of your family to town when you've produce to sell."

"I—I felt he was cheating me, but what could I do? My husband's got to have his morning coffee."

"Mistah Stone, he say he ready, naow, ma'am," announced the 'ninny, breathlessly.

"Bring your children with you next time, and have them offer your beans from house to house—at forty cents a peck," advised America, giving the black boy a nickel. "You'll find they'll sell like hot cakes. Dried butter beans keep."

"That's an idea"—admitted the country woman—"if my husband's willing to let us peddle things."

What was the use, America asked herself on the way upstreet, of trying to help farmers? They couldn't figure things out for themselves, they wouldn't stand together, and they let their inferiors bully them into a complaining acceptance of conditions which they might easily remedy if they as a class would stand up for their rights, instead of acting as if they might burst into tears the way this woman had just looked, if you crooked your little finger at them.

America next observed closer home among share-croppers this same tendency to abandon the field in acknowledged defeat or to accept crushing conditions with a serflike meekness. Two instances emphasized these traits sharply to her. In January of 1905 Hans Claussen had notified Stone that he was giving up the losing business of farming. His boys insisted on going to Cincinnati in search of factory jobs, Hans said, and to keep the family together he would accompany them back to the Wurlitzer plant, which followed a policy of giving preference to the descendants of their original employees brought over from Germany before the Civil War.

In the other case, a lank mountaineer named Jett Bell, with his pregnant wife Hannah and their two gaunt boys, had moved into Stone's tenant house vacated by the Claussens. One blazing July midafternoon, America rode her black gelding down the hill to see how the Bell crops looked. Nearing the tobacco patch, she heard an unfamiliar sound too loud for the whirring of a tree locust. At the same time her horse side-stepped, snorting as if it scented a snake. One look under the walnut tree at the edge of the patch, where on a blanket Hannah's young baby lay spellbound watching something, and America was out of her saddle, had caught up a stick, and was striking ground and snake in a frenzied attack. The Bells came running. Hannah picked up her infant, and held it to her sweaty breast.

"By doggie if hit ain't a rattler!" drawled Jett Bell, chopping off the reptile's smashed head with his hoe. "I reckon high water must 'a' brung hit daown from the mountains."

"Accept a mother's thanks, Miz Merry," quavered Hannah Bell, panting in reflex alarm.

"Maw, you must 'a' laid the baby's blanket daown acrost its run," one of the Bell boys felt obliged to have his say, while the other opened his bowie-knife to skin the snake.

"Yessum, Miz Moncure, we air shore obliged tuh you. Tom, you run ketch that colt fer Miz Merry," Jett Bell made proper acknowledgment before he turned back into the tobacco rows.

"Hannah, how many times must I tell you not to bring that baby to the field?" scolded America, when the two women were alone. "You know my husband doesn't approve of tenant women working in the crop—after they've done housework and maybe washed all morning."

"Effen I don't give Jett a hand after dinner, how's he an' aour two puny boys a-goin' tuh fill Mister Stone's barns, ma'am? You know we cayain't afford to hire no help in the crop—with terbacker prices as low as they was last year," Hannah answered mildly, and laid the baby on the blanket again while she unbuttoned her calico dress with fingers which still shook.

"Hannah, don't nurse that baby while you're so excited," cautioned America. "My husband won't even let his work-mares give suck until they're cooled off."

Hannah lifted her sweaty face to smile at all such indulgent ideas of landlords and their wives, before she remarked:

"Us pore women think we're lucky effen we don't have tuh born 'em in a corn row—like an ol' houn' bitch."

"No wonder you lose your health—and your children!" retorted America, knowing that Jett Bell would be ashamed to be seen on the turnpike with a coon-dog or a work-mare as lean as Hannah. "Put that child down—until you cool off."

"Jett's needin' me too bad fer sech notions—though I know you mean well, ma'am," Hannah smiled at her with the meekness of a field Madonna.

As she rode up the hill, America analysed her exasperation over Hannah's passive acceptance of what she herself considered serfdom. To pay taxes and interest on his debts, Stone had to have all his tobacco barns filled. Jett Bell, to have a roof over his family's head and to eat, must contract to fill these barns, to raise six acres of tobacco, a physical impossibility for one man and two puny boys unless his wife, already overburdened with housekeeping and child-bearing, would undertake to work also as a full hand in the field. Six acres—thirty thousand tobacco plants handled around the calendar, nurtured like flowers in a seed bed, transplanted to the hillside, hoed, topped, suckered, wormed twice a week, housed, stripped—to bring seven cents a pound for six thousand pounds of leaf—a pitiful total of four hundred and twenty dollars a year—two hundred and ten dollars a year for landlord, and two hundred and ten dollars a year for tenant family—less than Tugger Blake spent to take a dozen friends to a casual champagne dinner! What, America tried to reason, could Hannah and Jett Bell do to meet and overcome these conditions under which they seemed so completely submerged? Here stood a man and a woman bound to the tobacco patch, illiterate, without leadership, without hope and, what was most discouraging of all, apparently without even a desire to improve their lot, as oxen bent under a heavy yoke will look back without resentment at the goad which pushes them bleeding until they fall.

Thoroughly upset, on reaching home America wrote two letters. The first was addressed to the New York Stock Exchange. On her best stationery, she asked them why was Inter-Ocean Plug no longer listed on their big board? Her second letter was to Nicke. To her usual monthly account of family news—for Nicke did not like to answer oftener—America added the announcement that the Tobacco Trust had broken ground in Limestone next to the high school for a receiving warehouse. A man named Jim Payne, whom Steve doubtless knew, would act as agent, America's letter continued. "If General Tobacco intends to invade Mason County, which Stone and I have always regarded as our territory for handling hogshead tobacco," America used a little guile on Nicke, "you and

Steve will readily see how vital it is for us to know exactly how much of the tobacco trade the Lord interests really do control in this country. In other words, will their crumbs be profitable enough for us to keep on going? Do write me all you can find out, Nicke—or else Steve may have a mother-in-law to support."

With both answers in hand, America kept Stone indoors one hot August evening to hear the decision which had been forming in her mind all summer:

"Stone, I'm going 'to write a letter to the *Times.*'"

"The *New York Times?*" asked Stone, who had been preoccupied of late with correspondence of his own.

"No, my dear. The *Limestone Eagle*—and the *Lexington Herald*—and the Louisville *Courier-Journal.* All of them have free-press columns. All of them will take my articles—against the Tobacco Trust," she concluded, trying not to let the nervousness she felt creep into her voice.

"I—I suppose you realize what you're doing?" asked Stone, with the half-smile he used when he was dead serious.

"I've collected some facts—on the best authority," America continued the speech she had rehearsed all week. "The New York Stock Exchange writes me that Consolidated Tobacco—the holding company for the cigarette and plug combines—paid a dividend of twenty per cent in 1903 out of the profits they made the preceding year. In 1904, after the Supreme Court had dissolved the Northern Securities Corporation, Dan Lord merged these three companies into one corporation under the old name of the original cigarette combine, General Tobacco."

"'A rose by any other name—'" nodded Stone, his eyes bitter.

"Precisely. John Moody, financial expert and editor of *Moody's Manual,*" continued America, consulting her top letter, "is quoted here as saying that 'this remarkable group of men who stand at the head of this wonderful aggregation of consolidated industry . . . in fourteen years have acquired one hundred and fifty manufactories and have grown from a twenty-five-million-dollar corporation to a mammoth aggregation controlling a capitalization, in parent and allied companies, of five hundred and two million dollars.' "

"Figures like that never impress people," scoffed Stone, who none the less seemed strangely excited. "You'll have to simplify them."

"I got Nicke and Steve to do that for me," smiled America, surprised that Stone's mind had followed the same line of thought as her own. "Today the Dan Lord interests control over seventy per cent of the smoking tobacco manufactured in the United States; seventy-three per cent of the cigarettes; eighty-one per cent of the plug and twist; eighty-nine per cent of the 'little cigars'; ninety-six per cent of the snuff; ninety-five per cent of the licorice paste; and dominate British and world trade in manufactured tobacco products. How does that sound?"

"It'll make exciting reading for every Kentucky farmer who grows burley," Stone clipped off his words, "and the editors whom you mentioned ought to give you a rake-off as a circulation builder. I've just one question to ask: How are we going to pay the interest on my notes—and keep Children's Chance over our heads—when Dan Lord's buyers walk around my hogsheads on the Cincinnati breaks—or refuse to receive my loose leaf at their Limestone warehouse?"

"Stone, they wouldn't be so little—so contemptibly small and mean!"

"You're a smart woman, America Moncure," drawled Stone, as he might have conceded equality to another trader as shrewd as himself. "You saw what Stanley did to Henry Morris."

"You're right," she admitted, and dropped the letters which in her rash eagerness to do battle she had considered broadsides against Tugger Blake. "I—I guess I did go off half cocked."

"Last week I'd have said we couldn't do it—that we'd have to consider which side our bread is buttered on."

"Stone, you don't mean you're actually with me, now?"

"God A'mighty, woman, do you think I'm blind—or spineless as a tobacco worm?" His wrath, so long pent up, blazed at her: "Don't you suppose I've seen the treadmill we've been on ever since we got married—you churning and slopping around in the weeds day and night to make butter and raise poultry to keep this house running—me working in the field as no nigger ever sweated on this farm in slavery days! And for whom? For twenty or thirty fat slugs sitting around a director's table in New York City—for half a hundred absentee landlords who're grinding us lower than the peasants of Europe!"

"If we let them," whispered America, staring past the moth-encircled lamp into the darkness as if to call up the ghost of her statesman-father whose favorite phrase Stone's words had awakened in her memory: "The fighting Anglo-Saxon stock from which Americans spring has never yet permitted itself to be ground down to the level of a peasantry." Surely the strangle hold which the Tobacco Trust was tightening on the burley market somehow could be broken? "Stone," she began again, "there must be some way half a million tobacco growers can defeat Dan Lord and Tugger Blake? 'United We Stand,' Stone—that's the motto of the Commonwealth of Kentucky—"

" 'United We Stand!' " he repeated the words, while she watched the purpose forming in his soul freeze his face into set lines of resolution. "Merry, I believe we could do it—you with your newspaper articles—me with the job Kelly has just offered."

"Do what?"

"Organize an equity society of farmers—of burley growers who'd stand together to fight the trust until we force Dan Lord to give us a living price for our leaf—a price that would be fair and equitable for the labor involved, and the investment represented by our farms."

"Whom are you quoting, Stone?"

"A traveling delegate named Hawkins. He said he came

from the Department of Agriculture in Washington. He said that trust-busting Teddy Roosevelt in the White House had the interests of the farmer at heart; and that there was work still to be done following his victory in the Northern Securities case, if we are to keep 'the malefactors of great wealth' on the run. Hawkins said the only way we can help the government combat the abuses of the Tobacco Trust, is to organize an equity movement among the people—to fight Dan Lord and his crowd, now that they have secured control of every phase of the business," answered Stone, seeing again in his mind's eye big bluff Archibald Hawkins standing up in the Tuckahoe blacksmith shop.

"Stone, it's a magnificent idea!" America's excited voice jerked him back to the present, to the white cloth and the hot lamp which was attracting millers. Reaching out fingers grubby with tobacco gum, Stone picked up a dead moth by its scorched wings and held it over the chimney top until it shriveled into a blackened wisp.

"Two weeks ago, this is what would have happened to us —if we'd tackled Dan Lord and Tugger Blake—with newspaper articles," he smiled at her across the corner of the table. Reaching in his pocket with his other hand, he pulled out a crumpled letter and tossed it towards her to read, as he continued: "This letter from Kelly comes like an answer to prayer. In it he asks me to solicit hogshead tobacco for the Growers warehouse. Kelly aims to put on a death struggle against the trust's receiving depot in Limestone, which Payne will have ready to open in December. The salary Kelly offers me—a hundred a month, and three hundred for a new buggy which I can get along without—will help pay the interest on my debts. Best of all, nobody will suspect anything when they see me driving around the country soliciting leaf for the Growers warehouse."

"I know. All broken-down speculators come to that," nodded America, unaware of how she had catalogued her husband until he grinned.

"To all outward appearances, we'll go on raising tobacco here at Children's Chance—prizing it down—selling it on the Cincinnati breaks," declared Stone, "and at the same time I'll start interviewing every grower in this end of the state—first, to solicit for Kelly—then to talk them into joining our equity society—to pool our crops, and hold them off the market until we starve Dan Lord into giving us a living wage for our leaf."

"Is that the name Mr. Hawkins suggested—the equity society?"

"Do you like it?"

"Very much."

"Then that's what we'll call it—until somebody suggests a better one," continued Stone, his eyes shining, his voice gathering enthusiasm. "I'll go first to men I can trust—men who know how to keep a secret."

"Brother Ephraim ought to be able to help you," smiled America.

"I'll get Eph—and every other key man in this end of the state! Before you know it, we'll have so many burley growers signed in, we'll be too strong for the trust to smash us all. That's the way to fight—the way city men fight!" he cried, and she knew he was thinking of the directors of the old Growers Warehouse Company, Meiers and his money lenders who had tried to freeze him out of Children's Chance. " 'United we stand'—we the people of the Commonwealth of Kentucky—against a tableful of Wall Street hogs!"

As he paused for breath, she looked at him. Above his outthrust jaw and sun-reddened cheeks blazed his angry blue eyes. Into her memory flashed the picture of Stone as she had first seen him at the *Magnolia*'s rail nearly forty years ago, with the "limestone look" on his stolid young face. Hard work, anxiety and age had worn his once-chunky body to sinew, blood and bone, as the sweep of the seasons across the Kentucky hills wears them to their native rock. They, and he, she saw at a glance, were none the less strong and enduring because they were weather-worn.

"Where do I come in—in this tobacco war?" she asked, glancing at her letters.

"You shall be our John the Baptist—crying in the wilderness."

"Don't you mean Cassandra?" she modified the title to conform with realism and a love of the classics her father had inculcated in her as a child. "Nobody 'll believe me at first, anyhow—until you've talked secretly to the men. And by then Dan Lord and Tugger Blake will think I'm a huge joke—just another crack-brained crusader in skirts—like the Lucy Stone Leaguers or the Clafflin sisters."

"Cassy, my love, this is the first night in ten years I've gone to bed with hope in my heart!" exulted Stone, standing up with his face aglow.

And so, as ten years before, Stone Moncure, seated sideways in his weather-beaten buggy, his clothes shabby, his sun-streaked hair greying with age and dust, became a familiar sight again as his old black mares drew him less swiftly than the occasional automobile which they frantically encountered, up and down the hard limestone roads of Mason and her sister counties. His comings and goings at first appeared of scant importance to anyone except himself. The burley tobacco belt had become accustomed to seeing solicitors for the hogshead market—men who had risked their all, had lost, and must now be taken care of—driving through the pleasant autumn days to remind the faithful that the old Growers warehouse was still prepared to offer the best in sales and service on the Cincinnati breaks. The sight of such staunch derelicts, the eager shine rekindling in their defeated eyes, an ingratiating appeal in their humbled voices, put many a disgruntled grower into a conciliatory mood towards the warehouse men, made him realize that it was the trust, and not they, which was hammering leaf prices down to where a Kentucky farmer couldn't sleep nights for worry.

Another broken-down pensioner of the hogshead trade

Stone was called by the smart young men hurrying citywards from the moribund farms; just another has-been of a marketing system, itself soon to become as extinct as the dodo bird. For every ambitious lad who could read knew the Horatio Alger story of how Dan Lord and Tugger Blake, Thomas Fortune Ryan and R. J. Reynolds left their backwoods' farms to make of their Wall Street desks the hub of world tobacco trade.

To the fathers and uncles of these youthful deserters, to the burley growers left shorthanded in the tobacco patch, Stone Moncure brought the leaven of a secret hope. When he was lucky enough to find his man at the house for the noon meal, Stone sat down gratefully to whatever the flustered housewife and her girls could provide. After the always substantial meal, while the womenfolk sat fanning themselves with their aprons and congratulating each other on well-stocked canning shelves, Stone explained the equity movement to the men and boys stretched in the shade on the front lawn. More often, however, he drove on through the stable lot out across the ridge to the tobacco patch.

Stone could remember every crop of leaf which he had purchased off these rolling hillsides. Hearing the sound of a team and buggy, the men in the green rows straightened their backs to watch Stone's approach. With the silent fraternalism of the soil, the head of the house came to open the gate. After he had spoken in Kelly's behalf, Stone launched into the main purpose of his call. To see the vitalizing effect of his message on his listener always filled Stone with deep personal satisfaction. The stooped body leaning on hoe handle or against the buggy wheel seemed actually to grow taller. Under the sweaty skin, the relaxed facial muscles tightened, as jaws set resolutely while hearing mutually shared grievances so ably stated by Stone. In eyes at first friendly and sometimes even pitying—for the man one jump ahead of the sheriff considers his situation better than that of the debtor assignor, else why keep jumping?—Stone watched the personal emotion give place to a dreamy far-off expression, the look of dawning hope. Sighing deeply, as a plow horse sighs when the gear is pulled off over his tired haunches, the grower would look up and deliver himself laboriously of his opinion:

"Your scheme sounds reasonable, Stone—dog take me if hit don't! Provided you kin git enough of us growers to jine this thing—name hit agin for me."

"To join the pool."

"That's hit. How're you aimin' to hold us in, so's Dan Lord won't come around to the weak uns and buy 'em out agin?"

"Our idea is to have a contract. We'd all sign when the proper time comes. Can we count on you?"

"I'll study on hit—and tell you next time you come around."

"You do that," concluded Stone, reaching for his lines. "And, Will, talk this plan up with your neighbors, will you—with the substantial men in this community? We can't have rattlebrains in this movement—idle talkers who'd blab our names the first thing to the trust's buyers. You see what I mean, don't you?"

"I git yer idear."

"Will you do that—for me?"

"Well, yes. I'll go along with you that fur, anyhaow."

"I knew I could count on you, Will," nodded Stone, and clucked to his mares.

Simple as it was, the equity plan seemed to gather momentum. On every hand, Stone and America grew conscious of the changed attitude of country people towards them when they met—the quick look of anxious inquiry as if to ask "How goes it, comrade?," the knowing glance of admiration which followed them downstreet in Limestone.

"Wait a minute, Mr. Stone!" called Osman Humphreys, member of the Kentucky State Legislature from Mason County, one October afternoon in 1906 as Stone was about to enter Mose Dalton's livery stable on Second Street. "Stop and tell us about the Equity meeting at Cynthiana, will you?"

Pausing, Stone frowned at the Limestone lawyer-politician. Humphreys, Stone knew, had been darting straws into the wind lately to see which way public opinion was blowing before he took sides. If the Equity Society, clumsy vehicle of the farmers' hopes and purses, could be jacked up and shoved out onto the highroad to success, who could say how far it might not be able to carry its drivers and any town passenger smart enough to climb aboard early into a pleasant seat? After all, thought Humphreys, shaking hands with Stone, it is the county vote that keeps a man at Frankfort and sends him on to Washington.

"As long as farmers stay the way they are, we'll never get anywhere!" barked Stone, shooting a challenging glance towards the usual Saturday afternoon crowd of rustics gathered on the nearest street corner. Seeing that Stone wanted to make a speech, they obligingly moved forward to listen.

"What happened?" prompted Humphreys.

"We had a big meeting," Stone answered. "Growers came in by the dozens, listened to everything we had to say, and pledged themselves to support the pool. When the meeting adjourned, they slipped up the nearest alley with samples of their leaf under their arms, showed them to the trust's buyer, sold their crop, climbed into their buggies, and drove home."

"You mean they were carrying water on both shoulders—ha! ha!" laughed Humphreys.

"I mean there's no use trying to help farmers until they learn to stick together and help themselves!" blazed Stone. With a reproachful look at his country listeners, he entered the livery stable and ordered his buggy hitched.

By November, 1906, Stone felt that he and his assistants had sufficient leaf pledged in Mason County to show their hand to Dan Lord. To Stone's surprise, America declined to make the trip to New York and seemed mysteriously reticent about the wisdom of Stone heading the delegation.

"If we could stay at your sister's house, think of the hotel bill we'd save," hinted Stone, who still invited farm machinery salesmen to draw up their chairs to the table if they happened to call at Children's Chance at mealtime.

"We had a serious falling-out," answered America, unwilling to tell her husband Teena was in a private sanitarium and that Number 860 Fifth Avenue had been closed. "I'll give you a note to Tugger Blake, who can get you in to see Dan Lord—if he will. Is Eph going, too?"

"The reunion-crazy fool says he has to speak at Memphis. So there'll be just Ulysses Cary and myself—unless you'll change your mind? Think what a picnic we could make of it! I've never been to New York," Stone added, wistfully.

"Take John Willy Barnes with you—to draw up any papers you may have to sign," advised America, reluctant to see her husband enter the lion's den without able legal counsel. "You'll need him, because this trip isn't going to be a picnic for anybody."

When Stone presented his wife's letter to an alert-looking young man presiding over Tugger Blake's office in Wall Street, the country delegation was kept waiting an hour before they were admitted into the great man's presence. For a Tarheel too busy to welcome his sister-in-law's husband more hospitably, thought Stone, Blake's big desk looked bare. Around the wall, uniformly framed and at eye level, marched the originals of yellow-journal cartoons vilifying the Tobacco Trust and its key men. On the wall opposite Tugger's desk, a picture had been recently removed, for its outline showed on the panel where it had hung.

"America would have come, too, except she felt Mr. Barnes' services as a lawyer might be needed worse," Stone made pleasant conversation. "We hope you'll put us in position to draw up a bill of sale, Mr. Blake—a big bill of sale, I might add."

Tugger, gazing at this hayseed who had married America Moncure, curbed a natural inclination to utter his short mirthless bark of angry laughter. Here in this office which handled only million-dollar transactions, what did this clodhopper think he had to sell—a few hundred head of cattle, perhaps a thousand tons of clover? Behind his set smile which he hoped covered the initial shock of America's letter, primitive fighting emotions surged through Tugger's brain, upsetting his careful mental balance. Fearful lest his hands betray his tumultuous feelings, he dropped his arms below his desk, then bethought himself of segars. With a gold penknife unsnapped from his watch chain, he began painstakingly to open a fresh box of Corona Coronas.

"What kind of a deal did you have in mind?" Tugger heard himself asking, in his urbane trader's voice.

"We want you to introduce us to Dan Lord, Mr. Blake," interposed the old farmer who resembled Santa Claus.

"He's a life-long friend of mine," commented Tugger, busy removing the revenue stamp intact. "Let's see—what's your name again?"

"Ulysses Cary—at your service," beamed Santa Claus.

"And who're you?" Tugger shot his searching glance towards the youngest of the trio, who wore the cocky look of a small-town lawyer. No need to ask who Stone Moncure is! You're her cousin husband, you with the look of the land and the windswept sky so strong on your face I can almost smell its freshness—you with the field-hardened body of a young man while I'm soft as putty and have high blood pressure that's making me see red now—I know who you are. And I hate your guts, Stone Moncure, I hate your guts!

"John W. Barnes, from Limestone," the cock-sparrow was chirping. "I represent the legal end of this deal, sir."

"Limestone, eh?" Tugger caught and reechoed the familiar word. "Dan Lord tells me General Tobacco has just finished a fine new receiving warehouse in Limestone—a warehouse capable of giving you growers the top dollar on the market as soon as you get your leaf stripped and hauled to town."

"That's the object of our call on you, Mr. Blake—No, I thank you, I smoke a pipe," Stone declared in the tone traders use when they've skirmished for position long enough. "We represent a group of growers in Mason County who don't intend to haul their burley to Lord's new warehouse in Limestone."

"You'll get better service—at less expense—than on the Cincinnati hogshead market," grinned Tugger, leaning forward to offer the segar box to the others. If they wanted the new experience of smoking a dollar segar, let them get up and come take one.

"We don't intend to haul it there, either," was Stone's flat announcement.

"Where else, may I ask, do you hope to sell it?" smiled Tugger, unpleasantly.

"If we can't trade direct with Dan Lord—or you, if you're his accredited agent—we'll hold our leaf until we can."

"Now, Stone, ain't you acting a mite techous?" interposed Santa Claus, before Tugger could reply. "You see, it's thisaway with us, Mr. Blake. We can't make ends meet on the seven cents Dan Lord's been paying burley growers ever since he hog tied the tobacco business after the free silver stampede of '96. It just ain't humanly possible to keep body and soul together on seven-cent leaf. So when this boy here—his name's Stone Moncure—"

"I know his name!" snapped Tugger, his short temper flaring. A moment later, he had screened the rush of apoplectic blood to his face behind a cloud of segar smoke.

"When Stone got the notion for us growers to pool our crops, it struck us all as a mighty fine idea," Santa Claus finished, at a loss to understand the great man's anger.

"To pool your crops?" laughed Tugger. "As long as I've been in the tobacco business, I've never heard that one."

"We borrowed it from you big operators here on Wall Street," the small-town lawyer defended his cause.

"What d'you mean by it?"

"By pooling our crops and shipping direct to Dan Lord," continued Ulysses Cary, "we hope he'll give us a better price—because he'd be spared the expense of warehouse fees and maintainin' a string of buyers on the hogshead breaks. We'v read in the papers he claims it's cheaper to run a big business than a little un. The extra cents our pool could save him—if he'd give those coppers to us—would make all the difference in the world to burley growers."

"How much leaf have you gentlemen—uh, pooled?"

Santa Claus and the small-town lawyer looked uncertainly at each other and then at Stone. Watching them shrewdly, Tugger guessed that in rehearsal they had decided not to tell the exact amount of their shirt tail of tobacco, hoping they might bluff somebody into believing it to be more than it was. Tugger was thus unprepared for Stone's simple announcement:

"Fourteen million pounds."

"Fourteen million pounds? You mean fourteen thousand, don't you?" Tugger caught himself on the point of correcting the fellow. "That's a lot of burley, Moncure. Fourteen million pounds is one-fourth of General Tobacco's annual purchase for the British-American interests. I repeat, that's a lot of burley."

"Nobody knows that better than Stone!" interposed Barnes, enthusiastically. "He's worn out two buggies signing our butt-headed Mason County growers in."

"So you've got them under written contract?" Blake deduced, swiftly. "For how long?"

"Our local organization is immaterial, sir," Stone evaded with old-time courtesy. "We hope you'll see fit to introduce us to Dan Lord—or to handle this deal for him yourself, if you're so authorized. We can deliver our leaf wherever Mr. Lord wants it—in winter or summer case, as he prefers. We'll have to work out some method of grades and samples, but there's no need to trouble you with such details, now."

If America has put you up to this fool stunt, thought Tugger, measuring his adversary with his eye, she's coached you well. Who do you think you are, you tobacco yap, to throw down the gauntlet to Tugger Blake and Dan Lord? Even in the hills of northeastern Kentucky, where he vaguely remembered America had once said Limestone was situated, is there anybody left so ignorant they don't know that Dan Lord and the men who sit around his directors' table rule the tobacco business of the United States and of the world?

How can I best out-trade you, Tugger Blake asked himself. How can I crush you, send you humiliated—defeated—beaten—home to her and to your hillside tobacco patch? Boastful phrases describing the corporate strength of General Tobacco occurred to Tugger, but he rejected them as beyond the dull comprehension of these yokels. What he needed was a ruse, a "come-on" scheme which would lull this trio into a sense of false security. Then, when he chose to spring the trap, Tugger anticipated, he would leave Moncure and his two henchmen swinging in complete disorganization, exposed to the disappointment and ridicule of their followers. Nothing demoralizes a man or hurts a cause so much as to raise hopes high, and then dash them. With the neck of community confidence thus broken, it should be an easy matter to cut Moncure down financially and bury this whole outrageous scheme before its infection spread.

"What you gentlemen have said interests me very much—will interest my friend, Dan Lord, even more," Tugger launched his attack in his best trading voice. "I confess that at first you took me by surprise. Dan didn't tell me—if, indeed, he knows himself!—that discontent exists among you burley growers over the price General Tobacco has been offering for your leaf. What you choose to accept from broken-down speculators is of course your own bad judgment."

"Now, Blake, you're trying to beat the devil around the stump."

"That's what you say, Moncure!" Tugger's anger flared again. That doctor must be right about your blood pressure Tugger pulled himself up sharply, if you can't keep your head any better in a trade as simple as this one, a walk-away easy as taking candy from a baby. With an attempt to muster his old infectious grin, Tugger continued: "However, I'll not deny your plan to sell Dan Lord fourteen million pounds of burley all at once isn't without its attractive features—to us both. If for no other reason than its magnitude, your proposition appeals to me."

"We've been telling our growers you're that kind of a man, Mr. Blake," the small-town lawyer took the bait. Santa Claus beamed, but Moncure remained unimpressed.

"My only objection is that you haven't signed in enough tobacco," continued Tugger, watching Stone's face slyly. "Knowing Dan as I do, I—I wish you could have made it—say, twenty millions. Dan can use twenty millions of burley as readily as fourteen—"

"You mean you want us to go home, and sign up six milions more, Mr. Blake?" beamed Santa Claus.

"D'you think you could do that?"

"Blake, are you trading in good faith?"

"Why shouldn't I, Moncure? Dan and I have spent the better part of our lives manufacturing and merchandising obacco products from raw leaf."

"Could you give us a word to that effect in writing, sir?" nterposed Barnes, looking as if he scarcely dared believe their good fortune. "Just some little memorandum of our talk, and —and a general indication of about what you'd be willing to pay?"

"Mr. Blake couldn't do that before he consults with Mr. Lord," Stone answered, reasonably. The Kentuckian sensed, but could not identify the cause of the great man's evident personal dislike of him. America had been right as usual, Stone now appreciated, and arose to leave. When Moncure stood up, Tugger was pleased to notice, he seemed less of a man. His lothes were cheap and the tobacco patch had given a permanent stoop to his shoulders. "We're obliged to you for seeing us, Mr. Blake," Stone concluded. "You'll hear from us within a month."

"We honestly hadn't expected to find you so easy to approach, Mr. Blake," chirped the cock-sparrow, Barnes, venturing nearer for crumbs. "This is the best see-gar I ever smoked."

"I've made it a lifelong habit to be accessible to men just in from the field," confessed Tugger, rising to escort them to the door. "When we were in the thick of the cheroot war—but I mustn't bore you with an older man's tendency to reminisce."

"Fine office you've got here, sir—the purtiest I ever was in," expanded Santa Claus, enjoying himself. "I must confess, though, I'd get riled if I had to look at those funny-men's ideas of me day in month out."

"Dan and I are running a race to see which of us can collect the most," laughed Tugger, his hand on the doorknob. "They're the originals, y'know. And cartoonists make us pay through the nose for 'em now, I can tell you! See that fat Pharaoh over there? I bet I gave more for him than the worth of your three farms put together."

"That wouldn't be claiming a lot today—because land's worth only just as much as its produce brings," declared Stone gazing up at the panel from which the framed picture had been removed. "If I'm not being too inquisitive, Mr. Blake—that empty space piques my curiosity."

"I took that one down to—to let Dan have a copy made. It's the star of my collection," chuckled Tugger, his eyes expressionless. You yokel, you corncob bridegroom, you'll never know!

"America will never forgive me if I forget to ask about her sister," continued Stone, lagging so the others could precede him into the outer office.

"Didn't I tell you Teena's in Europe? She's in fine health and spirits, she writes. Sorry she's not in town—or I'd insist on you staying over and letting us show you the bright lights. Good-day, Moncure—I'll expect to hear from you shortly," Tugger ended the interview before one of the sudden spells to which he was subject these days thickened his speech and blinded his already blood-shot eyes.

Three days later, against his doctor's advice, Tugger came down to his office to keep an appointment with Tom Coyle.

"Tell me what you know about a fellow named Moncure," Blake suggested, after he had passed the Coronas now forbidden for himself.

"You mean Stone Moncure, of Children's Chance? Has he been up here to see you?" asked Coyle, a big man with straight blue-black hair and a bright brown eye which was never still.

"What d'you know about him?"

"He's another broken-down tobacco speculator who's out to roast Dan Lord on a spit. He's put himself in the lead of a bunch of Mason County growers who hope that by holding their leaf off the market, they can compel you Wall Street fellows to give them a higher price. Not a bad idea," Tom conceded, cocking his eye impudently at his host over the segar he was lighting. "He might succeed, if it weren't for one thing."

"What's that?"

"He's built up his entire organization—they call themselves the Equity Society—on the principle farmers will stand together for their own good. They never have. And they never will."

"Why d'you think so?" asked Tugger, hoping to pick up a stray arrow to put into his already full quiver.

"In the first place, all farmers are one-man workers—with no more sense of team play than a ground hog," declared Coyle, his voice authoritative. "There's something about cultivating a little patch of land all his own makes the average man feel as independent as a hog on ice."

" 'Better be master on your own dunghill than chief steward in the halls of an emperor,' eh?" Tugger quoted America, before he realized his source.

"Exactly. And there's something else, too. Farmers just can't bear to see other farmers get along too far. Oh, they'll help a neighbor out if he's been unfortunate—because that appeals to the big I in 'em, makes 'em feel like the Lord God-A'mighty—but just let some clodhopper prosper a little, and then watch his neighbors sharpen their axes for him!"

"I see you understand farmers," chuckled Tugger. "Now, about this equity idea—has it spread to the Blue Grass?"

"It's not as strong there as in Mason and the hill counties."

"Why is that?"

"Because as a rule, we operate on a bigger scale. When Dan Lord knocked down leaf prices another cent last year, we had our sheep and cattle to fall back on. In Mason and the river counties, burley growers went broke, because they were already down to bedrock."

"You talk like a member of the Equity Society," smiled Tugger.

"Maybe I'll have to be—some day."

"Then why are you in here?"

"Because I want you to intercede for me with Dan Lord, Mr. Blake," Coyle answered, earnestly. "This trip, when I offered him my customary hundred thousand pounds of leaf, he—he turned me down."

"Why?"

"He said his field organization objected to his buying hogshead tobacco over their heads. They claim, in buying from me, Dan himself is pin-hooking—and you know how the trust feels about that. Any buyer caught pin-hooking in the street outside the hogshead breaks is automatically left off the pay roll, I've been told. But you and I both know Dan Lord, Mr. Blake. If it amuses Dan to pin-hook my little shirt tail of leaf, the devil himself couldn't stop him! What I've got to find out is why—after all these years—Dan's decided to turn the screw down on me."

"Didn't you put your own finger on the sore spot?" hinted Tugger, studying a hangnail his valet had missed. "Maybe you've overplayed your hand, Coyle—maybe Dan's gotten fed up with the GawdA'mighty cheek of you struttin' dirt farmers."

"Looky here, Mr. Blake, I'll tell you something I never felt I could afford to tell Dan Lord—because—well, because I hoped to keep on doing business with him," confessed Coyle.

a note of desperation edging his voice. "The only reason I ever went into this one-man game—and stuck in it when Dan Lord was offering me a whale of a salary to come on over into the trust and work for him—was because I felt so damn' sorry for the pore devils, the growers I used to see on the Cincinnati hogshead breaks. This hundred thousand pounds of leaf Dan Lord refuses to take off my hands now—d'you want to know how I got it?"

"You got stuck with it—gingering the market at a dollar a hogshead," chuckled Tugger.

"So—you know?"

"Sure we know! We've known for years. What kind of suckers do you take us for here in Wall Street?" demanded Tugger unpleasantly, and slapped his hand down hard on his empty desk top. "Since you feel so damn' sorry for the growers, Coyle, that you choose to throw a monkey wrench every chance you can into our orderly trade practices, I suggest you go back to 'em now—"

"Tugger Blake, you don't mean that," whispered Tom Coyle, staring at the great man.

"I do mean it."

"But you couldn't—why, you come from the tobacco patch yourself! You know by actual experience a man can't feed his family—and keep a roof over their heads—on seven-cent leaf."

"I'm sick and tired of hearing you damn' tobacco yaps cry-baby about what you can or can't do!" shouted Tugger, forgetting his doctor's orders. "Get out of this office—get back where you belong—before I throw you out!"

"You're right about one thing," acknowledged Coyle, with ominous calm. "I have been a tobacco yap to keep on coming here to beg favors of you and Dan Lord—to coax a few coppers more for us growers out of you two hogs who've set your own price for five years on mine and everybody else's leaf. But this is the last time I'll ever come to you, Tugger Blake—or to Dan Lord. From now on, when you want burley tobacco—and it's seventy per cent of your mix, don't forget that, because we won't!—you'll come to me. And I'll be the one who sets the price."

"Now you're talking like a fool, Tom Coyle."

"I'm talking like the president of the Equity Society!"

"So you are in it?"

"From this moment on, until you come to our terms," declared Coyle. "Good-afternoon, Blake."

After the Kentuckian had closed the door gently behind himself, Tugger raised his eyes to the poster of America that hung in the panel opposite his desk. It was the original of the *Wild Honey* poster, and it showed America in a mood Tugger had never seen in the flesh—with her head thrown back, white teeth flashing, golden fingers clasped behind her ears, wrists and ears hung with gypsy gauds, the grave grey eyes haunted, a tender smile on her full red lips, the glossy hair tied into a polka-dot bandanna, the cheap calico dress unbuttoned to show the swell of rounded throat and brown lean breasts . . .

"So you've started this tobacco war, my dear?" he whispered to the poster. "Just the idea makes me sick—because I'm tired—and I need rest and quiet—and you, America—I need you. But if you will fight," he sighed, and leaned forward to pick up a telegram lying face downwards under the white jade elephant on his desk. After he had rung for a secretary, in the moment of waiting his eye ran over the telegraphic message: "We of the Equity Society happy to inform you we have twenty million pounds burley signed into our pool. We await your bid." Stone Moncure's name led three other signatures. Tom Coyle's was not among them.

"Answer this wire," Tugger instructed the secretary who appeared in response to his summons. "Tell them the deal's off—that I've changed my mind."

"Yes, Mr. Blake. Do you want to see it, sir?"

"That's not necessary. Just send it along."

"Will this be all, sir?" asked the respectful young man.

"That's all."

Like an old farm wagon left standing too long in the field until its wheel rims sun-loosen and its axles creak, the equity movement got slowly under way. Occasionally its unruly horses, the growers, backed and lunged. Horsemen and riders, inexperienced in handling such a multi-powered span, often tangled the reins. If a lash were needed, however, Tugger Blake's telegram calling off the deal for the poundage he himself had suggested served as that lash. And Tom Coyle's acceptance of the presidency presaged at least one experienced friend of the growers in the main driver's seat.

Organization was purposely kept as simple and local as possible. All matters of general policy were to be referred to a central board of control made up of forty directors, to be elected one from each of the forty counties in Kentucky and Ohio which were then producing burley tobacco. Each county was to have its local or county board, made up of its director and one member each to be elected from the voting precincts of the county. Stock in the Equity Society was to be issued annually to farmer-members in the amount of leaf which they grew and pooled.

At the first Equity assembly in Limestone, called to meet after tobacco-housing time in 1906, Stone was chosen Mason County's director on the central board of control. He then began systematically to call meetings in the schoolhouses of each precinct to ascertain the majority opinion there on the pool movement, and, if it was favorable, to hold an election of the precinct's delegate to the county's local board. America, whose newspaper articles against the Tobacco Trust were attracting statewide attention, accompanied Stone to write the poll on the blackboard and to keep minutes of the precinct meeting for Stone's reports to the central Equity office established at Winchester, some nineteen miles from Lexington.

On a mild Indian summer night, Tuckahoe's Equity meeting was held in the Glade Springs schoolhouse. Into the single room crowded sixty or more growers. Landowners took the benches, tenants stood at the rear and around the side walls, or sat in the open windows. After a twenty-minute speech explaining their water haul to New York, Stone recited Tugger Blake's telegram from memory, and briefly stated the objects of the Equity movement on which he was asking every landowner in the precinct to express an opinion. Picking up a tax list, he began to call the alphabetically arranged roll:

"Fant Annable? Will you please declare your acreage, and how you choose to vote it?"

"Against the pool!" called young Fant from among the Barnes men standing in the rear of the schoolroom. "Four hundred and seventy acres."

As she turned to write her son's vote in plain sight for everyone to see this split in clan ranks, America wondered briefly how Ishmael could have developed to such a striking degree his father's and her own most unlovely characteristics. Not even his voice resembled that of the man whose very memory tonight constricted America's heart with pain, momentarily almost unbearable. My son, you don't even look like your father, the gallant love of my youth—you with his blue-black hair you never brush, his fine-contoured cheeks you are too lazy to shave, his gay brown eyes which mirror your soul's sulkiness, his daring which in you is only bravado. Is it I, your mother, who have failed you? Or are you by nature so contrary-minded that in every issue you must needs take an opposing stand to progressive community opinion? All herds have at least one steer which to thrive must graze alone.

"The Widow Annable?" Stone was continuing.

"Ma gave me her vote in writing," spoke up Kate. Thrusting a sealed envelope into her left pocket, she continued with traditional Annable caution: "If it's the same to you, I'll hold it for a spell."

"I'm sure that's permissible, ma'am," agreed Stone, courteously. "Horace Bacon?"

"I'm a-goin' to vote my hundred and five acres into the pool—if it kills me!" cried a small farmer, with a give-me-liberty-or-give-me-death expression.

"Yee-eee!" screeched Ephraim from the window sill in the ear-splitting Rebel yell.

"Since we are all neighbors—and want to go on living together in peace and concord," smiled Stone, "may I ask that there be no demonstration following each vote?"

"That's more like it, young man!" grunted Aunt Polly Grove, the money-lender whose rich farm adjoined the Doggett place. "I purta near swallered my false teeth, that bobcat sciert me so."

"Ulysses Cary?"

"For the pool—nine hundred and twenty acres," voted Santa Claus.

"Thank you, sir. Major Chisholm?"

"I stand on ma constitootional rights, Stone," pronounced the Major, testily. "Nae Board o' Control in th' Blue Grass may tell me whin I can oor canna sell ma ain crop. Seven hundred an' six acres."

"Then you vote against the pool, sir?"

"Aye, mon, I do!"

"Major Chisholm—seven hundred and six acres—against the pool," repeated America, at the blackboard.

"Captain Doggett?"

"Against, sir—against all such centralized tyranny designed to check a man in the management of his own estate!" barked Ephraim's irascible father-in-law from his wheel chair. "I was born a State's righter—I broke my back for State's rights—and I aim to die a State's righter!"

"How many acres, sir?" inquired America respectfully, chalk in hand.

"Eight hundred and thirty-five! And I wish now I owned twice as much—to vote against this tomfoolery."

"The Widow Drake?" Stone continued, and checked his list.

"Ma sent her vote," declared Allilee, rising. "And while I'm opening it, I want to go on public record as in hearty agreement with Cap'n Doggett and Major Chisholm. Nobody

—least of all you, Stone Moncure, and you, America—can tell me how to run ma's farm!"

"Allilee, the understanding on which this meeting was called," interposed Stone, firmly, "was that tonight we would vote without further discussion—and then go home. What is the Widow Drake's vote?"

"Against the pool—three hundred and seventy acres!" snapped Allilee.

"James Fagin?" went on Stone's imperturbable voice.

"For the pool, sor. Ninety acres."

"Aunt Polly Grove?"

"For—on general principles—nine hundred and two," grunted the old lady.

"Adolph Klinger?"

"For de pool—sixty-tree acres."

"Solomon Liebman?"

"Vor de pool—because it's good business," snapped the other money-lender on Minerva turnpike, the little German Jew who had walked into Limestone fifty years ago with a pack on his back.

"What is your acreage, Mr. Liebman?" inquired Stone.

"In dis county—or precinct?"

"In this voting precinct, please."

"Vour hunnerd and ten acres in de Bledsoe farm—two hunnered and eighty-six in de Walton home place."

"James MacGower?" Stone continued the roll call.

"Against—till I pay ma debts," answered Jamie, from the rear of the room. "Three hundred and twinty-five acres."

"An' I'd like tae belt him for it, auld mon that he is!" protested Abigail MacGower.

"Andrew McCorkle?"

"For—but I dinna raise th' weed," declared the young blacksmith who had bought out the Widow MacGower. "Twenty acres."

"Stone Moncure—for—eleven hundred and forty-three acres," Stone was announcing, when Allilee cut in:

"I protest against Children's Chance being counted!"

"Why, ma'am?" asked Stone, raising startled blue eyes.

"Because everybody knows you don't own it—after you assigned in '96," Allilee declared with a toss of her iron-grey head which put America in mind of a spiteful old driving-mare. Allilee's next move should be to lay back her ears and kick over the dashboard.

"If you, Major Chisholm—or you, Mr. Cary—will take the chair, I would like to read the ruling the central board made on this point," began Stone, his face crimson.

"Damned if that ain't jest like a woman—al'ays gittin' personal!" muttered Jim Barnes audibly, from the window opposite Ephraim.

"Get on with your rat-killing, Stone—and stop this silly female chit-chat!" complained Captain Doggett, pounding on the floor with his gold-headed cane. "My back hurts—I want to go home."

"I move Allilee's back-bitin' be blotted aff th' record," interposed Abigail MacGower, with a hard look at her life-long neighbor.

"Second the motion," called Kate Annable.

"Are you all ready for the question?" Stone asked, tight-lipped.

"We want to count in Children's Chance!" roared the roomful of farmers, enjoying the short shrift Allilee's peers had given her.

"Contrary minded?" demanded Stone.

"Here!" began Allilee, until the boos of tenant youths silenced her.

"Stone Moncure—for the pool—eleven hundred and forty-three acres," America repeated, at the blackboard.

The poll of the Whitman brothers, who farmed below Jamie on Lee's Creek, brought two hundred and thirty-seven more acres into the pool.

"That ends it," announced Stone, while everybody began hastily to add up the two columns of figures before them on the blackboard. "Now, Miss Kate, if we may have your mother's proxy, please?"

"Ma said I was to vote her land with the majority," announced Kate, both hands in her tweed pockets. "Since she broke her hip, ma said, ever'body on the ridge has been mighty kind to her. Besides, she took pa's being an Abolitionist so hard during the last war, now she wants to side with the majority of you, she said. So ma gave me two proxies," concluded Kate, withdrawing a sealed envelope from her right-hand pocket. "She votes for the pool—four hundred and seventy-one acres."

"Yee-eee!" howled Ephraim again. "That more than clinches us a fat majority!"

"Order, please," demanded Stone. "You can see for yourselves, ladies and gentlemen. The vote stands forty-five hundred and forty-seven acres for the pool—twenty-seven hundred and six acres against it. Were Children's Chance not counted, Tuckahoe Ridge would still stand with a substantial majority for the pool. And, now, nominations are in order for your precinct delegate to Mason County's local board of control."

"I nominate America Moncure," called Ulysses Cary, beaming like old St. Nick.

"I move the nominations be closed," sang out Kate Annable.

"Hear—hear!" shouted the meeting.

"Are you ready for the vote?" called Stone, turning to smile at his embarrassed wife.

"Go on—elect her!" even Captain Doggett conceded, though as a non-pool man he had no moral right to express an opinion. "Maybe she can keep you puddin' heads on the right track."

"Vote—vote!"

By a roar which America found very gratifying, the vote was unanimous.

"Before we adjourn," began Stone, stepping from behind the desk and coming forward to the edge of the platform, "may

I say just two more things to you all? Tenants must sell their crops as their landlord has voted. In other words, my tenants—if they elect to stay on my farm next year—automatically become Equity men and must pool their half of the crop with mine."

"Didn't Major Chisholm just say those Blue Grass fellows up at Winchester will soon be tellin' us we can't raise black-eyed peas?" demanded Cap'n Doggett, shifting in his wheel chair as if in acute pain.

"The other matter I want to bring to your attention is this," Stone continued, his voice and eyes so earnest that he was able to hold rising emotions in check for a few minutes longer: "In the Civil War, although one was an Abolitionist and the other a Confederate, my father and Justinian Annable—by the grace of God in your hearts—were able to hold this community together in Christian fellowship. If our parents could accomplish this when flesh and blood were at stake, can't we follow their example when only our pocket-books are involved?"

"Ain't hit the selfsame thing, mister?" called a tenant's voice from outside, across Jim Barnes' shoulder.

"Yep, that's all right for you to say," drawled Fant Annable, who had hardly spoken to Stone since his marriage to America, "because you're top dawg right naow."

"Meeting adjourned," snapped Stone, his jaw tight.

"Folks, wait a minute!" called a voice from outside.

Around the rear door the tenants gave way to admit Os Humphreys. Hurrying up the aisle, he stepped onto the platform and swung around.

"Os, you're too late to make a speech tonight," grinned Stone. "We know you aim to get elected as a delegate from some precinct, but you're twenty minutes too late for Tuckahoe."

"Now, Stone, you will have your little joke," the Limestone politician tried to dissolve his disappointment in a sickly smile. "How'd the vote turn out?"

"Nearly seventy per cent in favor of the pool—"

"That's about the same as in other Mason precincts—and all over the burley belt, I hear," nodded Humphreys. "I just came from the Lewisburg meeting—would 'a' been here sooner if my old mare hadn't throwed a shoe."

Before Thanksgiving, 1906, the central Equity Society at Winchester called an open meeting to elect the society's permanent officers and to consider ways and means to handle and market the pooled crop. America, sick in bed with tonsillitis, waved Stone off with high hopes. When he returned, she saw from his manner that something had gone wrong. After she had put a warmed-over supper on the table for him, she sat down to hear an account of the meeting.

"Well," began Stone, "the meeting authorized the central society to take five per cent out of all county checks for selling the crop as a whole to the trust. The central society will set up standard types at Winchester, and the local county boards will grade and prize according to this scale. They elected me chairman of this committee to establish grades—with Tom Coyle and Scott Osborne to help me."

"That sounds like real work," smiled America. "What else did they do?"

"The Limestone crowd put over their plan to commingle," Stone answered, ducking his head to drink hot coffee.

"Is that all that happened?"

"Not by a long shot! When I got back to Limestone, I found Os Humphreys had called a meeting of the local board of control—"

"I didn't receive any announcement," interposed America.

"No, Os said he hadn't sent word out here because he thought he'd catch you with me on our way home from Winchester."

"How have they worked out their plan to commingle?" America determined not to stop for trivialities, to approach this difficult handling problem without prejudice, if she could.

She and Os Humphreys had argued long and heatedly about his plan to commingle. Os said such a method was the only modern progressive way to handle large quantities of leaf, and cited the lumber and pig-iron industries as cases in point. America had maintained that tobacco, unlike pig iron, comes off separate pieces of land which produces each a separate color and quality. In addition, added America, tobacco is stripped into a hundred varying grades and hues by thousands of farmer-strippers. When they had first started to organize the pool, the Moncures—Stone verbally and America in her free-press articles—had promised every grower who signed in: "You may prize your crop yourself, or get any expert tobacco man you choose, to do it for you." Os Humphrey's clique, with their plan to commingle, had already upset one of the underlying agreements of the pool movement, had sown a first seed of grower discontent. "Tell me the details—and I'll try to listen with an open mind," America concluded, unhappily.

"All pool growers in each precinct will be required to haul their crops to one central warehouse located in their largest market town," explained Stone. "There the local Equity board will subcontract the handling to an experienced tobacco man who will receive and grade all crops according to the standard Winchester grades my committee will establish."

"That won't be as easy as it sounds," America could not resist comment. "However, I suppose it can be done, if their subcontractors are experienced enough. What happened next?"

"The local board offered me the subcontract for the Tuckahoe precinct."

"Why, Stone! How very gratifying," cried America, calculating swiftly. Such a contract, if the ceiling were high enough and the Equity fight against the trust lasted several years, might make them rich. Even if Dan Lord capitulated quickly, the profits they could make should go a long way towards paying off Stone's debt on Children's Chance. He could stop hiring hands and raising big crops; she could put out fewer chickens and might even engage a competent cook. Her quick mind moved to the next important detail: "What's the figure at which the local board wants you to accept the Tuckahoe subcontract?"

"Humphreys said their other precinct handlers felt they could get by nicely—with a good margin of profit—for about seventy-five cents a hundredweight, and store for another fifteen cents a month per hogshead for as long as the trust makes us hold the leaf."

"That's fifty per cent more than the old-time speculators got rich on," America tried not to look too pleased. "I did very well charging fifty cents a hundred for the occasional crop I handled for service only—and that included hauling down to the wharf."

"Wait 'll you hear the rest," snapped Stone, his eyes hard. "What d'you think the local board aims to charge the grower."

"You just said seventy-five cents a hundred, with fifteen cents storage."

"Oh, that's only the price the subcontractors agreed to do their part for! The local board aims to charge the grower two dollars and twenty-five cents a hundred—and twenty-five cents for storage."

"Two dollars and twenty-five cents—why, Stone, that's sheer robbery! What does the local board expect to do with that dollar and fifty cents they'll be making off every hundred pounds—and a dime a month storage off every hogshead?"

"Build warehouses—organize a big pay roll—pay themselves fat salaries!" snorted Stone, his eyes gleaming to see how quickly his wife's business acumen had fastened on the salient facts of the complicated set-up. For two days he had been seething inwardly. Even now, his hand shook so he overturned his empty coffee cup into his saucer, as he continued: "You know Shad Chewe, that big livestock dealer who's a bank director in Limestone? Well, Shad Chewe has subcontracted the Sand Licks precinct. Shad actually had the gall to say to me: 'Come on in with us, Moncure, and we'll all make a barrel of money!'

And Os Humphreys asked: 'How d'you handle tobacco anyhow, Stone? You dump it into a barrel, don't you, and then turn a weight down on it, I'm told.' "

"What did you answer?"

"When I could trust my voice to speak, I said you and I hadn't organized the pool to make a barrel of money for anybody—for ourselves or for town grabbers like them. I said you'd racked your brains writing articles—and I'd worn out three buggies driving all over this end of the state—to try and help the growers get a living price for their leaf."

"Good for you! What happened next?"

"The meeting turned into pretty much of a free-for-all. A delegate from Dover and another scared rabbit sided with me. The rest voted us down—and awarded the Tuckahoe subcontract to Spence Martin, along with the Limestone contract."

"Oh, Stone!" whispered America and swallowed painfully with her still sore throat muscles. "Would it have done any good if I'd been there?"

"Not a damn' bit, Merry. Os Humphreys had everything all lined up before I got back from Winchester. They only waited for me because they knew I'd raise hell if they tried to put anything over on us while our backs were turned," he concluded wearily, and straightened the teacup in its saucer. An impulse crossed his mind to say that three times in the last ten years he had stood fighting across a table to save the fruits of his own and his neighbors' toil from being taken away by non-producers. In Cincinnati he had faced paunchy old Meiers and his moneylenders alone; and, thanks to his neighbors, he had come off at least with a fighting chance to regain his feet. In New York, confronting Tugger Blake, he and John Willy and Ulysses Cary had lost. And today at the Equity's local board, facing small-town politicians and bankers and traders, he had lost again for the army of growers he represented, the men and women of the fields, the tired country people with the "limestone look" on their faces, faces worn down to basic muscle, bone and soul—Hannah stooping in the furrow to pick up and nurse her young baby, her calico dress dark with sweat; the Bell children lifting unchildlike faces from the tobacco leaves they were conscientiously worming; Jamie MacGower resting on his hoe in the moonlight; and behind these known toilers, the nameless and the unknown and the uncounted, the ragged and hopeless army of tobacco farmers moving up and down the waving green rows in the hot Kentucky sunshine . . .

"America, say something!" cried Stone, his soul gripped in the icy clutch of panic. What if America saw this whole set-up differently; what if she, like the smart town men, felt that the time had come for the Stone Moncures to join the greedy circle under the Equity plum tree and shake down a rich basketful for themselves?

"What do you want me to say, my dear?"

"Tell me I did the right thing—to stick by the growers! Tell me you'll stick with me, though I know it means more back-breaking work for us both—you bending over that hot stove and slopping around in the wet weeds trying to raise poultry to keep a good table for hands—me slaving in the tobacco patch till I drop!"

The sudden change which came over America's face, transforming it, was answer enough for him. In addition, she reached out her strong work-coarsened hands and seized his before she declared steadily:

"You being you, Stone, you couldn't have done otherwise. Neither could I, if I'd been there. We just aren't the kind of people who go back on our pledged word to the growers, our friends—just to make a barrel of money for ourselves."

"Oh, Merry, you're the best wife a man ever had!" gulped Stone, his voice breaking, his eyes shining with relief. "I know I've saddled you with years more of drudgery—worse here than you ever had at Foxden."

"Don't you give another thought to me, my dear!" she smiled bravely at him. "Some folks make rocking-chairs for others to rock in, as Aunt Flora used to say. All my life it's been this way with me. And now, in this Equity fight, if you and I have to do it again, why, we'll just have to forget our personal grievances and go on as best we may—to hold the pool together until we can whip the trust. We've got to stick together, you see that. And we will stick together—town handlers and country growers—until we can present a solid front against Dan Lord and Tugger Blake."

" 'United we stand!' " he nodded, his hands still gripping hers across the red-checked tablecloth.

By the summer of 1907, the Equity Society reported that the pool had sixty million pounds of the 1906 burley crop prized and ready for sale. The General Tobacco Company entered no bid, and the handful of surviving independents dared not incur Dan Lord's displeasure by giving succor to his enemies. The unpooled portion of the crop continued to be sold over the Cincinnati and Louisville hogshead markets. With three-fifths of the crop lying untouched in Equity warehouses, the year's average price for 1906 climbed to ten cents a pound all around.

"Dan Lord's letting out the snaffle on you non-poolers just to make us poolers discontented," Ulysses Cary declared at the Tuckahoe post office on Christmas Eve of 1907, while the men stood about waiting for Mrs. McCorkle to sort the mail. Outside, snow had already begun to fall in the traditional holiday blizzard. "You as can afford a big Christmas this year, better thank your neighbors who can't," added Ulysses, shaking wet flakes off his worn beaver-skin collar.

"There's no law requires a man to be a fool, Squire Cary!" snapped Allilee, laying her mail on top of two bushel baskets crammed with holiday cheer for the tenant children on the Drake farm. As none of the younger men made a move to help Allilee, Stone carried her baskets out to the buggy for her, returned and backed up to the glowing cannon stove to await his due claim on the new post-mistress' services. Tuckahoe seemed another store, a far less interesting place, without Abigail MacGower to lean across the counter and peck verbally at all comers. After looking around to make sure he was speaking only to friends, Ulysses Cary continued:

"If the Equity don't sell some leaf soon—and make some kind of part payment to us growers before taxes roll around next March—I'll have to sell my south pike meadow to Major Chisholm. What you aiming to do, Stone, with all the interest money you owe staring you in the face?"

"I honestly don't know sir," answered Stone, fingering a pasteboard brick chimney full of hard candy. He would like to buy the entire lot of them, to hang one for each of the Bell and Schraedlich children on the Christmas tree America had trimmed with strung popcorn for the candlelight party she planned this evening at Children's Chance. His tenant youngsters would have to content themselves with the fruit cake and ambrosia America intended to serve tonight for refreshments. In the cellar Stone had a fresh-killed quarter of young beef to present to their parents. What on earth could he give to America?

"Santy Claus is a-leavin' a new buggy for that hawg who line-fences with me—that polecat who's a-gittin' rich off the sacrifices of his neighbors," spoke up small-farmer Horace Bacon, paraphrasing from America's most recent editorial carried above her celebrated Cassandra signature in the Limestone *Eagle*.

"A new pie-anner Cap'n Doggett's givin' Miss Betheny's little girls," Jim Fagin contributed his item of local news. "Whin Misther Eph saw it comin', he got so tarnation mad he had to go squirrel-shootin', he tol' me, to cool off. The Cap'n give me this piece o' money to help move it into the parlor, while the colleens were lookin' t'other way. I'll take fifty cents worth av yer cheapest Christmas candy, ma'am," concluded Fagin, pushing his coin across the counter.

"Last night John Willy read me Miss Merry's fine article in the *Lexington Herald* abaout starvin' the trust," spoke up Jim Barnes, hitting a bull's-eye in the open door of the cannon stove. "Ask her for me, Mr. Stone, if she ain't gittin' a wee mite mixed on who's adoin' the starvin'?"

"Let's hope it's a good year for rabbits!" Stone offered the poolers' threadbare but always appreciated joke.

"Here's a big box come out for you from the railroad office —and a package from Chicago—and a mighty important-looking letter to Miss Merry from New York City—from Zachary Taylor Blake, 48 Wall Street," announced the post-mistress, reading the return address on the long envelope.

"Don't reckon that could be Tugger Blake changing his mind again, do you, Stone?" asked Ulysses Cary, wistfully.

"Miracles have happened—but I doubt it," replied Stone, unconsciously feeling the engraving with his thumb. Every eye in the store was anticipating his next move with the intensity of hungry hounds watching their master's hands moving towards the pan of corn bread intended for them. "If he has, squire, I'll send Weed up the pike with the good news—so's everybody can have a happy Christmas," he added, and put the letter unopened into his pocket.

His buggy mares were eager to trot briskly home through the thickening snow. Weed came out to the lane gate, helped Stone carry in the packages and took the mares, their flanks steaming, on up to their stalls. In the dining room, America sat at the table filling paper cornucopias she had cleverly pasted out of scraps of colored magazine covers, with homemade candy spread out to cool on breadboards and platters.

"A person ud have to get up mighty early in the morning to get ahead of you," grinned Stone, thinking how much better the cornucopias would serve their purpose than the brick chimneys, filled with a third the amount of less nourishing candy. "Got an extra piece for a good lil fellow?"

"Help yourself," she flashed her brilliant smile at him. "There's black walnut fudge—and hickory nut caramels—and molasses taffy."

"Here's an express package from Nicke. Shall I open it?"

"Another of her cast-off wedding presents," America guessed, going on with her work. "Want to bet it's a piece of statuary—or a doorstop? I can't wait till she works her way through these—to the really nice candlesticks and book ends those rich New Yorkers gave her. Nicke wouldn't have any more use for a book end than she would for a book."

The gift, when carefully removed from its excelsior wrappings, proved to be a three-foot reproduction in pink marble of The Greek Slave.

"It's indecent!" snorted Stone, backing off from it.

"I'm only sorry it's not life-sized. Then I could set it against the cedar hedge in my rose garden, and try to keep all the old men on Tuckahoe from becoming rose fanciers," joked America. "What's in that other package?"

High Jinks, Bayard and their two girls had sent useful, charming gifts. After he had piled the boxes neatly on a chair Stone came over to the table, stole a caramel, and thrust his hand with a Napoleonic gesture into his coat pocket, declaring:

"Guess what I have for you, milady?"

"I hope it isn't much—because I haven't a thing for you, darling—except my love."

"It's the last thing in the world you'd expect—after what you told me about a family falling-out," Stone gave her a hint.

The last thing she'd expect, thought America, was to have Tugger Blake pay her the ten thousand dollars he owed her. All morning, as she beat and pulled candy, she had thought of what that ten thousand dollars would do at Children's Chance—on Tuckahoe—throughout the burley belt, sixty per cent of which was half starved this Christmas.

"I give up," she said, fitting a hickory nut into the bottom of another cornucopia.

"It's a letter from Zachary Taylor Blake."

"From Tugger Blake?" echoed America, looking up with a whitening face.

"Here it is!"

"My—my hands are sticky," whispered America, suddenly weak all over. "Open it, Stone—read it to me."

With shaking fingers he tore the handsome paper. Inside was a typed letter and something long and green.

"It's a check," he gasped, "a check for ten thousand dollars—payable to you."

"I don't believe it," she said, and snatched the check from him. For a moment, as she gazed at it, he thought she might faint, so pale was her tired face. Then into her cheeks came a tide of color, her hands and voice trembled as she declared: "I—I never have been so angry—or so insulted—in all my life—except once!"

"Blake says he owes you this money," reported Stone, reading the letter. "He says it's the final payment on that *Wild Honey* job you did for General Tobacco way back in '97. What does he mean by that?"

"In '97, I spied out a plug formula for him—dressed up as a Creole," panted America, moving around because she was too furious to stand still. "Just for a joke I had a picture taken of myself in that silly costume—and he used it on a poster."

Now I know what I'm going to give you for Christmas, Stone congratulated himself mentally, remembering the half a dozen *Wild Honey* posters of all sizes he had put away in the parlor years ago, because the poster girl had reminded him of America.

"What's so wrong about that?" Stone tried to soothe her. "I can't honestly see anything in this letter—and in what you've just told me—to upset you so, unless you've worn yourself plumb out."

"You can't see through Tugger Blake's trying to trap me—with ten thousand dollars he's owed me for years? To pay it now when I can't take it—when to take it would look as if I've accepted a bribe?" she demanded, almost beside herself with chagrin and frustration. "Don't you realize he's only paying me now to try to break up the pool? The minute he gets this check into his hands with my endorsement on it, he'll use

it against me—to try and prove that I—like plenty of other
in the Equity Society—can be bought off by the trust!"

"Damned if I'd thought of that, Merry—why, of cours
he would," breathed Stone, and dropped the check as if i
were poison. "That's just the kind of thing Tugger Blak
would most enjoy doing—to publicly discredit you and m
and everybody else who has anything to do with the pool."

"Well, for once the old fox has met his match," continue
America, in a harsher voice than Stone had heard her use
Rising, she went to the bookcase-desk, brought out writing
materials.

"What're you going to do, Merry?" asked Stone, startle
to see his wife uncork the ink bottle with shaking fingers an
insert the pen. "Don't tell me you're going to accept it?"

" 'Pay - to - the - order - of - the - Equity - Society - Relief
Fund,' " America pronounced each word as she wrote it, then
leaned back in her chair to exclaim: "There! I hope that'll
make him sick—as sick as it makes me glad. We'll hang this
check at the top of our Christmas tree, Stone—for everybody
on Tuckahoe to see. And then the first thing Monday morning—as soon as we can get to town—I'll release a simple statement to all my papers that Tugger Blake sent me this check,
which I've turned over to the Relief Fund. He'll nearly have
apoplexy when he reads about it, but it'll be too late then for
him to stop payment—without my making even more of a
scandal."

In view of the utter destitution facing the majority of
pooled growers after the 1907 crop had been delivered to
Equity warehouses, a strong sentiment to curtail the 1908 crop
began to percolate through the burley-producing belt. Early
in March, 1908, the central society called an open meeting in
Winchester to consider ways and means of forcing the General
Tobacco Company to buy the pooled crops of 1906 and 1907.

When they arrived at Winchester, Stone and America found
the small but ornate hotel ballroom overflowing with farmers

in rags. Sucking their knuckles chapped raw from doing barn-lot chores without gloves, they sat on the gilt benches around the ballroom walls, or on rented funeral chairs placed in rows on the waxed dancing floor; or they hung over the rails of Juliet balconies they had reached from the mezzanine floor. On the stage, gilt music racks of a local Apollo Club had been pushed back to make room for the speaker's table and gilt chairs placed for the forty county directors of the central society. Stone, in his patched street clothes, went forward to sit on the stage. America, who had felt no desire to don Teena's expensive hand-me-downs, slipped inconspicuously into a side-aisle seat in the rear of the ballroom.

After considerable whispering among themselves, the society's officers mounted the stage, joked about turning their backs on the county directors and composed themselves near the speakers' table placed behind the footlights. As Tom Coyle called the meeting to order, America was impressed anew by his restless energy and the impression he gave her of being a sharpshooter, a guerilla fighter such as Mosby had proven himself, rather than a general farsighted as Marse Robert. Without ado, Tom Coyle turned the chair over to Judge Pace, the society's vice president, who introduced Dwight Pembroke, Equity's able counsel and a leading lawyer from Winchester.

"Members of the Equity Society," began Pembroke, in his unemotional voice. "You are as familiar with the crisis which brings us here tonight, as I am. The basic idea of this pool is, as you know, to form an agrarian monopoly strong enough to gain absolute economic control of the burley crop, so that none of it can reach the hands of the General Tobacco Company until they agree to take it—and this means some of every grade that we have established!—at a price which will insure both grower and handler a fair return on his labor and his capital investment.

"As you know, your Judiciary Committee is trying to secure legal relief through the higher courts under the Sherman anti-trust law. On May 7, 1896, Dan Lord and the Board of the

General Tobacco Company were indicted in the New Jersey courts for violation of this law, but unfortunately for us the case was dismissed the next March. The only appeal left open to us now appears to be to the Supreme Court at Washington. And you all know how long and costly that may be. To give you an idea of how devious are the ways of the law—and how subject to half a dozen different interpretations—let me tell you that we, the Equity Society, have sixteen receivership suits directed against us under the same statute by which we ourselves are endeavoring to win relief from the trust. Another grave difficulty confronts us in this year of an approaching Presidential election: Our good friend in the White House—Teddy Roosevelt, the Trust-buster—is retiring from his high office; and we do not yet know who his successor will be, nor in what light he may regard our cause. So all that I can say to you growers is this: I believe the courts eventually will give us relief under the Sherman law, but how soon that relief may come, no man can say tonight."

"He sounds pretty down in the mouth to me," whispered the farmer next to America. "What's he tryin' to tell us, Mrs. Moncure—that we're licked?"

"No," she answered, her voice thoughtful. "I think he's trying to suggest—without saying it—that you take the law into your own hands."

"Mr. Chairman!" Tom Coyle asked for recognition. After the Chair had given him the floor, Coyle came forward to the front of the stage. Light from the crystal chandeliers in the ballroom shone on his blue-black hair and the satin lapels of his faultlessly tailored dinner coat. Like a flycatcher on the wing, his bright brown glance swooped among the farmers poised forward on their chairs to hear him, lifted to the Juliet balconies bulging with desperate men and came back to include the county delegates seated behind him on the stage.

"Members of the Equity Society," he began, in a controlled voice, "as you already know, we hold prized in Equity warehouses tonight over seventy per cent of the 1906 burley crop, and over sixty per cent of the 1907 crop. The General Tobacco Company has announced its firm intention not to purchase a hogshead of this pooled leaf, declaring that they can meet their trade requirements for raw burley from their surplus—"

"Dan Lord ain't got a hundred thousand pounds of usable leaf left on hand, and you know it!" shouted an angry voice from the floor.

"We all know it," Coyle quietly continued. "We also know that we sixty per cent in the pool are making an abnormal market for the forty per cent who have refused to come in with their neighbors for the common good—"

"We call a hawg a hawg whar I come from!" shouted a rough voice from the rear.

"My chillern are starvin', while my neighbors' brats ride to school in new buggies and buy piannies to play on!" cried an angry giant in the left stage balcony. "Yet no man works harder nor me in all Bracken County!"

This outburst called forth a babel of further protest:

"Hear—hear!"

"Hit ain't right, us without a cent from terbacker for two years, an' non-poolers sellin' their leaf plumb outa sight the minute they deliver to the trust!"

"Dan Lord's only stringin' 'em along to break the pool!"

"That's the Gospel truth, but I cayent eat it, kin I?" roared the giant from the left stage balcony.

"Yeah, an' the rabbits air gittin' mighty scarce in aour neck o' the woods!" another voice carried on the worn-out jest.

"What you gentlemen are trying to say from the floor," continued Tom Coyle, "became apparent months ago to us, the officers of your central board. We have been studying all possible ways and means at our command to remedy this unfortunate condition which makes one man rich and his neighbor starve. We realize better than you do, men, that this pool experiment which we have pledged ourselves to carry through to success, is unique in American and world history. When before has a majority voluntarily elected to starve themselves for two years, to pool their crops year after year without a cent of revenue—while their children call for bread and the shadow of the sheriff threatens their homes—in order that they may stand shoulder to shoulder demanding a living price for their leaf from the corporate interests which have fattened off the fruits of their toil until today they constitute one of the richest and most powerful combines the world has ever seen?"

"Mr. Tom has hit his stride," her neighbor nodded approvingly to America.

"However, the time for words, for moral suasion"—Coyle's voice deepened—"is passed. Now, we must act! The plan which we propose to you tonight—and we have asked your county directors to sit with us before you to show we are united in it—is a desperate plan, conceived to meet the desperate situation which confronts us. Rumors of it may have reached you in the form of a suggested cut-out of the 1908 burley crop. That is exactly what we have the courage and the vision to ask you to do tonight: to vote to cut out the entire burley crop for 1908, and then go home and see to it that the will of the majority rules!"

"You don't mean for us not to grow any terbacky atall this season?" called a puzzled voice from the right section of the ballroom floor.

"Not a leaf!" Coyle answered him. "Because only by creating an acute shortage in raw burley can we force the Tobacco Trust to buy our pooled crops!"

"But my family's starvin', naow!" called a ragged grower.

"How aire we goin' tuh live?" another protested. "The bank shet daown on me eighteen months ago."

"I've got land notes to meet!"

"My woman's sick, an' needs medicine."

"Looky here, how much d'ye think flesh and blood kin stand? We're starvin' naow, I tell you!"

"Order! This meeting will come to order!" called Judge Pace, hammering on the table with his gavel.

"Honest, Mr. Tom, we're on aour uppers, naow! Hit cayent

be you a-standin' up thar askin' us not tuh grow the only crop on the farm that'll bring us a little cash money in hand tuh pay aour debts an' buy coffee an' bakin' sody?"

"We are asking you not to raise a single leaf!" Coyle's voice rang above the discontent.

"That's the craziest thing you've said yet!" came a furious roar from the left center of the ballroom. "Do you think the rich old land hawgs a-fattenin' around me, are going to stop making money hand over fist just because us growers were fools enough to listen to you pool fellers in the first place?"

"When we recommend a cut-out of the 1908 crop, we mean an absolute cut-out!" Coyle shouted down the rising tumult. "And that includes every grower in the burley belt, regardless of whether he's an Equity man or not. Furthermore, you men have overlooked the second part of our recommendation." he rebuked his hecklers sternly, "I repeat: We are asking you tonight to vote a complete cut-out, and then *go home and see to it that the will of the majority rules."*

"Dammit, how?" called a puzzled voice from the center aisle.

"Ways and means will be suggested to you locally," Coyle repeated, with sinister meaning.

A moment of stunned silence greeted his reply. The eyes of every man in the audience sought the speaker's, before turning in bewilderment to their neighbors'. Audible whispers began to run through the rows:

"Naow, what in tarnation does he mean by that?"

"There's only one way I'll ever keep the hog who neighbors with me from growing the weed—and that's by violence."

"Mr. Coyle wouldna permit that!"

"Oh, wouldn't he? You don't know Tom Coyle very well, do you, Scottie?"

"Nae, but I canna think—"

"Hit plumb pleasures me tuh think what I could do!"

"The idea is mighty appealin' tuh me, too."

"An' me—"

"An' me! Hit's somepin a desp-rate man kin sink his teeth into, an' bite down on hard!"

Half turning, America looked back at the roomful of men behind her. A curious hush held them. Poised forward on their chairs, they reminded America of tense and weather-beaten animals crouching to spring. Others, among them Ephraim, leaned almost motionless over the rails of the Juliet balconies. Three hundred men held their breaths, it seemed, while Tom Coyle turned to address the Chair:

"Mr. Chairman, I put my recommendation in the form of a motion: That this convention, made up of delegates representing over sixty per cent of the tobacco growers in the burley belt, vote now to cut out completely the 1908 crop, and then go home, and see that this action is enforced for the common good."

"You have heard the motion," the Chair grimly responded. "Is there a second?"

"Second!"

"I second!"

"Here!"

"Is there any further discussion?"

"Naow, wait a minute, boys—"

"Vote! Vote—"

"Set down, you!"

"We don't aim tuh listen to yer jaw. Set down!"

"We aim to vote! Vote—"

"Order!" thundered the Chairman. "All in favor of Mr. Coyle's motion will please raise their right hands."

Hands, like foam on a choppy sea, came up.

"The vote is unanimous."

"Yee-ee!" screeched Ephraim, leaning far out of his balcony to utter again the earsplitting Rebel yell.

Pandemonium broke loose in the ballroom. The delegates rose, stamped their feet, thumped each other on the back, shouted, took up the Rebel yell, and repeated it until the violence of their demonstration put America in mind of a tidal wave surging shorewards to inundate alike rich and poor, powerful and weak. What, in our desperation, have we done, she asked herself. Yet what is left for us to do except to fight—and perhaps lose—or surrender and starve? If life had proven one truth to her, this truth was that to fight is always preferable to surrender . . .

Looking towards the stage, she saw Stone shaking hands with Tom Coyle. The position of the two black-clad figures—hands clasped, eyes locked in the first long look of victory—reminded her again of the Kentucky state seal and of its grim motto.

"United we stand—but divided we fall," she whispered, nerving herself for the bitter months ahead.

Chapter 17

With the sudden finality of lightning out of thunderheads, the news struck Tuckahoe—night riders have scraped Major Chisholm's plant beds! Hoes grasped in angry hands can make short shrift of tender green seedlings. Several rips of the ghostly canvas, the glint of steel rising and falling in the moonlight, and all prospects of raising a tobacco crop lay reduced to pulpy green, shreds of torn canvas, and the tracks of half a hundred horsemen vanished as swiftly as they had appeared. Before the community had recovered its breath, the same fate overtook Allilee Drake's and Captain Doggett's beds.

"Ma says this is the worst thing that's happened in Mason County since the Indians used to scalp the improvers," quavered Kate Annable, at the May meeting of the Christian Women's Board of Missions held at Timberlawn. "America, this pool idea of yours has split Tuckahoe far worse than the Civil War."

"You ought to be locked up, you rabble rouser!" Allilee Drake flung at America.

"You needn't think you can turn pa aside by a night-riding gang of hoodlums with rags tied across their eyes," sniffled Bethenia Doggett Moncure who with a head cold more than ever resembled a pink-nosed white rabbit. "He's already sent to the mountains for more plants. And if Ephraim won't defend them, pa says he better move—*kachoo!*" Bethenia's defiance dissolved into a watery-eyed paroxysm of sneezing.

"Major Chisholm has four Gatling guns upstairs at Charter

Oak, commanding each of the four approaches," Emarind McCord announced. "He told Cap'n McCord he intends to man them day and night with mountaineers who can really shoot—while hired hands from Limestone set out his crop in the pike fields around the house."

"Ladies, let us proceed with our program," young Anna Cary, the president, tried to pour oil on the rising waters.

"Just because you and Stone have lost two fortunes speculating in tobacco," Allilee spat the accumulating spleen of years at her lifelong rival, "is no reason why you should incite the lowest elements of the population against thrifty law-abiding citizens!"

"Kate, if you'll excuse me, I'll go now," America quietly declined to be drawn into name-calling. "Don't trouble to leave the meeting, please. I'll talk to Cousin Margaret while somebody brings my buggy."

That night America rode with Stone to one of his barns on the back of Children's Chance. As precinct delegate of Tuckahoe, by word of mouth she had called a meeting here of pool members. Built in pioneer days, the barn was supported inside by a log pen. Here young ruffians often gathered, in spite of Stone's threats to turn them over to the sheriff, to fight roosters and drink moonshine with which, to quote the irate law enforcement officers, Lee's Creek flowed.

Approaching the barn, through its wide-flung doors America saw perhaps forty men squatting inside the pen under the murky light of lanterns hung high on the log butts. Several youths had climbed the sides of the pen in an effort to see better, and clung there like monkeys. As Stone and America rode their horses into the barn, the men looked up. For the first time in her life, America gazed into the eyeless faces of a masked mob. When the cocks had been sacked and whiskey jugs set back out of sight, Stone secured silence for her. She spoke from her sidesaddle, her clear voice ringing above the roar of the Creek behind her:

"When you elected me your precinct delegate," America

began, "I felt honored to do anything I could do to further our cause. Before us now lies work ill-fitted to any woman. Yet I am unwilling to resign, lest such a move be misinterpreted by our enemies. So, with your consent, I will delegate certain duties of my office to my husband—"

"Lady, that don't make me mad," called a red-faced young hoodlum clinging like a bat near the top of the pen. "I never was one fer petticoat rule."

"Shet yer drunken mouth, Red," called Jim Barnes. "Go on, Miss Merry."

"Before I leave this meeting, I want you to see Dan Lord and Tugger Blake as I have often seen them," America continued. "Because of their millions—and our own abject need—some of you may have imagined them as more powerful than they really are—as giants! Forty years ago I met Tugger Blake in Charlotte Court House, Virginia, where he and Dan Lord came every autumn to sell rival brands of Durham smokin' mixture. Tugger Blake was a ragged No'th Carolina boy who sat on a cowhide blending chopped leaf—an ignorant mountain boy who boasted he had no use for education. 'Tradin's my pride!' he bragged. And that's all he is today—a greedy, shrewd, cut-throat trader who's grasped every nickel and every opportunity which has come his way until he has millions of dollars with which to fight you now—millions of dollars, but that's all! You aren't fighting Wall Street giants. You're fighting whip-sharp Yankee traders. Is there a man amongst you tonight who in his heart is afraid of a grown-up peddler boy? And now," America concluded, raising her hand to quiet the shout which had answered her challenge, because Stone had impressed on her the necessity of keeping her speech at a low emotional pitch lest the men get out of hand, "my husband will take over the meeting whenever there is work of this kind to be done."

America rode home alone, turned her horse into the avenue to graze and went to bed. Gazing at the pattern on her bedroom wall caused by moonlight shining through the newly leafed maple tree in the front yard, in her mind's eye she visualized the shadowy armies riding—great splay hoofs of work horses, spider legs of show stallions, sure-footed hoofs of sedate buggy mares hammering the hard white roads all over the state —in the dark-fired tobacco belt of southwestern Kentucky, down the wide straight avenues of the Blue Grass, along the high windy ridges and through the deep narrow valleys of the river counties, stirring up clouds of white dust which billowed behind them, drowning out the whistle of mockingbirds newly mated and singing in thickets silvery with dogwood, sweet with the heavy locust bloom that presages an abundant crop year . . .

Shoulder to shoulder with the embattled growers, America realized, might soon be riding the socially irresponsible—if indeed they were not already in the Equity ranks tonight! Idle share-croppers who had stealthily bridled a work mule or colt in their landlord's back pasture; ne'er-do-well sons of the impoverished rural gentry, weaklings who would rather ride by night than work by day; and the riffraff of the market towns, the bar-flies and ruffians who saw in the farmers' desperate last stand the chance for free sport livelier than any to be bought in gambling den or brothel on the wrong side of the tracks—all these also might be riding tonight! Even the men of conscience were praying for Heavenly guidance before they threw leg over saddle. She recalled a whispered conversation she had overheard in the waiting-room of Dalton's livery stable in Limestone, while her buggy mare was being hitched: "Thar in the stable loft a-kneelin' on the hay with his Sunday-go-to-meetin' clothes on, was Elder Simpson, askin' the Lord to forgive him 'cause he felt obliged to go chop up Cap'n Doggett's plant beds. Then with his face shinin' wet, he climbed down the ladder, hoisted himself onto his ol' mare, an' went clippity-cloppin' away!"

Life, thought America, watching the moonlight ripple in like water over her bedroom window sill, brings us back to where we started. She had spent her girlhood lying awake nights in terror lest the Yankees burn Golden Hill, lest her father and brothers be killed. Now, in her old age, she lay tormented by the same oppressive fear for Children's Chance, for Ephraim—for young Fant—for Stone—perhaps for all three?

I am not the only woman lying sleepless on Tuckahoe, she tried to rationalize her dread. Abigail MacGower and brown-eyed Jeannie are counting the hours while Jamie sleeps the sleep of physical exhaustion, if he can. Up at Foxden, Effie May with her wilted-flower face is trying to understand this God's country feud which divides mother and son. Even in far-away Chicago, High Jinks may be watching the clock for daylight to bring comparative safety to her twelve-year-old daughter Adelia, come at Major Chisholm's insistence to spend the summer at Charter Oak, but forbidden by him to ride down the pike to visit her other grandparents at Children's Chance.

Suppose the Night Riders start settling personal animosities under cover of the Cut-Out, as Ephraim had said unruly elements in the Ku-Klux Klan had done during Reconstruction? Stone had foes a plenty in town and county, as had she. "A man," she had proudly written only last week in one of her editorials, "is known by his enemies as well as by his friends." She thought again of Stone galloping his wild young horse at the head of sober farmers turned night rider, of cock-fighters, whiskey drinkers and town scum, the mob which had lifted its masked face to stare at her from the murky pen-barn floor . . .

Turning restlessly in bed, America told herself she would not sleep before dawn if she thus allowed her thoughts to follow her husband on his grim duties all over the county. Perhaps she could relax better if she tried to count sheep? In her mind's eye she saw Major Chisholm's flock lying dead in the pike meadow around the horseshoe pond which until last week had held sweet water for a hundred years. On her way to Limestone, from the road America had seen the Major standing in his field supervising the digging of a burial trench for his poisoned livestock. Beside the eighty-year-old man a little girl stood bareheaded, with the May sunshine bright on her chestnut curls. "You mustn't feel too badly if Adelia doesn't get down to Children's Chance this summer," High Jinks had written, apologetically. "Bayard one day shares the Major's opinion that all Equity signers are rabble-rousing outlaws, then after he has talked with Chicago conservatives pooh-poohs the Cut-Out as a tempest in a very small agrarian teapot. Both of us honestly wanted to keep Adelia home this summer. But after she and the Major begged so hard, it seemed a pity to deprive them of their happy summer together. Adelia has inherited more from you than her pretty hair. Even the Major admits she has your talent for farming."

Up and down Tuckahoe the bluegrass was rising to heavy-headed splendor, the hollows were white with berry bloom, vagrant breezes chased cloud shadows across the pastel hills. Yet where on Tuckahoe was spring's bright renaissance of joy, of kindliness and of the will to work mightily in the pleasant sunshine? On Tuckahoe in May of 1908 only women toiled heavy-hearted in poultry yard and garden, while their men slept by day or rode and watched the grim nights through . . .

As he eased his tired old body into his favorite chair placed near the Gatling gun in the upper front hall at Charter Oak, Major Alastair Chisholm told himself he was much too old a man to be carrying on like this with his neighbors. Neck deep in the Equity fight as he was, how could he back out now? He also regretted that he had insisted on Adelia's coming down to spend the summer with him. Sight of the poisoned livestock had almost put the sensitive child to bed. Adults, too, at Charter Oak were in crying need of a good night's sleep. Moreover, the loaded Gatling guns, one of which commanded each approach to his square Georgian mansion and overlooked the tobacco growing in his house fields, were damn' dangerous. He had given public notice that he had secured these fieldpieces, and crews to man them, as necessary to the defense of his constitutional rights, but he knew his announcement had been generally laughed off as an old soldier's boast. If he didn't watch sharp, somebody was apt to get hurt bad around here. Every mealtime he cautioned the mountaineers manning his guns, that no shots were to be fired until he himself expressly gave the command for each round. He knew those Rowan County wildcats, he had seen their grandpaps fight at Shiloh! Something about tonight put him in mind of the moon coming over the rolling Tennessee hills.

"It's the mockin' birds," he identified the memory, speaking his thoughts aloud in this old man's habit which he despised.

"Birds don't sing like that in Chicago," declared Adelia, appearing barefooted in her bedroom doorway.

"Delie, whit are ye daein' up at this 'oor?" scolded the Major, fondly. "Gang tae bed, chiel. Ye need y'r-r rest."

"I couldn't sleep—for the birds singing. Listen—they've stopped!"

"Gang tae bed, Adelia," declared the Major in a stern voice, although his heart sank. Birds have sharp ears, they can hear unaccustomed noises far away, such as the beat of many horses' hoofs pounding the hard white turnpike way down the ridge.

"Grandpa, don't you hear something—like drums a long way off?" insisted the nervous child.

"Mistah Majuh, dey's a-coming, de Night Ridahs is a-comin'!" called Uncle Ben from below stairs. A moment later, pulling on his white house coat, the old negro emerged out of the dark well of the stairs.

"Wha's comin' but pair white trash—wha run a' nicht wi' rags ower th' een they widna daur show in th' licht!" scoffed the Major, calm as he drew off the oilcloth laid over the gun to protect it from the damp night air. "Ben, haud th' lassie on y'rr lap in th' chimney nook, whaur ye canna be seen—or hit by a stray bullet."

"I can hear horses, now," announced Adelia.

"They're nearin' th' brig in Glade Springs glen," agreed the Major.

Like tribal drums the beat of many horses' hoofs reverberated hollowly on the ancient bridge timbers, then struck the hard roadbed beyond. Glancing around from his gunsight, the Major noticed with satisfaction that Adelia in her white nightgown was out of sight behind the jutting inside chimney and that Blaylock, the smartest of his three mountain men, stood in the north bedroom doorway awaiting orders.

"Dinna fire till I gi'e ye th' wor-rd," the Major repeated, "but dinna let 'em set foot on your-r step."

"We'll stop them bobcats cold in thar tracks," nodded Blaylock. "Shore you can manage aout here?"

"I dinna plan tae fire a shot!"

Watching through the opened front hall door that led out onto the ornamental iron balcony, the Major saw swift shapes racing over the crest of the hill to the northeast of Charter Oak. Like ghosts of John Peel, a few soared over the rail fence. Others wheeled sharply, their horses' shoes striking sparks on the roadbed, and streamed like dark water through the pike gate. All avoided the pale carriage road curving between the double line of oak trees grown from Charter Oak acorns planted by the Major's mother, a Wadsworth from Connecticut, who had also named the Chisholm stronghold on Tuckahoe. Streaking through moonshine and shadow, the heavy sod of the avenue muffling the sound of their approach, the horsemen raced for the stable lane to the left of the mansion.

"Major, kin I pick off them varmints one by one—as they come through the lane gate?" demanded Blaylock, appearing again in the north bedroom doorway.

"Nae, mon!" barked the Major. "Th' witless gowks hae wives an' weans."

"I cain't vouch fer that, but you're missin' a mighty purty shot," grieved Blaylock, and disappeared.

From the direction of the tobacco barns to the northwest of the house a rosy glow came creeping through the boxwood garden.

"Ben, whit aboot th' beasties?" called the Major, busy with the complicated cartridge cylinders.

"Dey's all pisoned, boss."

"Aye," agreed the Major. "It slippit ma mind."

On the wall of the upper hall, reflected from the north bedroom windows, pinkish light rose and fell. The Major hoped that Adelia could not see it, until he realized that from where she sat she could probably see the conflagration itself through the west bedroom windows. With the fire glow came the sound of men's ribald voices and of horses trampling on the shells of the boxwood garden. The trimmed forms gave horsemen shelter in which to gather strength for a frontal attack on the house.

"Come on, boys," shouted a drunken voice. "Le's smoke the old badger aout."

"Shore, an' reason with him."

"I've got a good persuader here. Hit's t'other end of the rope that fired his big terbacker barn."

Thirty horsemen, the Major estimated swiftly, were gathering in the boxwood garden to charge the lawn which curved in a wide semicircle around the mansion's front. Looking down through the iron grille of the small balcony, the pink-white columns of his porch, the hunter's green velvet lawn, the foam-flecked horses and masked men appeared as unreal to the Major as the scene and actors in a Walter Scott novel read before the library fire on a snowy winter's evening. As he watched, three Night Riders grouped together, then one came to the nearest boxwood, while the others spurred their horses through the farther darkness as if to charge the house from three sides.

"Stay, men—or I'll open fire!" called the Major in a ringing voice he had not used since Shiloh.

With scant heed to his warning, the Rider behind the boxwood trotted his horse crazily out onto the open lawn. Reining in with his left hand, in his right he raised an automatic and emptied its chambers point-blank at the iron balcony. Two of the bullets pinged into the ceiling above the Major. Something stung his right leg above the knee. It might have been a bullet ricochetting from some metal object in the upper hall wall, or one of the sleepy hornets, now aroused, which had wintered in the casing of the side lights. Too intent on watching for the other two Riders to come charging out of the shadows towards the porch, the Major paid no attention to his leg.

"Red, you drunken fool!" called an angry voice from the garden. "What d'you mean—firing like that? You know we never fire first—"

"Aw naow, John Willy, I was only a-shootin' into the air," answered the tipsy horseman on the terrace. "I jes' aimed tuh scare the ole coot, so's he'd come on daown hyah—an' we could use my persuader on him."

"Come back here, Red—before I ride out and get you!" warned John Willy's impatient voice.

As if encouraged by John Willy's threat, the two Riders in the outlying shrubbery charged for the front porch. Up the bright green lawn they came, the glare of burning barns on their masked faces. A moment more, and they might be out of range—at the front step. With an odd sensation of regret, something he had not remembered from his artillery stand at Shiloh, the Major squeezed the trigger.

The Gatling gun spat a long clicking stream of lead far more deadly than Blaylock's profanity, of which it reminded the Major. Four horses were down on the lawn. Two thrashed in death agony, one tried to rise on three legs, the fourth scrambled up and galloped whinnying with alarm off into the darkness. Apparently unhurt, two Riders gained their feet and made the shrubbery in safety. A third, the tipsy Red, lay motionless with his outflung hand still clutching his emptied revolver. With a stab of regret sharper than the pain in his own hurt leg, the Major recognized the fourth horseman whom he had downed, as John Willy Barnes. Raising himself on his elbows, John Willy tried to drag his body, helpless below the waist, beyond reach of the flailing hoofs of the wounded horses.

"Come help John Willy!" shouted the Major, and directed

several well aimed shots at the struggling horses, quieting them. "I'll haud ma fire."

Half a dozen Riders darted on foot out of the garden, seized John Willy and Red and carried them to a triangle boxwood to the right of the porch, the shelter nearest at hand. From the garden arose excited voices:

"Boys, le's burn the house!"

"I'll go git some kerosene daown to the store at Tuckahoe—"

"Look on the back porch. They's always a can of coal oil on the back porch."

"We've Gatling guns covering every entrance, and men to fire them!" warned Major Chisholm, from above.

"We don't believe you!" shouted back a Rider, in doubtful defiance.

"Hear the ol' rooster crow—"

"You, there!" challenged Stone's angry voice approaching from the stable lane. "What're you doing—fighting an old man and a little girl?"

"They're fightin' us, ain't they?" called back a defensive voice.

"Yeah, an' they've done fer Red—an' maybe John Willy, too," another Rider complained.

"Is John Willy seriously hurt?" demanded Stone, spurring his colt in full view across the lawn towards the shrubbery where rescuers squatted over John Willy.

"Purty bad," answered one, looking up.

"Take him over to Cary's Grove," commanded Stone, wheeling his horse and trotting towards the iron balcony, his unmasked face chalk-white as he called up: "Oh, Major! Throw us down some quilts, will you—so we can carry off our wounded?"

Attempting to stand, the Major felt his leg collapse under him. He would have fallen, had he not caught himself on the gun mount. Stone's upturned face and the lawn behind it swam dizzily before the Major's eyes. His leg must be bleeding worse than he had thought; but he couldn't stop to bother with it now, with the battle half won and Adelia there in the chimney corner. If the sight of the poisoned lambs had bothered her so, a little human blood might scare her out of her wits.

"Ben, bring some bedding—quick!" called the Major, supporting his injured leg.

"You ain't talkin' tuh me, boss—wid bullets flyin' 'round lak bees!" chattered the house servant.

"Y' damned auld crow, dae as I tell ye!"

"I'll get them, grandpa."

"Delie, bide whaur ye be!"

"Here they are, sir," Adelia spoke at his side in a surprisingly short interval. His head was swimming so, the Major could hardly see her. He struggled to rise, to carry the bedding out onto the balcony. His leg refused again to support him, and yet he hated to confess before Adelia that he was downed.

"I'll throw them out for you, grandpa," the courageous child volunteered. "You stick by your gun."

"Delia, stay awa'!"

Barefooted in her candy-striped nightdress, Adelia stepped out onto the balcony, bundled the quilts over the rail, ran into the hall and scurried to her chimney corner. Bracing himself against the sides of the gun mount, the Major watched through the balcony grille. On the grass below the bedding was spread out, the dead and wounded laid upon it. A man at each corner, while a fifth followed leading their horses, the impromptu stretchers were carried sagging in the middle across the lawn towards the carriage road.

"Come away, men! There's been enough blood shed here tonight," Stone marshaled his forces.

"You ain't aimin' tuh spare the ol' rooster, be you, Mister Stone?" challenged a Rider, plaintively.

"Didn't you see him save John Willy from under those horses' hoofs?" Stone called back across his shoulder, as he walked his colt down the lawn to follow the procession moving up the carriage road pale between the darker mass of oaks on each side of the avenue.

"Tha's so," agreed another voice. "If he hadn't finished those critters, one of 'em wudda struck John Willy shore."

"Wal, if you and Mister Stone say so—"

"Mister Stone's the boss."

"Hosses, shake a leg!"

Singly and in groups, the Night Riders darted from the garden across the strip of lawn towards the protecting darkness of the avenue trees. Like a single mourner, Stone plodded on after the stretcher bearers. The first had already reached the pike gate and was turning towards Cary's Grove. Along the avenue fences the Night Riders raced away as wraithlike as they had come to Charter Oak. On the front lawn, no longer hunter's green with white fire glare, lay the three dead horses, one with a hind leg grotesquely upthrust.

"Grandpa!" called Adelia, venturing out of her chimney corner. "Are they gone—is the battle won?"

"Aye, chiel—" whispered the Major, struggling to hold himself erect. "Bring a licht, Ben—an' some towels—for ma leg."

"Mistah Majuh, is you hurt? Is you hurt bad? Gawd-A'mighty, lookit that pool ob blood!" gasped the negro, striking a match. "Ketch him, Miss Delie, he's keelin' ovah! Doan' let him hit his haid—"

In the pink glow of the upper hall, Adelia and Uncle Ben eased the fainting Major onto the floor. Blaylock and his men came running from the bedrooms. Gatling guns, the Cut-Out, even ten acres of non-pooled tobacco seemed of little importance now compared to the ebbing life of one brave old man.

When she heard strange men's voices calling her from the side yard below her bedroom window at Children's Chance, America sat up rigid with alarm. So they have come to summon me, she tried to steel herself, to watch Stone die.

"Hit's John Willy, ma'am!" shouted Horace Bacon from below. "Will you ring up the doctor—an' then come yourself? John Willy's been a-callin' for you ever since he was first hit."

"Where is he?"

"At Cary's Grove. I'll get your horse."

Standing shivering in her kimona before the call box of the new Mason County mutual telephone, America ground until she awakened a sleepy Central, who promised to keep on ringing Limestone until the emergency summons was delivered to Doctor Gillespie. Tossing bandages and Stone's brandy flask into an egg basket, America mounted her horse and led the way up the pike. Clattering past Foxden, she was relieved to see its massive chimneys thrust against the eastern stars. Along the yard fences plant-bed cotton no longer stretched ghostly in the moonlight.

At his white front door, Ulysses Cary met her with a kerosene lamp held high. Its light fell over his snowy hair and the old-fashioned nightshirt he wore.

"His back's broke," whispered Ulysses, opening the doors into the handsome double parlors.

John Willy lay on a carved Federal sofa. Although he was still wrapped in Chisholm quilts, his teeth chattered and his lips bore the telltale stains of pulmonary hemorrhage. From the shallowness of his breath, America realized the end could not be far off.

"Are you in pain, John Willy?" she whispered, sitting beside him on a low chair someone thrust forward for her, and feeling in her basket for her flask.

"No, ma'am—not now," he gasped.

"Drink this," she ordered, slipping her arm under his head. "The doctor 'll be here any minute—Doctor Gillespie, from Limestone."

"You're the only doctor I need now, ma'am," whispered John Willy, smiling at her. "I've been lying here worryin' for fear you wouldn't get here in time—in time to hear somethin' I want to say to you."

She took his cold hand in her strong warm palms, before she asked tenderly:

"What is it, John Willy?"

"Miss Merry, you were the first person on Tuckahoe—who had faith in me," gasped the shallow voice. "When ever'body else was a-pushing me down, you held out a hand to me—you helped me pull myself up."

"I've always believed in you, John Willy," she declared earnestly, thinking of the difference between this eager soul and her own young Fant. With every man's hand actually against him, John Willy had reached for education and a high place in community regard. Her sulky Ishmael, imagining himself an outcast because he did not have faith even to trust his own mother, had turned his back on the birthright of his gentle blood and had sunk without a struggle to the level of his inferiors. John Willy had courageously faced greater obstacles and had risen far above them. "You've made a brave, hard fight—and you've won," she continued. "Only last night Stone was saying the growers mean to run you for the state legislature—for the unselfish way you've served them—and asked nothing in return but their gratitude and good will."

Watching the pleased light shine in his eyes, she wanted to say more. His time, she saw, was running short. What else could she say to console him? "You've been a true soldier, John Willy—"

"No, Miss Merry—you did the soldiering!" the weak voice contradicted her. "Many's the time—paw and I 'lowed on how game you were. You never said a word when ever'body was despisin' you. Now I can tell you—I used to call you—my good angel, like the storybooks said. All my hard fightin' years—I loved you—a long way off—for what you helped me make o' myself."

Dropping on her knees, she slid her arm under his shoulders and answered, winking away her tears:

"I've loved you too, John Willy. You were my star pupil. And I've never been so proud of you as I am tonight."

"Oh, Miss Merry! It's been my fondest dream to hear you say that—to live in a fine house like this—and hear you say that," gasped John Willy, struggling with the habit of years against the approaching darkness. "When I'd feel myself—slipping back—I'd ask myself—what would Miss Merry say? And just thinking about you—would help me pull myself up again—pull myself—up again—" The tortured body stiffened, the glazing eyes shone with a last swift gleam: "I can't—seem to pull—any more. Miss Merry, I—"

For a few moments America remained on her knees to gaze at John Willy's face majestic now in the frozen look of death. After she had drawn the quilt over his head, America arose and turned to the several persons whom she heard weeping behind her in the room. In the doorway stood a twelve-year-old girl with High Jinks' eyes, and her own bright hair under a Red Riding Hood bonnet.

"Adelia—my precious child!" cried America, stretching her arms hungrily towards the forlorn little figure which continued to stand motionless in the doorway.

"I'm sorry, grandma," declared Adelia, in the toneless voice of an obedient child. "But grandpa Chisholm made me promise not to speak to you."

"What is it, my dear?" asked Ulysses Cary, recovering his composure.

"Are you Mr. Cary?"

"That's me, missy. What can I do for you?"

"I'm Major Chisholm's great granddaughter, Adelia Langston. Will you please come over to Charter Oak—and help me, sir? The mountain men have run away—'cause Mr. Blaylock said they couldn't afford to have folks find them there. And Uncle Ben's so scared he won't set foot outside the house."

"Where's the Major?" demanded Ulysses Cary, his voice sharp with alarm. "What's the matter with the Major?"

"Gran'pa's dead," whispered Adelia, her set white face breaking down into that of a terrified heart-broken child. "He bled to death from a stray bullet, Mr. Blaylock said. He wouldn't tell us he was hit—and he wouldn't leave his gun—for fear the mountain men might shoot too soon and hurt s-somebody b-bad, he said."

Once the non-pooled tobacco crops were out on the hill-sides, little could be done except to let them grow. Everyone realized that Night Rider violence would break out again while the leaf was curing in the barns or when it was being hauled to market. America considered it her manifest duty during July and August to try and coax the non-pool growers on Tuckahoe to join the Equity Society. Approaching the Drake tobacco patch, America saw Allilee seated on an old kitchen chair with a shotgun across her knees. Among the spreading leaves, Allilee's two nephews, Kit and Theodore Gunther, were breaking out suckers.

"Allilee," began America, "don't you think you're taking a gross advantage of your sex? You know this crop wouldn't stand overnight if you were a man."

"It's a pity you didn't think of yours," lisped Allilee through her new false teeth, "when you flaunted yourself on the Cin-cinnati hogshead breaks—to wheedle a few extra pennies out of the buyers."

"You'll hurt yourself with that gun if you're not careful," sniffed America. Here she and Allilee stood calling each other names like two old fishwives at Billings-gate. Even their rivalry over Fant Annable hadn't been able to bring about this de-grading spectacle!

On her way home, America stopped at Foxden. Effie May was at the woodpile chopping kindling for her supper fire. Her three youngsters recognized America and charged her with whoops of delight.

"Why don't you make Fant do that for you, my dear?" America greeted the gentle mountain girl whose uncomplain-ing acceptance of Foxden's drudgery called to America's mind the years she herself had slaved here with every hand on Tuck-ahoe Ridge raised against her.

"I ain't complainin' none," smiled Effie May.

"Where's Fant?" continued America, distributing stick candy to her grandchildren.

"Oh, he's somewhars abaout the place," evaded Effie May, reaching for her axe again.

"He had plants to sell—and it would be just like him to try and grow leaf hidden away somewhere," declared America. "I've a good mind to walk out to the walnut grove—there's ground a plenty concealed in the middle of that grove to raise three acres of tobacco."

"In Breathitt County, feudin' comes nach'rel as mornin' dew," Effie May changed the subject. "What I cain't puzzle aout daown here is how families kin feud amongst 'emselves—like you and Fant."

"There are some things stronger than family ties, Effie May," America sought for simple words which none the less would convey the magnitude of the Equity cause. "We in the pool are fighting for something much bigger than money in our pockets—or clan loyalty. We're fighting for our homes and our farms—not just for this year, but for the future—for our children's and our grandchildren's futures. Isn't that bigger—and stronger—than mere family ties?"

"Fer a woman, thar ain't nuthin' stronger—or more lastin' —than her own flesh 'n' blood," contradicted Effie May.

"Fant must have talked to you so much against the pool," America replied, meeting the younger woman's eyes, "I suppose you just can't see there are two sides to this question."

"He don't talk much, ma'am. All he says is that Foxden's his castle—an' tuh let 'em come. Hit's a fine big log house," conceded Effie with a prideful glance towards the stalwart chimneys, "but I wouldn't call hit no castle."

"Effie May, will you do something for me?" demanded America, abruptly.

"That depends, ma'am—"

"If I send Weed up the pike with the carriage as soon as I can get home, will you bring your youngsters to Children's

Chance—and stay with me till the Cut-Out's over? The Night Riders won't hurt you while you're with Stone and me. And if you come, Fant might follow—"

"No, ma'am. He wouldn't."

"Then will you go home and visit your own people?" begged America. "I'll pay your way—and send you money every month to live on."

"An' leave Fant here?" Effie May rebuked her with a smile.

In mid-August, America rode down the pike to the Bierbower place which Jamie MacGower had bought with Abigail's help. Tying her bridle reins through one of the iron rings in the ancient retaining wall which kept the steep yard and stone house from slipping down onto the pike, America climbed the rough limestone steps up the hillside. When she paused occasionally to catch her breath, America noticed the beds of petunias, marigolds and asters Jeannie MacGower had coaxed into gay bloom in rock-held beds on the steep lawn. Looking down across the road, she approved the well-kept outbuildings and neat barn, until second thought told her that the patch of non-pooled tobacco which shone like an immense green postage stamp stuck on an envelope of brown wheat stubble in Lee's Creek bottom was paying for this husbandlike plenty. She found Jeannie and her girls shelling butter beans in the sun-dappled grape arbor.

"Good-afternoon, Jeannie," panted America, her back to the house. "How are you, girls?"

"Fetch Miss Merry a chair," Jeannie acknowledged the greeting without enthusiasm and bent her sleek brown head over her dishpan of beans.

"Where's your grandmother, Abbie?"

"Dinna ye come honeyin' around me as if butter wudna melt in your-r mouth, America Moncure!" called Mrs. MacGower, hobbling out on her cane. In her left hand she carried a scrap of paper which she waved indignantly in America's face, continuing: "Tell me th' truth—did ye or did ye not leave this in our-r mail box?"

America took the folded half-page of cheap tablet paper. On the outside was scrawled Jamie's name. Inside was a crude drawing of a barn in flames and of a black snake whip coiled around a human skull. Across the top of the page was printed by an unskilled hand:

"Join the pool or—"

"Abigail," began America, refolding the note before she handed it back, her steady gaze meeting the blazing eagle eyes of the old Scotchwoman, "if you really believe I sent this to Jamie, then our forty years of friendship have been in vain. Good-day to you, ma'am—until you come to your senses."

Throughout the burley belt, the promise of the heavy locust bloom held true. What tobacco crops were growing, yellowed early, were cut and cured in ideal dry hot weather without a trace of house burn. Like a mischievous child which has accomplished all the devilment it can devise, and then sits back to enjoy the discomfiture of its elders, nature rested in a long Indian summer. Over the pumpkin-studded fields, the harvest moon swung high.

Cloppity-clop! Cloppity-clod!

The drumming of horses' hoofs awakened America. Sitting up in bed, she listened. Far up the turnpike the staccato beat sounded without a break. Dressing quickly, America hurried downstairs and out onto the rear north porch. Around the corner of the house, Weed came buckling the belt of his ragged cotton breeches.

"Weed, where's my horse?" demanded America, knowing what she must do.

"In de fiel', ma'am."

"Then I'll have to go on foot—"

"Lawdy, Miss Merry, whar you gwine in shoes dis time ob night?"

"To the MacGowers," she answered, her head bent as she laced her oxfords.

"Gawda'Mighty, ma'am, you cain't do dat!"

"I've got to. Stay here and watch the house."

"I's comin' wid you—"

"Thank you, Weed, but this is no fight of yours."

As she ran up the stable lane, she glanced at the quarter moon. Yellow as cheese, it hung in the western sky over the ridgepole of Stone's big tobacco barn. Three o'clock—dawn would break in perhaps an hour, the blessed dawn which sends night hunters to cover. They had not stopped at Foxden, else she would have seen the fire glow up the ridge.

She ran out the ridge path and down the steep hill. In her nostrils was the smell of dust on ragweed, in her ears the sound of horses trotting swiftly down the grade. From where she slipped and stumbled, on the rough path, she could see the Night Riders moving against the opposite side of the hill. She reached the hollow, jumped across the stepping-stones laid in the branch and ran up the shoulder of the road. Ahead of her the Bierbower place lay a quarter of a mile farther down the pike.

In a black knot, the main group of Night Riders sat their horses below the limestone retaining wall. As America ran towards them, she saw others drag a struggling white-shirted figure down the top flight of hillside steps. That must be Jamie MacGower, in shirt and dark trousers, America decided. Behind the group, another Rider was picking his way down with a lighted kerosene lamp held aloft. Above the stamp and movement of horses in the road, America heard a mountain voice eloquently curse the darkness.

"Throw that lamp thisaway onto the crib!" shouted someone in the crowd on the road.

"Yeah, that'll give plenty of light!"

A roar of approval greeted these suggestions. On the steps, the lamp-bearer wound up with exaggerated precision, and flung the lighted lamp. Its chimney dropped off. With wick smoking and the kerosene churning inside, the lamp performed a graceful parabola over the heads of the horsemen, crashed against the tinder dry shingles of the crib roof and spattered in all directions what appeared to be liquid fire, so quickly did the kerosene ignite. Tobacco barn and outbuildings were doomed, America saw at a glance. While everybody was looking at the corncrib catch fire, America pushed her way through sweaty horses' shoulders and swung herself up onto the retaining wall. Between her and Jamie MacGower were half a dozen dismounted Riders and the well of the limestone steps.

The men who had dragged Jamie MacGower out of bed stood holding him quietly halfway down the hillside steps. They were too preoccupied watching the fire leap from crib to chicken house to notice him. The chicken-house door was padlocked, but from within came the excited cackle of fowls rising in a crescendo of alarm above the roar of the flames: *Cock-cock-cock-coo! Cock-cock-cock-coo!* Stooping, America seized several small stones lying loose on the top of the wall and hurled them through the glass in the chicken-house windows. Cackling frenziedly, a few hens flew out and disappeared in the darkness before the way of escape was choked by others. To the smell of wood smoke was added the reek of burning feathers.

Her stone-throwing drew the Night Riders' attention to where she stood on the wall beyond the steps. Someone recognized her with a ribald shout:

"Howdye, Americy Moncure!"

"We was sent daown hyar tuh wash your dirty clothes fer you, Miss Merry!"

"Next week you kin send yer menfolks up to do us a like favor, eh, boys?"

Embers from crib and chicken house sucked upwards by the flames were falling on the roof of Jamie's tobacco barn. Here the mossy shingles, powder-dry, were blazing merrily in a dozen places. The brisk little fires put America in mind of one of the Doré engravings of Dante's *Inferno* which she used to study in the Golden Hill library on Sunday afternoons when secular subjects were forbidden. Under her eyes, the barn roof seemed to gather itself and spring skyward in a single sheet of fire. The intense white light it shed illuminated sharp vignettes of barnyard life which were noted without comprehension and then forgotten. A white-faced calf panted with its head out of the smoking stable window, and a black sow and spotted pigs charged frantically around the narrow confines of their pen.

"Bring him daown onto the top o' the wall!" The Night Riders' attention swung back to Jamie.

"Thar's plenty o' light thar, naow," called the jocular voice which had suggested throwing the lamp.

Down the steps ahead of them the Riders thrust their prisoner. One of them, a masked giant, had Jamie MacGower's right arm. Outnumbered a hundred to one, the Scot was struggling silently with the courage of the desperate. With grunts and curses, his captors shoved him onto the top of the retaining wall, where he wrenched himself free and stood erect with what dignity he could muster, in the hot glare of his burning outbuildings.

"Make him join the pool!" yelled the group of horsemen on the pike.

"We'll fix it so you can't fatten off your neighbors this year!" growled the masked Rider at Jamie's right shoulder.

"Make him join the pool!" clamored other voices from the road. "Who's got the paper?"

"Make him sign the paper, Shad—"

"Make him join the pool!"

"Men, I canna," Jamie shouted above the fire. "I hae made obleegations tae pay for ma land. When 'tis mine, I'll gladly join wi' ye, but fur-rst I maun pay ma just debts."

"Maybe we better reason with him a bit, eh, boys?"

"What's the damn' furriner sayin', does anybody know?"

"He's no foreigner!" called America, and leaped onto the wall beside Jamie. "Men, I've known Jamie MacGower for over thirty years. He used to go to school to me. He's got a mistaken idea he's under some sort of conscientious obligation to meet his land notes—before he can come into the pool. Let him go, men—let him obey his conscience! You've taught him a lesson—look at his barns! There'll be no leaf sold off this farm this year—or for years to come."

"We ain't begun to lesson this schoolboy yet," interrupted the big Rider at Jamie's right shoulder. Before he realized what she meant to do, America stepped closer and jerked the mask from his face.

"You can't talk to me with a rag across your eyes, Shad Chewe!" she cried, hotly.

"Git goin', Shad!" reminded a voice from the road.

"Shore, what's keeping you?" came another.

Chewe turned to take something from the man behind him. America stepped closer to Jamie, whispering:

"Sign—for God's sake!"

"I canna, ma'am. Ma conscience—"

"They'll kill you!"

"I canna sign."

"Git busy up thar, or we'll lend a hand!"

"Step aside, Miss Merry. We don't aim tuh let this tight Scotchman git rich offa our misfortune."

"We won't hurt him none!"

"No, indeedy! You wouldn't hurt a flea now, would you, Shad?"

From all sides came the jeering cries. America looked down on the sea of faces upturned towards her. With black masks hiding their eyes, mouths dripping tobacco juice, teeth decayed, jaws unshaven and gaunt, the faces of the horsemen looked inhuman in the flickering glare cast by the flaming destruction below. Even the ribald-drunk appeared unnatural in their mirth. A moment later, two Riders seized America's arms from behind and pulled her away. She struggled to break loose from them but they held her good-naturedly, without paying much heed to her struggles except to make sure that she did not get free.

All eyes were turned towards what was taking place on the other section of the wall. Several Riders flung Jamie face downwards on the rocks, so forcibly that blood stained the grey limestone. While Shad was removing his coat, a hand reached up from below, and snatched off Jamie's torn shirt. Other hands clutched for it, tore out a sleeve, mounted it over a rifle butt and flapped it comically above the heads of the crowd. When Shad stepped forward with his whip, the crowd hushed its mirth.

As the blacksnake rose and fell, America turned away her head. There was no sound now except the roar of the fire, the impact of rawhide on flesh, and the gasping grunts with which the stoic Scot received the blows. Not since America's childhood, when once she had slipped away to watch a negro being publicly flogged for fault in the Charlotte courthouse yard, had she witnessed this spectacle of violence. What was the difference between black flesh under rawhide then, and this white flesh being cut to ribbons tonight? If the enslavement of black flesh for economic gain was wrong—and evil enough to plunge a nation justifiably into fraternal war—what about this monstrous system of profit and greed which was making wolves out of peaceable farmers, so that they ran in packs at night to pull down and destroy their own kind?

With the berserk strength which came to her in times of crisis, America wrenched herself free, sprang towards Chewe and, seizing the whipstock as he was swinging it for the downstroke, wrested it from his startled grasp. Turning onto the crowd below, she shrieked at them in a voice which she did not recognize as her own:

"You fools, you're killing the wrong man! It's Tugger Blake—and the trust—you're fighting—not a poor farmer like yourselves!"

"What's making you blow cold, Americy Moncure—against the Cut-Out you suggested yourself?" called someone.

"This isn't the Cut-Out—this is murder!" America shouted back. "I told you before—no leaf can be sold off this farm this year. Haven't you shed enough blood for tonight?"

"We ain't won, have we?" the man who had joked about the lamp heckled her.

"Dan Lord ain't give in—an' bought our leaf—like you promised he would do," complained another voice from the mob.

"Look, men, it's almost dawn," America tried another argument. Turning, with the whipstock she pointed to the greying east along the crest of the hill above them.

"Gawda'Mighty, Shad, lookit—hit's daybreak!"

"Come on, men, we can't be seen!"

"Your quickest way to the county line is through Dover," advised America, thinking fast that Dover lay in the opposite direction from Foxden.

"Hosses, shake a leg!"

"You can have your schoolboy now, Mrs. Moncure," Shad Chewe declared. "Give me my whip, please."

Wishing it were the other end, she flung the rawhide towards him. Below, on the road, the Night Riders were wheeling their horses. To America's relief, they took her suggestion and went thundering down the pike towards Dover. Chewe and two local men galloped up the hill towards Tuckahoe and Limestone. These three alone, America realized, would not dare challenge Foxden.

Down the long flight of stone steps Jeannie MacGower came running in her ruffled calico dressing gown. Firelight shone on the tears rolling down her cheeks. America, bending over Jamie to feel for a heartbeat under his striped left ribs, called up to reassure her:

"He's alive, Jeannie!"

Her field-calloused feet strong on the uncertain steps, Jeannie descended to the top of the wall. Without words, she bent at her husband's knees. America took his shoulders, and they struggled with Jamie's dead weight up the steep flight. Almost at the top, Jeannie eased her man's buttocks onto the ledge, and began to look about with anxious eyes.

"Catch your breath as long as you need," agreed America, thankfully.

"It's nae thot."

"What're you looking for?"

"He wudna want his bairns tae see his back like this."

"Here—take my jacket."

"I'm muckle obleeged," Jeannie panted with dignity, and they bent to their load again.

Big-eyed and solemn in their decent cotton nightgowns, the MacGower children stood aside to watch their father being carried into his house. Abigail MacGower went hobbling ahead with a kerosene lamp to light them into the family room. They laid Jamie on the rumpled double bed against the wall. With the lamp held high, the Widow MacGower gazed down at her son.

"I canna thole it," she whispered as if to herself, and then her eyes lifted to America's, blazed through her tears as she continued: "God's curse be on ye, America Moncure! Ye hae sown th' wind—but th' whirlwind's raged aboot th' heids o' th' innocent. May ye see your-r ain bairn lyin' some nicht as I see ma Jamie noo!"

"Abigail, I did all I could—I saved his life!" cried America, aghast.

"Dinna heed her, ma'am," Jeannie whispered at the washstand where she was pouring water into a basin to revive her husband, to bathe his bleeding back.

"I—I'll go telephone for Doctor Gillespie," America volunteered, miserably.

"Nay, Jamie wudna want th' talk," interposed Jeannie. "I can dae a' that's needfu'."

As America turned to leave, the MacGower children scattered before her as from a witch or a mad dog. She stepped down the long stone steps. Below across the pike, last year's corn which Jamie had husbanded so carefully, burned amid the still-blazing timbers of the crib. Uprights and joists of outbuildings and the tobacco barn would smolder all day, America knew. Blackened remains of farm machinery, the plow handles still smoking and the cutting discs red-hot, stood among the fallen timbers. In the farthest corner of the pen, huddled against the charred rails, lay the black sow and her spotted pigs, all dead.

Unable to gaze longer at the desolation before her, America started up the pike on the two-mile walk home to Children's Chance.

In late October a black frost set the color of the curing tobacco grown in defiance of the Cut-Out. When Captain Doggett, after inspection of his full barns, announced at the noonday dinner table that he would expect Ephraim to start stripping as soon as he could hire extra hands and adequate protection for them, Ephraim laid down his carving tools.

"I don't intend to handle a leaf of your crop, sir," he openly defied his father-in-law.

"Now, Eph—" begged Bethenia, twisting her napkin.

"Everybody who eats at my board must obey my orders!" Captain Doggett returned Ephraim's fire.

"Poppa, you promised me you wouldn't make a scene," whimpered Bethenia, patting her bosom frantically to locate the handkerchief she knew she would soon need.

"You offer me no other course, sir," began Ephraim, rising, "but to leave your house—and take my wife and daughters with me. Bethenia, I'll go to town at once and locate a suitable house. Please be ready to move by sundown."

"How can I leave poppa at his advanced age?" quavered the distraught Bethenia. "Yet Eph—you know I love you more than life!"

"Then you'll have to choose between us," Ephraim told her, gently. "In the meantime, I'll get my things together."

While his family argued, Ephraim packed and moved his personal belongings out into the front yard. In the tack room, from the sporting collection of twenty years he selected his favorite guns, saddles, boots and a complete camping outfit. While he was bridling his riding mare, Sue, his older girl, came running to the stable to beg him not to go. She failed to sway him, and returned in tears to the house. When he led his mare around to the front stile, his womenfolk and Captain Doggett were lined up against him at the front porch rail.

"Oh, Eph!" sniffled Bethenia, as he started up the new cement walk to say good-bye. "Poppa threatens to cut me out of his will if I g-go with you. We'll be poor as church mice—just when the g-girls need things."

"Beth, you don't have to come with me," Ephraim announced in his most reasonable voice. "The only stand I'm taking is that I can't honorably touch your father's non-pooled crop. Furthermore, I'm fed up with his insults to the Equity Society—especially when he knows I'm working tooth and nail to make that Cut-Out a success. If the trust gets the upper hand now in this Equity fight, Dan Lord will turn the screw down on us growers until we starve to death. It's not the Night Riders, it's selfish old land hogs like you, sir," Ephraim turned furiously on the Captain, "who're drenching this county with blood—and making widows and orphans out of happy homes!"

"Don't you dare call me an old land hawg, you damn' wild Indian!" sputtered Captain Doggett, snatching up Ephraim's gun lying across the top of his baggage. "I've a good mind to pump you full of lead—and save the sheriff the expense of hanging you—because you'll be the death of me, I swear! I won't last a month without Beth to take care of me—and you know it!"

"Cap, you are old—when you can't tell one end of a gun from the other—ho! ho!" laughed Ephraim. Stepping towards his father-in-law, he continued: "That's really funny—you one of the heroes of Kennesaw Mountain—and threatening me with the wrong end of a shotgun! Wait till I tell this one on you at reunion, ho!—ho! ho!" Laying a careful hand on the shotgun, Ephraim drew it gently out of Captain Doggett's shaking hands, broke it open, dropped the cartridges into his own palm, and handed the gun back to his father-in-law with a respectful: "There you are, sir! Now, nobody 'll get hurt. Beth, have you made up your mind?"

" 'Where thou goest, I will go—' " quavered Bethenia, in a martyred tone.

"Then step down to the stile with me," Ephraim smiled. When they were out of earshot, he continued: "Don't take it so hard, my pet. You know I don't really want you and the girls to leave your comfortable home here—especially to face the hardships I'm bound to meet during the next few weeks."

"Eph, you aren't going back to Texas, are you?" Bethenia anticipated the worst.

"I've been assigned to guard the Lawrence Creek bridge—where the Tuckahoe pike joins the Cincinnati road into Limestone," explained Ephraim, happy as a boy at the prospect of a camping trip. "My job will be to see that no tobacco passes across that bridge to market."

"Must you leave home to do that?" asked Bethenia, suspiciously.

"Night Riders will guard the bridge from dusk till dawn, when I'll take over. Rather than make you get up and cook me breakfast at such an ungodly hour, I thought I'd just go camp down there on the creek till the Cut-Out's over."

"But, Eph, you'll catch your death of cold sleeping out like that!"

"Maybe I will—but let me try, won't you, honey?" pleaded Ephraim, boyishly. "You know that big old cottonwood tree on the bank near the bridge—the one with its trunk hollowed out by the floods?"

"The one where the free nigger lived when I was a child?"

"That's the tree! Ever since you told me about him, I've been crazy to go live in that hollow tree myself. I—I even persuaded the boys to let me have the Lawrence Creek bridge, so I could camp out in that tree. It ud take me back to my old outdoor life in the West."

The weeks which followed proved highly agreeable to the Virginia lad now grown old. Bethenia kept him well supplied with choice food. On the wagon which had brought over his camping gear, she had even remembered to send his favorite ladder-back rush-bottom chair. Tilted in it against one or the other entrance to the bridge with his shotgun across his knees, Ephraim basked through the mild Indian summer days of 1908, smoked his pipe, pulled his old hound's ears and back-tracked in memory over the events of his adventurous life . . .

His sentry duties were light. Ephraim told himself realistically that something was bound to happen soon. Every night or so his relief, when they came on duty, had stories to tell of non-pool men trying under various ruses to deliver their tobacco in loose leaf to Mr. Payne at the trust's warehouse. A favorite hour to try and run the Night Riders' gauntlet was at twilight, when the river fog hung low in the gaps leading out of Limestone and when good farmers ought to be at home milking. Time and again wagons loaded with prime loose leaf creaked out of their home barns. Often within a mile of the town, masked men materialized out of the mist, sent the teams flying, tipped the top-heavy wagons into the creek or hollow, kicked the leaf about in muddy water until it was irreparably damaged, disarmed and lashed the non-Equity growers into semiconsciousness, and vanished like wraiths in the drizzle before another vehicle had come into view.

"Sorry to have to stop you, sir," Ephraim challenged a stranger one cold mid-November forenoon. "I know you're anxious to get on into town—with the feel of snow in the air. But I'll only detain you for a minute. What you got in that compartment there—in the back of your buggy?"

"Cain't you Kaintuckians read?" demanded the driver, holding his overheated team nervously. "I've been sellin' sewin' machines on Tuckahoe."

"That's what your sign says—but not your horses," smiled Ephraim, laying down his shotgun to rest his right hand on his revolver butt. "Seems to me a light sample sewing machine shouldn't make a well-conditioned team like yours sweat so hard—especially when the grade's downhill all the way from Tuckahoe."

"Naow, looky here, uncle, I'm in a hurry—"

"You're from Ohio, that's certain. On this side of the river, we call niggers uncle," snapped Ephraim. "Are you sure you haven't a thousand pounds of bright leaf in that rear compartment?"

"Why, you darned ol' fool! Whatever gave you such a notion?"

"Want to make a little bet with me, stranger?" drawled Ephraim. "If that's a sewing machine you've got in back there, then I'll apologize to you like a gentleman—after I take a look. If it's bright leaf—that you grew on some Ohio bottom and rowed across the river last night—and sweated this bay team brown to haul up the river rim on that old road yonder—then you agree to help me tumble it peacefully down the bank here into the creek—like a gentleman. That may not appeal to you on first hearing—but it's a damn' sight better than for you to get hurt or to mix it with the Equity Society. Even if you slip past me, they'll catch you at the bridge on the edge of town."

"You git out o' my way," advised the stranger in an ugly tone, although his hands were still on the reins. "I'm warnin' yuh—"

"Climb down out of that buggy," said Ephraim, in his tired voice of command.

"You'll have to plug him, Jake!" shouted the driver, and reached for his whip.

At the stranger's first motion, Ephraim fired, saw the man clutch his belly, then jerk on one rein. From somewhere in the rear compartment a rifle blazed twice. Taken by surprise, Ephraim was turned halfway around by the force of the two shots striking him. As the buggy lurched forward behind the crazily galloping horses, Ephraim was flung off balance. He toppled off the ledge where the bridge joined the road. Crashing down the creek bank, he would have fallen headlong into a deep pool beneath the bridge, had not his arm caught a boulder. With his legs knee-deep in the water, Ephraim pulled himself into what shelter the rock offered, raised his revolver.

Through dry leaves and underbrush his hound came bounding down joyously to lick his face.

"Serves me right," whispered Ephraim in agony, straining the dog's muzzle to his cheek, "for offering to bet with a Damyankee! Say good-bye for me—to Beth and Merry—good—old—dog—"

During the afternoon the snow fell like a still white blanket. A blizzardlike wind rising during the night rolled Ephraim's chair through the bridge and out onto the roadside beyond it, buried his shotgun in a drift of snow which sifted dry as powder through the planks of the covered bridge . . .

Stone had written America that he would arrive on the eight o'clock train the next morning at Limestone, and could she send in a rig? As she drove her sleigh towards the Lawrence Creek bridge, she noticed Ephraim's upturned chair, and then his hound shivering on the farther bank. The dog recognized her, barked excitedly but did not come running alongside as he usually did with Eph's friends. America was a few minutes behind schedule. Urging her horse into a faster trot, from the elevation of the Cincinnati road she noticed how black Lawrence Creek looked tumbling downstream between its snowy banks. All the way into town she remembered the creek-bank drifts, unbroken by Ephraim's footsteps leading back and forth to his tent pitched against the cottonwood which, like the creek, looked dark against the virgin purity of the snow. When she mentioned the oddity to Stone, concluding that Ephraim must have been relieved during the storm by a younger man, Stone's face grew grave as he asked:

"Was another sentry on duty when you drove through the bridge?"

"Come to think of it, I didn't see one," declared America, her heart missing a stroke.

"We'll go right out," Stone took worried command.

The old hound, pathetically glad to see them, led the way down the bank and under the bridge. There Ephraim lay like the recumbent statue of the leader with whom lie buried the war hopes and the heart of every loyal Confederate veteran. His booted legs were frozen in the shore ice of the deep pool. On his closed eyelashes, his grizzled brows and long cavalryman's mustaches lay feathery flakes of snow.

"He died like all the men of our family—with his boots on and a gun in his hand," whispered America, her lips against her brother's white marble cheek.

"He died like a soldier," Stone tried to comfort her. "Don't grieve too hard for him, my dear. He would have hated the inactivity—and the infirmities—of old age."

CHAPTER 18

OVER Tuckahoe supper tables speculation ran high as to what would happen to Miss Allilee Drake's tobacco when that doughty spinster tried to haul it to market. Kit and Theodore Gunther, orphaned sons of Minerva and Jonathan Gunther, had raised the crop for their aunt. Ten days before Thanksgiving a long-and-three-shorts, Allilee's call signal, caused telephone receivers to be taken off their hooks and held to curious ears up and down Tuckahoe's new party line. Would Kit come shoot birds up in Madison County, drawled a mountain voice, and bring his dogs?

With a pointer and setter muffled like gentry on either side of him, Kit departed an hour later in a buckboard. Hardly had he turned onto the pike, before curious ears inclined again to their telephone receivers, this time to hear Allilee calling Mr. Payne at the Tobacco Trust's receiving warehouse in Limestone.

"I'll be in the first thing tomorrow morning with six thousand pounds of burley in loose leaf," announced Allilee, too deaf to realize how reduced the current was by her uninvited listeners. Hanging up the receiver, Allilee swung a shawl over her grey head, strode up to the barn and bade her tenant, now working for day wages, to load her crop onto the wagon in readiness for delivery to town.

"You can finish stripping that shirt-tailful the first thing tomorrow morning," she said, waggling her father's gold-headed cane at the remainder of the crop lying on the table.

She and Theodore were breakfasting by lamplight when David, the white-headed negro who acted as general domestic, burst into the dining room to announce:

"Miss Allie, dar's two ob Dem paradin' up and daown wid guns in front ob ouah ba'hn!"

"Whom do you mean by 'Dem,' David?"

"Night Riders, auntie!" cried Theodore, called Tap by everybody except Allilee.

"Compose yourself, Theodore. How long have they been here, David?"

"All night, dey say."

"They must be cold and hungry. Go ask them in to breakfast."

In wornout boots and with chapped hands the Night Riders presented themselves sheepishly at Allilee's side-porch door.

"Warm yourselves, gentlemen," instructed Allilee. "David, lay their places here—on either side of mine."

When they were served, the elder Rider divided the platter of fried ham and eggs and a plate of hot biscuits with strict impartiality. As she handed him coffee, Allilee inquired pleasantly:

"What's your name, please?"

"You wouldn't hardly know me, ma'am. I'm from—from Pendleton County."

"And you are Clayton Beale, aren't you?" continued Allilee, turning to her guest on the left.

"Yes, ma'am."

At this confession, which identified the embarrassed young man as one of Mason County's best shots, Tap's eyes bulged over his glass of milk. The Night Riders ate, wiped their mouths on the backs of their hands, and arose.

"I'm obliged to you, ma'am," the Pendleton County man made his acknowledgments.

"That coffee shore tetched the right spot, Miss Allie!" Young Beale waxed voluble.

Tap accompanied them to the barn and returned to report that they had propped their guns against the stripping-room wall, and were assisting the tenant with the handful of leaf that remained unclassed.

"They want to earn their breakfast," nodded Allilee, approvingly.

By eight o'clock, men began arriving on horseback and in buggies, buckboards and wagons. To reinforce their one-time schoolmistress, Mary Dan Humphreys and Polly Dunlop, both of whose fathers were non-pool men, hurried over as fast as their dobbins would trot.

"Come in, girls," Allilee welcomed them. "Excuse me if I continue my knitting. I didn't know we were going to have so much company, and so I promised to finish these mittens today for a tenant child. What's that in your pocket, Mary Dan?"

"My revolver. I asked maw if I hadn't better bring my gun, and she said, 'Yes, Mary Dan, tote your gun.' "

"That was thoughtful of you, child. Put it on the mantel. It's pulling your dress out of shape."

"Miss Allie—"

"What is it now, David?"

"Maymie Ellen's aout heah. She's come foah dem mittens you done say she kin have."

"Tell her I'm just finishing the last one," answered Allilee, with the first gleam of anxiety her face had shown. "Send her in here to wait."

Maymie Ellen, a tow-headed child more diffident than frightened, sidled in and sat down by the fire. Through the open door, Mary Dan could see up the lane into the stable lot, where several hundred men had gathered before the sloping limestone grade to the closed doors of the tobacco barn.

"Stone Moncure's arrived," Mary Dan announced. "He's making a speech."

"He's a'nawful fine speaker," remarked Polly.

"Yes, ma'am, he is," agreed Maymie Ellen.

Allilee was too busy counting and dropping stitches off the wristband, to make any comment.

'Here comes three men to the house. They walk like a delegation."

Led by a weather-beaten young giant, the three presented themselves before their hostess.

"Be seated, gentlemen," Allilee bade them.

They took chairs and swung them forward into the traditional circle before the fire. In sitting down, one of them spat expertly over Mary Dan's knee onto the hearth.

"We come from wheah we live, ma'am," began their spokesman, "tuh reason with you—an' other folks araound here—who don't see eye to eye with the rest of us abaout the Cut-Out. The fustest thing we hear't is how good you are tuh pore folks. Naow, the pool is a pore man's movement—calculated to help us aout of the fix we're in—an' intended to improve aour lot. We don't want tuh hurt no good friend of the pore. At the same time we don't aim ter have nobody hurt the pool we've been a-fightin' fer these two years and more. So we've just stepped in here peaceable, ma'am—ter ask you kindly not tuh sell yer terbacker."

"Son, what's your name?"

"James Benjamin Todd, ma'am—only they mostly calls me Jim."

"Does your mother know you're here, James?"

"No, ma'am."

"You get back home, James," advised Allilee, her eyes on her needles, her foot tapping the floor, "and tell your mother I say you're a good boy, but you've gotten mixed up in mighty poor company. And furthermore," she continued, sweeping the others with her scornful eyes, "nobody is going to tell me what I can or can't do with my own land! Have I made myself clear?"

"Yes, ma'am."

Relieving himself of a quantity of tobacco juice, which caused Mary Dan to move her knee indignantly, the spitter tried his hand:

"We war sent in, ma'am, not with no idee of shootin' off

aour jaw, but maybe ter make a bad matter better. If you'll promise not to sell yer terbacker—"

"I'll promise nothing!"

"When did you figger on sellin' your crop?" asked the third member of the delegation.

"Just as soon as you busybodies get off my farm."

"Yes, and you'd better stop spitting all over me, too!" Mary Dan could contain herself no longer. "It seems to me if I'd come in here to see a lady as good to the poor as Miss Allilee has been to you all, I'd show some respect for her age and character!"

"We ain't intended no disrespect to her, miss—nor to you, neither," meekly answered the spitter.

"Don't go and excite yourself, Mary Dan," admonished Allilee.

"Well, ma'am, we might as well be goin', naow," announced Jim unhappily. "We ain't doin' no good here."

"No, we ain't doin' no good here," sadly agreed the third member.

At the barn, Jim Todd mounted the driveway and announced the delegation's entire lack of success.

"Let's throw her terbacker intuh the pond!" shouted someone from the midst of the crowd.

"Come on, Clayt, give us a hand!"

"I'll tell you what, boys!" shouted Stone, and sprang up beside Todd on the driveway. "Let's unload her tobacco and rebulk it in the barn. I'll take her team and wagon—so she can't haul it into town. When Kit comes home—he's her nephew, and a man grown—we can grasp this problem by the other end of the stick. What d'you say?"

From the crowd below came shouts of approval:

"I side with Mr. Stone!"

"That's not a bad idea—"

"I'm for hit, too!"

Within an hour, the tobacco had been carefully unloaded from the wagon. and the last Rider had disappeared. Wiping the perspiration from his forehead, Stone reported to the ladies in the family room.

"I didn't expect any trouble," snorted Allilee, and with a final emphatic nod tied the last stitch before concluding: "Here're your mittens, Maymie Ellen. I hope you enjoy them."

The next day Allilee rented a wagon and four stout mules, loaded her six thousand pounds of leaf onto it, mounted the tarpaulin spread on top, shook the reins and started to town. Tap, his rifle over his knees, sat facing backwards on the rear of the load. Mary Dan and Polly, also armed, tagged along behind in their buggy.

As Miss Allilee neared Limestone, farmers appeared beside her wagon wheels, laughed and joked with each other and with her. If they were pool men by night, in broad daylight they did not betray their identity even by undue yawns. In the rear, Mary Dan and Polly found themselves the center of more flattering attention than they had received before in their not-unpopular young ladyhood. The eight-mile trip took on some of the aspects of a royal progress.

When the idea first occurred to Tugger Blake to go personally and see for himself just how serious this tempest in the burley belt really was, he thought it might be pleasant to make the trip in one of his new Winton Sixes. He had friends a plenty to visit in the Blue Grass, and they might enjoy driving with him to the tobacco market towns such as Cynthiana, Winchester, Georgetown and Limestone. With the Winton's top down, and a chauffeur and that good-looking new office man on the front seat to open doors with his Harvard accent, Tugger felt he would cut quite a figure when he was driven up to the shabby hill-county farm where America now lived with that corncob husband of hers.

In the afternoons and at night, when high blood pressure seemed likely to split his head wide open, Tugger fumed against America as furiously as he did against "that buffoon in the White House." Through subscription to a clipping bureau he read every word that Cassandra hurled against him. Breakfasting in bed according to his doctor's orders, he pictured himself as an old man imprisoned in a wheel chair pushed by the hands of mercenaries. To bolster his forlorn hope that reconciliation with America might someday be possible, he told himself that women go where they are treated the best, are given the most. Surely somehow and somewhere America, after punishing him long enough, would find a place for him again in her presence, would let him warm his starved soul at the fires of her strong and loving nature? Thus, the Kentucky trip, ostensibly to report first-hand to Dan Lord the conditions he found in the burley belt, was linked with Tugger's secret thoughts of America. It became the one glowing objective on his otherwise laborious horizon. Unfortunately, as had so often happened before when his heart's desire seemed almost within his grasp, unforeseen difficulties arose in his path to keep him in New York. Throughout 1907 and 1908 he found himself caught in the troublesome coils of litigation.

In 1906, the federal government's prosecution of the licorice combine had opened what was to be a five years' legal battle. Officers of the Tobacco Trust were subpoenaed, and directed to produce papers and documentary evidence. They refused, and were held in contempt of court. On January 10, 1907, the case was decided on two counts against the two licorice defendants, and heavy fines were imposed.

Six months later, on July 10, 1907, the Department of Justice brought suit in the United States Circuit Court in New York against the Tobacco Trust for violation of the Sherman anti-trust law. An able young lawyer, James C. McReynolds, was the government's special representative. Before he was called upon to testify in the widely publicized case, Tugger Blake studied Dan Lord's deposition. "We did not buy out rival concerns to get rid of competition, but as investments," Dan declared. "We don't gain anything by getting rid of competition. If we started to buy them out with that idea, they would start to build them faster than we could buy them."

To the charge that the Tobacco Trust had bought or acquired a large stock interest in various concerns which were continued in operation under their former names with their new ownership kept secret, thus producing a public impression that they were still independent competitors, Dan replied:

"I was always opposed to that from my standpoint. I thought it was foolishness. But to the man who is going to run a business, I say: Here, go ahead and run it any way you like, so you make profits; that is all I care. I thought it was foolish to run a business secretly. I would rather not do business than have to do it that way."

To the charge that he had eliminated competition on the Virginia, Carolina and Kentucky auction floors, Dan answered:

"The farmer has got to have a good price for his tobacco, or he won't grow it. We are just as interested in the farmer as we are in the consumer."

More angry than embarrassed to find himself named an individual defendant in this legal tobacco war, Tugger stayed on in New York first to testify and then to await the court's decision. He felt that the very foundation of his liberty and of his millions was at stake. Since Ben Franklin's time, the American ideal had preached Poor Richard's axioms that "early to bed and early to rise makes a man healthy, wealthy and wise," had enshrined the lad of modest origin who had saved his pennies, toiled mightily and prospered. Were not most of Wall Street's overlords, now called "malefactors of great wealth," once penniless country boys who had possessed the stamina, the wit and the foresight to come to the big cities and wrest their fortunes out of the disorganization of the post-Civil War period, or out of the virgin wealth of a new continent? Was success a crime, that millionaires as a class should now be haled into court and stripped of the fruits of their herculean labors, of their thrift and of their vision by rabble rousers, political scoundrels and moral cranks? What was the country coming to, when a cheap demagogue in the White House dared use the newspapers as no other President heretofore had lowered the dignity of his high office to do, to create and hold public support for his own ambitious schemes? Soon the merest outline cartoon of the man of "teeth, glasses and fire" was enough to send Tugger's blood pressure soaring, before he had read a word of Teddy's ringing phrases. Reading in a newspaper the prophecy of one minister speaking before a convention of Christian Socialists in Buffalo—that "some day after the trusts have with great labor and difficulty taken the cart up to the top of a long hill, we will relieve them of their labors; we will say, 'This is our cart,' and take it"—Tugger became so upset that his doctor ordered him to Poland Springs to have the choler boiled out of his system.

On November 7, 1908, the United States Circuit Court in New York decided against the Tobacco Trust, the snuff combine and others, and enjoined them from engaging further in interstate commerce, but withheld the injunction pending possible appeal to the Supreme Court.

"We'll damn' well appeal!" swore Tugger at the *Wild Honey* poster of America hung in the wall panel opposite his desk. "We'll fight this thing through if it takes years—and millions—to win. You, America Moncure—with your glib phrases of starving the trust—we'll show you tobacco yaps what starvation really is!"

"The boss must have gone nuts over losing his lawsuit," whispered Matthews, the new secretary in Tugger's outer office. "He's talking to the pictures on the wall."

"Oh, he's been doing that for the last ten years," yawned Conway, at the confidential files. "Did he look like he's fixing to leave?"

On the morning of November 17, Tugger swung off the Cincinnati train at the Limestone depot. Carrying his Gladstone bag, as forty years ago he used to carry his sample cases of smokin' mixture, he walked briskly from the station up the single main street of the old river town. On the hillside, like the rocking-chair brigade on a summer resort veranda, sat substantial brick houses among frost-blackened gardens. Under shrubbery and north walls, patches of snow still lingered, but the air was mild and wet, an ideal season for handling stripped leaf. Boyhood habit caused Tugger to sniff. Where was the fragrance of burley in high case which should hang over this market town, receiving center for the second largest tobacco-growing county in the United States? And where was the bustle of trade which should follow the grower hurrying to spend his tobacco check in time to get home and milk during the shortest days of the year? Limestone's stores were empty.

Wondering if he had been wise to come to this hotbed of lawlessness without even a revolver, Tugger decided not to stop at café or hotel to quiz the natives while he ate breakfast. Striding on up the main thoroughfare of the narrow four-streeted town, he noticed the railroad tracks running parallel with him on Front Street. Beyond them was the dull morning shine of the river. At Market Square he saw the welcome sign of the General Tobacco Company painted above the entrance of a new receiving warehouse beyond the high school, which was housed in a yellow frame building.

Feeling very much the New Yorker, Tugger set his bag down at the office door of the warehouse, and knocked for admittance. Through the shuttered window near by, he could see the business end of what looked like a field gun. A pair of anxious eyes appeared between slats of the blind, a patient voice inquired his business. Tugger passed in his letter of introduction and a moment later was being cordially received by a thin man named Payne, who said he was General Tobacco's agent in Limestone. Payne's first suggestion to Tugger was that they walk around the empty but well-manned warehouse to inspect its defenses.

"Where'd you get these things?" chuckled Tugger, examining a second Gatling gun mounted at the double driveway entrance of the receiving deck. At the exit, he could see a third gun and its skeleton crew.

"I bought 'em out in the county—from the heirs of a non-pool man," explained Payne, unhappily.

"What happened to him?" asked Tugger, fingering the trigger. He'd been wanting to shoot off one of these things ever since he'd read about them in *Popular Mechanics.*

"The Night Riders got the old fellow."

"Old, was he? Well, he'd probably have died soon from hardening of the arteries. Now—what did you say your name was?"

"Payne—Robert Payne, sir."

"Now, Payne, this whole thing is just a tempest in a teapot—or a tobacco patch, I might say," began Tugger, smiling pleasantly. "What you want to do with these people is to treat the outlaws with a firm hand—and our own people with generosity."

"I've another gun in the balcony overlooking the alley," Payne interposed. "One of the worst things we have to fight here is the fire hazard. These mountaineers have a way of charring a rope in their cook stoves—and then dropping it in the chaff alongside a tobacco barn. Hours later—when you aren't looking for trouble—everything goes up in smoke."

"We'll make an example of the next fellow who tries a sneaky trick like that!"

"That's easier said than done, Mr. Blake—if you want to stay alive—and do business later on in this town."

"Now, Payne, you're letting this thing get on your nerves," declared Tugger, giving the worried agent a heartening slap on the back. That was the trouble with little men; they could never see the forest for the trees and the blackberry bushes. Tugger felt glad he had come to Limestone. When he got back to New York, he could honestly recommend to Dan Lord, without feeling he was doing anybody an injustice, that Payne had better be replaced with a steadier, less imaginative man. For the present, Tugger decided he might as well make himself comfortable, and so he inquired: "Can't you send out for some coffee? I haven't had breakfast."

"Would you rather have country ham and hot biscuits—or homemade sausage and corn-batter cakes? The hotel does both pretty well," vouched Payne, in his tired voice. "I've been sleeping here since June, so I know."

Over his delicious breakfast, Tugger outlined to Payne his ideas for the winter campaign. To congratulate Payne on his Gatling guns, and the use he'd made of the warehouse floor as a roller-skating rink, didn't cost General Tobacco any money. Admissions had cut down overhead appreciably. At the mid-morning recess the gatekeeper took in enough change to pay for the juice necessary to keep the electric lights going all night, a precaution Tugger heartily endorsed. Seventeen high school students trooped in at noon and went clicking around the floor.

Chuckling over the pastimes of small towns, Tugger slouched in Payne's desk chair with his feet high, dozed, congratulated himself on having left Durham when the going was good, and dozed again. Had it not been for the competition *Lord's Mixture* had given his *Fighting Cock,* and Eph Moncure's refusal to work any longer for nothing, Tugger thought nostalgically, he might himself have dropped into the financial oblivion which had swallowed Dan's other small-town competitors. The first milestone in Dan's extraordinary success, Tugger reviewed his friend's career, had been Dan's decision to make cigarettes. Second was Dan's recognition of the potential value of the Bonsack machine, and his mechanical genius in helping O'Brien make it work, which had led to the mechanization of the cigarette industry. A third milestone was Dan's use of advertising on an unprecedented national scale, which had created a taste for cigarettes at a time when American tobacco users were in occupational transition. "I have spent more money," Tugger remembered Dan's favorite boast, "in advertising than any other living man. I have given out fifty millions to make my goods known." The steepest part of Dan's uphill climb lay across the battlefields of the five ruthless trade wars he had captained against his competitors. Dan's genius, Tugger was ready now to concede, iay not so much in his ability to bring his trade antagonists to their knees as in his shrewdness in prevailing on them to get up and reenter the tobacco business as his lieutenants. Too bad the same methods couldn't be applied to judges, in this sixth tobacco war of litigation!

Without knocking, a sentry stuck his head through a slit in the door of Payne's office and bawled.

"There's an old woman drivin' a wagonload of loose leaf this-a-way—with abaout a hundred growers follerin' along behind!"

Through the slit in the front office shutters, Payne recognized driver, load and escort:

"It's Miss Allilee Drake. When she telephoned me night before last, I heard receivers coming down all along that party line, and I knew we'd be in for trouble."

"That's no way to receive customers!" joked Tugger. "You evidently don't appreciate just how badly we need burley tobacco."

"Open up!" shouted several farmers, pounding on the roll-down galvanized iron doors of the driveway.

"We ain't fightin' women and children—like you are, Payne," shouted another good-natured voice, finding himself surrounded by youngsters on roller-skates who had come clicking down the alley onto the sidewalk.

"Looks like you fellers ain't very anxious to buy a load o prime burley," jeered another grower.

"Maybe the trust don't need it, eh, Payne?"

"Like hell they don't!" one joker became grim.

"Open up—and receive the lady's leaf!"

"What'll I do?" Payne appealed to the New Yorker.

"Whatta you think's best?" Tugger followed his lifelong custom of consulting the man in the field before he made any important decision.

"I—I think we'd best humor them," Payne advised, courageously. "If we do, they may pass the whole thing off as joke. If we don't, well—they tore down the warehouse over in the next county."

"I'll tell you what," decided Tugger. "Open up, and pay her twice—three times what her leaf's worth. That'll give the others something to think about! Because if there's one thing makes a farmer spit green, it's to see another farmer get more money for his crop than he did. Wait till the word circulates around what this old lady's leaf brought. You'll have more growers hustling their crops in here—while the market's still hot—than you can handle!"

"I hope so, Mr. Blake—especially now that we're also responsible for your safety," sighed Payne. "For your own good, sir, I must ask you to stay inside this office—where nobody 'll recognize you. Will you promise that?"

"Oh, sure—if you're going to fuss like a Miss Nancy," grinned Tugger, enjoying himself.

"You don't know these Mason County farmers as I do," Payne overlooked the jibe. "All right, boys—open her up!"

The heavy iron doors rolled upwards and back over the inside driveway. Standing on her load, Allilee drove her nervous mules in and swung them towards the receiving deck. As if this were part of an ordinary day's work, and the growers who gathered around were the good-natured country jakes they appeared to be, Payne and his assistants unloaded Allilee's crop, sorted it by type and piled it onto baskets, and weighed it in the scales booth. Knowing that Tugger was listening from behind the balcony gun, Payne cleared his throat anxiously, glanced at the duplicate weight bill and took the plunge:

"The market's strong this morning, ma'am. Will you—will you take thirty-three cents all around for your crop?"

"Thirty-three cents—why, Mr. Payne!"

"Thirty-three cents!" the whisper ran through the ranks of listening growers. "Thirty-three cents, did you hear that?" farmers exchanged promissory glances over the heads of the watching children.

"This is a—a mighty nice crop," gulped Payne, taking out

check book and fountain pen. "Well handled, too. Will you let it go for thirty-three cents?"

"I—I'd hoped for thirty-five," Allilee saw her chance and took it.

"Haw! haw!" guffawed Tugger from the balcony. A hundred heads swung around and upwards.

"It's a deal, ma'am!" Payne's hasty assent brought the heads back to the transaction at hand, before anybody could see who had laughed up there.

"What did I tell you, Payne?" rejoiced Tugger, as the agent reentered his office. "This whole affair has been grossly exaggerated."

"I don't like the way those farmers looked at one another," worried Payne.

"All we've got to do now is to find an example," continued Tugger, examining the mechanism of the Gatling gun with the curiosity of a schoolboy.

"An example of what, sir?"

"Of how tough we can get, when we have to," concluded Tugger, grimly.

The November afternoon wore on. High school was dismissed. Students lucky enough still to have a dime trooped into the warehouse to roller-skate. On the new gramophone, the whine of a popular song drifted into the office over the clicking of many wheels around the echoing warehouse floor:

> Honey-boy, I hate to see you leaving,
> Honey-boy, you know my heart is grieving—

Tugger began to think about time-tables. The F.F.V. came through Limestone at eight o'clock at night. Tugger wondered whether he could flag it to stop for him at Dover, seventeen miles westward down the line. America, Tugger knew, lived with that corncob husband of hers on a hillside farm between Limestone and Dover. The road maps which Matthews had secured when Tugger was planning the trip by auto car, had shown a passable turnpike with a country post office marked Tuckahoe halfway between Limestone and Dover. Unwilling to confess he couldn't leave Limestone without seeing the petticoated ringleader of the Equity Society, Tugger began to wonder how he could best shake Payne. He had already spotted a livery stable on his way upstreet this morning. The thing to do now was to tell Payne he was going around to that hotel which made the real corn-batter cakes, and engage a room for the night.

"Mr. Payne!" a sentry poked his head into the office. "There's a Night Rider sneakin' down the alley—with something hid under his coat."

"It's a charred rope," whispered a pimply faced clerk. "He's aiming to burn the warehouse!"

"Shut your lily-livered mouth!" Payne took command with surprising firmness. "Come up to the balcony window, Mr. Blake. We've a gun there overlooks the alley. You men here in the office, stay at your posts, understand? But whatever you do, don't fire into the crowd!"

"I'm the last one to contradict a man in charge, Payne," Tugger protested, almost treading on the agent's heels in his eagerness to follow him upstairs, "but that's a damn' queer order to give against hoodlums fixin' to burn the company's valuable property."

Without answering, Payne stood back for Tugger to go ahead of him onto the balcony. The gunner had the best place to see down the alley. Pushing him aside, Tugger squinted along the sights into the gloom of the mid-November twilight. No street or alley lights had as yet blinked on through the white fog curling up from the river. At the end of the alley Tugger made out a horse and buggy tied to the cross alley lamppost. Down the cobbled passageway between the blank brick wall of the hardware store opposite and the warehouse shadows, a man came forward furtive as an alley cat. Under a slouch hat pulled low across his eyes, Tugger could see his unshaven chin, with hollow cheeks above, as the fellow kept turning his head first to one side and then to the other to see if he was being observed. Under his thin overcoat he appeared to be carrying something bulky.

"Looks like he means to burn or bomb us out, sir," grinned the gunner whom Tugger had shoved aside.

"I'll take charge here," declared Tugger, voicing the first step necessary to clear decks for the action he had been ruminating all day. "I want no cowards around me!"

"Naow looky here, mister—"

"Get on the gun in the front office, Tom," interposed Payne, his eyes speaking volumes. "I need you worse down there, with those yellow-bellied clerks my friend's talking about. Get goin', Tom—we haven't got all night."

Alone with Payne, Tugger carefully sighted the fellow in the alley. Payne was right, in half a minute that damn' Night Rider would be too close for range.

"Who is he, d'you know?"

"From this distance—nobody to worry over, I'd say," answered Payne, squinting to get a better look at the man in the alley below them. "His father was quite a public character, I believe—a river-boat gambler."

"He's just the man for us—to teach these hillbillies a lesson!" cried Tugger, and squeezed the trigger.

Out of the gun muzzle with surprisingly little commotion for the destruction it carried, leaped a fiery spray of steel. Before Tugger could experiment again, Payne with an oath pushed him away from the gun.

"Dammit, man, have you lost your senses? That poor devil down there—"

"He's the very chap we needed—to scare these tobacco yaps back to the field!" barked Tugger and looked into the alley. Sprawled on the cobblestones, the fellow lay with his coat open and bundles of something dark around him.

"Good Lord, he was only trying to sell us his leaf!" whispered Payne, and looked at Tugger with a whitening face.

"Sell us his leaf?"

"Can't you see his samples spread out down there? That's what he had under his coat—his samples! He had to hide 'em like that to keep the pool men from telling his maw— Mr. Blake, this is terrible!"

"You don't mean he isn't a Night Rider?"

"He's not even a pool man. He's young Fant Annable—"

"Not the son of—of—"

"The son of America Moncure! I clean forgot Mrs. Stone Moncure was married to that river-boat gambler, this man's paw. Mr. Blake, what's the matter with you. Are you sick, sir?"

"No—no, but I've got to get out of this town!"

"You bet you have, before these Equity men get hold of you. They swear by Miss Merry! Number Ten—the F.F.V.—comes through here at eight o'clock—"

"How can I get aboard her?"

"You can't wait for her in this town. Your only chance now is Dover. Come on, man. I'll tell you the rest on the way!" cried Payne, pushing Tugger towards the open window.

They scrambled down the fire escape, crouched in the shadow of the warehouse wall. At the Main Street end of the alley, a crowd was gathering. Fists pounded hollowly on the galvanized iron doors, voices were calling for the warehouse to open up and explain those shots.

"See Annable's horse and buggy, Blake?" Payne whispered, pointing up the alley. "Run for it, and drive it quietly out of town—quietly, do you understand? Pretend you're a travelin' salesman—or somebody from Winchester come to see Stone Moncure on Equity business. When you're in Dover, lay low at the depot till train time—"

"How'll I know the way in the dark?"

"Keep driving west. There's only one fork—turn right and go through a covered bridge. You'll see the sentry's fire on the bank. Hurry, sir—and good luck!"

By the fading sky, Tugger trotted the willing horse westwards on a narrow upper street past the back doors of houses. He was safely out of Limestone before the gelding slowed to walk up a long icy hill. Better let the animal go his own gait, choose his way home, Tugger decided with teeth chattering from nervousness and the cold. If his head wasn't splitting so, he could think more clearly. To get past that body sprawled on the alley cobblestones, Tugger had had to step over a dark pool spreading among the familiar bundles of tobacco. The still white face upturned to the light from the balcony window had been handsome, in a romantic storybook way—

"Who goes there?" a man's voice penetrated through the confusion of pain and memories in Tugger's reeling mind. "Stop an' be searched, mister— Oh, it's you, Fant?"

"Annable lent me his rig," Tugger tried to make his voice sound natural. "I'm—I'm from Winchester on official business—to see his maw."

"How come Annable lent you his buggy, then?" demanded another long face emerging out of the fog. "He 'n' Miss Merry ain't hardly speakin'. Sorry, mister, but we'll have to search you."

"Go right ahead!" agreed Tugger, wondering what identification he had to betray him. Fortunately, the New York newspaper he had read on the train out was in his overcoat pocket back in Payne's office. What a break for him Payne had forgotten to return him that letter of introduction from Dan Lord!

"Keep him covered, Ollie—and shoot you know when," ordered the talkative sentry, stepping to the rear compartment of the buggy. "Sorry tuh seem so unfriendly, mister, but last week we lost one o' the best men ever come intuh this country. Right here at this very bridge—"

"Too bad! Wasn't he getting on in years, though?"

"Hell, no! Eph Moncure was in his prime."

"Eph Moncure—"

"Yep, mister. Shot in the back an' froze stiff as a mac'rel!"

"Did you know him?" asked the glum sentry with the upraised gun at point-blank range.

"I shore did," Tugger found himself slipping naturally

into his North Carolina drawl. "I knew him back in Virginny, an' I'm mighty sorry to hear he's gone."

"The trust's made this the wurst Thanksgivin' we've had in Mason Caounty since the Injuns," continued the talkative sentry, slamming the rear compartment shut and walking around front again with several bundles of leaf in his hand. "They got aour brother John Willy—the flower of aour flock."

"Where'd that leaf come from? Honest, boys, I never knew it was there," declared Tugger, trying to keep his hands from transmitting his nervousness down the reins to the horse restive to get home to his stall.

"We know you didn't, stranger. Young Fant likely as not was totin' hit araound jest tuh be contrary. All right, Ollie rest yer gun."

"Where'll I find America Moncure?"

"Second big brick haouse on the left—abaout two mile on daown the pike."

"Am I apt to find her at home?" persisted Tugger, wondering at himself for asking all these fool questions.

"She ain't hardly been aout o' the haouse since Eph got kilt," spoke up the glum sentry. "She jes' cain't seem tuh git over it, paw says."

"Thanks, boys. And good-night to you."

"Good-night, mister."

At a brisk clip, the horse trotted up a gentle hill and quickened pace along a ridge. What good did it do him now to know that America was at home, Tugger's thoughts began whirling around again inside his aching head. If he thought for a minute he could go see Sister Merry without blurting out to her what had happened, about her son lying back there in that dark alley with his blood spreading out over the cobblestones, Tugger told himself he'd better think again—he'd better go lie down somewhere till his blood pressure quieted or he'd have a stroke sure, just as the doctors had said . . .

The horse, throwing his head, had stopped at a gate across a lane which curved to the right up through a meadow to a light burning in a window on the hill crest. That light couldn't be America's, Tugger told himself. Those tobacco yaps on the bridge had said America lived on the left side of the pike, in a big brick house on the left side of the pike—

"Giddap, mule," clucked Tugger, as if he were on his peddler's wagon.

Willing enough, the patient animal started down the pike. Tugger wondered what time of night it was. He felt as if he'd been driving all his life. He located his watch, drew it out of his vest pocket but could not see the dial in the darkness. It wasn't worth trying to strike a match, somebody might see his face and recognize him. He mustn't be recognized, Payne had said he must lie low in that depot at Dover until the F.F.V. came pounding through, pounding through—like his head like the crazy wild pain in his head . . .

Those two lights must be the depot windows, Tugger decided with relief. The horse had stopped on a rise of ground in front of two lighted windows. Stiff with cold, Tugger got out of the buggy, stumbled up a patch cleared through trodden snow to a closed door pale in a brick wall between the lighted windows. Pushing against the door, Tugger opened it and found himself in a warm old kitchen lighted by a well-polished kerosene lamp. At a table a familiar-looking woman was slicing side meat for supper with a butcher knife worn crescent-shaped in the middle of the blade by years of sharpening on a hand whetstone.

"Merry, I had to come—" gasped Tugger, closing the door behind him and falling back against it.

"Tugger Blake!" the woman cried, knife in one hand, white slab of country bacon in the other. She was America, all right, that was America's melodious Eastern Virginia voice. Above somber mourning garb was the unforgettable heart-shaped face, the dear steady grey eyes, the tender yet resolute mouth.

"Tugger, what are you doing here? Don't you know the Night Riders will kill you if they catch you in this county?"

"That's why I came—"

"But I can't help you now, Tugger Blake—even if I wanted to!"

"I didn't come for myself, Sister Merry. I came because I had to—to tell you I've killed your boy."

Staring at her through the red mist before his eyes, Tugger saw her face whiten, her eyes dilate. Knife and chunk of meat fell noisily onto floor and table, as she reached for support.

"You've done what?" she whispered, wetting her lips with the tip of a small tongue that looked pink against her spreading pallor.

"I killed your boy—by mistake. I thought he was going to fire the warehouse—one of Payne's men said he was! But he'd only come to sell us his crop. He had his samples—not a charred rope or a bomb—under his coat."

"So he raised a crop after all—in the walnut grove," whispered America. "He had to go against everybody just like his father. And now he's died like his father—you killed him, Tugger Blake! You shot him down like a sheep-killin' dog—in an alley, you say?"

"Go ahead, talk to me any way you like, America. I deserve it—and I haven't long to live anyhow—even if I should get to Dover to catch the F.F.V. Without you, I don't want to live—life just doesn't mean anything to me any more. Does it to you, Sister Merry?" asked Tugger, looking at her from under his brows in the way she remembered he had first looked up from his cowhide. "Does life mean anything to you these days? Are you happy here in this kitchen—cookin' for your hayseed husband? Where is he now?"

"He's up at the barn, milking. He'll be coming to the house any minute now—and if he catches you here, he'll feel it's his bounden duty to turn you over to the sheriff—for the bloodshed you've caused—my boy's—and John Willy's and Eph's blood you've shed!"

Her voice breaking, she looked at him, at the face which

neither sickness nor thirty years in Wall Street could rob of its powerful attraction. Below the domed forehead the searching hazel eyes blazed out of putty-colored lids. The once firm blue cheeks sagged with rich man's fat. The close ruthless mouth twitched with regret, not with true remorse because he had killed an innocent man, but because that innocent man happened to be her son. For the first time, as if the starvation months of the Cut-Out had sharpened her faculties, she was able to see Tugger Blake stripped of the pleasant and stormy associations of their long-shared past. Instead of the mountain lad raising his circuit-rider face to solve the problem of her economic future; instead of the successful New Yorker whose business acumen matched hers—here before her stood only a whip-smart Yankee trader, another Mudston who with greedy hands had drained away her birthright, her way of pleasant country living, another Mudston come to her now with the blood of her only son, her first-born, upon his hands.

She took a step towards him, her shocked white face flushing with righteous anger. On the floor her foot struck the butcher knife she had dropped, and she stooped mechanically to pick it up. Seeing her with it, the thought flashed through Tugger's mind that she was going to kill him, as years ago she had struck down that carpetbagger. Somehow, he didn't mind. Nothing seemed important now except just to be able to look at her again, maybe to reach out and touch her. Only once in all their years together under the same roof had he kissed her, only once—

The feel of the knife handle in her palm turned America's thoughts backwards to the day of Golden Hill's destruction. Her refusal then to accept defeat had not saved Golden Hill, had instead hounded her own and her family's lives with the consequences of her rebellion. What was it that Tugger had once said about their having both been cut from the same cloth? Once before, when as now she was almost beside herself with heartbreak, on the night when Tugger had asked her to help him put Teena away so that together they might enjoy his millions—on that night of utter fatigue, despair, and absence of souls' understanding, Tugger had said that they were both tough, that they could stand wear and tear, that "if we stretch a little now and then, we can still snap back." So tonight why not stretch to make a last trade with this arch sharper, why not forget your dead son long enough to trade his murderer out of the one possession uniquely his, the influence he has which you must, for the present, control and direct if the blood of your own and other farm women's sons is not to have been spilled in vain?

"What you and I feel tonight—doesn't matter," she heard her faltering voice begin. "We've had our day—and so has my poor unhappy boy. What matters now are the growers—and this tobacco war you and Dan Lord have pushed us into fighting to keep from starvation. You'll do us no good dead, Tugger Blake—you've got to go back to New York and tell Dan Lord to quit fighting—to give up. Will you make one last bargain with me, Tugger? Remember how you used to boast 'Tradin's my pride'? Will you trade once more with me, Tugger Blake?"

"Le's hear what you've got to offer—"

"Your life tonight—against victory for the Equity Society!" she cried, her voice steadying. "If you'll influence Dan Lord to buy our leaf—the two crops the Equity has pooled—if you'll do that for me, Tugger, I'll save your life tonight—I'll drive you down to Dover and put you safely on the F.F.V. Will you do that, Tugger Blake—will you do that?"

"How'll you know I—I won't change my mind when I'm on the train—when I'm safe back in New York?" he jeered with a flare of his old buccaneering spirit.

"You can telephone Dan Lord right here and now!"

"On a rural party line? Payne told me how the busybodies jump to their receivers every time the telephone rings. You couldn't get me out of your front gate before the Night Riders ud be after us."

"That's so," she agreed, and stared at him while she made up her mind to accept the only alternative: "I'll have to trust you just once more, Tugger—against my better judgment. I'll have to trust you to keep your side of this trade, because I can't help myself. But I'm warning you, if Dan Lord doesn't buy our leaf by Christmas Eve, I'll come to New York and—and I'll kill you both!"

"I expect you could, Sister Merry," he smiled wanly at her standing there like that French girl in the peaked cap Palestine had mentioned, with the thin-bladed knife in her hand.

"Is it a trade, Tugger?"

"It's a trade," he agreed, stretching out his hand to clinch it.

With its headlight blinding them, the eastern flyer came pounding down the double steel track which had once reminded Tugger of the way his and America's minds worked together. Looking away, he wondered how one thin circle of red lanternlight could stop this clanking iron monster long enough to let him swing aboard. In the pit of his stomach Tugger felt the old boyish horror of being sucked under the trucks and ground to pulp by tons of living steel above him. Engine, baggage cars and coaches tore at America's skirts, blew hot air in Tugger's face as they thundered by. Air brakes were screaming, a long blur of lighted Pullmans ground to a stop. Out of an opening vestibule came a white-jacketed porter, with a trainman's worried face hanging above him. Tugger reached for the moving hand rail, pulled himself up the steps feeling, as he did so, the coach gather speed under him.

"Tugger, if you break your bargain—" America's voice and white face trailed behind.

"It's a wonder he stopped for you," marveled the trainman, disgustedly. "Why didn't you get on at Limestone—up the track?"

"Help me into the nearest compartment!" gasped Tugger, knowing himself to be on the verge of collapse.

Stretched out on the couch, with pillows under his head and shoulders, Tugger felt the blood recede from his brain, felt his head clear so that he could think straight again. Whistling mournfully for grade crossings, the Fast Flying Virginian pounded eastwards through the darkness. A slick black ribbon beside it, the river appeared to roll backwards ahead of the train into the mountains. Beginning to feel the need of food, and especially the stimulus of black coffee now that liquor was denied him, Tugger made his way unsteadily to the diner. The steward, after a respectful look at his Bond Street clothes, pulled out the forward chair at the best table in the car. Feeling better already, Tugger unfolded his snowy napkin, ordered lavishly and sat back to take stock of his situation.

Your luck's nolding, Tugger Blake, he congratulated himself. Two hours ago, I wouldn't have given two cents Mexican for your chances. And just look at you now, safe and sound and about to eat a good hot supper in this brightly lighted familiar dining car! I'm glad to see you haven't lost your way with women, either. Without half trying, you fooled a clever trader like Sister Merry into helping you out of a damn' bad mess, as safe and sound, as quiet and easy as you used to pull the wool over country jakes' eyes who would follow you up the Wilmington tracks . . .

Under him, Tugger felt the train slowing to a stop. Telling himself that vegetables were good for him, Tugger chewed patiently at his celery stalk. He'd have to learn to like vegetables, they were all he could eat these days. The doctor said they'd keep him from seeing red. Hell-damn, what's this pink light on the tablecloth— Is my blood pressure coming up again?

"We's slowin' in de ya'hds for Limestone, boss," announced the soft-voiced waiter. "Dar's a big fiah in town, an' de cap'n's deecidin' whethah we kin run fru all right."

"A big fire—where?"

"Hit seems des Kaintucky taowns is fightin' de war all ovah agin, suh—some kin' ob a terbacker wa'h, dey say. What's de matter naow, boss—whar you want, suh?"

Thrusting through the extra flat silver, the sugar bowl and condiment bottles, Tugger shot up the diner curtain nearest him. Beyond the window several blocks up the street, an inferno was raging. Flames two stories high shot up from the warehouse next to the doomed yellow-frame high school. Why, that was Dan Lord's tobacco warehouse, Tugger realized, and sprang up to stop them, to show these hoodlums they couldn't destroy valuable property like that! In the half-opened vestibule the trainman was leaning out to watch for a signal ahead.

"Now I understand why you flagged us at Dover, sir!" he declared with an anxious grin at Tugger. "These Kentucky hotheads are at it again. Look at 'em sittin' there watchin' as if butter wouldn't melt in their mouths! I'll bet there's a thousand of 'em lined up there like dummies—without liftin' a hand to help put out that fire."

"They must be the Night Riders!" gasped Tugger, staring.

Less than half a block distant from the track over which the train was moving cautiously ahead at a snail's pace, the motionless army was drawn up. Few wore masks. The majority appeared indifferent to the gaze of anyone who might recognize them and be reckless enough to remember them afterwards. Tall mountaineers in ragged overalls bestrode mousy grey mules. Frock-coated landlords sat their saddles sedately. Young blades in boots and spurs struggled for mastery over animals shown in county fairs all over Kentucky. The rank and file of the Night Riders were farmers, plainly dressed and unassuming, mounted on work horses as unkempt and seemingly as tireless as themselves. A few had pitchforks or corn knives across their saddle bows. The majority carried rifles or shotguns. One common attribute characterized them all—their silence, the most awful silence he ever felt, Tugger afterwards remembered. With the "limestone look" on their set white faces, with eyes fixed straight ahead and glittering in the moonlight—the wan street lamps picking out high cheekbones and forming pools of shadow above unshaven jaws—they watched in complete silence except for the clatter of an occasional horse's hoof on the paving brick, and the nasal whine of a gramophone still playing, forgotten somewhere:

> And if ever you should take the notion,
> To come sailing home across the ocean—

"That's a terrible sight!" exclaimed a fellow-traveler to Tugger. "Why don't they call out the police?"

"What good would the police do against the whole county —against an entire state?" whispered Tugger, staring. Where was tired old Payne and that good man Tom whom he had pushed aside from his gun? Where was that pimply faced clerk and those half-dozen sentries ready to die for Dan Lord's property? Where was that dark-sprawled body in the alley, with the storybook face turned upwards towards the death spray that had come at him from the balcony? Without a warning, without a chance to fight back or even to turn and run, in cold blood you killed an innocent man, Tugger Blake. He was trying to sell you his honest burley, the good White Burley you and Dan Lord need so desperately if you're going to keep manufactured tobacco products moving into the world-trade channels you have established. With courage and sweat he raised that leaf. And you didn't even stop to find out who he was, or what he carried tucked under that shabby coat, until it was too late. When you ran past him frantic to save your own hide, he didn't call out to accuse you, he made no move to reach out a dying hand to clutch you. With his white face turned wonderingly towards you he lay there in the widening pool of his innocent blood—

"All right, folks, you can go back to the diner, now," declared the trainman, swinging around into the vestibule. "Track's clear—we're going through."

"What's de matter, suh?" asked the waiter solicitously after he had placed Tugger's dinner before him. "Ain't everything all right?"

"This roast beef's too rare—for my taste." Tugger smiled

up at him, trying not to make the good nigger feel bad. "Never mind about another piece. My doctor says I shouldn't eat meat, anyhow. High blood pressure, y'know. Just bring me some good strong coffee."

"Now, suh—wi' youah dinnah?"

"The sooner the better!"

After he had gulped down his coffee, Tugger paid his check, nodded to the waiter grinning white-toothed over his tip, and went to the Pullman. The shiny cubicle of his drawing room reminded Tugger of a coffin—or a jail.

You shot a man and ran away, leaving that tired chap Payne to face the consequences of your crazy act. You made fun of his caution, you called him a Miss Nance and implied he was a coward. You are the coward, Tugger Blake, you are the fugitive, now . . .

Walking back to the observation car because he couldn't endure to lie any longer alone in the shiny compartment, Tugger sat down by a rose-shaded lamp and reached for a copy of a Cincinnati evening paper some one had left.

They've brought your dead son home to you by now, America. Limp as a rag doll, they've laid him on the sofa in your unused parlor and tiptoed out, leaving you alone with your first-born. Here is the man-child you nearly froze to death to bring into the world, Nicke told me; here is what I've left you of your brown-eyed baby boy . . .

So you thought it was a tempest in a teapot, eh, Blake? Rather is it a holocaust, a consuming flame that once started may sweep the entire nation like wildfire skimming the prairies, leaping from hillside to mountain range until it reaches Washington and even Wall Street. What have you done, Tugger Blake? In your criminal folly and your greed, what have you done?

When he arrived in New York, Tugger went directly to his club, had himself wrapped in hot fomentations to bring down his blood pressure, was properly massaged and crawled into bed. The next morning, still feeling shaky, he hurried to his Wall Street office to start putting his affairs in order before some travel-stained deputy sheriff arrived from Kentucky to tap him on the shoulder. New York had never looked so sleek, so gay, so full of Thanksgiving spirit as when he arrived back in the city after seventy-two hours absence, although it seemed a century.

Alone in his office, Tugger put in a long distance telephone call to Robert Payne in Limestone. With his heart beating like a trip hammer, he listened while the necessary connections were made across key cities to Cincinnati. A nasal voice twanged:

"This is Limestone, Kentucky . . . There's no such party here now, Cincinnati. We've had a big fire."

"I want to speak to Robert Payne!" cut in Tugger. "Locate Robert Payne—"

Ten minutes later, he heard the tired voice:

"Hello—this is Payne. Mr. Blake? You shouldn't have bothered to call me—"

"Payne, are you all right?" cried Tugger, feeling his eyes smart with relief. "Where are you, now?"

"The sheriff brought me back to Limestone this morning—for the coroner's inquest," explained Payne over a surprisingly good connection. "I guess you and Mr. Lord saw in the papers about the warehouse getting burned? I—I had to shoot a man, and the Night Riders went on the warpath."

"I know all about that," cut in Tugger, without noticing the personal pronoun the agent had used. "Are you where you can talk?"

"I'm in the jailer's office," answered Payne, as distinctly as if he were in the next room. "I've decided to plead guilty—on the grounds of justifiable homicide. Seeing Annable—the chap I had to stop—coming down that dark alley with something under his coat—well, I naturally supposed he meant to burn down or blow up the warehouse. The two men on that gun had gone for their supper. I was the only person on guard, so I had to stop him. I—I guess I lost my head and squeezed that trigger before I realized what I was doing."

"You squeezed that trigger?" echoed Tugger, foolishly.

"I lost my head," repeated the patient voice. "There's enough sentiment gathering in Limestone, my lawyer says, to give me a good chance for acquittal. Tradespeople here want General Tobacco to build another warehouse—to make Limestone a real tobacco center—so maybe the jury won't be too hard on me. Besides, townfolks and the county alike are shocked at the amount of bitterness this tobacco war has created. Everybody is getting sick of all this killing."

"Do you honestly believe that, Payne?" demanded Tugger, hopefully. "Do you suppose that they're ready to come to terms?"

"Mr. Blake!" rang Payne's voice, sharply. "I'm not discussing the Equity movement with you. I'm just trying to make you understand what my chances are for acquittal in this Annable mess."

"I—I see," Tugger gulped, accepting the rebuke. "Have you good counsel?"

"These country lawyers are mighty resourceful."

"Wouldn't you rather I'd bring my own lawyer out to defend you? Maybe you could get the trial postponed till we get there—"

"That ud be the one sure thing to make these farmers see red again!" Payne's alarm came crackling over the wire. "You and Dan Lord stay out of this, do you understand? Otherwise, the Night Riders may string me up to the nearest lamppost—trying to get at you two. My best chance for acquittal rests on these folks feeling sorry for me. They know I'm just a salaried man trying to do my duty—to protect the valuable property left in my care."

"I get your point," agreed Tugger, and pulled at his collar because he felt as if he might choke from relief.

"Good-bye, Mr. Blake—and thank you for calling."

"Thank you, Payne! I won't forget—" Tugger tried to

make proper acknowledgment before the connection was broken.

After he had hung up the receiver, Tugger leaned back in his chair and thanked his fool's luck, or God, that there still existed one loyal man, one faithful servant in this money-grabbing world. Ringing for his secretary Matthews, the Harvard chap who knew all about the laws of supply and demand and the theory of the leisure class, Tugger began:

"Take a letter to Dan Lord. 'Dear Dan . . . Robert Payne, agent for General Tobacco at Limestone, Kentucky—is a man who deserves every opportunity your organization can give him . . . Payne is energetic, has great capacity for initiative and hard work, understands local conditions and human nature, knows when to be flexible and when to stand firm . . . In addition, he possesses loyalty and discretion to a rare degree . . . Writing as a director of the Company, I recommend that his salary be immediately increased to $25,000 a year . . . and that he be transferred, as soon as such a move seems indicated in Payne's own judgment . . . to a larger field of activity than Limestone offers.' That's all. And, Matthews, underline 'in Payne's own judgment,' understand?"

"Yes, sir," answered Matthews. "Do you wish to sign it yourself, sir?"

"Hell-damn, yes!"

Safe in the outer office, with the door closed behind him, Matthews made a grimace of relief. Returning to his desk, as he rolled a sheet of paper into his typewriter he said to Conway:

"Golly, but the boss is sore this morning!"

"Now you see what's made an old man out of me before my time?" croaked Conway.

When the letter was ready, Matthews took it in and watched Tugger sign it with a shaking hand. Bracing himself, the secretary ventured:

"Mr. Lord's office 'phoned us twice yesterday, sir—asking where you were and when could Mr. Lord expect a confidential report on your Kentucky trip. What shall we tell them when they call again?"

"Don't bother me now, Matthews—"

"I'm sorry, but Mr. Lord said he would hold lunch open today until he hears from you."

"I'm a sick man, son. Get out and let me alone."

"Yes, Mr. Blake."

The door shut quietly on the young man's trim back. At Tugger's left the ticker began to chatter like a scared guinea hen. It had chattered like that the first time America had come into this office, that breathless July afternoon of '85 when he was leading a stock market raid. He had dropped everything to listen to her, to hear the truth about Palestine which had stopped his worry for the twins' sanity, had let him sleep again. What wouldn't he do now, he asked himself as he turned off the ticker, for one good night's sleep? In this big rich city full of doctors who everybody else said knew their business, to whom could he go now to get one good night's sleep, to get freedom from worry and a quickened zest for life such as America had given him of her own abundance years ago?

He raised his eyes to the wall panel opposite his desk. There hung the outdated *Wild Honey* poster. Was it moving or were his eyes playing him tricks again? America, my dear, in your funereal black as I saw you last, with your face grey from sleepless nights and your eyes red with weeping, have you pushed your way into my office again? Now you are sitting down opposite me, America. What is it you're saying, my heart's only love?

Once we were friends, Tugger Blake, as few men and women have enjoyed friendship—

We could have been lovers, America, but you wouldn't have it that way.

You made a trade with me, Tugger. I kept my side of the bargain. Aren't you going to keep yours? Lift up that receiver, and call Dan Lord.

You forced me into this trade under duress, my love. I

was shaken by an accident, by the accidental killing of my own man, your son whom you never really loved because he was too much of an Ishmael to let anyone love him, as you once told me yourself. In your kitchen, when my head was splitting open and I was sick at heart because I'd killed my own man, you took advantage of me. You would have done as I did, America. Any smart trader would have shaken hands at a time like that on a deal any other smart trader would have known I didn't intend to keep. And when it comes to tradin', America, that's your pride, too!

Then let's forget our trade, Tugger. Consider this tobacco war that's ruining us both. You and Dan Lord aren't fighting men alone, Tugger. Now, you're fighting women and children. The men can hold out as long as you can.

Then there'll never be peace in the burley belt, America Moncure!

There won't be peace until you and Dan make the first move, Tugger. Be generous, you two who can so amply afford it. Be generous, and let my people go! Surely to be generous is not to surrender? Buy our leaf, because until you do there can never be happiness for women and children starving in the burley belt. Christmas is coming, Tugger—

"I beg your pardon, Mr. Blake," Matthews' scared voice penetrated through Tugger's whirling thoughts: "It's Mr. Lord again—on the telephone. Will you talk to him, sir?"

Tugger reached for the instrument, began to speak in gasps, laboriously:

"Dan? Is this you, Dan? Yes, this is Blake, Tugger Blake. Sorry, but not today. The doctor says I've got to go off somewhere and rest . . . my voice sounds queer? Never mind how it sounds, just listen to me, will you? I haven't an encouraging report to make, Dan . . . Nope, no signs of weakening. Yes, I was at Limestone—I saw the whole thing—I've mailed you a letter about Payne . . . I saw the Night Riders, I tell you, over a thousand of 'em in front of that new warehouse of yours they turned into an inferno! Those men can hold out longer than you can, Dan . . . But I tell you they can—and will! Right now, the brunt of this fight isn't on them, it's on their women and children . . . Yes, Dan, I do recommend you give in and buy their leaf . . . Dan, what's surrender—compared to peace by Christmas time? . . . No, I'm not softening. I tell you I saw local conditions—desperate men! Militia from twenty states couldn't stop those farmers—it didn't at Bunker Hill, did it? . . . All right, Dan, you think it over. But mark my words: Buy their leaf now—while you can—or you'll regret it to your dying day!"

He hung up the receiver. It's all over, America. You've won. I've let your people go.

When a little boy, he had thought that only women cry He knew better, now. Dropping his head on his arms, he began to sob. His clenched right fist struck the mahogany desk several times, then relaxed and lay still, empty palm upwards.

A button on his coat pressed against one of the buzzers connected with his outer office. In response to its continuous ringing, Matthews came running with notebook and pencil, his scared face set to receive his employer's abuse. One look, and he turned and fled to the outer office.

"Conway, the boss has collapsed!" exclaimed Matthews. "He's fallen across his desk—he's crying like an old woman—"

"Sooner or later, nerves get 'em all," barked the senior secretary. "If I've seen it happen once here in Wall Street, I've seen it a dozen times. Keep your eye on him—so he doesn't hurt himself—while I call his doctor to come on over with an ambulance."

In the family room at Children's Chance, America sat before the bright fire she had rekindled to make the twilight seem less forlorn for Stone's home-coming. It had been snowing all afternoon. He would come from town hungry and cold. with his shoulders stooped in discouragement. Only this morning, America recalled, she had noticed at the breakfast table how old and tired he looked. Fear stirred in her frozen heart.

What if something should happen to him? Other good Equity men had fallen. What if on one of these early winter twilights Stone fails to come home and is found the next morning frozen by the roadside as together you and he found Ephraim?

This morning before he had left, America tried to control her sinking spirits, Stone had made her promise not to grieve any more. You're acting like an ignorant resourceless tenant woman, America reproached herself, instead of as the wife and daughter and sister of good soldiers. If you can't keep your mind off your troubles, get up and work. If busy fingers can't turn your bleak thoughts outward, open your Bible and read until you feel beneath you again the everlasting arms . . .

"The Lord is my shepherd; I shall not want. He maketh me to lie down in green pastures; He leadeth me beside the still waters. He restoreth my soul . . . Yea, though I walk through the valley of the shadow of death, I will fear no evil: for Thou art with me . . ."

Someone was running up on the front porch steps, calling her name. Something had happened to Stone! Only strangers—and messengers in terrible haste—used the front porch. Now that they hadn't money to pay Weed, Stone drove his buggy around the lane to stable his horse himself before he came to the house.

"Merry, where are you?" shouted Stone's dear familiar voice as, snowy-shouldered and red-faced from the cold, he burst into the family room waving a telegram and crying, "Dan Lord's surrendered—he's come to our terms!"

"Oh, Stone—"

"He's bought our leaf! Merry, we've won," Stone was crying, tears of relief or from the cold coursing down his ruddy cheeks below his shining blue eyes. "On the Louisville hogshead breaks the Tobacco Trust just bought seventy million pounds of the Equity pooled crops for twelve million dollars—paying fifteen cents all around for the 1906 crop and seventeen cents for the 1907 crop, because they said it's the better of the two!"

She stood in the middle of the room staring at her husband. It was over—the penny-pinching economies, the threat of dispossession by the sheriff, the enmity of lifelong neighbors and friends, the pressing weight of discouragement which was slipped off at night for only a few hours of broken sleep and had to be shouldered resolutely again in the morning, nearer and nearer the approach of failure, tighter and tighter the heart-squeezing fear for the safety of loved ones!

"It just doesn't seem possible," she whispered, caught in the sense of unreality which comes to all soldiers when they hear the order to cease firing. "I can hardly believe that we've won. 'Thou preparest a table before me in the presence of mine enemies,'" she continued the quotation from her favorite psalm, "'my cup runneth over. . . .'"

Chapter 19

Three years later, on May 31, 1911, America sat on the front porch at Children's Chance and listened while Stone on the step below read the decision of the Supreme Court which outlawed the Tobacco Trust. Chief Justice White had written the opinion of the court, which decided against the sixty-five American corporations, their two English allies and the twenty-nine individual defendants. The Tobacco Trust and the licorice combine were found guilty of violating the Sherman anti-trust law. Strong words were used to describe their methods, methods clearly showing a purpose to acquire control over the entire tobacco industry, "methods devised to monopolize the trade by driving competitors out of business, which were ruthlessly carried out upon the assumption that to work upon the fears or play upon the cupidity of competitors would make success possible—methods exhibiting a conscious wrong-doing by the form in which the various transactions were embodied from the beginning, ever changing but ever in substance the same."

The case was remanded to the lower court in New York for the purpose of working out within a few months' time some method or plan of dissolving the half-billion-dollar combination, and of "recreating out of the elements now composing it, a new condition which shall be honestly in harmony with, and not repugnant to the law."

Around the porch at Children's Chance, early summer was everywhere in evidence, in the tender green of leafing trees, in great white clouds tumbling across the blue horizon, in the weedless bluegrass fields where young lambs frisked. Up the stately avenue, black boughs of locust trees which Charles Moncure had planted nearly a hundred years ago, dripped ivory bloom like rare old lace. Freshly painted, newly repaired, Children's Chance reminded America of some gallant old lady dressed in her best to celebrate her ninetieth birthday, to receive the loving congratulations of family and friends.

You will soon be an old lady yourself, thought America, while Stone read on. Like other women of your time you will sit dressed up in your own chair on portico or hearth, and call up memories

> Of old, unhappy, far-off things,
> And battles long ago.

Now, you are hearing the terms of victory imposed on your enemy worsted in battle three years ago. Battle is no new thing to you, America Moncure! By now, you should be well used to victory. Your first great struggle was for Golden Hill and to save Palestine. The second was to win the man you loved, and to keep your marriage vows through the hermit years at Foxden—for better, for worse, till death did you part. Then your life circle widened to include all Mason County, the hogshead breaks of Cincinnati, and New York. On Fifth Avenue, you gambled and won to give your girls the place in life you coveted for them. When Tugger Blake took you to the housetops and offered you the world glittering below you, if you would only help him put Palestine away, you rejected his millions and his love, to remain true to your ideal of a great Virginia lady.

That is all very well, swiftly thought America, but strong women have always accomplished these same things. What else have you done which would make you worthy of this last great victory?

I came back to the land which bred me, she answered her

soul's questioning. I came back to the good brown earth and the windswept sky, to rain and snow and sunshine, to crop failures and rich harvests. I chose the free country way of life—until it became serfdom. Then, instead of abandoning it to the new industrialism which was trying to strangle it, I fought my greatest battle to break that grip. And I won, we all won together. At long last, this decision of the Supreme Court vouchsafes an enduring victory for the Equity Society, for the small-town merchants and resourceful country lawyers. John Willy and Ephraim, do you hear? Victory for you, sleeping in your grass-grown graves. Victory for you, Hannah Bell, for all you gaunt women, you men and children moving up and down the waving green rows with the "limestone look" on your tired faces. And for you, lush green fields and wooded hillsides, pleasant farmhouses and well-filled tobacco barns. Victory for you, my beloved country way of life, victory for you over crowded city streets leading to the factory gate, over a machine-driven existence of meager security bounded by grimy walls and punctuated by the jangle of a time clock!

"Stone—"

"Yes, my dear?"

"Now that the Supreme Court has outlawed the trust, do you think all this bloodshed was necessary?"

"You mean could we have won at a cheaper price?" he rephrased her question, and thought before he answered: "Who can say, Merry? If it's true the Supreme Court follows public opinion, then it required the fully aroused anger of this Commonwealth to reach as far as Washington."

"How do you suppose Dan Lord felt when he read that decision? It took him—and Tugger Blake—a lifetime to build up the industrial empire this court in Washington wiped out with one stroke of the pen. I'm glad Tugger is dead, because this decision would have been the final blow."

" 'I have seen the wicked in great power,' " Stone was moved to quote, " 'and spreading himself like a green bay tree.

Yet he passed away, and lo, he was not; yea, I sought him but he could not be found.' "

"Until he takes root somewhere else!" smiled America, and added with weary satisfaction in her pleasant Virginia voice: "Then we—our children—will have to cut him down again."

THE END